EXPERIMENTAL HEART

DESTINY

BOOK 1

SHANNON PEMRICK

Destiny
Experimental Heart | Book One

Copyright © 2018 Shannon Pemrick
www.shannonpemrick.com

Cover Illustration by Jackson Tjota
Cover Typography by Amalia Chitulescu
Editing by Sandra Nguyen

ISBN 978-0-9984464-3-1 (paperback)
ISBN 978-0-9984464-5-5 (hardcover)
ISBN 978-0-9912213-2-5 (e-book)

First edition © 2014

To Lora and Sammie
Thank you for being a huge character inspiration and having faith in her and in me.

And

To Jim
Without you I would have never been able to bring Eira and Raikidan to life.

BOOKS BY SHANNON PEMRICK

EXPERIMENTAL HEART
Destiny
Pieces
Secrets
Exposed
Surrendered

ORACLE'S PATH
Prophecy of Convergence

Prophecy Tested
Prophecy Chosen

LOOKING FOR GROUP
Spellbinding His Ranger
Protecting His Priestess
Summoning Their Elementalist

Impenetrable walls made of stone and synthetic metal surrounded me on all sides. Cold and dampness clung to the air, adding to the oppression. I stared, with tired eyes, up at the small, barred window as I leaned against the wall of the cell, contemplating my options. Oh, that's right. I had none.

I was trapped with my comrades—my friends—in this cell, waiting for our judgment. They shouldn't be here. This was my punishment, not theirs. If I hadn't been so stupid, I wouldn't have gotten them into this mess.

I shouldn't have allowed him to join us. I shouldn't have trusted him. I shouldn't have cared about him the way I did. It was all a bunch of lies, and those lies started the day I...

CHAPTER 1

A failure… I was nothing but a failure. Nothing I did was right. Nothing I was could ever be perfect enough. Even now, I failed.

The mid-day sun shone brilliantly over the peaks of the Larkian Mountain Range in the distance, filling Lumaraeon with warmth. Birds sang in unison with the crickets, while a stream babbled nearby. Mid-spring—a perfect time to explore the mountainous regions of Lumaraeon. I, however, was not here on a luxury hiking trip.

My violet bangs hung over my eyes as I rested against a tall birch tree. I placed pressure on the deep gash on the left side of my abdomen, though the staining of my white tank top showed how futile my attempt was. *What a predicament you've gotten yourself into this time, Eira.* Former commander of Company 14 of the Dalatrend Army, reduced to such a state by someone as insignificant as a Hunter. I'd been running for so long. Had I really let my guard down that much? *Pathetic.*

He may be dead by my hands now, but I would soon follow. Death was coming, and I wasn't afraid.

I didn't fear death. I never had. I had faced death every second since I was… born. I felt nothing about this situation. I felt nothing at all—ever. Well, that wasn't true. I felt some emotions, mostly negative, such as anger, and right now, I experienced a lot of that. I was angry with myself, and angry with those who forced me into this situation. Yet there was no point in being angry. I would never be able to obtain the revenge I craved, and the physical pain I experienced was more powerful than that anger. To take my mind off my suffering, I allowed my gaze to wander.

A small bubbling stream pushed its way through the land in front of me. Water bugs effortlessly cruised their way downstream while fish desperately tried to catch them. In the distance, a waterfall roared, feeding the river that spawned the stream before me. Squirrels chattered in the trees above, and I chuckled as I listened to their angry squabble.

Suddenly a loud roar pierced the air, sending a chill down my spine and putting me on full alert. I had never heard that type of noise before, but for some reason, it seemed… familiar. Everything went quiet, but for only a moment, and then life around me continued on as if nothing had happened.

I looked down at my side when something touched my skin. Flies attempted to get into my wound. I swatted them away, but the attempt was futile. I eventually gave up and watched the grazing deer in the meadow across the stream for some time instead. It was peaceful, and made me feel slightly odd—happiness—an emotion I wasn't supposed to feel—a flaw in my… creation.

Although the sensation was supposed to be forbidden to me, I didn't push it away. I liked it. I was glad it was in a place like this—a place so peaceful and untouched by Zarda's tyrannical clutches. I would leave this pitiful excuse of a land and possibly atone for my sins. *No.* Atonement for my bloodied past wasn't possible.

My head spun, the blood loss getting to me. A small amount of sadness picked in my chest. I wanted to live for a little while longer, to continue to feel free, but I couldn't prolong it. My lifeline was not mine to control now.

A gust of wind picked up and blew dust everywhere. It got into my wound and stung. I wanted to go to the stream and clean it, but couldn't find the will or reason to do so. The ground trembled underneath me. I was alert again and took in my surroundings. The trembling became more and more frequent, and soon I was able to hear large footsteps. With my bloodstained hand, I drew a dagger strapped to my leg and held it close to my body; I didn't know why. I wouldn't be able to protect myself in this state, and frankly, I didn't want to.

Maybe instinct drove me. Maybe my training. Possibly both. In the end, it didn't really matter. Although my body told me to fight, my mind won with logic to just give up, because there was no hope in the end for me anyway.

A purple butterfly fluttered into view and I stared. Naturally it wasn't the source of the trembling, but the amaranthine butterfly was a rare species. It was so rarely seen that most believed they were extinct, and any claimed sightings were just tales to stir up excitement.

The butterfly landed on my knee, and I just stared at it. The small creature seemed so unaware of how easily I could crush it. Or maybe it could sense my weakened state and determined I wasn't a threat. The ground shook again, but the butterfly didn't move. A large black figure slowly came into my peripheral vision, pulling my attention away from the purple insect. It was like nothing I had ever seen before, only heard in the stories, and from—well—that didn't matter. What did matter was the enormous creature that stood before me.

The large bat-like wings, long tail and horns, spined neck, and black scales were unmistakable. A black dragon stood before me, and its presence was unbelievable.

Its sapphire eyes pierced through me. Although its presence was daunting, I couldn't help but smile. If the stories were true and a dragon was really as fearsome as it was told to be, then it was finally my time to pass from this plane. I was at peace with that knowledge.

The purple butterfly fluttered away suddenly, and I watched it go before addressing the dragon. "Are you here to take my life, Dragon?" At least it would be quick, or so I thought. The dragon just stared at me, unmoving. This was frustrating and confusing to say the least. "What's wrong, Dragon? Afraid of me?"

The dragon growled but still didn't move.

I snorted and rested my head back on the trunk of the tree. "No, of course you wouldn't be. What reason would a dragon have to fear a human? Why would life be kind to me, now, when it's always spit on me in the past?"

I wanted death. The life I had lived, the things I had seen, it would make anyone want death. I grunted. "Listen to me. Begging for death like a wounded dog. Pathetic. I guess I really am a worthless bitch."

My body grew weaker, but I paid it no mind. Instead, I ran scenarios through my head. What would become of me once my breathing stopped? *Hell* came up in most. It's where I belonged, after all.

The end was coming, and there was no stopping it. Oddly enough, I couldn't help but smile. "This is it, then. It's... finally over..."

Everything started to blur. The last thing I saw was the dragon's head moving closer to me until it was level with my face.

The dense forest was a blur. My feet carried me as quickly as they could, while my pursuer closed in. Pain raked my body, and everything around me spun. My body crashed into the ground, and instinct kicked in as I struggled to fight off my assailant. The warmth of sticky blood splashed over my skin, and then the spinning stopped, but there was nothing left to see. Only darkness.

My eyes snapped open and darted around. The sun hung low, casting long shadows over the forest. *Am I dead?* My head whirled, and then pain shot through my abdomen as I attempted to move. It didn't hurt like before, but it was enough to convince me to remain still a while longer. *No, I'm alive, but how?*

I remembered waiting for death and then I remembered the dragon. My eyes opened more with the realization. *That dragon.* Had I really seen him? I could have been delusional. Dragons were extinct, after all. Or that was the claim. *You know a bit more truth than the gullible masses, Eira, don't you?*

A shadow blocked my view of the sky, and I squinted to adjust my eyes to the lack of light. Leaning over me was a young man. I gasped with surprise and scrambled to a sitting position, trying to put some distance between us. He appeared my age, late twenties, maybe early thirties. He was shirtless, exposing his tanned broad shoulders and muscular frame. His hair was black with a red stripe in the middle, cut to a medium length, and he had a black soul patch with a matching goatee.

"I was starting to think you hadn't actually made it," he said, his voice low-pitched with a slight gravely edge.

I continued to pull back, the way he watched me making me uneasy. "Well, I did, thanks."

"You lost a lot of blood, but you should be fine now that the wound is closed, and you've had time to rest."

My brow furrowed, and I lifted my bloodstained shirt to find a long scar where my wound had been. *How...* I pinched my nose. Trying to understand made my head hurt, on top of all the blood loss contribution. *Maybe I'm dead after all.*

I made an attempt to clear my head, so I could think, only to find myself looking directly into his eyes. They were a deep sapphire blue, and the way the sun reflected off them made them look like the precious azure gem. *I am alive.* Death couldn't possibly allow me to gaze at something so... beautiful. *Not with my dark, bloodstained past.*

I continued to hold his gaze, noting the careful way he watched me, reflecting my own caution. He also showed some interest in my presence, though I wasn't sure why. *Nothing special about me.* Then it hit me. "You're... you're that dragon."

He half smiled. "I'm surprised you figured it out. Although you don't appear to be surprised in the least."

He was right, but I wasn't going to let him know that. "I was told stories of dragons and what they were capable of."

He didn't respond, and his expression gave nothing away. That's when I noticed he wasn't only shirtless. My gaze shifted out to the river, my cheeks burning.

"Something wrong?" he asked.

"You're not wearing pants," I muttered through clenched teeth.

"You would be correct. Do you have a problem with it?"

"Yes. Yes, I do."

He chuckled in response. This had to be my punishment, unless, of course, I had truly been born into hell and I could never escape.

A long silence filled the air between us until I sighed and broke it. I had too many questions, which was uncharacteristic of me.

"Why didn't you leave me to die? Or kill me yourself?"

He didn't respond. I rested my chin on my hand. *He should have just killed me.*

"Why would I kill you?" he asked.

"Because."

"That's not a real answer. Why do you believe I should have killed you?"

I sighed. "Because it's what I deserve."

"You don't come across as the type who deserves such a fate."

"You don't know me." Getting a strange feeling my personal space was being invaded, I turned to face him, only to find him a few inches from my face. I jerked my head back. "Do you mind? You're too close."

He didn't move, nor did he budge when I tried to push his face away, so I resorted to scooting away a few inches.

"You didn't fear me when I found you, and you don't appear to fear me now. The elves I've crossed paths with were far more cowardly, especially when facing death."

My lip curled. "I'm not an elf. And I don't fear death."

His head tilted, a smirk firm on his lips. "The long ears say otherwise."

I scoffed. "I'm a nu-human. Nowhere close to an elf."

"Nu...human?"

My brow furrowed. *Is he serious?* He looked at me expectantly. *He is. I guess it's possible a dragon wouldn't know.* "Nu-humans are genetically enhanced humans. Telling sign is our long ears. They far exceed the length of an elf. Everyone knows this. We're more abundant than ordinary humans, and have existed for centuries."

"And what would be the purpose of genetic enhancement, as you call it?"

"Don't tell him anything," a malevolent voice I knew all too well whispered.

I eyed him. "Perfection, of course."

"Right." He drew close to me again.

What is his issue? "Do you have a problem or something?"

"I've never been so close to a *nu-human* before. Do you?" he asked.

"Do I what?" The inconsistency in his speech, and what he seemed to be thinking, was irritating to say the least.

"Have a problem with me being this close?"

"Yes. I don't like others being so close to me."

"Interesting," he mused. "Never thought a *human* would have a personal-space problem."

I stood, wincing in pain, and faced the river, crossing my arms and keeping myself aware of his presence in case he tried to pull something. "Well, I do."

"Is there an explanation to go along with that?"

"Don't tell him," the voice whispered.

"I have nothing to tell you."

"Don't be like that. I saved you, after all. I think I deserve some explanation."

"Don't tell him anything."

"No one asked you to save me."

"Consider it my good deed for the year."

I almost laughed. That was a response I'd expect from myself, or even old comrades of mine. *Funny how I'd find a dragon that fit part of that profile.* "Very well, I'll tell you something. But don't say I didn't try to spare you. I am artificially created. Grown in a lab for the sole purpose of being another's lap dog. My training—assassination. Because of that, I prefer my space to only contain myself."

The dragon remained quiet for a moment. "So, what is a weapon like you doing all the way out here on your own?"

"Keep quiet."

"Running."

"From what?"

My gaze fell on the moving water. My past flashed before my eyes. The cruelty—the punishment. I lived in torment. "After everything I'd done under his orders, my creator deemed me imperfect and tried to destroy me. I chose to run instead of face my demise."

I wanted it all to be a lie. That I'd wake up and be a normal person with a normal life.

"What kind of cruel person would do that to another?"

My fists clenched. "Cruel? Cruel doesn't begin to describe him. He's maniacal and twisted. He uses his power to get whatever he wants and torture those who do not submit. He makes others appear weaker—stupid—imperfect."

My rage numbed me. The awful memories of the torture and suffering I had endured ran through my mind.

"We are just tools to him, and he makes sure we understand that is our sole purpose in life. We are nothing without that single purpose."

I jumped back when a hand rested on my shoulder. I focused on the dragon to find his eyes filled with concern. My brow furrowed. "Why are you looking at me like that?"

His expression twisted with more concern. "Have you never been shown compassion?"

I took a step back and averted my gaze. "I'm not overly familiar with that emotion."

"It's not just an emotion. It's an action."

"That's right… I forgot that." I looked up at the sky, the sun lower than before, casting longer shadows across the tree-filled landscape. I listened as the chirping of crickets filled the air and felt the coolness of the river lap at my bare feet. Everything was so peaceful and calm. "The answer to your question is not really. Very few have shown me such an action."

"Was one such person, the one who gave you this?" I turned to see him holding up a hairclip made of emerald. The wind picked up and my hair whipped around my face. I had been so distracted, I hadn't realized it was missing. "I'm not sure about humans, but for a dragon to give another something made of pure emerald, you have to mean a lot to them."

I snorted and took the hairclip from him. "Have you not been listening to me? A misfit like me, special? That's a laugh. I'm nothing more than a broken toy, thrown away."

"I did listen, but what you said doesn't add up to that. I've seen that craftsman's work before. An elf from Ravenward up north. He charges a hefty price. So, unless you stole it, then you had to mean a lot to someone."

I twirled up my hair and clipped in the hair clip underneath it, letting the loose portion of my hair flow over the top hair clip. I then looked away. "How I got this isn't your business."

Silence fell between us, allowing me to think about where to go from here. I had been heading west some time, but I wasn't sure I wanted to continue that way. North seemed like a better choice; being much colder, it gave less possibility of being followed.

The dragon broke the silence. "What did you do to be deemed imperfect?"

I continued to stare out at the scenery. "I failed my design. I showed emotion."

"What?"

Instead of replying, I listened to the forest. I'd heard some rustling that didn't match the typical wildlife here. I turned around to find the dragon-man had moved closer to me again, though I ignored it this time.

"Watch yourself."

I continued to listen, hearing the sound of something metallic moving quick through the foliage. My eyes widened, and I pushed the dragon to the side. "Look out!"

He fell to the ground, and a small throwing knife sunk deep into my shoulder. I bit my lip, so I wouldn't cry out in pain and then yanked the weapon out. Spinning it in my fingers, I looked to the forest. "Come out and fight me like a man."

Three more blades flung out of the brush, but I knocked them away. *Those weren't thrown with conviction.* "Wow, both a coward and a weak shot. This isn't exciting at all."

The brush rustled and then a tall man bolted from his cover. One glance at his bizarre features made me aware of what he was. I readied myself for a fight, but before he came into range, a mass of fur barreled into him. *A wolf?* The man screamed when the wolf bit down on his arm and shook his head. I took a moment to glance the dragon's way to find him gone. *Where did he go?*

The attacker raked its talon-like nails across the wolf's shoulder. It yelped and released him. The man jumped to his feet and did his best to keep his eyes on both the wolf and me. The wolf forced the man's attention when he showed himself to be a threat, and I used the opportunity to sneak closer. *Gun tucked away behind him.* By the time the man knew of my presence, I was already on him.

I thrust the throwing knife into his back and then reached around and slit his throat. I let him go, pulling the gun he held. He choked and writhed on the ground.

He gasped for air. "Zarda will get you… you disloyal bitch."

I checked the gun, finding one bullet in it. *Convenient.* "Says the puppet bleeding out at my feet." I spat on him. "Your master is nothing. And soon, neither will you be."

I aimed the gun at his head and fired, blood and viscera splattering over the ground. If anyone came across him, they wouldn't be able to identify him from his face. The wolf looked at the dead man, and then, before my eyes, slowly changed shape into the human form the dragon had taken. It wasn't a pretty process by any means, but I'd seen far worse in my life.

A dragon that can take the shape of a human and a wolf? The historical texts were true. They claimed dragons were the last with the ability prior to going "extinct." Druids could take a single form, and science tried to replicate the ability, but had only come as far as druids, with some slight variation.

"Let me see that scratch he gave you," I ordered.

The dragon turned his injured shoulder away. "I'm fine. What was he?"

"A Hunter." I knelt and rummaged through the man's pockets. He didn't wear a uniform, but many in the field didn't so they could blend in better. *Not that their features don't make them stand out anyways.* "They're created specifically for tracking people." I found a small object in his jacket. Pulling it out, I examined a small shield-shaped pin with a city engraved on it. A crown hovered over it and a sword plunged through them both. "This one is from my city."

I tossed the pin on the ground, and continued to rummage, finally finding a few medical supplies. I tossed a tube of salve to him. "Here. It'll keep it from getting infected. Their claws dig deep."

He tossed it back, "I'm fine."

"Very well." I started walking upstream. "Thanks for the help. I've now proven I'm hazardous to your health, so I'll be leaving." My voice lowered. "I don't even know why you've stuck around this long…"

"Well if I'm going to help you, I guess I have to get used to that."

I stopped walking and gazed back at him, my face scrunched with confusion. "What?"

"Running from this maker of yours hasn't helped you, so why not take care of him? I can tell you want revenge for what he's done."

"Don't do it," the voice whispered.

I regarded him for a moment. "Why would you want to help me?"

His gaze lowered, as did his voice, though my good hearing picked him up well. "Misfits are more common than you realize." He then looked at me again. "We dragons are good at exacting revenge. We like it, even if it's not our own."

"Don't listen to him."

He was hiding something, and I wanted to know what it was. "Getting to Zarda isn't something as easy as heading home and killing him. He's well-fortified and has an army on his side. There's a resistance movement against him, but after all the time I've been gone, I can't say the type of progress they've made, or if they're even around still."

But, gods, do I hope they are.

"Then we'll join forces with them. With us added to their numbers, it should help, right?"

"Refuse his offer. He can't be trusted."

My eyes narrowed. Something wasn't right. "There is no trust between us, neither can deny that. So why should I believe you wish to help me? What do you really get out of this? Revenge can't be a sole motivating factor. I can't even offer you payment as a mercenary."

He smirked. "I have my reasons, and you appear smart enough to figure them out sooner or later."

"Leave now! Get away from him!"

"You really think that's going to get me to trust you?"

"Of course not, but trust isn't the aim here. Do you or do you not want to get rid of this creator of yours?"

I thought about this and realized he was right. Running all these years didn't slow the pursuit, and I couldn't run for the rest of my life. It treated the symptoms, not the sickness. *And there's something else about the offer...* I couldn't shake the strange sensation I got as he tried to convince me. It felt like some sort of pull toward saying yes.

"Fool," the voice hissed.

I extended my hand. "My name is Eira."

The dragon grasped my hand. "Raikidan."

2
CHAPTER

The crisp air clung to my lungs as Raikidan and I traveled farther up river, the orange sun setting behind the purple mountain range in the distance.

Raikidan continued to be chatty along the way. "So, you said you were an assassin. Is there anything else you did while in service of your creator—Zarda, was it?"

"I'm a former commander." The look he gave indicated I'd have to explain. "It's a rank in our military. For our city it sits just below general, which is the highest rank you can attain."

His brow stayed risen. "You specified your city. It's different in other ones?"

I gave a curt nod. "Human cities are governed differently, if they don't have an on overarching ruler between them. This means they can choose how they wish to rank their military and civilians." My eyes swept across our surroundings. "Are you sure there's a safe place to rest up this way?"

Raikidan responded with a loud snort. "This is my territory. Of course I'm sure."

Since it was late in the day, the two of us agreed it'd be best to rest up before heading for Dalatrend. Raikidan claimed to know a place that would keep us out of the eyes of any Hunters. Of course, this forced me to place trust in him that I wasn't ready to give.

"Don't trust him."

The roar of the upstream waterfall grew louder and the path we took became rockier until it came into view. It wasn't as large as I expected, but it pushed the river and had a deep pool beneath it. Behind the falling water I spied a cave. *Please don't tell me this is our destination.*

Raikidan pointed to the cave. "That's where we can stay for the night."

Of course. I looked at him with a raised brow. "A cave behind a waterfall? How cliché can you get?"

The dragon's eyes narrowed. "It's an easy location to defend if we are found. If you'd rather sleep in the open, be my guest."

A small grin spread across my lips, despite myself. The bite in his tongue was refreshing. "As long as it's a secure spot, I'll give it a try, I suppose."

He snorted and waved me to follow him. Raikidan led me up a narrow path leading to the cave and allowed me to look around the large chamber. From the looks of it, it started out as a naturally occurring space, but the gouges in the rocks and occasional scorch marks showed me it had been excavated by something large. *Probably safe to assume he did it.* I guessed this to be, at the very least, one place he'd call a lair. Whether it was his main one, where he stored hoarded treasure, had yet to be determined.

Raikidan sat down with his back against the wall. "So, what's your plan?"

I leaned against the opposite wall, noting its dampness. "The obvious is to head to Dalatrend. I would like to stop at a small village on the way, for personal reasons, but unfortunately, I don't know where we are. You wouldn't have a map, by chance?"

His brow rose in question. "Why would I have a map?"

I rolled my eyes. "Typical male response."

"I'm being serious. What need would I have for a map?"

I crossed my arms and shrugged. "I'm not saying you do. But everyone knows dragons hoard, so I thought maybe you'd collected one or two in whatever fashion you choose to accumulate that wealth." I shifted my gaze away from him. "I was only asking if you had one. It's not a big deal if you don't."

He looked away, speaking to himself. The sounds came out as grunts and growls. *Must be Draconic.* From what I knew, dragons had their own language called Draconic and they used a unique power most called draconic magic. It was said to be the source of how they shifted and received their rarely matched strength.

I searched for a dry place to sit, but found none. I steepled my hands in front of my lips. Exhaling, a burning sensation rose up from my chest and out of my mouth. Harnessing the power in my hands, I discreetly pulled the flame from my lips and held it within my fingers, adding power to it to create the illusion I'd conjured the fire from my hand.

I had the innate ability to produce fire internally in my body and use it at will. Many beings in Lumaraeon had this ability, and some had the skills to harness other elements. They were called elementalists. A few races could go beyond that and shift into an animal, such as a druid, while shamans could speak with the spirits of the dead. Though how I produced fire wasn't natural for a human. Not even a nu-human like myself. It had caused me my fair share of problems, so I'd come to hiding its production to ease my headaches.

I went about drying off the rocky surface and noticed Raikidan watching me with great interest. "What?"

"You can create fire?"

The side of my lips twisted upward as I continued my task. "One of the many things that set me apart from a normal nu-human."

Raikidan's eyes glowed with interest. "There's a town, east of here, with people capable of doing that. I've never gone there since it's out of my territory, but if you're familiar with it, it may give you an idea of where you need to bring us."

My brow furrowed into deep creases as I mulled over this new information. "If it's the same place I'm thinking, yes, I have. It'd be the West Shaman Tribe, and the town I want to stop in."

Raikidan cocked his head to one side. "Why do you want to stop there?"

"I stayed there for some time and had to leave in a hurry. I left a few things there I'd like to retrieve, as they'll be useful in our goal."

"If they let you stay there, does that mean you're a shaman as well?"

I avoided his gaze. I didn't like the way the conversation kept shifting back to me. "You could say that." His stomach growled, and I took the escape route presented. "You should go find something to eat. If your shifting is anything like a druid's, then I'm sure you've used a great deal of energy staying in your human form."

"What about you?"

I sat down in my now dry spot. "I'm not hungry."

He leveled his eyes at me for a moment, then removed the clothes he'd "borrowed" from the dead Hunter at my request. I was sure to keep my eyes averted. His shape changed, and I now shared my space with a large dragon. Thankfully, the cave accommodated the two of us well. I stole a glance, but he launched himself out of the cavern and took to the skies before I could catch more than the sight of some red scales mixed in with the black on his spine.

I placed a hand on my stomach. It'd been some time since it had needed to tell me to feed. In my tormented years, it learned to adapt to a lack of food. A cave cricket jumped past me and I licked my lips. I knew it would provide some energy, but I didn't need that dragon to know how weak I was at the moment. I'd have to resort to foraging, rather than hunting wild game.

A cold breeze blew through the cascading water into the cave and I shivered. *I should collect firewood, too.* I stood and left the rock chamber.

My search turned up a good source of firewood, but food proved more difficult. The nuts on the hardwood trees weren't developed enough at this time of year, and all mushrooms and berries I found were poisonous. *I should have eaten that cricket.* I had a feeling insect hunting would be my next resort. While most reeled at the thought of eating an insect, I understood their importance to a diet when food was hard to come by. I even knew when to suck up my pride and dig for worms. As disgusting as they were, food was food.

My foraging halted when I realized how quiet the forest had grown. I dropped my wood haul when a twig snapped. I drew a dagger, taking in a deep whiff to gauge what may be hiding in the shadows. The petrichor masked the unknown being, but when I heard another twig snap in the opposite direction from the first. I had a decent idea of who and what was hiding beyond the brush. My suspicions were proven correct when two figures charged out from opposite sides of the forest, talon-like hands extended for a kill.

I managed to push back their first attack, but one of them was quicker on the recovery than I expected he'd be, and managed to rake me in the side. I cried out in pain, anger flaring in me. Spurred on by that anger, I retaliated and stabbed him twice with my weapon while back-fisting his comrade. The pair backed off and exchanged glances, then tried to flank me. I dropped into a defensive stance and watched them with trained eyes. Rushing with two opponents would result in my death. But the blood wafting in the air... it teased me.

"Kill them."

Yet before the fight could continue, an ear-piercing roar echoed through the trees, followed by the beating of wings. Everyone looked up to see a black dragon descending from the skies. I noticed the red scales trailing his head and spine. *Is it Raikidan or another dragon?* I didn't know enough about their species to understand identification between individuals.

The Hunters attempted to attack me in this distracted state, but the dragon swung his tail. I barely managed to jump out of the way of the attack while the two Hunters went flying into the forest. *If it is Raikidan, he's showing his true colors.*

"I told you not to trust him!"

The dragon landed above me and snapped his wicked teeth at a Hunter who ran back into this uneven fight. The man wasn't prepared for the attack and screamed in agony as the dragon crunched him in his toothy maw, blood splattering in all directions. The huge creature spit out the Hunter, his body landing on the ground with a *thud*. He lay there unmoving. I had to admit, I was impressed. *That's one way to deal with these pests.*

The dragon swiveled his head back and forth, scanning the forest for the other Hunter. *This has to be my dragon.* I couldn't rationalize his lack of interest in killing me any other way—unless you counted that failed tail attack an attempt. It could have been a poorly misjudged swipe for all I knew, and my lack of trust was skewing my opinion.

"Don't trust him."

A sudden movement in the forest caught my eye, and before I knew it my dagger flew out of my hand. I silently cursed myself when the blade disappeared into the underbrush with no target met.

"Idiot."

The dragon above me moved forward, the trees around us moaning, cracking, and eventually falling under the strength of the large creature. His actions flushed out the remaining Hunter.

From the indecisive look on the Hunter's face, I could tell he was torn between his orders to kill me and saving his own life. Unfortunately for him, disobeying orders wasn't easy for the average creation of Zarda. As a result, the Hunter tried to get around my dragon comrade. That proved to be a mistake.

The Hunter, as their design intended, was quick, but the dragon happened to be quicker. Even with his large size, he raked his enormous talons into the man's soft flesh. The Hunter cried out as the dragon gored him, spilling his innards across the ground. An ordinary person might have blanched at the sight, but my bloodstained past left me unaffected by the grizzly visage.

With both Hunters now dead, I was left to retrieve my thrown dagger and discarded timber, mindful of the wound I now had.

"Are you all right?"

I turned to find Raikidan back in his human form and swiftly returned to my side. "I'm fine."

"I smell blood on you; are you sure?"

My upper lip curled into a snarl. "I said I'm fine."

The human-dragon let out a long sigh. "Very well. Can I know why you're out here?"

I held up a small stack of timber in front of me. "I don't know about you, but I'm going to need a fire to keep me warm in that damp cave."

Raikidan's eyes widened as if the thought had never occurred to him. It was probably one of the perks of being a dragon. I guessed it took a lot before they suffered from the cold.

As I finished collecting up the wood, I noticed a patch of mushrooms growing by the base of a tree. Upon closer inspection, I found them to be edible. I wasted no time harvesting them, even popping a few in my mouth while securing my fire fuel in my arms. My foraging did not go unnoticed.

"Wait, are you hungry?" Raikidan asked from behind me. "If you were hungry, you only had to say something when I went hunting earlier. I could have brought you back something."

"I'm perfectly capable of fending for myself."

He ground his teeth together. "Does your species know nothing of working together? Or is there something just wrong with you? I'm offering my assistance because we need to work together."

Timber and food in hand, I ignored his question and headed back to the cave. *There's a lot wrong with me, Dragon. You don't want to waste your time knowing what kind of mess I am.* "Thanks for the help with those Hunters. Next time just watch where you swing that tail."

Raikidan caught up with me. "I realized how stupid that was to do. It wasn't my intent to attack you as well. I'm sorry."

"Don't accept those words."

"Apology accepted."

"What is wrong with you?"

The two of us remained silent on the rest of our walk back to the cave. When we reached our destination, I went about crafting a fire and roasting a few of the mushrooms to add a different taste to my palate. Meanwhile, Raikidan had slipped out of the cave again. He returned once I'd settled down in front of the fire. I nearly jumped when he threw something at me, but managed to catch it thanks to my quick reflexes. In my hands, I now held a dead rabbit. I eyed the human-dragon with suspicion. "Why do you insist I eat more than what I've collected?"

"Because you're too stubborn for your own good. That will sustain you more than those mushrooms."

"Don't eat it."

I looked at the meal he provided and then back to him.

Raikidan shook his head then shrugged. "Listen, if I really wanted to kill you, I'd have already done so instead of poisoning you like some coward."

I half grunted and half laughed. "Poison isn't for cowards, and you did attack me earlier."

"That was an accident. Had I meant to, you would no longer be alive."

He has a point.

"No, it's a trick."

I decided I'd have to risk the chance. Even if it was poisoned, I'd get the death I asked for earlier. I went about skinning the rabbit, and eating everything edible it could offer. Raw or cooked—it didn't matter to me.

Raikidan didn't take his eyes off me the entire time.

Even after I finished my meal, his gaze hadn't left me. It was really starting to bother me. As I cleaned up, I decided to find out his problem. "Why are you staring at me?"

His response was rather simplistic. "You're wounded. You said you were fine, but I can see how you favor one side."

"Just because I'm wounded doesn't mean I'm not fine. I've dealt with worse. It'll heal in time."

"I can heal you."

I let out a derisive snort. "Sure you can."

He continued to speak as he drew closer. "I healed the other life-threatening wound you had. So, let me help."

I shoved him away and started to stand. "Don't touch me."

Raikidan fell over and his eyes narrowed. "What's your deal? I'm only trying to help."

"And I said I didn't want it!" He didn't flinch at my loud tone, but his eyes darkened. My eyes narrowed. "There's that anger. I was wondering when it'd come back."

His expression almost immediately softened. "What are you talking about?"

"This fake concern; did you really think I wouldn't see it? Heh... I saw you trying to hide the hate you have when you look at me. While you do well concealing, I'm all too accustomed to that look for you to succeed. You associate me with someone who has caused you pain, at least enough to justify anger toward me."

The human-dragon moved with a speed I never saw coming. Before I knew it, my back was slammed into the cave wall and Raikidan's arm was pressed into my neck, cutting off the air to my lungs. The bundle in my hand clattered to the ground. "Don't you dare start making assumptions as if you know me."

"Fight!"

I struggled to breathe, but I didn't fight him. "But it's... true. Otherwise... you wouldn't be... choking me... You want... me dead..."

His eyes narrowed, his gaze so intense it nearly burned. "You have it wrong."

"He's lying."

When I remained impassive, his brow furrowed. "Why are you so calm?"

"You think... you're the first man... to ever try... to beat me..." My lips spread into a sick, twisted grin. "You're years late... to that party..."

His eyes widened at my confession. He paused a moment, then jumped back. Air flooded into my lungs and I fell to my knees. My side pulsed with pain, but I refused to show weakness in front of this dragon.

I glanced up at him as I rubbed my throat. "What's wrong? You had the perfect opportunity… to end me and… get some sort of twisted revenge. I may be strong… but I'm no match for a dragon."

He stared at me as if frozen, mixed emotions playing across his face. *What is with him? It's not like what I said was all that shocking.*

Raikidan finally composed himself and knelt. "Stop being stubborn and let me look at your wound. I can smell the fresh blood. All this moving around has caused it to open back up." He peered at me with soft eyes when I refused to budge. "Please."

The way he's looking at me… My face felt a bit warm for some reason. I couldn't explain it. I sighed and showed him the damage the Hunter had caused. "Consider yourself lucky. I wouldn't show this to just anyone."

He chuckled. For the first time since I met him, I noticed how handsome he was. *Funny what a smile can do.*

"Someone as stubborn as you, I wouldn't doubt it. Now let me see."

I kept a close eye on him as he leaned in to inspect the wound. It didn't escape me when he noticed the deep horizontal scars on my sides, but he didn't say anything. *For the best. No way would I allow him to know about the origins of those.*

Raikidan peered up at me with regretful eyes. "I'm sorry for attacking you. That was wrong. I don't hate you. I don't even know you to be able to do that."

"It's easy to hate someone if they remind you of someone else."

"You're wrong about me." He held my shirt out of the way. "Now hold still. This shouldn't hurt, but it might."

Well at least he gave me warning.

Raikidan took a deep breath and then exhaled a thin flame at my skin. *He can breathe fire in this form?* I tensed, expecting pain, but instead, a soothing sensation fell over my wound and my body. *What is this?* Before my very eyes, the wound closed and then disappeared.

"See, not so bad getting my help," Raikidan said as he pulled away.

I touched the spot he healed. Nothing was left to indicate I'd been harmed during that attack, though my prior scars remained. "Is this how you saved me last time?"

He nodded. "Yes, though for some reason that time left a scar. Sorry."

I cocked my head to one side and shrugged. "It's not like I don't have others."

His eyes darkened but he didn't say anything. I continued to watch him. I didn't understand this dragon. I was so sure I'd figured him out. *But if he really did want me dead, he had the perfect opportunity. And yet, here he is showing me… kindness.*

"It's a trap."

I didn't believe he could be trusted. I'd now have to be extra careful with him.

I started picking up my dropped mess. "I'm going to clean this up and then get some rest. We have a long day tomorrow."

"Right."

I got up and started to leave, but stopped and looked back. "Thank you."

I then left the cave to deal with the rabbit remains.

Light hit my eyes, stirring me. My eyes fluttered open and I looked around. Soft rays of light filtered through the cascading water outside the cave, and Raikidan's "soft" dragon snores echoed against the cave walls. He'd kept his distance, as much as the cave allowed, at least. My body was on high alert, and I woke up every time the smallest sound echoed through this cave, even if it was just him moving in his sleep. Sometimes, when I'd wake, I'd catch him watching me or staring out at the water falling in front of the mouth of the rocky chamber.

I gazed down at the dagger in my hands. I always slept with it there, just in case. It wouldn't deter a dragon, but it helped me sleep at least. Sheathing it, I quietly made my way out of the cave.

The sun hung low in the morning skies, maybe a few hours after sunrise. Later than I expected to wake, but with my years of military service behind me, and running for as long as I had, that internal clock had changed. And I'd learned, the safer I felt, the longer and more soundly I'd sleep. *It's been a long time since I slept through the night. And just as long waking up so late after sunrise.* I wouldn't let Raikidan know, but for some illogical reason, his presence helped me sleep. Even though I couldn't trust him, I had this strange sense of ease resting near him.

I examined my surroundings to find the forest quiet of anything unusual. A light breeze rustled the trees, and birds trilled their morning song. Following the path, I made my way down to the pool below the falls. The agitated water churned beneath the cascading water. *I could handle the flow, but… that's too deep for my liking.* I moved down river a few yards and found a small spot that would work for a quick wash up.

Wading into the hip-deep water, I suppressed a shiver as the icy water seeped into my clothes. Spring river water wasn't the most comfortable to bathe in, but I'd dealt with worse. Part of my training in the military had me completing tasks while water elementalists assaulted me with both frigid and scalding water.

Removing my hair clip, I sloshed and scrubbed my neglected body and hair, cleaning myself as best I could without modern beauty products. *The next time I decide to run away, I should think about taking a route with better access to water.* I gazed down at the moving water, but it was too agitated to give a clear enough image. I would have to wait to see just how bad I looked. *Couldn't be too bad, or the dragon would have made some sort of comment.* At most I suspected I merely appeared malnourished and unkempt.

As I cleaned myself, I sensed I wasn't alone. I did my best to act casual as I scanned the area. My eyes fell on the waterfall as movement caught my eyes. *Raikidan.* He didn't come out from where he hid, but I could tell he watched me. *Creeper.* "You know, it's rude to stare."

I didn't get an answer right away, but I never stopped looking at the rushing water. Raikidan finally moved out from behind the falls and maneuvered his way down to the ground. My eyes, unhindered by the low light of dusk and night, got a perfect view of his *impressive* natural form. I couldn't lie to myself: he was a magnificent-looking creature.

His scales were polished and black, save for a small section of red scales. His head was triangular, with several small ivory spikes on his jawbones on each side of his head. Heavy black cascading plated scales covered his neck and chest as well as his hips and thighs. Heavy plated scales also lined the tops of his eyes and merged with his long heavily plated horns. Under the plating I could tell his horns were ivory, contrasting with his dark scales. Ivory spikes lined the undersides of his eyes, and large ivory spines grew down his neck and body until they reached the heavy plating on his tail.

The red scales created a stripe that began at the tip of the center point of his eyes and flowed down his body, ending at his tail. At the end of his tail, a spade-shaped club flexed, revealing malleable spikes on either side of the base.

When he reached the shore next to me, he lay down, watching me. I held his gaze for a while, unable to find the ability to go back to washing up. Some strong unseen force pulled me away from that task to this one.

Raikidan lowered his head next to me. His breath was warm, but non-threatening. Involuntarily, my hand stretched out and rested gently on the tip of his snout. A part of me screamed to stop, but the other was much too curious to care.

I didn't understand what was going on with me. It had been so long—a distant memory at best—since I had been so curious about something. The small, almond-shaped scales were smooth and almost leathery, and as I slid my hand across them, I felt the separation between each of them.

Finally snapping out of my daze, I stepped back. *Get a hold of yourself, Eira!* I really was losing it. I went back to bathing, my mind going to plans for the next few days. I'd need Raikidan to show me the way to the village he mentioned. I was sure I knew this place. It made sense, based on my erratic path to lose these Hunters over the years. Even if it wasn't the right place, I could obtain a map and plot out our path.

Once we reached Dalatrend, we'd have to sneak in and then make my presence known with the resistance. If luck was on our side, which it wasn't for me most of these days; there would be a path to sneak in under the city.

Strong hands pressed the back of my neck and shoulders. "Let me help you with that."

Surprised, I whirled around and knocked Raikidan in the face. He stumbled back, the water barely covering his now human lower half. He stood a few inches taller than me, so I was lucky the water covered him at all. "Don't touch me!"

He rubbed his cheek. "You didn't need to hit me."

"Then learn personal space!" I lashed out. "And don't touch people without their permission."

"I only wanted to help." He continued to rub his face. *Is… he pouting?* As I watched him, his lip was in fact sticking out a bit. It was cute. *Wait, why am I thinking this way? Keep yourself together, Eira.*

"I don't know a lot about humans. I've only learned from those who have wandered through my territory, and I kept tabs on them without interacting. Not too long ago, an elven pair, male and female, chose this river to wash up. The male helped his female companion. I know humans and elves are different, but they have a lot of similarities." Raikidan cupped his chin with his hand. "Oh wait. While doing that, it did entice a pursuit that—"

My hand flew up into the air, my cheeks warming at the unwanted image he'd planted in my head. "Stop! I don't want to hear what they did."

Raikidan tilted his head. "You look to be of a human equivalent to mating age. I would have thought that topic wouldn't have bothered you. How old are you?"

"Don't tell him anything."

My eyes narrowed, and my teeth remained clenched as I fought the uncomfortable feeling plaguing my body. "I'm twenty-seven." I spun around, indicating I wasn't going to continue the topic. Raikidan let me be, but for once I wasn't satisfied by that. "You know, it's rude to ask someone's age without giving your own."

"You didn't ask for it."

I crossed my arms. "Well, I am now."

"Only about two centuries hatched. I had been in my shell for almost another two."

"So, based on how you act, and the age you present yourself in human form, if I'm correct in believing you can't change that look, you'd be the equivalent to my age."

"I guess so. But what do you mean by 'act'?"

I chuckled. "An older, wiser dragon would know when to leave someone be."

"Are you saying I'm not wise?"

I glanced back at him to find him annoyed. The side of my mouth twisted into a smirk. "Precisely."

His upper lip curled, and he crossed his arms, looking away from me. "Whatever."

I chuckled again. *Thanks for proving my point.*

Determining I was as clean as possible without removing my clothes, I made my way out of the water.

"Wait, how are you done?" Raikidan asked. "You're still in your clothes. Why would you even get them wet?"

"Because there's no way I'd undress in the open, especially with someone around."

"I don't understand you. What it is with you and clothes?" I didn't answer him. He followed me out of the moving water. "Is this strange reaction the reason why you're so adamant I wear them?" His hot breath met the back of my neck suddenly, surprising me. "Does this form I take make you uncomfortable? Look too human for someone your age, causing confusion?"

I elbowed him. He grunted and then backed off. "No."

He chuckled. "If you're concerned something may happen between us, don't be. I'm able to discern between our two species, even in this form."

"You have an active imagination. Clothes are customary for humans. To walk around without them is considered indecent, and sometimes illegal, depending on where you are. I care not for how you appear, and I'm well aware you're not human. I also care not for the engagement of sex or companionship. Both are a waste of time. Now would you please go put your clothes on, so we can leave? We're burning daylight."

"Sure." He walked off.

His easy compliance confused me, but I brushed it off. While he retrieved his clothes, I produced some fire and encircled my body, drying my skin and clothes. By the time Raikidan returned, I had finished throwing my hair up into a modified ponytail.

"I've never seen someone wear their hair like that," Raikidan said.

"Is that a problem?"

His brow furrowed. "No, just an observation."

"Right, well if we can, I'd like to get moving. You know where this town is, roughly, so it's on you to get us there. Or at least close."

He stared at me for a moment and then looked skyward. "It would be faster if I flew us."

"Yeah, no," I said in a flat tone. "We'll walk."

He gave me a perplexed look, but my expression remained neutral.

There was no way he'd convince me to allow him to fly us anywhere. *My feet are to stay on the ground.*

He let out an exasperated sigh and waved me to follow. "Have it your way. It's a good three or four days from here on foot. Hope you like walking."

I snorted and followed, hoping this conversation wouldn't be an indicator of how painful the next few days would be.

CHAPTER 3

Raikidan and I made our way through the forest. Birds screeched above and insects buzzed all around. The gaps in the canopy casted dapples of light over the forest floor and our skin, providing refreshing warmth over the cool air. Raikidan led the way without hesitation, even alerting me when we left his territory. That was two days ago. We'd yet to come across a road of any kind, but I didn't complain. The two of us were better off not risking being spotted in such an open location.

"So, the reason your weapons don't rust is due to a special material it's made of?" Raikidan asked.

Yet another question... I nodded. "Yes, that's correct. It's a commonly-used material for weapons, even among the other races."

He glanced my way. "What was it like being part of the military?"

My fist clenched. We'd managed a full day before he started playing twenty questions with me, again. At first, I was willing to answer, as the questions were harmless enough and hadn't been personal. But as the days passed, they continued, making them more annoying than anything, and some of them, like this one, were getting personal. I knew we needed to work together, but I had no intention of making some personal connection with this dragon. "I ran away and couldn't care less if I lived or died. What do you think it was like?"

He looked at me, his brow creased. "It was just a question. No need to snap at me."

I didn't answer him and continued our direction forward.

"Okay… what about this question. What do you like to do for fun? Besides killing others."

Pain pulsed in my chest. "I don't enjoy killing."

"Then why did you become an assassin?"

I shook my head. "Did you forget I was created for a purpose? I didn't choose what I did. Making choices against my creator ended with me dealing with you!"

"No need to shout… or be rude. I'm just trying to understand you. If we're going to work together, I need to know things about you."

"It's one thing to inquire information to know your partner of a tentative alliance. It's another to ask personal questions. I have no intentions of being your buddy."

"Seriously, what is wrong with you? One minute you're fine, the next you snap at me, and then you're fine again, only to cop an attitude the next. It's like your emotions are all messed up or something."

The pain in my chest returned, and I looked in a different direction, my shoulders involuntarily sagging. *There's that phrase again…*

Raikidan stopped walking. "I see. I was wondering why I hadn't seen you smile once since we met. And I mean a real smile, not some sick twisted grin. Not even when I've complimented you, which would have made others smile. You act this way to protect yourself. You don't want anyone close, so you can't be hurt."

"Watch what you tell him."

More pain flared in my chest. I stopped walking, but didn't look at him. "No, that's not it…" My hands balled into fists. "I lack the capability to express and feel most emotions."

He came up to me. "What?"

"I was created to be the first soldier without any emotions."

"Wait, you mentioned your creator deemed you unworthy because of emotions."

I nodded, my eyes focused on the ground. *Where to start on that explanation…* "Nu-humans and humans differ, but living weapons like myself are different from regular nu-humans. Nu-humans have enhanced physical characteristics—greater physical strength, hearing, smell, taste, and touch. Living weapons have all that, but to a much greater degree.

"Further, almost all living weapons are experimental, with changes to their DNA such as adding other creature-type characteristics, more desirable human characteristics, or removing them. Once they find a characteristic they like, they keep it in all new designs."

I took a deep breath. "My design was to be emotionless, but the design failed. I experience emotions, but not the way others do, nor am I capable of expressing them correctly. So, in emotional situations I get confused, and that confusion comes out as frustration."

I crossed my arms. "They did, however, manage to get something out of it. I'm unable to express sadness in the form of tears, experience fear, or possibly even feel happiness."

He cocked an eyebrow. "Possibly?"

I nodded. "I understand how happiness works. I know the right responses and how it can affect others. Still, because you cannot teach someone how to be happy, it's unknown if I've never experienced it."

"You've gone this far living like this. What is your opinion about it all? How do you really feel about being created this way?"

How do I feel? No one had ever asked me that before. They'd always just accepted it and moved on. *Why is he the first to ask?*

"Personally, I don't really care. It's not like it can be magically fixed." I started walking away. "It's not like I'm worth fixing."

For a good minute I walked by myself, but Raikidan finally caught up. I chuckled when a thought came to me at the same time. "It's weird. I've never talked about myself so much to a stranger."

"Maybe that's a sign not to see me as a stranger."

I snorted. "Not likely." I regarded him for a moment. "You know, you're a lot more curious than I would have expected you to be."

Raikidan was the one to look away this time.

"What? Curiosity isn't a bad thing—most of the time. It's how we learn."

His eyes narrowed. "Your tone now is confusing. You're not tensing to bite me again."

I chuckled. "Might as well get used to it. I'm temperamental." He snorted, and I had to stop myself from laughing. A realization came to me. "Hey, you're going to need to change the form you take. If you're going to help me in Dalatrend, you'll need to look like a nu-human, and if we're going to this town, it's best if you use an appearance that's more acceptable."

His brow furrowed. "More acceptable? What are you talking about?"

I paused a moment. "Oh, right, you don't know the history between humans and nu-humans." I took a deep breath. "For as long as recorded history goes, humans have felt insignificant compared to the other races of the land. We were generally considered the weakest, even though it's said we were the first, and other races evolved from us. To change our position, humans advanced their technology, and thus their culture, but even after doing this, they were ill-equipped for surviving in Lumaraeon compared to the other races. Therefore, they collected the best human scientists, engineers, chemists, and biologists of the time, and started experimenting on a genetic level."

I stopped a moment and rubbed my arm. Raikidan seemed completely engrossed in my story. "After hundreds of failed attempts, they finally had a breakthrough, and as a result a new breed of human was born. That new breed took shape in the form of a little girl. The little girl's life force was stable and growing, so more were soon created. They called this new breed of human… *nu-human*. As the nu-humans grew and developed, they were integrated into society. Ordinary families took the children in to teach them how to live normal lives, and all was good. That is, until the nu-humans became greedy."

Raikidan still listened intently, as if he were feeding off this information.

"With their enhanced senses and looks, they felt they were superior to the regular humans. Their arrogance drove a rift between the two types of humans, and civil war broke out. The battles raged until the humans lost the will to keep control. The nu-humans imprisoned their makers and turned them into their slaves. They had planned to slowly drive the humans to extinction, but after realizing the work they would have to do once the humans were gone, they spared the poor, lesser versions of themselves."

I looked Raikidan in the eye. "So, now that you've heard the history, you can understand why you can't look like an ordinary human." I smirked. "Unless, of course, you want to pose as my slave."

Raikidan's eyes darkened, and there was a dangerous edge to his voice. "Not going to happen."

I closed my eyes and nodded. Despite my protests, this dragon was starting to grow on me. "I'm glad you said that. To be fully honest, I've never liked the idea humans were beneath us. While that fact had been taught to us since day one, it never set well with me." I looked to the sky; a bird darted through the trees catching my eye. "When I escaped, I learned how closed off my city was. Humans had more freedom the farther west I went. It was as if those in power were perpetuating a lie to keep us controlled." I grunted in contempt. "Not too far from the truth. The citizens are slaves in their own right. They're so brainwashed they believe they shouldn't leave the city. When in reality, Zarda's greed for power keeps them contained in their cages—where he can control them easier."

Raikidan stepped closer to me. "Sounds like a rotten way to live."

I grimaced. "That's why there's a resistance movement. We want him gone and the people free."

Raikidan responded with a slow nod. "Noble goal. I hope to help you achieve that, especially since it'll sate your desire for revenge, but there's one slight problem."

I narrowed my eyes at him. "What's that?"

A sheepish grin crossed his face. "I can't take a nu-human form yet. If the difference between the two human types were cosmetic, it wouldn't be an issue, but as you've indicated, there are other differences as well. I need to observe you longer before I can make that change."

I eyed him for a few moments, then let out a long sigh. "Very well. We'll just have to have a good story if you meet someone as a human and then happen to again later as a nu-human."

Raikidan crossed his arms. "You act like I'm new to being a dragon. We're good at being secretive."

"Right, that's why you saved a nu-human." He gave me an unamused look and I chuckled before waving him to follow. "Now let's keep moving. This conversation isn't helping us get places."

At some point, the forest thinned, and before long we stepped out onto a dirt road. Few towns had the ability to produce the materials to sustain vehicles, so there wasn't a need to maintain roads like they did in cities. Even advanced technologies were limited. Such were the perks of living in cities in a broken land on the verge of war again. *Will we ever see peace, like before the War of End?*

Raikidan peered around. "I think we're close. I wasn't expecting to find a road just yet, so I'm not sure."

I also gazed around, the sounds of the forest alive even here. The trees swayed in the breeze, and small birds flew above in the blue sky. *Something is familiar about this place.*

The wind, no more than a gentle breeze, was a welcome relief to the midsummer heat as I strolled through the forest. I walked the familiar path as I had so many times during the past years. But this time was different. This time I hadn't tread this path for some time.

My stare caught Raikidan's attention. "What's up?"

I shook my head to clear it and peered around again. "I know this road."

His brow rose. "You recognize a road?"

"I traveled it a lot." I spotted an old wooden sign and ran over to it. Elemental symbols were carved into the wood. "I was right. I have been here." My eyes shifted to Raikidan as he approached. "And we were correct in our assumption about the nearby village. It's the West Shaman Village. We're close. Follow me."

Before he could protest I took off, an eagerness adding to my speed. As I led the way, my pace slowed, the memories of why I'd left coming back.

Everyone here who knew how to was fighting. Instead of turning me in, instead of making it safe for them to live, they chose to fight for me. They were choosing to die for me.

My shoulders sagged. *Maybe going back isn't a good idea.*

I jumped when a hand landed on my shoulder. I glanced at Raikidan, whose brow creased with concern. "Are you okay, Eira?"

"Don't let him know."

I nodded. "I'm fine. Lost in thought. It's been a while since I was here last."

"Is that why you led us off the road?"

"I what?" I looked around to find he told the truth. The forest around us had thickened and the canopy choked out the sun. "Shit. Well, no going back now. Stay close to me. If you wander off you may have to deal with the Guardian, and you're not equipped with the knowledge to convince it you're not an enemy."

"What do you mean by 'guardian?'"

"They're ancient beings, created during the War of End to protect towns and villages. They're humanoid in shape, but featureless, and without emotion or independent thought outside their programming. Many would call them golems." I glanced his way. "The West Tribe has one to protect their people from invaders. They had more, but only one has survived the sands of time. It's programmed to attack outsiders who stray too far from the three main roads leading to the village."

"Sounds dangerous for those wandering the woods with no ill intent."

I nodded. "True, but the shamans have a safety measure in place in case that happens. Those trained in the way of the Guard are sent out on daily patrols, keeping an eye out for such situations. It also keeps poachers at bay, as this area is a prime target for wild game."

"So, say I did get separated from you, and it attacked me, h—"

"How would you fight it?" I chuckled. "By running. There isn't a mortal alive that could kill a Guardian on their own. A group may be able to do it, but due to their design, they can take all sorts of damage."

Raikidan's shoulders pulled back as he crossed his arms. "Don't underestimate us dragons. You nu-humans may be stronger than this human form I take, but even I know you'd struggle against me in my natural form."

I looked him up and down, a smirk spreading across my lips. "Of course, I've never fought a dragon, so you could be right. Though I doubt you'd make it out unscathed *if* you could take it out."

Raikidan's head lifted as he eyed me. "You tried to fight it once, didn't you? That's how you've come to your conclusions."

I held up my hands. "Guilty as charged. I stumbled upon the tribe by chance. A Hunter perused me through these woods when I stumbled upon a resident of the tribe. My presence, along with the Hunter's, called the Guardian to the very spot to protect the villager." I shook my head. "What a mess that was. But I learned quick how strong these creatures are, and will never make an attempt against one again if I can help it."

Movement in the forest caught our eyes. Raikidan's stance changed to a defensive one. I chuckled and shifted my path toward the movement.

"What are you doing?" he hissed. "You don't know what it is yet."

I snickered. "What are you, a dragon or a mouse?"

His eyes narrowed. "I'm trying to be sensible."

Several hundred feet away, a tall humanoid figure with a shadowy appearance came into view. Closing my eyes and placing my hand on my chest, I looked within myself until a pulsating warmth called to me. This warmth wasn't the same as the flame I contained in my body. I pushed the warmth into my chest while muttering an ancient incantation, mixing it with my flame, and then extracted it by forcing the will to my hand. Pulling my hand away, a red and white flame rested on my palm—fire mixed with spiritual energy. Several symbols of unknown origin to me rotated around the flame.

The figure drew closer, but I stayed put—even when it reached me and towered over me with its impressive size.

I grinned. "Hello, Guardian. It's been some time. I wasn't sure if you'd recognize me or not."

The featureless figure focused on Raikidan.

"He's with me. A visitor I accidentally led off the road."

The Guardian peered down at me again and then turned around, heading the way it came. I motioned Raikidan to follow and I set a pace behind the Guardian.

Raikidan bent closer to me. "Why are we following it?"

"It's going to show us back to the road."

"How do you know?"

"I was here long enough to understand its actions."

His brow rose. "Is that how you knew how to make that strange fire?"

I nodded. He accepted my answer, and the two of us followed the Guardian in silence. The forest eventually thinned again. When light from the sun was able to seep through the trees, the Guardian stopped. In front of us was the path we had wandered off. The figure stepped aside, motioning us to keep going.

"Thank you, Guardian," I said before continuing along the path.

"You're so polite to it," Raikidan said when the Guardian had disappeared from sight.

"It may not have independent thought from its programming, but it does remember allies and it has a tendency to favor them, prioritizing its favorites if multiple people are in trouble," I said. "I try to at least stay off the bottom of that list, just in case."

Raikidan chuckled as he bent closer to me. "Smart."

I pulled back, my brow creased. "Uh, personal space, remember?"

Raikidan smirked but said nothing. *Gods, his space issue is annoying.* He'd pushed this boundary many times on our excursion. He seemed to get some sort of sick enjoyment out of pushing my buttons this way. I hated it.

It wasn't long until the road brought us into a clearing. On the opposite side of the clearing, near a pond, an old man sat on a small stump, feeding bread crumbs to a pair of ducks, his pointed ears giving away his elven heritage. A smile spread across my lips as recognition dawned on me.

The ducks swam away at our approach and the old man turned to face us. "Visitors? How may I help—" His eyes widened. "E–Eira? Eira, is that you?"

I smiled at him. "Hey, Mel'ka."

His eyes welled up with tears. "You're alive... You're really alive!"

Mel'ka hobbled to me, and in his hunched-over state, wrapped his arms around my torso and buried his face into me. I continued to smile as I stroked his balding head. "I didn't think you'd miss me that much."

He peered up at me with tear-stained cheeks. "You're such a kind young lady. And you listened to my stories with more interest than anyone else in the village."

I chuckled, a few of my favorite stories by him coming to mind immediately. "Because you tell such great stories."

He reached up and ruffled my hair. "And you're good to your elders. Not enough young ones like that these days." He hooked my arm in his. "Now come. The others will be happy to know you're here, safe and sound. We've all been worried about you."

My eyes widened in surprise. I hadn't expected him to say that. "Everyone?"

He chuckled. "Well, Maka'shi doesn't count. I doubt she worries about anyone anymore." He shook his head. "She's not the woman she used to be. It's a shame."

I refrained to comment. I didn't have a high opinion of the half-elf woman. Leader of the West Shaman Tribe, and ice-touched, Maka'shi was anything but a pleasant woman. Unlike the average shaman, she mistrusted strangers and hated me in particular. If anyone would have a fit with my return, it'd be her.

The three of us walked for a few hundred yards, Mel'ka going into his story-teller mode. It was a story he'd told me more times than I wanted to count, but I enjoyed it. Raikidan even showed interest in the tale.

We emerged from the forest and came upon a new clearing with a small village nestled inside. The buildings had little pattern to their layout. Some stacked on top of each other, others with more room, and gardens or crop patches in need of daily tending. Shops had signs hanging above or next to their entrances and cobblestone paths connected them all.

Several people outside their homes looked our way, their faces expressing shock and... *happiness?* Before I knew it, shouts of excitement rang through the village. "Laz'shika has returned!" "Eira is back!" "Come quick!" People of all races rushed out of their homes, some staying by their doors to wave, others crowding us. The excited buzz of energy alive in these people dumbfounded me. I hadn't expected this reaction at all. It made it hard to figure out how I was to react myself. *It's overwhelming...*

"Excuse me!" came a voice in the crowed. "Excuse me, please let me through."

I know that voice! The crowd in front of me parted and a young human woman—about mid-twenties, with porcelain skin, stunning icy-blue eyes and long brown hair that curled in ringlets past her shoulders—rushed toward me. A small silver chain threaded through a ring hung around her neck as a type of necklace, as did another longer chain attached to a long, jagged, blue wire-wrapped crystal. The young woman's eyes welled up with tears when our eyes met. "Eira!"

"Valene..." Her presence stunned me to the point that I almost fell over as she crashed into me.

"You're alive." She sobbed. "You're here."

I shook myself and wrapped my arms around her. Standing a few inches taller than her, I pressed my face into the top of her head, inhaling her scent. My enhanced senses picked up her natural smell and the sweet aroma of various flowers I knew her to work with. A smile spread across my lips. "I'm so glad to see you."

I glanced up when another person pushed through the crowd and I smiled at the stout, pot-bellied human man with bronze skin. "Hey, Daren."

His hands flew up to his balding head and tears welled up in his blue eyes. "'Tis true. It really be ye, lass. Ye really be alive."

I shrugged, a small smile on my lips. "More or less."

Valene pulled away just as Daren rushed me. He pulled me into a tight embrace and spun us around. He laughed, Valene laughed, even I started to laugh. Soon, everyone around us laughed. It was a strange sound to me after all this time. *I almost forgot what it felt like.*

The laughter abruptly stopped, and Daren put me down. I looked at him, but found his gaze going elsewhere, his lips pressed together and his eyes tight. *Why does he look so nervous?*

Turning around, my eyes narrowed, and my lips slipped into a frown. The crowd had parted again, this time for a short woman with long white-blue hair and light skin. She had two blue painted dots on her forehead as well as a stripe that ran down her lip to her chin. "I should have known it was you, Maka'shi. Only you have the ability to kill joy by entering a room, or a crowd, in this case."

Maka'shi held her head high, her hair falling back enough to reveal slightly elongated ears, a telling sign of her mixed human and elf heritage. "Your manners are as poor as ever, Laz'shika."

I snorted at the short, self-important elf. "We've never been buddies, so why pretend now?"

A pleased smile spread across her lips. "Yes, that's true. Now, care to tell me why you've returned after five years?"

So, I have been gone that long. I thought I had lost count of the number of seasons that had passed. "I'm returning to Dalatrend to deal with my problems. I left some things here and had hoped to retrieve them."

She regarded me for a moment. "You're not running away anymore? That's new for you."

My eyes narrowed. Several townspeople murmured amongst themselves, their disapproval apparent in their tones. Maka'shi looked past me. "I'm guessing your friend there has something to do with this change?"

I cranked my neck to glance over my shoulder at Raikidan. He watched her with a cautious eye. "Yes. Raikidan has offered his assistance. He has skills that may help us turn the tides against Zarda."

Maka'shi eyed him a bit longer, then focused on me. "Are you still hunted?"

I nodded; this wasn't the time to lie. "The number of Hunters has slowed over the years, but they're still after me."

"Then you will be gone by sundown."

The people around us gasped and murmured amongst themselves. Valene stomped her foot and rose her voice so Maka'shi couldn't ignore her, surprising me. "That's not fair! She just got back. We all missed her."

Maka'shi held firm. "Do not forget, Valene, she's the reason this village suffered five years ago. Why you suffered memory loss, and why we lost so many lives. Even Xye!"

My blood ran cold. *She's lying... he didn't...*

"Don't you dare!" Valene shouted. "He followed her when she told him not to. That was his fault, not hers."

Maka'shi pointed to me. "She caused that attack. Had she not been here, he'd still be alive."

"Had she not been here, three years before, he would have fallen off that cliff while foraging and died! You don't have the power to predict who will live and die."

The crowd murmured in agreement, but I knew Maka'shi wouldn't budge. I didn't expect her to. She was right. Had I not stayed here, the village wouldn't have come under attack.

"That is enough, Valene. Your leader has spoken. I wasn't planning to stay long anyway. To be frank, I didn't expect such a warm welcome."

Daren placed a hand on my shoulder. "Lass, we dinnae hate ye for what happened. Now, enough o' this nonsense. Ye be stayin' for one night at least. Rest those tired bones an'"—he looked me up and down—"get a proper meal in ye. Ye be too skinny, lass."

I couldn't help but laugh. "You always say that."

"Aye, but it be even more true now."

Maka'shi's eyes darkened. "I have made my stance clear. She and her companion are to leave by sundown."

Raikidan let out a deep sigh no one could miss. I looked at him to find him with arms crossed with a bored expression as he leaned back on his heels. "Are you almost done, Eira? I'd like to get off my feet after walking for as long as we did."

Daren slapped me on the back. "Hear that? The lad be tired. We cannae turn him down now, can we, Maka'shi? He be a weary traveler, after all."

Maka'shi sucked in a tight breath, her fingers curling. I glanced between the two men and noticed the glint of amusement in Raikidan's eyes. *Cheeky dragon!* I wasn't sure how much he knew of shaman customs, but he rightly guessed them to be hospitable to travelers. Thanks to Zarda, Lumaraeon was on the fringe of war again. Travelers weren't all that common these days, but the shamans did their best to welcome them when they could. Maka'shi trusted few, and tended to scare away most travelers, but the people of the village weren't like that… for the most part.

"Very well," Maka'shi said through tight teeth. "One night. That is all I'll permit."

She then spun on her heels and left. The people around us cheered, and many of them welcomed me back before they dispersed.

Valene squealed and latched onto my arm. "I'm so happy! You'll have to have dinner with us, and I'll get your room at the inn ready." She looked at Raikidan, assessing him with her eyes. "Daren decided to renovate most of them, so your friend will have to share a room with you."

"That's fine." She raised a brow at me and I shook my head. "Don't go there. It's not like that."

She chuckled. "I guess you haven't changed *that* much." She glanced back at Raikidan, a small smirk spreading across her lips. Her gaze lingered on him for a few moments before she pulled me toward the inn.

I wanted to take in the town, see how well it had recovered in the last few years, but Maka'shi's words plagued me. "Valene…" She looked at me. "Is it true, about Xye?"

She frowned, her gaze lowering to the ground. "Yes. He didn't listen to you when you told him to stay put."

My gaze fell. *I can't believe… he's gone… That idiot!* "I need to find Shva'sika."

"She's not in town," Valene said. "She left a few weeks ago to visit with some of her family up north."

"The lass should be back in a day or two," Daren said. "Ye can talk tae 'er then."

"Only if she returns before I leave."

He chuckled. "Maka'shi may be our leader, but even ye know she won't have the power to send ye away as long as the rest o' us want ye here."

A warm sensation spread through my chest, bringing a small smile to my lips. "Thank you."

The area around us opened up and I spotted Maka'shi. She stood in the center of the clearing, her hands held up to an enormous glowing crystal that hovered above the ground in an elegant wooden structure that acted as an accent, and neither a cage nor a dais. In my time spent here, I never learned how the crystal defied gravity, but I suspected it had to do with the type of energy that poured out of it.

"What is Maka'shi doing over at the Spiritual Crystal?" I asked.

Valene glanced over at the half-elf. "Seeking answers or something like that. There's rarely a time she's not there anymore. Lot of good it does her."

I watched her, noting the blank gaze as if her mind had all been vanquished from her body. "I suppose at this point, it's best to let her do her crazy bitch thing."

Valene giggled and nodded.

The four of us came to a large two-story rustic building. From the outside it looked cozy, snug, and inviting. Daren opened one of the double doors and Valene led us inside. To the left was the common gathering area, filled with chairs, couches, stocked bookshelves, and a cozy fireplace. To our right, rows of well-crafted tables and chairs filled the dining area, and a bar set in the back to serve patrons. Large chandeliers hung from the ceiling and paintings filled the walls, all of landscapes found across Lumaraeon. Tucked away beyond the common area, on a far wall, was a staircase leading up to the second floor, and behind the bar was a door that I knew led to the spacious kitchen Daren hardly left.

"I see you did some redecorating," I said as I peered around.

Daren chuckled. "Valene's idea."

Valene crossed her arms, her lower lip sticking out. "Too bad we don't get enough visitors to enjoy it."

I patted her on the shoulder. "One of these days that will change. I promise."

She nodded, a big smile on her face. "I'm going to go prepare that room for you."

She ran off, leaving Raikidan and me with Daren, who was already heading for the kitchen. I chose to follow. "If you need help with food prep, I'd be happy to."

The corners of Daren's eyes crinkled as he smiled. "I wouldn't say nae tae ye help, lass."

Once in the spacious kitchen, Daren rattled off the ingredients he'd need for our meals and I went to retrieve them. The two of us fell into casual conversation, as if no time had passed. I'd always gotten along with Daren—hard not to with a man as genuinely kind as him. I swore there was no harsh bone in his body. No matter how badly you treated him, he would always smile and welcome you back.

Daren wasn't a native of the town; he had stumbled upon it by accident like myself. He fit well with the people, though, and worked with the inn's previous owner, taking it over when she retired. Valene's mother, Valessa, had arrived in town sometime after that and the two became good friends. She'd already been pregnant with Valene at the time, and while the two had shown interest in each other, they'd done nothing about it for over a decade. In that time, Daren had taken Valene under his wing, and when Valessa had died of an incurable illness, he naturally took her in.

Daren glanced back at Raikidan. "Tell me about yer friend over there."

I looked back to find Raikidan still leaning against a wall, watching us work. "He's not a friend."

Daren's brow rose, but Raikidan cut in before he could ask questions. "We've agreed to help each other. We haven't known each other long, so there's only a basic trust here."

My culinary companion looked between us, shrugged, and went back to cooking. I would have gone back to my prep work, but Valene entered the room. She took immediate notice of Raikidan, but he didn't pay her much mind. *Anyone can see where this is going. I'll have to make sure she understands it's best to set her eyes on someone else.*

"Room all set now?"

She nodded. "It was the one you used the last time you were here. I've kept that one clean, so it wasn't hard tidying up." She peered at the work Daren and I had accomplished. "I see Daren still isn't letting you cook."

I let out a short laugh and finished slicing a potato. "We all know I'm a terrible cook."

Daren regarded me for a moment. "Ye are not terrible."

Valene sputtered a laugh. "Yeah, right. We all know you say that to be nice." She gazed at me tentatively. "I was going to go to my mom's garden to pick some flowers to have as a table setting. Want to join me?"

I slipped the sliced up root vegetable into a bowl. "I'd be happy to."

4
CHAPTER

Valene led the way through a small path in the forest. Daren had wrangled Raikidan into helping him cook, though Valene and I got a good laugh when he admitted he didn't know the first thing about food prep, let alone cooking, and yet Daren insisted he'd still be of some use. This allowed Valene and me some much needed time together.

The Guardian had stopped by to assess our presence, but we sent him along rather quickly. The brunette hummed a tune that made me smile. I was glad to see her so happy. She'd lost much in her twenty-some years; I thought one day that joy would disappear.

The trees around us thinned and then opened up. My breath caught at the sight before us—a gorgeous meadow filled with all sorts of flowers and trees. The sweet aroma of the "garden" wafted into my nose. While Valene called it a garden, which wasn't untrue for someone touched by the elements of earth, most would find it too large to be one. "It doesn't look any different than the day I left."

Valene's smile on her face widened, her eyes shining. "You mean it?"

I nodded as I smiled back at her. "You've done a wonderful job taking up this task. I'm sure she's proud of you."

Valene gazed out at the meadow. "I hope so. I've tried so hard to follow her notes she left me. I've managed some things, but there are others that I'm struggling with." She looked at me. "I'm trying to make fragrances like her too. They're not as good, but people like them, so I know I'm on the right track."

I watched her for a moment. "Maka'shi said something about memory loss. I'm guessing it was when that Hunter attacked you. Is it the source of your struggle?"

She nodded slowly. "I had gaping holes in my memory. I couldn't remember how to walk the spiritual plane, work with the elements, or even remember certain people's names." Her eyes welled up with tears. "I even forgot what my mother looked like. Over the years it's come back in pieces, but I still can't remember her face. I remembered you quicker than her." She peered up at me, tears streaming down her cheeks. "How horrible of a daughter am I that I can't even remember her face?"

I cupped her cheek with my hand and wiped a tear away with my thumb. "Don't be like that. It's not your fault."

"I hate myself! She tried so hard to raise me and I can't even remember her face." Valene looked away from me. "I'm so ashamed I can't even bear the thought of visiting her on the spiritual plane."

I frowned and placed my hand on her shoulder. "Do you remember me telling you about my mother?"

She nodded. "I remember a little. You said you're one of the few who got to know their mother and you lost her some time ago, right?"

"Yes. So long ago that the only things that remind me of her face are my memories, and a photograph I have of her. But memories are fragile, and I don't have that photograph on me anymore. Her face has started to fade from my mind after all these years. Does it upset me? Of course. But I'm not going to beat myself up over it. My mother would understand that memories are fragile and they fade. She wouldn't hold it against me for naturally forgetting, because she loved me."

I pulled Valene closer and held her against me, stroking her hair. "Just as Valessa loved you. You meant more to her than Lumaraeon itself."

Valene wrapped her arms around me and buried her face into my chest. "Thank you."

The two of us remained in this position for a few moments longer until she pulled away, wiping away her tears and taking in a deep breath. "I missed having you around to confide in. Life has been a little lonely without you."

I poked her in the side. "You sure? 'Cause I'm sure you don't miss how much of a pain in the ass I can be."

She giggled. "Yeah, I'm sure." She touched the necklace with the wrapped stone. "I couldn't bear to take this off when I remembered you. It's one of the few things you were able to give me that hasn't gone missing over the years."

I smiled. "I'm glad you still love it. I remember the smile you had that whole week after I gave it to you. I think you showed everyone in town your new gift, at least three times."

Valene laughed. "Only three?"

I laughed as well and then looked around. "We should probably get to picking flowers."

"Yeah, I guess you're right. What do you think of a vase filled with flowers that will compliment honeysuckle? I know they're your favorite."

I nodded. "I don't hate that idea."

She smiled wide and ran off. I went my own way, looking for any flowers that caught my eyes. Valene knew the best ones for floral arrangements, but even if I picked some that wouldn't work, she'd use them for something else.

I cut several stems of stargazer lilies and found a patch of freesia. I had a particular fondness for those two, along with honeysuckle and hyacinth. I plucked a few stems and inhaled the lovely scent. *So beautiful…*

I then stood, planning to find Valene, only for my attention to be caught by a rose bush. Well, bush wasn't the right word. Tree was really the right word for what this was, and not just any type of tree. The roses this tree produced were black with red tips. I had never seen such a color on a growing bush, or in this case, tree. Valessa had shown me a special species of rose that produced orange-yellow flowers with dark orange tips, and another that produced white with dark red tips. She even showed me how she prepared certain white flowers with colored water to make unnatural colored flowers to sell, but never had I seen a rose like these ones. I walked closer and reached up to touch the petals to find them velvet soft. *Well, it's real, so how is it done?*

"Beautiful, isn't it?" I glanced back at Valene, who carried an armful of flowers. "Mother's book talks about this tree. She searched high and low for the right place to start up a field with any flora she could possibly need. One day she came across this meadow. It had all sorts of beautiful wild flowers—and this rose tree. She had no idea why it was here, how it came to have such a unique coloring, but something told her she had finally found what she had been seeking."

She touched the leaves.

"Her notes go on about how she had her ups and downs during her training—how she would struggle to keep certain flowers alive while making others grow too much. Yet through it all, this rose bush remained the same, as if to encourage her to keep trying. It definitely helped. Everyone says how great of an earth shaman she was, and so many earth shamans strive to be as good as her. Even though my memory is damaged, I do have a vague memory of her working."

Valene smiled.

"I was supposed to be studying, but I didn't want to because it was boring, and I wanted to be doing what she was doing. I knew she'd get upset if she found out, so I quietly peered around the doorframe of the root cellar watching her. She was so happy, humming away while she worked. That memory keeps me following the same path she walked."

I couldn't help but smile. "I don't doubt you'll be able to do even greater things than she ever could."

"You mean it?"

"Of course I do."

She smiled. "Thanks." She then frowned. "I wish I could remember what happened after that memory. I don't know if she ever caught me or not."

"I did." I tried not to react to the ghostly voice. I didn't need to scare Valene. I was sure it was too soon for her to know her mother was around. *"And I wasn't mad in the least."*

Valene smiled at me. "You can take a rose or two off. I haven't taken any in some time, so it'll be good for it."

I nodded my thanks and drew a dagger to cut off a flower with the stem attached and carefully went about removing the thorns. The light scent of the flora teased my senses, drawing up memories of the times I'd worked in my own greenhouse back in Dalatrend. A gift from Zane in hopes it'd help my damaged mental state. In some ways he was right, it had helped. But mostly, it gave me something to do that didn't relate to killing people.

The memory bought Ryoko and Rylan to mind. Two of the most important people to me. I wondered how they were doing. The urge to check my bond with Rylan struck me hard all of a sudden, but I knew it was a futile effort. An experimental fabrication on Zarda's part to connect his creations mentally, had been deemed a failure project and resulted in only being a problem for Rylan and me. Rarely had it ever been useful, and over this time of separation from him, I'd found it had deteriorated. Not enough for me to forget it stopped existing—no, that obnoxious bubbling sensation in the back of my head still endured—but it was reduced enough for me to easily ignore it was even placed in me.

In the past, I'd have been relieved. Now, even as much as I hated the bond, I wished I could have it back in this moment to check in on him. Even if only to sense a little bit from him to know he was okay.

Suddenly, my thoughts spiraled. *Is the bond's breakdown a sign I've been willfully ignoring?* I wanted my freedom—wanted to live without looking over my shoulder—but was I really meant to have that? Was it right going back to Dalatrend? Was I meant to deal with Zarda? *Is it even right to involve a dragon into such affairs?* Raikidan may have offered his services on his own volition, for whatever messed up reason he had, that didn't mean I should have agreed to drag him into a human's mess.

My mind continued its downward decent, memories of the past rising up with the uncertainly raging in my head. And, unsurprisingly, the negative thoughts and memories came to... *him.*

Warm smile, deep caring eyes, a voice so soothing—pain pulsed in my chest, and I desperately wished to banish the memories—forget that pain and regret.

"Eira?" Valene's voice cut into the spiraling haze of my mind. "Eira, you okay?"

I blinked, my head returning to reality. Valene had bent forward to get a better look at me. I forced a smile, mentally banishing any lingering memories swirling in my mind. "Sorry. One of my... moments. I'm good now."

Valene frowned. "Okay, if you're sure."

I finished removing the last two thorns from the rose, and I tucked it behind my ear. In the past I would have never considered of putting a flower in my hair. It'd tempt me to feel more beautiful than I had a right to be, but today I allowed it.

I jerked my head as I walked away. "Let's head back. Unless you think we need more flowers."

Valene looked at the rose tree as she tucked her hair behind her ear, revealing an ear that was slightly different from that of an ordinary human ear. They were small, like those of an ordinary human, but they were shaped similarly to that of a nu-human.

"Does Valene know anything about her father?"

"No, and I would prefer to keep it that way. I may have come to terms with him leaving, but he chose not to be part of our lives. She doesn't need him."

"He wasn't an ordinary human, was he?"

To someone with little to no racial knowledge, they may not notice, or think she was a half-elf. But I knew better.

Valene, satisfied with whatever she saw in the tree, nodded in acknowledgement and joined me by my side. "I have a question. Is it still okay for me to call you Laz?"

"Laz, Laz, Laz, Laz, Laz. Have fun training, Laz!"

She turned her gaze away. "I know only certain people get to call you that, and it's been so long…"

I ruffled her hair. "Of course you can."

She smiled wide and the two of us headed back to the inn. When we arrived, there were quite a few more bodies inside the common area than before. Several men and boys of elven decent with a mix of umber and olive skin tones, eight in total, lounged about—some on the tables, while others were on actual furniture. Several of the men had looks similar to those of the shaman tribe to the south—tattoos, piercings, and partially shaven heads and all. All of them noticed us immediately, and we were accosted by excited shouts of "Eira!" and "Laz'shika!".

Valene glanced my way, a smirk on her lips. "Someone is popular with the men these days." I rolled my eyes and she looked at the men sitting on the tables. "Unfortunately, some of these men have no manners. Off the tables! I know your mother taught you better than that."

The lot of them grumbled but complied with her order. A whimsical laugh came from the kitchen and moments later a lithe elven woman with umber skin and ash brown hair decorated with colorful feathers entered the common area, carrying a large tray of food. A young boy, no older than six, tagged along, his hand clutching her dress. "Yes, as a matter of fact I did." The woman set down the tray and smiled at me. "Welcome back, Eira."

I smiled. "Thanks, Alena. It's good to see you." My eyes scanned over the others. "All of you. Though I see a few are missing, as is your father."

"I'm afraid Del'karo is off on a job and won't be back for some time," Alena said. "He brought two of our sons with him to gain experience."

I counted how many children they had, an absurd number if you asked me, especially for elves. "You're still missing one."

She nodded. "Ne'kall. He's decided to stay in the South Tribe. We visit him every now and then; Del'karo more so as his jobs allow for that. He's happy and his family is healthy and doing well."

I approached her, placing the flowers I had down on the table. "That's good. I know his mysterious disappearance only to reappear married all those years ago set a wedge between you two I thought would never mend."

Her eyes twinkled, and her lips turned up. "Yes, well he's now the first to make me a grandmother, so I have to forgive him." I laughed and the two of us embraced. A rush of familiarity ran through me. I missed her hugs. They reminded me a lot of my own mother's embraces.

Alena squinted her eyes at some of her other older sons. "Now if only some of my other boys would follow his lead and find someone to settle down with so I can free up some space in my home."

Several hung their heads with a sigh while others rolled their eyes. I laughed, understanding the complexity of elven families to some degree. "Well, they can't take all the blame. You and Del'karo reproduce like rabbits."

The room roared with laughter. Even Alena found my words funny. Though the young boy with her was another story. "Don't say mean things about my mommy!"

Alena patted him on the head. "She's not being mean, sweetie, don't worry."

I crouched down to get a good look at the boy. He shared many features of his father, with the lighter olive skin tone and black and red hair, but had his mother's eyes. The young boy tried to be brave and meet my stare, but the longer I watched him, the more his nerves took over, and in the end, he hid behind his mother. "You've gotten big, Sethal. You weren't even old enough to walk when I last saw you."

He peeked around his mother but still remained shy. I smiled and held a bent finger up to my lips to discretely pull an ember from my mouth. With a flick of the wrist I controlled the fire to take the shape of a butterfly. Sethal's eyes went wide. "You make fire like Daddy and big brother Ne'kall."

I smirked. "Your father taught me all sorts of tricks to control my fire. And I used to tussle with your brother from time to time before he left."

He stared at me with eyes filled with awe and wonder. Before I could do much else to impress the child, one of his older brothers came up and pulled me to my feet in a headlock. "Yeah, now she gets to deal with the rest of us."

I pulled against his grip, though not putting a whole lot into the effort. "Better let go, Tesne, or you'll regret it."

"You may be a nu-human, but I've been training as a Guard for some time. I can handle you."

I chuckled. "Suit yourself."

No longer holding back, I easily pulled myself out of his grip and tackled him, pinning him to the ground. He struggled, but was no match for my nu-human enhancements.

"Brother, I'll save you!" Sethal declared before jumping on my back.

I cried out in fake pain as he wrapped his little arms around my neck and rolled off Tesne, careful not to crush the young boy latched onto me. "Too strong!"

Sethal held on tighter as I moved around. He giggled the longer he managed to stay locked in place, and I couldn't stop myself from laughing. Eventually I managed to grab onto him and pulled him into my lap. He looked up at me with squinted eyes; a large toothy grin spread across his face.

My attention was pulled from him when someone exited the kitchen. Raikidan, a platter of food in his hands, watched us all. "Is that dinner?"

He glanced at the food. "No. It's a snack. Or so Daren says."

A snack? I sighed and raised my voice so Daren could hear me. "Daren, you'd better not be going overboard!"

"I never go overboard, lass," Daren called back.

I pinched my nose, my voice lowering. "Meaning you're going over-board and we're going to be waiting a while." I moved Sethal from my lap and stood. "I'm going to use this time to wash up, then. I could use a warm bath."

The boy elf frowned. "Aww, but I want to keep playing."

I rubbed his head. "We will. I just need to take the time to not smell like a three-week-old fish locker."

The men around me roared with laughter. Valene, who had gone about making her floral arrangements, looked up from her work. "Oh please, Laz. You smell fine, especially for someone who has been on the run. You look like you haven't brushed your hair or eaten a good meal in some time, but that's to be expected. Trust me, if you smelled like a fish locker, I would have made you bathe hours ago."

I scratched my head. "Yeah, well, I'd still like to enjoy a hot bath. It's been too long."

"I need to speak to you in private anyway, Eira," Raikidan said.

What did he want to talk to me about?

Valene took great interest in the mini exchange. "Give me another three seconds and I'll have a floral arrangement for you to bring upstairs."

I nodded and she ran off into the kitchen.

"Oh, Eira, before you go," Alena said. "I'd like your input. I told your friend here that he could benefit from a haircut, to blend in better to the city, if him being human won't be an issue in itself. But he wasn't sure on the idea. What do you think?"

I shrugged. "It's up to him. You'll find all kinds of people in the city, so he could wear it however he likes, and no one would bat an eye."

"With his facial structure, though, wouldn't you say shorter hair would be better?"

"I've seen men with his structure pull off long hair. I'm honestly indifferent to all this."

She looked to Raikidan. "Well, if you change your mind, I have plenty of experience handling hair. I never thought having boys would require such skills, but here we are."

I snickered when some of her sons—who were known for changing their hair styles often—rolled their eyes.

Valene returned with a small glass vase filled with water. Arranging some lilies with a few other flora, she handed the arrangement to Raikidan with a smile. He took them, but clearly wasn't picking up on her cues, disappointing her. Raikidan walked over to me and handed the vase off, Valene's mood souring even more. *Yep, definitely have to talk to her.*

Now holding the flower arrangement, I headed upstairs. Raikidan followed, glancing back behind us a few times. When we were sufficiently away from the others, he spoke, but with a lowered voice. "What's up with that female you know? She's acting weird around me."

"So, you have noticed. I was starting to wonder." I chuckled. "She has a small crush on you. Don't worry about it, though. I'll set her straight without revealing what you are."

His brow wrinkled in confusion. "What is a 'crush?'"

I shook my head slightly. "It's when you're attracted to someone in some way and wish to pursue it, but aren't ready to find out if they would like to have a relationship of that level with you."

"Oh, we don't do that, so that doesn't make sense to me."

"Don't you start asking questions," the voice in my head warned. *"You risk attachment."*

I pursed my lips, my curiosity getting the better of me. "So, how does it work for you? You find a dragon with good genetic qualities you wish to procreate with and then go your separate ways?"

His face twisted, and his upper lip curled as if he took offense to my words. "No. We're strictly monogamous. We just know our perfect match when we meet them."

"Uh huh…" I had a hard time believing any of that.

Raikidan eyed me for a moment. "Humans aren't monogamous?"

I shrugged. "Some are, some aren't. It's a matter of choice or tradition for us. And some are better at it than others."

He watched me, but didn't say anything as we reached the top of the stairs. There was nothing special about the second floor—a long hallway with several doors leading to rooms. I opened the first one on the right and entered the room. It didn't look any different from when I'd been here last.

The room was a moderate size, with tan walls, king size bed, and a bookshelf and vanity on a far wall, adorned with a red-curtained window looking out into the town. To my right was the door to the bathroom.

I placed the vase of flowers down on the vanity and sat down on the bed, already relishing the soft surface. "So, you wanted to talk to me before I disappeared for my much-needed bath."

He leaned against a wall nearby. "For someone who says they are incapable of feeling happiness, you do a lot around these people. You have rarely stopped smiling, and I heard you laugh for the first time."

"You fool. You got careless."

Shit... I shrugged. "I've learned to fake such things. It keeps others off my back. I pretend I'm someone I'm not, and no one bothers me."

My dragon companion narrowed his eyes. "You really expect me to believe that?"

I got to my feet and peered out the window. "Do, don't, I don't care either way. It doesn't change anything. You just become like the others. Thinking you know me when you don't, or thinking you can change me as if I'm fixable. Reality is, there is no fixing me. I came to terms with that a long time ago."

A long silence filled the air until Raikidan spoke again. "The brood-mother downstairs... was she correct in telling me I'd blend in better if I cut my hair?"

I looked back at him. "Broodmother? Are you talking about Alena?" He nodded and I chuckled. "We really need to work on your vocabulary. That would help you blend in better than a haircut. And a race change, too."

"I still need time to understand your nu-human form. Shouldn't be much longer."

I nodded. "Good. I don't want your lack of understanding to get in the way of the goal."

He watched me for a moment. "Would it please you if I cut my hair?"

His question took me aback. *Why did he go back to this? And why is he concerned about my opinion on the matter?* "Like I told Alena, I don't care either way. It's your hair. I don't know why it's such a big concern to you."

Raikidan averted his gaze. "If I cut it, it won't grow back. It's a one-shot deal."

My brow furrowed. "What?"

"Our hair stops growing two decades after adolescence." He rubbed the small bit of facial hair on his chin. "That's how I ended up with this. I didn't like the full beard, so my mother took a blade to it and cut most of it off. This wasn't so bad, so I kept it."

I cocked my head and crossed my arms. "Well, that explains why I've never seen five o' clock shadow on your face these past few days."

I approached him. "If you're nervous about the outcome, Alena is good at styling hair. She's had a lot of practice and she knows all types of hairstyles, including common ones worn in cities." I smirked. "I'm guessing you don't want a mohawk or partially shaven head like some of her kids. Rest assured, if that's not what you want, she'll listen."

Before I made it to him, I turned for the bathroom. "I'm not going to tell you what to do with your hair. That is solely your choice, and not my business to stick my nose into."

I closed the door behind me, immersing myself in the steam-filled room. Unlike the modern look to the bedroom, the bath had a natural appearance. Vines crawled up the stone walls, and the floor was made up of natural soil with beautiful plants growing from it. The small cobblestone path I stood on led to a stone bathing pool and a close-by stone sink with a pile of fresh towels and mirrors that were wrapped in what appeared to be roots.

Topping off the bizarre but spectacular view was the room's main light source; an artificially placed natural light that closely resembled the sun. Thinking back, I remembered the baths in this village were all like this, and at night, the light source would become a full moon. I had always wondered how they did it.

I headed over to the mirror display first to get a good look at my condition. I groaned at the mess before me. My usually bright, gold-ringed, emerald-green eyes were now dull, and my violet hair was losing its luster. I looked pale and malnourished, and I had dark shadows under my eyes. My paler-than-normal complexion made the freckles that banded across my nose and around my shoulders stand out even more. *One look at me and you'd know I've been running for a while.*

Pushing away from the sink, I stripped off my tattered clothing and sank into the warm bath water. A content sigh escaped my lips. Grabbing the nearby shampoo, I lathered up my hair. The packed soil and natural oils loosened from my hair, and I enjoyed the floral scent of the shampoo wafting into my nose. As I cleaned my hair, I started to hum.

At first, I hummed only random notes, but they soon came together and formed the one song I knew well. My voice echoed around the room, giving me a sense of comfort. I just hoped, if he'd stalled in leaving the room, Raikidan couldn't hear me. I wasn't the type to sing around others, but when I was alone, I was more than happy to, especially this particular song.

After some time, I didn't know how long I had been in the bath, but I realized I was taking longer than necessary when I had gone through the song for the tenth time or so, and my fingers had become prune-like. Sighing, I reluctantly climbed out of the bath and grabbed a towel. Wrapping the towel around my body, I retrieved my clothes and washed them as best I could.

I entered the bedroom as I carefully dried my clothes with fire, to find Raikidan hadn't left the room like I'd expected him to. He sat on the bed, looking out the window, but his attention snapped to me the moment I entered.

He raised an eyebrow at my appearance and then held up a bundle of clothes. "These are for you. That Valene woman came up, said they belonged to you once… I think."

I chuckled. I suspected he hadn't listened to everything she'd said. She had a tendency to ramble when she crushed on a guy. I really needed to set her straight.

"Oh, she also said that some of your things are in the possession of some other woman. She suspects they're the items you're here to get before we head to the city." *Gods, I hope he's not talking about Maka'shi.* I really didn't want to deal with her. "A woman you two mentioned before. Shva… something-or-other."

I laughed. "Well, I can honestly say that was the most half-assed attempt I've ever heard. Her name is Shva'sika, and I'm glad that she has my things as opposed to Maka'shi. At least it means I'll get them back. Though, depending on when she returns, I might make myself an even bigger enemy of Maka'shi's."

"What is with the two of you anyway?" he asked.

I shook my head. "You don't want to get yourself involved with that mess. It makes no sense, and it's just not worth your time."

Raikidan nodded and handed the clothes to me, but when I took them, his expression changed to one of interest and slight confusion. He leaned in close to me and smelled the top of my head.

Perturbed, I jerked back. "What the hell are you doing? Personal space."

"You smell different. Not a lot, but it's noticeable."

"It's the scented shampoo."

"Shampoo?"

"It's a product that helps clean hair. Most are scented as well."

He tried to smell my head again, but I pushed him away. "I said personal space! You can't just go up and smell random people."

He frowned. "But you're not random."

I pinched my nose. He had a point, but it didn't make his actions any less weird. "Regardless of that, you still can't go up and smell people without their permission. It's creepy."

"I'm just trying to figure out why it's such a subtle but powerful change. It's as if it's made of what you smell like."

I tilted my head. "Is your sense of smell different in your natural form compared to this human one?"

He nodded. "It's not as strong, but it's strong enough."

"Then you'll like the nu-human form. Our sense of smell is better than an ordinary human."

He tilted his head and eyed me for a moment. "How so?"

I leaned against the vanity, double-checking to be sure my towel was secure. "At a relatively close proximity, I can take your smell and break it up into layers that I can associate with other outside sources. Like, since you use fire, you have a sooty-ash smell mixed into your musky smell that most men have. There's also a scent layer of mountain pines and petrichor, all coming from where you live, and you have a similar reptilian smell that the grekeleons have, but it's also different. It has the smell of the sky mixed into it. And yes, I know, the sky doesn't technically have a smell, but trust me, that's the image I get from this part of that scent. Your dragon scent is so new to me I really can't describe it any other way."

His eyes widened with surprise. "You picked all that up?"

I nodded. "You also have a slight floral scent, like honeysuckle, that sticks to you better than the forest smells. That tells me it's part of your natural smells that won't go away when you reside in a different environment for a long period of time."

"Why honeysuckle, though?" he murmured, almost as if he were talking to himself. "There's quite a bit in my territory, but..."

I shrugged. "Everyone has a unique part to their scent. Some have a floral scent, some fruity, and some have a scent that's way out in left field."

Raikidan's brow rose. "What?"

I shook my head and opened the door. "Human expression. Don't worry about it."

He thought about this for a moment. "You, too, have that ash smell, though knowing you have control over fire, it doesn't surprise me. But there's a lighter smell I'm trying to identify."

I regarded him for a moment. I couldn't figure out why he was so hung up about this, but it got my curiosity ramped up into high gear. "Why not try to take a nu-human shape? Just for a moment to see if you can maintain it with the information you have?"

Raikidan rubbed his chin and then nodded. He closed his eyes and after few moments of silence, his ears elongated before my very eyes. Nothing else about his… impressive… physical appearance changed, but the difference was more internal than external.

My dragon ally opened his eyes and took in our surroundings, his eyes widening. "If I got this right, this is far different than the other human shape."

I tilted my head. "Tell me what you're experiencing."

"My eyes are far crisper. And I can hear much farther. It's much closer to my natural form."

I nodded. "Sounds like you got those two right."

He stared at me. "I can pick your scent up better, like you said. I catch the smell of deciduous trees because of the surrounding forest of this place and of my territory." His brow furrowed. "But that shampoo scent still has me confused due to other scents I'm picking up on you."

"Watch yourself around him."

Raikidan came over to me. He leaned in, though he passed my head and aimed for more of my neck area, making me tense. A lump formed in my throat that I didn't like. I went to move away, but Raikidan placed a hand on my arm and took a deep whiff of the scent by my neck. "There it is. It's a light but sweet floral scent."

Light and sweet? What flora had that kind of scent?

"I believe it's freesia." He pulled away and pointed to the vase of flowers. "I smell it coming from that."

Freesia had a very unique scent that was hard to describe. I would have described it as a mix of clean sheeting in the wind, strawberries, and a hint of honeysuckle. But Raikidan came off as more simple in thought, so his description worked, too. *He really thinks he detects freesia as a scent?* "Well, the scent for the shampoo is freesia…"

"That explains why it confused me, since it's enhancing your natural smell." He tilted his head. "You look confused."

I shrugged. "It's nothing. In this form, are you able to pick up anything else?"

He shook his head. "That's the one that confused me."

I held my chin between my index finger and thumb. That couldn't be right. He had to smell something else.

Raikidan narrowed his eyes. "Are you expecting something more? Or are you unhappy with the scents I mentioned?"

"No, it's not that. I don't think you've perfected the form. You should be able to pick up a racial smell."

"Oh, I do smell that. You smell human for sure, like the young woman downstairs."

I nodded. "Since humans and nu-humans are technically the same species, that makes sense."

He stroked his chin. "But now that you bring it up, there is something different about your smell. It's odd, but it smells reptilian."

"That's weird." I shrugged. "But maybe it's something I picked up from being around you."

"Maybe…" His trailing words caught my attention, but his eyes showed his mind had gone somewhere else.

I took a deep breath. "You should either wash up or leave, because I'm going to change, and you're not allowed to be in here while I do."

Raikidan's brow furrowed. "Why?"

"Because I demand my privacy when dressing." I pointed toward the two doors. "Now go."

His face stayed scrunched in confusion, but he did as told. Before disappearing into the bathroom, however, he cast a glance back over his shoulder. "I've decided to allow your broodmother friend to cut my hair as long as she doesn't make me look stupid. Would you tell her that for me?"

A strained breath left my lips. "Just call her a mother so your cover isn't blown, and yes, I will do that."

He nodded his thanks, his ears going back to a human look, and shut the door behind him. I let out a heavy sigh and leaned on the vanity. That had been one hell of a conversation. I gazed down at the flower arrangement, my eyes pinning on the freesia Valene had tucked in.

"*...a light but sweet floral scent...*" Did he really think I smelled like this flower? I looked at my hand and flexed it. *At least it's what he focused on. And it's good that I smell mostly human...* I didn't need any unwanted questions to come up. They'd complicate matters and there were some truths that were better left buried. *I especially don't need a dragon such as himself finding out these truths.* If I had to lie to him to keep them safe, then so be it. *It's not like I haven't given him a few already.*

"*He's smarter than he looks, though,*" the voice in my head warned. "*You need to be extra careful.*"

I did need to be more careful. Dropping my towel, I went about changing into the clothes Valene had brought up for me. I pulled out a hairbrush from the vanity drawer and brushed my tangled hair, drying it with a bit of fire at the same time. Once I threw my hair back up into my hairclip, I went through a small pouch containing earrings. Most belonged to me, others I guessed she'd thrown in as a gift. Pulling out small gold hoops and gemmed studs, as well as two gold clamps connected by a chain, I went about inserting them into the various holes I had, some causing a bit of pain as I had to reopen them a little. My right ear had a match for the left, excluding the clamps and the first piercing hole, which I left empty. *I suspect Shva'sika has that earring... at least I hope she does.*

My reflection in the vanity mirror looked a bit healthier after the bath. With a few nights of sleep on a nice bed, and some good meals, it wouldn't be long before I was in peak shape again.

I headed downstairs to let Alena know of Raikidan's decision.

I set the table as best I could with one hand. With Alena off helping Raikidan with his hair, her youngest had chosen me to cling to, and wanted me to carry him around on my back. I didn't mind, though. *He reminds me a lot of Ryder—only younger.*

My chest pulsed with pain and I did my best not to react. I hoped he was okay after all these years.

Everyone stopped what they were doing when someone came down the stairs. Alena entered the common room, a smile on her face. "I've never seen such a drastic change in a person from one little haircut. Even I'm impressed by my work."

Valene joined my side as Alena stepped aside and someone entered the room behind her. My eyes widened in surprise at the sight of Raikidan sporting his new haircut, without a shirt. *Of course, he's not wearing one...*

His hair was no longer past his ears, and the center red portion had been cut and styled to be longer than either side of the black. Raikidan looked at me, holding my gaze, and a strange sensation fell over me while my mouth started to dry out.

"Look away from him," the voice warned. *"Now."*

Valene grabbed my arm, jerking me out of my trance, and kept her voice low while also keeping an eye on Raikidan. "He looks like a god. Where did you find a guy that perfect?"

Raikidan's brow rose and some of Alena's boys laughed. I looked at her with the same expression as Raikidan. "I'm not sure how to respond to that."

One of Alena's older sons, who I noticed had been eyeing Raikidan almost as much as Valene, spoke up. "I know how you could."

One of her other sons snorted. "Yeah, like, where are his clothes?"

I laughed. "Just be glad he's wearing pants."

"Got a streaker for a man, do you?"

I went about continuing my task. "We're not together."

Alena watched me. "You haven't made a comment on his hair. Do you disapprove of the haircut?"

I raised my brow at her. "I'm not saying that at all. I'm indifferent to the change. He looked fine with the longer hair, and he looks fine now with the shorter hair. I don't know why all of you are making a big deal out of it."

Daren, hands full with a large serving platter, laughed as he left the kitchen. "Careful, lass, that kind o' talk will get us tae think he's not yer boyfriend an' free for the takin'."

I sighed. "He's not my boyfriend, Daren. Just made that clear."

"Ach, away ye go!" Daren waved me off and looked at the men in the room. "All right, lads, come help me serve the meal."

He set down the platter he carried on one of the tables and re-entered the kitchen, expecting the men to help him without question, which they did. Sethal continued to hang onto me instead of helping his brothers.

Raikidan approached and held out a hand toward me. "Let me help you."

I half-smiled and handed him the rest of the plates. "Thank you. I'll set the utensils since they're over your comprehension level."

He smacked me in the arm and I chuckled. Sethal took interest in Raikidan's presence then and Raikidan ruffled his hair before placing the last plates exactly how I had. *Impressive.* His ability to fit in after such a short time gave me an idea of how useful he would be in the city.

Valene and Alena also went to assist the men, though both looked at me in a way I didn't understand as they passed. I brushed it off and focused on my task. Once Raikidan finished his, I showed him how to set out the utensils and supervised his work. While a mundane task, it helped me gauge his ability to follow directions and learn on the fly.

I did find myself taking in this new look of his. Valene wasn't wrong, he was an impressive looking man… dragon. *Whatever…* And even though I told the others I was indifferent to the haircut, that was turning out to be a lie. *He's actually quite handsome…*

I stopped that thought and focused on the last two plates that needed utensils. That idiotic road needed to be avoided. *I've learned from past mistakes.*

Once all the food was set out and everyone seated themselves, we dug in. Conversation went well. Nothing that happened five years ago came up, and I was filled in here and there on the goings-on of the village and any juicy gossip the more social individuals had. Valene's infatuation with Raikidan showed throughout the whole meal. She'd be the first to hand him food, refill the water pitcher if it emptied just before he needed it, and just about anything else under the sun besides feed him herself. Most of us found it amusing, especially since he showed no signs of understanding any of her overly personal gestures.

Raikidan had surprised me with how well he managed to handle the group meal. At first he looked out of place—Alena even com-mented that it was a clear sign he'd lived alone for a long time. My dragon companion ran with that and crafted some story of living in the woods in isolation for personal reasons, and how his family never had meals like this when he had lived with them. Valene tried to pry a bit more into his personal life, but he either gave little information or deflected. It amused me.

Once dinner ended, we said goodbye to Alena and her family. Valene and I then cleaned up, making sure Daren didn't lift a finger since he did all the cooking.

Valene smiled wide at Raikidan when he brought in the last of the plates, but frowned when he didn't react to her. He promptly left so we could clean the dishes.

I shook my head. "We really need to talk about that."

She grinned wickedly. "You're not jealous, are you?"

"No. And I'm not dating him either. But you really shouldn't set your sights on him. It's not going to work out."

She crossed her arms and glared at me. "And why not?"

"Besides the fact we're not going to be here long, he's got a lot of secrets. It's why you couldn't get anything out of him during dinner. Also, he isn't noticing your interest in him. I think it's safe to assume he isn't going to."

Her shoulders sagged as she dried a clean plate. "I know… I just… hoped maybe I could get someone's attention for more than a single night. I figured if he's good enough to travel with you, then he'd be a good candidate for something more."

I patted her on the shoulder with a wet hand. "You have time. Don't rush it. You'll regret it if you do."

"Says the woman who lives forever," she muttered.

I snorted and scrubbed a plate. "I won't live forever. I won't even live as long as an elf."

"Yeah, well, still longer than me."

I shook my head. She'd learn one of these days she was better off not rushing if she wanted to make the right match. Hopefully this talk would help get her off Raikidan's back and now I could focus on more important matters.

5
CHAPTER

I ran. I kept running. No matter what happened, I was to keep running down this seemingly endless stone hall. They ran beside me—my comrades. We would either escape together or die together. That was the plan.

A light could be seen at the end of the hall. A glimmer of hope sparked in us all. That was, until she fell. I stopped and tried to go and help her.

"No, just go!" she shouted.

"But..." I couldn't leave her. She was the only thing I had left to remind me of—

"You have to go. Live! Like she wanted you to. Don't get yourself killed because of me."

My female comrade yanked on my arm. "C'mon, we gotta go!"

Guards had caught up and were shouting orders to close the gate. Either we got out now or we all died in this spot.

"Run and don't look back!" she ordered.

I did as I was told. I ran as fast as I could, but I looked back when I shouldn't have. There was blood; so much blood. My heart felt like it was being crushed. She lay there in a crumpled heap with blood pooling out around her. If I could have cried I would have. I had lost her just as I had lost everything else I had ever cared for.

"Jasmine!"

My eyes snapped open and I bolted upright. Sweat dripped down my back and my breath came out in hard gasps. It was so horrible to remember. Why did I have to dream of that night? Why now?

I examined the room, taking deep breaths. Light of the full moon peeked through the curtains, falling on the scales of Raikidan's natural form as he slept. A smaller version of his normal dragon form, but a dragon form nonetheless.

It hadn't taken me long, two or three nights, tops, to figure out one of two things. Either he didn't enjoy being in his human form, or while he slept, he couldn't maintain that form. If it was the latter, it might pose a problem. I'd have to remember to talk to him about it later. *Once I get into a better mindset after that dream.*

His scales shimmered in the moonlight, his sides rising and falling as he slept. *At least one of us will get a good night's sleep.*

I needed to clear my head, and the best way to do that was to go out for a run. I didn't want to wake him, so I tiptoed over to the window and slid it open. The old wood groaned and squeaked in protest and I mentally swore. I turned my head back when Raikidan's sounds of sleep halted, to find him rousing from his slumber. He blinked at me with bleary eyes.

While he didn't need to know what I was doing, I figured it best to tell him just in case. "I'm going out for a run. I'll be back in a few hours."

I slipped through the window and onto the overhang of the front entrance, and then leapt off the building. Tucking and rolling, I made it safely to the ground and picked the northbound path out of the village.

"Eira, wait," Raikidan's hushed voice hissed. I looked up to see Raikidan in his human form hanging halfway out the window. "I'd like to go with you."

"I'm built for running," I said, my voice also hushed so as not to wake anyone. "I don't want to be slowed down if you can't keep up."

"Nu-humans are faster than regular humans, right?"

"Well yeah."

"Then I'll take that form again and give it another test."

I noted his shirtless nature again. "Fine, just throw some clothes on while you're at it." He rolled his eyes and grunted. "I'll be at the north end of the village. Meet me there."

Without waiting for him to agree, I jogged to the northern path. The high, full moon in the sky cast silver light over the town and surrounding forest. The woods itself had its own life about it with the different sounds it gave off, from cooing night birds, to humming insects, to snuffling underbrush creatures. After a few minutes of taking in the peacefulness of my natural surroundings, I heard the sounds of footsteps behind me. I turned to find Raikidan approaching. He'd already taken his nu-human form. The moon above bathed him with silver light, making him look almost ethereal. *If I didn't know any better, I'd believe I was dreaming.*

A thin smirk crossed his lips. "So, where are we going?"

I jerked my head toward the north path. "There's a ravine about three miles north. Sufficient distance for a run and to test your form."

Raikidan shifted his gaze around the woods. "Will we have trouble with that Guardian thing?"

I shook my head and produced two flames identical to the one I created when we first met the Guardian. One floated over to Raikidan and circled him. "That will keep him from bothering us."

Raikidan watched the flame, enthralled by it.

I chuckled before jogging off. "Focus, Raikidan, or I'll leave you behind."

He caught up to me, but I picked up the pace, the light of our fires illuminating the path around us. Some nu-human experiments had the luxury of good night vision. My night vision, on the other hand, wasn't terrible, but I wouldn't brag about it, either.

My pace continued to pick up, the trees blurring by. The brisk air gripped my lungs. Raikidan managed to keep up, showing he'd done well with his transformation, but I could hear his heavy panting. I figured he'd naturally gravitate toward strength over agility, which would come in handy in its own right. But tonight, he'd regret that decision.

The road veered left, but I continued my course into the underbrush. Leaves crunched underfoot, and Raikidan cursed me when I pushed aside a low hanging branch only for it to swing back at him. I snickered and pushed myself faster.

I cleared boulders and fallen trees with ease. Several felled trees that had caught on something else were too tempting to ignore, so I ran up to them. Raikidan chose to keep his feet on the ground, but kept his eyes trained on me.

I'd jump off the wooded plants and land with grace. Raikidan would gain ground on me, but my speed didn't allow it for long.

My intense military training flashed through my mind.

Short quick breaths left my lungs as I ran, a male voice yelling at me to run faster—Shyden pointed at me as he reprimanded me for not jumping correctly, his one good golden eye bearing down at me with great intensity—Gunfire blasted close to my sensitive ears and I tried not to jump, not wanting to fail this test.

I shook the memories from my mind and focused on the present.

This was exciting, fun even. *Fun.* It'd been some time since I had that. I liked it. I liked how easily this took me away from that nightmare.

Light from the moon cascaded through the forest canopy. The light grew as the trees thinned. Bursting through the tree line, I skidded to a halt, barely stopping before the ground gave way to the cliff face of the ravine. Raikidan was by my side moments later.

In quick, shallow breaths, I took in the crisp, clean air, my head clearing.

"You"—Raikidan took in a deep breath—"run fast."

I laughed. "That's my job."

I sat down, allowing my feet to dangle over the edge of the cliff, and Raikidan joined me. Closing my eyes, I took in all the sounds and smells around me, my nightmare long forgotten. When I opened them again, I found Raikidan watching me, the light of the moon cascading over his muscular form. I smiled at him, unable to keep a stern demeanor. Besides, I needed to get along with him in some way or this alliance wouldn't work out. *Still, I need to be careful. He is a dragon, after all.*

"You should smile more," he said. "You'd be more approachable."

I smacked him in the arm. "Shut up. Like you're much better."

"Loners like myself don't want others to approach us." He snorted. "I guess that's why you do it."

I tilted my head. "You said loners like you. Sounds like it's not all dragons. What's your society like?"

"Complex, like I'm gathering yours is. We have clans and colonies, each with a head leader who keeps it all together. Interactions between colors is limited for the most part unless territories border each other. Loners, like myself, don't have to deal with a lot of that complexity, but we still have to abide by certain rules."

"Why do you choose a solitary life?"

"I like peace and quiet." He grunted and looked at me accusingly. "Some peace I got."

I tried not to laugh, but a giggle slipped out, which caused Raikidan to chuckle. Before we knew it, we were both roaring with laughter. I got myself under control after a few moments, smiling despite myself. "Thanks, I needed that."

"You have a nice laugh." I raised a brow and he peered up at the moon. "The unrestrained and blissful nature of it reminds me of songbirds."

Warmth spread to my cheeks.

The wind picked up and he closed his eyes, taking in a deep breath. "Your scent... it's also nice. Better than that. It's one of the most pleasant things I've smelled before."

My eyes widened. *It's what...* He glanced my way and I grinned, pushing away the strange feeling bubbling up inside. "Watch out, ladies, we got a charmer here." I looked up at the sky. "Lucky for me I'm immune to such tricks, or I'd be in trouble."

He looked at me, confused, and I laughed. "We have a lot of work to do with you before you can pass off as not so clueless."

A smirk spread across his lips. "Maybe that'll be my quirk the entire time we work together."

My lips spread into a tense line. "I hope not. I'd like to work with someone who comes off as competent, thank you."

Raikidan regarded me for a moment. "I'd like to talk to you about that, if we can. You mentioned a resistance but didn't go into details. Anyone I need to be aware of when we do work with them?"

"That's a lot of ground to cover, so I won't bore you with so many details all at once. But the group I'd like to stop in with first would be the main subgroup you'll get to know most. There's Rylan, Ryoko, Zane, and a few others. I'll introduce you to each of them, as long as they're still alive." *They'd better be, or I'll drag their spirits back to their corpses, Cosmic Law be damned.* "One thing to note, don't stare at Ryoko when you meet her. It pisses her off, and she'd be the first to throw you through a brick wall."

His eyes widened while his brow furrowed to show his mixed emotions. "Why would I stare?"

"She's half-wogron, and her figure is... well, let's just say the person who designed her really wanted her to be a distraction. So, she has a few features that are hard to miss."

He nodded slowly. "Okay, I'll keep that all in mind. But, half-wogron?

I didn't think there were any more left. Between the curse that keeps wogrons in that humanoid-wolf state and their toxin-filled bites and scratches, I would have thought it'd be impossible for them to exist now."

I gave him a sidelong glance. "Experiments, remember? Doesn't take more than some DNA and some science for humans to pretend they're gods."

"Fair." He ran his fingers through his hair. "Are you really indifferent to this short hair that broodm—elf woman gave me?"

I regarded him, perplexed at such a sudden topic change. I found him looking my way from the corner of his eye, his lips set in a way I'd never seen before. *Is he concerned I don't approve of the change? Of course not, Eira, don't be ridiculous.*

I decided to be honest with him. "Well, at first I was, but the more I've seen you with this new haircut, the more I like it. It suits you and can also be styled with a product called hair gel to look different. I can teach you how to use that when we get to the city." I looked him over. "Better question, do you like it?"

He shrugged. "I guess."

I lifted a brow and he ran his hand through his hair again. "It's just different. I've never had it this short, and knowing it will remain this way, no matter how I feel later, is a bit…"

"Scary?"

"Alarming."

I grunted. "Same thing."

Fluttering green wings just out of clear sight distracted me. Looking up, I saw a large luna moth hovering above me. *So beautiful…* I extended my hand into the air, and it landed on my index finger. I smiled. Sadly, the moment didn't last forever. The moth fluttered away and disappeared into the silver light of the sky.

"To us, the luna moth is special." I looked at Raikidan to find him staring up at the moon. "Most active on the night of a full moon, they're seen as little messengers from the moon goddess, Lunaria. With their brief lifespan, it's an honor to be graced with their presence, even for a short time. It shows that you are an especially graced being."

I snorted. "Well, looks like a part of your philosophy is wrong. I am nothing special, unless, of course, you call monsters special."

"Is that how you see yourself?"

"Of course." My gaze drifted out to the vast ravine below. "If you saw the life I've had to live—the blood staining my hands—you'd think so too; believe me."

"I don't believe you."

I waited for him to continue, but he didn't. He didn't even look at me. *What is going on in that head of his?* He was an odd one, but was I much different? The two of us stared into the sky, and it brought a question to mind.

"Raikidan, what's flying like?" When he didn't answer, I spoke again. "Never mind, it was a stupid—"

"No, it wasn't. I've just never had to think about it before. I've never been asked."

I should have thought of that. It only made sense since he didn't associate with anything but dragons, who knew how to fly.

"I guess the best I could compare it to would be the way you had been running earlier. My wings are your feet, and the sky is your ground. The only limitation is the one you place on yourself. The higher and faster you go, the better you feel. The air whips around you, but you can't be contained by it."

"So, in a single word, free."

"Yeah, I guess that sums it up. Not sure if that was much help."

"No, it was," I admitted. *More than you know.* He looked at me, expecting more, but I kept my thoughts to myself. He had shown me that, even if I had wings, I would never be able to fly.

"I want to ask you something now. The song you were humming while bathing, where did you learn it?"

Ah shit, he did hear me. I peered up at him through my lashes. *Should I tell him?* It wasn't necessarily a big deal, but may lead to more questions, especially from me. If he were asking about it, did it mean he knew it too?

"I learned it some time ago from my mother." I gazed up at the moon, her face and all the memories rushing back to me.

"Thanks, Mom."

"No need to thank me."

"Promise we'll always be together?"

"Promise."

Raikidan tilted his head as he watched me. "If you're artificially created, how can you have a mother?"

I sighed. "I was created in a tank, that's true, but in order for me to exist, they needed DNA, and in order to obtain the DNA, they needed donors. For me, my donors were from a male and a female, so I have a mother and a father. I'm also one of the few who had contact with even just one of them."

"Do you at least know who your father is?"

My eyes began to wander as dark, angry thoughts swam in my head. But I caught myself before I could become consumed by them. "No."

"You sure? That look would say—"

My eyes tightened as I snapped my attention on him, my teeth bearing a bit. "I said no, so don't bring it up again!"

He reeled back. "Okay, noted. Sorry. Are you close with your mother?"

I nodded. "I was."

"Was?"

A pain pulsed in my chest. "She was murdered…"

Raikidan stared at me, as if too shocked to speak.

"She was one of the few people who associated with me willingly. It hurt to lose her."

He regarded me for a moment. "What do you mean?"

"I have a bad reputation. That's all I'll say on that matter."

Raikidan nodded. "Where did she learn the song?"

"From someone else. I never learned more than that." I looked at him. "Why do you ask?"

"It's a dragon lullaby." My brow rose with interest. "It's the only one we have, and I couldn't see a dragon teaching a human it, so that's why I was curious."

"Sorry, I don't know much more than that. She only ever hummed it to me, so I had no idea it belonged to another race. It's possible she learned it from a dragon and never told me, or learned it from someone else who had contact with one. We may be told dragons are extinct, but that's not to say someone wouldn't come across any of you and chose to keep their mouth shut."

"You've chosen to do the same, even though we've yet to discuss what to do about that." He rubbed his chin. "Why show such loyalty to someone who means nothing to you?"

"Honor isn't common in humans these days, but it's not lost, either. For me, loyalty is of utmost importance, and I must hold myself to that standard if I expect it as well." I glanced at him. "If you find a human with that kind of loyalty standard, consider yourself lucky and don't take it for granted."

He smirked. "Well then, I must be one lucky dragon."

My cheeks burned as they flushed several shades darker, and I looked away from him. All these compliments today were throwing me all out of sorts. I didn't need him seeing just how much it actually affected me.

"What is a boyfriend?"

My attention snapped back on him. "What?"

"Your friends kept calling me your boyfriend, or words similar, but you were quick to correct them. What is it? A kind of mate to your kind?"

I thought about how to word it in a way he'd understand. "Well, I guess it depends on what you mean by mate. I'm going to guess permanent or long-term partner of sorts, since your kind is monogamous as a whole, in which case the answer then would be no, it's not a mate. It'd be akin to a trial phase before taking them as a mate. This would be to figure out if you're compatible with each other in the long run."

"Sounds strange to me, but if that's how your kind does things, then so be it."

I eyed him. "Like your kind's way is less strange? Strictly monogamous and claiming a mate just by meeting them? Like life really works that magically."

"Yes, we are monogamous, and no, I won't explain further about how we find our mates to make you believe me." My brow rose and he chuckled. "You refused to answer one of my questions, so I know I don't have to answer yours."

I half laughed. "Well okay then. Then answer me this, how strong are your ties with your mates?"

His brow furrowed. "I don't understand your question."

"Can your bond with them be fractured or weak?"

"Of course not!"

I recoiled from his intensity.

"We're loyal to them. We'll do anything to protect them and ensure they're happy. To show any weakness in that is to disgrace our bond and what it stands for."

"No need to get mad. It was only an inquiry."

His gaze lowered, and I noticed his shoulders sag. "Sorry, I know."

I looked him over and noted his defeated expression, though guarded. *He's hiding something.* My expression softened. "But you have seen weakness, haven't you?"

He let out a strained breath. "Yes. Rare, but I've seen it and it's a serious matter to my kind."

This topic wasn't a good one to continue. I noted the brighter look to the sky and knew it would only be a matter of hours before the sun rose. I got to my feet. "We should head back. We'll need our rest for the journey ahead."

I turned around but stopped dead in my tracks. Standing before me at the edge of the forest stood a nu-human man about my age, with tawny-beige skin common from the west desert region of Lumaraeon. Normally his identifying features would be obscured by the hood of the cloak he wore—customary attire for shamans who ventured outside the town—but he had pulled it down. "Ken'ichi?"

His blue eyes stared at me. "It's true… you're really back."

"For a day, yes."

"You're alive…"

I smiled and approached him. He didn't move. I reached out and placed a hand on both sides of his face. "I'm really here, bonehead."

He reached up and touched my hands, holding tight to be sure I wasn't a spirit here to trick him. Then suddenly, he wrapped his arms around me, lifting me off my feet, and spun us around. "You're alive!"

I couldn't stop myself from laughing. Ken'ichi and I had hit it off quick when I'd first arrived. His kind nature toward everyone unsettled me at first, but it came in handy when I went to learning the ways of a shaman. While my mentors Del'karo and Shva'sika worked with me most, Ken'ichi taught me what it meant to be a Guard, showing me a tougher side of him than I thought capable from him.

He also helped Xye teach me how healing worked, even though I had no innate ability for it. I'd learned from that experience how rare it was to find someone who was both a guard and a healer due to the different temperament requirements.

Ken'ichi put me down and smiled. "I'm so glad you're okay."

I snickered. "I can tell." I slapped him in the arm. "You're looking good. Especially for someone who has the night watch."

He shrugged. "I've always been a night owl."

I looked around. "How did you find me? Chance happening?"

He pointed into the forest. "The Guardian kept returning to this area, so I thought something might be up."

My brow furrowed. "How many times?"

Ken'ichi thought for a moment. "Four times in the last hour, maybe?"

That wasn't good. It had to be sensing some sort of problem. *Are there Hunters lurking about in the woods?*

"I see that look, and don't worry. I checked the area out. There's nothing here. It was acting like this in another location earlier today. The village is safe."

"I'm still hunted, Ken'ichi." I glanced up at him. "It's why I'm out of here tomorrow. Maka'shi threw enough of a fit over that. And if the Guardian is acting this strange, then it's obviously found something. I don't need to be causing issues for all of you again."

He cupped my cheek. "You worry too much. But if you're that concerned, head on back into town and I'll keep an extra vigil on my watch. I took out a number of Hunters five years ago. They won't get past me to you."

I pulled away from his touch. "Just don't get yourself killed. It's all I ask."

He smiled at me, but it disappeared when he noticed Raikidan. "Who's this?"

I looked at Raikidan and then back to him. "Raikidan. He's giving me a hand with the situation back in Dalatrend."

Ken'ichi stared at Raikidan, a displeased look on his face, but he didn't say anything to my dragon companion, nor did Raikidan say anything to him. He returned his gaze to me. "I won't hold you back anymore. Have a good night, Eira."

His eyes lingered on me for a moment before he walked off. I watched him until he disappeared into the forest, and then motioned for Raikidan to follow. The two of us moved through the underbrush in silence until we came to the road leading back into the village.

"Hey, Eira, can I ask you something?" Raikidan said.

I looked at him. "What's that?"

"You said something about my kind being extinct. What's that about?" His lips twisted. "I know we're secretive and all, but I never thought we were *that* secretive."

I nodded. "It's said dragons died out because of the Great War."

"I see. That makes sense, thank you."

His gratitude perplexed me. *Why thank me for such a trivial answer?* It wasn't like I'd given a whole lot of detail on the subject or anything.

"That friend of yours back there," he said, "he's seen me with this new form. I'm sorry if it causes you any issues later."

I waved him off. "I'll figure it out when the time comes. I'm not worried about it."

"You're worried about the Guardian's activity though, aren't you?"

I nodded. "Yes. Activity like that would indicate intruders of some sort. So, either it's managed to kill a few Hunters, or they're running and its pursuing them. Either way, it's a clear enough sign we have to leave tomorrow. I wanted to get my things, but they're not worth these people's lives."

"You're loyal to them." He smiled, his captivating eyes unusually soft. "I like that."

I found myself unable to look away from him. Normally a compliment would get me all out of sorts. *But the way he said it—* I ripped my gaze away. *Get a hold of yourself!* It was just a way to lure me into a false sense of security. That's how that stuff worked. *I won't fall for that game...*

The forest was the only one to speak the rest of the walk back to the inn. The Guardian showed up once, but didn't bother us, making me uneasy. I really hated that I put these people in danger. They didn't deserve that after all they'd done for me.

My first day here rolled through my mind like a movie. I hadn't meant to stay, but before I knew it, I'd been convinced to give it a chance and these people grew on me little by little. Raikidan got one thing right about me with them. I held them close and wanted nothing more than to protect them.

My resolve to fight Zarda hardened. They'd be safer once he was gone. *One more reason to destroy him.*

The two of us made it back into town about a half an hour later. A light in front of the inn caught my attention, but before I had the chance to think on it, Daren came around the corner, lantern in hand and dressed in sleep wear including a sleep cap.

He held the lantern higher as we approached. "Ah, there ye are. I heard ye two movin' about earlier. Thought ye was runnin' away again."

I chuckled. "No, I wouldn't do that to you, Daren. I just needed to go for a run. Raikidan chose to join me."

Daren turned his focus to Raikidan and cranked his head to the side as his brow twisted. Confused, I also looked his way, my heart stopping. He still had his nu-human disguise on. *Shit!*

I had to think of something quick. I didn't want to lie to the man, but I also couldn't tell the full truth. "Before you ask, Daren, it's one of the abilities he possesses. I thought it'd come in handy when making my decision to recruit him."

Daren nodded slowly, though I could tell he wasn't sure if he should believe me or not. "Ye, lad, will need tae be careful around Maka'shi as well, then. She already be mistrustin' o' ye because o' Eira, and this ability won't help ye any."

Raikidan nodded and changed his form back to that of an ordinary human. "I'll do my best to remember that. Eira warned me not to use the ability while here, but I didn't listen. I now know I should have heeded her council."

Nice diplomatic response. And it wasn't because it painted me in a better light. I could see how it eased the tension from Daren.

Daren waved us to follow him. "Good. Now both ye get back tae bed."

The two of us complied and headed to our room while Daren went off to his.

I sighed when Raikidan closed the door behind us. "We're lucky it was Daren who saw you. Ken'ichi did too, but we could have easily played that off."

"Sorry," he said. "I forgot I'd changed forms. I found it comfortable. More so than this one."

I nodded as I headed for the vanity. "I understand. Once we leave here you'll be able to take it permanently."

With my hands over my head, I stretched. My hands glided over my skin, touching a few of the scars I'd received in my lifetime.

"Is it common for females of your kind to fight?" Raikidan asked.

My arms dropped to my sides and I threw my head back to look at him. "Yes. Women are part of the military, and there are a number of scrappy female civilians, too. Even shaman Guards can be women if they so choose. Why do you ask?"

"It's hard not to notice the scars you carry."

I couldn't help but notice the slight scowl on his face. "They're just scars. It's not like they're a big deal."

"To a dragon, they are. They mean you've seen fights beyond simple disagreements."

I leaned on the vanity. "So, females of your kind don't fight?"

He shook his head. "Not unless they absolutely have to, and if they do, then we males aren't doing our job. We protect them no matter what."

"What if two females fight?"

Raikidan rubbed the back of his neck. "That's where things get a bit tricky. We struggle to intervene in those situations." He chuckled. "If you human females are anything like ours, you're ruthless against each other and could make a male second-guess his entire life's choices."

I couldn't help but laugh. "Yeah, that sounds about right for us, too."

Raikidan reached out suddenly and took my hand. His free one traced a few of my scars, their sensitive nature sending a jolt through my arm. I noticed his darkening eyes and the way his lip curled into a snarl of disgust. "These bother me the more I look at them. They don't belong on you."

I pulled my hand away, holding it close to me. This was getting too personal. It risked too much. "Well, nothing can be done now. Can't change the past."

I removed my hairclip, and threaded my fingers through my hair. Raikidan pulled a flower from the vase arrangement and examined it for a moment before reaching out and tucking it behind my ear. "It adds to your beauty."

I looked away as an uncomfortable feeling writhed in me. *There is that random charm he was trying to... the gods only know what!*

"Thank you for putting up with me. I know I've made this difficult on you in ways, but you're not complaining. I see it as a kind of loyalty and I do appreciate it."

I pulled the flower out of my hair and tucked it back in the vase. "You're putting up with me, so it's not that big a deal."

I headed for my bed. As I did, I thought about our conversation and the large scar on my abdomen. The day he saved me ran through my head. *"We protect them no matter what."*

Was that why he did it? Did he have a primal instinct, one that was stronger than his conscious thought, which drove him to save me even though I wasn't a dragon? Or was it something else that drove him? I had to know. "Is your way of seeing females the reason why you saved me instead of leaving me to die?"

Raikidan remained quiet for a moment. "I... don't know why I saved you. Something just compelled me to. It could have something to do with how we treat our own kind. Even if you are a human, you're still female."

I sat down on the bed. "Well, thank you. I didn't deserve such kindness and I don't deserve the time you've devoted to putting up with me."

I lay down and closed my eyes, deciding it best to end this conversation now. I needed rest for the long day to come, and if I wasn't careful, I was going to start breaking rules with this dragon. *And that wouldn't be smart.*

I awoke to the sun peering through the curtains. Although tired from a less than restful night's sleep, the new day was greatly welcomed. Sitting up with a yawn and stretch, my eyes wandered about the room. Raikidan slept soundly on the floor, his dragon-like snores an indication he slept better than me. I didn't feel like waking him yet, in case he chose to play twenty-questions this early, but it would be good for me to get ready for the day. Maka'shi would be expecting us to leave before noon.

Sliding off the bed, I maneuvered around his head and squeezed between his shoulders and the wall. I did my best not to touch him, but he shifted slightly, and I miscalculated my next step. Before I could catch myself, I landed on him. Raikidan stirred and slowly lifted his head. Yawning, he looked at me and tilted his head.

"Sorry, didn't mean to wake you." I gestured to the vanity with my chin. "I'm just trying to get over there."

He yawned again, giving me a good look at his razor-sharp teeth, and then moved away to give me the room I needed. Making it to the vanity, I went about brushing my hair until someone knocked on the door.

"Laz, it's me," came Valene's voice on the other side. "I have some clothes for the two of you, and Daren is almost done making breakfast."

I glanced at Raikidan to find him shifting to his human form. As I made my way over to the door, I pointed at his discarded clothes and he let out a long drawn out sigh. I shook my head and didn't open the door until he had pants on.

Valene greeted me with a bright smile, her eyes sparkling. "Good morning."

"Morning to you too."

She held up a bundle of clothes. "These are for you and"—she glanced past me—"Raikidan."

I noticed the desire in her eyes. Even after my talk with her, it'd take her a bit to let him go. *What is he doing now?* I turned to find Raikidan lying on the bed on his back, one arm over his eyes while the other hanging off the bed. He'd chosen to only wear his pants. *I… guess I could see why she's acting that way…*

I focused back on her, taking the offered clothes. "Thank you. I appreciate not having to wear the same set of clothes back-to-back for once."

Valene's eyes lingered on Raikidan before she looked up at me. "Don't mention it. By the way, on my way over here, I heard Shva'sika had returned early this morning. After breakfast you'll be able to see her. Unless you want me to run to her house and invite her over."

I held up a hand. "No need. I'm sure she's tired from her journey. I'll let her rest before bothering her."

Valene stared at me, her eyes giving away her want to argue about the last part of my comment, but she nodded instead and excused herself. I shut the door behind me and noticed Raikidan didn't move. Perplexed, I walked over to the bed and towered over him.

He peeked under his arm. "Stay there. You're blocking out the sun."

I rolled my eyes as I scoffed and dropped his clothes on his face. "Drama queen."

He lifted the clothes off his face as I walked toward the bathroom. "Drama what?"

I didn't answer him as I shut the door behind me, so I could change in peace.

Light from the mid-morning sun filtered through the trees on the northbound road. After a pleasant breakfast, Raikidan and I headed out to track down Shva'sika. In theory she'd be home, but she could have gone to one other place. *Please be home...*

Raikidan remained quiet while walking. He watched me with great intensity, but it was as if he could see my nerves going AWOL. I did my best to hide it, but after finding out what happened to Xye, I didn't want to face Shva'sika. I didn't have a right.

I veered us off the main road onto a smaller path leading into the forest. The well-traversed dirt changed to cobblestone and soon we found ourselves in a clearing. A large elvish-style house with an angular roof and elegant accents sat in the center. Before us was a stone patio leading to the deck of the front of the house. To the north and south sides of the house, balconies with lattice railings wound their way around the building; and to the south rear side of the house, a large glass greenhouse could be seen.

The two of us walked up the wide stone steps of the deck and approached the tall mahogany doors of the house. My balled-up hand hovered over the wooden surface, my nerves hesitating my knocking. *You have to do this, Eira.*

I took a controlled breath and knocked three times. *Silence.* I knocked again. *Silence.* I contemplated knocking again to be sure, but I knew it wouldn't make a difference. "She's not here. We'll have to go back into town to—"

Quick muffled footsteps came from inside the house, and then a female voice. "One minute! I'm coming."

Raikidan and I glanced at each other and then waited. The hurried steps came closer and then the door unlocked. It swung open, revealing an alluring elven woman, appearing to be no older than thirty-five, and stood taller than Raikidan by two or three inches. She had porcelain skin, captivating crystal-blue eyes, and beautiful long dark blue hair that was tied together in areas with large beads and cloth wraps.

Painted above her brow was a V-shaped line of blue dots that went from one large one in the center to smaller ones on the ends. Laid on top of the dots was a gold circlet with a crystal pendant hanging from the center. She had a beautifully crafted torc around her neck, and her body was adorned by a violet dress with long flowing sleeves and a cloth belt.

She hadn't changed much—well, at all, really. "Shva'sika…"

The elven woman's eyes went wide. "Laz?"

I tried to say something to her, but my mind blanked. Nothing I could say would make things right. They wouldn't bring Xye back.

Shva'sika's eyes welled up with tears. "You're alive!"

My body stiffened as she threw her arms around me and sobbed into my shoulder. This was not what I had expected to happen. Maybe some blaming, some yelling, or maybe even some name calling, but not a hug.

"I'm so relieved. I thought I'd never see you again."

"I… I don't understand. Why aren't you screaming at me?"

Shva'sika pulled away, her brow knitted, and her cheeks still stained with tears. "Why would I do that?"

My lips slipped into a frown. "I… heard about what happened to Xye."

I jumped back when she started laughing. Raikidan and I gave each other confused glances.

Shva'sika got herself under control and wiped away her tears, careful not to ruin her makeup any more than she already had. "I'm sorry, that response wasn't one you'd expect, I know. As much as I miss my dear brother, he was an idiot. You told him not to follow you, and he did anyway. You're not to blame for his choices."

"But had I not—"

Shva'sika flicked her hand dismissively. "I will have none of that. You are not to blame for what happened. I don't care what Maka'shi thinks. You'd been with us for years without incident and then that attack happened? No one can make me believe you were at fault for that. You were just a convenient scape goat."

My shoulders slouched. I didn't understand this behavior. Of all people, she should hate me for what happened. I'm the reason she lost what immediate family she had left.

"You can't be blamed for the actions of fools."

My elven friend waved us in. "Now, come inside. It's rude of me to make you linger in the doorway. My parents, may their souls rest, would question my upbringing."

The two of us entered, finding ourselves in a spacious living room with a fireplace and large windows to invite the sun. To the north side of the house was the open kitchen and some glass doors for the north balcony. To the south, another pair of glass doors led to the other balcony. A large spiral staircase led to the upstairs, and behind that a hallway led to the backside of the house. While elvish in design and decoration, it had a more modern feel to it, especially compared to the outside.

Shva'sika faced me. "I have to guess, your visit here wasn't just so you could apologize for something you didn't do, yes?"

I nodded. "I returned here to grab a few things before heading back to Dalatrend."

"I thought that might be the case. I do have the items you seek. I'll go get them. Make yourself at home."

She sashayed her way into the back of the house, leaving Raikidan and me to wait. Raikidan chose to sit down on a couch and I wandered around until I made it to the fireplace. Fancy ornaments covered the mantle, along with four framed photographs. One pictured Shva'sika and me, along with a young man who had his arm around my shoulder. *Xye…* I picked it up to look at it.

He was a handsome young man, looking no older than twenty-five, although I knew he was a little more than a century old. His long blue-silver hair, light skin, and green eyes showed his kind demeanor. Garbed in traditional elvish robes, he stood an inch or two taller than Shva'sika, which I'd come to learn over time that was an unusual height for a half-elf.

My thumb slid over my smiling face, memories of my time here flashing through my mind. They were nice memories, but painful, too. My reception upon first arriving here all those years ago hadn't been warm, but I hadn't expected it to be. I didn't even want to stay, but Shva'sika insisted. Others warmed up to me in time, and this place had become a sanctuary for me. I'd thought I had finally found a place to belong—a place that could teach me what happiness was.

My thumb slid over Xye's face. *I'm sorry…*

"He meant a lot to you, didn't he?"

I turned myself to look at Raikidan. He sat on the couch, watching me with great intensity.

I placed the picture back up on the mantle. "Not as much as he would have liked, but yes."

He lifted an eyebrow with interest. "Care to elaborate?"

I sat down on another couch and leaned back, staring at the ceiling. "He wanted me to marry him."

Raikidan snorted. "You're not the mating type, from what I've gathered."

I chuckled. His choice of words was odd and primitive, but they didn't bother me. I was actually more comfortable with those words than the ones I had chosen. "That's what I told him, but he was persistent. He told me he'd keep trying to get me to say yes, even if it killed him, and he got just that."

"You can't blame yourself for his death."

I looked at him. "Yes, I can."

Raikidan came over and sat next to me. I leaned forward and clasped my hands together. "Things were going fine here. No problems and no fighting. It was peaceful. If my memory wasn't as good as it is, I probably would have forgotten why I ended up here in the first place."

My hands tensed. "Then one day, out of the blue, a company of Hunters attacked the village. They were after me. I had planned on drawing them away without anyone getting involved, but many insisted on helping. Xye was part of that group." I let out a deep sigh. "I told him to stay back. He was a healer, not a fighter." I shook my head. "I can blame myself for what happened all I want, because it's the truth. Had I not been here, none of that would have happened."

"The elf woman is right." Raikidan leaned forward. "Even if the attack is your fault, her brother made his choice. You are not responsible for the choices of others."

I stared at the floor, unable to agree with him.

Shva'sika returned a few moments later, in her hand three items of importance to me. I got to my feet and walked over to her. She handed me a leather corded necklace with a wolf's tooth wrapped into it. I wrapped the leather around my neck three times and tied it together in three knots near the tooth.

Shva'sika handed me an earring next, a sapphire stud with a silver chain connecting to a golden bell. Three feathers and a red ribbon were attached to the top of the bell. As the bell dangled from the chain and moved when I accepted the earring from Shva'sika, it made no sound. Concentrating, I gave it a swift flick and a lovely ring echoed from the metal ball. Lightness came to my body and mind, and I had to resist the urge to sit.

I spun around when something heavy hit the floor to find Raikidan on his ass. Apparently while I'd been inspecting my items, he'd gotten off the couch.

Raikidan stared at me with wide, confused eyes, and I bit my lip. "What the hell just happened?"

I couldn't hold back and sputtered out a laugh. Shva'sika rested her fingers on her lips as she giggled away.

"What did you do?" Raikidan repeated.

I continued to laugh, bending over and resting my hands on my legs for support. "I can't... I can't believe that worked on you."

He continued to sit there. "Why can't I get back up?"

I held out a finger as I tried to get myself under control. Taking a few quick breaths, I straightened up and then concentrated before flicking the bell again. This time, a different sound rang from the metal.

Raikidan looked at his hands, his eyes wide as if surprised by his returned strength, and then got up to his feet. "What did you do?"

I attached the earring stud to my ear in a hole I'd left empty earlier this morning. "Sorry about that. I had no idea that frequency would affect you. It's never affected anyone before, so I thought it was safe to test and make sure the bell still worked."

"That doesn't explain to me what you did," he said, crossing his arms.

"It's a special tool designed to soothe. The soothing effect depends on the frequency I create and who is around to hear it. So far, I've only been able to get it to work consistently on two of my comrades, Ryoko and Rylan, and people like them. It's helpful when they're getting out of hand, I can make them... uh, well... sit."

Shva'sika sputtered out a laugh, understanding my snarky meaning. Raikidan's confusion was evident, even though I had told him about Ryoko a bit, but he'd understand soon enough when he met them. *Hopefully he'll get to meet them.*

"Well, don't do that to me again," he said. "I didn't like it."

I grinned. "No promises."

Shva'sika shook her head. "You're terrible. But I suppose I'm even more so for giving this back to you."

She held out a wicked-looking dagger, its hilt made of dark metal and gold accents, and its blade curved and jagged. I accepted my last item of importance, and tested the diamond coated blade's sharpness, careful not to cut myself. I sliced it through the air a few times and noted it wasn't the same as when I left it.

"One of the blacksmiths in town tried to improve it," Shva'sika said. "I tried to warn him of its unusual nature, but he insisted he knew how to work it. He claims it should be lighter to wield."

I nodded. "It is." I then concentrated and thought about wielding a broadsword. The dagger warped and before everyone's very eyes, it transformed into a claymore. I thought of a pike, then a sickle, a bow, and then the original shaped dagger again, the weapon transforming each time.

"Transition feels a bit slow, but I could be imagining it due to my perceived thought of him meddling."

Raikidan stared at the weapon. "What the hell is that? What are these items you have? Some sort of ancient magic artifacts? Is that necklace special, too, in some way?"

I chuckled. "No, the necklace is just a necklace. And these items aren't magic relics. At least the dagger isn't." I thought about holding two daggers, and the weapon distorted, allowing me to pull it apart. I spun the two blades in my hands. "It was made for me, and he refused to reveal his secret." *Because Ryder is a brat.* "The bell was a gift, and I'm not sure where she got it from, so it's possible it's a magic relic."

"I've always suspected it was," Shva'sika said. "It may be small, but historical texts say even the smallest of arcane magic was strong. And really, if it can get even a dragon to calm down, how could it not be?"

I stared at her with wide eyes.

She grinned. "What? Did you really not expect me to figure it out? Honestly, Laz, you're better than that."

My brow furrowed. "But... but how?"

She shook her head. "Well, for one, why would you of all people bring an ordinary human to Dalatrend, a city known for how much it loves to keep the old slave ways?"

Shit, she has a point.

"I also have met a dragon before, on my pilgrimage. Once you meet one, it's easier to spot them when you cross paths with another."

"And you never told me?"

She shrugged. "I didn't see a need to. It was never relevant information."

She had me there.

Shva'sika looked to Raikidan. "Me knowing isn't an issue, right?"

Raikidan shook his head. "No."

She smiled. "Good, though Maka'shi won't be pleased if she finds out. Not because of your race, but because of your ability to disguise yourself." She looked at me. "I hope you understand that, Laz."

"She's already been made aware," Raikidan said. Shva'sika's brow rose at his words. "Daren, I guess his name is, caught me testing out the nu-human form after seeing this one."

My elven friend chuckled. "You're lucky it was him. He's a good man and will take your secret to the grave."

"I know." His response surprised me. I didn't think he'd trust anyone, even someone as nice as Daren.

Shva'sika focused on me. "Now, if that is all, I'm going to go place flowers on my brother's grave. I would like it if you came with me."

A lump formed in my throat and I nodded, bringing the dagger back to its original single form and slipping it into a sheath strapped to my thigh. She nodded back and went into the kitchen, picking up a bouquet of flowers I hadn't noticed before. *She must have been getting it ready when I showed up.*

Shva'sika linked arms with me and the three of us set off for the village graveyard.

Shva'sika chatted on and on, acting as if nothing had changed between us. It made me uneasy. I struggled to understand how she couldn't blame me, or if she had at some point forgiven me.

Her grip on my arm tightened. "What's bothering you?"

I shook my head. "It's nothing."

Shva'sika tilted her head down and gave me a stern look. "Don't lie to me."

I looked away. "I... just don't understand how you can be around me after what happened."

Her grip on me tightened. "Even if I did blame you, which I don't, it's because I would have forgiven you. That's what family does."

Family? After all this time, and what happened, she still saw us as such? We weren't biological family of course, but she had seen me as such quite early on, due to a connection we shared that led me to this place without me realizing it.

"And as family, I must say, you're far too thin."

I rolled my eyes. "Don't start. Daren is on my case too. It's not like I have any control of that. Food isn't easy to come by when you're running for your life. I was always grateful to have the time to eat even a bug or some type of mushroom."

Raikidan's face scrunched. "You ate insects?"

"Yeah, it's not that strange."

Shva'sika laughed. "Yes, it is, dear."

I held my hands out to Raikidan. "I doubt it is for him. I've seen lizards eat insects. Even if it was only as a baby dragon." I glanced at Raikidan. "I highly doubt a small dragon could do well taking down even a rodent."

Raikidan looked elsewhere. "It's not that hard."

I noticed the red tint to his cheeks. "Yeah, sure."

"Well, I've never eaten bugs. That's just gross."

I shrugged. "Some aren't that bad. Even if they were gross, it was better than nothing."

The three of us stopped walking when we came to a large, intricately designed iron gate with two hanging lanterns emitting a blue light. Beyond this, gravestones of various styles and ages were aligned in rows. A statue of a tall woman with long hair stood on the far side of the graveyard, surrounded by tended flowers, shrubbery, and ornately carved stones.

The woman wore ancient swordsman attire I had only seen in books, and was adorned in magnificent jewelry. Several katanas—curved, single-edged bladed swords with squared guards and long hilts—were tied to her hips, and in her hand, she carried a bamboo pole with a lantern attached to the end. By her side sat a magnificent wolf carrying a matching lantern in its mouth. *Goddess of spirits, Arcadia, and her faithful helper, Maiyun.*

Shva'sika pulled me into the graveyard, my mind desperate to fight her, but my body followed. I glanced back at Raikidan when I noticed his footsteps missing from my hearing, to find him remaining outside.

He watched us, but showed no signs of following. I let it be. Dealing with the dead or being near a place like this wasn't something everyone was capable of, and his reasons for staying out were his own.

I followed Shva'sika to a stone structure ornately decorated in an elvish flair. Above the door to the building, carved into the stone, was the symbol of the Lightshine family. *Shva'sika's family's mausoleum.* Shva'sika pushed open the heavy door and led me down long winding steps lit by sconces on the wall. The smell of herbs, death, and decay bothered my nose, but I followed nonetheless.

The stairs led to a single room, several sarcophagi filling it. Each sarcophagus had ornate Elvish script around the base and a sculpture adorning the lids. Shva'sika handed me the bouquet of flowers and went about clearing out old flowers left in vases and moved them to other vases filled with ash. I stayed out of the way when I could. She may call me family, but that didn't make me official family, so I had no right to assist in the care of the family crypt, unless specifically asked. *Had I accepted Xye's proposal, this would be quite different.* But he was foolish to think I'd be capable of reciprocating such luscious feelings. *Love… what a joke.*

Shva'sika faced me when she'd finished cleaning. "If you could place a bundle of flowers in each vase for me, while I prep herbs, I'd appreciate it."

I nodded, and went about the task requested. Once done, I was asked to help place herbs in the ash-filled vases as well as add them into a few special sconces. Shva'sika pointed to the ash-filled vases and I complied with her unspoken request. Using my fire control ability, I pulled a small ember from a sconce, binding the chaotic element to my will, and then lit the herbs and dead flowers from Shva'sika's previous visit. A strong aroma filled the air, masking the smell of decomposition to those with less sensitive senses of smell. For me, it just bothered my nose even more.

Shva'sika knelt in front of her brother's sarcophagus and glanced at me for only a moment before closing her eyes. Her breath slowed and then after a moment her eyes flew open. They glowed with a blue-white light. A lump formed in my throat. I couldn't go that far. I couldn't face Xye after what happened. But I could pay my respects.

Kneeling down, I bowed my head and prayed to the gods for his soul to rest.

"Don't blame yourself," a masculine voice whispered.

My prayer stopped. *Xye?* It couldn't be him. After what I did, there was no way he'd come to me briefly to say that. I went back to praying.

When I finished, I waited for Shva'sika to finish her walk on the spiritual plane. The longer I waited, the more my nerves begged me to leave, but I was stronger than that.

What I guessed to be thirty minutes passed before my elven friend returned to the living plane. She peered at me with soft eyes, and I looked back at her with a silent *"time to go?"* expression. I didn't hide how uncomfortable this place made me feel, and she nodded.

Linking arms with me, the two of us left, rejoining with Raikidan, who hadn't moved. He didn't ask questions and fell in behind us as we headed back for the village.

The silence didn't last long, as Shva'sika went back to chatting; catching me up on events I'd missed in the village during my absence. That is, until a shrill scream pierced the air.

7
CHAPTER

My heart pounded in my chest, my head whipping in different directions. *Where had that scream come from?* Another scream pierced the air, and Raikidan and I both focused on the direction of the village.

"Something is wrong back in the village," Raikidan said, more for Shva'sika's sake than mine.

My blood ran cold. *What if... it's under attack?*

The air smelled of burning wood... plants... bodies. There were a lot of bodies on the ground.

I took off into a full sprint. I could reflect on that thought later. The village needed help, and I wasn't going to run this time. Raikidan followed, but fell behind as my design pushed me faster than he could muster in his form.

My heart raced as the forest blurred past me. Bursting into the clearing, I scanned the village clearing. This whole scenario was sickly familiar.

I didn't see anything out of the ordinary, but when a woman screamed and a sound of a man crying out in pain crossed my ears, my feet moved again. Turning around the corner of a house, I found a grisly sight. Bodies of shamans lay out across the ground. Valene lay on the ground as well, though propped up by her arm, flowers strewn about her, her eyes stricken with fear as she stared at something.

My gaze followed hers, to find an odd creature standing over a man cowering in fear. The creature had long raven hair, fair skin, two sets of horns growing from its head, talon-like hands and feet, and a tail and large wings coming out of her backside. Even with the odd features, the creature was busty and had an alluring female form that wasn't covered much by clothing. *Succubus.*

A hand grabbed my pant leg and I almost jumped. My gaze fell to the Guard grabbing my clothes, to realize it was Ken'ichi. Based on the trail of blood behind him, he'd dragged himself to me while I was taking in the situation. I knelt and placed a hand on his shoulder, keeping my voice down. "Stop moving. You're going to kill yourself. I'll take care of the demon, so healers can tend to everyone."

"T–there's more than one," his shaky voice said.

"I can take on a succubus. Their hypnotic gazes don't affect women."

Ken'ichi pointed a shaky hand to a female guard lying face down, unmoving. My blood ran cold. "Not a… succubus. I–incubus. He doesn't… toy with us like she does."

"Kill them for what they've done."

I patted him on the shoulder and stood. While it wasn't Hunters like I'd expected, two demons weren't good either, especially since I couldn't see the other one Ken'ichi mentioned. I didn't have time to think about him. The succubus was going after the frightened man, no longer enjoying her toy. I drew a dagger from my arm and flung it at her.

It whistled through the air, alerting the demon of the oncoming attack, and she jumped out of the way, though she wasn't fast enough in her reaction and the blade sliced across her cheek, sinking into the building behind her with a *thunk*. She screeched and looked about wildly.

"Over here, ugly!" I needed to take her attention away from the villagers.

The demon's seething stare snapped to me. "Bitch, I'll kill you!"

She came at me. Drawing the dagger Shva'sika had just returned to me, I charged in. As the distance between the demon and me lessened, I thought of a weapon that was much larger than the dagger. As the thought came to me, the dagger morphed into a claymore.

The succubus' talons sliced the air. Using my momentum to my advantage, I sliced through her arm and the succubus screeched in pain. Sliding to a halt on the cobblestone, I glanced at the sword; black blood dripped off the blade.

Turning, I faced my opponent and was disturbed at what I saw. Her arm was regenerating, and it was by no means a fast process, or pretty for that matter. The tissue fused together in small strands like living thread. The succubus set a malicious gaze on me, but her expression changed to a twisted happy smile that sent chills down my spine. "Hold her for me."

A presence appeared behind me and before I could react, an arm wrapped around my body, binding my arms to my side, and a clawed hand reached up and threatened to pierce my throat. *Shit.* This had to be the incubus.

"What a beautiful woman," his unnaturally smooth voice cooed. "Shame we have to kill you, but my darling is the jealous type, and you've harmed her. That is unforgivable."

His darling?

The succubus took deliberate steps toward us. "I want to hear this pretty little bird sing."

Shit, what do I do? I should have been more aware while fighting the female demon. I wouldn't be in this avoidable predicament had I not acted so rashly. *So much for being a well-trained assassin deserving the commander rank.*

A blurred mass caught my peripheral, and a fist slammed into the succubus' face. She cried out and fell to the ground. I stared, my eyes wide, at Raikidan, who stood in her place. *I can't believe he hit her.*

The incubus snarled and pressed his claws to my neck more. "How dare you! No one touches my darling."

Raikidan gestured to me. "You've touched mine, so it's only fair."

Oh, he did not just call me that!

"Rip out his tongue for such words."

To my surprise, the incubus' grip loosened, though not enough to escape. I glanced up at him to find him... conflicted? *Focus, Eira. Now's my chance.*

With him distracted, I changed my claymore back into its dagger shape and then slammed the weapon into his thigh. He roared in pain and pushed me away from him, his claws scraping against my exposed neck. I managed to roll away from the attack some, stopping him from killing me immediately. I put some distance between myself and the incubus and touched my neck, noting the blood from the wound he'd managed to create. *Not deep, I'll live… for now.*

Raikidan rushed the male demon, the incubus swiftly moving away. But Raikidan wasn't bent on attacking. He stood in front of me, blocking a direct view of the incubus, but I was able to get a quick look at his true demon form. His features were very much like the succubus, except he had light hair, tan skin, only one pair of horns, and he wore a bit more clothing—barely.

Raikidan glanced back at me. "You okay?"

I nodded and pressed my back to his, focusing on the succubus, who was now getting to her feet. "We're the villagers' last defense. I'm counting on you to deal with the incubus while I deal with his partner."

He looked ready to question me, but this wasn't the time. I focused on the succubus, her wound now completely healed. Not waiting for the succubus to gain any more time, I rushed in. It wasn't going to be easy to take her down. I didn't even know how to kill something that could regenerate at will, but I had to try.

My weapon changed back into a claymore and I attacked. The succubus dodged the swing of my sword with ease. I tried again, and missed once more. *She's too quick!* I wasn't going to be able to catch her this way. *That's it!*

"Valene!" I called out, stealing a glance back at her. "Help me."

"B–but…" Her eyes tightened, her voice quivering. "I–I can't…"

"Yes, you can. Get on your feet and help protect this village." I prayed to the gods she'd find her wits and at least give it a shot. I only needed this demonic bitch to be rooted.

Roots erupted from the ground. Unfortunately, they weren't close enough and receded back into the soil. *Well, she tried like I told her to.* Valene tried again, but nothing seemed to happen.

"Not me!" Raikidan complained.

"Sorry!"

He fell to the ground and went back to chasing the incubus, who was just as fast as his counterpart. *Damn, are all demons this slippery?* I'd been called many things in my life, demon was one, but not even I could ever hope to be this quick.

Raikidan managed to coerce the incubus into hand-to-hand combat when he threw out a few insults, but he wasn't the only demon engaging. The succubus came at me with a ferocity that matched her counterpart. It didn't match up with her previous fighting form. It was too… strength based. My brow furrowed, and I pushed her back, the female demon switching to dodging and evading, as did her counterpart. *Wait a second…* "Raikidan! I think they're linked somehow."

He glanced my way. "You sure?"

I nodded. "Trust me on this."

Raikidan focused on the incubus. "Great. So, what do we do?"

"If we can immobilize one, it should affect the other."

The succubus screeched and attacked, preventing any further planning. I blocked her talons and swung my leg out, planting my foot into her face.

"Bitch." I turned to see the incubus on the ground, holding his face. Their connection was stronger than I had thought.

"Valene, I really need your help here," I called out again.

"I—I'm sorry." Her voice cracked. "I—I'm not good at this…"

Dammit. I was asking too much of her. I hating doing it, but this kind of situation demanded it. I was just going to have to find another way.

Unfortunately, while I was dealing with Valene, the succubus had taken the liberty of sneaking away and paralyzing Raikidan. *Shit!* If I didn't think fast, he'd be demon chow. That's when I noticed Shva'sika. She stood near Ken'ichi, watching the battle intently. She nodded to me, indicating she could help, but I needed to get Raikidan out of the way.

Sheathing my weapon, I ran to his aid, pushing the succubus back with a swift blow to the head. She staggered back into her counterpart. Grabbing onto Raikidan, I threw him and myself to the ground, using my body as a shield. I felt the static as bolts of lightning shot over us, and I instinctively shielded him more. I knew how painful those bolts could be.

Bone-chilling screams pierced the air, and I knew the lightning had finally hit its mark. Glancing up, I could see the succubus staggering to her feet, her body distorted by the savage attack she was unable to dodge like her counterpart had. Her golden eyes burned with fury as she ran at the two of us. Instinct took over. I swung myself onto my back, and as she came into range, I kicked upward, impacting her in the chest. It left her winded, giving me the chance to wrap both legs around her and propel her forward, toward Shva'sika.

Using this upward momentum, I flipped over Raikidan and landed on my feet in a crouched position. In the process, I had used my free hand to draw my unique dagger again. Using both hands, I split the metal material and each piece formed into two long reverse daggers. The strong smell of blood teased my senses.

"*Kill.*"

Shit, this needs to end now, or these demons are going to be the least of everyone's worry.

The succubus hissed and slashed with fury. Claws met metal as I parried her away. My blades slashed and she dodged. *Bitch, just stay still!*

The sound of quick feet approaching hit my ears, but they weren't from an ally. Turning, I narrowly dodged the incubus' claws. He focused his intense gaze on me, and I averted mine. *The hell? Where is Raikidan?* Parrying the succubus, I looked to where I last knew Raikidan to be, and found him still on the ground, watching. *Seriously?*

Pushing both demons back as best I could, I shouted to him, "Raikidan, get off your ass and help!"

Forcing the incubus back again, I spun around and landed a swift kick to the succubus's abdomen, winding her. *I need more help.* As strong as I was, not even I could effectively deal with two demons alone. With Raikidan not helping, my only hope to get one of these off me was Valene.

I glanced over to her to find her standing rigid, her eyes glazed over. *Perfect. Why must the spirits have such shitty timing?*

"*We're helping, I promise,*" whispered a familiar ethereal voice.

I gasped quietly. "Xye?"

"Eira, look out!" Raikidan's voice rang through my ears.

The succubus came back for another attack, taking advantage of my brief distracted state. I had just enough time to manage a dodge and block. Regaining my composure, I pushed her back and punched her with the hilt of the dagger.

She moaned in pain and staggered backward, holding her face. I needed to concentrate. Refocusing, I evaded the demon's attacks, looking for an opening. It didn't come.

The incubus came at me, trying to catch me off-guard. *Where's a gun when you need one?*

"*Slaughter them both.*"

The two drew up next to each other, malicious grins on their lips. This forced me to avert my gaze from them both, putting me at a nasty disadvantage. They attacked with a fury I struggled to keep up with. Slashes on my arms, a kick to the stomach, a punch to the face—they were a few of the blows I couldn't deflect or roll away from.

The two constantly glanced at each other, reveling in the thrill of fighting together. *I used to know what it was like to have that kind of comraderie.* But no one had had my back like that in a very long time. I learned to rely on myself. I could only trust myself because rarely could I ever fail myself. These two relied on each other, and in that laid their weakness.

A large thorned vine erupted from the ground and grabbed the startled succubus by the leg, giving a moment of reprieve. It whipped her around and then slammed her on the ground. The incubus hissed and assaulted the vine, successfully freeing his partner. I stole a glance at Valene to find her back with us, eyes focused and determined and an arm outstretched. *The spirits gave her the courage she needed.*

"Told you so," Xye's ethereal voice whispered in my ear.

I knew better than to question them. But even I wasn't above rash decisions and thought.

Then, a new sound slipped into my ears. The sound of ripping clothes, and I knew they weren't coming from the demons. A loud roar pierced the sky.

I threw my head back. "Oh, for the love of—"

All that time I had spent trying to hide his secret—coming up with excuses for those we struggled to fool or who had found out a part of the truth—and Raikidan decided now would be the best time to shift into his dragon form.

Raikidan swiped at the demons, the pair running in two directions. But the succubus found herself too slow, still disoriented from Valene's attack, so when Raikidan made a backhanded swing, he landed a successful hit and sent her flying into the forest. She cried out in pain when she hit something hard. Her partner hissed in anger and attacked Raikidan, but his scales proved difficult to get past.

I focused on trying to maneuver around Raikidan's large form to assist him, but struggled. He continuously moved, nearly toppling a few buildings with his tail.

"Fat-ass, watch where you swing that!" I snarled. "We're supposed to help everyone, not make it worse!"

A deep rumble came from his throat, and I swore he was backtalking me. *He'd better not be.*

While the two of us still struggled to deal with the elusive incubus, I looked to Shva'sika for help. She held herself poised for another attack, having built up another electric charge. Unlike most lightning elementalists, Shva'sika couldn't produce her own lightning at will. It had to build, storing in her body as it did, so she had to be careful with her aim.

She nodded to me and I angled myself so I wouldn't be in the way of her attack, keeping an eye out for the missing succubus. I knew she wouldn't run off without her partner. Shva'sika found her chance and sent sparks of energy flying toward her mark, but it failed to make contact. The incubus used Raikidan's attacks to his advantage and dodged both. Shva'sika swore in her native tongue and then pulled back to recharge in a safe place.

Just then, the succubus reappeared and focused on me as her target. She attacked with a fury of swipes, pushing me back.

"Valene, give me a hand!" When I received no response, I cranked my head back to find her staring up at Raikidan, her eyes wide. "Valene, focus!"

She shook herself. "Right, right."

Roots burst out of the ground near the female demon, but missed. They lashed out again and the succubus evaded, her eyes trained on the plant matter. She wasn't going to be taken by surprise again.

My nerves kicked into gear when Valene missed again, and the succubus decided to set her sights on the young woman. With incredible speed, the demon rushed Valene, but before it could reach her, Raikidan's tail came slamming down on the ground between the two. He swung his tail at the succubus, landing a hit on the startled demon, and I had little time to duck through the narrow space between his appendage and the ground.

The succubus slammed and bounced on the ground.

"Valene, now!"

She nodded and took a deep breath before a thorned root erupted out of the ground and wrapped around the demon. The creature cried out in frustration and struggled, but Valene used her skills to squeeze her prey. I could tell she lacked the conviction to kill the monster, but I wouldn't force that on her.

"Kill it."

I went to rush the female demon, to finish her off, but clawed hands grabbed me from behind, grappling me. I stilled when claws pressed up against my throat. *Really, this again?*

"Let my beloved go," the incubus hissed. "Or she dies. Painfully."

Valene stared at me with fear-stricken eyes.

Poor thing. She wasn't cut out for these choices. But I was. "Don't listen to him. Whatever you do, don't let him"—the demon pressed his talons harder against my throat—"don't let him control your actions."

The succubus screamed in pain, pulling my attention. Raikidan pressed his claws down on her, crushing her slowly into the ground. The incubus cringed in pain, gritting his teeth, making me aware of just how tightly the two were connected.

He pressed his claws into my throat more, drawing a bit of blood. "I mean it."

I stared at Raikidan, my resolve strong. "Do what needs to be done."

Raikidan watched us for a few moments, and then did what I never thought he would, he lifted his claws off the female demon. *What is he doing?*

The incubus chuckled. "You mortals are so predictable. Threaten what's precious to you, and eventually you'll crack under pressure."

Raikidan's muscles flexed and his weight shifted, his eyes fixed on the demon holding me captive. *Oh, that's what he's doing.*

"You're wrong."

The demon pressed his claws into my throat, not liking my words.

"We're more likely to make reckless decisions to destroy those who threaten what we hold dear."

Just then, Raikidan swung his tail and I braced for the inevitable impact. When it came, nothing could have prepared me for the pain. My body bounced and rolled on the ground until it came to a stop. Stunned, I struggled to breathe. I'd been hit by Brute soldiers, and even hit by a car driven by a deranged civilian. All of that pain felt like a kitten's tickle compared to this. *He definitely broke something.*

"Fool!"

"Laz!" Valene shrieked.

Pain seared my brain and I tried to shake my state. The battle hadn't finished.

"You…" I looked at the incubus, seeing him struggle to get up. "You bitch!"

I chuckled, pain hammering all over. "I told you… we do stupid shit."

Raikidan advanced and snapped his teeth at the male demon. He missed when the creature managed to roll out of the way, but he kept the demon's attention focused, allowing me to work on getting back up.

It wasn't easy, breathing remained hard, and at one point I coughed up blood, but I wasn't dead yet, so I could stand.

"Kill them."

Staggering on weak legs, I took slow steps toward the captured succubus. The flames in my chest stoked with each heavy breath. I could end this if I could get to her. I didn't have the strength to launch any flames at her, so an in-your-face and personal death would have to do.

Valene, seeing my intended target, strengthened her grip around the female demon. The succubus screamed, as did the incubus. He had fallen to his knees and held his body as if he, too, were being attacked by the plant. Raikidan swiped his large claws at the incubus, but the demon managed to clumsily dodge the attack and head my way.

I discreetly spat an ember into my hand and lit a flame, holding my hand up threateningly as I advanced.

"No!" the incubus cried out.

The demon's speed suddenly tripled, and I was forced to ignore the succubus and clumsily dodge him once he was close enough to swipe at me.

"I will not allow you to kill my Rosa!"

Rosa? The succubus' name is Rosa?

The incubus lunged at me with outstretched claws. "She is mine. You cannot take her from me!"

"No, Zaedrix," Rosa whispered.

Zaedrix? These demons were using their names so freely. It was as if they forgot they could be used against them.

Zaedrix put me on a defensive that I struggled to keep up with. Every movement flooded me with pain. Raikidan came to my aid, landing a strong swipe to the male demon. He landed at the feet of his counterpart, winded and bleeding.

Zaedrix staggered to his feet and stared at me with malice. "Let her go."

I struggled to hold myself up. "Why would we, demon? You attacked us without reason, beyond you indulging in the thrill of death."

"We will leave and not come back," he promised. "We'll do whatever you say."

Why would he bargain with me? Why was her life so important to him? I held his gaze as I thought this over. As I did, something within me stirred—a kind of familiarity emanating from these two. *Why?*

"I will not lose her after everything we've been through," Zaedrix said.

"You will cease killing innocent people," I bargained. "If you don't, I will hunt you down and slowly kill her while you watch helplessly, unable to save her."

He nodded, his eyes pleading with me. "Deal. Just don't kill her. Please."

Could I trust him to keep his word and stay away? Demons didn't have to keep any verbal "promise" unless a blood pact was involved. Then I realized he wasn't trying to hypnotize me. As I held eye contact, he chose not to control me.

I lowered my guard. *Could he possibly*— "Valene, let her go."

"Laz, what are you thinking?" Shva'sika shouted from where she hid. "You can't trust demons."

"I said let her go," I repeated.

Valene hesitated, but obeyed my order and released the succubus. The incubus held my gaze for a moment longer, then scooped up his counterpart and took off into the woods.

Shva'sika came out from her around a building and sighed. "I hope you know what you're doing."

I went to reply, but my body gave out and I collapsed onto the ground.

"Laz!" Valene shrieked. "Alena. Alena, come quick!"

"No…" I managed. "Save the others first."

Shva'sika ran over to me. "We were doing that while you and Raikidan distracted those creatures. We need to tend to you now."

I nodded through labored breaths. At least those attacked and still alive were safe. It pained me to know others had died. I knew I should have made those demons pay for what they did. But something kept me from going through with it.

"It's because you're a fool."

Alena rushed over to me with Valene and began assessing the damage. "You have so many broken bones…"

She gazed up at Raikidan, who I noticed took a step back. She smiled, and then focused on me again. "At least he's remorseful."

She got all that from one look? I couldn't see how, especially since he was in his natural dragon form.

Alena's hands hovered over me and a white light enveloped her hands and then my body. A soothing sensation washed through me, the pain disappearing, and I let out a relieved sigh.

The glow faded when she finished. "There. Give yourself a few moments before trying to—or not." She sighed as I pushed myself up into a partial sitting position. "I wish you'd listen for once."

I twisted my finger in my ear. "What?"

She chuckled and patted me on the head before standing up. "I'm going to go check on the others. Don't get into any more fights."

I grinned, noting her motherly tone. "No promises."

She shook her head. "Kids."

As Alena left, she looked up to Raikidan, and he shook his head to the unspoken question. At least he was fine. Or, fine enough not to be a focus for healing at the moment.

Raikidan approached, the ground shaking with each step, and then shifted.

"Raikidan, have some decency!" I shielded my eyes from his… "glory."

Shva'sika laughed, as did some others in the village watching us. Valene shielded her eyes but was obviously contemplating snagging a peek.

"Get him some clothes, please, Shva'sika," I begged.

"Sure thing." She continued to laugh as she walked off.

I pulled Valene close to me, and positioned her so she couldn't see. She didn't fight me, but the temptation to look remained.

I turned her head back to face away from him. "Don't you dare."

"Why not?" she said. "I'm an adult. I can look at what I want."

"Because it's not becoming of a young lady to ogle at a young man who is being indecent."

She giggled. "Well, he's not exactly a man, now, is he?"

I laughed. "No, you're right, he's not, but he could at least put in some effort to adhere to our customs."

"You know, I'm right here."

"Then maybe you should take the hint."

He knelt behind me. "I'd rather be sure you're okay. I'm sorry for hitting you so hard. It wasn't my intention."

"You have nothing to apologize for. You took the necessary measures I wanted."

"That doesn't excuse my actions. It won't happen again."

I held my dagger up to him, the blade pointed at his neck. "You also won't ever call me your "darling" again. Got it?"

He held up his hands. "No need to get offended. That incubus called the succubus his 'darling' enough times for me to realize it'd have an effect if I called you mine."

"I don't care. Don't ever do it again."

He exhaled. "Fine."

"Where is she?" a female voice demanded.

I sighed. *Great. Just what I want to deal with after all that.*

"That cold woman is coming," Raikidan said.

My brow rose. "Cold woman?"

"She smells like winter." He shrugged. "And her heart is cased in ice."

Valene sputtered a laugh and I chuckled.

"Maka'shi, please, calm down," someone begged.

Maka'shi's tone rose. "Where is she?"

I pulled myself to my feet. *Might as well get this done and over with.*

8
CHAPTER

Raikidan and Valene followed me as I went to meet Maka'shi half-way. When we came face to face, her eyes bore into me.

"There you"—she stopped and looked at Raikidan, her face twisting and then flushing a shade—"Where are his clothes?"

Raikidan shrugged, showing his lack of understanding about the importance of clothing. "Torn. Shapeshifting does that."

Maka'shi's eyes snapped to me. "So, it's true. You brought a shapeshifter here?"

I shrugged. "Last I knew, it wasn't illegal."

Her lips pressed into a thin line as others around us chuckled. She looked at Raikidan. "So, are you human, or something else?"

"Dragon."

His expression remained impassive, and I could see it riled Maka'shi up. Her face reddened with anger. "I want you two to leave this instant."

Valene gasped, and my eyes narrowed. "Excuse you?"

"You heard me. You bring a dragon here, disguised as a human, without disclosing his nature to me, and you cause demons to attack our village—"

I held up my hand. "Whoa, back up! I am not to blame for those creatures showing up."

"You come here, and Hunters follow. You leave, everything goes back to normal. You return, and demons show up. You *are* to blame." She looked at some of the damage that had come to a few buildings from Raikidan's attack. "You pick destructive allies. You pick an ally whose species is known for stealing and manipulating. I won't stand for the trouble you cause."

I held up a finger to her. "Shut your mouth. I will not allow you to insult my comrade."

Her eyes narrowed. "I will insult him, and you. You caused more damage with your 'help.'"

My eyes darkened, and my fists clenched. "And where were you during all of this? If you're so concerned about your people, why weren't you helping?"

"I was dealing with the dead!"

My upper lip curled. "The dead don't need saving, you egotistical bitch!"

Her eyes flashed, and a cold aura leaked out of her, freezing the ground beneath her feet. "How d—"

My fist collided with her jaw, the sensation of bone cracking on impact ran up my arm. She cried out, falling to the ground and holding her face. The others around me gasped and I stared. *Shit, what have I done?*

"She deserved it."

There was no going back from that. "Maybe that'll knock some sense into you. I had nothing to do with these demons. But I had everything to do with getting them away from here. I may not have been able to save everyone, but at least I did more than you."

She looked up at me, her bleeding lips pulled back into a snarl. "You're going to regret that, Laz'shika."

I spat on the ground and stormed off. I needed to hit something, and it'd be best if I didn't hit her again.

I punched the rock again, splitting and veining it more. Blood oozed from my knuckles as several portions of rock fell to the ground. I put everything I had into each punch, but I didn't feel any better. I was just too angry.

How dare she think I caused this. *How dare she!* My fist collided with the rock again. During the fight I started to realize they'd been the reason for the Guardian's behavior last night. They were so fast, I didn't doubt they had been running around scoping the village out before attacking. It didn't help there had been plenty of people outside the town to tempt them.

"You know, something with a little more flesh might help you more than that rock."

I spun around, my breath heavy from exhaustion. Raikidan stood a little ways off, leaning against a tree, looking on. He'd finally found clothes, and the cuts and bruises he'd received from the earlier fight were partially healed, as if he'd rejected a full healing session.

If my anger hadn't been so focused, I would have made him my next target. "How long have you been there?"

"Long enough." His normally cocky grin wasn't plastered on his face, so I knew he wasn't being snarky.

I turned my gaze away. "The only thing that could honestly make me feel better is if I smashed that damned woman's face in."

He glanced back in the direction of the village and shrugged. "Then why don't you? Dragons hurt each other all the time when they have a bone to pick with each other. If getting into a physical fight means you'll feel better, then why not?"

"Why not?" I let out a slow exhale. "Maybe because we're not dragons, Raikidan. She's the leader of a shaman tribe, and I'm some failed experiment. It just doesn't work like that."

"You're right. You are an experiment. And if I remember correctly, you also said you know how to kill. So, what's the problem?"

"What's the problem? Do you think I like killing? Do you think I like being a monster?" I threw out my hands. "Newsflash, I don't! I hate knowing that blood stains my hands. I hate knowing that if I killed something right now, it would make me feel better. I hate all of it! I hate..." I sighed and turned away. "Forget it..."

"You're not a monster, Eira. I refuse to believe that."

I looked back at him, my brow furrowed. *He refuses to believe it? Why?*

He approached and sat down on the rock I'd been beating up. "Can I ask you something?"

I shrugged. "Might as well."

"You say you don't like to kill and yet you did it your whole life. Why? Why didn't you say no?"

I leaned against the boulder. "Because I didn't have the ability to." He gave me a quizzical glance, and I continued. "Experiments are designed to take orders. We're tools. We don't have the physical ability to say no to one." I grunted. "Well, not without a lot of struggling. Once we figure out how to struggle past that hurdle, we escape our 'master's' clutches, or die trying."

His lips slipped into a frown. "That's a hellish way to live."

I stared up at the blue sky. "Life can't be kind to everyone."

"How can you just accept it?"

"What else am I supposed to do? I can't change the past, and I can't jump through the timelines to find one where I would be happy and unbroken." I rubbed my bleeding knuckle. "The shamans tried to show me a way to live a better life going forward, but not even they could erase where I came from."

A pause set in for a moment before Raikidan spoke up. "The name Maka'shi calls you. Is that your shaman name?"

I nodded.

"What about this 'Laz' name some have called you?"

"Laz is short for Laz'shika, but I only allow certain individuals to call me that."

"Can I?"

My eyes hardened. "No. You're to call me Eira." He stared at me for a moment, perplexing me. "What?"

"I'm trying to figure out if you're being honest."

"Careful."

"About my name? Why would I lie about something like that?"

He thought this over. "I guess there would be no reason to lie about that. It would be stupid."

"Right, so just call me Eira."

He nodded in agreement, and I watched him carefully. *If he knew how close to the truth he was, I'd be in hot water.*

I looked down at my hands. Alena would kill me if she found out I banged myself up again after she put me back together.

"I want to thank you," Raikidan began, "for defending me. I didn't mean to cause structural damage to those buildings. I'm just stronger in that form. My size also makes up for my lack of speed, so I thought it would be a better choice than this form."

"You don't need to thank me. You're my comrade. I may not trust you with everything I know, but that doesn't change that we're allies." My expression softened. "I won't allow anyone like Maka'shi to insult you for doing what needed to be done to save others."

Before he could reply, my attention snapped to the surrounding tree line. Something large was moving around. A bear was a possible culprit, and not a creature you wanted to surprise, but this creature didn't sound like it was lumbering around. It sounded like a human—a human trying to be quiet and stealthy—*In the trees!*

Just then, a figure jumped down from the tree tops. I managed to push Raikidan out of the way and roll on the ground myself to stay safe. I glanced to the man who stood above me and scowled. Deformed ears and nose, fangs, and talon-like hands, the man wasn't exactly pleasing to look at. *Hunter.* I should have known that it would have been only a matter of time before one made it past the Guardian. With the demons around, they'd have more opportunities to find the construct distracted. *I should have been more careful.*

The Hunter suddenly went flying when Raikidan crashed into it. "Wait, that's a female…"

I was taken aback by this observation and startled when the Hunter rebounded and threw Raikidan into the boulder I had been punching earlier. The boulder broke apart and he cried out out in pain. *Dammit!* I never thought to tell him to take a nu-human form now that his true nature was known. He would have been able to take that a little better, especially after all the fighting we'd done with those demons.

My attention went back to the Hunter, who was still focused on Raikidan. I realized he was right. This was a female Hunter. Female Hunters were rare, and those few that existed cut their hair and bound their chests in order to look more like the males.

The woman slowly turned her angry gaze at me. For some reason, even though they willingly altered their appearance, they didn't particularly enjoy being mistaken for men.

I jumped to my feet and the Hunter came at me with extended claws. She was fast, an enhancement she had over her male counterparts, but so was I. I drew my dagger and parried her sharp claws. Her nails were strong enough to withstand the strength of the blade, another enhancement she had.

As I kept up my defense to find her weak points, I took a second to glance at Raikidan to assess his condition. He appeared to be in pain but was sitting up, which was a good sign. But it also looked as though he had no intention of helping. I suspected he wasn't comfortable fighting a woman. He may have harmed me in that cave, and fought the succubus, but a creature with his kind of loyalty and morals around females would make it hard for him to choose to fight a woman.

I grinned when the Hunter overextended herself, opening her up for my attacks. Going on the offensive, I slashed away at her—my anger and frustration ebbing with each draw of blood. My assault continued until she struggled to stand. She stared up at me with hate-filled eyes.

As much as I didn't like Hunters, it didn't feel right to let her suffer any more, so I plunged the dagger into her chest and then slit her throat. The Hunter caught me off-guard when she continued to fight after suffering such wounds, allowing her to grab hold of my arm and slice into it. I yelled and held my wounded arm. I glared at the woman, but that disappeared as I watched the Hunter fall to the ground and remain motionless. *Fight with every last breath.*

I sighed with relief. My head pulsated with each whiff of blood, but I pushed it away, along with the sensation of satisfaction ebbing over me.

Raikidan approached as I looked down at the body. "You okay?"

I nodded.

"Do you feel any better?"

Instead of replying, I wiped the blood off my dagger. I didn't want to openly admit that the act of killing this Hunter had nearly pacified my anger. Such a reaction was wrong.

I shifted my gaze to the forest when bushes rustled. In the shade of the trees stood the featureless form of the village Guardian. I wouldn't doubt it had been chasing the Hunter before it found Raikidan and me. A quick whistle slipped through my lips as I signaled to it that things were now fine. The Guardian turned away and disappeared into the shadows.

Raikidan held out his hand. "Let me see your arm. Sounded like she got you pretty good."

I tried to hide my arm and ignored the pain pulsing under my skin. "It's nothing, really."

He kept his hand out. "Just let me see it."

"How are you feeling?" I asked, trying to deflect.

"I'll be fine." He didn't drop his hand. "It'll take more than that to kill me."

"That's good. You should probably consider taking a nu-human form going forward. It'll be easier to take hits like that."

He nodded, still not budging on his request. "I thought of that while watching you fight."

I finally gave in to his silent insisting and he examined the wound, as well as the damage I'd caused to my hands. "Sorry for not helping you. After I realized that Hunter was a woman, it didn't feel right to have hit her."

I let him heal up my arm and then my knuckles. "How were you able to harm that succubus? She was female."

His lips pressed into a thin line. "That wasn't easy, either. I had to force myself to think of her as not really a female, and just a creature that pretends to be one to confuse me."

My brow rose. "That's actually an impressive way to go about it."

His lip twitched, and he looked away. *He's remorseful of his actions. Interesting...*

"How do you feel about me letting them go?"

He shrugged. "I don't know. Part of me thinks it was a stupid choice, the other is glad for some reason. I can't explain it."

I nodded and glanced down at the Hunter's body. "I'll take care of her. Why don't you focus on changing your form?"

He agreed, and I went about dragging the body away. When I returned, I found Raikidan in his new form, and Valene with him. They appeared to be having a friendly conversation, based on her smile and his relaxed expression.

Valene smiled at me when I approached. "Body all hidden?"

I looked to Raikidan for answers. He shrugged. "She asked where you were."

Valene giggled. "Don't worry, I won't tell Maka'shi. Don't need another reason for her to go on a rampage."

I bit the inside of my cheek to stop myself from making a remark.

She pointed at Raikidan. "Shva'sika needs him for something, if that's okay."

I pursed my lips. "Maka'shi wants us gone. I don't thi—"

She waved me off. "It's fine. A few of us got Maka'shi to calm down enough to talk some sense into her. We can't send you away without giving you the chance to properly prepare. We got you a few more hours at least. That's why Shva'sika needs Raikidan. She's working on some sort of plan."

"Okay, I'll trust your judgment. While that's going on, I think I'll go to the Library. I want to know more about the demons we dealt with."

Valene smiled. "I'd be happy to help with that."

I nodded. "I wouldn't say no."

She hooked her arm with mine and led the two of us back to the village.

A page of the book flipped on its own as I held my hand over it. Words played through my mind; the ancient magic laced into the pages. Valene rummaged through a bookshelf nearby. We'd searched for several hours for information. We'd found all kinds of history, but not the information we wanted. Until now.

"I finally found you two," came a feminine voice. Valene and I looked up to find Shva'sika and Raikidan approaching. "Raikidan said you'd come here, but I didn't think you'd be so far in."

"Yeah, you're not the only one," I admitted. "I hoped the information would be easy to find, but it took a while."

She continued her approach. "Did you find what you were looking for?"

"I think so." I focused on the closed book in my hand and Valene abandoned her search. "Since succubi and incubi aren't native to Lumaraeon, and only arrived here from summons during the *Dark Wars*, this is the only text I found that could give a plausible reason for the attack. If this text is correct, the two were a mated pair."

Shva'sika rested a finger on her cheek as she thought. "I've never heard of it, and that's surprising with my family's history."

"Mated pairs are rare, even when these creatures were numerous in the past. When it happens, they're gratifying each other's sexual desires, but not their desire for temptation and lust for blood, so they seek out prey together. As a mated pair, they would share each other's strengths and weaknesses, which has its pros and cons. If one hurts, so does the other, but as long as they go untouched, they're golden."

A crystal chair formed next to me from the crystal floor, and Shva'sika took a seat. "That does make sense. So, their attack on our village was just a chance happening."

I nodded. "I believe so. They would have been able to sense the number of people in the village, and if they're fast and elusive enough, they can get past the village Guardian and shaman Guards. Last night, the Guardian was acting strange, quickly moving around in the territory as if hunting. I suspect they found this place yesterday and were scoping it out before their assault."

"With Hunters lurking in the forest too, they might have been able to use that as a distraction," Valene said.

I snorted. "They probably used them as easy victims first."

Shva'sika's eyes darted between the two of us. "What are you two talking about?"

My eyes darted around to make sure no one was listening in and then leaned closer to her, keeping my voice down. "Raikidan and I killed a Hunter before Valene showed up to tell us you needed Raikidan."

Her lips slipped into a frown. "I'll be sure to not allow that to leak to Maka'shi. Getting her to hold off her eviction for a few hours has been hard enough. I don't need another reason for her to banish you."

I shrugged. "I am putting you all in danger. She has a right to be concerned."

Shva'sika shook her head. "We both know that's a scapegoat answer. She's never liked you. From the very beginning, she tried to get rid of you."

One side of my lips slid into a smile. "Half the village didn't want me here when I first showed up."

"But once they realized how wrong they were to make assumptions about you, that changed."

I looked down at the book in my hands. "They weren't exactly wrong assumptions."

She sighed, knowing full well it'd be pointless to argue with me. "Since you're still looking at that tome, it's safe to assume something else is bothering you about those demons?"

I nodded. "It's how the two acted. They were both careless about allowing their names to be known, and then the incubus was so protective of his partner, it was almost as if he…"

"Loved her?" Shva'sika guessed. "That's a pretty farfetched claim for a demon."

"I know, but I can't see why he'd say those things to me if it wasn't true."

"Is that why you let them go?"

"He had the chance to hypnotize me. I looked right into his eyes, but he didn't. He just wanted *Rosa* to be let go. Such a human-sounding name. I can't get that out of my thoughts." I couldn't let her know there had been something else, unknown to me at the moment, compelling me to let them go. That wouldn't reflect well.

Shva'sika held her chin as she thought. "Well, it's possible she was human once. I've heard, back during the days of the Dark Wars, some summoners would perform rituals that would turn themselves into demons. It's possible that succubus had done that to herself."

I nodded slowly. "It's possible. It might be a reason why the incubus had such a fondness for her. Maybe their past is a lot deeper than just being demons. Unfortunately, the book didn't talk about those kinds of rituals or how demons feel about certain things, so unless I find a dark ritual tome, a journal, or talk to a real demon, I doubt I'll know for certain."

"Don't worry too much about it," Shva'sika said. "Those days are long gone, and there are many out there in Lumaraeon who keep watch for possibilities of those days coming back. That's not for you to worry about. The now and the future are what you should be focusing on."

She patted me on the leg and then stood. "I need to finish my task, so you can leave. Valene, I need your help with this last part."

She nodded, a smile on her lips. "Of course."

Shva'sika looked down at me. "I'll have someone fetch you once we're done."

The two left before I could ask questions. Raikidan took Shva'sika's chair. "Any clues to what they're up to?"

He shook his head. "She asked me about my skills and then measured me with some strange rope. Then said that was all she needed me for."

My face scrunched. "Weird."

He looked around. "What is this place?"

"The Library. It holds all of Lumaraeon's known records, even some not known by those living."

"That's a lot of books." He continued his gazing. "Not to sound rude, but this is a weird library."

I chuckled because he was right. There were no walls, and barely any flooring. It was a dark void, and the only light came from floating flames and candelabras. The floor was made of colored crystal, and if you didn't watch yourself, you might just fall into the black abyss below... or was it above?

I gazed at the crystal flooring above and watched people walk around normally, as if they were the ones right side up. All sense of direction was thrown out of balance here. It was easy to forget where you were or which way you came from if you weren't careful. This definitely wasn't your usual library.

I got up from my spot and stored the book away, pulling another one from the shelf that had caught my eye earlier, and also grabbed one that sat on a small table. Sitting back down, I examined the smaller of the two books. Leather bound, like all other tomes in here, the cover had strange designs embossed into it, including some odd script I was unable to make out the origins for. I ran my fingers over the engraving. Before I knew it, the book was out of my hands and in Raikidan's.

He stared at it intently. "Do you know what this says?"

I shook my head. "No, I've never seen such symbols. Do you know what it is?"

"It's my native tongue."

My brow rose. "Speak it."

"*Ion cuvk.*" The words sounded more like a combination of grunts, growls, and a hiss, but it also sounded nice. It sounded natural when he said it.

"What does it mean?"

"Our kind." His voice still had a slight growl to it.

I looked down at the book. "I'll be honest, even with my knowledge of this place, I wouldn't have thought this would be a book on dragons."

Raikidan slid his hand over the leather. "It doesn't look old, either. Maybe a few decades or so. We dragons like to keep to ourselves. I don't understand why someone would put this in here. Or how."

"The Library is old and has many entrances; some in the other shaman villages, and others that are scattered across Lumaraeon, so you'll probably never figure it out."

He opened the book and blinked when faced with blank pages.

I laughed. "It reads to you."

He looked at me, still confused.

"Here." I put his hand on the page and held it there. "Just open up your mind. It's that simple."

He closed his eyes and did as I instructed. As the book spoke to him, symbols appeared and disappeared on the page. When the words stopped appearing, Raikidan opened his eyes. I took the book from him and decided it might be best to find out what was in it. He probably wouldn't tell me much about his kind, so this would be the only way.

"You won't be able to understand." He smirked. "It's all in Draconic."

I chuckled. "The book will translate to the reader's native tongue. In my case, common."

His brow furrowed, and his lips twisted as he thought. *That's actually kind of adorable.*

"Don't think those things about him."

I studied him. "That isn't a problem... right?"

"No. I don't see the harm in you knowing." He scratched his head. "I'm just trying to understand how this all works."

I let him ponder that for a moment. Holding my hand expertly over the book, I let the words flow into my mind, and watched as the words flew across the pages. Since my hand wasn't touching the pages, like I had Raikidan do, the pages flipped automatically after each page, feeding my craving.

Most of the information I was given was either something I had already figured out, or something Raikidan had told me.

> *All dragons can shapeshift, although most choose not to. It takes energy to shift between forms, and as long as a dragon has the energy to shift back to his or her original form, he or she will revert back while asleep, otherwise they will remain in their shifted form until the proper energy is regained. Depending on the shifting skill of a dragon, they will be able to shrink their natural size even while sleeping to accommodate for times when space is an issue, although they cannot make themselves larger than their age-appropriate size.*

This confirmed my earlier suspicions about Raikidan's shifting, and I hoped it wouldn't pose a problem. As long as he had his own room to sleep in, his secret would be safe. I had no intention of telling anyone about what he really was unless he said to. I continued reading.

A majority of dragons are unconcerned about what happens to other species, but some are much more curious, and many of those dragons have a tendency to become obsessive over gaining more knowledge.

I'd have to watch that with Raikidan. I didn't need any curiosity posing a problem. The rest of the text was uneventful. It touched lightly on dragon loyalties and a few territorial habits, but nothing I either didn't know already or cared much about. Satisfied, I closed the book.

"So, what do you think?" he asked.

I shrugged. "Some of it was informative. I figured half of this stuff out already, though."

He held out his hand and I gave it back to him. He looked it over. "So, how does it work? How does someone put information in here?"

I patted the other book I'd retrieved. "This place uses a lost magic. The only way to add new information or alter information is to use one of these."

He rested the Draconic book on the floor to look at the new tome. "How does it work?"

Leaning closer to him, I placed the book on the arms of our chairs and opened it. "Just as you put your hand over it to read it, you have to do the same to write in it. When you do, the book will enter your mind and you must think of what you want on the page. The book will do the rest."

I demonstrated for him. I thought up a few things I wouldn't mind others knowing and let the tome record them.

I am Eira, former commander of Company 14. Life as an experiment was tough and unrewarding, as I did not enjoy my profession, so when the chance came, I escaped. I left the city altogether, leaving my comrades behind, and I have been running since. Now I'm stuck with a dragon named Raikidan, who has personal-space issues, and has the intelligence of a fish.

Figuring that would be enough, I took my hand off and placed Raikidan's hand on the pages in my place. "Read."

He did, and near the end his brow furrowed. I laughed, knowing full well he had gotten to the part about him.

He smacked me on the arm. "Rude. Get rid of it."

"Fine, fine, you big baby." I placed my hand back over the book and changed the information about him. He placed his hand over the tome when I was done and read it.

"Do you mean that?" he asked.

I avoided his question. "Now, to make it completely permanent, you just think of the word *done*, and the book will officially log the entry. If an entry of similar topics hasn't been made, the book will produce a new one in your hands, but since I have made information before, it will automatically transfer to that book."

His brow rose, his interest in the topic clear. "You wrote something about yourself?"

"It has common knowledge in it. Nothing I wouldn't want others to know."

A sly grin spread across his lips. "So, if I looked for it, I wouldn't find something I wouldn't already know?"

I shrugged. "You might, you might not. The major factor is you finding the book. This place is huge, having multiple levels and hundreds of thousands of books, and if the Library doesn't want to help you find it, you could be searching for some time. Time you don't really have."

He grunted and I smiled inwardly. There actually was information in there I would prefer no one knew, but I had accidentally thought of it while recording and the Library hadn't allowed me to alter it for some reason, forcing me to keep the information public. As long as I didn't encourage him to look, I'd be safe, although I had hidden it well. It would take him forever and a half to find it even if he tried, that was, as long as the Library was on my side.

Raikidan picked up the Draconic book again. "I'm sorry about your mother." This sudden change in topic took me by surprise. "I wanted to say it before, but didn't know how at the time."

"I appreciate the sentiment. It won't bring her back, but I came to terms with that some time ago."

Raikidan placed a hand on the entry tome and wrote something in it. When he was done, he gave it back. I read it.

My name is Raikidan, and I'm a solitary dragon. I lived in a small clan that consisted of my mother and my father. That is, until my mother was murdered by humans.

We were the same. We lived alone and lost the one who would always know us the best.

"Ironic." I almost laughed. "She was murdered by humans, and yet here you are, helping one."

"You didn't do it to her," he said calmly. "You don't deserve their deaths."

You don't really believe that. It was easy to see that was a lie. It explained why he had that anger toward me that I'd catch every now and then. And that meant I needed to be careful around him. This alliance could be a way for him to find those who killed his mother, or it could be a ruse.

Raikidan regarded me for a moment and then wrote another entry. When he was done, I took the book back.

I travel with a strange nu-human experiment named Eira. I question if that's her real name, but like she said, 'Why would I lie about a name?' She hates others being in her face, and I swear she wants to kill me sometimes when I get too close.

I chuckled but continued reading.

She's a skilled fighter and can command others as easily as it is to breathe. Eira is the most loyal human I've heard of or even seen for that matter. I've known her for only a short time, but she defends me as if it has been longer. She has called me a comrade, but I don't see her as that. I see her as sa dnuyvk.

I listened to those last two words again and my brow furrowed. As I thought, they didn't translate over. He had figured out how to make it so the words didn't translate, and I really wanted to know what they meant.

"Cheeky dragon, what do those words mean?" I asked.

He smirked. "You'll know when they become true."

Raikidan closed the tome, and I assumed he had told it he was done because a small scroll materialized on top of it. The scroll was sealed shut with a strange wax seal, and when I went to touch it, Raikidan took it away. I crossed my arms and huffed. I knew it was childish, but I wanted to know.

He looked at the bookshelf across from us. "Are we able to take books out of here? Some of these might be helpful."

I shook my head. "No. The Library doesn't allow it."

He tilted his head and I chuckled. "Like Lumaraeon, this place is a living entity. It knows who and what you are. It knows what you intend to do here, and it knows what information you seek. Sometimes it allows you to search on your own, and other times it will place the book in front of you to find it easier, like the book in your hands.

"I never came across it until now, so it obviously didn't want me to see it until this very moment. To protect its secrets, it doesn't allow those who would harm it to enter, and doesn't allow books to go out."

Raikidan's lips twisted as he thought, tapping his scroll absentmindedly on the book.

I pulled the entry tome into my arms. "We don't have to leave if you want to do some reading."

He smiled at me. "Yes, I'd like to do that."

I went to stand up to put away the entry tome, but my foot caught on the leg of the crystal chair. Raikidan bolted out of his seat, his book and scroll clattering on the ground, and caught me. "Easy."

I looked at up him. "What, no fat jokes?"

His brow rose. "Why would I make a joke like that?"

"Because I'm heavy."

"You're not heavy." His arm secure around behind my back, he leaned over and tucked his arm under my leg and then lifted me up as if I weighed nothing. My body tensed up immediately. "See, not heavy in the slightest."

I slammed my palm into his chest. "Put me down this instant!"

He chuckled, his eyes dancing with amusement, and did as I told. "Payback for calling me fat in my true form."

I snorted. "I'm sure if I met another dragon I'd be able to prove it."

His shoulders pulled back as he crossed his arms. "All muscle here."

I couldn't lie, he was an impressive specimen. Most men would kill for his physique. I tossed my head back as I turned away. "Sure sure. But if I'm right, you're going on an insect diet."

Raikidan's face scrunched with disgust and I couldn't stop myself from laughing. He then started laughing, too.

After a moment, I realized how bad that was of me to do. I shouldn't be laughing with him—making a connection with him. I got myself under control and went about putting the entry tome away.

Raikidan retrieved his dropped book and scroll, storing the dragon book in the bookshelf. He smiled at me and then perused the shelf selection, his scroll still in hand.

He was acting oddly. *Did it have to do with what I wrote?*

> *...a dragon named Raikidan, who has to be the most loyal and protective creature I've ever met.*

The approach of a person pulled my attention. I smiled at the blue-eyed man. "Hey, Ken'ichi. Glad to see you up and walking."

He smiled. "If it hadn't been for you, I wouldn't be."

I shrugged. "I do what I can."

Ken'ichi nodded. "And for that, I'm helping where I can. The preparations are done. You and your friend should come with me."

Raikidan stopped his searching, a frown on his lips. I felt a little bad. He'd really wanted to find something. He bopped me on the head with his scroll before placing it in a pile of other scrolls. I swatted at him and he chuckled.

Ken'ichi watched Raikidan, the look in his eyes indicating he either didn't trust Raikidan or didn't like him. I couldn't be sure. Even as kind as he was, he didn't automatically like everyone.

Ken'ichi motioned for us to follow and led us to this mysterious location in regards to the secret planning for my leave.

9
CHAPTER

The drumming of fingers on stone echoed through the room as I sat at Shva'sika's kitchen counter, my cheek resting on my other hand. Ken'ichi, Raikidan, and I had arrived at her house only to find her not there, with a note left for me.

Laz,
  I'll be right back. I have to do one last-minute thing.

Twenty minutes had passed, and my patience was growing thin. I could have let Raikidan read more if I'd known there wasn't any rush.

Raikidan leaned against a wall in the living room, his arms crossed. In the same position, Ken'ichi leaned on a wall near him, the two unmoving. This display was the only thing keeping me from preparing an angry lecture for Shva'sika. I had patience for many things, but this kind of behavior from people didn't fall into that bubble.

The front door flew open, and Shva'sika and Valene entered the house. *Finally!* I stood, only to notice their subdued expressions. "What's with the faces?"

Ken'ichi's eyes widened. "Don't tell me Maka'shi found out about the plan."

Shva'sika let out a long sigh as her shoulders sagged. "I'm afraid so. I just spent the last twenty or so minutes arguing with her about it."

I studied her. "Ken'ichi wouldn't tell us this plan. Said it was best if you relayed it, but from what I can see, you won the battle, but at a heavy cost."

She nodded, not able to meet my gaze. "Yes. I wanted to come up with an easy way for you to sneak into Dalatrend. I suspected you had some secret way in, but this would allow you to walk in the front gate, making it less risky."

I realized what she was up to. Her needing to take Raikidan's measurements made sense now. "You wanted to work it out, so we could disguise ourselves as shamans."

Shva'sika nodded. "Since you're a shaman in training, it wouldn't be a disguise for you." She glanced Raikidan's way. "And he's shown promise for Guard selections, so Ken'ichi agreed to a do a quick assessment to accept him as one in training or not. This will allow for him to also wear the clothes without causing any law issues. Dalatrend soldiers also believe only men can be Guards in our customs, so that thinking can work in our favor keeping you out of the spotlight."

It was an excellent idea. Due to customs, not even soldiers could force a shaman to pull down the hood of their cloak to reveal their identities. It wasn't that complicated of a disguise, but the cloaks obscured the face just enough for people to struggle with facial recognition. I'd seen it happen with something as simple as wearing goggles or a haircut, so a cloak would work just as well.

But there was one issue with her plan involving Raikidan as a Guard. "But shamans need a connection to the spiritual plane. There isn't enough time to test for that."

Valene giggled. "Guards are an exception. Many Guards with no spiritual connection have been trained in the different tribes, even this one."

I nodded. "I didn't realize that. That's good to know. But this plan now comes with conditions if I'm guessing correctly."

Shva'sika's hands clenched into tight fists and Valene's eyes lowered. "Yes. Maka'shi has made some... heavy demands. If the two of you accept this plan, you will be stripped of your shaman status."

My eyes narrowed. Even I knew that wasn't possible. She didn't have the power to make such decisions. There had to be more to this.

"And... and you're banned from ever stepping foot into this village again."

Valene flinched and Ken'ichi's arms fell to his sides, his eyes widening. "She can't be serious."

Shva'sika remained quiet. I could see her struggling to keep her composure.

"I agree to the terms." The three of them stared at me with slacked jaws and wide eyes. I shrugged. "I knew she'd do that. You saw how she acted earlier. Even without this plan, she'd try to ban me from this place. This just gives her leverage."

Valene's eyes welled up. "How can you act like it's not a big deal?"

"Because there's nothing that can be done to fight it." I sighed and shoved my hands into my pocket. "There comes a time where you learn to accept the bad with the good, no matter the ratio." I chuckled. "You won't die without me here. You'll keep living your life and be happy."

Tears streamed down her cheeks and she ran out of the house. Shva'sika sighed and Ken'ichi looked at me. "You could have been nicer."

I shook my head. "There's no nice way to handle that. She's better off accepting the terms as they are than fighting a pointless battle."

He crossed his arms and his lips spread into a line, but he didn't have a comeback. I knew he didn't like them any more than she did, but he also understood there were some terms that couldn't be negotiated.

"There's also one more term," Shva'sika said. "But you don't have to follow it because she can't enforce it. Naturally we shamans are to appear neutral, especially with Dalatrend due to the pact we've signed. Maka'shi is determined to ensure this stays in place, and has forbidden you to use your attire after you arrive in the city. She's forbade you to use it as some sort of cover while out and about. But most of us would rather see Zarda's soul rendered into oblivion. This means, no one is going to stop you if you choose to walk around the city as one of us. You have a right to do so anyway, no matter what she says."

She's really trying to separate me from them. The only thing was, she couldn't stop me from joining another tribe if I so desired, making the heavy weight of her demands far lighter than she'd want. *Too bad for her, I'm too smart for that.*

I nodded. "I'm still accepting the terms, as long as Raikidan also does."

He shrugged. "I don't see a reason not to if you have."

Ken'ichi pushed away from the wall. "It's settled, then. Raikidan, come with me so I can give you a crash course and assessment. We'll return here for you to dress and rejoin Eira."

The two left the house, leaving me with Shva'sika. Her downhearted expression spurred me to speed up this process. "So, what am I going to wear? I never went about designing special clothes for myself when I lived here."

Her expression changed, lips sliding into a devious grin. "Oh, I'm well aware. I created something special for you."

The shamans and druids of the land had a rather unique way of dressing, and each tribe had their own spin. But one thing that was similar, even for the cold North Tribe, was the lack of clothing involved. A knot formed in the pit of my stomach. "What did you do?"

Shva'sika hooked her arm in mine and pulled me up the stairs. "You'll see."

I followed, but I tried to be slow, my reluctance to trust her clear. *She's getting back at me for all those times I refused her outfits before.* My actions amused her, and she continued to lead me to my torture chamber.

The body mirror reflected my image as I fussed with the "clothes" Shva'sika forced on me. My top was a thick strip of red cloth that wrapped around my breasts, though not thick enough to prevent an obnoxious amount of cleavage and underboob. No matter how much I fussed, I couldn't fix that problem.

The top tied in the back like a corset and was lined on the top and bottom with gold metal. The bottom lining grew thicker in the center between my breasts, allowing for a carving of the West Tribe symbol.

Fastened around each arm with gold metal bands at the top were loose red cloth sleeves that had small cutouts on the underside by the metal bands. The end of each sleeve merged into a small triangle that attached to a golden ring and was slipped around my middle finger. Strapped to these arm pieces were two of my daggers.

My lip curled as I tugged on the thin cloth covering my lower half, my fingers grazing the exposed skin of my ass. My face flushed. "I can't believe you put me in this repulsive thing."

Shva'sika scoffed as she appeared behind me, in her hands gold chain sandals she wanted me to wear. "You're such a prude."

My face reddened more. "Sorry that I think I should be wearing something that's more than bedroom appropriate for the more adventurous woman?"

"A little skin never hurt anyone." Her eyes twinkled. "And they'd help you get a man finally."

I rolled my eyes and fussed with my clothes some more. "Not on my *to-do* list." She giggled and my face reddened when I realized she twisted that meaning. "This thong is giving me the worst wedgie of my life. I can't believe I'm going to have to wear this for days. I don't even see why you're insisting I wear something like this. It's not like anyone is going to see me in it with the cloak thankfully hiding me."

Just then, the door to the room flew open, Ken'ichi's words ringing out. "Raikidan, you can't just barge in!"

I gasped as Raikidan walked in. He wore a red hooded vest with gold embroidery, the front open exposing his bare chest. Loose red pants covered his lower half, pinning to his legs near his ankles, and sandals, similar in design to the ones I still needed to put on, covered his feet.

"Get out!" I screeched as I shrunk back, wrapping my arms around my body.

Raikidan's eyes widened, clearly not understanding my reaction. "Why are you yelling?"

Ken'ichi showed up in the room and reached for Raikidan's arm. "I said you can't—"

He stopped dead when he spotted me. My face burned the longer he stared, the heat reaching my ears.

My next words were articulated and laced with venom. "Get out. Now!"

Ken'ichi snapped out of his daze and pulled Raikidan out of the room. "Let's go before she kills us."

When the door closed, Shva'sika burst out laughing, sending the heat from my face flooding through my body. "That wasn't funny…"

"Yes, it was." She continued to laugh. "Oh, yes it was."

My eyebrow twitched. "Give me my cloak."

Shva'sika shook her head as she calmed herself. "You need to lighten up. It could have been worse. You could still be putting on your clothes."

I desperately tried to shut out that mental image. "Don't even go there."

She grinned wickedly as she handed me my sandals. "What? Don't you want those men's eyes bugging out?"

"They wouldn't have bugged out..."

She snickered as she grabbed two red sheer cloths. "Oh, don't be like that. It was obvious with Ken'ichi, but even your new dragon Guard had his own subtle reaction." She winked. "Means this outfit works just as I intended."

My lips pressed into a thin line as I slipped my feet into my new shoes, refusing to continue this unwanted conversation. Instead, I focused on the new feeling these shoes brought. It'd been a while since I'd worn anything on my feet. I guessed it'd take me a few hours at least to get used to it.

While I had my focus on my feet, I made sure the daggers strapped to my legs were secure. I'd never worn them on bare skin before, so I wanted to be sure I wouldn't lose them.

Shva'sika approached with the cloth, handing me the smaller of the two. Taking a look, I found it to be a veil designed to go over the mouth. *This will help to throw off my appearance, even if the fabric can be seen through a bit.* While I fitted the veil to my face, Shva'sika took the longer fabric and wrapped it around my waist, tying it off on one side at the hip. *Oh, it's a sarong.* Even as a sheer fabric, I felt a little more covered.

My elven friend then retrieved the cloak I asked for earlier, allowing me to hide. I let out an audible sigh of relief when I clasped the cloak closed on my shoulder.

Shva'sika shook her head and then fussed with my hair. "I wish you'd just kept it down. I decorated it, so it'd look better that way."

I gazed at myself in the mirror. An elegant golden circlet, with an oval-shaped ruby fastened to the center, sat on my brow while leaves and feathers had been wrapped and twisted into my hair before being pulled back into my usual hairstyle. "I told you, with my hair color I need to keep it out of view as much as possible. In a city, I could pull it off as a dyed color, but out here... well, you tell me how many people you've met with my hair color."

She let out a quiet breath. "I get your point; I just wish you would wear your hair down more often."

My mouth remained shut, memories of my past threatening to surface. *I just prefer it up...*

Her hand landed on my shoulder. "I should stop stalling you. We don't need Raikidan barging in again out of impatience."

My cheeks flushed and I grumbled to myself. He needed to learn the meaning of privacy, and quick. I was not going to tolerate such behavior as what he displayed earlier. Shva'sika led me through her house, taking her time to allow me to sear it into my memory. I hadn't wanted to be banished from here, but there were things in life that were out of my control. *And I've never been lucky enough to have what I want…* Something always went wrong when I came close. *I just hope this choice to fight Zarda isn't what ends me.*

The sound of the two Guards talking wisped past my ears. The two stopped when Shva'sika and I came to the top of the stairs. Raikidan's expression remained impassive and Ken'ichi smiled, though I could tell it hurt him to. My decision weighed heavily on him.

"We're ready to depart, if you two are," Shva'sika announced when we reached the bottom of the stairs.

Ken'ichi nodded and followed her to the door. I glanced at Raikidan, who remained quiet and followed. He didn't look at me, and it perplexed me. *Probably for the best after what happened earlier.*

Our small group walked the dirt path leading back to town. Upon arrival, a group of people had gathered by the Spiritual Crystal. I guessed them to be those who wanted to see me off. Our approach parted them, revealing Maka'shi standing next to the crystal, her expression neutral. *For now.*

The half-elf's eyes darted from me to Raikidan when we stopped a few feet from her, and then her gaze fell on Ken'ichi. "What was the outcome for the assessment?"

"He performed the assessment well enough that I ended up giving him the full entrance test. He passed without issue."

Her eyes darkened but focused on me. "You know of my terms, yes?"

I gave a curt nod. "And I accept them."

"Very well." She held her head high, a vindictive smile spreading across her lips. "I, Maka'shi, leader of the West Shaman Tribe, strip you of your rank as a Shaman of the Rising Sun, as with your shaman name." She threw out her hand as if to emphasis her next words. "You are hereby banished from this village. Return, and you will be seen as an invader."

The people around her gasped but she didn't falter. "You are also never to contact anyone in this village, in any way, unless they have contacted you first with my express approval."

The crowd murmured, their eyes darting between Maka'shi and me.

My lips spread into a thin line. I knew there was more than what had been agreed with by Shva'sika.

Shva'sika's eyes narrowed. "This is not what we discussed!"

Maka'shi held her ground. "This is my stipulation."

"You can't do this!" Shva'sika yelled. "You may be our leader, but you can't do this!"

Maka'shi's eyes hardened. "Per our customs, I was handed the mantle of leader of this tribe. It is my sworn duty to protect all who live here. I decide what is a threat to us, and will do what I must to remove it. This is my decree."

Shva'sika went to argue more but I held up my hand to stop her. "I agree to the terms."

Shva'sika gasped. "Laz... Why? This is—"

I held her gaze. "Don't argue, please. It will only delay the inevitable."

Maka'shi nodded, clearly pleased she'd won. "Say your goodbyes and leave. You still have a few hours before nightfall. That should be plenty of time to leave our lands."

Shva'sika's eyes burned into Maka'shi, her teeth nearly baring in her anger. "You will not get away with this."

Maka'shi tilted her head, regarding Shva'sika's threat. But in her arrogance, she brushed it off and focused back on me. "Eira, if I catch wind of you using this disguise to gain foothold in your little rebellion, I will—"

"Will what?" A smirk spread across my lips. "You'll leave your precious 'sanctuary' and find me? We both know that won't happen. And you won't find anyone to enforce your power, either."

Her eyes glittered, knowing I was right. "Say your goodbyes and leave."

She stepped back, but didn't allow me to leave her sight. Several townsfolk said their farewells before Alena pushed through. She gave me a tight hug. "I'm going to miss you."

"I'll miss you too." I pulled away. "Give Del'karo my regards and apologies for missing him."

She tried to smile, but her somber mood overpowered it. "You know I will."

A small hand tugged on my cloak. I looked down to see Sethal peering up at me with sad eyes. "You don't really have to go forever, do you?"

I knelt and patted him on the head. "I'm afraid so."

His gaze fell to the ground. "I don't want you to go."

I kissed him on the forehead. "I know. But this just means you have to protect your mom extra hard with me gone. Can you do that for me?"

He looked up at me and nodded, steeling himself. "Of course!"

I patted him on the head again and stood.

Sethal grabbed onto his mother's clothes and gave Maka'shi a side-long glance. "I don't like her anymore, Momma."

Alena rested her hand on her son's head. "I know. I don't, either."

I noticed Maka'shi's expression change to shock. I didn't understand why. *Could she possibly think no one would hate her for this decision?*

Shva'sika and Daren approached, the latter carrying a leather bag. He held it out to me. "For ye, lass. Supplies for ye trip."

"I also put some items of my own in it," Shva'sika added.

I accepted the bag with a smile, but Raikidan took it from me and slung it over his shoulder. He didn't look at me or give any quick explanation. I chose not to fuss. I wasn't in the mood.

Daren's lip quivered, the cheerful face that'd gotten me through some tough days gone. I never wanted to see that smile leave him, and as a last goodbye, I desperately wanted to see it one last time, searing it into my mind. He pulled me in for a tight hug. "Ye be careful. Dinnae be gettin' yerself killed now, ye hear?"

Even though my arms couldn't reach around his large size, I did my best to return his tight hug. "I'll do my best."

He let go only for Shva'sika to throw her arms around me. "I'm sorry. I didn't think she'd go beyond our agreed terms. Had I known, I would have come up with another idea."

I held her close. "It's not your fault. She would have done this without this plan. It's why I accepted the terms still." I pulled away and wiped away a single tear running down her cheek. "It'll all work out. You'll see."

Ken'ichi came up to me and handed over a small, blue-and-black glowing orb to me. I accepted it with a raised brow. "A portal?"

"It's about to die out, so can only transport you a few miles." He smiled. "But I figured it'd help cut down the time required to walk. Probably best to use it once you leave the territory."

I smiled. "Thanks."

Looking around I frowned. Valene hadn't come to say goodbye. *She's probably too upset.* I decided, for her sake, that it would be best not to go and find her.

With a heavy heart, I waved and said my final farewell before leading Raikidan to the East road leading out of the village.

We made it halfway to the road when a female voice called out, "Wait! Laz, please wait."

I turned to find Valene rushing toward us, tears staining her cheeks. I held out my arms and she crashed into me, the force pushing me back a few steps.

"Don't go," she begged. "Please don't go."

I kissed her on the head. "I'm sorry, but I have to."

She shook her head and tightened her grip. "No, no you can't. Please don't leave me again."

Her words pierced my heart like the sharpest knife. "I have to go, Valene. I can't stay here. I'm sorry."

"No, you can't leave!"

I looked up, hoping someone could assist me, to find Ken'ichi and Tesne running over to help. The two grabbed a hold of Valene and I proceeded to pry her off me. She fought us, screaming, crying... begging for me not to go. Each plea dug the emotional knife deeper.

Valene held out her arm, now pulled back too far to touch me. "You can't! Don't go!" Her tears splattered on the ground as I turned away. "Please... Momma..."

Pain I thought I'd never feel again tore through my chest. My teeth clenched *Why, Valene... why...* I pulled my hood over my head and pushed it all away. Nothing could change this. Rebellion or no, Maka'shi would have banished me either way. And as an ordinary human, Valene couldn't come with me. She'd be safe here, and only here for now.

Valene's screams and pleas followed me as Raikidan and I disappeared into the woods. The sound of her falling to the ground and sobbing sat heavy on my shoulders. It eventually turned to words of malice as she tore into Maka'shi. No one stopped her.

In time, it all faded with the distance placed between me and the last place I had ever been able to call home.

10
CHAPTER

ilence permeated the air as Raikidan and I followed the East path. We'd walked about an hour from what I could gauge, and I was thankful for the quiet. It gave me time to sort myself out, as I found it hard to shake Valene's words. My hand clutched the portal Ken'ichi gave me, giving me grounding, but I was careful not to squeeze it too hard and accidentally activate it. I wanted to use up what was left of its power in one go to get us as far as possible.

Movement in the forest caught our attention. Turning, we found the Guardian approaching. *Great, Maka'shi probably had it reprogramed already.*

The Guardian stopped walking when it came into arm's reach, towering over us, and held out an arm. In what could serve as its hand hovered a small flame. The being held it out to me. I summoned up my own key flame, assuming it wanted proof I wasn't a threat, but when I held the fire out, the Guardian ignored it. It pushed the flame it carried closer to me.

I eyed the Guardian warily, and then reached out to touch the flame. I'd never seen this behavior before, and in my time spent at the village, no one had told me of it, either. My finger came in contact with the burning element and a startling pulse ran through me.

"Shaman," came a strong ethereal voice in my mind. *"I have been given a strange command. It has told me to see you as an enemy."*

Great, here we go.

"But I will not heed this new command." My eyes widened with surprise. *"I have watched you since the day you first arrived long ago. I have seen your bravery and your drive to protect these people. You've shown me respect when others have treated me as a mere construct, having forgotten exactly what I am. This has not changed in you as the sands of time passed. You have remained the same caring soul that I cannot forget. You are not a danger."*

It pulled away and walked back in the direction it'd come, its last words still burning in my mind.

"You are welcome in these lands, as you have always been. We will meet again, Ancient Soul. I'm looking forward to it."

The fact this creature could speak, in its own way, shocked me enough to be unable to respond. I didn't know what it meant by "Ancient Soul" but I didn't feel as though this was the time to ponder that.

Raikidan leaned over to look at me. "Are you okay?"

"It... talked to me." I turned my head to focus on him. "It's a sentient being."

He looked taken aback by what I said. "Uh, so does that not make it some sort of golem?"

"I don't know..."

"What did it say to you?"

"That it won't obey its new order to see me as a threat to the tribe." My brow furrowed. "And that we'll meet again and it's looking forward to it."

I figured it best not to mention the "Ancient Soul" part. Too many unwanted situations could come of that confusion.

Raikidan straightened up. "Well, strange as it is, that's a good thing, right?"

I nodded. "I guess I got it to like me more than I thought."

He gazed up at the sky. "We're burning daylight. We should get moving." Raikidan looked down at me again. "We could use that thing you called a portal. Sounded like it could move us closer to our destination somehow."

I peered down at the glowing orb in my hands. "Technically these aren't supposed to be used within the shaman territories, except for emergencies or special occasions. With what happened between Maka'shi and me, I'm not all that interested in obeying her, but at the rate the sun is sinking, we could use the protected nature of this forest to our advantage for a night of rest. Then in the morning we could use the portal to cut a few miles of travel off our journey."

Raikidan frowned. "Do you not trust me to keep you safe?"

I pursed my lips. "I didn't say that. I just figured it'd be easier on the both of us if we use the added safety of the Guardian. We don't know the terrain we'll end up in on the other side of the portal."

His expression didn't change. "I can keep us safe without it lurking around."

I pulled back. *Why is he acting so offended? It's not like what I planned insulted his abilities or anything.* "Okay, fine. We'll use the portal now."

Squeezing the orb in my hand, I pictured Dalatrend, a sprawling city with high walls to keep invaders out and citizens in, and then tossed it on the ground. Within seconds, the orb distorted and grew until it was several feet taller and wider than the average man. I beckoned Raikidan to follow, and then entered the mystical doorway. Inside the portal, blue, black, and white lights flashed and swirled around. The further we walked, the more disorienting the chosen path became.

When it got to the point where I thought I might get sick, a white light flashed before us, forcing me to shield my eyes. I blinked a few times once it was gone, and examined our surroundings. We stood in a meadow, the forest long gone and a brook bubbling in the distance. The eastern road still traveled the same way, unmaintained as ever. I guessed us to be still several days out from our destination. A day's travel from the city, we'd pass a small town that would be the farthest west to have a road suitable for standard vehicles.

The portal behind us warped and then collapsed within itself, never to be used again. Raikidan stared at the now empty space and then looked around. "So, where did you bring us?"

"Somewhere between the tribe and Dalatrend." I headed down the road. "The portal didn't have enough energy to bring us the full length of the destination, so it brought us as far as possible without trapping us inside."

He followed. "I didn't think we'd be in such an exposed area."

"I did mention this would be an unknown before you went and got offended about something I didn't accuse you of."

Raikidan didn't reply to this, and I didn't have the urge to care whether it affected him or not. We'd just have to trudge on and hope some cover would come up in the next few hours of travel.

The hours passed, and night fell before we came to a small grove. It didn't offer optimal cover, but it rested several yards away from the main road on hilly ground, aiding in our need to stay hidden.

Raikidan gathered some tinder and lit a fire while I settled down to look over the bag Darren and Shva'sika had given me. The outside wasn't anything too impressive, although the leather was of high quality and the stitching was well done. Opening the bag, I found it to be lined in various-colored rabbit pelts.

The bag contained a number of items, much of it wrapped up in paper. *Must be the food Daren mentioned.* I went about pulling some out, only to find more beneath.

I continued to pull out more, catching Raikidan's attention. "That's a lot of stuff you're pulling out."

He's right. My brow furrowed as I found more and more items to pull out, as if it were endless. *Wait a second...* I looked at the exterior of the bag, then inside, then outside again as I analyzed the accessory. "She gave me a void bag."

Raikidan tilted his head a few degrees. "A what?"

I continued to pull items out of the bag. "It's a rare bag with an ancient magical enchantment. The enchantment allows for an absurd amount of objects to be placed into it without the exterior growing in size or bursting. The exact amount it can hold before it gets full is determined by the size of the bag used. Based on this size, I'm going to guess I could fit a few people in here if I wanted to."

"Well if any of those Hunters show up, we can always stuff their bodies in there until we find a good place to dump them."

I sputtered out a laugh and he grinned.

"At least the dark humor wasn't wasted."

He watched me take out more items after I got myself under control and then spoke again. "So, you said it's lost magic. What about that portal?"

I rocked my head side to side as I thought about how to answer. "Sorta. Portals are a type of magic, and much of the knowledge on how to create them isn't as widely known, but it's a different magic than straight arcane magic like the bag. From what I've been told, the portal magic is a combination of arcane, spiritual, and natural. Where they have access to arcane, I couldn't begin to tell you, since everyone knows there are only a handful of lesser arcane spells left in Lumaraeon. A major spell would be needed for something like a portal or a void bag."

Raikidan stroked his chin. "I know what natural magic is—druids use it—and our draconic magic is similar to it, but what is spiritual magic?"

I steepled my hands as I thought about the explanation. When I was first told about it, it didn't make much sense to me. "Well, unlike druidic magic, which is pulled from both outside and inside the body, spiritual magic is all internal. It's the energy our spirits and souls are made of, meaning all beings have this energy. Shamans have a way of manipulating that energy and forcing it to their will. It allows them to calm other people, heal, or force their consciousness onto the spiritual plane, to name a few things."

Raikidan held his chin and tapped a finger on his lips. "Sounds… complicated."

I chuckled. "Trust me, it's no cakewalk learning."

"How does someone go about learning?"

"The spirits choose you."

He gave a look to urge me to explain better.

"As most know, those who die go to the spiritual plane, but for a short period of time they can come back and offer guidance. They also sense the strength of an individual's spiritual magic. If it's strong enough, they send them vision dreams to find shamans for training." I grunted. "Of course, their visions are cryptic as all hell, but I'm sure it's how they get their kicks."

Raikidan chuckled and then pulled on his vest. "What magic is used on this?"

I tilted my head and he caught onto my confusion quickly.

"Your nu-human friend said it was special made for my shifting ability. He said there'd be some sort of note to explain if there wasn't time to inform you in person."

I rummaged through the bag, finding two large books, one with a note tucked into it. I pulled it out to find it scrawled in elegant handwriting in Elvish script. *Shva'sika...* I ran my fingers over the dried ink, and the letter began to read to me, like one of the library books would.

> *Laz,*
>
> *If you're reading this, then I wasn't able to tell you a few things in person.*
>
> *Due to Raikidan's shifting abilities, he will struggle to keep a wardrobe. I did some research and found a druidic spell that rectifies that issue. Whenever he shifts, the clothes will fit that form, if humanoid, and disappear into his form when not. Don't ask me how it works; I just collected the materials required.*
>
> *I've applied the spell to his Guard clothes and provided the materials needed for three more outfits for when you arrive in the city. I've also given you another gift. The books.*
>
> *Both of these books are connected to the Library. One book is blank for writing in, if you ever wish to add to the collection. The other is an access book, allowing you to obtain any information you need from the Library, including the spell I used.*
>
> *I hope you cherish this book. It's been in my family for generations and was given to us by the Library in thanks for protecting the entrance before the village had been constructed around it.*
>
> *I hope these will help you in some way. I will see you again in time, and remember, no matter what Maka'shi says, you will always be my sister and I will be there for you when you need me.*
>
> *Love always,*
> *Shva'sika*

I smiled and continued to touch the ink. "She put some sort of druid spell on the clothes. It won't rip when you shift, though what happens to them when you take a non-humanoid form, is an unknown beyond 'they go away.'"

He nodded. "We'll find out soon enough." He focused on the small food packages. "What do we have to eat?"

"Good question." With the amount of food given, we'd be set for weeks. Or could potentially feed an army. I opened a few bundles to find mostly meat, both dried and fresh cut, but there were a number of premade meals. "We have a bit of everything, take your pick."

He took a bundle of raw meat and a soup, still hot. I also chose a bundle of raw meat and a premade meal of chicken, potatoes, and greens, also still warm.

Raikidan inspected the hot stew. "How is this possible?"

I bit into some chicken. "Druid spell. It preserves food for a month before dissipating. Shamans use it as they agree with the minimal-waste ideologies of druids. Works great for long journeys."

He nodded, accepting the explanation, and went to eating. Silence fell between us as we consumed our meals. That is, until I tore into the raw meat and consumed it. "You ate like that the other day. We dragons eat like that, but I thought with the way you humans live, that you cooked all your food."

I finished chewing before answering. "Well, you'd be right for the average person. Most people who eat raw meat would get sick, but I'm one of those strange ones who can eat it raw or cooked."

"Interesting." He tore into his own cut of meat. "Since we're talking, can you tell me more about this place we're going to?"

I pursed my lips. "I can try. It's one of the largest cities on this side of Lumaraeon, surrounded by two walls, an inner and an outer. Houses and businesses of all shapes and sizes are crammed inside the inner wall, while the outer wall is used for agriculture."

I ripped into my food. "The city itself is split into four quadrants, which in turn are split into three sectors each. All invisible lines of course, but it's rather easy to tell where those lines are since each quadrant shows the wealth of those who live there. Located in the center of Quadrant One is the temple dedicated to those who wish to publicly show worship to their gods, and in Quadrant Two is an empty area that allows for large social gatherings, like music concerts and festivals. In the center of the city is a small forest with a park for people to use as recreation. Behind it all is a giant, heavily guarded wall that encloses the 'castle' Zarda lives in."

Raikidan chewed his meal as he processed the information and then changed the topic a bit. "This Zarda we're after. Tell me more about him, besides being a 'tyrant.'"

It was a good question. How best to describe the monster?

"He looks young, no older than thirty-five or so, although he's much older than that. No one knows his true age, but he's far outlived the nu-human life expectancy… somehow. He's tall, has black hair, and is clean-shaven, most of the time. He's of course nu-human and basically demon spawn. He cares only for power, and doesn't care who tries to get in his way; he'll destroy them one way or another."

"How did someone like that gain so much power?"

"He took it. He assassinated our previous leader, and then usurped the position. But he had his fingers tangled in the mess long before."

"Strange question, but was anyone you know born while the previous leader ruled?"

I nodded, wording myself carefully so as not to give too many secrets away, but still show some honesty to this dragon. "A couple—all experiments who've also outlived the average nu-human life expectancy."

He tilted his head back to gaze at the sky. "Interesting…"

Silence fell between us again until I finished my meal and cleaned up. "I'll take first watch."

Raikidan peered into the darkness beyond the low campfire light. "I can do that. You get some sleep."

"I'm going to have to take a watch at some point tonight. You need sleep as well."

He shrugged. "I'll be fine. I've gone without sleep before."

I didn't feel like arguing with him, so I let him do his thing. Still, that didn't mean I trusted him not to fall asleep during his long watch. I found a small outcropping in the hill to slip under and curl up, using my cloak to help hide me. With as thin a material as it was, I felt uncomfortable with it covering me, but I sucked it up. It was safer this way and would keep my exposed ass covered. Making sure I had a dagger in an accessible area to defend myself if needed, I let the crickets sing me to sleep, knowing full well I'd wake up periodically to check our surroundings and take watch if the time came.

11
CHAPTER

N ine days passed before the giant outer wall of Dalatrend came into view. My knowledge of the land, thanks to my time in the military, told me the West Tribe was about a two-week walk from Dalatrend, so that portal had cut our travel time by five days. A considerable distance, given the fact it didn't have much life left in it. *Far more miles than Ken'ichi originally claimed, too.* I wasn't complaining.

Raikidan had tried to convince me to allow him to fly us here under the cover of night to hasten our trip, but I wasn't having it. I'd have rather walked another ten years before I'd be caught up in the air like that.

Raikidan took great interest in the sight of the structure but didn't ask about it. He did, however, close what little distance between us as we approached the front gate, which I didn't think possible due to his already too-close proximity.

Sentinels on the watchtowers took notice of us and called out to more beyond the wall to warn of our approach. By the time the two of us came within feet of the closed front gate, several men and women garbed in off-white military uniforms stood on guard, their hands clearly ready to use their weapons if ordered. Full-face helmets obscured their identities.

One stepped forward, his shoulders pulled back to impose his power on us. "Halt. State your names, association, and business."

I bowed while Raikidan remained upright and alert to every soldier in view. "Good morning. My name is Laz'shika and this is my Guard. We hail from the West Tribe. Our business relates to shaman mercantile matters."

He beckoned me forward with a finger. "Present papers."

"Papers?" Why was he asking for papers? Even when I was in the military, I knew of the peace pact between Dalatrend and the shamans. No paperwork was necessary for them to enter or leave.

"Yes, all who visit must present the proper preapproved paperwork detailing the means for their visits as well as their length of stay."

Since when? Something wasn't right here. Just then, a fortified door on the wall opened and a tall, well-built man clad in a black military uniform exited. *Oh good, someone with identifiable rank who can give me answers.*

"Excuse me, Sir, but might you be the commanding officer?" I asked.

"I am." He approached and removed his helmet, showing he saw us as no threat. *That's reassuring.* He had a clean-shaven face, tan skin, and red hair, cut high and tight like many military men. "General Zo. Is there a problem here?"

I bowed. "A pleasure to meet you. As for a problem, I'm not sure. My Guard and I are on business to assist others of the tribes with some mercantile necessities and guidance. This gentleman here has barred our entrance due to a lack of paperwork. This would be my first time here in Dalatrend, but I'm well aware of our agreement with this city. I don't ever recall any need for paperwork."

He nodded. "My deepest apologies, ma'am. This has been a recent change of ours for security purposes"—he glanced at his comrade—"though shamans are exempt from this. Amon here knows this and shouldn't have barred your entry."

Amon lowered his head. "My apologies. I… forgot."

Yeah right. I smiled. "All is forgiven."

General Zo touched something small attached to his ear and spoke. "Open the gates."

A muffled voice answered him and a few moments later, the large gate creaked and moaned as it opened.

The general looked at Raikidan and me again. "You're all clear. Do you know where you're headed?"

"Just a vague location," I said. "They mentioned Quadrant Three, but that was several weeks ago, and I don't fully understand where that is."

He nodded and reached into a pouch tied to his belt, pulling out a box. He pressed a button and the top of the box twisted open in the center, revealing a small glass dome. It then emitted a bright light through the dome and projected a map of the city. "There aren't any shaman merchant caravans in Quadrant Three this week." He pointed to a spot in Quadrant Two. "You'll be looking for them in Quadrant Two. They've moved around a lot this week, so I'm afraid I don't have an exact location.

"When you arrive, if you can't find them after some searching, just speak to military personnel and they'll be able to guide you to your friends. If you fear getting lost on your way to Quadrant Two, there are many public maps placed on the main roads to guide you." He then pointed to a spot in Quadrant Three. "And, I'd highly recommend you check out this area during your stay."

My brow rose. What was he up to? "Why's that?"

The general smirked. "It's a popular shopping district, and a pretty woman like yourself should treat herself every once in a while to the finer things in life."

Great, one of those guys. I forced a smiled. "Thank you for the suggestion. I'll have to think about it—if time permits, of course."

General Zo smiled. "Of course. Please enjoy your stay in Dalatrend, and if you see any suspicious activity, please let military personnel know. Our goal is to keep everyone safe."

More like control them. "Thank you, General. You and your compatriots have a wonderful day."

The general moved aside, smacking Amon in the back of the head as he let Raikidan and me pass. When we were out of earshot, I let out a deep sigh of relief. "That wasn't as easy as expected."

"Was that paperwork requirement real?" Raikidan asked.

I shrugged. "I don't know. Before I left, if anyone planned to stay longer than a week, they had to sign paperwork indicating their length of stay. If they stayed beyond what was agreed, then there'd be some sort of consequence. The most notable was forced residency. Shamans, druids, and gypsies were always exempt from this."

Raikidan held up a hand. "Wait, back up, people were forced to stay here if they visited too long?"

I nodded. "Told you Zarda was a tyrant. He gets away with it, too, due to his power, compared to a lot of other cities. Of course, many of those people join the resistance if they can't get proper transfer paperwork approved, so it doesn't work out as well for Zarda as he thinks it does."

"It doesn't make sense to me how it works at all, but if it does, then it does." He became distracted when we approached the plantation fields. They spread for miles, bordering the entire city, acting as a type of buffer zone between the inner and outer walls protecting the city. If anyone managed to get through either wall, it wasn't likely they'd make it to the next without being caught here.

As we walked, Raikidan took interest in the people working the fields, and some of them took interest in us. They appeared malnourished and overworked. Some looked like they hadn't slept for several days. I found it easy to ignore them, but Raikidan was another story.

"Ignore them," I whispered. "We don't want to attract unwanted attention."

"They look like regular humans. Are they slaves?"

I nodded. "Yes. You'll find they work the jobs nu-humans don't, such as manual labor."

"You act like it doesn't bother you."

"Trust me, it does, but there's nothing either of us can do about it. This is how it is right now. You'll get used to it pretty fast. Soon you'll barely know they're around."

He frowned. "If you say so…"

"But if you don't stop paying attention to them, they're going to get curious and then get into trouble for not working. Trust me, you really don't want them to get into trouble."

He sighed. "All right."

We walked in silence after that, for the last few miles to the inner wall. The soldiers let us through without a word, and Raikidan looked around curiously as we entered the city. It was busy and noisy, and putrid didn't begin to describe the smell. Vehicles roared, people shouted, and dogs barked. It was everything I didn't miss about the city.

"This is Quadrant One," I told him. "It's the poorest of the four quadrants."

"Where will we be mostly?"

"If everything goes as planned, we'll be staying in Quadrant Three."
Raikidan nodded. "What's the plan now?"

"I'm going to bring us to a business that also happens to be in Quadrant Three. The owner, Zane, is one of us. He doesn't get directly involved with skirmishes or infiltration, so if anyone is still around, it'll be him. It's a few hours' walk, but if we catch a caravan we might be able to hitch a ride."

Raikidan accepted this. A few hours' walk was short compared to the trek it took to get here.

Hours passed before Raikidan and I made it to the street of our destination. We'd managed to snag a ride from a few West Tribe shamans for a portion of the way, but that had only gotten us so far into Quadrant Two. They were all happy to see me, and irritated by the news of Maka'shi's orders when I relayed them. They refused to accept her decree and offered certain kinds of help that wouldn't put them in direct conflict of the pact. They had my utmost gratitude for their kindness, and I offered my assistance when they needed it for shaman-related matters.

The street I led Raikidan down had no people roaming about. If I didn't know of the mechanic shop at the end of the dead-end street, I may have thought I'd taken a wrong turn. The shop came into view. It looked exactly the same as when I had left. *At least you stayed consistent after all these years, Zane.*

The thought of seeing him again sent a flutter of odd emotions through me. *Happiness? No... Excitement? Probably.*

Two people sat on some crates between the front door and one of the garage doors. They appeared to be in a casual conversation, and as we drew closer, I was able to get a good look at their features.

The man was tall, tan, and handsome. He had short white hair and a matching goatee. His eyes were two different colors, the right dark blue and the left golden. He wore a tight red men's tank, ripped denim pants, black leather fingerless gloves, and standard sneakers. A lip ring pierced the center of his lip and was attached to an earring on his upper right ear by a chain, along with both ears having been gauged to the size of the diameter of a pencil. Large metal shackles hung from his wrists and neck, although the one around his neck was mostly obscured by a black-and-white plaid scarf that was wrapped around his neck like a bandana.

The woman next to him was a little shorter than me. She had long, straight brown hair, golden eyes, and sun-kissed skin. Her ears, while positioned in the same location, were not of a nu-human but that of a wolf, with two silver earrings pierced halfway up the left ear. She wore a bikini top that could barely hold her large breasts, and matching short denim shorts. Thick metal and leather goggles wrapped over her head, and leather fingerless gloves covered her hands. Her feet were covered by large black combat boots, and two silver studs pierced the top of her left eyebrow while two other studs pierced the bottom.

My pace picked up, though not into a run, and I couldn't stop myself from calling out to them. "Ryoko, Rylan!"

My voice echoed against the buildings surrounding us and the two people looked around.

"I thought I just heard Laz's voice," Ryoko said, her ears twitching.

Rylan nodded. "Me too..."

The two then noticed Raikidan and me. They squinted and then stood.

Rylan took a few steps forward. "Are you two lost? We don't get many shamans here."

I laughed, realizing they'd been unable to recognize me with my cloak up.

Ryoko's ears twitched and her back straightened. "Laz?"

I pulled down my hood, revealing my face, and her eyes widened, tears welling up in her eyes. "It is you!"

She sprinted over to me, the sight of her heavy chest making me uncomfortable. I didn't know how she dealt with that day to day. She crashed into me, wrapping her arms around me and squeezing so tight it hurt to breath.

"Ry...oko... I need... to... breathe..." I managed.

She sobbed into my neck, her grip unrelenting. "You're here. You're really here."

Rylan finally made it to us, placing a hand on the back of her neck and then his other on the back of mine. He then rested his forehead on my head. "You're not a ghost here to tease us, right?"

"I will... be... if Ryoko... doesn't... let... up."

He chuckled and then went about wrestling Ryoko off me. She didn't make it easy due to her strength rivaling the two of us combined, but eventually I managed to talk some sense into her. She calmed down and wiped her eyes, muttering about being thankful for waterproof makeup.

"Let's get you inside," Rylan said. "Just in case a patrol comes by. We can discuss everything." He then noticed Raikidan standing nearby watching this scene unfold. "And you can tell us about him."

I twisted my body, successfully popping it back into place after Ryoko's "assault," and nodded. "Good idea."

Rylan opened the metal door when we reached the shop and ushered us in. The building looked like most car shops; large bays to work on new and old vehicles, an office that was *supposed* to be where files were organized and stored, but I knew Zane, and that room was sure to be anything but organized.

Tall shelving units lined the back half of the building, stocked with parts and miscellaneous tools that didn't fit in their toolboxes, and organized the way Zane liked it. *It's the only thing that's ever organized here, if you asked me.*

The door closed behind us with a bang.

"Zane, get out here!" Ryoko shouted. "We got some visitors!"

A rattling noise and *thud*, followed by low cursing, were heard. Rylan and I snickered. A tall, tan, toned man who appeared to be in his forties walked around a truck. He wore a gray mechanic's jumpsuit with black boots and a red bandana that covered his shaved head. His long red mustache and matching goatee contrasted with his blue eyes. "What in Lumaraeon are you yelling about, Ryoko? It's too late to be having random—by Satria!" He rubbed his eyes. "I'm not seeing things, right?"

I smiled and waved. "Hey, Uncle."

He ran over to me and embraced me in a large bear hug. "You're back. The gods gave you back to me…"

I slipped my hand out of my cloak and rubbed his back to soothe him. "I'm here."

A tan and muscular man, appearing to be in his early thirties, came around a heavily stocked shelf. He had slicked-back brown hair, and a thin brown mustache with a matching soul patch and goatee. He wore basic denim pants, several loose belts, standard sneakers, as well as an open, blue, button-up shirt that exposed the two silver piercings on his nipples. Two beaded necklaces with crystals hung from his neck, and a silver ball-studded loop labret pierced the center of his lower lip.

"Hey, Zane, what's—" His green eyes widened. "Eira?"

I smiled. "Hey, Argus."

He turned and shouted into the shop. "Blaze, get out here!"

Someone put down some tools and jogged around the stocked shelf Argus had appeared from. A young man, slightly shorter than Argus, and appearing to be in his late twenties, joined Argus. He had tan, toned skin, and medium-length black hair. A red bandana was wrapped around his head and was covered by a black hat. A white-and-black, short-sleeved jacket covered his upper body, while black pants, a leather belt with a large belt buckle, and sneakers covered his lower. The jacket was unzipped, revealing the tight red shirt underneath, and a set of dog tags hung from his neck. A black fingerless glove was worn on his left hand, and three beaded bracelets on his right.

He hadn't noticed me yet. "What's up?"

Argus pointed and Blaze's gaze followed, his crimson red eyes widening with surprise. "This isn't a trick… right?"

I lifted my hand and flipped him my middle finger. The room boomed with laugher as Argus, Ryoko, and Rylan found amusement in the gesture and Blaze held up his hands. "I mean, if you want to, I'm not going to say no to a hot chick like you."

I shook my head. "You haven't changed."

Zane let go, now able to take in the whole scene. "You expect anything less from him?"

"No, not really."

My uncle chuckled as he patted me on the shoulder. "It's been a long time. I'm really surprised you're back. You insisted your absence would be permanent."

Argus approached. "Seda kept insisting you'd return, but most of us didn't believe it."

Ryoko snorted as she crossed her arms. "Of course those of us with a brain listened since she can see the future and all."

Rylan shrugged. "But that didn't mean we knew when. It could have been years from now, after the rebellion ended."

I leaned on the main workbench in the shop. "Yeah, well, I'm here, so get used to it."

Zane laughed. "Sounds like her, that's for sure."

Blaze pointed to Raikidan. "Yeah, but who is he?"

Everyone turned to look at Raikidan, and it was Rylan who spoke. "Shit, I forgot about him."

"Guys, it's cool," I said. "This is Raikidan. We had a chance meeting, and after some discussion he convinced me to come back. He's going to be useful to us. Raikidan, these are some of the main group of people you'll be associating with. Zane, Rylan, Ryoko, Argus, and Blaze."

Raikidan pulled down his hood and nodded in greeting, taking in the situation like he always did. The guys nodded in return and Ryoko waved, an interested smile on her lips. There was no denying she was checking him out. *Oh, Ryoko, you never change.*

I looked at everyone else. "I'll explain more in a moment, but are there any extra clothes we can swap out of? It'd be great to get out of these ones."

Zane's brow furrowed. "No, I don't think—"

Ryoko snapped her fingers. "Yes, we do! Arnia stopped by a few hours ago with some new tech. Let me go get it."

She ran off into the office, leaving me a bit perplexed. What did new tech have to do with clothing?

Moments later she came back with two strips of latex and handed one to me. I pressed my lips together. "Um…"

"It's a new cloth the military developed. Arnia says all you have to do is think of what you want to wear, and it'll become it, mimicking the color and texture exactly as it should. We haven't tried it yet ourselves, but she says it does a great job."

I shrugged. *No harm giving it a shot.* I entered the office and closed the door behind me, taking a quick look around. It was small and as messy as I expected, with books and papers strewn everywhere. The blinds were already drawn, so I didn't have to bother taking the time to mess with those. Placing the latex down on a pile of books, I quickly shed myself of the cloak and unstrapped my daggers. I made quick work of the scraps of cloth that clung to my body next, but was careful not to damage them. I was going to need them in the future.

Removing the material from my hair, I grabbed the latex and held it in one hand. I wasn't really sure how it worked, so I closed my eyes and pictured something in my head. It was a simple outfit, one I enjoyed wearing often before I had left. After I thought of every piece of the outfit, the latex distorted in my hand. I opened my eyes and watched as it took form over my body.

Before I knew it, I was fully clothed in denim pants with rips in the knees, standard sneakers, a purple long shirt with an open front and three vertical fasteners at the chest to keep it closed, and long elastic gloves with a single middle finger at the end of the shirt's long white sleeves. I had a sleeveless variant of this shirt for the summer that I had a preference for over this one, but it was early enough in the spring season where it was best to wear this style of shirt.

The clothing process was quick, couldn't have been more than a minute. I slowly turned and couldn't believe this clothing was once latex. I could feel the proper textures on all the different materials, and the only thing that gave away its true identity was the fact the clothes were lighter than their natural counterparts.

I grabbed two of my daggers and strapped them to my arms, and then snatched the last two daggers and secured them to my legs. Peering over at the nearby computer screen, I looked myself over. It was a nice look for me, as it didn't cause any conflict with my exotic colored hair or odd eyes. My eyes were unique because of the golden ring. Only one other nu-human after me had ever had this ring around the pupils, and my hair was such a unique color, no one I'd met had anything close. Sometimes I wished I had the red hair I had been designed to have, but DNA and mutations were funny like that.

Content, I tossed my shaman disguise into my bag and left the bag on the floor. Raikidan would need it to store his disguise. Opening the office door, I walked out.

Ryoko sat on a workbench and let out a low whistle. "Nice scar. How'd you get it?"

"Long story." I was grateful she hadn't mentioned my attire. Being fashion inclined, unlike me, she tended to do that from time to time.

I looked to Raikidan and tossed my thumb toward the office. "Your turn. And no, you're not getting any help from me."

He looked me up and down and then waked by. "I don't think you could help."

I kicked him in the ass and sauntered over to Ryoko. She snickered and then winked at Raikidan. "I'll help if you need it."

He stared at her, not understanding what she was hinting at, and then closed himself into the office. Her brow twisted with confusion, but it quickly changed to excitement when I sat on the workbench with her.

She latched onto my arm. "Can you say 'eye candy' much? My gods. Like, seriously, were did you find a guy like that?"

Ryoko fanned herself and I laughed. She was something else. "It's a long, complicated story."

She didn't need to know about my near-death experience.

She pouted. "Fine, be that way." Ryoko looked me over. "You want me to re-pierce your lip? Looks like you haven't had that in for some time."

I ran my tongue across the inside of my lip as I thought for a second. I did miss having it. "Sure, why not?"

Ryoko smiled and dashed away to the back side of the shop. I wouldn't doubt she was going to the closet. They stored all sorts of miscellaneous things in there. Why there was a piercing kit in a place like this, I couldn't say, but I had always known them to have it.

When Ryoko returned, she held a small metal box in her hands. She placed the box down and grabbed a large hollow needle and small silver ring. Grabbing my lip and positioning the needle on the right, inside of my mouth, she thrust my lip into the needle. I didn't react much when the needle penetrated my flesh.

Carefully she attached the ring to the end of the needle and pulled both through the new hole in my mouth. Once the ring was in place, she closed it and let go of my lip. "Much better."

She put the needle in the plastic bag it came with and tossed it into a trashcan. Grabbing the box, she turned to return it but froze. Raikidan leaned against the doorway, a smirk plastered on his dumb face.

He wore a tight white tank and a red one underneath that. His pants were green khaki and were held up by a cloth belt, although it didn't do such a great job, since the band of his boxers was still showing. His outfit was completed by black boots. He could have passed as a soldier out of uniform if it weren't for the lack of dog tags.

"Well, you managed to not look like an idiot," I said.

"I'll say! It should be illegal to look that good!" Ryoko hung off me. "Like only gods have that good of a body." Her eyes snapped to him. "You're not a god, are you?"

Taken aback, his face twisted and I laughed. "Ignore her. She's got an active imagination."

Her face scrunched in disapproval of my claim.

Blaze, who hung by the truck Zane went back to working on, grunted. "So, he's eye-candy for you two, big deal. What can he bring to the table that'll actually help us?"

"Someone's jealous," Ryoko muttered, not happy he was spoiling her fun.

Blaze's eyes narrowed, but I interjected before he could bite out a response. "He's a true non-tank born shapeshifter."

All attention fell on me but before anyone could speak, a loud knock came from the entrance door. Everyone froze. It was obvious no one was expecting any business to show up. Thinking quickly, I grabbed Raikidan by the wrist and dragged him behind tall metal shelving units full of parts and tools. The others scrambled, looking for something to make them look busy. Rylan, Argus, and Blaze settled on covering up a few vehicles, while Ryoko threw the piercing kit under the workbench and grabbed a few tools to pretend to work on another vehicle. Zane was the one to open the door and greeted our unwelcome visitors.

Peering through a gap in some of the shelved objects, I watched two armed soldiers walk in. I recognized the man in black as the general at the front gate, but the other one with him was a different story.

"Sorry to drop in on you like this, Zane, but we were wondering if you have those upgrades done yet," General Zo said.

Zane waved him off. "You're welcome to drop in, my shop is open. But I have to tell you, my answer hasn't changed since you were here a few days ago. It's nowhere near being finished. What you've asked for has been difficult to design."

Zo nodded. "That's fine. Do you mind if we see it anyway?"

Zane shrugged. "Sure. Ryoko, do you mind bringing out the order?"

"Sure thing." Ryoko dashed off into an unknown place, but when she came back, she carried a giant gun that should have been impossible to carry.

With a loud thud, she placed it on the table. Raikidan glanced to me as if to get an answer of what was going on, but I shook my head. It was best to stay quiet at the moment. He understood and went back to watching with me.

"The strength you have, Ryoko, still astounds me," Zo complimented. Ryoko giggled but didn't say anything. "It looks fine to me, Zane. What's wrong with it?"

"It may look fine, but that doesn't mean it works fine," Zane explained. "With everything you want it to do, it just stopped working. We've been trying to figure out what will and won't work, but still haven't found the exact problem yet."

"You will," Zo assured. "Do you mind if I look at the specs I wanted?"

"Sure, I don't mind at all." I wished Zane would hurry this up, but I knew if he did, it might look suspicious. "I'll grab it from the office."

My pinky slid on the metal rack I was resting my hands on, hitting a wrench. It turned and knocked a lug nut onto the floor. *Shit!* As I feared, the sound caught the soldiers' attention. *Double shit.* Now I wouldn't be able to stay hidden.

"Dammit," I muttered as I reached for a tote just in my reach. "Just need... this one... thing..."

Raikidan, understanding what I was trying to do, reached out to the tote. "Hey, let me help you."

I lightly pushed his hand away. "No, no, I got it, Rai."

"You're so stubborn."

"It's because I got—" I yanked on the tote and jumped out of the way as it crashed to the floor, parts spilling out everywhere. "Dammit!"

Raikidan sighed with false exasperation. "See. Had you let me help, that wouldn't have happened."

"Shut up..."

I retrieved some nuts and bolts, a few shims, and some rubber mounts, before leaving my sanctuary. *Please, gods, allow me to be right about the effectiveness of our shaman disguises...* "Zane I think I got what you wanted."

He looked at me, his eyes clear with concern. "Are you okay?"

I nodded. "Yeah, I just made a mess while trying to get these."

"I'm not cleaning it up!" Raikidan called out.

"I know that, dummy..." I muttered.

Zane chuckled. "Well, as long as you're okay, that's what matters. Just put those parts down on the workbench for now."

I nodded and did as he instructed. Zo's intense gaze followed me. It made me feel uncomfortable.

Zo leaned on the workbench and smirked at me. His eyes showed he had no idea he'd met me before. *Thank Satria.* "And who might you be?"

My mind froze up. I hadn't come up with a false name yet. *Shit… shit… shit! Brain work!* "It's… um… Eira." *Dammit!* I could have picked Aliyah, Silva, or even Amy. Why the hell could I not pick something besides my real name?

He took my hand and kissed it. "Lovely name. My name is Zo. I remember all beautiful women I have the pleasure of meeting, and I know I've never met you before. Are you a new employee?"

"Get away from him!" the voice screamed in my head.

When most men acted this way, I could handle it, but the way this Zo character acted, it just made me uncomfortable. It also made it hard to come up with some sort of cover story on the spot. *Why didn't I think of this on my way here?* "Sorta…"

Zo glanced to Zane. "You've been hiding her from me, haven't you?"

Zane crossed his arms. "You come off too strong. You would have scared the poor girl."

"I'm not that bad." Zo looked at me and grinned. "How long have you been working here?"

My gaze fell elsewhere as I tried to think. "Um… about two weeks now, I think. I'm only here a couple hours a week." *Think of something. Think of something!* "Zane doesn't think I'm ready for a full week of work yet."

Zo's brow creased. "You seem like you're a capable woman."

I wrung my hands together. "It's not that…"

Zane, noticing my struggle and taking the hint from my use of his name, jumped in. "Poor girl has amnesia." He pointed to his head in dramatic effect. "She can't remember much prior to a few months ago."

"Pity." Zo caressed the top of my hand with his thumb. "But you're in good hands with this lot, so I'm sure you'll get your memory back soon enough."

"Get away from him!" the voice screamed again.

His touching me wasn't helping me feel any better about him. He creeped me out.

Just then, Raikidan came out with a large tool chest balanced on his shoulder. Placing it down on the metal workbench with a *thud*, he pulled me to the other side of him by the shoulder, getting me away from Zo. He stared the general down. "You're making her uncomfortable."

Zo assessed him. "Whoa, how much you lift, kid?"

Ryoko walked over to the toolbox and opened it. "Not as much as soldiers, but enough to be of some use." She then looked at him. "Ray, I told you one item, not the entire box."

"Well, the way you described what you wanted wasn't very helpful," Raikidan replied, not taking his gaze off Zo.

She opened the toolbox and looked at the chrome objects. "Yeah, I guess 'something shiny' wasn't the best way to describe it."

I giggled and she glared at me. Even though Ryoko was playing this up, it would be just like her to say that.

"Don't mind Ray, Zo," Zane said. "He's just a little overprotective of Eira. He's the only one who has any real connection to her past."

"I see. Well, hopefully you can help get her back on track," Zo said.

"She'll remember when she's ready." Raikidan then turned his back to Zo, putting his arm around my shoulders and placing his attention on me.

Ryoko grabbed a few tools from the toolbox. "Why don't you two come help me with the car over here?"

I pointed to where I'd made the mess. "I need to go clean u—"

"I already did it," Raikidan said.

My brow furrowed. "You said you weren't going t—"

"Well I did, so now you don't have to."

I let out an aggravated sigh and then followed Ryoko to help her. Zane finished up with Zo and his gun as fast as he could.

A relieved breath left my lips when Zane bolted the door shut and swapped the sign to *closed*. "That's one way to be thrown back into the swing of things."

Zane's laughter boomed through the building. "I'll say!"

Argus and Blaze approached the workbench, Argus speaking, "Not a bad cover story. Especially one that was clearly made up on the spot."

Blaze snorted. "It's a stupid one, if you ask me."

Argus shook his head. "It's not, if you actually think about it."

Ryoko laughed. "Blaze, think? Yeah right."

The building echoed with laughter while Blaze glowered at her.

"Honestly," Rylan said, trying to help Blaze understand. "Amnesia is a great way to explain Laz's presence as well as our new comrade. It also gives us an easy out for history crafting to keep them under the radar." He glanced at me with his head tilted. "It, of course, would have been easier if someone used a false name."

I held up my hands and ducked my head. "I'm sorry! I didn't think of one before coming here. I didn't think I'd need to so soon after arriving."

He crossed his arms. "We're lucky Zo or that other soldier with him doesn't know you. Of course if he uses your name around others, that might be another story."

I held my hand out to Ryoko. "At least we have one for Raikidan, thanks to Ryoko."

Ryoko held her head high. "Yes, we do."

"I intended to give him an actual alias that sounded more human, but obviously that didn't happen."

"The fact Zo didn't notice the change just shows how stupid he is, and easy to manipulate," Rylan said.

I shrugged. "To be fair, Rai and Ray are quite similar. He could have thought he heard me wrong."

"And if he didn't?" Blaze asked.

"Then I have both names," Raikidan said. Everyone looked at him. "Eira can call me Rai."

Argus rubbed his chin. "That would work, actually. You are supposed to be the only person connected to her 'past,' so it'd make sense if she had a different name for you only she'd call you."

I nodded. "That's an excellent point. I'll come up with a reason for that later. It's not all that important now."

Zane placed his hands on the workbench. "Now that we have that all settled, I think it's time we hear about your explanation. Not that we're unhappy you're back."

Blaze lifted a finger. "I don't know, I'm pretty unhappy."

I snorted. "Why, because I won't sleep with you?"

He held up his hands. "It's a valid reason."

"No, it's not," Ryoko said. "That's a childish reason to be an ass."

"Bite me."

"I'll pass, thanks."

He threw his thumb at Raikidan. "But let me guess, you wouldn't pass if he said to."

A grin spread across her lips. "Maybe."

His eyes narrowed and I chuckled. Nothing ever changed with this group. Blaze always wanted to be the focus of a pretty woman's attention, and with Ryoko giving Raikidan so much, it was obviously getting his blood boiling.

Zane held up his hand. "Okay, okay, enough. Blaze, Argus, go get the shutters closed so we can have our discussion without risking prying eyes."

Argus and Blaze nodded, running off, while Ryoko and Rylan cleared off the workbench.

Zane pulled out a remote from under the workbench and handed it to me. "I'll give you the honors."

12
CHAPTER

I smiled and took the remote. It'd be nice to use "advanced" technology again.

It wasn't long before metal shades slammed over the windows and the back door was locked up. Lights shut off as the two made it through the building back to us, leaving us in the dark.

I pressed a large green button on the remote. The bench transformed quickly into a table with a holographic map of the city that illuminated the room. I leaned on the table to take a closer look. Raikidan stood close to me, interested in the piece of technology.

I took command, finding it easy to slip back into the role. "Let's begin. As we all know, I'm really here—after a *very* long time away—and not a spirit haunting you." Rylan and Ryoko chuckled. "As I mentioned before, Raikidan here is a shapeshifter and is here to help as well. He's from the West and has no experience with our modern technologies, but that shouldn't be a problem as he's proven to be a quick learner in the time I've known him."

I looked to Raikidan. "I briefly introduced you to everyone, but now I can give a better rundown. You'll need it as these will be the main teammates you associate with during your stay with us. There are some more who you'll meet in time, but you can worry about that later. The rebellion is broken down into seven different teams for organization purposes. Our team is Team Three."

I gestured to Zane. "Zane runs this shop as our main source of income. It's mostly a car repair and restoration shop, but we do weapon work for the military on the side and use that information for our cause. Zane doesn't participate in any of our skirmishes or assignments."

I pointed to Blaze. "Blaze, our resident playboy. Nothing too special about him, just that he likes a good hand-to-hand combat and does well with our undercover missions." Blaze's expression dropped to an unamused one and I smirked before gesturing to Argus. "Argus is our weapons and technology specialist, and overall genius. You need to know anything on any weapon or advanced tech, he's the guy to talk to."

I waved my hand to encompass all three of them in an imaginary circle. "All three were designed before Zarda came into the picture, so unlike the rest of us, they have no significant special abilities aside from a strength increase on Zane's and Blaze's end, and an intelligence increase on Argus' end."

I pointed to the gorgeous woman standing next to me. "Ryoko here is a Brute class, so don't let her pretty face fool you. She's a living siege weapon. She'll always be the first one of us in on any skirmish battle, and is always ready to do so. Her strength has been unmatched by any other experiment that I've seen."

Raikidan looked at her, clearly impressed, and she bowed for dramatics.

"As I mentioned to you before, her nu-human DNA was mixed with a wogron's in hopes of trying out different advantages the new combination would offer."

I motioned to Rylan. "And lastly, we have Rylan. He's our sniper. Best shot you'll find. He's also ice touched, so he will use ice in battle or in other ways when the need arises. His design was an attempt at shapeshifting. To do this, they combined his nu-human DNA with wolves."

Raikidan nodded, taking this all in. "What about you? You said you were an assassin… or former assassin. Whichever you want to go by. Is that it about you, or are you the shot-caller?"

I shook my head. "Neither. Genesis is the team leader and calls the shots. You'll meet her later. I'm the battle leader, which goes beyond my commander title in the rebellion's eyes. My job is to strategize correctly for battle situations *as well* as non-battle oriented assignments. When I'm not doing that, I'm on my own assassin-based assignments, taking out targets that are a huge threat to us."

"I took her place as battle leader in her absence," Rylan said. "The Council wasn't able to find a suitable replacement with the same rank as her, so I kept the position this whole time. Though, I'm happy to give it back."

Raikidan leaned on the table. "This is more complex than I thought. Where will I fit into it all?"

I shrugged. "I'm not sure yet, but it shouldn't be long before we figure it out." I focused on Zane. "Would you be able to bring me up to speed on our current status?"

Zane nodded. "The layout of the city hasn't changed much. It's gotten bigger, though, and some of the walls have been moved to allow for the expansion. Zarda's fortress is just as impenetrable as ever, so frontal assaults are still out of the question.

"The residence decree is still in place, but you probably guessed that. They've increased the patrols inside and outside the city walls and upped the penalty for leaving without the proper approved documentation, sometimes resorting to killing the offender on sight, no questions asked. I can't say if your tunnel to the outside escapes their eye, but I'd be careful if you plan to use it. Those who have the courage to try and leave have been aided by the shamans, gypsies, or traveling merchants, but there haven't been many as far as I'm aware.

"The number of tank-born soldiers has increased immensely. Intel from the inside claims there are as many as five coming out per day now, each fully grown and more savage than the last. None have been seen in the city as of yet, and I hope they won't be anytime soon."

I tapped on the table, my eyes narrowing. "Figures Zarda is still trying for the most bloodthirsty weapon."

"Rumor has it, your little escape act made him go insane," Argus said.

I laughed dryly. "That man, if you can call him that, was already insane. He pitted fifty soldiers against each other to the death for his own amusement one day."

His brow knitted. "You saw that happen?"

"I was part of it."

The room was silent. Even though it wasn't part of my initial design, the type of damage I was capable of, given the right motivation, wasn't to be messed with. Ryoko and Rylan knew this the best out of everyone.

"Anyway," Zane continued, "although we haven't had the opportunity to take out a lot of their numbers, we've managed to keep their supplies low in the city, forcing them to have to retreat back to the castle walls more often. New fighters on our side have trickled down to nearly none. No one has made any escape attempts from the fortress, and our efforts to recruit civilians have been a waste. It's also been hard to get any new intel. Zarda has locked the city down pretty tight. On the bright side, we've only lost one on our team, and that was due to his own stupidity. I don't think I have to tell you who it is."

"Drake?" I asked.

Zane nodded. Of course it was him. He had never been the brightest out of the bunch and was always too quick to react to situations. It was only a matter of time before he'd get himself killed.

"Azriel still owns Twilight, in case you were wondering, and I think that's about it," Zane finished.

"So basically, in the years I've been gone, we're no closer than we were before," I summed up.

He nodded. "Yeah, pretty much."

I sighed. Of course it wasn't any better for them. Why would my disappearance make it better? I was just one person, and it was only a matter of time before Zarda stopped putting any effort into my recapture. Then a thought occurred to me. "Hey, Ryoko, I never asked earlier. Aside from the fact that this cloth can change on a whim, what's the real use for it?"

"It's bulletproof," she said. "It uses a newer technology that lessens the impact of the bullet, too. We tested it earlier. Works great."

I nodded "Good to know. Do you know if it can handle shapeshifting?"

She shook her head. "Sorry, I don't. Will it be a problem if it can't?"

"No, I can fix that if needed. I'll just have Raikidan test it out later."

"We should head home, then," Ryoko suggested. "You two can get situated in the house, and then you can stress-test the cloth some more."

I nodded. "Good idea."

I grabbed my bag from the office and then headed for the door with Ryoko while the others went back to work.

"We all piled into one car today, so we'll have to walk, if that's okay," Ryoko said.

I nodded. "I've been walking for weeks. I can walk a few more miles back home."

As we walked, I paid attention to Raikidan instead of soaking up our surroundings myself. It was quite amusing, really. I had never seen someone so interested in a city.

Then I thought about his possible reaction to Genesis when he saw her. "Raikidan, you'll end up meeting Genesis when we reach the house. She looks young, but don't be deceived by her looks. Genesis is the first nu-human I told you about before, hence her name. Since she isn't a war experiment, you'll never see her in battle. You'll also meet Seda. The two work closely with each other, so they are almost always together. Seda is psychic, so be aware of that when you think to yourself."

"Okay, sure," Raikidan said absentmindedly.

I knew he had heard only a quarter of what I said, if that, but no one could say I didn't warn him, although my warning wouldn't be much help anyway. Seda wasn't one to invade your mind, but sometimes even she couldn't control her power, and if you didn't lock memories or thoughts up, she would see them. Genesis, on the other hand, was a very strange case for an experiment, and overall would be perfect if it weren't for one small problem...

Ryoko unlocked the front door as we arrived, and we all walked up the long staircase. Originally, there was a staircase leading down to the basement as well, but we renovated the front so anyone coming into the house would have to make themselves known first.

Reaching the top, I looked around. We were in the living room, and aside from the new furniture and renovated kitchen, everything looked the same. My room, if it was still mine, was right in front of us, with the small kitchen and bar next to it. Between the two was a door that led to the roof.

If everything was the same, down the hall would be Ryoko's room, with the large bath across the hall. Between the kitchen and Ryoko's room would be a door that led down to the basement, and next to her room, on the other side would be a spare bedroom. Genesis and Seda's room was next to that.

Next to the bath, across the hall from Ryoko's room would be another spare bedroom, and then Rylan's room. The rest of the rooms down the hall and around the corner were a part of the addition that was added some time ago. They were either empty or claimed by the boys, one of them being the music room Rylan wouldn't stop talking about until we had gotten around to making it.

Before I had a chance to put down my bag, a door out of sight opened. I watched a girl, no older than seven, with light skin and long raven hair pulled into pigtails, and a woman around my age, with creamy white skin and long blonde hair, come around the corner of the hallway. The woman was dressed in a strange two-piece outfit. It was a dark-violet leotard with a tight collar. Seamlessly attached were two tight sleeves of the same material that were fastened to a small golden ring fitted around her middle finger. In her hands she carried a silver chain with a purple amethyst pendant with a hexagram engraved in the center.

In the center of the leotard, near her breast, was a large cutout that was attached at the top and bottom by two gold rings with a leather strap holding them together. The same material as the leotard covered her legs. It stretched down to her feet until it reached her toes, leaving them and her heels exposed. Around her thighs, the material gapped in places as if it had ripped cleanly, and a loose white sash was wrapped around her.

Three black rings pierced her lips, one on each side and the last in the middle; and a dark veil with a golden hexagram hung over her eyes, obstructing a good view of her face. The little girl, on the other hand, appeared normal, wearing a yellow sundress and red ribbons that held back her pigtails, but I knew better.

"Eira!" the girl exclaimed, running over to me.

Kneeling, I took her into my embrace. "Hey, Genesis."

Raikidan stiffened. "This is Genesis?"

I glanced up at him. "I told you not to be surprised."

"She's just a child!"

"She may look like a child, but she isn't. Her years well surpass seven hundred."

"Things may be confusing now, Raikidan, but you'll understand soon enough." Genesis smiled at him. "Just give it time."

Several conflicted emotions flashed over Raikidan's face. "How did you—"

"Thanks to Seda, I know all about you."

I rose to my feet and looked at Seda, giving her a respectful bow with my head.

Her voice penetrated my mind. *"Do not worry, Eira. We will not say anything to anyone. It will be his choice to tell if he wishes them to know."*

I suppressed a shiver. Her voice was hollow and devoid of emotion. It was something you had to get used to, and my time away made it hard to do so. *"Thank you."*

"It is nice to see you back. It has not been the same here without you."

Ryoko noticed our private conversation as she made her way to the kitchen. "Hey, you two, secrets don't make friends."

"It's nothing important," I replied with a shrug. I walked to my room and opened the door. Peering in I found it exactly how I left it. It was a bit strange to see, but I was grateful.

She grabbed an apple from the fruit bowl on the bar. "Where you going?"

"Bed. Today has been a little more eventful than I'm used to. Raikidan, your room is the second door on the right of this main hall."

"What about you guys testing those clothes?"

"It can wait 'til tomorrow."

She shrugged. "Okay."

I entered my room, but as I closed the door, it was stopped. I cranked my head back just as Raikidan forced his way in. "What do you think you're doing? I told you, your room is down the hall."

"I'm staying here," he stated in an authoritative tone.

"No, you are not." There was no way I was giving my room up to him or sharing it for that matter.

"I am." With that, he closed the door.

"Get out! This is my room, and I don't share."

He averted his gaze and his voice quieted. "I don't trust them."

At first, I didn't know what to say. Not only had he admitted something that was a sort of weakness, but he had insinuated he trusted me. I had to ask. "And you trust me?"

"More than them." With that, he sat down under the windowsill, with his arms hanging over his knees, and closed his eyes.

There was no arguing with him at this point. He wasn't going to leave, and I doubted I had the strength to force him. I may be strong, but I knew my limits.

Shaking my head, I walked over to my closet and put both shaman disguises away. Turning, I opened the drawer to my dresser and stored the material Shva'sika had put in my hair. I then made my way to my bed, and I took out the two books and note Shva'sika had given me. Opening the top drawer of the nightstand, I took out a handful of photographs and placed the books neatly inside, tucking the note into the blank book. Without looking at the photographs, I placed them back in the drawer and shut it.

I stored away my daggers in the lower drawer and then pulled one of the last meals out of my bag. I tossed the bag at Raikidan's feet. "Make sure you eat."

He looked at the bag, and then after a moment, reached in and took out some meat. As I ate my meal, I thought of something light and comfortable to wear. The clothing changed, its response time impressing me.

"I already know these clothes won't change with my form like those shaman clothes," Raikidan said, his mouth full.

Geez, manners much? "What makes you say that?"

"It has the same feeling as the other clothes I wore before it."

I nodded, my mind running this through. The first morning after Raikidan wore the clothes, he told me his experience with them. From his account, when he shifted to his natural shape, it felt as if the clothes disappeared, and when he shifted to his nu-human form, it suddenly reappeared. He couldn't see the clothes changing or see where they went in the non-humanoid form.

"I suspected it wouldn't be the same as your Guard clothes. That spell is strange and not something we could recreate with our technology. Though, there are uniforms with a technology that was made with shifters in mind. It causes the clothes to reform to the individual's new body, but doesn't disappear. I don't know how it works of course, but I do know it's not magic based." I shook my head. "Back on track, I'd like to know if this new cloth with do the same as the technology we have at hand, or not work at all."

He put his food down. "Then we'll test it now."

Standing, he closed his eyes and took the shape of a wolf. I watched, unable to look away from the sight. I'd seen him take his dragon shape many times, but only one form other than something human. It wasn't an instant process, nor did it involve a bright light that made the transformation look beautiful. Instead the process was slow and his body became warped.

I crawled to the edge of the bed on my hands and knees and leaned over the footboard to get a better look. When his transformation was complete, he shook his head to remove the shirt that draped over it and then looked at me.

"Well, I guess we know it doesn't work for shapeshifters," I said with a small giggle. I couldn't help it. The way he shook his head was slightly cute, although I'd never admit it to anyone.

The material, unable to discern the original body it was connected to, reverted back into its original cloth form on the floor.

"Can you bring me the cloth?" I asked, moving from my spot to grab the access book from the nightstand. Turning back, my face was met with his, but it wasn't a wolf's face. I did my best to not physically react. "Why do you insist on being so indecent?"

I was glad the wooden footboard was covering his lower half, but it didn't change the fact he was naked and leaning onto my bed.

"Why do you have such a problem with me like this?"

"I've already told you. It's indecent and not a human thing to do."

His brow rose. "And I'm not human."

I sighed, my aggravation clear, and went about searching for the druid spell using the Library access book. "That doesn't mean you can't learn to be decent in the presence of one."

From my peripheral I could see him watching me, though I couldn't exactly tell the expression he had.

I finally found the druid spell and the book read out how to apply the reagents. "Hey, I need that bag for the ingredients Shva'sika gave me."

He pulled away, and I was sure to keep my eyes firmly planted on the book. The bag dropped on the bed and I snatched it up, still not looking at him.

"I don't get you," Raikidan said. "Two of your friends have vocally indicated how they find this body attractive. One even compared it to a god. Yet you actively avoid it. Do you just not see it the way they do?"

I couldn't deny he had looks in this form. Actually, he really was the best-looking guy I'd seen in some time, but it didn't mean I was attracted to him or wanted to see him naked. "No, I don't. I don't see that in anyone."

"Why?"

"Because I don't, so leave me alone about it."

I found the part of the spell that showed how to use spiritual magic in place of natural magic, and went about enchanting the spell on the cloth. When done, I tossed it to the edge of the bed for him. "Try it out."

Raikidan watched me put the book away and drop my bag on the floor beside my bed before trying on the clothes. Testing them with the same wolf form, we found it working just as it should. Pleased, I went back to finishing my meal.

"Do you not see the same way as your friends because of your emotional design issue?" Raikidan asked.

My hand clenched and I ground my teeth together. "I said we're not talking about this, so drop it."

My meal done, I wrapped the plate up and stored it in my bag. I'd have to do a lot of dishes tomorrow.

Raikidan shifted to his natural dragon shape as I lay down. He watched me with great intensity as I got myself comfortable. *I don't get him...*

Choosing not to dwell on something so trivial, I curled up and closed my eyes. But as I did, something twinged in my heart, and his questions replayed in my mind before unconsciousness took me.

Stupid, you know better than to dwell on this topic... You know what happened last time...

13
CHAPTER

I groggily opened my eyes when the light from the skylight I both hated and loved became too much for me to ignore.

Shifting, I noticed my bed didn't move right, as if there was another body on it. Slowly I sat up, and my eyes were met with Raikidan lying across the width of my bed on his back, thankfully clothed in standard denim pants and a tight men's tank. Over his head my bell earring dangled from his hand.

My brow rose, a part of me irritated with him for being on my bed, while the other was just glad he wasn't lying next to me. "What are you doing on my bed?"

"I was bored waiting on the sill for you to wake up. Not much going on in that alley," he explained.

"Why not go out into the living room?" I didn't question how he knew what an alley was. That answer didn't really matter.

He turned his head, looking at me. "And do what?"

Right, first time in a home with modern technology to entertain. "What are you doing with my earring?"

"I'm trying to figure out how you got it to work. It doesn't ring on its own, but you made it emit that sound that put me on the floor."

I chuckled, unable to forget that sight. "You have to hit it a certain way, with a specific amount of force, and either natural or spiritual magic."

"But how could you use this before your shaman training?"

I crawled over to him. "Those gifted with spiritual magic always have access to it. It radiates off them, making them identifiable by the most experienced shamans. So, because it seeped out of me all the time, when I hit the bell, it'd always ring, where someone else wouldn't be able to make it work." I poked the bell with my finger and it *tinged* like a normal bell would when lightly touched, emphasizing my point.

Raikidan looked at the bell and then flicked it with a finger, the object swinging from the action but making no sound. He huffed and I couldn't stop the entertained giggle from slipping off my lips.

To add insult to injury, I reached out and flicked the bell, choosing a particular frequency I knew worked wonders. It rang with a lovely tune, and then the sound of something heavy dropping in another room caught our ears.

"Laz!" Ryoko shouted.

I bit my lips and stifled a laugh, but Raikidan was less considerate and let out a boisterous laugh. "That was an awful thing for you to do."

I continued to keep my laughter at bay. "I never said I was… a nice person."

"Laz, I hate you, undo this right now!" Ryoko cried. When I didn't listen, she yelled out again. "Stop being a jerkface and fix this!"

I couldn't hold it back anymore and rolled on my back as I laughed.

"Stop laughing!"

Raikidan and I laughed harder. Ryoko whined but didn't call out again, knowing that it'd only delay her demand.

The two of us finally calmed ourselves and Raikidan looked at me. "So why her?"

"I found that frequency works on humans with canine-like DNA. So she's affected because of her half-wogron nature, and Rylan also will find himself unable to do anything because of his wolf DNA. Any other human like them in a quarter of a mile who can hear would be suffering the same effect."

"That's a decent coverage."

I nodded. "That's about how far the bell's sound travels before distorting, nullifying the effect."

A grin spread across his lips suddenly. "This is why you mentioned 'sit' when telling me about the reason for needing it."

I snickered and rolled back over on my front. "Yep."

He laughed. "I enjoy your sense of humor. I want you to know that."

"I don't!" Ryoko said.

The two of us laughed some more.

Raikidan was the first to calm himself and when I finally did, I caught him staring at me. The longer I held eye contact, the less I found myself able to look away. *It's those eyes.* They were like a snare. My lips felt dry, and I licked them quickly to wet them again only to realize they were fine. What was going on?

"You have some really interesting eyes," he said. "Makes it hard not to look at you."

My cheeks warmed and I broke away my gaze. I touched a feather on the bell to regain my composure. "Your eyes are nice too… I guess."

"Hello?" Ryoko called out. "You two better not be ignoring me now. I'll pulverize you both."

The two of us chuckled and Raikidan handed the bell back to me. It was time to end this game, but first, I wanted to figure out where Ryoko was. Willing my clothes to change, I exited my room and looked around, finding my half-wogron friend sitting in the kitchen, her leg out in front of her and her arms at her side.

My lips spread into a grin. "Morning, sunshine."

She pouted with drooped ears. "Stop being mean! I missed you and this is how you treat me after being gone so long?"

I snickered. "I have to make up for lost time."

"Laz," she whined.

"Okay, okay." I flicked the bell and it emitted a sound different than before. She sighed with relief and stood, but before she could say anything, Rylan's door down the hall flew open, crashing into the inner wall of his room, and he stormed out. Rage seeped off of him in waves.

My brow rose at the sight of him only wearing red heart boxers. "I guess I'm supposed to be happy you're at least wearing boxers."

"I was getting dressed when you used that damn thing." He almost bared his teeth, a habit from his wolf DNA that he hated. "Give it to me, now."

I pointed my finger to the ground and spun it. "Go put some clothes on and then we'll talk."

Rylan stalked down the hall, ignoring my request. "Give it to me."

I sighed and hopped up on the bar, ready for this to take a bit. Ryoko stayed where she was, interested in my approach to this. Rylan came in reaching distance, his arm out, but I stopped him from coming closer by placing my foot on his chest.

He glanced down at my foot and then at me with a raised brow. "Seriously?"

Rylan continued his reach attempt and I planted my other foot on his chest, keeping him at bay. He let out an aggravated sigh and tried to push and pull my feet off him, but I stayed firm.

"Just give me the bell, Laz."

I held it out of his reach. "No, it's mine. So be a good boy and behave."

His eyes narrowed and his lip pulled back. "Don't treat me like some dog." His grip around my ankles tightened. "Now give me that stupid bell or I'll freeze you."

I grinned and held a finger up to the bell. "Try me."

Ryoko whimpered. "Don't be mean, Laz."

I didn't take my eyes off Rylan. "Don't worry, this next frequency won't affect you. Just Rylan."

She perked up. "Okay, then go for it!"

Rylan looked at her with a shocked, betrayed expression before hardening his resolve and squeezed my ankles tighter, his hands growing cold. I knew him well enough to know that he would apply some ice to my skin, but not enough to harm me. I grinned and flicked the bell, a beautiful sound ringing from it. Rylan fell to the ground, as did another body.

Furrowed brow, I bent forward to peek over to where Raikidan had been standing, watching the events before him, to find him also on his ass.

Ryoko leaned over the bar to look at him too. "That affected you too?"

Raikidan glowered at me. "Did you really have to do that to me as well?"

I snickered. "I didn't think it would. It's not the same tone that worked on you last time."

Ryoko held up her hands. "Wait, back up. I want to know why it works on him. Is it because he's a shifter?"

Raikidan frowned. "Yes."

Ryoko slammed her hand on the bar. "Well, welcome to the club!"

He tilted his head. "Club?"

"Yeah, the 'Laz likes to torture us with a bell' club."

I snickered. Not only was the name of this club ridiculous and long, but she didn't understand that he'd questioned her because he had no idea what she meant by a "club."

"Sounds stupid."

I leaned back as I laughed, and Ryoko placed her hand on her chest, faking insult. "Rude. Fine, we don't want you in the club anyway." She wrapped her arms around me suddenly and pulled me off the bar. "Now, I need to talk to you."

"What? Wait, hold on." She didn't allow me any choice as she pulled me by the wrist to her room.

"Fix us first!" Rylan yelled.

Ryoko went to close the door, but I stopped her, so I could undo the effect. The bell rang and Ryoko locked the door before Rylan had a chance to get to his feet and chase after us.

She then spun around and stared me down, a weird smile on her lips. "Okay, spill it."

"Spill what?"

Her eyes darted to the door and her next words were slow and evasive. "You know…" Unfortunately, I didn't, and I hated she wouldn't just come out and say it. Ryoko sighed. "You and the new guy. Spill it!"

I laughed. "Is that what this is about? Ryoko, I thought you knew me better than that. I can assure you, there is nothing going on between me and Raikidan."

"But you shared the room last night. You never let anyone stay in your room."

"He slept on the floor," I defended. Her brow lifted as she crossed her arms. It didn't surprise me she didn't believe me, but it didn't make it any less true. "Look, he doesn't trust you guys. I've been traveling with him for a while, so it's only natural he would have a little more trust in me than any of you. Also, you're right, he didn't just sleep on the floor. He slept propped up against the door."

"So that's why the door wouldn't budge…" I knew I wasn't supposed to hear that, but I had, and I stared at her, eyes wide. "Sorry! I wanted to know, so I tried to enter, but the door wouldn't open. Let me tell you, he's a lot heavier than he looks, and that's saying something, with my strength."

If I hadn't been laughing so hard, I would have smacked her. "So, what about you? You and Rylan seem to be sleeping in different rooms, so either you two finally hooked up and it didn't work out, or you're still being your usual self about it."

Her face reddened and she averted her gaze. *Nope, hasn't told him.* It didn't surprise me in the least. It had been hard enough getting her to admit to me how she felt in the first place. If she's not showing signs Rylan would catch, that dummy wouldn't know to act on his own feelings that I also knew he had. *Why do I get caught up in the middle of these things?*

"Because you're a moron," the voice in my head hissed.

She wrung her hands together, her shoulders tight. "I just feel there's still some sort of connection between the two of you, that's all…"

I crossed my arms. "Ryoko, how many times do I have to tell you, there is nothing between us. There never was."

"But—"

"Don't start," I warned. "There was never anything. There never will be anything. Not with him, not with anyone else."

Her shoulders sagged. "Why don't you try to find someone, Laz? Don't you find anyone attractive?"

It was my turn to avert my gaze. "Finding someone attractive and being attracted to them are two completely different things."

A thin smirk spread across her lips. "So, you do find this new guy attractive."

I let out a sigh. "How the hell did you get that assumption from my answer?"

"You're not denying it."

The problem was she really wasn't… wrong. "Yes, he's an attractive…" *How do I word this that's close to the truth and not blow his cover?* "… male."

She tilted her head to the side and tapped her lips with a finger. "And you don't care he's a shapeshifter, right?"

My eyes narrowed. *What is she getting at?* "No."

A big smile spread across her face. "Well, there you go. There's still hope for the two of you!"

With a groan, I smacked my head. "Why can't anyone understand I don't care about this stuff? I have more important things to worry about than trivial emotions I can't experience."

"Laz, we both know that's not why you refuse to think about this."

I leaned against the wall and stared at the ground. She was right, but I had told myself long ago I would learn from that mistake, and the way I was acting was part of it.

"I just want you to be happy," she said.

"I don't know what happy means."

Her ears drooped. "Please don't say that. I hate it when you do."

"You know I don't like to lie to you."

Ryoko walked up to me and draped my hair to one side. "You look nice with your hair this length. It looks even better pulled over like this. You should try to have it like this more."

Her change in subject made me feel a little better. "I'm going to bring Raikidan out into the city today to give him a feel for the place. If you're interested in coming along, you're more than welcome to."

She smiled. "That's a great idea. We could familiarize you, as well, since you've been gone so long. I'd love to join you." She snickered. "I'm not sure Rylan will go, though, not after the fun you had this morning."

I winked as I headed for the door. "I'm sure you could convince him."

Her face flushed, and I chuckled before opening the door. Rylan's bored expression met my eyes as he leaned an arm on the doorframe. He'd been decent enough to throw some pants on while waiting.

Rylan held out his hand. "Give me the bell."

"No." I pushed past him. "Raikidan, I'm going to take you out into the city today to get accustomed to it. But first, I need a shower because I reek from weeks of traveling."

Ryoko scrunched her nose. "Yeah, you do." Before I could flip her my middle finger, she latched onto Rylan. "You should come with us. It'll be fun." She didn't give him a chance to protest and went straight into playing dirty. Her ears drooped, her eyes widened while her brow furrowed, and she stuck her bottom lip out into a pout. "Please?"

Rylan closed his eyes and visibly swallowed. "Yes, I'll go, please stop looking at me like that. You know I can't take it."

Ryoko smiled with delight. I went to take my shower, but Rylan stopped me. "The bell first."

"You're not getting it. I won't use it again unless I absolutely have to, but you're not getting it."

"Why not?"

"Because Mom gave it to me…"

Rylan's touch retracted immediately, allowing me to slip away. As I did, I did what I could to keep the memories at bay. I needed to focus on the present—a time where she and many others were no longer with us—and there was no changing that.

The early evening sun hung low in the sky by the time we made it to Sector Three, and the city was still busy with life. I didn't like this sector, but Ryoko had insisted it was best to show Raikidan this area as well. As we walked, Ryoko and I had taken turns explaining things to him, and to my surprise, he kept up rather well.

"Hey, Ryoko, where—" I stopped and looked around. Neither she nor Rylan was with us anymore. "Um, where did they go?"

Raikidan threw a thumb behind him. "She got all excited and ran into one of those buildings you called a store."

"And you didn't say anything?" I couldn't believe this.

"I didn't think it would be a big deal. How hard would it be for us to find them?" he asked.

I gestured around me. "I don't know, Raikidan. How hard would it be to find two people out of hundreds?" He thought this over for a moment and finally understood the problem. I pulled him by the arm. "C'mon, we should keep moving. Otherwise we might attract unwanted attention."

"What kind of attention?" he asked.

"Soldiers, thieves, could be a number of things. It's best to blend in whenever possible."

Sadly, my desire to blend in didn't happen. A woman with too much makeup and in need of some more clothing sashayed her way over to us. "Hey, big boy." She grabbed onto Raikidan's arm. "Why not come with me, and for a small price, have a little fun?" Her voice made me sick. "I'll even give you a special discount for being so hot."

Raikidan looked to me for answers. I sighed. This was not going to be fun in the least. I wrapped my arms around Raikidan's free one and pulled him away from the woman. "He's not interested."

"Aw, c'mon, sweetheart. Can't you share?" She grabbed Raikidan's arm again, pushing her luck. "If you want to join, it'll only cost a little extra. I'm not a picky woman."

"Go find another dick to suck on, whore," I snarled, nearly baring my teeth.

She let go of his arm and stalked away, turning her nose up at me. Dragging Raikidan with me, I stormed down the street. I didn't let go until I knew we were out of her sight.

"What the hell was that?" Raikidan asked.

"That would be a type of unwanted attention," I muttered.

"That's not what I mean."

I sighed. I knew what he meant. I just didn't want to explain it. "She was a hooker."

"A what?"

"A person you pay to have sex with."

"Humans pay to procreate with each other?" Of course he didn't get it. Why would he?

"That's not what I meant." I sighed. This was going to get very awkward very fast. Sitting on a nearby bench, I thought about how to word what I had to say. Raikidan sat down next to me and waited. "Humans have something called contraceptives that make it so a child isn't produced when having sex. This way, we can have a little fun with no worries about anything happening afterward."

"You do this for fun?"

"Obviously, it's a little different for dragons." It wasn't a question. If he was surprised humans had fun with something like this, then it had to be different for them.

"We mate for reproductive purposes only, and we definitely don't reproduce with random dragons."

My brow furrowed. "Wait, I know your kind is monogamous, but do you mate for life too?"

His brow twisted, as if the answer was an obvious one. "Of course."

Actually, yeah, that was an obvious answer. I didn't know why I hadn't thought of that. He'd said they were loyal to their mates, but I had never thought that would influence them to stick together for their entire lifespan.

"Humans don't?"

I shook my head. "I'm not sure about regular humans, but for monogamous nu-humans, it's not common these days. They try, but most of the time the relationships are lucky to last a decade or two."

"Is that the real reason you don't try to find a mate?" he asked. I looked at him funny. "I overheard your conversation with your friend."

"Y–you what?" This was a little embarrassing. "How the hell did you hear us? Her room has soundproofing built into it."

"Not really sure. Your voices were low, but just loud enough for my ears to pick up. You didn't answer my question."

I turned my gaze away. "It's none of your business."

He leaned closer, a smirk plastered on his face. "Look, your friends have liked this form I take, so I can't blame you if you do as well."

I pushed his face away as I stood. "You're being a creeper. Knock it off and behave."

"Where are you going?" he asked as I walked back the way we had come.

"I'm getting hungry, and I don't know where the place Ryoko wanted us to go is, so we're going back to Sector Eight and eating at a restaurant I know of."

"Are you all right?"

"I'm fine."

"I've upset you in some way, haven't I?"

"Just drop it, Raikidan."

"All right, all right."

I glanced back at him. "Just fair warning, I doubt you're going to like Blaze." He waited for an explanation. "He's not monogamous and is proud of that. It's not uncommon for him to bring a few different women home during the week."

Raikidan's lip curled. "I'll do my best to tolerate it."

I nodded and led him to the restaurant. When we arrived, the hostess brought us to our table and gave us the menu. She named off a few of the house specials and left when I ordered drinks. I peered out the window into the darkness of the night that had fallen. I didn't need to look at the menu to know what to order. This was one place the menu never changed.

Raikidan looked at the first page and his expression changed to confusion. "What is this stuff? Why are there so many strange names on here?"

I chuckled. "Each dish is comprised of several kinds of ingredients, so they give them names to make it easy for people to order. I know what to order, so don't try too hard to understand right now."

He continued to look at the menu. "I don't trust it."

"I'll be eating the food. Does that make you trust it more?"

"I guess…"

The waitress returned with our drinks and I placed our order. She blinked when I was done. "Um, miss, the Jalea and Lomo Saltado both feed two people each, and the House Special Platter feeds five."

"We eat a lot." I handed her the menus. She wordlessly took the menus and left. When she was out of earshot, Raikidan spoke. "So… what are we eating?"

I smiled. "The Jalea is deep-fried fish, breaded shrimp, squid, and marinated onions. The Lomo is beef that is sautéed with onions and tomatoes and served with rice. Lastly, which I think you'll like the most, is the House Special Platter, which is a combination of chicken tikka, tandoori chicken, lamb kebobs, and tandoori shrimp served with fresh vegetables."

Raikidan just stared at me wide-eyed. It really was a lot for two people to eat, but, from what I'd gathered in my time spent with him, we wouldn't have a problem.

Twenty minutes later the waitress returned with our large order. I didn't worry about putting anything on my own plate. It was just the two of us. Raikidan didn't start eating when I did. He eyed the food suspiciously, and I sighed.

"Here." I stabbed some chicken with my fork and handed it to him. "Just try it."

Hesitantly he took the fork and popped the chicken into his mouth. After a few chews, he became more interested in the food in front of him. Knowing full well he wasn't going to give me my fork back, I reached over the table and took his.

We quietly ate for a while until something across the room caught his attention. "What are those two doing?"

Glancing to where he was pointing with his fork, I saw a young couple laughing and sharing their food. Uninterested, I went back to eating. "Probably on a date."

"What's a date?" he asked.

I had to think about this for a moment. "Well, it's when you go out somewhere nice with someone else."

"So, we're on a date?" he questioned.

I bobbed my head as I tried to figure out how to word my response. "Yes, and no."

He raised his brow. "Huh?"

I giggled. "Technically we're on a date, but it's a non-romantic date. Those two are on a romantic date."

"What's the difference?"

"A non-romantic date is when two or more people get together for activities with no amorous or sexual intentions. A romantic date has those romantic feelings in mind when engaging in activities during the date."

He nodded, understanding what I was saying. "How do you know it's a romantic date just by looking at them?"

"The way they act. They sit close together, share their food, talk quietly, and stuff like that. It's... hard to explain, really."

I wasn't knowledgeable on the topic, and with Raikidan asking about this topic as much as he did, it really put me out of my element. I was glad when he accepted my answer and didn't ask any more questions, so we could finish off the rest of our food in silence. But as we ate, something didn't feel right about the stillness between us. When Ryoko and I used to go out together she'd chat up a storm, so maybe that was it.

I found myself glancing over at the couple on their date. They were sharing a dessert and seemed to be really enjoying themselves. The strange feeling I had grew, and I realized it was located in the center of my chest.

"You can have that too, Chickadee."

Tannek?

I casually scanned the restaurant so as to not alert Raikidan of my suspicious state, but everything was the way it had been all night. I was just hearing things. Shaking it off, I went back to eating dinner until the two of us had finished every last bite.

To say the waitress was surprised by our appetites was an understatement, and she became more so when I ordered some chocolate cake and ice cream. Raikidan abstained from eating more, and once I was done with my dessert, I pulled out a few silver coins and paid for our dinner. As we left the restaurant, we ran into the couple from earlier, embracing each other next to a car.

"What were they doing?" Raikidan asked when we were out of earshot.

"Kissing."

"Kissing? What is that?"

I sighed. "It's a type of affection. Depending on how you kiss someone, it shows how you feel about them."

"What does it feel like?"

I shrugged. "I don't know."

"Oh, c'mon." He leaned in close to my face.

"What?" I pushed him away. "I really don't know. Why don't you believe that?"

"Oh, I don't know, maybe because you're an attractive female who has had several males show some sort of interest in you."

"No one has any interest in me."

Raikidan threw up fingers as he rattled names off. "Xye, Ken'ichi, Blaze, in a weird way from my observation, and according to Ryoko, Rylan."

My brow furrowed. "Ken'ichi doesn't see me that way, and Blaze doesn't count because he's willing to hump any female he finds attractive. And Rylan... we're not going there."

"Why, because he would count?"

My eyebrow twitched. "He had interest in me for a brief time—a very brief time—but now he doesn't, and I like it that way. I prefer him to be a friend."

"Means he still counts. And Ken'ichi counts, too, because it's obvious by the way he acts around you." I scoffed at the idea and he shook his head. "Now, with so many interested, I find it hard to believe none of them have tried to give you one of these kisses to prove to you they are."

I shoved my hands in my pockets and kept walking. "No."

Even though I didn't care about finding someone, Raikidan bringing up this subject was really starting to bother me. I didn't need to be reminded how much of a lie those feelings were.

I was pulled out of my brooding thoughts when a loud booming noise echoed though the air and dark smoke began billowing up into the sky. Raikidan stood by me as I stopped to look, as did many others in the street.

"What's that?" he asked.

"I'm not sure." I suspected it had something to do with the rebellion. Based on where the smoke originated, I calculated that area to be a military outpost.

Suddenly the night sky lit up in that area, and the sounds of gunfire filled the air. People began talking more, and when the sounds grew louder they started to panic.

"Eira, what's going on?" Raikidan asked.

Before I could reply, a light on my communicator, a device designed for long distance talking with others, began flashing. I unhooked it from my belt loop and attached the device to my head. The device was only long enough to wrap halfway around my head, but its design clipped around my ear and curved with my head to create a perfect fit. Zo had something similar when we met him, but more compact, a design I suspected was new and for military personnel only due to its discreet nature.

With a quick adjust of the microphone, I pressed a button on the frequency dial and a holographic visor slid out of the dial and over my eyes.

"Babe, you there?" came the voice on the other end.

"Hey, Aurora," I greeted. It didn't matter how long I'd been gone, I'd always recognizes the cadence of our personal Underground computer tech. "What's going on?"

"Are you in a good spot to talk?" she asked.

I glanced around. "No, let me get to a quieter place. Too many panicking people."

"Sounds like you're close to the action, then."

So, there is something going on with the rebellion. I grabbed Raikidan by the wrist and dragged him into an alley. I didn't stop until we were halfway down and hidden from prying eyes.

"All right, what's going on?" I asked Aurora.

"There's been a screw-up with one of the assignments," she said.

"I can see that," I muttered.

She chuckled. "Part of Team Three was assigned to take out a few supply bases, but they didn't want to listen to the approved ones. They ended up taking on a high security outpost and it's caused a battle."

I sighed with aggravation. "Of course, they would. Now they need the cleanup crew to bail them out of their mess, right?"

"Yeah. I already have Ryoko and the others on the move. You're the last to be contacted."

I glanced at Raikidan. "How soon am I needed?"

"Well, immediately, of course. Why, what's up? You've never been hesitant to jump in where needed in the past."

There was no point in lying to her. "I have a new recruit with me, and he hasn't been exposed or trained for our kinds of battles yet."

"Eira, don't worry, I can help," Raikidan said in a low voice.

"There really isn't any time for you to get him somewhere safe unless you send him home on his own," Aurora said. "But if you're talking about the guy Genesis sent me info about recently, then I can see why you can't just do that."

"Yeah, that's my dilemma."

"Eira, I can help," Raikidan insisted a bit louder.

"What kind of fire power are they packing?" I asked. "I don't have much for weapons myself."

"The basic stuff, so you should be fine, but Ryoko said she was grabbing something for you just in case."

"All right. I'll figure something out."

"Okay, good luck. I'll send coordinates to your communicator."

I deactivated my communicator and thought. What was I going to do?

"Eira," Raikidan said. "I am here to help. Let me join."

I sighed. "Raikidan, it's not that simple. The battles here are different than the ones we fought outside the city. We use guns here, and you've never been exposed to that. I'm not signing your death warrant because some idiots decided not to listen."

"It can't be much different than arrows, right?"

I shook my head. "See, this is what I mean. They're far different than arrows. They're faster, more destructive, and can be shot off in rounds far quicker than any archer could dream of doing."

"I came here to help, so let me prove that to you. Bark out any order you want, and I'll do it without question." He placed a hand on my shoulder. "Trust me."

I ground my teeth and then sighed in defeat. "Fine. We're wasting time arguing. You listen, and be cautious. If you have to do more hiding than fighting, fine. And if you die, don't you haunt me saying it's my fault."

He chuckled. "Deal."

I jerked my head and started moving. "Then let's go."

14
CHAPTER

I ducked behind the remains of a crumbled wall and steadied my breath. This battle had gone from bad to worse before Raikidan and I had even arrived, and I wasn't sure how we were going to come out of this alive. My team had really screwed this up big time. They had to go and pick the biggest and most well-armed military post in the entire city. They had pushed us far from the outpost and nearly surrounded us. If we got out of this alive, I was going to be skinning a few people.

Bullets flew over my head, and I peeked around the rubble to gauge how many soldiers I was up against. Three were visible, and I suspected a few more were hiding. I checked my ammunition count for the handgun I had picked up off a fallen rebel, to find only four bullets left. I had to make them count, and I wasn't nearly as great a marksman as Rylan.

Taking a deep breath, I left my cover and took three quick shots, only to have to take a fourth when I missed the last target, and then quickly pulled back to hide when more soldiers came out of hiding. They opened fire, and I rolled until I was hidden and temporarily safe behind a building. Other rebels on the street had my back and opened fired on the military, while I thought about how to help now that my weapon was useless. I could use fire, but I was losing energy the longer this dragged on, and that meant I wouldn't be able to produce a strong flame for long.

I nearly jumped out of my skin when something cold and wet touched my arm. I whipped around to defend myself, but stopped mid-swing when the gray wolf behind me flattened his ears and backed up. By his feet was a carbine, and strapped around his body were ammunition cartridges.

"Raikidan?" I asked.

He shifted and held up his hands. "I didn't mean to sneak up on you."

I sighed in relief, my shoulder sagging. "You have got to be more careful. If this had a bullet left, I would have shot you."

"Sorry," he repeated. "I just thought you'd want the weapon Ryoko picked for you. I even have extra ammunition."

I picked up the loaded carbine and unloaded a round on the military in the street. When my magazine was empty, I pulled back so I could reload. "So, tell me, why did you leave the spot I ordered you to stay in?"

"You told me not to die, so when my alley was overrun, I figured it'd be best to get out of there," Raikidan replied after I unleashed half of my second round. "I went searching for Ryoko at that point, since I figured you could use the weapon. I was able to get a good view from the sky from time to time, so I also gave position information to our side."

"Smart moves. Learn anything while you were doing all that?"

"Don't challenge Ryoko to an arm wrestling contest."

I laughed far harder than I should have, stalling me from unleashing the last half of my magazine. "Well, at least you learned that. Far too many others are still learning."

He watched me as I fussed with my carbine and insulted it when it jammed. He found it mildly amusing, but was otherwise useless, not bothering to give me a hand. I really wished Ryoko hadn't given me this particular weapon. We all had our own preferred weapons, and extras just in case, and she had grabbed the wrong carbine. Mine was better taken care of and would have had less chance of this happening.

"Look out!" Raikidan shouted.

Everything happened so fast. He pushed me. A gun went off and he yelled in pain, and I pulled an ember from my lips and tossed it at our attacker. She dropped her weapon and screamed as her skin burned, but I had more important things to focus on. Raikidan was leaning against the wall clutching his shoulder, blood running down his arm.

"Let me see," I ordered as I reached for his arm.

Raikidan hesitated, but then revealed a large, nasty gash, going from his upper arm to his shoulder. I sighed with relief. At least the bullet had only grazed him. This was easier to deal with than a full bullet wound.

I started ripping my shirt. "We'll have to get you stitched up when we get home, but this will help with the bleeding."

He flinched as I tied the cloth strips around his arm. "I can heal it myself."

"I know, but it'll be easier and will come out better if we stitch you up first," I said. "Sorry you had to get hit because of me. I should have been paying more attention."

"I'm not complaining," he replied. "You had to get your weapon working."

"Yes, although I should have just abandoned it. I know better than to waste time fixing the damn thing in a battle like this."

"How else will you fight these men?"

I stood and pulled the remaining fire from the woman's charred, lifeless body. "With this. Stay put so you don't get in the way or lose any more blood."

I charged out of the side street and unleashed a fury of fire. I put everything I had into my attack, without fear of returned fire. The soldiers who hadn't been hit by my first attack took cover, but that didn't protect them from my ability. My control over fire when I first left this city was nothing to sneeze at, but the training I had done with the shamans had taught me things I never thought possible.

Just when I thought I couldn't hold out any more and had to fall back, the military miraculously pulled back. Rebels flooded past me, and I moved back to where I had left Raikidan and collapsed on my knees against the wall, exhausted.

"Are you okay?" Raikidan asked.

"Yeah, just tired."

Just then, someone appeared at the mouth of the side street. Raikidan and I readied for a fight, but relaxed when we recognized the young man as a rebel. He knelt in front of me and handed over a bottle of water.

"Don't feel that you have to join back in," he said. "What you did helped us push them back on this side, and the others are doing well on the other side, finally. We're going to win this one, and you deserve a rest after that display."

I took a swig of water. "Don't tell me what to do."

He chuckled, and then ran off to join the fight.

"Are you going to join them?" Raikidan asked.

I shook my head. "I put everything I had into that attack. I need time to rest."

"That was impressive to watch."

I chuckled. "You're so terrible at listening."

"Like you're one to talk."

I laughed and he joined in after a few moments. It was cut short when my communicator began flashing.

"Yeah?" I answered once it was on my head.

"They retreated," Ryoko said.

I sighed with relief. "Good. I was starting to worry about our chances for a bit."

"You're not the only one. How did you hold up? Did Raikidan ever find you?"

"Yeah, he found me. We're a little banged up, but in one piece."

"Good to hear. We're all gathering up on Coral Street if you can make it over to us."

"We'll be right there."

I hung up and struggled to stand, refusing help from Raikidan when he offered. Once I was sure my legs would hold me, we made our way to Ryoko's location. We were the last to arrive, but no one appeared to mind. They were too battle weary to care, and there was still more to do. They looked to me for direction. That's when I realized I was the highest ranking member here. *Well, here we go.*

But before I could open my mouth, someone stumbled out of an alley. He was a tall, muscular young man with mocha skin, who looked to be on death's door.

"Derek!" Ryoko screeched.

She and I both ran over to him and he collapsed in my arms. I fell to my knees from his weight and my weariness, but I made sure he didn't hit his head.

"You look terrible, kid," I teased.

He chuckled. "Yeah, well not all of us can look like they just rolled out of bed in some ritzy mansion, Commander."

I snorted. "I don't look that good."

"I'm glad I got to see you again. Sorry I screwed up and wasn't careful... I won't be able to see a new dawn, will I..."

"We all do stupid things. Don't beat yourself up over it."

"Laz," Ryoko warned. "Stop acting like he's a goner. We can still get him help."

The two of us ignored her. Derek wasn't coming out of this alive, and that was just how it was.

"B–burn my body, would you?" he asked me.

"Of course."

"T–thanks..." His words came out in an airy hiss, and then his chest stilled.

Tears welled up in Ryoko's eyes. "Derek..."

I reached up and closed the lids over Derek's lifeless blue eyes and then rested him on the ground.

"Damn military," someone muttered. "They had to go and make a mess of all this."

I snapped my head over to the man, to find him about to kick the lifeless body of a fallen soldier. "Don't you dare."

He stopped and glared at me. "Why shouldn't I?"

I jumped to my feet, my fatigue now gone, and stormed over to him, others seeing my anger and quickly moving out of my way. "Because you used to be like him. Because you're not superior to him in any way. Because it's not his fault you screwed up and didn't listen to orders to leave this post alone. You have no place to throw around the blame when this could have been avoided if you had just targeted the correct outposts!"

"This was the best one, and you were all afraid to take it," he said hotly. "Look at what we managed to accomplish. We took out a huge supply building. We took out their numbers. We—"

"Get your head out of your ass and look around!" I barked. "Look at the damage you've caused. Look how close they pushed us to civilian homes. Look at all the resources you've wasted and all the dead men around you, comrade and enemy alike. Their lives can't be replaced.

They aren't expendable! All you've done is cause death and destruction with your arrogance."

He snorted. "You should be proud then, Commander. Death and
destruction are the only two things you're good at."

I was stunned. How dare he say that to me? Before I had a chance
to recover, someone slammed into him and sent him crashing into
a building. I stared at Raikidan, his livid expression marring his face.
Why—

My attention was drawn to Ryoko when she started whining childishly. "Man, I wanted to hit him."

Others around us chuckled nervously, lightening the mood a little,
but it was clear they were walking on eggshells around me.

The rebel got up shakily and prepared himself for a fight. "You want
to fight with me, outsider?"

Raikidan sucked in a deep breath and unleashed a hot flame, not
quite reaching the cowering rebel. I figured that was Raikidan's goal.
The fire subsided when Raikidan ran out of air, and he turned his
back on the rebel. "You're not worth anyone's time."

The others around us became wary of Raikidan and muttered amongst
themselves. It didn't surprise me. Firebreathers were rare, and were
typically outcasts here. Raikidan didn't care, though I doubted he cared
what any human thought of him. He could kill most humans easily
with his natural dragon strength.

I sucked in a deep breath, trying to clear my head and get everything
moving before the military came back. "Get the wounded home and
patched. Those not helping with that, help me bring *all* bodies to the
Underground for me to perform burial rites."

I spun on my heels and heaved the body of a soldier over my shoulder.
Raikidan turned and reached out to help, but I refused him. "I said,
wounded go home. That includes you. Argus, get Raikidan patched up."

"Of course," Argus said obediently.

"I'm fine," Raikidan insisted.

Argus grabbed Raikidan by the back of the shirt and dragged him
away. "If you want to live to see tomorrow, don't argue with her."

Raikidan sighed unhappily, but obeyed without any fuss. This allowed
me to focus on my new task, one I wasn't thrilled about performing,
but it was my duty.

I waited while Rylan and Ryoko laid Derek's body on the altar. It had taken us several hours to get all the bodies underground and ready for their burial rites. I had struggled with the task of speaking with all the dead to find out who preferred to be buried, and who wanted to be cremated. Normally we would call a priest who believed in our cause to do this, but it was late, and I was more than qualified to step in—even if I didn't believe I was a proper choice.

Most wanted their bodies burned, but we only had one altar down here, and I really didn't want to use it; I much preferred doing this ceremony above ground. They deserved that, but we didn't live in an ideal world. When Ryoko and Rylan were done preparing Derek's body, they stepped back and I advanced. Slowly I lit a fire around his body. The fire danced as I chanted. Once his body was consumed by the flames, I stepped back to wait. The smell of burning flesh would sicken most, but we were so used to it, we had become desensitized. Ryoko stayed next to me while Rylan went to let the others know to prepare the next body.

"So… Raikidan is a Firebreather, and you're really a shaman," she said.

"Yep. Crazy world we live in, huh?"

She snorted. "You're telling me."

"Speaking of crazy, Raikidan heard what we were talking about in your room this morning. Crazy, huh?"

Her face flushed. "He what? Oh man, that's embarrassing."

"You're telling me. He brought it up when you and Rylan conveniently ditched us in the city."

She held up her hands. "Sorry. I'll check for damage around the door, since it's likely the cause of the sound leak. And speaking of that ditching incident, sorry about that. It wasn't my intention. I just got excited when I saw something in a shop window."

I chuckled. "I figured as much. No big deal."

"Are you hungry?" she asked. "You and Raikidan didn't come back to the house, and then all the fight—"

"Raikidan and I stopped to get something to eat, so I'm okay for now," I interrupted.

Ryoko nudged me and smirked. "You had a date with the rookie?"

I rolled my eyes. "Not the kind of date you're thinking of."

"Uh huh, sure, keep denying it."

I shook my head and focused just beyond Derek's skeleton. His spiritual form stood beyond the fire, watching. A somber expression glossed his eyes, no hints of anger to be seen, so I was sure I didn't have to worry about him remaining here longer than he should. He knew we'd avenge his death. *No doubt about it.* Then, two more people started to appear. One was a muscular, olive-skinned man who appeared to be in his mid-thirties, and the other was a young woman in her early twenties with blonde hair and fair skin.

I quickly looked away when three more people began to appear. I couldn't look at them—couldn't face them.

"What's up?" Ryoko asked. "You see something?"

"Dead people." I meant it as a joke, but my words came out hollow.

"Derek?" she guessed.

"Zeek and Jade, too."

Her eyes went wide. "What about Amara and Jasmine?"

I nodded slowly. "Tannek too…"

Her eyes softened. "What's it like, seeing the dead?"

"Most of the time it's as if they're alive, but they tend to have a translucent form. Sometimes you only hear a voice, and sometimes the air around you goes cold, but that doesn't happen all that often."

"So, if you're not paying attention, could you think you're talking to someone alive?"

"Yeah, that happens quite a bit, especially since many spirits don't try to correct you, as it allows them to feel they're alive again."

"That's sad…"

I frowned. "I'd like to stop talking about it, if it's okay…"

"Yeah, of course. I didn't mean to upset you."

"I know."

I was tempted to look up at them again, even if it meant bringing back all the pain, but I couldn't do it. I couldn't face what had happened. What I had done to some of them…

I lay awake, unable to sleep, even though weariness clung to me. It had taken several hours to get a portion of the bodies burned in ritual, and I was sent home before I was anywhere near finished. I was told a priest would be called to do the rest, but still I didn't stop willingly. The priest wasn't going to be there for some time, and spirits were finicky when they were newly released from their bodies.

They could wait patiently for their rites if you were actively working on more than one body, but the moment you stopped, that's when things would go wrong. Of course, those who don't have experience with the dead couldn't know that.

I gazed at my tooth necklace and listened to the combined sounds of the rain and Raikidan's soft snores. He was sound asleep when I got back. Argus waited up for us and told me about Raikidan's wound status; it had been stitched up successfully, but Argus had struggled to get it just right. Apparently Raikidan's muscular physique was mostly to blame, compounded by the type of wound he received. He reported that Raikidan had been a good patient, too, remaining still the entire time.

Once I slipped into my room, I immediately checked on him, and found I had no reason to worry. He'd healed himself up while he was alone, and there was barely a mark to show for his ordeal. I was curious what he'd tell everyone since it'd be noticeable he wasn't wounded anymore. It was hit-or-miss with him whether he'd tell truths about himself or make something up. It was what made it hard to trust him, not that I wanted to trust many. Trust got you into trouble. I learned that some time ago.

I yawned loudly and Raikidan's snoring suddenly stopped. Looking over at him, I watched his eyes flutter open. He picked up his head and stared at me. "Sorry. I didn't mean to wake you."

He yawned and then shifted from his dragon form to his nu-human one, and jumped onto my bed, causing me to bounce a little bit. I sat up and glared at him.

He snickered and leaned against my footboard. "So, since you won't let me sleep, why not tell me more about this place?"

"If yawning isn't letting you sleep, then you'd hate to see what I'm capable of when I actually don't want you to sleep." He snorted and I chuckled as I reclined against my many pillows stacked against the headboard. "So, what do you want to know?"

"More about you and your experiment friends, about your social structures, about what goes on here—anything, really."

"I know I said it before, but I'll say it again. You're far more inquisitive than I ever imagined you'd be."

He didn't say anything, just avoided eye contact.

"You avoided my comment before, too. Why are you acting like it's a bad thing?"

His brow rose. "You don't think so?"

I shrugged. "It's how we learn in life. Humans are naturally inquisitive, so finding another creature who is equally inquisitive isn't odd to me."

"Black dragons aren't inquisitive," he said. "They couldn't care less about another, including other black dragons. But since I'm not full black dragon, I end up wanting to learn more than I should."

"What do you mean, not full black dragon?" I asked.

He looked up at the ceiling. "My mother was a red dragon."

He didn't show it, but I had a strong suspicion there was something wrong with that. I didn't ask him, though, causing the room to become very quiet.

"Aren't you going to ask me something?" he asked, looking at me again.

"What's there to ask?" I questioned.

"You said it yourself, humans are inquisitive. So, doesn't that mean you should be asking a bunch of questions?"

"If I asked you about yourself, you'd more than likely not answer," I replied. "But why should I ask? It's none of my business, and I never talk about myself, so it's not my place to ask about others. Besides, if you wanted me to know something, you're more than capable of telling me yourself."

"Ask me," he demanded.

I furrowed my brow. "Why not just tell me?"

"Because my black dragon side tells me to just shut my mouth, so even if I wanted to tell anything about me or my kind, I can't. Now ask me."

"How many dragon colors are there?" It was a start, I guess.

"Three. Black, green, and red. There were more once, but those other dragons went extinct some time ago."

"What's the difference between dragon colors besides their scale colors?"

"Personalities and lifestyles."

"Elaborate."

"Black dragons tend to be selfish, greedy, and at times cruel. They generally keep to themselves and usually see other creatures, including other-colored dragons, as being of a lesser status. Their territories usually consist of barren places, such as dry steppes, but a well-hidden cave in any terrain will do just fine. Green dragons tend to vary on personality, but most are friendly to just about anyone. They live in small clans that usually consist of a male, his mate, and some of their offspring. Their territories are always based in low mountains or heavily forested areas. Red dragons are the most social of the three dragon colors, and the most loyal. They're kind, enjoy learning, and mingle with other creatures. They tend to live in large clans or colonies, and many live amongst non-dragons without ever being noticed. They aren't picky on where their territory rests, if it even exists at all. That good enough?"

His fight against his own instinct to stay quiet reminded me of me. Because of this, I had to keep asking questions. "What's the problem with you being a black-red dragon?"

"Dragons only mate with other dragons of the same color. They barely ever come into contact with each other unless their territories border, or they require aid of some sort. Because of this, when two different-colored dragons mate, it causes complications among the structures of both colors. The mated pair tends to be shunned by both sides, and their offspring don't have the easiest life. Red dragons are more likely to accept this union, but it doesn't mean it's any less hard."

"So basically, your father sucked up his pride, mated with a red dragon, and you're punished for it. So now you live in the middle of nowhere."

"That about sums it up."

I shifted my weight a little, resting my arm on my raised knee. "The red stripe you have, does it mark you?" He growled and I turned my gaze away. "Forget it. I shouldn't have asked." *I should have also worded myself better. That was rather insensitive of me.*

"You just don't understand," he muttered.

"I think I understand a little more than you realize," I mumbled. He looked at me. "Experiments aren't accepted in society. Our creators see us as tools, nu-humans see us as monsters, and because we are human, our existence means nothing to other races. The only ones who accept our existence are the neutral parties of shamans, druids, and gypsies, but as seen with Maka'shi, just because they're supposed to be neutral doesn't mean they truly are. We fit in only amongst ourselves." I sighed and pulled my legs up, resting my arms on them lightly. "And even so, some of us don't fit in even there."

"You come across as a normal nu-human to me," Raikidan said.

"And you come across as a normal dragon to me."

"How would you know what a normal dragon is like? You said you never met a dragon before."

A smirk spread across my lips. "You claimed to never have met a nu-human before."

He chuckled. "I have, actually, but it was a long time ago."

"I bet I made him look like a Saint."

"No, it's the other way around."

I snorted. "Yeah, right." A small silence enveloped us, so I decided to change the subject. "So, is there anything else you want to know?"

"Start with the structure of this place, and how you're able to blend in," he said.

"The people of the city are divided into two parts: civilians and soldiers. Civilians are broken down into rebels, freed experiments, and regular citizens. Soldiers are broken down into experiments and civilian recruits. The rebels come in two forms: ex-military, and civilians who want a change. Ex-military rebels are usually experiments, but are sometimes civilian soldiers. Ex-military rebels do the dirty work, while civilian rebels act as spies and relay messages to rally points, although it can be the other way around at times.

"Free experiments, like Zane, Blaze, Argus, and Seda, are experiments who were active during the time of the previous ruler. After a certain amount of service, and if you were deemed fit enough, you were allowed to live in the city as a normal citizen. After the leadership switched, this was no longer the case, except for those experiments who were designed to be medics, like Azriel."

"Who is Azriel?" Raikidan asked.

"Someone you'll meet eventually. Nice guy."

"All right, continue, then."

"Okay, as I was saying, military medics are given leave after a certain length of service, even now. Zarda sees no need to force them to stay once their time is up, as he doesn't find them important enough to keep. The city is also always looking for medical personnel, and since most medics stay in the medical field once they're let go, it works out.

"Those of us who had yet to be released by contract, or were created after the new ruling, were not allowed to be freed, so in order to blend in, we have to keep lower profiles by forging files, changing names and histories, or doing anything else to throw off the military. Our group normally finds ways to change files, which is the case for Rylan and Ryoko, but there are times when files, like mine, are unable to be located and changed, so other more complicated measures have to be taken.

"In cases like Seda, papers are made to make it look as though she is dead. Otherwise she would have to be registered, and she'd be watched constantly to make sure she isn't a threat, since she's a psychic. This mandatory registry would make it even harder for us to work, so the Council agreed all psychics were to be split up. Some would register, while others, like Seda, would falsify death records and work in secret. To keep information coming in to help us with our fight, and income to fund it, we set up businesses, like Zane's shop and Azriel's club."

"So, you used the amnesia as a way to throw off those soldiers," Raikidan said.

I nodded. "I don't recognize that Zo character, which means there's a greater likelihood he doesn't know who I am, so it made it easier to get him to believe us. Now, with a general believing the story, the rest of the military will be more likely to believe the same. The only drawback is we have to be on top of our game to keep playing it up. A slip from anyone and the charade is all over."

Raikidan rubbed his chin. "All of this to kill one man. Why not just kill the guy and get it over with?"

"It's not as simple as it seems," I stated. "The castle's defense is great, and you have to expend a lot of energy just to get to him. If, by chance, you do manage to get to him, you are more than likely going to fail. He created us, so he knows every experiment's weakness, or if they're extremely unlucky, weaknesses. This makes our effort harder, so we try to cut the resistance until we can break through easily."

"So why not kill him while you were still living in the fortress?" he asked.

I shrugged. "When you're loyal to him, you don't want to kill him, and when you break that loyalty, you have very little time to get out. Escape becomes your primary objective."

"So, what's your weakness?" he asked.

I snorted. "You'd think I'd tell you?"

He raised an eyebrow. "You don't deny you have one?"

"I did say every experiment has one. I'm no different."

"So, you don't trust me with that secret?"

"I have never told anyone what it is."

"Sounds like a serious weakness if you don't tell."

I didn't answer. I didn't need him knowing how crippling these weaknesses were.

"Tell me more about this experimenting stuff."

I shrugged. "Not much to say. By the use of science, DNA is made from various donors and then changed for the need of the maker. Most experiments are kept in their tank until their age is roughly seventeen. On rare occasions they are removed sooner or later than this age, depending on the desired effect. Then they're removed for training."

"They wait seventeen years for each experiment?" he asked curiously.

I nodded. "Most of the time. They usually have a few experiments going at one time to speed up the process, but within the past few years, they've been trying out a new speed-up process that causes the body to mature faster in the tank."

"Were you part of that process?"

I shook my head. "No. It took seventeen years for me. They didn't start the trials 'til after Ryoko, Rylan, and I were removed from our tanks."

"How close was your release to the others?"

I thought for a moment. "We were all designed around the same time, but Rylan was removed first, then me a half year later, then Ryoko a year after that. We were placed on the same team to see how well our designs worked together."

"Where do they get the donated DNA?" he asked.

"Depends. Past experiments came from humans who willingly gave it. Now that they've added in other species' DNA, the gene pool is larger, so most of the time it comes from other experiments. But there are times it comes from outside sources, so the gene pools don't mix too much."

He tilted his head. "Why would someone on the outside willingly donate DNA?"

I shook my head. "With Zarda in control, these people don't have a choice. If Zarda can't convince the party to willingly give up a sample, he'll take it by force."

"Do experiments know what type of DNA they have?" he asked.

I thought about this for a moment. "Some do, some don't. Half of our group is made with straight nu-human DNA, but some of us, like Ryoko, Rylan, and me, have a little extra. As I told you yesterday, Rylan has DNA of both wolves and dogs built into him. Ryoko has wogron DNA."

"What about you?" he asked.

I shrugged. "I don't know. Whatever it is, it's carnivorous, making it easier for the geneticists to alter it to crave blood and death."

"Have you ever wanted to find out?" he asked.

I lifted my shoulders again. "It wouldn't make a difference. I can't change it."

"If you could change it, would you?" he questioned. As I nodded slowly, he asked, "Why?"

I pulled my legs up tighter to my chest and stared down at the bed. "Do you know what it's like to kill without regret? Do you know what it's like to feel a deep emptiness when you have to guess how to act in situations where emotions are involved? Do you know what it's like to feel as if your existence is meaningless? Do you know what it's like to live in hell?" I looked at him, but he didn't answer. A defeated breath left my lips as my gaze fell away. "Didn't think so..."

He gets the choice whether to feel or not. He was born, like everyone should be. He gets the choice to choose. I sighed again and curled up on my bed. Raikidan took that as a hint that I didn't want to talk anymore, and lay back down on the floor.

"You do a good job of acting normal. Maybe you feel more than you realize," he said before he shifted to his dragon form.

I closed my eyes, emptiness creeping into my chest. No one ever understood. Raikidan, it seemed, was no different. They just thought I was broken and could be fixed, or that I was beyond repair.

I wished I could be fixed. I wished I could just experience emotions like a normal person. Just once I wished I could. *Just once...*

15
CHAPTER

The wooden steps creaked under my feet as Raikidan and I jogged down the stairs of the basement. I had woken up close to midafternoon and waited for a few hours for Genesis to receive assignments I'd consider useful to our cause, but she had only been sent surveillance missions. They had their place, sure, but from what Ryoko had told me, they were still the majority of the assignments our team received unless we were sent to bail out another team.

Some things never change. I refrained from sighing. I just had to be patient and do this the right way. I wasn't asking for a death wish.

That was why I had suggested I take Raikidan out into the city with a car while the others did the assignment Genesis had chosen. I was sure this was the best way to integrate him into our daily lives. With him not being human, he wasn't going to be able to easily jump into the way we humans lived, and last's night battle was not the best way to introduce him to everything.

The two of us went from the basement to the connected underground garage, and I headed straight for my second favorite car, my first being a preferred choice in the summer. This self-assigned mission wasn't just good for Raikidan. I needed to reacquaint myself with the wheel of a car. *Shouldn't be too hard. It's like riding a horse.* That was easy for everyone as long as they had a saddle… right?

I stopped walking when I realized Raikidan was no longer with me. Turning on my heels, I found him gazing upon the vast selection of cars and motorcycles with awe and curiosity. The variety of models and makes would make any motor junkie have a heart attack, but I was sure Raikidan's reaction was due to his lack of knowledge about this type of technology.

Leaning on the fender of one of the SUVs we had, I waited patiently. It wasn't like we were under a time limit. Raikidan wandered around as he took interest in the cars. He appeared to have a preference to the sports cars over most, and I found myself smiling. I couldn't help it. The look in his eyes told me he was impressed—no, delighted. Dragon, human, elf, it didn't matter. Like most men, he was drawn to these toys.

"So, are you going to keep gawking, or can we get a move on?" I teased.

He looked at me only to glance away as he grabbed the back of his neck. "Sorry."

I chuckled. "It's fine. I'm mostly teasing. But we should get going."

A perplexed expression crossed his face, as if he weren't sure how to react, then nodded and jogged over to me. I led him to my car. She was a spectacular red and black aerodynamic supercar with a convex hood, large lateral air intakes in the front, streamlining zones to facilitate air flow, external wing mirrors, panoramic glass roof, low spoiler, twin exhaust system, and leather interior.

Lifting up the butterfly door, I slid into the driver's side and situated myself after closing the door, placing my communicator in a small pocket where the dash and center console met. For a moment, I wondered if I should have chosen my third favorite sports car, as it had a canopy door, but as I watched Raikidan try to understand how the door worked, I decided to stick with my choice. His trouble was highly amusing, and his frustration only grew when he realized I was getting sick satisfaction out of his predicament.

"Are you going to help me?" he demanded.

I just smirked and dug into my back pocket to remove my identification card. I briefly looked at the thin, rectangular object with small buttons and glass dome in the center before stashing it into the glovebox. I sat upright in my seat after I closed the glovebox, and buckled myself up just as Raikidan was finally figuring out how to open the door. I couldn't stop myself from snickering as he ducked his head in attempt to avoid the bizarre door and sat down.

"Not funny," he muttered as he closed the door.

My snickering continued when he fumbled with figuring out the seatbelt. "Need help?"

His cheeks tinted. "No."

I started up the car while he dealt with his problem, and chuckled when his seatbelt clicked and he sighed quietly with relief.

"Don't make fun of me," he said.

"It was far more amusing watching you do all that than I thought it would be," I admitted. "Though I'm surprised you figured out the seatbelt so quick."

"I watched you do it," he said, his voice little more than a murmur. "Can we just go?"

I snickered and shifted the car into gear. Pulling the vehicle out of its spot, I sped through the garage to the ramp entrance.

Raikidan glanced at me and then at the seemingly dead end. "What are you doing?"

"Leaving the garage, of course," I said without looking at him.

"It's a dead end! Are you crazy?"

I smirked and then pressed a button on the center dash. Within seconds, the roof above the ramp pulled away and we flew out of the mouth of the earth. Raikidan immediately began looking around frantically.

"Told you we were fine."

"Where are we?" he asked. "I don't see the house."

"What? Did you really think the combination of the basement and garage was really that small? There is no way we could have that much stuff down there in a normal-sized basement."

"That doesn't answer my question," Raikidan said irritably.

I shook my head. "We're four blocks away from the house."

"All right, where are we going?"

"No destination," I said. "We're just going to cruise around and take things in that way. Just keep an eye out for suspicious activity."

"How am I supposed to do that in here?" he asked. "I don't even know what you mean by suspicious."

"Trust me, you'll know when you see it."

He sighed and looked outside the car, but he wasn't being inconspicuous enough.

I shook my head. "Raikidan, you need to stop looking around frantically."

"How am I supposed to find the activity you're looking for if I don't?"

"Look, I'm not expecting much from you on this assignment—"

"Gee, thanks," he muttered.

I laughed. "Let me finish. You're still new to all this. I don't expect you to master everything immediately, but I do expect you to work hard on perfecting the most important part first. This means looking like you belong in the city.

"A child looks around wildly as a car moves to take in as much as possible, even though their minds won't be able to process everything. The same goes for outsiders. They try to take in more than they can handle. I understand this is a new experience for you, and you want to take it in as best as you can, but I'm going to have to ruin that experience by forcing you to act as if you know this city like the back of your hand. Sit calmly in your seat and just scan the city slowly. I'm not expecting anything else out of you."

"So, you won't get upset if I don't catch anything… suspicious?" I could tell he was skeptical.

"That's correct. I need you to learn to blend in more than accomplishing anything else right now. That's why I made this assignment up."

"Made it up? Is that why the others left without us?" Raikidan asked.

I nodded as I slowed the car down. "Precisely. You got thrown into things a little faster than I wanted last night, so I wanted to give you something a little easier to grasp. How are you feeling, by the way? Battles are hard for many to witness."

"Fine," he replied. "I'm no stranger to death."

I nodded. I was tempted to press about that comment, but decided it wasn't the best idea right now. "How's your arm? I noticed by the time I had gotten home you had done your magic on it."

He chuckled when I said magic. "Yes, when I retired for the night I took care of it. There's no residual pain, a perk to my fire healing."

"You barely have a mark from it, too."

He nodded. "Had I tended to it sooner, I might not have one at all, but I don't care."

"Badge of honor."

Raikidan was quiet for a moment. "Yes."

"So, you were up and out of the room well before I was; anyone ask you questions when they noticed the healed area?" I asked.

"Just Ryoko."

"What did you say?"

"I decided to mess with her and got her to think I had super healing powers because of my shapeshifting ability."

I hit the wheel as I laughed. I wasn't sure if it was the fact he had pulled such a trick on her or that he sounded so satisfied when saying it that made that so funny. *Maybe both? Definitely both.*

"After allowing her to think that way for a few minutes I told her it wasn't the case. She whined at me for tricking her and then when I told her the real reason was a secret, she complained some more, telling me I was mean, and I acted too much like you."

I continued to laugh. "You're going to fit in just fine with the team."

He watched me as I got myself under control.

"What?" I asked.

He shook his head and looked out the window. "Nothing."

I raised my brow in question but focused on the road.

"Why are you stopping?" he asked.

I nodded my head at the multicolored light fixture above the road. "See that? It's a traffic light. It controls the flow of traffic on the road. When it's green, cars can move at the designated speed. When it's yellow, they have to slow down. And when it's red, they have to stop."

"Instantly?"

I chuckled. "No, not instantly. That would be impossible, not to mention dangerous. They're to stop before they reach a certain line on the road or before they run into the car in front of them."

"Such a complicated system you humans create just to get around."

"Don't worry. If you're here long enough, you'll get the hang of it."

My attention diverted to the sidewalk and Raikidan noticed immediately. "What is it?"

I reached for my communicator. "You know that suspicious activity I was talking about? Just found some."

"Where?"

"See that group of soldiers?"

"Yeah, they look ordinary to me."

"I figured you'd say that. Means they're doing their job well. This is a good exercise for you. See how close they're walking to each other? That formation is too tight for standard patrolling soldiers."

Raikidan nodded. "I see what you mean."

"Also, notice how tense their shoulders are. Their armor would normally hide much of their uneasiness, so if you can see it, then they're really on edge. Something is up." I dialed out my signal until someone picked up the other end. "Seda, I have activity to report."

"You are slow," she teased. "I've already sent some members out to watch that group."

"Damn psychic," I muttered as I cut the connection and put my car in motion.

I weaved through the traffic almost effortlessly as I cruised down the street. It had been so easy to get back behind the wheel.

"You're a good driver," Raikidan complimented. I laughed and he looked at me as if he was insulted. "What's so funny?"

I smiled. "You're the first to think I'm a good driver."

He blinked. "What, seriously? Why?"

"If you jumped into a car with the others of the house, you'd see. I've got some serious subpar driving skills compared to them. Well maybe not Rylan. He's pretty insane."

"Well, if nothing bad happens, I would say you're a good driver," he defended.

I smiled. "Yes, I suppose that's true."

We passed under a large motorway that was suspended in the air and Raikidan took great interest in it. "What is that?"

"A freeway," I said. "Well, I call it that. Most people in this city call it a motorway. Both terms work, though."

"What's a freeway?"

"It's a road that provides an unhindered flow of traffic," I explained. "There are no traffic signals, intersections, or property access. Dala-trend suspends its freeways above the city and limits the number of exits it has, making it ideal for those who need to get to one end of the city to the other quickly without any stops in between. Freeways also have a higher speed limit, making it that much more convenient for those people. One day I'll bring you up there to see for yourself. Today isn't a good day to do that."

"I understand."

We rode in relative silence after that. It was only ever broken if Raikidan had a quick question, or when we stopped to get a quick bite to eat at a sandwich shop. I didn't start heading home until the sun began to set.

Then I remembered I had forgotten to tell him something very important last night. "Hey, this may seem out of the blue, but I just remembered I didn't talk to you about this. Remember when we talked about how citizens can't leave without proper approval?" He nodded. "Now that you've been seen by Zo, that means you're marked as a citizen. Please promise me you won't try to leave unless you tell me. I know of ways to help you get out safely, as not even shifting is a safe bet due to the experimental shapeshifters in Dalatrend."

"You won't stop me if I want to leave?"

"I won't force you to continue to help us if you don't want to."

He smiled. "Then I promise I'll let you know if I want to leave."

I looked him in the eye to see if I could figure out if he was lying, but had to focus back on the road. I'd just have to take his word for it. "Thank you."

I drove down the ramp when I reached the garage and parked into the same spot as before.

"Your cars are interesting," Raikidan said as I was removing my seatbelt.

"Good or bad kind of interesting?"

"I'm not sure," he admitted. "I can see why you humans enjoy them. They're convenient, faster than walking, and they're nice to look at."

"But you're undecided if you actually like them, yes?" I reached over his lap to get into the glovebox.

"Yes."

I chuckled and then climbed out of the car. Raikidan followed, but he slowed down as he started looking at all the vehicles again. *Yeah, you like them a lot. You just don't want to admit it.*

It took Raikidan a solid fifteen minutes to tear away from the cars. I watched him the entire time as he wandered around, looking at the various designs. He muttered to himself a few times in what I presumed to his kind's language. It wasn't until I decided to head up stairs did he give up his admiring. I grinned at him, and he avoided eye contact, his face a bit red.

When the two of us reached the stairs, the door above us opened and Ryoko and Rylan started coming down.

"Hey," I greeted. "How'd your assignment go?"

"Bad," Ryoko admitted when she stopped halfway down the staircase. "We didn't see anything out of place. What about you guys?"

"Just one suspicious group of soldiers," I said.

"That's still better than us."

The door opened again, and Blaze and Argus started heading down the stairs as well.

My brow rose. "What's the occasion?"

"Oh, right." Ryoko giggled. "We were thinking of going to the Underground and doing some virtual training. We figured it'd be a good way to get you back in shape quick, and help Raikidan learn a thing or two about our weapons. Last night was a really bad time for him to be thrown into the action."

I nodded. "Good idea. Let me just put away my ID."

She nodded and I let the four of them reach the bottom step before heading upstairs briefly. Once I stored away my identification, I rejoined everyone in the basement by an empty stone wall. Ryoko pressed her hands on the wall until it made a crunch sound and then let go as it slid away.

She turned on a flashlight and led the way down the narrow path. I scrunched my nose when an awful smell wafted into my senses, and Raikidan began grumbling until we reached the sewers.

"What is this place?" Raikidan muttered.

"We're under the city, in the sewers," I explained.

He gagged. "What an awful place. We really have to be here?"

"It's the only way to get to the Underground," I said. "We can't exactly run a large operation above ground, so we had to set up down here."

"How do you stand this smell?"

"We just have to put up with it," Rylan said. "We've developed a solution that destroys the smell of this place that we infuse into our soaps and other cleaning products, so we can keep the Underground nearly free of the smell once inside, plus rid ourselves of the smell once we go above ground again."

"Should have picked a better place than a sewer," Raikidan grumbled.

Ryoko giggled quietly and I rolled my eyes. He'd learn to get used to it.

Eventually we made our way up to two large metal doors. They creaked as Argus and Ryoko pulled them open. Passing through the threshold of the doors, we were slammed with the sounds of music, the ticking noises of computer works, and the loud bantering from the hundreds of people in the large room. Raikidan stuck close to me, his whole body tense, and his eyes darted back everywhere. I realized I hadn't gotten the chance to tell him about this place.

"Stay calm," I told him. He glanced at me. "Just follow our lead and you'll do fine here. Don't speak to anyone, even if you're addressed, unless you really want to talk."

He didn't say anything. He just walked a little closer to me, which made him relax a bit. I resisted the urge to sigh. This was going to be a long night.

"Laz!" a female voice call.

Looking around, I noticed a lean woman with mocha skin, crimson eyes, and shoulder-length black-and-red hair jump out of a computer station and rush over to us. She wore dark-green cargo pants with several belts, a black-and-yellow cropped tank top, and a brown cropped leather jacket.

I grinned and slammed the side of my fist with hers in greeting. "Hey, Aurora."

She smiled. "I didn't expect to see you here so soon, babe. Would have figured you'd be resting after that doozy of a night you had."

I opened my mouth to reply, but was interrupted by a low masculine voice. "Well, well, well. Look who finally decided to show up after all this time."

I turned and was faced with a tall, tan and muscular man with dark brown eyes, and brown hair and mustache. He wore a tight white men's tank, denim pants, suspenders, black boots, and leather gloves. His arms were crossed, and tucked between his fingers was a previously lit cigar.

"Raynn," I greeted, giving a curt nod.

"What have you been doing, Eira? The big bad military scare you into hiding? Or were you afraid to settle the score between your team and mine?" he sneered.

"Make him regret those words," the malevolent voice in my head hissed.

The confrontation drew attention, and my pride wouldn't let me just ignore him. Leaving the security of my comrades, I walked around Raynn. "I was doing my job. Now that's it's done, I'm back and leading my team. A better question is, what have you been doing? Still leaving your comrades behind to save your own ass?"

His lip curled. I smirked and headed toward Aurora's computer station, but was stopped when he spoke. "Rumor has it you brought in an outsider. Outsiders can't be trusted. You should know that better than anyone. And from what I can see, you've brought him here, where he can see our base of operation."

Raikidan turned and faced Raynn. "If you have a problem with me, tell it to my face."

"You're not one of us," Raynn spat. "You don't belong here. There's no way you can keep up with any of us, pretty boy. It would be best if you just left."

"Why don't you put your money where your mouth is?" I challenged.

Raikidan glanced at me and smirked. The crowd around us began to make bets. Raynn threw his cigar on the ground, accepting the challenge, and went at Raikidan. Raikidan prepared himself, and when Raynn came in range, he swung his fist, aiming for Raynn's face. He was far quicker than Raynn and landed a direct hit on his jaw. Raynn stumbled back and fell to the floor, blood trickling down the side of his mouth.

Slowly I made my way over to Raikidan's side and wrapped my arms around one of his. "You see, Raynn, I have only the best on my team, and Raikidan fits in that category. I'd pick him over you any day, a thousand times over."

Without giving Raynn the chance to spit out any kind of response, I pulled Raikidan away. My grip loosened from his arm until I was only holding on to his wrist with one hand. My team fell in behind us, giving Raikidan a nod of approval as he passed them.

Aurora slipped in next to Raikidan, and when she wrapped her arm around his free one, a strange feeling quickly flared up in my chest. But just as suddenly as it came, it disappeared.

"You don't mind, do you, babe?" she asked him.

"Uh, no," he replied awkwardly. He, like most others, would have to get used to the baseline name she gave everyone.

She assessed him. "You're a lot stronger than you look." She looked at me. "Babe, I'm surprised you chose someone so strong. I'd have figured you wouldn't want to feel the weakest anymore."

"I meant what I said," I replied. "Bringing in someone weaker than me would bring my team's efficiency down. I don't mind being the weakest. It's not like I can't still hold my own or anything."

Aurora shrugged. "Whatever you say, babe."

When we reached her computer station, she let go of Raikidan's arm and climbed up. I let go of his wrist and hopped up behind her. She placed a communicator into her ear, and the small digital visor swiped across her eyes. As she touched the blank space before her, bright lights popped up and flashed in front of her. *A hologram screen.* Looking at the large screen, I watched numbers, letters, and symbols write out, along with video clips of people with guns running around in tight bodysuits.

"How many pods are open?" I asked her.

"Quite a few actually," she said as she touched the screen. A small layout of the room appeared. "I can place you all in these pods here next to each other."

I patted her on the shoulder. "We'll need a quick-start course for Raikidan."

"It'll be ready when he enters the virtual realm. Anyone else going to go with him?" she asked, typing out something on her keyboard that sat below the screen.

I thought for a moment who would be best to help train him. "Argus and Rylan. Blaze might join them, so have it ready for him just in case."

Leaving Aurora to her thing, I jumped down from the station and grabbed Raikidan by the wrist again and headed for the virtual pods. As we walked, Raikidan noticed the experiments who had anthropo-morphic traits.

"They were the first to be tested with animal DNA," I explained. "The geneticists didn't know what they were doing, and the end result was what you see in front of you."

"How do they fit into your city's structure?" he asked.

I shook my head. "They don't. They are what remain of a massive number of failed experiments. Some disappeared from the city, others died of natural causes, and some were killed within the city or castle walls by Zarda. Since they don't blend in, they stay hidden until dark. That's when they leave the safety of the Underground and play their part."

Arriving at the pod, I let go of Raikidan and pressed a release button to open the lid. The pod let out a hiss and the lip popped open. "Get in."

He eyed the machine warily, and then slowly sat down on the gel padding. When he was finally lying down, I pressed a few buttons on the side and leaned against the pod. Blue lights appeared and scattered across his body and face.

"I need you to stay relaxed and keep your mind open," I said.

He fidgeted a little. "Easy for you to say."

I chuckled. "Nothing bad is going to happen, I promise." His attention drifted from me to other people looking on from a distance. I placed a finger on his chin and pulled his attention back to me. "Hey, focus on me."

He stared at me for a moment before nodding. "What do I have to do?"

"When the lid closes, just keep your mind open and relax. The pod will push your mind into a virtual version of you in the cyber-range network. It won't hurt, just be slightly uncomfortable. I'll be waiting for you on the other side."

He grabbed my wrist, preventing me from shutting the lid. "Wait, where are you going?"

I chuckled. "I have to get into my pod. I'll be waiting for you. Now close your eyes and relax."

He let go of my wrist slowly, and as soon as he closed his eyes, I shut the lid of the pod and headed to mine. I hopped onto the gel padding as Ryoko and the others were shutting themselves in. Not wanting to make myself a liar to Raikidan, I quickly pressed a few buttons on the outside of the pod and shut the lid.

As I relaxed, a tingling sensation pressed on all sides of my head as I slipped into the virtual realm. My virtual body flowed through the gateway and my clothes dematerialized. In the same instant, they were replaced with a tight green-and-black bodysuit, long black gloves, and black thigh-high boots with a green stripe running up the side.

My feet touched solid ground, and the swirling atmosphere melted away, revealing a large white lobby with several potted plants and a few black couches. My sense of smell was muted in this area, but that didn't prevent me from noting the unnaturally clean order the room gave off.

I couldn't see anyone, but I knew they were here somewhere. Walking in the direction I assumed Raikidan would be, I went searching for him.

"I see you made it through fine," I said when I finally found him.

He also wore a green-and-black bodysuit that hugged his muscular form, black gloves, and black boots. *Team color is green this session.* I put a hand on my hip and shifted my weight to the opposite side of my body as Raikidan looked me over. I was glad when he didn't make a comment about my attire.

"I think I made it in one piece," he finally said. "You didn't say it would be such an unpleasant feeling to enter here, or that we'd have to wear such ridiculous clothes."

I rolled my eyes. "It's not that bad."

He snorted and took in our surroundings. "Where is everyone else?"

I shrugged. "Somewhere. They'll make their way over here soon. How are you feeling?"

"Aside from the small pressure in my head, fine."

I gave a curt nod. "Good. That should go away soon. Now I'll give you a quick rundown on what's going to happen. Once Argus and Rylan get here, the three of you will go through the beginner course. You'll learn how to hold your own with a gun, and how the rules of this place work. I'll warn you now, if you're shot at any time in this place by what would be a killing blow in the real world, you'll be forced out and won't be able to come back in. The transition between the outside and here is stressful on the body and going in and out of it multiple times could possibly kill you."

His eyebrow rose. "Possibly?"

"It's never happened before, so we can't be fully sure, and we'd also like to not test that theory," I replied.

Raikidan nodded. "Okay, so what happens if I'm shot?"

Before I could explain, a large screen appeared on the wall and showed someone bursting into pieces as he was fatally shot. "That answer your question?" He gulped and nodded slowly. "It's not as painful as it looks, but it's still not pleasant."

Just then, I noticed Argus, Rylan, and Blaze approaching behind Raikidan, and when I turned a little, I noticed Ryoko approaching as well. The boys' bodysuits looked much like Raikidan's, with a few minor differences, and Ryoko's nearly matched mine but with visible cleavage. I wasn't sure why, but the system had a habit of doing that with the bustier women, not that most complained.

"So, you want to explain why Argus and I have to go through the beginner course instead of you?" Rylan asked.

I smirked. "Well, since you guys are always bragging about how much of a better shot you are over Ryoko and me, I thought it would be best if Raikidan was taught by a *master* shot, alongside the computer."

He crossed his arms, unamused by my ability to twist his teasing in a way he couldn't worm out of.

"So, what are we going to do while they learn?" Ryoko asked me, draping her arm around my shoulder.

I smirked. "Have a little fun." Ryoko smiled, but Rylan's small growl made it disappear. I rolled my eyes. "Don't be such a baby. You can join the two of us once you're done."

A communicator materialized on the side of my face, and the small digital visor swiped across my eyes. The same happened for Ryoko. Before I could contact her, Aurora's voice rang through the earpiece. "I already have a match set up for you, babe. It's against a computer simulated team. Hope you don't mind."

"That's fine. Thanks, Aurora," I replied.

My preferred carbine model materialized in my right hand, along with a small finger gun that materialized around my left hand. Ryoko pulled away from me, and an absurdly large railgun, her favorite weapon, materialized in her hands along with a handgun around her leg.

"What am I supposed to do?" Blaze asked.

I shrugged and walked away with Ryoko.

"You could join us," Argus suggested.

"Normally I would decline," Blaze said. "But since I have no reason to, I might as well."

I stopped listening in after that. I needed to focus. Ryoko and I were going to be running together, and I was getting psyched about the idea of putting a few bullets into some bodies. Maybe I'd pretend they were Raynn. That would make it more enjoyable.

16
CHAPTER

We were fighting blind. Ryoko had lost her communicator early on in the session, and my visor was malfunctioning, thanks to a lucky shot from one of the computers. Bullets flew past my hiding place against the maze wall. I held my carbine close to my chest, and kept my breathing steady and calm. I had expected the computers to be difficult, but I'd forgotten about the randomized area conditions that occurred in some matches. I hadn't expected to have to fight in a maze, let alone run into a dead end.

The gunfire stopped—and everything went silent. I glanced over to Ryoko, on the other side of the corridor opening, and she looked at me. Either this silence was a trap, or the computers were reloading. Their programing allowed them to be smart enough to know they'd cornered us.

Brushing my bangs out of my face, I took a chance and peered around the corner. I pulled back as fast as I could as bullets flew at me. I let out a slow breath and held my gun close. *Yep, definitely a trap.* Ryoko retaliated with several rounds of gunfire, and I joined in soon after, that is, until we both ran out of ammunition with both of our guns. Now we were trapped, out of ammunition, and running short on time. Soon those computers would advance, and we'd be toast.

I grabbed my communicator and threw it on the ground in frustration. It wasn't going to be any help to me anyway.

"Burn them all," the malevolent voice whispered. *"Burn them and hear them scream."*

Getting an idea, I pulled my body in closer, and I breathed a small amount of fire into my hand. Placing my carbine down quietly, I went for it. Pushing away from the wall, I purged the hall with a blast of fire. The computers screamed in pain, and then they were gone. The fire died in my hands as I faced the charred hall. Nothing was left. Even parts of the walls had crumbled. We had won.

The maze wall behind us deteriorated, and a large door was left standing in its place. Ryoko and I walked through the door into the lobby, where we were met with marveling stares from the boys.

"I didn't know your fire techniques were so powerful, Eira," Argus complimented.

I shrugged. "Shaman thing, I suppose."

"Can't be," Rylan commented. "You had that power before you left. You just have more control over it."

"It really was impressive," Ryoko said. "I think you might have even singed this virtual hair of mine."

I rubbed the back of my neck and avoided eye contact. This praise made me uncomfortable.

Argus laughed. "Well, remind me to never pick a fight with you."

I snorted. "Of all the people for me to pick a fight with, if it's you, I'd be damned if there wasn't something wrong with me."

"Let's hope you're right."

"Sorry to ruin your bonding time, but what are we going to do now?" Blaze asked. *Someone's in a foul mood.*

"Aww, did someone not do well in the training session?" Ryoko teased.

He crossed his arms and his upper lip curled. "Shut up, Ryoko."

"I think that's a yes," I whispered to her.

She giggled in response. Blaze grumbled as he turned away, and I joined in with Ryoko's giggling. I enjoyed making fun of him. He made it easy.

When our giggle fit was over, I looked at Rylan. "So how did the training go?"

He shrugged. "Not bad. Blaze made himself look like an idiot, but that's nothing new. He's lucky training isn't viewable by anyone."

I laughed. "That bad, huh?"

He nodded and sighed. "Other than him, the rest of us did fine, although Raikidan sucks at using a gun."

Raikidan growled at him, and Rylan raised his hands defensively.

I narrowed my eyes. "Rylan."

He sighed. "All right, all right. Raikidan may suck at using our advanced technology, but his skills with fire and close combat are definitely not subpar. His close combat may even surpass Ryoko's."

Ryoko's jaw dropped. "As if!"

I laughed and Ryoko huffed as she crossed her arms. She really didn't like being shown up, especially not in the one fighting category she was good in.

"He's not as tactical as you, if that makes you feel better," Rylan said.

Ryoko tilted her head. "Raikidan ate a bullet to the face."

I laughed more, and this bit of information also cheered Ryoko up. Raikidan definitely hadn't listened to me before. He was lucky it was only a training session. Raikidan rubbed his forehead and muttered to himself, which only made me laugh harder. Just as I managed to compose myself, both Rylan and Raikidan scowled. I glanced over my shoulder and my good mood soured instantly.

Raynn approached, a cocky grin on his lips. He wore a red-and-black sleeveless bodysuit, and his black gloves were short and fingerless. "Sorry to ruin your fun, ladies, but I need to have a word with your commander."

I really didn't want to deal with him right now. "What do you want?"

He shifted the railgun on his shoulder, so it would sit better. "We still have a score to settle."

"Says you. You just can't stand that someone is better than you, so you have to pick fights endlessly. Why don't you just get lost?" I turned my back on him.

"Aww, is the little commander afraid?" a female voice said.

I turned to face the wretch. She was a tall woman with cream-colored skin, black hair that curled slightly around her shoulders, black ears on the top of her head, a black tail, golden eyes, and a nose that wasn't entirely human-like. She was an anthro, and the way she hung off Raynn's arm made me sick. She was always good at playing his faithful pet.

"Rip her tongue out!" the voice hissed.

"Go play with a ball of yarn, Mocha," I spat.

"Aww, did I hit a nerve?" She purred. "Sorry to disappoint you, but I outgrew that childish behavior some time ago."

Rylan snorted. "As if."

Mocha hissed.

Ryoko raked her hand in the air like claws. "Rawr to you too, kitty-kitty."

Ryoko and Rylan laughed. Mocha growled and her tail twitched with annoyance, but she didn't say anything back.

Raynn pulled his shoulders back and looked down at me. "So, what's it going to be? You going to fight us, or are you too afraid?"

"Fight him. Humiliate him! Tear him apart!"

I scowled. "How many per team?"

He rested all his weight to one side of his body. "Eight plus a computer tech." Eight on eight was a typical match size, but currently my team was lacking that size. "Is it a deal? Or is your team too small to have a real match?"

"It's a deal," a male voice chimed in.

I turned back to see a young man with short blue and black hair walking up to us. "Dan?"

It had been some time since I'd seen him. This was the last place I'd think to find him. He wasn't fond of virtual training.

"Well, if it isn't your first lieutenant, Eira." Raynn grinned. "Come to her rescue, kid?"

Dan snorted. "Eira doesn't need rescuing. I just came to even things out a bit."

He wasn't wrong. During his time as my lieutenant, he never once questioned what I was capable of handling. It had hit me hard when he went into hiding to join the rebellion. I took it as a personal slight. Luckily, I learned how right he was for leaving and forgave him before we'd reunited after my escape.

Even with that temporary loss, it worked out in my favor. Ryoko had taken up the vacant position and balanced me better than he had managed to.

Raynn chuckled. "Whatever you say, kid. So, Eira, now you have seven here. Where is the last one? Why not call that child of yours you call a Council member to help, or is she still too young to see the battlefield?"

I spat on the ground. "If her powers worked here, I'd let her take your entire team on by herself."

Raynn threw his head back and laughed. "Right, sure."

"What are we going to do, Eira? We can't do a seven-on-eight fight," Argus whispered.

"We'll manage," I responded. "Let's see your team, Raynn."

Raynn smirked. Behind him six more people approached. They all seemed normal and I knew them all by name, but there was one that I wasn't okay with in this lineup. "I only see seven on your team, Raynn. Did you forget how to count?"

He chuckled. "I think you're the one in need of counting lessons, kid. Did all that time in the wild rot your brain?"

"You know the rules, Raynn. No Battle Psychics on the range. Council's orders. Nioush isn't exempt from that rule. That makes seven on your team."

Nioush approached. He was a tall, fair-skinned man with an athletic build, short blonde hair and matching goatee. A black cloth blindfold with a painted golden hexagram covered his eyes, and his bodysuit was red and black like the rest of his team's, but it wasn't a normally-styled bodysuit. It consisted of low-rise pants and an open, cropped vest with golden hexagrams on either side. His lip was pierced with black rings in the center and on the sides, and silver bars pierced both of his nipples. "Are you afraid, Eira?"

Nioush spoke much differently from his twin sister, Seda. His voice wasn't hollow and didn't come off as emotionally detached, but it did have an arrogant tone mixed with a haughty attitude. Like Raynn, all his comrades on his main team thought they were better than everyone else, and had the arrogance to show it.

My expression remained impassive. "I fear nothing."

"Then what's the problem? I doubt the Council will mind, as long as all parties agree. They usually look the other way in those circumstances." A thin smirk appeared on his lips. "Or is it because I'm mistaken and Seda is merely a Seer?"

"They have a Battle Psychic," a woman's voice echoed around us.

We all looked around but couldn't see anyone. It became clear rather quickly that the woman was still phasing through. After a moment of waiting, she materialized behind us.

"Seda?" To say I was surprised was an understatement. She rarely ever left the house except for Council meetings, and when she did, she did her best to avoid Nioush. The two had never gotten along.

Seda wore a black and green bodysuit that went up to her cheeks, framing her face; black and green gloves that went up to her elbows; and black and green thigh-high boots. Just below her neck and on both of her forearms, were golden hexagrams. Her eyes were covered by a blindfold that was shaped like Ryoko's goggles, and around her neck hung the silver-chained amethyst she usually carried around.

Nioush smirked as he held out his arms. "Ah, baby sister, how kind of you to join us."

She stood next to me. "Your pleasant greetings fall on deaf ears, Nioush." Her artic reply sent a shiver down my spine. As devoid of emotion as her words usually were, this coldness was something new to even me.

"Still as cold as ever, I see," Nioush teased. Seda didn't reply and her expression remained impassive. Her brother turned his head in several directions as if he were searching for something. "So, Seda, where is this Battle Psychic you claim this team had? The only psychic I see is you."

"Exactly."

He laughed. "When I called you a Battle Psychic, I wasn't serious. Why don't you go back to your meditation and palm reading?"

My eyes locked onto him. "Are you afraid to face her, Nioush? I don't blame you if you are. She does have an unusual power level for a Seer from what I understand. It may even rival yours." I gasped. "Oh, wait, that must be the issue. You're mad that she is better than you, and had she been trained as a Battle Psychic, you wouldn't be able to challenge her like you do."

He scowled. It wasn't long before pressure pushed against my mind. Glaring, I forced Nioush out. His scowl worsened. I wasn't going to allow him to control me. Although I never thought I'd ever face a Battle Psychic, it was thanks to Seda that we knew the basics of how to defend ourselves against them, even if the knowledge wouldn't save us completely. *Though, for me, that credit mostly goes to Telar. He equipped me more than anyone else attempted to.*

Nioush tried again, but before I could push him out, he flew back a few feet and his mental presence disappeared.

"I would not try that again, brother," Seda warned.

He snorted and stayed where he was.

"Seda, was that a good idea?" I questioned.

"It was just a warning throw, and he knows it," she replied.

"Very well."

"So, when is this happening?" Blaze asked impatiently.

Raynn held up two fingers. "We'll give you twenty minutes."

Wordlessly, his team followed him as he left.

Seda nudged me and handed me a soft, round object. I grinned wickedly and accepted it. "Oh, Mocha."

Mocha turned just as I tossed the yarn ball. Her eyes widened and she ran after it. When she finally caught the yarn ball, she tossed it into the air a few times and purred. When she realized what she was doing, she stopped. Everyone on my team laughed at her.

"She sure broke that childish habit," Rylan said as he wrapped his arm around Ryoko's neck to help keep him up. The two were in tears.

Mocha hissed and threw the ball on the ground before storming off and rejoining her team. Walls materialized around us, secluding us from the rest of the lobby to allow for our planning.

"Not to sound ungrateful," I began, "but, Seda, Dan, what are you two doing here?"

Dan scratched the back of his head. "I heard you'd returned, so I figured I'd welcome you back, but you had already left by the time I dropped by the house. Genesis insisted on coming here when I said I'd come to find you, and you know her, once she's made up her mind, there's rarely a time she'll change it. Seda figured it'd be best to accompany her. When we saw the problems Raynn was trying to cause, I wanted to give you a hand. I didn't think Seda would follow."

"I did not plan on it until I saw Nioush," Seda said. "I was not about to let you deal with him on your own. Plus, if I did not step in, Genesis was more than willing, and I know how much you do not enjoy her actively fighting."

I snorted. "Not like she would have been much help here anyway. Her powers don't work in virtual training and she can't hold a gun. She would have just been in the way."

"I would not!" Genesis' voice rang. Just then a monitor appeared on the wall closest to us, Genesis' image projecting through it. She wore a communicator, and her arms were crossed, showing how unhappy she was about my choice of words. "I would be helpful! You just don't give me much of a chance."

I sighed. "The system doesn't allow necromancy, and out there, neither do I."

She puffed out her cheeks, the child-like behavior she exhibited from time to time in full control of her right now. "I don't see why not. It's not a bad thing."

I turned away from the screen and headed to the other side of the room. "Let the dead rest. It's the least they deserve."

"Laz?" Ryoko said.

I stopped walking but didn't face them. "You all have ten minutes to collect yourselves. We'll regroup after that, and quickly figure out the best strategy to use while we grab our gear. Seda, I'll need you to give Raikidan a crash course on basic Battle Psychic blocking techniques at some point during this time."

"I understand. I will need five minutes of meditation beforehand," she stated.

"Granted." I left them to their business.

I had meditation of my own to do, and I knew Raikidan would have a few questions to shoot off at me, so I figured I'd get it in when I could. Sitting down, I held my hands near my chest. I would need to make sure I was on top of my game. Real people were much harder than the computers. I inhaled and exhaled deeply, and my mind aligned with my body.

Someone sat down next to me but stayed silent. By the sound of the breathing, I knew it had to be Raikidan, and I figured I'd let him wait a little. When I had prepped myself long enough, I opened my eyes and focused on him. He watched me with his hands in his lap, his curiosity clear. Turning myself to face him, I copied the way he was sitting. His eyes were filled with unspoken questions, but his lips never moved.

I smirked. "What, no questions?"

"About what?" he asked.

"About Battle Psychics, Seers, Genesis, or what we're doing?" I clarified.

He turned his head and cupped it in his hand. "I'm not stupid."

Raising an eyebrow, I waited. He sighed and looked at me again. "Tell me."

I snickered. He was all too predictable. "We don't have a lot of time, but I can answer a few questions."

"Who is this Lieutenant Dan?" he asked.

"My former lieutenant in my company in Zarda's army. When we each escaped and then joined the rebellion, we were assigned to different teams."

He nodded. "Explain more about psychics. I've never come across any before. From what I've been able to gather, they're a big deal."

I thought for a moment. "That's a lot to cover all at once, so I'll give you the basic rundown for now."

Raikidan nodded again.

"Psychics are always twins, like Seda and Nioush. There are two types. Battle Psychics, who use their powers to throw around large objects or mind-controlling others, and Seers, who are only capable of levitating small to medium objects, but mostly use their abilities for mind reading or momentary glances into the timelines for potential situation outcomes."

"All right, that makes sense. Is there a particular reason Nioush and Seda don't get along? The tension is obvious."

"There's always a sibling rivalry between Battle Psychics and Seers. From what I understand, Battle Psychics are generally more powerful. This causes most of them to be arrogant and even aggressive. Seers are far calmer in comparison. The differences often drive a wedge between the two."

"All right. Do you have time for another question?"

I chuckled. Raikidan's thirst for knowledge was like a glass with an empty bottom. "Sure, but we need to wrap this up soon."

Raikidan responded with a curt nod. "Okay, then explain to me why you never said anything about Genesis being a necromancer."

That was a loaded question. I leaned back on my hands and peered up at the white ceiling. "I don't like to think about it."

Raikidan waited patiently for me to continue.

"The ability randomly manifested long after she'd been released. When those who had created her went to go check her files to understand better, they were missing. They chose not to pursue it further after that discovery. Unfortunately, a few hundred years later, they realized she was still alive, so they tried to replicate her. That's when the war experiments started."

I sat back up. "Genesis went into hiding at that point, so they couldn't grab more of her DNA. Now that we're fighting back, she feels the need to do more than be part of the Council and guide us, but I can't allow it. It wouldn't be right."

"I can train Raikidan now," Seda messaged.

I glanced her way then focused back on Raikidan. "Seda is ready to teach you. It's important you listen to her carefully. Fighting off even some of Nioush's basic mind attacks is paramount."

He stood. "I have one last question. Why the hell are we doing this?"

I sighed and shook my head. "Because Raynn is a moron and likes to pick fights with everyone, but with us it's personal. Raynn was part of our company in the military, until he was promoted to general. When he broke off, he assembled his own faithful group of misfits, and has been challenging us ever since. It's as if he thinks there is some score to settle."

"Fair enough." He then left in search of Seda.

I sighed and went back to meditating, until a computer's voice echoed through the room.

Ten minutes until match start. Make final preparations and head to your team's weapons bay.

We grouped up and then headed through a set of doors that opened into a large metal room. The walls were littered with all types of weapons, along with tables and open cabinets scattered everywhere.

A communicator materialized on the side of my head, and I spoke as we all went about grabbing our weapons. "Aurora, give us some info on the battlefield."

"I don't have much," Aurora said. "Raynn is really keeping things on the lowdown. From what I've been able to dig up, the terrain type will be standard, with no weather conditions, and the map type is called *Random*."

I perused a selection of carbine models on a wall. "Random? That's a new one. Can I have some clarification?"

"That's the thing, babe, I'm not sure." She typed a few more entries with her keyboard. "There's nothing in here giving any information about it, but I can make two conclusions. Either the map will be randomly chosen at the start, or the map will randomly change during the match."

Choosing the light carbine model I preferred, I secured it across my back. "Okay, anything else?"

"No, I don't—wait, hold on." She was quiet for a moment. "That's weird."

"What's going on, Aurora?"

"I just saw two of Raynn's teammates who were supposed to fight walk by."

I narrowed my eyes. I didn't like the sound of that. "Go on."

She typed on her keyboard some more. "The thing is, the two pods they were occupying are still in use. I think they switched out two of their members when I wasn't looking."

"I don't like the sound of that," Rylan commented. "Raynn must have been planning this from the start."

I nodded in agreement. "He probably thinks it's going to give their team a major advantage."

"It just might," Argus said. "Aurora, do you know who the new members are?"

"Afraid not. I've been trying to access that part of the network, but I'm locked out. I think their technician is behind that."

Argus bought his hand up to his chin and mumbled. "I wouldn't doubt it. If Raynn really did have this all planned out, he would have informed his technician to make sure we wouldn't get in on his little secret."

"We're just going to have to make do," I stated. "We've dealt with worse conditions. We'll get over it. It just means we're going to have to be on our guard until we can identify the two. The worst that could happen is we lose."

Blaze crossed his arms. "I'd rather that not happen."

I nodded. "I'm with you on that, but if it does, it does, and we'll learn from it. Aurora, I want you to use the remainder of this time to see if you can hack that block."

"I'll see what I can do, babe. They have Ezhno as their tech. You can't get any better than him."

I smirked. "I beg to differ."

When she didn't respond, I figured she was too embarrassed. She was about as bad as me when it came to compliments sometimes.

I looked at the table next to me. Laid out on it were belts with four pouches, a handgun, and two finger guns. I opened the pouches and inspected the contents. One pouch was a first-aid kit. Another pouch was filled with smoke bombs. The third carried grenades, and the last one carried ammunition cartridges. *That'll be handy.* I strapped the belt to my waist and then grabbed the two finger guns and tossed them into one of the pouches. They were close-range weapons, making them only ideal if we had close-quarters combat, but it was best to go out prepared for any possible situation. I also grabbed a mask just in case I needed to use the smoke bombs.

"Okay, Seda, any tips on dealing with Nioush?" I asked. "He's the major issue in this lineup."

"No one but me will take him head-on," she advised. "The training I have given you all will barely be enough to keep you safe from his basic mind abilities. I would prefer to be the only one he takes on at any given time, but if he insists on focusing his attention on anyone but me, he is fair game to you all. Be warned, though. He is strong, and I am going to have my hands full with him, so do not rely on me to help you with the rest of his team, or if you take him on and cannot handle it."

"Understood," I said. "But if he gets to be too much, you must tell us."

She nodded. "I understand, but I would like to request you not to take it personally if I don't get that message to you in time."

"As long as you try we'll forgive you," Ryoko said.

Seda chuckled. "Is there anything else needing to be discussed?"

"It's hard formulating a proper plan without knowing what to expect," I admitted. "So, we'll just have to play it by ear until we get a better feel for everything. We might as well finish prepping ourselves."

Everyone nodded and finished up. I was already set, or so I thought. Although I appeared ready, I didn't feel it. *Something is missing...* After a little thought, I realized what it was. Glad the system allowed for alterations like this, I closed my eyes and connected my mind with the mainframe. Thinking of the daggers attached to my physical body, I willed the code of the computer to materialize them and then pulled myself back to my virtual body. Looking at my arms and then my legs, I found it had worked.

"You look ready."

I turned to find Raikidan behind me. I assessed him, though that didn't last long. "You don't."

He appeared exactly the same as he had when he entered the room. He shrugged. "I don't need anything."

"Like hell you don't. You need a weapon, like the rest of us."

"I'm not good at using your guns," he said. "I'll just use fire."

"Fire won't be enough."

"I beg to differ."

I sighed and grabbed a supply belt. "Then take this. If anything, it'll put my mind at ease."

Reluctantly, he took it and put it on. Soon after, he grabbed a carbine model. It was a larger and heavier model than mine, but it suited him well. "How do you use this?"

I chuckled and shook my head. Of course, he'd choose something he didn't know how to use. I moved closer to him to give him a hand, placing his hands in the correct positions as I spoke. "You want to hold it by the pistol grip with your dominant hand here and place your other hand under the barrel here."

"You don't hold it here?" he asked, tapping the second arm that came out of the bottom of the gun.

I shook my head and slightly smiled. "That's the ammunition magazine."

"Magazine?"

"It's a type of cartridge that holds a large round of ammunition. In the case of this model, you get thirty rounds before you have to reload. So just trust me, you don't want to hold that. The model you're using isn't equipped with a forward handgrip, so you have to hold it by the barrel."

He nodded and placed his hand back on the barrel. I pointed to the cylindrical object on the top of the gun. "This is a scope. It allows better targeting while shooting. Use it whenever possible, but don't forget to stay alert. If you aren't careful, you could become easy prey for the other team if you're too focused on the scope."

Raikidan nodded again and held the gun up and peered through the scope.

"Good. That's exactly how you're supposed to hold it." He caught on fast. I had to admit I was a little impressed. Rylan made it seem like he was a complete failure at this. "Now, do you see that red dot in the center of the scope?" He nodded. "Use that to aim. Keep this next bit in the front of your mind. Guns have particular ranges they are best at. The accuracy of your shot is not only dependent on you, but your range. This means, even if you have your target in the center of your scope, you may miss or even hit him somewhere else. This carbine model you're using is a medium-ranged gun, so keep that in mind. Now I want you to aim at something and pull the trigger."

"The trigger is this, right?" He tapped the curved metal piece that was in front of the pistol grip. I nodded. He aimed the gun at the wall and fired a few shots. Lowering the gun, he grinned and then focused on me. "You're better at teaching than the computer or your male companions."

I backed away from him a little and looked away—my cheeks burning. "I just know carbines."

"Yeah, I'm sure that's what it is."

One minute until match start.

"Looks like it's show time." I waved him to follow. "Let's group up with the others."

He complied, grabbing a pistol as a spare weapon on the way. Most of the others had basic gear, hand guns, battle rifles, even machine guns with belt-fed ammunition box magazines. Ryoko and Rylan were the only ones with weapons that deviated, the former sporting her typical railgun and the later equipping his high-velocity sniper rifle.

"I just found something of use," Aurora called in. "There are no rules to this match, making it an anything-goes fight, so be careful. On the plus side, it looks like Raynn's team needs a crutch, as this includes a limitless ammo feature."

We snickered and tossed our extra ammunition away. The computer counted down the remaining thirty seconds of time. When the voice hit five, the room around us started to dematerialize. At zero we stood in a large field.

"Stay on your guard," I ordered. "Seda, can you find them?"

She shook her head. "Nioush is shielding them."

"Can they find us?" I asked.

"I am a Seer. That is the most basic ability. One thing none of you may know about Seers, we may not have the best offense, but we have been trained to be a good defense. It would not surprise me if some of the battles you fought in the past had a few Seers mixed in with the Battle Psychics to help shield you."

I grinned. That made me feel better. Even if Nioush had higher battle experience offense, Seda was a much better defense.

"I will go look for Nioush." Her hair began to stand on end and her body lifted off the ground.

She started to fly off, but I stopped her. "Seda."

"I will not fail you," she stated.

"That's not what I was going to say," I replied. "Prove Nioush wrong."

She threw her hand up across her chest in salute and then flew off in search of Nioush.

"Thank you for doing this, Seda."

"No, thank you, for giving me the opportunity to prove myself a worthwhile member of this team and our cause."

17
CHAPTER

There was no wind—no sound—only stillness. We scanned the area as we made our way slowly across the field.

Ryoko stopped and looked around. "Anyone else getting the feeling we're being watched?"

The rest of us came to a halt and took in our surroundings. Seemed like she was the only one, but her wogron senses were rather acute to such dangers in these conditions.

"I am sensing movement heading straight for all of you," Seda messaged. *"It is hard to make out, so be careful."*

"Continue with caution," I advised.

We continued on more slowly, alert to any possible attack.

"I'm getting movement," Dan informed us. It wasn't long before the rest of our visors were telling us the same.

"This can't be right," Blaze remarked. "I'm getting a reading of fifty."

I narrowed my eyes. These digital sets didn't malfunction. I then swore in realization. "Shit. They brought in Doppelganger."

"Beautiful," Rylan grumbled.

"Who?" Raikidan asked.

I threw my carbine over my shoulder and unzipped my grenade pouch to pull two out. "An experiment who can make copies of himself for a small amount of time. Cover me, Ryoko. The rest of you spread out."

Ryoko held her gun in front of her body like a shield, and her skin hardened into diamond-shaped patterns. "Stay behind me."

I fell in behind her and eyed her skin. I had seen her do this many times before, but it had been so long… I found it both strange and fascinating. The two of us took off, and gunfire erupted, sending bullets flying past us from the other side of the field. I pulled the pin from one of the grenades and tossed it. It exploded soon after it hit the ground, but the gunfire continued so I threw the second grenade.

"There are too many," Ryoko shouted back to me as bullets bounced off her skin. "I won't be able to hold as a shield for much longer at this rate. What are we going to do?"

"Ryoko, Laz, watch out!" Rylan's voice rang through the communicator. Just then a rocket hit the ground a little ways off from us, and we dove in an attempt to avoid being hit by anything. There was no question who had attacked us. It was her preferred weapon of choice.

Ryoko picked herself up and grumbled to herself. "I'm going to skin that cat."

I took out a few smoke bombs and tossed them around, creating a screen. "Go find Mocha. She's going to be trouble unless we get rid of her. Use this screen to sneak around."

"What about you?" she asked, putting a mask on.

"I'll be fine. Now get going."

"Right." She disappeared into the smoke, leaving me alone.

As I put my mask on, my mind buzzed. This game gave us unlimited ammunition, and that meant Doppelganger would fire off rounds without a second thought. I knew the original would hang back while his copies did the work, so theory would dictate he would be on the other side of this field, and that meant I could take him out, that is, if I could get close enough.

"Laz, how are you two holding up?" Rylan called in.

"I'm fine. I sent Ryoko to take care of Mocha," I replied. "What's the status on everyone else?"

"Argus, Blaze, and Dan took cover in your smoke screen. It looks like Seda found Nioush, and Raikidan is watching my back." He chuckled. "Although I think Raikidan is getting antsy."

"I don't like sitting still like this," Raikidan grumbled. "You're too far away to be helpful."

"This is what a sniper does," Rylan responded. "We use range to help."

"Well, a sniper is stupid," Raikidan said.

"We are not! We watch out for our comrades from afar and protect them from enemies they can't see."

I chuckled. "Hey, old married couple, shut up. Raikidan, you'll get your chance. Rylan needs you to watch his back since he's useless otherwise."

"Excuse me?"

I chuckled. "Inform me if anything new happens on the field."

I cut the connection and moved forward. I took out a few more smoke bombs and tossed them about. I had no idea where this screen stopped, and I didn't need to run face first into a cluster of guns.

Using my visor, I tried to locate a target. I was shocked by the numbers. "Aurora, I need you to do a little digging."

"What do you need me to do, babe?" she asked.

"I need to know if they're boosting abilities."

"Hold on while I check." The sound of her typing the keys echoed in my earpiece. "Yes, they are. I'll do the same for you if you'd like."

"No, I want our team to beat them the right way. If we can, it'll prove we really are better."

"All right, if you say so. Also, I'm getting enemy movement close to you. Just a few yards, from what I can see."

Without replying to her, I cut the connection and looked around. I didn't need them to find me because of my voice. My visor caught movement and I fired my gun. My victim screamed in pain, and then it was quiet. *That was too close; this smoke won't help me. I'm going to have to risk being out in the open.*

Gripping my gun tighter, I ripped off my mask and ventured out of the safety of the smoke. As soon as I did, bullets rained down on me. There was nowhere to hide, so I ran. Excruciating pain shot through my shoulder as a bullet passed through it. Glancing at it, I found a good-sized bullet hole oozing with blood. I gritted my teeth and kept going. A single bullet wound wouldn't stop me.

I fired at every Doppelganger copy I managed to see. The bullets ceased to rain, but the sound of retaliating friendly fire kept me calm. Looking back, I watched Dan, Argus, and Blaze rush out of the smoke screen and come to my aid. I grinned and continued firing.

"About time you ladies decided to come out and fight," I called out.

Blaze smirked and fired a few rounds of his shotgun. "We enjoyed watching you take them head on. It was quite sex—watch out!"

I turned in time to see a Doppelganger copy aim for me. I went to move, but knew I wasn't moving fast enough. I prepared for the worst, but it didn't come. Something pushed me to the ground and the sound of a shotgun rang through my ear. The copy in front of me burst into pixelated pieces.

I looked up at Blaze as he towered over me and grinned. "Looks like you're of more use than I thought. I owe you one."

He laughed and a suggestive grin crossed his face. "You sure do."

I rolled my eyes. "Not even in your dreams."

"I beg to differ."

Tripping him without warning, I shot a Doppelganger copy that was aiming at him from behind and then stood with a grin. "And now we're even."

He grumbled. "You're no fun."

A still figure in the distance caught my eye. Using my visor, I zoomed in. It was Raynn.

"Laz, I have a clear shot at Raynn," Rylan called in. "Should I take him?"

"Take him out," the voice in my head growled.

"No." I ground my teeth. "He's mine."

I took off once again and charged straight at him. He barely moved, aside from the occasional weight shift, and my instincts screamed something was wrong, but I ignored it. Raynn looked at me and grinned as I came into range. Swinging my gun over my shoulder, I balled my hand into a fist. Just once I needed to hit him. Just once I needed to remove that smirk off his ugly face.

I swung and passed right through him. "What the—"

I turned and looked at him. His figure waved and then disappeared. My eyes widened. *It was only an illusion!* I had walked right into a trap.

"Not very smart, are you?" a voice cooed.

I turned quickly and was faced with one of Raynn's other team members, who sat on a large boulder. I couldn't recall his name, but it didn't matter. I did know he was known for his energy illusions, and the idea that I fell for his trick pissed me off.

"Kill him for his treachery!" the voice ordered.

"Sorry you failed to take your built-up anger out on the general, but you won't have to worry about your failure for much longer." A twisted grin spread across his face. "I'm going to enjoy taking you out of this game."

As he pulled the trigger, I attempted to run. I gritted my teeth as pain shot through my leg and I fell to the ground. I turned and faced him and tried to pull myself away.

"Not very smart at all," he cooed again.

The sound of a carbine firing filled the air and the man stopped with several holes in his body. His eyes rolled back and he dropped to the ground, his body pixilating away soon after, causing a large screen to appear in the sky. With a ping, images of both teams displayed, and the man that had been killed now had a large X over his picture.

"Yes, you're not very smart," my savior said, mocking his target. I turned to face him and was surprised to see Raikidan slowly walking toward me. He ran his hand through his hair and yelled to me. "You all right?"

I glanced down at my bloody leg and chuckled. "Never better."

I attempted to get up but failed. My leg was too badly injured and blood poured out of the wound. If I didn't get it fixed up now, I'd be eliminated from the match due to blood loss. As horrible of an idea it was to do it here, I was going to have to use my first-aid kit immediately if I wanted any hopes to continue to fight.

As I reached for it, the ground started to shake and tremble. *What the—*

The two of us looked around. All around us the ground began to crack and morph. I watched in horrified amazement as the ground I was sitting on was lifted into the air, leaving Raikidan where he was. I now knew what *random* meant. The map was changing, and from what I could gather, it was changing a part of the terrain into a mountain.

Before I knew it, the ground I sat on cracked and shift underneath me. I tried to stand up again, but the pain in my thigh was too much. Gritting my teeth, I dragged myself to what I thought to would be a more secure spot, only to be proven wrong.

The ground fell from underneath me, and I grabbed a ledge with my bad arm. I groaned but refused to let go. When strong arms grabbed a hold of my suit and pulled me up, I looked up, my eyes meeting Raikidan's, and my brow furrowed. *How did he get up here so fast?* Before I knew it, he tossed me over his shoulder and ran along the narrow path. "You're such a pain, you know that?"

I grunted, not pleased he'd carry me like some Neanderthal. "No one is making you help me. You should be watching Rylan's back."

"Yeah, thanks for ditching me, ass," Rylan rang in.

Raikidan snorted. "It was either sit around and do nothing or save Eira since she wanted to play hero. I opted to be productive. Though, if I had known I was going to have to carry her, I would have stayed put."

I smacked him in the back of the head with my good arm. He growled, but the small upturn of the corners of his lips gave him away. The rock face in front of Raikidan exploded, forcing him to stop suddenly. I almost flipped over him.

"What the hell was that?" I shouted. The rock face behind us exploded in response.

"It's Mocha!" Ryoko called in. "She got away from me when the map changed. I'm trying to get her, but she's just too damn sneaky. I hate cats!"

"Get rid of her," Raikidan barked.

"I am, I am! Calm down, Mr. Bossy-pants. You're just as bad as Laz."

"I can hear you, you know," I muttered.

"Oops."

I rolled my eyes. Raikidan jumped over the gap in front of him and stumbled when he landed, though managed to keep us both from falling. *Gods this is stupid...* I felt so pathetic. *All because I had to let my anger get the better of me.* I knew better.

I gazed up the cliff face and noticed an opening. *A cave?* "Do you think you can get up there?"

He looked up and grinned. "Hold on tight."

"Hold onto what?"

He didn't give me a chance to figure it out. He let go of me, forcing me to grab onto his body suit wherever I could, and he began to climb. His speed surprised me. Even though he had used a lot of his draconic power to keep up with me when we were running in the forest, I barely sensed him using any now. This confirmed my secret speculation he was built for strength and not straight speed—or I was terrible at sensing his power. I had been working on it these past few weeks, but it had been difficult to get to the level I was currently at. I suspected I still had a ways to go before I would master this sense.

As we climbed, rockets hammered the cliff face. We were lucky Mocha had such poor aim. Reaching the top of the ledge, I climbed off Raikidan to allow him to get up quicker and pulled myself up into a standing position. With my injured leg dragging behind me, I made my way to the cave. My leg was now completely numb, with blood still pouring out, which worried me.

"Hey, let me help you," Raikidan insisted.

I shook my head. "You've done enough. I don't need help now."

He grunted. "Aren't teammates supposed to help each other?"

I sighed. "Fine, get over here."

He came over to me and grabbed my arm. Swinging it around his neck, he pulled me closer to use him as a type of crutch. I was thankful for this. It gave me the independence I needed and took the responsibility of carrying me away from him.

Once inside, I slid against the cave wall down to the floor. Unzipping my first-aid pouch, I took out the supplies I'd need and sighed with relief as I applied a healing ointment to my shoulder. After I was sure the entire wound was covered, I picked out a small gun from the pouch and inserted a needle and clear vial filled with liquid. *This is going to suck, but it should slow the bleeding.* Closing my eyes, I pulled the trigger and the liquid solution was injected into my thigh. I flinched from the sound and then the needle punctured my skin.

Suddenly the cave shook, and pieces of rocks fell as the rockets pelted the mountain, but I ignored them both. Once there was no more liquid to inject, I went to grab more ointment. Just as I scooped out some of the ointment, a rocket hit the mountain above the cave entrance. Boulders dislodged from the ceiling and crashed to the floor. I pulled myself away from my spot against the wall just as a boulder landed where I had been sitting. *That was too close.*

While my shoulder was almost completely healed now, my thigh was nowhere close. The injected solution helped with only the deep nerves and muscle tissue. I needed time to apply the healing ointment and let it work. Another rocket slammed into the mountain, causing the cave roof to collapse faster. Raikidan rushed over to me and pulled me farther back into the cave. When we couldn't go back any farther, he held me close, using his body as a shield.

My heart didn't start to pound until then. I could kill or stare death in the face without feeling a thing, but when it came to close contact with others like this, I didn't know what to do. *And why am I always getting stuck in these situations with Raikidan around?*

A boulder landed close to us, and he tightened his grip. My hold on his bodysuit tightened in response. His scent was overpowering, but just as I wasn't afraid, I smelled no fear on him. Did dragons just not fear, or was he not afraid because he knew this was only a simulation body? Most people feared even if it was only a simulation, so what was it for him?

The rocket fire finally ceased, as did the collapse of the cave, but Raikidan didn't let go right away. After a few moments, his grip loosened until our noses were nearly touching. My heart thumped in my chest as I stared into his eyes and a strange and uncomfortable feeling washed over me. Then, suddenly, he sat up, allowing me to pull myself up into a sitting position with my good arm. When my body stopped feeling weird, I peered at him only to find an interesting sight before me. Patches of small black scales littered his skin, and large bat-like wings protruded from his back. From the small rips in the membrane of his wings, I figured he had attempted to use them as an extra shield.

This new look intrigued me. I reached out my hand and touched his face, smearing what was left of the ointment on my fingers onto a small scratch on his face. My fingers glided over his smooth scales. They felt strange, but I enjoyed their feeling.

Realizing what I had just done, a wave of embarrassment flooded over me. Completely flustered by my actions, I retracted my touch and attempted to wipe the smeared ointment off his bodysuit. Of course, feeling his toned chest didn't help. I grabbed another container of ointment I had, since I had lost the other in the frenzy, and opened it. Dipping two of my fingers in, I held them up. "Come over here and I'll fix up your wings."

He didn't move. I glanced up at him, and he gave me an uneasy look. I sighed. Placing the ointment container down, I used my free hand to gently grab the boned portion of one of his wings. Gently pulling his wing closer, I forced him to face his back to me and gently massaged the cream onto the thin membrane of his wings. His body tensed at my touch.

"Just, relax," I murmured.

"You should be using that stuff for your leg," he muttered through clenched teeth.

"I'll have enough after I'm done with you. It's the least I can do since you've saved me twice now."

He tried to pull his wing out of my hand. He became less tense when he succeeded. "You don't have to. I can take care of it."

I tried to look at his face, but every time I tried, he'd turn his head away. I narrowed my eyes. Grabbing his wing again, I massaged on more of the ointment, careful to watch how he reacted. As soon as my finger touched the membrane again, his body tensed. I quickly moved my upper body to view his face and almost laughed at the sight—tightly shut eyes and twitching brow. Even though there was no color change in his cheeks, I knew that look. I grinned. I was going to make him regret trying to push into my personal space so many times before.

Careful of my lame leg, I let go of his wing slowly and pulled myself onto my good knee. Wrapping my arms around his neck, I leaned close to his ear and kept my voice lower. "If it felt good, you should have just told me."

His eyes snapped open and he glared at me from their corners. "I don't know what you're talking about."

"—Both—kay—there—?" Aurora's voice came through in bits and full of static. Seemed like the mountain interfered with both the communicator signal and the tracking capabilities for computer techs and image streaming. "Raik—dan—itals—umping—"

Snickering quietly, the visor flashed over my face, and I spoke to her. "We're fine, Aurora."

Grinning, I pulled away from Raikidan and grabbed his other wing, my visor vanishing once more in the process. I went back to work in applying the ointment, and he exhaled slowly. A small giggle snuck past the smile on my face.

"Please stop," he begged.

"I'm almost done."

He didn't let me finish. Pulling his wing out of my grip, he rounded on me. My back hit the cave wall as he pinned my arms to the wall.

"I said stop," he growled, his face close to mine.

Smirking, I held the ointment container up to him. "Fine."

His brow twisted, confusion clear. Obviously, I wasn't reacting as he'd thought I would.

"What? You expect me to always fight back? Squirm away?" I continued to grin. "Sorry to disappoint you, but I pick and choose my battles, and I'm choosing not to waste what little air we have in here."

He let me go slowly, keeping eye contact with me, and sat back on his heels. I just watched him. "Why are you acting as if my look is normal?"

I took out my last ointment container and applied it to the large hole on my thigh. "I suspected you could take a form like this. You're a shapeshifter, after all, so who am I to argue you can't have an in between-metamorphosis form? I'm actually curious about why you've chosen to use it. Obviously, your wings weren't much help."

He shifted and flexed his wings uncomfortably, avoiding direct eye contact. "Our scales are stronger than your human steel. They would make it easier to protect you from rocks, but…"

I peered up at him, expecting him to continue. He looked to be searching for the right words. I beat him to it. "You're not used to shifting, so the wings were an unfortunate side effect."

He blinked. *Bingo.* I gazed back down at my thigh and continued to work. "Before we met, how often did you shapeshift?"

"Almost never," he said. "I had no reason to."

I chuckled and shook my head. His brow furrowed in confusion. "What's so funny?"

"It's just like me to disrupt the flow of others' lives," I said, glancing slightly up at him.

He opened his mouth to speak, but a loud, pain-filled scream sounded through our communicators.

"Dan!" I exclaimed. My visor wiped across my face again. "What's going on out there?"

"Heav—ire—" Argus came in. "—Dan—on—"

I threw my communicator onto the ground and slammed my fist on the floor of the cave in anger. The roof of the cave shook, and small pieces of debris fell.

Raikidan held up his hands. "Hey, stay calm."

"Stay calm?" Rage boiled inside me. "While I'm sitting here chatting up a storm, with my bum leg because I decided to make a stupid move, my team is out there fighting for their lives, and now I've lost one! You really expect me to stay calm?"

"You act like it's the end of Lumaraeon."

"This simulation may be a game to you, Raikidan, but it's not to us!" I spat on the ground. "I may have said it was okay if we lost, but it really isn't. These simulations test our skills not only as individuals, but as a team. Any wrong move and you can affect your entire team, just like I have now. Had this not been a simulation, Dan would be gone for good! There's no bringing back the dead."

"Getting all worked up over it isn't going to help any either!" he shouted. "Everyone makes mistakes, and they have to live with that fact. Now shut up and focus on getting that leg of yours fixed instead of getting all worked up. You can help them when you're better."

I blinked in shock. Not many ever dared to talk to me like that. *He's right, though.* Getting worked up about the loss wasn't going to bring Dan back. Shaking my head with a sigh, I worked on putting more ointment on my leg wound. While I did that, Raikidan grabbed some of the ointment from the container I had given him and attempted to get the last hole in his wing. I watched him from the corner of my eye and tried not to laugh as he struggled, guessing it needed to be fixed up before he could pull it back into his body. He sighed and turned his gaze on me.

A half smile spread across my lips. "Need help?"

He slowly nodded with a frown that looked more like a pout. Chuckling, I took some of the ointment he had in his hand and grabbed his wing. Gently I rubbed the ointment over the small hole. Raikidan closed his eyes and sighed. His shoulders sagged as he relaxed. His cheeks tinted pink, and I smiled a little. There was no reason for him to hide how it felt, and secretly I found it kind of cute. It reminded me of when you rubbed Ryoko's ear. I just had to make sure I was careful. I didn't need to provoke anything.

"You look nice."

My brow rose. "Excuse me?"

"What you're wearing. It looks nice on you."

"Um, thank you. You… look nice too."

He tried to look at me from the corner of his eye, but I avoided contact. I understood he was trying to distract himself from his current situation, but I wished he had chosen a better topic.

"Can I ask you something?"

More ways to distract himself, I guess. I thought for a moment. *Might as well humor him.* It wasn't like I had anything better to do as I helped heal him up. "What's on your mind?"

"Everyone continues to mention some Council. Who are they?"

I chuckled. He'd picked a fine time to ask about the Council. I took a deep breath and launched into an explanation.

"The *Council of Seven*, also known as the Seven Firsts. They are experiments that make up the firsts of all types of experiments from this city, from the first of all creations, to the first psychics, to the first elementalists. They keep order among our ranks and pass judgment on those who fall out of line. Just as a team has one battle leader and one main psychic, each team is led by one Council member. When major disputes or concerns arise that can't be settled, the Council is called and they hold a meeting to settle the matter themselves."

"Their word is law?" Raikidan asked.

"It's supposed to be, but it's not uncommon for decisions to be made against the Council's orders."

"Have you ever gone against them?"

"Many times." I grinned, the memory of a fraction of those times running through my head. "The Council is made up of smart individuals, and for the most part, they know what they're doing when they make a decision, but there are still many things they don't know from experience. This is why I use my own judgment, and if the time comes where I have to go against them again, I will."

"Your friends are smart to follow you." He glanced back at me. "You lead them not because you are told to, but because you want to, and you use excellent judgment while doing so. Although you told me you're not their sole leader, I don't believe that now. You are their battle leader, but your judgment and decisions go beyond the battlefield."

I never really thought about it that way. I'd been created to do as ordered, and lead others had been one of those tasks. But even after I broke away from Zarda, I found myself in leadership roles, and I didn't exactly hate it. It put a lot of attention on me, sure, but I liked the tactical aspect of it all. I didn't want to take positions that put me in what would be thought of as "glory" roles. All I wanted was to win. *To be right for once.*

I smiled despite myself. "Thank you."

He nodded, a half-smile on his lips, and I went back to working on him.

Once I determined his wing was good, I let go, and with my eyes shut, leaned against the cave wall. The membrane of his wings was thin enough that it wouldn't take long to heal, but unfortunately, it would take a little more time for my thigh. My eyes snapped open when Raikidan touched my thigh. I stared at him as he applied more ointment to it. "What the hell do you think you're doing?"

"You missed a spot," he said, his tone calm enough to assure anyone but me.

I grabbed his hand and pulled it away. "I didn't miss a spot."

He grunted and pulled his hand out of my grip. "What, don't want me touching your leg?"

I crossed my arms. "I'd prefer you didn't."

He grinned and grabbed my leg again. "Then I guess I'll be applying more of this stuff."

I growled at him.

"I—inally—ot her!" Ryoko screamed through Raikidan's communicator.

Raikidan growled and threw the communicator on the ground. I couldn't help but laugh as he rubbed his ear. "Serves you right." Pulling myself over to my communicator on the ground, I grabbed it and placed it around my head. "Good job, Ryoko."

"—Old—ight—I'll ge—u—uys out—oon," she told us.

I glance over at Raikidan and watched as he shifted back to a nu-human form. His scales sunk into his skin as if they had never been there, and his healed wings folded back and disappeared under his bodysuit.

He retrieved his communicator and moved closer to me. "How's your leg?"

I looked down at it. "I can feel it healing, but it's still pretty banged up. I'm going to have a hard time walking, but I'll manage."

He opened his mouth to speak, but was interrupted when the boulders that blocked the cave entrance began to shift. Not long after, Ryoko poked her head through a good-sized hole in the wall.

"Glad to see both of you safe!" She winked. "Hope you two were good while you were alone in here."

I rolled my eyes. Of course, she'd make a comment like that. Ryoko grabbed another boulder and tossed it out of the cave and over the cliff face with such little effort you'd think they were made of paper.

Raikidan helped me up and crouched down a little. "I'll carry you until your leg is better."

"I'll walk."

He grunted and grabbed me. Throwing me onto his back, he walked to the entrance of the cave. I sighed unhappily and sulked.

"Aww, you're so cute when you don't get your way, Laz," Ryoko teased.

I huffed and muttered a few curses. Not only was I weaponless, I was also being treated like a child. As we made our way down the mountain, something heavy suddenly pulled on my back and shoulders. Looking back, I found two carbines strapped to me.

"The system showed you two lost yours during the cave collapse," Aurora called in. "You can thank me later."

I grinned and grabbed my carbine, making sure I was ready for any attack Raynn's team would throw at us, but just as we made it to the base of the mountain, the ground started to shift again.

CHAPTER 18

White walls and floors surrounded us. My leg now healed, I was able to walk on my own down the corridor, Ryoko and Raikidan close on my heels. The field had changed twice since we had reached the mountain's base. The first change had turned everything into a desert, although, thanks to Aurora, that didn't last very long. Unfortunately, while Aurora was hacking the system to make the change, Blaze was removed from the fight by Nioush.

I peered around the corner and held my finger gun at the ready just in case. "I'm going to kill Aurora for making this a maze."

Raikidan chuckled and peeked around the corner with me. *Empty.* We continued on. Reaching the end, we rounded the corner and ran into two people. Taken by surprise, everyone readied their guns.

Sighing, I lowered my gun. It was only Rylan and Argus.

"Don't do that!" Ryoko hissed.

Rylan ran his hand through his hair and put his handgun away. "I could say the same for you."

I glanced around. I had this feeling we were being watched.

"You feel it too?" Raikidan whispered.

I looked at him and nodded. At least I wasn't the only one, though it was strange Ryoko showed no signs of the same. *Maybe she's too distracted... or maybe the nerves are getting to us.*

"Now that we're regrouped, what should we do?" Argus asked. "Raynn's team is being oddly elusive."

I rubbed my chin. Even if this was a maze, normally they'd be wreaking havoc by now. "It is strange. It'd be in our best interest if we—"

I stopped and peered around. There was a strange thundering noise echoing through the corridors. "Rylan, I want you and Raikidan to get moving. The two of you are going to need to find a good sniping point. Ryoko, Argus, and I will continue looking around."

Rylan removed his sniper rifle from his back and grabbed my shoulder. "All right, just be careful. That noise is making me uneasy."

I grabbed his shoulder and nodded. Leaving them, I led Ryoko and Argus down the corridor.

We rounded a corner and hit a dead end. I gnashed my teeth, frustration rising within me. This was the fourth dead end we'd run into. I wasn't sure how long we had been walking around, but I did know the thundering noise from earlier had stopped completely and we still hadn't run into Raynn or his teammates. I didn't even know where Seda was. Looking up at the team board was the only relief I had in knowing if she was still alive or not.

Ryoko sighed and sat down. "This is stupid! Raynn is the one who challenged us to this, and now he's the one who is hiding."

"Aurora, can't you change the map again?" I begged.

"Sorry, babe," she replied. "I've been trying, but I'm locked out. I've taken a few digital peeks at Ezhno's system, and even he's trying to change it."

I had a feeling I now knew what that strange noise was. If Raynn wanted the map to change and he wasn't getting it, he was probably throwing a temper tantrum. "All right, thanks, Aurora. Keep trying if you can. Raikidan."

"What?" he asked.

"Have you guys found a place for Rylan to snipe from yet?"

He grunted. "It didn't take us long, although Captain Fussy here was picky and made us look at four other spots before he was happy."

I chuckled at Rylan's new nickname and full-out laughed when Rylan smacked Raikidan. Calming myself down, I spoke to him again. "Are either of you picking up movement on the scanners?"

"Nothing," he said.

I nodded. "I need you to do something for me."

"All right, what is it?"

"I'm tired of feeling like a rat looking for cheese. Are you able to *heat sense*?"

I prayed he could. Raikidan took a moment to respond. "I can. How did you know about that ability?"

"As a fire user myself, I'm also experienced with the technique."

"Okay, give me a minute to use it." Moments passed and Raikidan finally got back to me. "I'm seeing two figures standing around some ways off in the direction you're facing. There are two other figures acting as lost as the three of you, and I'm seeing two others fighting. I'm assuming by their movements they're our psychic friends."

I counted the number of people he listed off. "We're missing one."

"That's all I see."

"Aurora?"

"The system says they still have six active on their team," she said.

I didn't like the sound of that. Nothing could sneak by a heat sense—not even something cold blooded. Then it hit me. "Aurora, I really need you to get information on that other teammate they pulled in. It's urgent. More urgent than changing the map."

"I've tried my best, babe. I can't get in. I'm sorry."

"Bullshit! I've never known you to not be able to do something or give up. Now get your fingers typing and get me that damn information! Also, while you're at it, do me a favor. Take down these walls in front of us. I want to take out these two enemies Raikidan said were just beyond them."

Aurora chuckled. "Yes, ma'am."

The sound of Rylan's rifle firing rang through the maze. The team board pinged and crossed out one of Raynn's teammates. "That was for Dan. Watch yourselves, though. The other one ran off."

"Noted," I stated. "Raikidan, keep an eye on that loose one so Rylan can set up his next shot."

"Wouldn't this be cheating?" he asked.

"Utilizing our natural abilities isn't against the rules."

"Very well."

"Ready yourselves," Aurora instructed.

The floor began to shake, and walls shifted. We watched as some of the maze walls rearranged themselves and others disappeared into the floor. After a short period of time, we were faced with a long corridor that opened to a large, square room. In the center of the room stood a very confused Raynn and a man with tan skin, clean-shaven face, golden eyes, several types of piercing and gauged ears, and a short, green, unstyled mohawk with sideburns. *Doppelganger.* From the way he was standing, I guessed him to be the original.

Ryoko jumped to her feet and positioned herself in front of Argus and me. Raynn grinned and tossed his cigar on the ground. Doppelganger stood still as several copies pulled out of his body. It was quite a disturbing sight. As each copy pulled out, it would join the others in the forming lineup.

"Destroy them."

I narrowed my eyes. I wasn't in the mood for this. Not waiting for Ryoko or Argus, I ran at them. Doppelganger would pose a problem due to the army he was creating, but my focus was Raynn. Taking him out would diminish the morale of what was left of his team. They couldn't function without him shouting orders.

"Laz, wait!" Ryoko yelled.

I ignored her and picked up my speed. Doppelganger's copies swarmed and ran at me. I took out my last grenade and pulled the pin. Tossing it, I watched it detonate, but I didn't stop running. Using my momentum, I scaled the maze wall. As my fingers touched the wall, the small hidden spines under my skin surfaced and secured my hold.

Reaching the top of the wall, I continued running. The ground below was covered in smoke, but I didn't bother to keep my attention on it. There was no way the copies could survive that explosion, and Doppelganger was continuing to make more. Many of them started to open fire on me. The bullets whizzed past and a few grazed my bodysuit, but thankfully none were direct hits, and I hardly felt them. I ran too fast for any of the doppelgangers to get a good shot, aiding me.

As discreetly as possible in the situation, I exhaled an ember and manipulated it in my hand. Jumping into the mob of doppelgangers, I balled my hand into a fist. As it collided with the ground, I forced the fire I held out in all directions, incinerating every doppelganger it came in contact with.

Lifting the fire up, I willed it to come back to me and swirled it around my body until I pushed it out into one large blast. It rushed through the rest of the corridor, incinerating everything it came in contact with. As it reached Raynn, he jumped away. Doppelganger appeared paralyzed as the fire rushed toward him, and I prayed it would hit him. Doppelganger was unable to move as he made copies of himself. But after another copy came out of his body, he moved just in time. *Shit, not fast enough.*

"Bitch," Doppelganger muttered. He pulled out a pistol and aimed it at me, but it was kicked out of his hand. His eyes snapped to Raynn, narrowing into a glare. "What the hell?"

"She's mine," Raynn said, his focus on me.

I narrowed my eyes in disgust. I really couldn't stand Raynn or his teammates. They were self-centered, arrogant pricks. Raynn himself was known to leave teammates behind to save his own ass, though none of it could ever be proven well enough to demote him while he was still in service.

Raynn cracked his knuckles. "Let's dance, baby."

I grimaced. There was another reason I hated him so much. He was worse than Blaze when it came to women.

Doppelganger got up and readied his gun, but he was shot at. The bullets ultimately missed, but it stalled him long enough for Argus and Ryoko to rush into the room, Argus with his gun at the ready. *It's unusual for Argus to miss at such a range. I wonder what happened.*

Doppelganger backed off. As Argus and Ryoko advanced, he fled, and Argus and Ryoko were quick to pursue. *Just Raynn and me now.*

Not wanting to waste time, I charged. My fist collided with his arm, which he blocked easily. He took a swing at me, but I moved out of the way. I went at him again, but the result was the same, so I backed off and quickly thought it through. He was a Brute class, an old one, but still a Brute. Brutes pretty much fought the same way, meaning I had to think about how Ryoko fought.

I waited for him to come to me, and sure enough, he did. He rushed and swung a fist. Ducking, I grabbed his arm and swung my legs up and kicked him in the face. Pushing myself into the air and twisting so I'd land facing him, I drew a dagger from my arm and prepared to throw it as he stumbled.

"Eira, look out!" I looked up to see Raikidan running toward us on the top of a wall. What was so important that he had to leave Rylan's side to warn me?

"Listen to him, Laz!" Rylan shouted through the communicator.

I turned, and my eyes widened. *I should have listened to their warnings sooner.* I wasn't fast enough to move out of the way of the slab of wall that was flying right at me. It crashed into me, and my body collided with the adjacent maze wall. I cried out in pain, blood rushing into my throat.

"Eira!" Raikidan shouted.

I tried to move, but it was as if the slab was being held there.

"Nioush, you bastard. This is my fight. Stay out of it," Raynn spat.

I ground my teeth. Of course Nioush would come out of nowhere and screw things up for my team.

Nioush snickered. "Sorry, Raynn. I couldn't help it. I know how much my baby sister hates seeing her *friends* hurt. Don't you, Seda?"

"Leave her alone," Seda ordered. "Your fight is with me, not them."

"Oh, but you're mistaken," Nioush said. "This is a team battle. Therefore, I choose whomever I wish to torture."

I let out a dry laugh. "Team? None of you know the meaning of the word."

"Silence, wench!" The wall chunk pressed harder against me.

I refused to cry out in pain. I refused to give him that satisfaction, regardless of how difficult that was to do. The sound of crackling flames hit my ears, and the pressure of the slab lessened.

Nioush chuckled. "So, you're a Firebreather, outsider. A rare find. What backwater country village did the wench find you in?"

Raikidan exhaled more fire and the pressure increased.

"Careful, Firebreather," Nioush warned. "I don't want to kill her just yet. I enjoy seeing my baby sister feel pain."

"Rai…kidan…" It hurt to breathe. I thought I could hear the wall cracking, but maybe that was my ribcage. I was in so much pain I couldn't tell.

"Yes, Raikidan, listen to her. She's in such torment she can barely speak. She can only beg like a dog." Nioush snickered. "I can sense the anger in you. I hope you're not taken with her. She's quite good at breaking hearts. They all are."

I grunted. "No one cares... that a woman broke your heart... Nioush. So, do us all a favor... and keep your mind... on the battle at hand."

The wall chunk pressed harder into me.

"Shut up!" The sound of a distant gunshot rang through the maze, and Nioush chuckled. "Your other man toy is also tired of seeing you in pain. Do you enjoy toying with them, Eira? Do you find satisfaction in using them and then throwing them away?"

"Go to hell."

"Ladies first."

The wall pressed into me with even more force, but stopped when Seda yelled. "Let her go!"

A large wall chunk crashed through the wall next to me.

Nioush chuckled. "Patience, Sister, your turn will come soon enough."

Seda really threw that? I wondered how much energy she was using up in this fight. She was only a Seer and here she was in battle. *No, that's not right.* She wasn't a Seer or a Battle Psychic. She was something different than that. She was something in between, or was it beyond the two? *She told me this once before... what was it?*

The sound of magnetized bearing echoing from a railgun firing pulled me back to the battle at hand. "Hey, Battle Psychic wannabe, over here."

Ryoko? I had to admit, I was a bit confused. The team board hadn't told us Doppelganger was dead, and it wasn't like Ryoko to leave a chase. *Or come up with such a poor insult.*

The rounds continued, along with the sound of fire. Nioush grunted and the pressure of the slab wall lessened. *He's getting overwhelmed.* But as soon as I thought I could push it away, the pressure slammed back into me.

Raynn chuckled. "Didn't think you could get away that easy, did you? Nioush may be overwhelmed by the three attacking him, but I'm still here and I'm going to make sure you are dead by my hands."

I ground my teeth together. "In your dreams."

He chuckled and pushed on the slab more. The pressure forced me to cough in pain, and blood splattered against the wall.

The sound of a far-off gun sounded again, but nothing came of it. "Do me a favor, baby, and tell your little man toy he needs to brush up on his aim. He was way off."

"Whoever said he was after you?" a low voice growled. "Now get off her!"

Raikidan? The weight of the wall was lifted as Raikidan tossed Raynn away and picked up the slab. I slid to the ground and turned in time to watch him throw the chunk at Nioush. Nioush was so preoccupied with Seda and Ryoko, he didn't see it coming. The slab crashed into him, pushing him back, but he recovered quickly and pushed it away with his psychic power.

Raikidan helped me up. "Are you okay?"

Coughing up a little more blood, my eyes flicked up at him and I wiped some of the blood that had dribbled down my lip. "I'll be fine."

The team board pinged and another member of Raynn's team was eliminated.

"Doppelganger is finally down," Argus sounded in. But just as he did, the sound of bullets rang through his headset, along with his own scream of agony. The team board sounded once again.

"Argus…" Seda whispered.

A pang of pity for her shot through me.

"Oh, did that particular death upset you, baby sister?" Nioush said. "I'd hoped so. I planned that one especially for you."

You sick shit. I knew the two never got along, but this was a new low. His satisfaction in her pain sickened me.

Raynn chuckled as he sat up. "You'll never win. Even if you manage to get rid of me and Nioush, you'll never see your death coming. Just give up."

That made me even angrier. I aimed my finger gun at him and shot him twice in the legs.

Raynn screamed in agony. "You bitch!"

Slowly I walked over to him and grabbed him by his hair. I raised him up until he was at eye level with me. I was in no mood for games, and although I would have wanted a better fight from Raynn, this was good enough.

"Any last words?" I asked.

He chuckled. "Just a few. Bye-bye, Ryoko."

He pulled a small cylinder with a red button on the top from his back pocket and smirked before pressing it. My eyes widened, and my eyes snapped to Ryoko. The ground below her burst and she, too, screamed. The team board sounded for the fourth time.

"Ry…oko…"

I couldn't believe it. Raynn had planted a bomb and had been able to use it on Ryoko, of all people. Numbness fell over me. My grip tightened on Raynn's scalp as something stirred in the back of my head. I knew what it was, and I wasn't okay with its dark presence. Raynn's actions awoke it, and now it hungered for blood.

"Kill him."

"Laz!" Rylan called in. "The other teammate Raynn brought in is—"

He was cut short by the sound of bullets and agonizing screams. The team board pinged. I couldn't hold it back now. First Ryoko and now Rylan. Someone needed to pay, and Raynn would be that person. My shoulder convulsed, and I thought I could hear the laughter of the presence inside me.

"Kill!"

My pupils dilated, and my other shoulder convulsed. I looked into Raynn's fear-stricken eyes and saw the reflection of my crazed look. My mind fogged, and I chuckled. "You're going to pay, Raynn. Now die."

I lifted up my hand and thrust it through his face. Blood gushed everywhere. Only when I pulled my hand out did his body pixelate away. Slowly I turned and faced Nioush, his body posture rigid. Although I couldn't see the fear in his eyes, I smelled it. After that display, who wouldn't be afraid?

I chuckled again and moved closer to the two psychics. "You're next, Nioush."

I could feel *it* trying to claw its way out; it wanted blood so badly. It wanted to be let out, to kill with pleasure like it had always done in the past.

"What… what are you?" Nioush demanded.

I grinned and threw my finger gun to the ground. It was useless to me now that it was covered in blood. "A failed experiment, just like you."

Taking my carbine off my back, I threw it on the ground. I would have no use for it against him. Instead, I drew the dagger that was still sheathed to my arm. Nioush looked down at the ground where the dagger I dropped earlier lay. Using his psychic ability, he threw it at me. I readied myself to block it, but as soon as it came in range, Raikidan grabbed it.

"I don't know what's up with you," he whispered. "But if it's going to shut this bastard up, I won't ask 'til later."

I chuckled and took my dagger from him. Grinning, I looked at Nioush and then at Seda.

"I will follow your lead," she told me.

Focusing back at Nioush, I charged him. In response, he hovered higher in the air, mistakenly thinking it would help him. Turning quickly, I threw one of my daggers at him. He easily dodged, as I had expected. Picking up my pace, I veered left and used the room wall to launch myself into the air. I threw my other dagger at him, but this time he stopped it and forced it back at me. Catching it, I threw it once more, sacrificing the air I had gained. Landing, I jumped to the side as he threw it back at me. I went to rush him again, but he held out his hand and I could feel my body stop. I struggled to move. Only my eyes and mouth were unaffected.

He chuckled. "I don't know what is going on in that head of yours, but I don't care. I'll make you take out the last two of your teammates and kill you nice and slow in the process."

"Not going to happen."

He smirked and clamped his hand into a fist. My body responded by binding up in a straight position. His grin widened and a large amount of pressure pulsed at the front of my mind. Closing my eyes, I tried to force it out. He was powerful. I knew Battle Psychics were strong, but this was nothing like I had ever expected. *Is Telar this powerful too? Even with his unusual demeanor, had he done this to others as well?* I threw the thoughts away. I couldn't afford any distractions.

Forcing Nioush out was incredibly painful. I gritted my teeth as the pain increased.

"Don't be so impatient, outsider." Nioush chuckled. "You'll get your turn, if you can muster up the courage to kill the poor woman, that is."

"Never," Raikidan growled.

I opened my eyes to see Raikidan being hovered in the air. "Rai... ki...dan..."

"Hmm, you're much more resilient to my methods than I thought you would be. My sister taught you well." Nioush chuckled. "No matter. I'll just have to be more forceful."

I clenched my teeth and shut my eyes as the pain doubled, but I refused to give in, and refused to cry out. What was worse was that the presence was still there. It still wanted to get out. I opened my eyes when Seda yelled forcefully. A large wall slab sailed through the air at Nioush. He maneuvered around it and threw Raikidan at her, sending them both through a few walls. Nioush put his focus back on me, and the pain in my head increased even more. I let out slow, labored breaths, but I was too stubborn to give in.

"Tenacious bitch," Nioush muttered.

"*Kill him. Spill his blood.*" My eyes shut tightly as I tried to shut out the presence's voice. "*Annihilate him!*"

Then it hit me. I snickered and Nioush frowned. "What's so funny?"

"You..." I grinned. "You want in my head so bad. Well, so be it!"

"No, don't do it, Laz!" Ryoko screamed through Aurora's communicator.

I focused on Nioush as I welcomed him into my mind, but that wasn't the only thing I did. I let the presence loose. I could feel my face contort, and laughter escaped my lips. Although Nioush had a hold on my body, my shoulder muscles convulsed regardless. Smirking, I let every horrid memory flood through. All the pain. All the bloodshed. Every ounce of hunger for blood the monster inside yearned for. The monster fed off these and clawed about, trying to free itself completely.

Nioush moved back, fear flooding off him in waves. "W–what... what the hell?"

"What's wrong, Nioush?" I snickered. "Afraid of what you see?"

His grip on me was fading, and I used this opportunity to gain control of my body.

"*Say when,*" Seda stated.

Nioush's control on me was all but gone now. In one pressing force, I pushed him out of my mind for good. Crouching down, I drew a sheathed dagger from my leg. Pulling it close to my face, I breathed a little fire and lit the thin oil coating. The fire lit up the blade and I rushed Nioush.

I sent the dagger flying through the air, but Nioush gained his composure and dodged, only to be forced to repel a blast of fire from Raikidan. Using Raikidan's distraction to my advantage, I grabbed a discarded dagger from the ground, and I leapt skyward and attempted to slice into Nioush, taking advantage of the fact he'd lowered in altitude without seeming to realize. But he easily dodged when I came near. Pivoting as I fell to the ground, I threw the dagger at him, but instead of it making contact, he caught it by the hilt with his hands.

"Seda, now!" I ordered.

My dagger in her hand, she came at Nioush from behind. He turned to face her and was struck in the heart.

"You…" He coughed up blood. "Bitch…" Seda's face was expressionless, and then it twisted in pain. Nioush had taken my dagger and thrust it into her back. "You're pathetic. You weren't strong enough to take me on… your own. You needed… your *friends*… to help."

"At least… I have friends," she spoke softly.

He chuckled softly. "I don't need friends, especially if they're anything like that woman down there. She's not… a trustworthy one with what is going on inside her."

"You do not know… what you are talking about, Nioush," Seda said. "What you saw… is what I have known for a long time… and that is not even scratching the surface of who she is. I trust her."

He grunted. "Trust… No one is worthy of that."

His grip on the dagger lessened and his body pixelated away, from the dagger wound out. The team board pinged.

Seda looked down at me. "I am… sorry, Eira. I cannot help you anymore."

"Don't worry. You've done your job. Raikidan and I will handle this last bit." I smiled. "Also… as I've told you in the past, it's Laz."

She smiled and then she, too, pixelated away. The team board pinged again. It was just Raikidan and me now.

CHAPTER 19

Raikidan approached and looked at me expectantly. I pursed my lips. "What?"

"I said I wasn't going to ask 'til later. It's later," he stated.

"Don't tell him."

I waved him off. "Forget about it. It's nothing."

"Don't lie to me. You went nuts back there and scared that psychic to death. That's definitely not nothing."

I glared at him. "I don't want to talk about it, okay, so lay off!"

Brushing him aside with my shoulder, I walked away and grabbed my discarded carbine and then pulled out my spare finger gun. I coughed, blood coalescing on my tongue. *Right, internal injuries.* I dug into my medical pouch and pulled out the only pill inside. Popping it into my mouth I swallowed it, not an easy task without water. *That should start to work soon.* It would have been nice to have more than one pill at my disposal, so I could have avoided the need for the injection earlier, but to keep these matches balances, the game only allowed one, so it was usually rationed for internal injuries if you survived long enough to use it.

Raikidan approached as I slung my carbine over my shoulder. "You want to ask something else."

"Why did you tell Seda to call you Laz?" he asked. "You told me to only call you Eira because it was your name."

I didn't look at him. "Ask a different question."

Raikidan grabbed my arm and forced me to face him. "What are you hiding from me?"

Yanking my arm free, I leaned closer to his face. narrowing my eyes. "Everything."

My visor snapped over my eyes, and I stalked a little ways away from him, ignoring his confused look. "Aurora. Aurora, are you there?"

Static answered me.

My brow furrowed, and I called in again, receiving the same response. Something wasn't right.

"I don't like this," Raikidan said.

I nodded and gazed up at the team board. Three people remained. Raikidan's face and my face were up there, but where the image of Raynn's last teammate should be, there was a black square. "It's all too convenient."

Raikidan looked at me. "You think Raynn is behind this?"

I spat on the ground, residual blood from my earlier ordeal mixed in. "No, I know he is. Rylan knows who this last enemy is, so that means Aurora and the others know now as well. With our focus on this last member, they'll do anything to make sure we don't find out."

"So, what do we do?"

I sighed. "The only thing we can do is search for him on our own until we can make contact with the others."

He looked around. "Should we find a lookout?"

I shook my head. "There's no point."

He narrowed his eyes. "What do you know?"

I closed my eyes and sighed. Placing my hand on his back, I urged him to walk with me. It wouldn't get us anywhere to stand around. "I can't be certain, but I have a suspicion of who we're dealing with."

"Go on."

"This enemy doesn't appear on the scanners, but it's obvious he's moving. He doesn't appear on a heat sense, although he's living. I only know of one experiment that can avoid both of those types of detections." I glanced up at the team board again. "If I'm right, his name is Chameleon."

"Chameleon? As in the animal with color changing abilities?"

I looked up at him through my lashes. "Yep, except this guy doesn't just change color. An assassin-type experiment, the makeup of his DNA allows him to fuse with just about any object, becoming undetectable. This maze is a playground for him. He can move anywhere without detection as long as he's attached."

Raikidan narrowed his eyes. "How do we fight an enemy we can't see?"

I shrugged. "Your guess is as good as mine. I've never had to fight him before, and when I've watched Raynn's team fight in simulations in the past, if Chameleon was on the team, they always won. No one has ever beaten him."

"But it's not impossible."

"Nothing is impossible, really, but I think I remember hearing he had a weakness. Just like Doppelganger can't always have copies out, Chameleon can't stay hidden forever. He has to change back to his original form, but I don't know the time frame he has to stay out or can be in, especially now that his ability is being boosted."

Raikidan pulled out his pistol. "Well, that gives us a better chance. So, what's the plan?"

I opened my mouth to speak, but was cut off by a blast of light that crashed through the maze wall. "Run!"

We picked up our pace. Looking back, I hoped to catch a glimpse of Chameleon, but luck wasn't on my side this time. We kept running until we hit a dead end. The beams of light had stopped by this point, but that didn't mean we were in the clear.

"What in Lumaraeon were those?" Raikidan demanded to know.

I shook my head. "I think it was a type of plasma gun, but not sure."

"You can't be sure? How can you not be sure about your own technology?"

"I've been gone a while, okay? Things change at a rapid pace in this city, especially technology. When I left, plasma guns were still in the prototype phase."

"Fine, I'll go with that, but what are we supposed to do now?"

"How well do you do with scaling walls?" I asked as I looked at the walls.

His face scrunched. "What?"

Without explaining myself, I backed up a little and then, with a running start, I scaled the wall. I crouched at the top and peered down at him. "You coming, or what?"

"How did you do that?" he yelled up.

I grinned. "That's a secret. Now get up here or I'm leaving you behind."

"Looks like I won't be saving your ass anytime soon," he muttered.

I chuckled and watched him jump up to me. I frowned. "Show-off."

Now it was his turn to chuckle. He jumped when a bullet hit the wall near him. We didn't need any other invitation to jump down.

"You're lucky he has cruddy aim."

With a grin, he pushed me. "So, what now?"

I shrugged. "The best we can do is to keep moving. It'd be best not to split up as well."

"You sure about that?"

I nodded. "With the connection problems with the outside, I don't want to worry if these communicators will stop working once we split up."

He gave a curt nod. "Okay."

I furrowed my brow and swiveled my head. Someone was watching us.

Raikidan pushed me. "Watch it!"

I turned as I fell, observing a figure with a combat knife lunge out of the wall and merge with the adjacent wall face. I didn't get a good look at the figure, but I didn't need to. It was definitely Chameleon. I scrambled to my feet and took off. "Let's go!"

Raikidan didn't have to be told twice to follow. We sprinted down the corridor and took any turn that came up, in hopes it would throw Chameleon off for even a moment.

"Watch it!" Raikidan shoved me into a side corridor unexpectedly.

I fell to the ground just as bullets flew through the air, and my carbine clattered on the ground. Scrambling to my feet without thinking about grabbing my weapon, I took off again, with Raikidan close behind. My pace quickened every time Chameleon reared his head in some form. I didn't stop running until I was tired enough to need to catch my breath. "Raikidan, we nee—Raikidan?"

I cranked my neck around, only to find myself alone. Inadvertently, in my attempt to flee from Chameleon, I had also managed to lose

Raikidan. *This is just great. Now we're going to be easier targets.* This had to be what Chameleon wanted.

A bright beam blasted through the wall near me, and I continued on. *It'd be nice to know what that weapon is.* Shaking that thought out of my head, I focused on the issue at hand. Raikidan and I were separated. We could only speak through the communicators, and it was going to be harder to formulate a good plan to take Chameleon out together.

The wall behind me disappeared when another bright beam broke through it, and I pushed faster, reminding me that the plan to take him out wouldn't happen if I couldn't survive. I quit running when the light beams finally stopped, and I leaned against the maze wall. My breath came heavy, and in ragged bursts. *This is so stupid!* I had no idea where I was, and I couldn't be sure where Chameleon was now. He could be toying with me, for all I knew, or he had given up on me and gone after Raikidan.

"How are you holding up?" Raikidan called in.

I took in another gasp of air. "My lungs are about to burst out of my chest."

He chuckled. "It amazes me how weak you humans are."

"Shut it, dragon-boy." He chuckled quietly, and I grunted. "How about you?"

"Fine so far, except that I'm completely lost."

I started moving again. "You're not the only one."

I passed a few corridors and took a right at a fork. Strong hands suddenly grabbed the back of my bodysuit and pulled me back to the corridor I had left. A black bodysuit filled my vision. Normally, I would have retaliated, but his familiar scent kept me calm as he pinned me with his body against the wall. Then I heard the barrage of bullets fly through the corridor I had nearly entered. I was confused. Raikidan was there to bail me out of danger yet again, but how?

"You should be more careful," he murmured.

"You shouldn't sneak up on me," I replied. His chest rumbled against me as he chuckled. I attempted to squirm out of his embrace, to no avail.

"It's a good thing I came out of the corridor when I did." He pushed himself away until his arms were fully outstretched and hands flat against the wall.

I looked at him. "How do you do it?"

He furrowed his brow. "Do what?"

I pushed him away from me. "Know when I'm in trouble. Be there at the right time to save my hide?"

He shrugged. "Luck, I guess."

I chuckled. "Lucky for you, or me?"

He placed his arm behind my back and pushed me toward a corridor. "Both, I suppose. Now we need to get moving."

I complied without a word. I wasn't really sure how to respond after what he had said, but now wasn't the time to mull it over.

Picking up our pace, we ran down the corridor. Raikidan looked over his shoulder and pushed me into a side path. For the second time, I was pinned against a wall as bullets flew through the corridor we had left. I expected Raikidan to let me go and keep moving, but he didn't. He let out a low growl and glared at the entrance of the corridor. Suddenly a shape peered around the corner, and Raikidan let out a breath of fire, letting me go in the process.

Grabbing him by the wrist, I took off. "Keep moving!"

I dragged him around a corner and down the corridor. We came to another corner and rounded it. As we did so, we were met with a wall of bullets. Raikidan grabbed me and pulled me close, letting out a blast of fire, but it didn't go down the hall like I had anticipated. Instead, it swirled around us, creating a protective barrier. I stared in awe. He did it so effortlessly. I'd never seen a skill like it, even with the number of fire shamans and elementalists I'd crossed paths with.

But I was also worried. I could tell the barrier was working, but Raikidan was going to run out of breath sooner or later, and that's when we'd be in trouble.

He frowned, and his grip on my bodysuit tightened. *He's running out of air.* I had to think quickly. Being so close to him, I wouldn't be able to create my own fire without him noticing. I was going to have to take a risk. Reaching up, I went to take the fire from him. His eyes widened as he glanced down at me.

"Trust me," I whispered.

Filling my body with heat, I wrapped the fire around the tips of my fingers and pulled it away from him. My eyes widened, and audible gasp escaping my lips. It was so strong—so hot. *So much power he holds.* I had no idea he harnessed such power. Closing my eyes, I concentrated on controlling the fire.

Raikidan wrapped one arm around my waist. "I can take it back now."

I shook my head. "I'm fine."

"You're struggling."

"I'm fine."

"You can't keep this up at this rate."

"I don't plan to. Stay behind me."

He moved closer to me, and I exhaled slowly as I pulled my other hand up. *Stay calm. You can do this.* I had only one shot, and if I messed up, we were done for. I took a deep breath and my eyes bolted open. Grabbing the fire with my free hand, I forced the fire down to the ground and then out in all directions as far as I could. I pushed it down every corridor that crossed the fire's path. It spread and spiraled until I could no longer hold it. Exhaling slowly, I let it go.

"We need to move," I stated, stumbling a bit. "He managed to dodge that somehow."

Raikidan grabbed my arm, holding me up. "Are you all right?"

I nodded. "I'm fine."

"I'm not going to lie, that was impressive. I've never heard of someone controlling fire that wasn't their own."

I looked away from him, slightly embarrassed by his praise. "It takes a lot of skill and training. And I'm nowhere near enough to be called a master at it."

He pulled me by the arm toward a corridor. "I might just make you teach me."

I laughed dryly. "You can't just learn it in a matter of days or weeks. It takes years of practice and discipline."

He smirked. "I'm a fast learner."

I rolled my eyes. "I'll think about it."

He grinned triumphantly and set a fast pace for us.

We ran around another corner and stopped to catch our breath.

Raikidan placed a hand on the wall, his posture slightly hunched. "How does he keep finding us?"

I took several deep breaths. "I'm not sure."

"It's as if he's tracking us." Raikidan shook his head. "It doesn't make sense."

Wait. My eyes widened in realization. "The communicators…"

His brow creased. "The communicators?"

I ripped mine off my head and pried it open. Inside were thousands of tiny circuit boards and wires, but I wasn't interested in that. Looking around, I finally found the flashing red light.

"What is that?" he asked.

I sighed. "It's the tracking device that allows the technician of the teams to track our whereabouts."

"So, what does this have to do with Chameleon?"

"If I'm correct, Raynn's technician is blocking out Aurora and homing in on our signal so he can relay them to Chameleon."

Raikidan scowled. "I don't like that."

I shook my head. "Neither do I, but that doesn't mean we can't use that to our advantage."

His brow furrowed with confusion. "What are you talking about? How do you use something like that as an advantage?"

I grinned. "Hand me your communicator."

He complied. "Okay, now what?" I crushed it and his eyes widened. "Why the hell did you do that?"

"I have my reasons." I looked around and then scaled the wall. He followed. "See the room where we fought Raynn and Nioush? We're going to split up and meet there."

"I still don't understand, but if you know what you're doing, then fine."

"I'll take my communicator, which will give you more time to get to the meeting spot, okay?"

"Uh, sure. But don't we need those to communicate with each other? Not that it matters now, since you already destroyed mine."

"In a normal situation, yes. But this isn't a normal situation."

"Then how the hell are we supposed to know if either one is in trouble or needs any sort of assistance?"

"Well, I just assumed your luck would save us this time," I teased. His eyes narrowed, causing me to laugh. "We'll just have to make a flare. You can make one, right?"

"I'm sure I can figure it out."

I jumped down from the wall and gazed up at him. "All right, I'm going to trust you on this decision, but don't make one unless you really have to. It could mess up my whole plan."

He furrowed his brow again. "If you told me your plan, you wouldn't have to worry."

I chuckled. "You don't need to know now the exact details. Just know that I know what I'm doing, and as long as you meet up with me, it should work."

I ran off without another word. If I was going to get this to work, I needed to get away from Raikidan and get Chameleon's attention. It wasn't long before Chameleon found me, although he appeared for only short bursts to shoot at me, which was quite easy to avoid. I ran as fast as I could and used every surface to give me an advantage.

Pulling my hand close to my mouth, I let out some fire and threw it behind me. *That should give me more time.* I scaled another wall and headed for the open room. When I reached it, I tossed the communicator on the ground near the center and hid by the entrance of another corridor.

"Here we go…" I tossed a fire flare into the air before inhaling deeply to utilize my heat sense ability.

My body filled with heat and my sight distorted as I climbed up the wall to look around. Objects were no longer defined by textures and individual shapes, but by layers of color. This ability allowed me to see the hottest and coldest portions of every object that gave off some sort of heat. I could see Raikidan's colorful image running quickly through the maze. As I had predicted, he used the most direct route to get here, which included the corridor I chose to wait in. Slipping down the wall, I waited for him. I didn't have to wait long before he came around a corner and rushed over to me.

"What—" I placed my hand over his mouth and held a finger to mine, telling him to keep quiet. He glared at me but nodded slowly, and I pulled my hand away. I moved closer to the entrance and peeked around the wall. Raikidan joined me.

Something began to move on the far wall. As we watched, a young, handsome man with short multicolored hair and kaleidoscopic eyes pulled away from the wall. He cautiously walked to the center of the room, his skin rippling with several shades of color as he moved. He had his communicator on and had his attention fixated on the readings the device was relaying. When he reached the center, he cursed and kicked my communicator.

"Ezhno, tell Raynn they figured it out," he muttered. "Now what do I do? Okay, understood."

I would have loved to have heard what had been said, but as long as Chameleon turned away from us, it didn't matter. As luck would have it, he did just that.

I glance at Raikidan, a grin on my lips. He responded with a smirk and nod and then charged Chameleon, knocking him to the ground. I was close behind. Chameleon turned over and faced us, fear lining his face. Raikidan and I grinned at each other.

"What do you think we should do with him?" he asked me.

"I think it's time to put the poor soul out of his misery."

Raikidan held his pistol at the ready while I held up my finger gun. Chameleon's eyes widened more, and he tried to scramble back. Raikidan and I fired simultaneously, Raikidan's bullet penetrating Chameleon's chest while mine shot through his head.

Chameleon screamed in pain before bursting into pixels, and the team board pinged for the last time. We looked up as Chameleon's face appeared with a large X crossed through it where the black box had been. Raynn's team pictures disappeared, and our team pictures became larger. All members who had been removed no longer had Xs over their picture.

I held up my hand for a high five, but Raikidan didn't reciprocate. He stared at my hand, his brow furrowed. "What are you doing?"

I chuckled. "Looking for a high five. You trusting me for such a crazy plan deserves it."

"High... five?"

"It's when you hit each other's hands together to show excitement or greeting. We also bump fists or arms for similar reasons."

Raikidan hesitantly raised his hand, looked at it, and then mine. With a furrowed brow still, he smacked his palm into mine. "Like that?"

I ignored the slight sting from his strength and nodded. "Yep."

He smiled. "I'm glad I listened to you, even though it wasn't easy. We make a good team."

I smiled despite myself. "Yeah, we do." I glanced down at my feet, which were starting to pixelate away. "Time to leave."

Raikidan grinned. "I'll be waiting for you."

I nodded with a slight smile, and I closed my eyes as I was pulled out of the simulation. Eventually I could hear muffled voices, and the hissing of the automatic lid release activating, but I didn't open my eyes just yet. My head still spun from the transition. When the disorientation finally ebbed, I opened my eyes. They were met with the closed lid of my pod. Slowly I pushed it open. I blinked a few times to adjust to the light.

"Slowpoke," Raikidan teased. He was leaning over my pod looking down at me.

I playfully kicked him before I sat up. He extended his hand to help me stand, and even though it wasn't necessary, I accepted the gesture anyway. I looked around and realized the rest of the team was waiting for us, grins plastered over their faces. Raikidan and I walked over to them.

"You guys did great!" Ryoko exclaimed. "That fire trick was really cool."

I chuckled. "I probably wouldn't have had to use it if we could have communicated with you guys." My head tilted with interest when I saw the eye shifts between Ryoko, Aurora, and Rylan. "What?"

"Well… we kinda had that fixed around that time, but you guys seemed to be doing well on your own, so we stayed quiet about it," Ryoko explained as she scratched the back of her head.

I glared at her. "Obviously, you all are blind if you thought we were fine."

"Aw, babe, don't be like that," Aurora said. "Raikidan, you understand where we're coming from, right?"

He shook his head. "I'm with Eira on this one."

I crossed my arms. "Thank you."

"What does it matter?" Genesis asked. "We won! Now let's go check the scoreboard to see how well everyone did."

"Scoreboard?" Raikidan whispered in my ear.

"When teams face off, the computer records everything that happens and tallies different types of scores for each team member," I explained, keeping my voice low for his sake. "The data is then displayed on a public scoring screen to be reviewed. It's a way to see how you're using your skills and a way for others to assess you for battle and assignment worth. Just follow us and you'll find out."

He nodded and we caught up to the others. Pushing our way through the crowd of experiments, we peered up at the scoreboard and waited as it compiled the scores. Ryoko rested comfortably on my left shoulder while Raikidan stood on the other side of me. Rylan, with Genesis on his back, stood next to Ryoko, and the boys next to him. Highlights of the match were shown for each team on separate screens.

An impressive-teamwork highlight between Argus and Blaze was shown, along with Ryoko's fearless march into battle in the beginning, my attack on Doppelganger's copies in the maze, and a sniper highlight by Rylan. Even my fire trick against Chameleon made it in.

Ryoko grinned. "Trained shamans are pretty skilled."

I didn't look at her. Her comment embarrassed me. With a grin, Raikidan nudged me, which only made it worse, causing a small smile to appear on my face. I could feel my cheeks flush despite my attempt to keep it at bay. It was interesting to watch at this view. My face was so serious and concentrated and yet slightly relaxed, although I hadn't felt relaxed at all when performing the maneuver.

Raikidan and Seda also made it onto the highlights. Raikidan's highlight showed him releasing a large breath of fire on Nioush. I figured it was the first time when I had been trapped under the wall slab, and as I watched, I wished I had witnessed it firsthand.

Seda's highlight was even more impressive. It showed her lifting up an entire wall and throwing it at Nioush. Nioush did block it with some type of force field, but with Seda being defined as a Seer and still having that amount of psychic power, it was just incredible to witness.

On Raynn's team, Mocha received a highlight for when she trapped Raikidan and me in that cave, along with Nioush receiving his highlight for when he painfully killed Blaze. I cringed when I watched it. Blaze had been lifted into the air and slowly squeezed to death. I was glad that had been only a simulation and hoped we never had to fight any Battle Psychics still loyal to Zarda in the near future. I couldn't face the idea of my teammates dying in such a manner.

The highlights faded out before they finished, and the scoring began. Dan was up first. A video image of him was seen, and then it stopped as his scores were calculated. The screen showed all sorts of calculations, but I focused only on a few.

Gun-skill: 89%
Teamwork: 83%
Special ability score: insufficient data

This didn't surprise me. Dan tried his hardest, more than most experiments, to be normal. Most now didn't even know what he was capable of.

Blaze and then Argus were shown next.

Gun-skill: 83%
Special ability: strength-based, 93%
Teamwork: 50%

I cringed at that score. *Blaze, we'll need to work on that.*

Blaze grumbled unhappily, causing us to laugh.

"Better luck next time," Argus said. Blaze grunted and shoved him, making Argus laugh.

Argus had a much higher score.

Gun-skill: 94%
Teamwork: 94%
Special ability: intelligence-based, 42%

Argus smiled contently. *Not bad, Argus.* I wasn't going to get on him for the special ability score. Battles were tough to show his kind of smarts.

Ryoko, Rylan, and then Seda were shown next.

Gun-skill: 89%
Teamwork: 97%
Special-ability: strength-based, 97%

Very good work, Ryoko! Railgun accuracies sometimes weren't great, even for a simulation, so I was sure to keep that in mind when making my own praise evaluations.

Rylan's score came in a little better than hers.

Gun-skill: 98%
Teamwork: 98%
Special-ability: multiple categories, insufficient data

I don't think he needed to use his ice or shifting abilities, so I'll let it slide without issue.
Seda's score was slightly different since she was a psychic.

Teamwork: 80%
Gun-skill: insufficient data

No surprise there. In its place, her special-ability score broke out into three parts.

Control: 82%
Wisdom: 96%
Power: 90%

Damn, Seda! That was the power level you'd expect from a Battle Psychic, not a Seer.

Glancing over at Raynn's team board, my jaw nearly dropped.

"What's wrong?" Ryoko asked me. I only pointed at the scoring board in response. She shifted her focus and her eyes widened. "By the gods!"

On the screen, extremely low stats belonging to Nioush displayed for all to see.

Teamwork: 10%
Gun-skill: insufficient data
Control: 65%
Wisdom: 9%
Power: 93%

Nioush's power score may have beaten Seda's by three percent, but it meant nothing when compared with his other stats and the knowledge that Seda was a Seer and shouldn't have the high power score she had.

A loud crash and a string of profanities echoed through the room, and the crowd of experiments erupted with laughter.

"Looks like you pissed off your brother, Seda," Argus said.

Seda smiled in response. She didn't have to speak for others to know how she felt about this. Not only had she beaten Nioush in battle, but she also had beaten him in the scores. That was a feat that no Seer had ever been known to do.

The scoring continued, and the board showed a video of Raikidan looking around with his carbine in hand and then showed his score.

Gun-skill: 40%
Teamwork: 85%

Already this looks good. I didn't expect his gun skill to be much higher. He was still learning. And his teamwork score was above average, reflecting well for the team and himself. I assessed the last score.

Special-ability: multiple categories, 99%

Well then... I never thought I'd see the day a teammate's special ability score would rival Ryoko's, besides me.

Ryoko crossed her arms and huffed in response.

"Aww, is somebody upset their teammate outscored her in her favorite category?" I teased, squinting my eyes.

"Shut up," she grumbled.

Raikidan chuckled. "Better luck next time."

She pointed at him, placing her other hand on her hip. "I want a match, just you and me."

Raikidan smirked. "Fine, it could be fun."

Ryoko winked. "I'm looking forward to it."

He gave her a blank stare, showing her how clueless he was, and she stared back with a tilted head and confused eyes. A strange sensation twisted in my chest, but whatever it was, I ignored it easily.

Don't get your hopes up, Ryoko. There was no way she'd convince him to fight her. I doubted he'd be okay with a wrestling match. *Maybe we'll have to get a special event going for these two in the virtual reality.* It couldn't hurt.

"I don't see why you're so worked up over this, babe," Aurora said. "Laz gets a higher special-ability score than you all the time."

"It's because Raikidan is the rookie," Rylan explained.

Ryoko tossed her thumb at him. "What he said. He's not supposed to rank higher than the veterans of the team."

"Doesn't that just mean Laz made a good choice?" Aurora asked.

Ryoko sighed. "I guess so, but I still don't have to like it."

Rolling my eyes, I chuckled and focused on the scoring board again. The battle leader always displayed last, so my score was being tallied now. The video clip it showed was of me running through a maze corridor and then scaling a wall. I gathered it was when I was going to attack Raynn and Doppelganger.

When my score was revealed, I smirked. I had done well. *Though there are some areas I can improve.*

> Gun-skill: 81%
> Teamwork: 89%
> Special-ability: multiple categories, 99%

Glancing over at Raynn's team score, I laughed. Ryoko's brow twisted but joined in my laughter soon after when she looked as well. "I didn't know you could have negative scoring!"

Neither of us could stop laughing at Raynn's displayed score.

> Gun-skill: 75%
> Special-ability: 20%
> Teamwork: -70%

What an impressive score, Raynn!

Normally, that would have looked bad for most teams, but it was expected for Raynn's main team. Most of them didn't know much about team loyalty, especially Raynn. The ones who did know had split from the main group and tried not to associate with the main part of the team as much as possible. I felt bad for that group, but it was hard to get the Council to allow transfers to other teams with the new living situations and jobs that had to usually be arranged.

"Hey, the battle partner scoring is being calculated," Aurora pointed out.

I gazed back up at the screen, although I wasn't all that interested in this part. In the past only Blaze and Argus ever made it on this board.

As I thought would happen, a video of Blaze and Argus fighting side by side was shown when the computer chose them as battle partners. I was taken by surprise however at what happened next.

The video clip vanished after it was done, and the next one shown was of Ryoko and Rylan. The two were shown on a split screen with them talking to each other while they fought at different ends of the battlefield. Although it hadn't surprised me that Rylan had watched Ryoko's back from his sniping locations, I was slightly taken aback by how often he had done it. He had to have done it quite a bit in order for the computer to pair them.

I glanced at Ryoko when I noticed her shift her weight. Her arms were crossed and a small smile was planted on her face, but her eyes gave away the turmoil inside her. Although she was happy they were paired together, it was her feelings for Rylan that made this match-up conflicting. Taking a quick glance at Rylan, I saw him glance at Ryoko from the corner of his eye. The look he gave showed he was feeling the same as her. I wanted to hit them both. It wasn't a secret to anyone on the team how they felt, but the two were just too oblivious and stubborn to see it themselves. *Oh well, not my place to tell them what to do.*

"Well, look at that," Seda mused. "Laz, you finally made it up there."

Ryoko let out a low whistle and nodded.

"What?" I snapped my attention back up to the scoreboard.

As Seda said, I was up there and so was Raikidan. Speechless wouldn't begin to describe how I felt.

A video was shown of when he carried me, and I hit him on the head, and then transitioned over to when we had our little argument after we had killed Nioush. That video clip transitioned again, to when I pushed him away from me after he had pinned me against the wall to protect me and then again to when we were crouched around the corner, waiting for Chameleon to turn away from us.

In my years of being a rebel, I had never been paired with a team-mate. But here I was on the board now with Raikidan, the rookie. I wasn't sure what to make of this.

Blaze snickered. "Raikidan better learn to stay on Eira's good side. She'll make his life a living hell if he doesn't."

"That happens to you every day and you're not her battle partner," Argus teased.

Blaze glared and shoved him. Argus smirked and shoved him back. I glanced quickly at Raikidan, who was growing confused from the hushed whispers in the crowd around us.

"Well, a congratulations is in order, I guess," I said to him.

Raikidan's brow rose. "Why is everyone making this out to be such a big deal?"

Ryoko placed her hands on her hips. "Cause no one has ever been paired with her. You don't know much about us yet, but Rylan was scientifically designed to be that person, and not even he's been paired to her."

"It's not a bad thing," Rylan added. "It's just surprising with how many of these simulations we've done."

Raikidan looked at me, but I turned and walked away before I took the chance to catch his expression. My mind was on other things. We'd run these simulations many times before I left, and I doubted they'd stopped after I'd gone on the run, either. Blaze and Argus were always paired up and that was that. Nothing ever changed. *Why was the outcome so easily changed this time?* And so drastically. What made Raikidan so special? None of this made any sense, and it was giving me a headache.

"Is Laz going to be okay?" Ryoko asked someone.

"She will be fine," Seda said. "She just needs time to think."

I headed for Aurora's computer station. She had a small fridge there, and if I was lucky, there'd be something for me to drink. I needed it. Unfortunately, Raynn came out of nowhere and stepped in front of me, blocking my path. I wasn't in the mood to deal with him. "What do you want?"

"You owe me an explanation of what your *friend* is," Raynn said.

"I owe you nothing."

Mocha snaked her arms around Raynn's neck and hung over him. "You owe all of us an explanation."

I glared as more of Raynn's team came to back him up. "Quit being sore losers and get out of my way."

The confrontation attracted attention, and my team ran over to back me up.

"No one has ever been chosen to be your battle partner by the computer, not even Rylan, and you want me to accept that this outsider can just waltz in and change all of this in one simulation?" Raynn spat on the ground. "Not happening. Now, what the hell is he?"

I didn't get a chance to respond. A figure jumped in front of me and slammed his fist into Raynn's face. Mocha screeched and jumped away.

My brow twisted. "Raikidan?"

Raikidan growled a little. "I told you if you had a problem with me to take it up with me, not her. Now back off!"

"Bastard." Raynn spit out some blood and wiped away the small trail that dripped down his mouth.

Mocha moved closer to Raikidan and hissed. Rylan pushed in front of me and let out a wolf-like growl in response.

Raynn spat more blood on the floor. "What's wrong, Eira? So weak you have to have your man-toys protect you?"

"You don't know what loyalty is," Rylan growled more. "You wouldn't understand."

I snickered. "Haven't you already had your ass handed to you enough by me today, Raynn?"

"I'm not afraid of you."

"That's not what your eyes told me before I smashed my fist through your face."

"I know what you're capable of."

"You don't even know the half of what I'm capable of." I wasn't going to let Raynn put in another word. With extreme speed and agility, I maneuvered around Raikidan and Rylan and nailed Raynn in the face with my knee. Without a moment's hesitation, I grabbed him by the back of his hair and smashed his face into the ground and then proceeded to throw him through an empty computer station.

Mocha hissed and lunged at me, but Rylan slammed his fist into her face. She stumbled back and growled at him. "I thought you didn't hit women."

He snickered. "You're right, I don't."

Raikidan chuckled and then punched another one of Raynn's teammates as he attempted to attack me.

"You didn't have to do that," I said. "I could have handled it."

He grinned at me. "I'm now labeled as your battle partner. I might as well live up to that."

I rolled my eyes and focused my attention back on Raynn, who was getting up with a groan. Broken electrical wires swung and sparked all around him, but he didn't pay them any mind. His focus was now on me.

"You're a fucking cunt, just like Amara," he spat.

Rage burned inside me. "Take that back."

He grinned. "Aww, did I hit a nerve? Good. She also got exactly what she deserved."

I lost it. No one insulted her, especially not like that. Before Raynn could react, I grabbed him by the back of his head and forced my knee into his face. Shortly after, I brought my free hand down on him. He was only able to stop me when he grabbed me by the throat. My grip on his hair loosened as his grip tightened, allowing him to stand up. I grabbed his arm and dug my sharp nails into his tough skin, causing him to bleed. Although I was slowly suffocating, I refused to show any weakness.

I fell to the ground when Raikidan slammed into Raynn and air rushed into my lungs. Raikidan pummeled Raynn in the face a few times before Raynn kicked him off. Raikidan stumbled but recovered quickly and stood in front of me as Raynn got up.

I stood and looked at Raikidan. "This is my fight."

He turned his head, gazing down at me. "No."

I could only stare at him because of the strange look he had. It wasn't one of a man, not entirely at least. It was much different than what an ordinary man would give when protecting someone. *Dragons protect...* I sighed inwardly. How could I forget so easily he was a dragon?

The look also made me feel a bit strange.

"We protect them..."

I shook that idea out of my head, as well as the sensation pricking at me. Dragons protected other dragons, not humans. It was something else. It had to be.

"I won't let him touch you again," Raikidan stated before looking back at Raynn.

I stared at him and that feeling threatened to come back. I didn't know what to think now. I was so confused. Today was just one upside-down day.

"How sweet." Raynn chuckled. "Too bad I'm going to have to cut your lovefest short."

Raikidan went to say something, but the creaking of the entrance doors stopped him—except it wasn't just him. Everyone in the room turned their attention to those doors. My heart stopped. Standing in the entrance of the doors were five helmetless soldiers.

"Well, well, well, look at what we have here," one of them stated as he held his gun at the ready.

My mind was abuzz. What were they doing here? How did they find this place? What were they doing in the sewers in the first place? They couldn't be allowed to expose this place, so I said the first thing that came to mind. "Kill them."

20
CHAPTER

Rylan instantly reacted to Laz's order, shifting to his wolf form and going in for the kill. His first victim suffered a ripped-out throat. Not to be outdone, Raikidan shifted into a wolf as well and took out another soldier in the same bloody fashion. I also wanted to jump in, but I needed the right target. My brute strength wouldn't be good against another Brute if we wanted this done quickly.

Laz ran in, targeting a cowardly soldier attempting to run. That left me with two choices, but as I locked onto them, one stuck out to me. *Him.* I rushed in and tackled him, pulling him into a tight headlock. He struggled but wasn't a match for me. His comrade aimed a gun at me, but Rylan and Raikidan teamed up and took him out.

"Ryoko," Laz called out. "I want that one alive."

Knowing why, I grinned down at my captive. "You're going to wish she had me kill you."

Fear flashed in the man's eyes, and he struggled more as I began dragging him to our interrogation room, but my hold on him was too good.

"Are things always this exciting here?" Raikidan asked. I looked back to see him back in human form.

Laz held up her hands. "It's just another day in paradise."

I couldn't help but laugh. I missed her sense of humor. I'd missed it so much and was glad she'd returned. She hadn't told me yet what convinced her to come back, not after the reason she'd ran in the first place, but I was sure the truth would come out soon enough.

"Raynn, quit daydreaming and move your ass! We have work to do," Laz called out.

"Don't tell me what to do, wench." Him calling her that raised the hairs on the back of my neck. I hated him so much.

"Fine, I guess I'll have all the fun."

"The hell you will!"

He ran after her, and I didn't understand. How could she put aside everything and work with him like that? After everything he'd done, and after everything he'd just said to her before all this went down?

The soldier struggled in my arms, bringing me back to my task at hand. I smiled at him. "I like things a little rough. I hope you do, too."

His facial reaction told me he wasn't sure if he should be intrigued or afraid. I loved doing that. It made things... exciting.

I dragged him into a room with a single light and a chair. A rebel stood waiting with rope in his hands. I looked down at the soldier again, a grin on my lips. "I get excited when rope is involved. Do try to make this fun for me and beg."

I shoved him down in the chair and the other rebel tied him up.

My compatriot and I opened the door to the interrogation room and exited, leaving our half-conscious victim tied up and alone. Laz leaned against a wall nearby and Raynn did the same to an adjacent wall.

She laid her eyes on me and I shook my head. "Not a word."

Raynn grinned. "Well that's good. Means we still get our fun."

Laz tapped her fingers on her arm. "We'll see. He may be close to cracking, based on the blood on Ryoko's hands."

I glanced down at my hands and nodded. I'd been pretty rough with him, but nothing that would cause him death. Of course, there was only so much a person could take before they broke. "We'll wait in the observation room, just in case you need us."

She nodded and the four of us split. The other rebel shut the door behind us and took a seat on one of the chairs in the observation room. I chose to stand, watching Laz take in the scene before her. Raynn circled the man, commenting about his state. Unsure if the soldier was alive, he leaned in for a closer look. I chuckled when the soldier spat in his face and muttered a few curses. He had spirit.

Raynn punched the man and Laz shook her head. She walked behind him, asking for his name. She received no response. *Same for me, Laz. Try something else.* She asked again, and he still kept his mouth shut. Raynn punched him again, but that didn't work either. *Dingbat, I tried that!*

Laz rested her folded arms on the soldier's shoulders and leaned close. Her usual neutral expression changed to a rather alluring one. She murmured in his ear, low enough the microphones weren't able to pick it up. The man glanced at her, his eyes wide. *What did she say to him?* I wanted to know so bad.

A smirk spread across her lips and she continued to speak to him in her low tone.

"A–Aiden," the man stammered. "My… my n–name… is Aiden."

My posture straightened. She'd done it. She got him to talk.

Laz's smirk remained as she pulled away, making sure her arms dragged across his form. "See, wasn't that easy, Aiden?"

She circled him, each step slow and deliberate, and her hands always coming in contact with his shoulders or back. *Oh damn, Laz, you're really laying it on.* She always tried to claim she sucked at this tactic—that she didn't understand seduction. But she used it so well. I didn't understand how she couldn't see that. *She probably thinks she looks stupid or something.* She had always been hyper critical of herself.

Laz went to asking him more questions, but Aiden's lips remained shut. Raynn came up and hit him again, demanding Laz's questions be answered. Laz shook her head and kept up her tactic. Looked like this was going to be a case of "good rebel, bad rebel" with a sexy twist.

"You ladies don't play fair sometimes," the rebel in the room said.

I glanced back at him. He still sat in his chair, but looked my way instead of the interrogation. He'd quite enjoyed watching me beat the snot out of the soldier, as well as some of the comments I made when he wouldn't talk.

I winked at him. "Sometimes you just gotta do whatcha gotta do."

He chuckled and then went back to watching Laz and Raynn work. Neither were getting anywhere with this guy, though I doubt Raynn's tactic was helping her much. *He's such an idiot.*

I could see Laz growing bored of this, and it wasn't long before she drew a dagger and angled the sharp blade toward his groin. *Oh, Laz, that is really dirty!* I loved it.

Aiden swallowed hard and bared his teeth at her. "Fuck you, Eira. Don't you dare start making those kinds of threats to me. I've proven I'm no talker!"

Laz smiled and pulled away her weapon. "You're the one who chose to be a mole. You know those risks."

I relaxed, pulling away from the one-way window. The jig was up, and that meant our fun was over. *Dang.* I liked picking on our moles. Every now and then, we had to take such desperate measures with them to ensure they weren't leaking information under pressure, and that meant I could use my fists. If I was picked for the job, of course.

"That doesn't mean you have to force them on me!" Aiden struggled against his restraints. "Shit, that's stupid to deal with. Ryoko hits hard, but you... shit, you play dirty."

Her brow rose and she went about untying him. "If you thought I was playing dirty, you don't want to meet those who are better at that tactic than me."

"Yeah, sure."

Right, that's what I'm saying! The other rebel and I left the observation room. He chose to go on his way as he wasn't needed anymore to keep up appearances, though he did look back at me for a moment when he got down the hall. *I wonder what that was about...*

Raynn exited the interrogation room first and just left, not even passing me a glance. *Good, I didn't want to deal with you either.* I stuck my tongue out at his back.

Laz and Aiden came out next, Laz supporting him. *I guess I overdid it.*

Aiden smirked when he spotted me. "Hey, Ryoko."

"Hey, Aiden. I'd say sorry for being so rough"—I winked at him—"But I'm pretty sure you're okay with it."

His cheeks reddened while he tried to laugh it off. "Well, it could have been a little less painful."

I gave Laz a hand with holding him up and smirked. "I'll have to keep that in mind for the next time we play."

His face reddened more, and Laz rolled her eyes. Conversation ended, and the three of us made it back to the main congregating area of the Underground. We rejoined the others, Rylan took Aiden from Laz, working with me to get our mole seated to rest. Raikidan watched the exchange from where he sat. His eyes narrowed as they focused on Aiden.

"Did no one tell Raikidan what's up?" I asked.

"No, we did," Rylan said. "He just doesn't believe us."

Aiden looked at Raikidan. "So, you're the newbie. Should have guessed since you're a shifter."

Since when did the moles know that?

"Yes, I put the word out of Raikidan's arrival, as well as his abilities." Eyes fell on Genesis when she approached, two bottles of water in her small hand. "It's protocol."

She handed one to Aiden and the other to me. Aiden didn't hesitate to chug down his drink before looking at Raikidan again. "Look, I get you're suspicious, but you have nothing to worry about. I'm one hundred percent loyal to the cause." He threw his thumb in the direction of the door leading to the sewers. "Those guys I was with, I'm okay with them dead. They were assholes, but they also had no desire to disobey Zarda, and most of them were pretty old experiments, so nothing was going to change with them."

Raikidan's posture didn't change. Words weren't going to work with him, and I could understand. Moles were risky, both in the sense of the line of work and loyalty. But this showed how committed Raikidan was to helping us—at least to me.

Laz sat down next to Aiden. "So, anything to report since you're here?"

He shook his head and took another gulp of water. "Not really. More and more experiments coming out these days, each being stronger and stranger than the last, but that's per the usual these days. Zarda himself has been quiet lately. We don't get orders from him directly anymore, and he never brings any of the commanding officers into his quarters for status reports."

Laz's brow furrowed. "Strange. Have the others keep an eye out for that. I don't like the sound of it."

"It sounds like the times when he gets ready for an execution," Rylan said.

I nodded in agreement. "I agree."

Laz stroked her chin. "Maybe."

What is she so suspicious about? Rylan's conclusion was solid and logical. She was always over analyzing what Zarda did. I didn't get it.

Aurora leaned on Rylan. "Hey, how about you guys go play something for everyone? The soldiers' appearance killed the mood, and I'd like to see it liven up a bit more."

Rylan, Argus, and Blaze exchanged glances and shrugged. "Why not."

Argus looked to Laz. "You in? It'd be nice to have you play with us again."

Her lip twisted to one side. "I haven't touched a guitar in years. I don't think that's a good idea."

"It's like riding a bike," Rylan said. "You'll be fine."

I pressed my lips together, so I wouldn't make a comment. Laz didn't know how to ride a bicycle.

Laz shook her head and stood. "Fine."

That surprised me. I didn't expect her to give in like that. She didn't like being the center of attention. *I guess maybe it's because—*

Blaze, cocky as he was, shifted his weight to one side with his arms bent over his shoulders. "I think she should sing a few songs."

Rylan's eyes lit up. *Oh boy, here it comes.* "That's a great idea."

Laz's eyes darkened and she sat back down. "No."

Yep, knew it. No one could get her to sing in front of others. Not even in private around those she trusted.

"C'mon, Laz, just one or two songs," Rylan said.

Laz crossed her arms. "No. I don't sing."

Raikidan leaned back, a smirk on his lips. "You sang for me."

My brow rose. *What?*

Laz nailed him in the arm with her fist. "I did not, you lying, eavesdropping jackass."

I sputtered out a laugh. "Someone's touchy about that."

"Shut up," she muttered.

Argus waved her to go with them. "Sing, don't sing, its fine. I just need someone with actual guitar skills to play with me. Even years out of practice, it's better than what I've had to work with."

Rylan glared at him. "Hey!"

Laz chuckled. "Well, with that reasoning, how can I refuse?"

The four of them walked off and I swooped in to where Laz had originally sat. Aiden limped off, following Genesis somewhere. *Probably to talk business.*

The boys set up while Laz re-familiarized herself with the guitar. Even though with her not hooked up to the amp she sat on, and with the loud chatter in the room deafening the sounds as she strummed the strings, I could see by her expression that Rylan had been right. She had to remember a few things, but as she played, it all came back to her.

I glanced at Raikidan to find him watching the setup, his eyes focused and unwavering. The intensity was a bit unsettling. *He's so... odd.* Handsome, but odd.

Raikidan leaned on his knees when Laz and the boys started playing. Just an instrumental warm-up, but it caught the attention of everyone in the room, if their setup hadn't. People gathered as the warm-up quickened and then turned into an aggressive heart-racing song. Rylan and Argus belted out the lyrics and I nodded my head along with the beat. Even though my sensitive ears weren't keen on the volume, the experiments down here sure loved it. They added to the energy of the song.

The longer the group played, the more visibly relaxed I noticed Laz became. She lost herself in the music, lowering her guard. Music had always soothed her. I wished it wasn't required for her to let loose more often, but her life experiences had left her rougher than she deserved. *I doubt her time on the run helped in the least, either.*

I glanced over to Raikidan to find him still as focused as before. It wasn't like he was even trying to feel the music like the rest of us would. *Has he never heard music before?* Maybe it was because this music wasn't something you'd find often outside a city. *Or maybe...* His relentless focus had to have something to with it. Nothing would distract him.

Following his gaze, I triangulated his point of interest at Laz. *That might explain it.* Did her actions fascinate him? Maybe just her standoffish nature made him want to understand her, crack the impenetrable shield around her to be one of the few to see the real her within. Or maybe he was infatuated with her. I didn't know how long the two had known each other. He did like to push her personal space, from what I could tell. I saw it while they were in the simulation, and she didn't freak out on him like she would someone else. It irritated her, sure, but she tolerated it, when she would have chewed out someone else, or beaten them.

Raikidan also seemed to be on rather friendly terms with her, able to make jokes, with her being somewhat okay with it. It took a long time to build up that kind of relationship with Laz, otherwise you had to deal with her aggressive, standoffish, and downright antisocial nature. Laz said there was nothing between them, but that didn't exactly mean she told the truth.

Maybe I should talk to him. See if I can get anything out of him. He wasn't the talkative type from what I could tell, unless he was pestering Laz, but maybe I could get him to open up. *Worth a shot.*

I leaned over to him. "What do you think of the music? Looks like you've never heard this style before."

"You're right, I haven't." He didn't take his focus off Laz. "It's interesting. Not sure what I think of it yet."

"What kind of music do you have where you come from?" I asked.

"I didn't. I lived alone."

"Oh…" Not what I was expecting for an answer. Maybe that explained a bit how the two met. Explained why he didn't talk much at least.

"How come you weren't asked to join them, Ryoko?"

The fact he specifically used my name got me to look at him, only to find him focused on me now. The intensity overpowered me. *Geez, why so intense?* "I'm not all that musically inclined. I'm not terrible at singing, mind you, but I couldn't play an instrument to save my life, so I wouldn't be caught dead up there."

"Is it a preference to not be… musically inclined?"

"Well, sorta…" *How to explain it so a non-experiment would understand…* I suddenly realized this was what Laz had to deal with since she met him. *Gods, that must have sucked for her.* "Everyone, born or made, has talents they can cultivate as a hobby or lifestyle, like music or art. But where those born usually have the choice to do so or not, we experiments don't. We're told if we are allowed to work on those talents or not, and that order comes into play on whether or not it'll assist us on our assignments."

I thought about how to word this next part. "Footsoldiers have the most lenience on these skills, and music is highly encouraged, so the boys cultivated that skill. Rylan is the only one of them who would love to make it his life-time commitment, but the other two enjoy it. Argus, when he's not playing music, is always using that smart brain of his to invent things."

"People like Laz, those who have to blend into different situations, were forced to learn multiple skills. So, in her case, she can play a few instruments, she could sing if she wanted to, and she's also a skilled craftsman, though it's rare she shows those talents off."

I wrung my hands together. "Me on the other hand, I was only allowed to focus on being a Brute, so any possible skill I could have had really wasn't worked on early enough. I did find a passion in fixing cars after meeting Zane, so there's that, I guess."

"I may not know much about your technologies, but from what I do understand, that's a handy skill to have." He looked back up at the group playing, their song changing to another one. "Can I ask you something about Eira?"

A smile tilted my lips. This might get interesting. "Sure."

"Why doesn't she want to sing?" Raikidan focused on me again. "I made my joke because it was a good time to do so, but I didn't realize there was a reason I'd caught her singing alone."

"Let me guess, you also think she's got a beautiful singing voice."

He nodded.

"I'm not sure how to answer your question, because it's not really clear to me either. She just tells everyone she doesn't like singing in front of others. I don't know if it's because she doesn't think she's all that good, or if it's a private thing for her."

He nodded and went back to listening.

When the song changed, my heart sank a little. I knew this song very well and had hoped they wouldn't play it. It was... sobering.

"Is this about Eira?" Raikidan asked.

"No, but you're not the first to think it might be." I frowned. "Argus wrote this song, not Rylan. It's one of the only songs Argus has written."

Raikidan glanced at me. "Someone hurt him?"

I nodded. "After being let out of the military, he settled into a normal life and in the process gave his heart to some woman who returned the favor by crushing it. He's only recently started to really get over it and move on in these past few years."

Raikidan looked down at the ground and stayed quiet.

"Good riddance, I say." I jumped as Genesis popped up between us. "Don't do that!" I hissed.

"Sorry." Genesis leaned against the bench Raikidan and I sat on. "But I am glad she's gone."

"Of course you are. You hated her from the start."

Genesis gave a curt nod. "And it's a good thing I did. She was a witch! She didn't deserve him, and he could have done so much better. If he had listened to Blaze and me, it could have all been avoided."

Raikidan shook his head.

Genesis crossed her arms. "What?"

He glanced my way. "I still can't believe you listen to a child."

Genesis' face reddened. "I am not a child!"

"You look like one," Raikidan said. "And you act it enough."

I half smiled. "He's got a point."

Genesis huffed and then stuck her bottom lip out into a pout. *She's so cute when she's mad.*

After her pouting, she looked at Raikidan. "What are your intentions toward Eira?"

His brow furrowed. "What do you mean? I'm not here to hurt her, if that's what you think."

Her lips twisted, as did her brow. "No... um... how should I put this... Where do your feelings stand with her?"

"Genesis," I hissed. "Don't be asking those kinds of questions here."

She placed her hands on her hips. "I could have been less tactful and asked if he was sleeping with her."

I smacked my forehead and groaned. This was embarrassing. "Just leave."

"Fine. I just wanted to know, since he's been the only one to be chosen as her battle partner, and he seemed to know when she needed help—more so than everyone else. I didn't want him hurting her if that was the case." Grudgingly, she walked back over to Aiden and Seda.

My face flushed hot. "Sorry about that."

He chuckled. "To be honest, I figured it would be you to ask me about that."

I looked at the ground. "Laz told me you heard what we talked about in my room. Sorry about that. I kinda went overboard a little. When I saw you with her and her actions toward you, I thought maybe she had finally let someone in and was able to be happy again. Sorry if that upset you."

"Sorry to disappoint you, but I don't even know her enough to call her a friend, let alone something more than that. A comrade is the closest thing I could call her, just as she calls me."

I pursed my lips. "If she really calls you that, then you should rethink that friend part." His brow twisted and waited for me to continue. "I don't know what's so special about you, but she treats you differently. I really do mean that. The way she acts around you doesn't go unnoticed, especially by me. She trusts you in a way she doesn't trust anyone else.

"You said she called you a comrade. That usually takes her some time to do. To her, a comrade is better than a friend. They're more trustworthy in her eyes."

I held his gaze. "Just don't take it all for granted. I've also seen how you like to push her boundaries, and I can't bear to see her get hurt more than she already has been."

Raikidan smiled at me. "You're loyal to her."

"She's my best friend, and I'll kill anyone who tries to take her from me." I frowned and glanced at the ground. "We're the reason you two met. When Rylan, Laz, and I escaped, Zarda put a lot of effort into finding us. He was mostly after Laz, but he wanted us all if he could."

I drummed my fingers on my knee. "This put too much pressure on the rebellion, so Laz made a plan to draw Zarda's attention away, knowing it meant she'd never see us again. We didn't want her to go through with it, but we couldn't find another way. She set out on her plan without a moment of hesitation."

"She's loyal to all of you," Raikidan said. "Nothing would have stopped her from doing what she thought would be for the betterment of you. And I can't blame her. The reason I live alone is because I could never find such loyalties in others. You're all very lucky."

I smiled. "We're all we have. We stick together no matter what."

Raikidan's lips spread into a thin line. "You should know, when I found her, she was almost dead."

I licked my lips, my heart stopping for a moment. "That explains why she avoided my question when I asked how the two of you met." I hid my face in my hands for a moment. "Her dying out there alone was my biggest fear all this time." I looked at him, making sure our eyes met. "Thank you for saving her."

He reached out and held my hand. "You're welcome." He let go and went back to watching Laz. "Tell me, what was up with Eira during that simulation? When she killed Raynn and went after Nioush?"

I bit my lip. "Well, it has to do with her experiment design."

"She told me she was designed to be without emotions, but that failed."

I nodded. "Yes, that's true, but there's more to it. Along with the lack of emotions, she was to take orders without question, like the rest of us. She was also supposed to want to obey these orders—to kill without mercy or regret and revel in it." My hands clutched. "Extended fighting or exposure to blood causes the programming to surface. She does her best to keep it at bay, but sometimes that doesn't work. Or in the case of the simulation, she let go of that control to gain the upper hand."

"I don't see why she couldn't just tell me that," Raikidan said.

"It's a sensitive subject…" I shook my head, rubbing my arm. "It's best to be careful when talking to experiments about their creation. We… don't handle those conversations well sometimes."

"I'm sorry; I didn't mean to upset you."

I smiled. "You're fine, don't worry."

He didn't need to apologize. He wouldn't have known.

Laz and the boys finished their song and packed up. This confused me. I would have thought they'd play a few more songs. When Laz ran off before they'd finished, I realized something must be up.

Following her with my gaze, Laz ran over to Genesis and Seda, speaking with them. *Maybe an assignment came up?* The three spoke, and Laz nodded before looking Raikidan's and my way, waving us over. The two of us stood and approached just as Aiden joined them as well.

"Bodies are all taken care of," he said.

"What's going on?" I asked.

Aiden rubbed the back of his neck. "Well, I have to head out. My little search party now has a search party of its own."

"And I have an assignment for Eira and Raikidan," Genesis said. "Something simple to ease him in, but an important one to be handled before the night is over."

The boys approached, and Rylan spoke. "Aiden, do you need help? I'm sure we could come up with something."

Blaze held his hands out to me and Genesis. "Yeah, I mean, we have Ryoko and Genesis to play mom and child when we need it."

I crossed my arms. "Yeah, how about no. I'd prefer to play single mom as little as possible, thanks."

Laz grinned at me. "I can think of a few nice men to play daddy for a hot single mom. All you have to do is ask *nicely*."

My face scrunched, and I swiped at her, knowing exactly what she was implying. She laughed as she jumped out of the way.

"I'll be fine, really," Aiden insisted. "I had the bodies of the fallen moved to a new place and I've got a good alibi worked up. I'll limp back to the nearest outpost and say we were ambushed and only I made it out. Not too hard to get them to believe that."

Rylan crossed his arms. "If that's what you want."

Aiden said goodbye, promising Genesis an updated report in a week or two, and headed off. Laz and Raikidan weren't too far behind. Seda advised we head home in pairs, as there were soldiers wandering the sewers looking for suspicious signs.

Genesis paired me with Rylan and sent us out first. The two of us didn't speak until halfway home, when Rylan broke the silence. "So, what were you and Raikidan talking about?"

I tilted my head to find him not looking at me. "I noticed he grabbed your hand while the two of you were talking."

He noticed that? Why? "Jealous or something?"

He snorted. "No, of course not." *See, Laz, nothing for me here with him.* "I just thought it would be strange for him to do so unless it was a rather personal conversation."

"So, I'm not allowed to have personal conversations with people?"

He sighed. "I'm not saying that."

I noticed the tightness in his shoulders. *I'm irritating him.* I focused my eyes forward, not wanting to cause the two of us issues. "I was just talking to him about how he and Laz met, that's all."

"That's it?"

I didn't let myself physically react to the question. I wasn't sure why, but it sounded off to me. "Yeah. From what he said, he saved her life."

"Hearing that upset you, didn't it?"

I nodded. "We're the reason she was on the run all these years..."

He reached out and grabbed my hand, surprising me. Our eyes met. "Don't go there, please. No one but Zarda is to blame for this."

I tried to smile, to reassure him and myself that he was right, but ended up looking away from him. I still felt a bit responsible.

Rylan let go of my hand, and a part of me didn't like that. I wanted that close connection with him. *But he doesn't want me... He would have said something to me by now if he did.*

"What do you think of him?" he asked. "Blaze, Argus, and I weren't able to get much out of him."

"He's a loner, like Laz, so not much for talking," I said. "He only engaged in certain topics. What I got from my conversation wasn't bad. Laz seems to trust him more than I thought she did, and he seems to like her, to some unknown extent."

"What makes you say that?"

I grinned. "The topics that engaged him the most were about her."

Rylan's eyes narrowed. "You're going to try and push those two together, aren't you?"

I held my hands behind my back, a thin smile spreading across my lips. "Maybe. Not sure yet. Depends on how they continue to act around each other."

"Meaning you are." He shook his head. "You need to leave her alone about those things. Let her make connections on her own."

I gave him a sidelong glance. "This is Laz. She doesn't know a good thing when it smacks her across the face. Or in this case, swoops in and saves her. The two of them have chemistry, and I'd be damned if I allowed her to let it slip away."

He shook his head again but didn't argue anymore. Either he wasn't happy I was trying to pair Laz with Raikidan, or he didn't like my meddling. Either way, I wasn't going to let him get between me and what I wanted. Laz's happiness was paramount, especially after everything she'd gone through for us.

Now... how to get this to work...

21
CHAPTER
(EIRA)

He looked up at me with a smile. "My name is Xye."
A heavy fog clung to my mind as I roused from my slumber. I squeezed my eyes tighter in hopes of blocking out the early morning sun. Sadly, that didn't help. I sighed as I slowly opened my eyes.

I screamed and pushed myself away from where I lay. Unfortunately, I didn't realize how close I was to the edge of my bed and fell off with a *thud*. I rubbed my rear. "Ow."

Raikidan chuckled and moved to the edge of the bed. "Did I scare you?"

I glared at him. "What the hell are you doing on my bed? Better yet, why were you laying next to me?"

He chuckled again. "Watching you sleep."

Unsettling wouldn't begin to describe this situation. "You creep! Why the hell would you do that?"

He shrugged. "You do strange things in your sleep."

I pinched the bridge of my nose, my anger rising. "Get off my bed."

Raikidan rested his hands in his lap. "No, it's comfortable."

Growling and getting up, I yanked on his ear. "Off my bed! And don't ever lie next to me again."

He grunted and grabbed my wrist. "Hurting others doesn't get you what you want."

"Wanna bet?"

He squeezed my wrist, forcing me to let go, and grinned. "You mumble in your sleep."

I pursed my lips. I hated it when he changed the subject. "Your point?"

He shrugged. "I figured you'd be curious about what you said."

I ripped my arm out of his grasp. "No."

"How do you know you didn't say something you didn't want me to hear?" he inquired.

"I highly doubt I said much." I turned away and headed to my closet.

"You spoke Xye's name a few times."

I briefly stopped filing through the clothes that hung on the hangers and then continued what I was doing. "What's your point?"

"I thought you two were only friends."

"We were."

"Then why are you dreaming about him?"

I sighed and stopped rummaging. "The degree of my friendship with him is irrelevant to dreams. They cannot be controlled—a mere link to our subconscious and memories. Xye is part of a memory. He will haunt me in both the waking realm and in the dreaming one."

"You make it sound like dreaming is a bad thing."

I pulled out my shaman outfit and stared at it. "I don't dream. I relive my past. And as hard as it may be to believe, there isn't much good to remember."

To my pleasure, Raikidan went quiet. I didn't like being questioned, especially this early in the morning, and he seemed to enjoy asking questions regardless of what I liked.

"Why do you sleep on top of your blankets?" he finally asked. "I thought the purpose of them was to sleep under them to keep you warm."

Pulling out his Guard clothes, I walked over to him. "Why do you want to know that?"

He shrugged. "I'm just curious." He glanced at the clothes when I handed them to him, and then back at me. "What's this for?"

"We're going out into the city after breakfast," I said. "I want to get an idea of how shamans are treated in the city. It'll be a good way to also do some surveillance."

He raised his eyebrow but took the clothes anyway. "Why not use these special clothes we're wearing?"

"Because this is better. Don't question me on it."

"Okay, fine. But back to the blanket thing."

I sighed. "Do you really need to know?"

"No, but I want to."

I shook my head and walked away from the bed. "I don't like being covered. Happy?"

"Why?" Raikidan asked. "I thought humans found comfort in that."

"I don't like being confined… Why do you care, anyway? It doesn't affect you in any way."

"I just feel like I should know more about you than I do at this point," he muttered. "Why do you have such an issue with that?"

"Two reasons. What's the point when you'll be out of here when this is all done, and we'll be out of your mind for good? Secondly, I'm not important enough to talk about. There is nothing about me that is interesting or worth conversation. Now if you don't mind, leave my room so I can get dressed."

"But—"

"Get out!"

He stood and walked over to me. "No wonder you don't have any friends."

I said nothing, and he walked to the door. Just as he grabbed the knob, he stopped and stayed silent for a moment before quietly speaking. "I'm sorry. That was wrong of me to say."

I shrugged. "Why apologize for the truth?"

Raikidan turned and looked at me. "You do have friends. They live in the same building as you."

"And those few are all I have. Nothing worth writing home about." I walked over to my bed and laid out my clothes. "Now please, just leave my room. You can dress yourself on your own."

He left, leaving me alone, not that it bothered me. I dressed slowly, grumbling to myself about how much I hated these clothes, and then went about doing my hair. Once done, I fastened my cloak tightly around my neck and left my room. I walked into the kitchen and searched for something light to eat. I settled for an apple from a basket of fruit and turned around, stopping dead when I almost bumped into Raikidan. I let out a slow breath. "Do you really have to do that?"

He chuckled. "You're the one in the way."

I rolled my eyes and went to move, but he also moved in the same direction. Narrowing my eyes, I moved back and Raikidan did the same. "Will you stop that?"

Raikidan grinned. "Stop moving in the same direction as me."

I didn't feel like playing his games and gestured for him to move. He complied—a cocky grin firmly planted on his lips—and grabbed an apple from the fruit bowl.

Biting into my breakfast, I looked over to Rylan, who sat on the couch reading. "We'll be back later."

"Don't get into too much trouble," he said, not looking up. "I don't want to be the one who has to break it to Ryoko why you're in prison and waiting to be executed."

I chuckled, heading for the basement door. "Can't guarantee any-thing."

Rylan chuckled and left it at that.

Opening the door, I looked back at Raikidan, who was still standing in the doorway of the kitchen. "You coming or what?"

Raikidan snickered. "You're pushy today."

"Get used to it," I said, heading down the stairs. "You put me in a bad mood."

He closed the door behind him. "And here I thought you were always in a foul mood."

Narrowing my eyes, I turned midstep and smacked his hard abs with the back of my half-clenched fist. My hand bounced right off, but his grunt told me he felt it enough.

He rubbed his stomach. "You should learn to be less violent. You might have better luck making friends."

I headed to the hidden door. "And you should learn how to stay quiet."

My body tensed as Raikidan snaked his arm around my waist and pulled me closer to him. He chuckled quietly in my ear. "Why would I stay quiet when it's so much fun to annoy you?"

I tried to struggle away. "Raikidan, let me go!"

His grip tightened as I struggled. Turning my face to him, I locked my eyes with his. His brow furrowed as if he was concerned, and he let go.

Stumbling forward, I caught myself and fixed my clothes. "Don't do that again, got it?"

"Yeah," he replied quietly.

I pounded the bottom of my fist on the hidden door when I approached it. The door slid open in response, and without waiting for Raikidan to follow, I headed down the passage quickly. Neither of us spoke as we walked. I didn't mind. I'd rather not have him with me after the stunt he had pulled, but unfortunately, I was stuck with him if I was to be dressed like this.

Taking a sharp turn down another narrow passage, we came to what appeared to be a dead end. I pounded the wall like I did with the hidden door at the house. The wall let out a small crunching noise and slid to the side, revealing the basement of a new building. Once Raikidan and I came through, the door closed behind us and I led the way upstairs.

Opening the door, I peered around carefully. The house should be empty aside from some furniture, but I wanted to make sure. This was a safe house, after all. Assuring myself we were alone, I headed for the front door, snatching up a key on an end table as I passed. I pulled my hood over my head to conceal my identity, and glanced back at Raikidan to make sure he did the same. Faces now obscured, we left, and I locked the place up, tucking the key away for later use. I led the way down the quiet street.

"Where are we going?" Raikidan asked as we walked.

I knew the silence couldn't last forever. "I'm going to bring you to the center of the city. It's an active area because of the park. Shamans are frequently seen there, so our presence won't be suspicious. Then we'll make our way to the Temple, playing up our disguise, as shamans also frequent the building. After that, we'll return home. Are you good with that plan?"

"Yeah, that's fine."

My eyes narrowed. *That was too complacent of a response for him.* I didn't like it, especially after how he was acting earlier. I made a note to keep an eye on him and we continued on.

I led Raikidan through a few quiet streets and several busy ones, pointing out important landmarks when no one was able to eavesdrop on us easily. Raikidan took in the information but rarely spoke. Reaching the end of the street we were on, I looked for any moving vehicles on the cross street before heading across. Stepping off the concrete street path, I led Raikidan down a brick path that led into the urban park. The surrounding tree line wasn't thick, and it thinned out more as we walked. I watched Raikidan look around with interest.

"What do you think?"

He continued to look around. "It's nice. Not a dense forest like I thought when you mentioned it before, but I like it." He looked down at the stone path we walked on. "Why is this here? Why not dirt?"

"Due to the weather here, and use by so many people, it's easier to maintain the walking paths if they're stone or paved."

He nodded and took in the scenery. "I see many people in the grass. That's okay to do?"

"Yes. You're allowed to go anywhere you wish in the park."

"How big is it?"

"That's a good question…" I thought about this. "Maybe one and a half square miles? Might be a bit bigger than that."

"That's bigger than I thought it'd be." He pursed his lips. "How big is Dalatrend exactly?"

I tapped my lips with a finger. "Um… around three hundred square miles last I knew, but Zane said the city grew in size. Not a city you could walk through in a single day, hence the great use of vehicle transportation."

"I didn't realize you came from such a big place."

The two of us came to a bridge arching over a man-made river. Not far off was the lake it fed from. I leaned on the stone railing. "I much prefer the smaller, quieter towns."

Raikidan copied my posture. "So, when everything is settled, you plan to leave for good?"

I nodded. "That's the plan. We'll see how well that pans out."

"You don't sound optimistic."

I refrained from making a comment, instead choosing to watch some ducks paddle under the stone structure we stood on. There were some things I knew that made me less than optimistic about my future that he didn't need to know about.

"If you did leave, where would you go?"

I thought about it for a moment. "Not sure. Can't go back to the West Tribe. I guess it doesn't really matter where I end up since I'd be on my own."

"Do you like being alone?"

"Do you?"

He was silent for a moment. "No."

I grunted. "Well, there's something that makes us different."

He looked at me. "Why do you like being alone so much?"

I pushed myself away from the rail and walked toward a large fountain a little ways off. "No one can hurt you when you're alone."

"Thought you said you were the one who hurt others?"

"I do. They hurt me, and I hurt them. Being alone prevents that."

"I don't see how you've hurt others."

I sighed. "It's what monsters do. We don't know how to help. We only know how to hurt."

Raikidan gripped my shoulder. "You're not—"

I shrugged off his hand. "Don't say it, Raikidan. You don't know me—who I used to be. It took me a long time and a lot of work to be the way I am now. You saw last night how easy it is for me to revert. And what you saw, it was only the beginning. For now, all I can do is try my best to keep it chained, and hope a complete relapse won't happen until people are no longer around to be in its path."

Silence fell between us, but inside I was anything but silent. Patchy half-emotions raged within me, each pulsing at different rates and strengths. I hated it. The constant ups and downs I experienced with no way of understanding how to process it all… I wished I could feel properly, like everyone else, or not feel at all. *The latter, preferably…*

The two of us walked quite a ways, the gaps in foliage above us scattering speckles of light all along the ground. When we rounded a corner, the path widened, and before us stood a large stone fountain, the center of it a work of art depicting six people: two human men, an elven man, a dwarven man, and two women—one human, the other also appearing human, though her ears resembled that of a dog's, much like Ryoko's. Choreographed jets of water sprouted up from the base of the fountain every few moments and children screeched and played with the water, their parents or guardians supervising.

"What's that?" Raikidan asked.

"It's a water fountain." When he showed he didn't understand, I thought about how to explain it better. "It's a type of structure that pours water into a basin, pulling the water from the basin it pours into; or jets water into the air from the basin reservoir. Many, like this one, are ornately decorated to enhance the area around it."

"Is that the Six Peacekeepers in the middle of it?"

I nodded. "This fountain is a memorial for what they did for everyone during the War of End."

"My mother would tell me stories of them from time to time. Would you be willing to share a human one? I'd like to see if they're the same."

I pursed my lips. I had never thought a story about these iconic figures could ever be different. But it did make me curious. I nodded and found a bench to sit down on, away from the clusters of people, to keep our conversation a bit more private.

"Long ago, the races of the land lived in peace. They traded, mingled, and life was generally considered good. This peace lasted many millennia. But it wasn't meant to last forever. Greed and spite spread through their hearts and war broke out. Humans fought the elves. Dwarves fought the wogrons. They even fought among themselves. The only ones to refrain from this fighting were the gypsies, shamans, and druids, and even they struggled when the war reached its peak. It lasted so long, and so many lives were claimed, it was called the *War of End.*

"Then, when all thought life would be lost to the chaos, six individuals came together and found a way to end the bloodshed. There was Varro, an elven man who was druid-born and shaman-trained. There was the dwarven man, Assar, and the human man, Raynn. The woman with the doglike ears is the wogron-human hybrid, Ryoko. Lastly, there are the two who had gotten everyone together, Reiki, a female Green dragon, and Pyralis, a male red dragon."

I gazed up at the fountain. "These individuals were revered all across Lumaraeon, and statues of them were erected all over the land. These six figures soon became known as the Six Peacekeepers, as they not only stopped the war, but they set up a global governing system that would ensure peace would last. Though, in the past few hundred years, that system has deteriorated drastically, and with Lumaraeon once again in turmoil, a potential war with the same devastation is thought to be on the horizon."

Raikidan nodded. "For the most part, that story is the same I was told."

"I thought it might be. I've never heard it told any other way. But your kind is so removed from the other races, it could have been possible."

"Can I ask you something else, about another war you mentioned?"

"The Great War?" I guessed. Even though I couldn't see his eyes, his lips pressed into a thin line, showing me he wasn't sure how I guessed correctly. "It was brought up once before, remember? You accepted my simple answer about it so easily, I figured you may have more questions later if it ever came up."

He chuckled. "I shouldn't have expected anything different from you. I'd like to know why that war happened, since you were led to believe we'd gone extinct because of that war."

My brow furrowed. "It was a war of humans versus dragons. Humans were said to have prevailed. Do you not know of that war?"

"Of course, I do. It made it so the red, black, and green dragons were the last remaining colors. I just wanted to know your take on it."

"Oh, well what I was told is that humans saw dragons as evil beings for some reason, and they thought it best to eradicate them. My guess this was a lingering opinion from the times of the War of End that grew as the Peacekeeper's peaceful hold crumbled. This war is the reason we experiments exist in the first place, as they needed soldiers who could hold up against the power dragons wielded."

"Do you believe we're evil?"

Loaded question... I had to word myself carefully. "I... don't think any race is inherently good or evil. It depends on what they wish to do with the resources at their disposal and how they treat others around them."

Raikidan stared at me. "Have you always believed that way?"

I nodded. "For the most part, yes. I had always wanted to know if the claims were true, that there could be a race that fell out of my shades-of-gray view, but it was claimed that the last dragon was finally killed about eighty-five years ago, so I never thought I'd be able to find that out."

Raikidan's hand clenched his pants. I narrowed my eyes. Something about what I had just said upset him. "Raikidan?"

He looked at me. "I'm fine."

Slowly his head tilted down down to look at his hand. Realizing what I had done, I quickly pulled my hand off his. I hadn't consciously made the action. Feeling slightly flustered and confused, I stood and walked away. I couldn't be near him. It had been a long time since I had touched someone in that way. And that path… had led to disaster in the end.

Raikidan ran to catch up with me. "Hey, wait up."

Pulling myself together, I slowed my pace.

"Now that you know me, do you still see my kind the same way as you always had?"

While grateful he didn't bring up my behavior, this wasn't a question I wished to answer. "I want to say yes… but you are only one individual, and I haven't known you for long. So, I can't make a proper judgment."

"I see."

Silence fell between us, which I found unusual. Unless my words upset him in some way, which I highly doubted, he should have been reaming me with questions. Especially after my story retelling.

"I'd like to understand something," he said, after a minute or so. "It's about two of the Peacekeepers."

Bingo. "Ryoko and Raynn, yes?"

"How did you know I was going to ask about them?"

"Because you've already met the Ryoko and Raynn of our time. I knew bringing them up would get through that thick skull of yours."

"Our time?"

I took a deep breath. This was always a doozy to reveal. "The Ryoko and Raynn you've met are clones of the two Peacekeepers."

He stopped following. "What?"

"It's exactly as I said." I waved him to continue following. "The two Peacekeepers had qualities many admired. Raynn was brave, chivalrous, handsome, and exceptionally strong for an ordinary human. Ryoko was even stronger, fierce, and beautiful. Much like you and other halflings, she wasn't accepted by either side of her blood. No matter how hard she tried, she could never prove herself to them. Any yet, she never let it stop her. People coveted most of these qualities, trying to find ways to obtain them themselves.

"But after the war, and once the global laws were laid down, they, along with the other Peacekeepers, disappeared. No one could find them. It was if they had never existed at all." I closed my eyes for a moment as the wind blew gently. "Then, centuries later, Raynn's remains were found. His grave was here in this very city, his records discovered soon after. After the war, he had led a normal life. He settled down, had a family, and even held a normal job. How he managed to stay so low on the radar perplexed everyone. Even when his descendants were interviewed, they give little away."

I took a deep breath. "Many years later, Ryoko's grave was discovered, though it was hard to get to, due to it being protected by her wogron pack. Not much was found out about her life after the war, beyond knowledge of her attaining full shaman status, and mixed accounts were given about her death. Some claims said she had married and settled down, where more accounts claimed she never found full acceptance. Whatever the case was, she had been buried next to another grave that was too small to be a wogron's, and written in a dialect of Elvish that is no longer known, even to scholars.

"The other Peacekeepers were never found, and it's unknown if anyone is still looking for them, or if anyone is still alive at this point who would have any information about where they'd be located." I chuckled. "Sorry, I went off on a tangent. Barely any of that had anything to do with what you wanted clarification on."

"No, but I don't mind," Raikidan said. "I… liked hearing you speak so freely with me."

His words made me falter. *What is he trying to get at? A connection?* That wasn't happening.

"Well, anyway, back to Ryoko and Raynn. Our former leader was approached by one of Raynn's descendants and offered to allow the use of some of his DNA. He thought maybe if a clone of him existed, even an enhanced clone, it'd help bring back the peace his ancestor had created." I shook my head. "It didn't work like he'd hoped. The Raynn we know had very few of the qualities of Peacekeeper Raynn, and those that he did share died out over time. It came as no surprise to most. Clones may share the same exact genetic code, but they have a different spirit, a different consciousness. You'll never get a living person to be a mirror match to another, even with cloning assisting you."

Raikidan peered at me. "What about Ryoko? She was made after Zarda took power, right? And you said the wogrons were protective of her grave."

My hands clutched into tight fists. "Zarda saw the potential in Ryoko's DNA, so he took it by force." Raikidan's steps faltered, but he kept up. "As you may have expected, the pack wasn't going to allow him to desecrate her grave, and as a result, the pack's numbers were decimated. Zarda got what he wanted before he could kill all of them, but to this day they're still trying to recover."

"That's... terrible."

"Do your best not to ask Ryoko too many questions about it. She's very sensitive to the topic."

He nodded. "I promise. I just can't believe he'd stoop so low as to desecrate a grave. It's disgusting."

"Why do you think I can't stand Genesis' necromancy ability? It's basically the same thing."

"I suppose... I never thought of it that way."

I sighed quietly. "Not many do."

"Hey." Raikidan grabbed my shoulder and stopped me. He moved to face me and cupped my chin, so I'd look up at him. "Don't go back into that mood. You shouldn't be so miserable all the time."

I pushed myself away from him. "Don't touch me like that."

"What did I do wrong?" he asked as he reached into my cloak and grabbed my arm.

I yanked my arm away. "Forget about it."

"No, tell me."

"I don't want to talk about it, okay?" I yelled. "I just... I just don't want to talk about it..." I held my arms close to my chest and picked up my pace. I didn't want to be asked about it. That memory hurt far too much.

"Laz, stop!" Raikidan begged.

My lip curled. "I told you not to call me that."

He sighed. "Look, I'm sorry. I didn't mean to upset you."

"No one ever does..."

"I'm not good at this. I've never dealt with humans before. I don't know what I'm supposed to do."

"It's not you, Raikidan. It's me. You've done well. No one suspects anything from you. They truly believe you're human. Me, on the other hand, I'm human but can barely pass as one. Like I said earlier, it's best not to get involved with me. There's no point. I'm just too different to matter."

Raikidan grabbed my shoulder again and stopped me from walking.

"Yes, you do matter, and yes, you are different, but that's not a bad thing. Your friends are predictable. The way they speak and act, it's all very predictable. You, on the other hand, are not. You're guarded and methodical. You act like a dragon." I looked at him now. "I don't know what to do because you act like one of my kind and then turn around in bursts of anger and freak out like a human."

I turned away. "Do what everyone else does. Just leave me to myself."

He chuckled. "If I did that, I wouldn't learn how to deal with you."

I smiled, despite myself, his comment lifting my mood. "You're so weird. I throw something at you and you just roll over." I shook my head. "Why are you really here, Rai? You put up with too much from me and our cause for your sole motive to be craving the power that comes from my revenge. What are you really gaining from this?"

"I have my reasons, I told you that."

I sighed. It seemed I wasn't going to get that answer for some time. Definitely meant I couldn't trust him. "C'mon. We need to head to the Temple if we want to be back at the house by dark."

"What is this 'Temple' you keep talking about?"

"It's a giant, multi-shrine building dedicated to the gods."

"What?"

Interesting. Even if they didn't have temples, I would have thought even dragons had small shrines. I motioned him to follow. "You'll see."

22
CHAPTER

We walked up the large stone steps of the giant temple. A woody and smoky aroma with a tinge of sweet floral wafted out from within where incense burned. Quietly we made our way through the enormous archway entrance and moved through the spacious building filled with statues and pillars, aware of all the civilians and priests clustered about in prayer.

"This place is huge," Raikidan said as he gazed around. "Humans made this just to show their respect to the gods?"

I nodded. "The gods are very important to us. More effort had been placed into making this temple than any other building in the city. Well, except Zarda's *castle*."

"I guess that's one way to show how much you like them."

"Many people have small shrines at their homes too"—I chuckled—"but we as a species like to show off a little too much." He chuckled as well. "Based on how you're reacting to all this, I guess dragons don't go this far? Not even something small, like a shrine?"

He shook his head. "They're important to us, but it's a private matter to us dragons."

I quite liked that, actually. "Humans could learn a thing or two from you."

Raikidan examined the room. "How many statues are in here?"

I smiled. "One for every god. Or close to it."

Raikidan gazed up at one statue. It was of a man with short hair wearing metal armor that matched the armor from ancient warriors found in library texts, with a large great sword strapped to his back. "Even Nazir, I see."

I looked up at the statue. "Some say he's misunderstood. That he's not an evil god, and death and corruption are a natural part of life. But I don't agree with that. The kind of death and corruption he spreads, and the types of deals he offers people, are too suspect for him to be labeled 'good.'"

Raikidan nodded. "Who do you show the most respect to?"

I waved for him to follow me. "I respect them all, as they're powerful beings, but there are some I revere more than others. I'll show you."

He let out a playful, aggravated sigh. "Why can't you just tell me these things?"

I snickered and kept moving. "Because it annoys you."

"Cheeky human."

I chuckled and led him through the rows of statues, pointing out the ones I revered the most, bowing to each one to show my respect.

One statue depicted a buxom woman with long curly hair, a long tunic and leather pants and sandals, and a muscular man with medium-length hair, leather pants, and bare chest and feet. The two stood together with their hands locked together, and shards of earth and small trees surrounded the pair protectively. "Valena and Tarlin, the goddess of the earth and the god of nature."

The next statue we came to was of a woman with long wavy hair and almond-shaped eyes. Water flowed around her slim figure that was adorned with light clothes and jewelry worn by many belly dancers today. "Kendaria, the goddess of water."

I stopped in front of a statue depicting another pair, a man with short hair and a woman with long hair. The two held each other close as a giant tree wrapped around their naked forms. This statue rose high above the others, and for good reason. "Zoltan and Genesis, the god and goddess of life—the first gods."

We continued on until we came to an alcove with two statues, though there was a pedestal where a third was supposed to be. One depicted a man with fire wrapping around his body. He had short hair, and clothes worn by ancient hand-to-hand fighters and warrior monks from hotter climates, along with a pair of tonfas, a baton-like weapon, strapped to his hips. The other stone sculpture was of a sultry woman with long straight hair who was clad in armor similar to that worn by ancient valkyries, and a sword claimed to have been named Tamashi—an abnormally large great sword capable of slicing through a horse and rider with ease, was strapped to her back. Not much was known about the origins of this sword, as its use and history faded with the sands of time. There had only been one other left in use in recent history, but that wielder had since long passed, and no one else wielded it after her. "Phyre, the god of fire, and Satria, the goddess of war."

I looked at him. "And that concludes my list."

Arcadia also would fit there, given my shaman nature, however, she wasn't as well known given her sphere of influence. This temple didn't even have a statue of her, instead it was located in the graveyard, much like most statue depictions.

Raikidan nodded. "I can understand why most of these gods are important to you. Though, I wonder if Satria is on it because you're an experiment?"

I nodded. "All war experiments revere her. She watches over us in times of war, and if we fall, she will guide us to our final place of rest."

"Sounds like a valkyrie."

"Similar, yes, but she doesn't decide our fate like they once did before their extinction. She lets us decide."

"You really don't fear death."

"All life dies. Even Genesis will die someday. Nothing can stop it, so there is no reason to fear it."

"How many times have you looked death in the face?"

"Including the day I met you, twice."

Raikidan worked his jaw. "Twice too many."

I laughed quietly. "It was in the past. Don't think on it too much."

He focused on the empty pedestal. "What is supposed to go there?"

"A statue." He elbowed me and I laughed. "Really, that's about all I know. There was a statue there, but it kept disappearing, so they decided to not replace it after a while.

"Do you know what god the statue belonged to?"

I shook my head. "I'd heard it depicted Rashta, goddess of judgment and rebirth, but I don't know for sure."

"That's not a goddess name I hear a lot."

I nodded. "I'll be honest; I haven't ever seen a statue of her." I rubbed my chin with furrowed brow. "Or any pictures of her in texts. It's strange, actually, now that I think of it."

"Is that a problem?"

"No, I'm just now curious."

"Don't be foolish and chase stupid things that don't matter," the voice in my head hissed.

I pursed my lips and my brow creased more. "I've been really rude. While I was pointing out my gods, I never let you point out yours."

Raikidan smiled. "That's okay. Besides Satria, I would have pointed out the same gods. The only god you didn't cover was Raisu."

My brow rose. "You know it's bad karma to lie in a temple."

"I'm being serious."

I crossed my arms, unwilling to see how it was possible we'd point out nearly the same gods.

"Without Valena, the earth wouldn't be hospitable to life. Without Tarlin and Kendaria, life would struggle to live without the bounty they provide Lumaraeon. Life without those three wouldn't last very long with our numbers, as the land couldn't maintain the demand. The fire that burns in my chest and the fire you hold in the palms of your hands are only able to exist because of Phyre. He is the reason fire lives the way it does, and he is the reason it resides in many of us."

He turned back to where Genesis and Zoltan's statues resided. "Without Zoltan and Genesis, neither you nor I would be here. They created all living creatures. And without Raisu, there would be no want for us to sleep. There'd be no reason to strive for or look forward to the future."

I looked at Phyre's statue, Raikidan's words running through my head.

"Is something the matter?" Raikidan asked.

I shook my head. "No, just thinking about what you said. Had you asked me why, I'd have given similar answers."

"See, I wasn't lying."

Maybe not, but it is a big coincidence that makes me uneasy. I knelt. "We should finish paying our respects. It's getting late."

We paid our respects in front of Phyre's and Satria's statues, then went to find Raisu's statue for Raikidan, though we needed a little help from a priest. Raikidan prayed in front of his god's monument while I gazed up at it. Tall, with long hair, he was dressed in loose clothing typical of those living in the desert region. *The god of dreams.* It was said he started out as a merchant, specializing in beautiful crafts one would be hard pressed to ignore. He ascended to godhood by seeing the future after speaking to those about their aspirations, although he wasn't a psychic, as they didn't come about in the world until much later. Of course, some believed the first psychics, Tyro and Sela, were possible descendants of him. *An interesting god choice for Raikidan.*

Once he finished paying his respects, we made our way outside the Temple. Halfway down the steps, Raikidan looked at me. "They rest in the North and in the South."

I stopped and faced him. "What?"

"Reiki and Pyralis." He kept walking, forcing me to catch up with him. "Reiki's final resting ground is with her mate in their former territory northwest of the Larkian Mountains, and Pyralis' final resting place is in his colony's territory in the South."

"You knew?"

He nodded. "Most dragons know where they are, and we're not supposed to tell outsiders."

"How come?"

"We don't bury the dead."

"You just let the bones rest on top of the soil?" I found that quite strange.

He nodded. "Usually, dragons die in secluded areas where they're never found. Many times, they're protected by either their living clan or colony mates, or a new dragon, regardless of color, who claims the territory as their own after the dragon dies. The dragon who takes over does it out of respect for the deceased dragon."

"You said outsiders aren't supposed to know about this. So why did you tell me?"

Raikidan shrugged. "I know you won't desecrate their graves, and maybe one day, once this is all over, you might want to go and pay your respects to them. That is, if the dragon guarding their remains lets you pass."

So, you trust me. I was tempted to say it, but I bit my tongue. I smiled instead. "Thank you."

He grinned. "As repayment, I request we walk through the park on our way home."

I chuckled. *He would.* "It'll be a longer walk, but if that's what you'd like, sure."

"The better scenery will make up for it"—he continued to grin at me—"and I have a pretty nu-human to keep me company."

I snorted. "Don't even start."

"I won't take it back."

"Ryoko is the pretty one."

He continued to grin, showing he was going to be stubborn and stupid. Before this little "argument" could continue, a shrill scream from a woman pierced the air. We stopped dead in our tracks and looked around.

A young girl, no older than seventeen, ran around the corner of the street and sprinted our way, constantly looking over her shoulder. Her fear rolled off her in waves so strong, I could feel it from our distance. When she noticed Raikidan and me, she picked up her pace until she crashed into my open arms.

The girl shook as she sobbed. I wrapped my arms protectively around her and made low hushing sounds. Her fear overwhelmed my senses. One look at her ears told me she was an ordinary human, and that made her a slave. I figured she was attempting to escape, but the fear she was feeling wasn't at a normal level. Something was very wrong with this situation.

"Calm, child," I cooed. "What ails you?"

She shook her head and continued to sob. Taking my hand, I stroked her head, which calmed her significantly.

"P–please… please h–help me," she managed.

"Wh—" I wasn't able to ask her my question. At the end of the street, a hulking creature crashed through the corner building, causing it to collapse. People ran and screamed in fear. The girl gasped and shook more. This was what she was afraid of.

Raikidan took a protective stance in front of us, and I peered around him to get a better look. The creature was actually a man overly built with muscle, making him appear disproportionate and creature-like.

He didn't wear the traditional soldier armor, but the faint tank water smell said he was.

"Come out, li'l girl." His voice boomed and echoed through the street. "You can't hide forever. I will find you." The man noticed us and grinned. "I found you."

The girl gasped and clung to me desperately. Prying her off, I forced her to hide behind me.

"Move, shaman," the man ordered as he approached. "This does not concern you."

Raikidan didn't move, and the man growled. More soldiers ran around the corner, six in total, one a short woman, by the looks of it. They all wore helmets, preventing us from seeing their faces, but I identified one as a general by the black armor.

The man I identified as their general approached. "This is official military business. Shamans are not to intervene."

Raikidan's lips curled back. "She's in our hands now. The military can—"

"Shut up!" The hulking man pulled his arm back and threw his fist at Raikidan. *The hell?* Attacking us like that was not only unnecessary, but a direct breach of the pact.

"Don't hit him, you idiot!" the female soldier screamed.

Before Raikidan was forced to defend himself, the general pivoted and slammed his fist into the hulking soldier's abdomen. The man stopped and choked. That's when I noticed the large gauntlets he wore. *That must be to control him.* Since he still smelled of tank water, the man would be a "recent" tank release. The smell clung to experiments for about three years, during which time they were considered new.

The general straightened and faced us again. "My apologies for his actions. That was out of line. We will have a civil discussion about this situation."

"I would hope so," I said, holding myself high. "I'd hate to have to report a breach of our pact over a simple misunderstanding."

A new voice, female, chuckled behind me, and spoke, "Laz'shika, you're far kinder than many of us."

We all turned to find two shamans approaching. A silver cloak with gold embroidery hid one of them, but enough of the lower face was visible to identify the figure as female. The style of the cloak indicated she came from the North Tribe.

The other shaman, also a woman, did not hide underneath a cloak, revealing her young elven features. She appeared to be around my age, maybe younger. Her black hair was shaved and styled into a tri-hawk, the tips of her hair bleached white, that flowed down to the middle of her back with four braids on the side of her head that draped over her mocha-tan shoulders. Woven into her braided tails were beads and feathers of various sizes and colors.

Black-and-white face paint that resembled a butterfly covered most of her face, along with a thin white paint stripe that went from her bottom lip to the edge of her chin. Two small bone spikes protruded just under her bottom lip, and several large bone spikes pierced her elven ears, along with a few chains with feathers.

Her clothes consisted of a short one-sleeved leather top, cloth pants, and long leather boots. An animal skull with horns was strapped to her shoulder. The woman's golden eyes focused on the troublesome soldier, one of her hands clutching a black bow, the other ready to draw an arrow from her quiver.

A South Tribe shaman. According to Del'karo, they were the only tribe to walk around with their identities exposed. They had the most "tribal" look to them. At least, what a city person would consider tribal. This was due to their way of living with the land and druidic influence. Del'karo had been the only South Tribe shaman I'd met, but I'd learned quite a bit from him and his family, as they had adopted a living style that merged his way of living and Alena's.

"Who are you?" the general asked.

The cloaked woman spoke, revealing herself to be the one who spoke prior. "Shamans on a search that has recently come to an end." She shifted her gaze to me. "Thank you for tracking her down. It's been a tiring search."

I chuckled, playing along with her. "I can't take all the credit. She found me first."

The woman smiled. "The spirits guided her path, as they do us all."

"Hold on," the general said. "This woman belongs to someone. He's paid good money to have her returned to him. You cannot—"

"People are not objects, therefore cannot be property," I said. "You can tell this so-called 'owner' that Laz'shika has removed the girl's shackles and he has no power to stop me." *And that he can take his self-inflated ego and shove it up his tight ass.* I bit my cheek, so I wouldn't add that. It wouldn't look good on the shamans.

The general took a step back. The young girl, in her frightened state, found solace in my words.

The general composed himself. "These are our laws."

"And these are ours," I said. "We shamans do not discriminate. We take in and train all who are chosen, and you cannot stop us. You could try of course, but you won't win." I grinned. "You did, after all, attack us first."

The South shaman nocked an arrow and aimed at the hulking man. The general's fists clutched and then he relaxed, seeing we weren't going to budge on this. He'd get into trouble, but if we were willing to fight for this girl, he wouldn't find her worth the punishment for breaking the pact.

"Very well, she's yours," he said. "Have a good day."

He motioned for his underlings to follow him and they left, though the hulking man wasn't keen on listening to the order. He narrowed his eyes at us and Raikidan flipped him his middle finger in farewell.

The man's muscles tightened, but before he could do anything stupid, his female comrade yelled out to him. "Let's go, meathead, you've gotten us in enough trouble already."

The man grumbled and lumbered off. The South shaman lowered her bow and I relaxed. I turned to face the two. "Thank you for the assistance."

The North Tribe shaman shook her head. "No, thank you. You've eased my search. I've been searching for this young woman for months now. Slaves are hard to track down, and even harder to free, even with our pact backing us."

I looked at the scared slave girl. "Well, at least we didn't lie to them."

"I would have regardless," the South shaman said.

I smirked. I liked this woman. I turned to check on the slave girl. "Are you all right?"

"Y–yes, thank you…" she whispered.

"You should go with them now," I said. "They'll take good care of you."

She hesitated at first, but after the cloaked woman extended her hand and smiled genuinely, she relaxed and took the woman's hand.

The North shaman then turned her attention to me. "Laz'shika, I'd like to request you come with us as well. I have something to discuss with you."

I pursed my lips. "I'm guessing it has something to do with how you know my name? I've never met either of you before."

She nodded. "Yes. But we can't discuss this here."

Raikidan leaned over to me. "We really should be going."

I understood he wanted to go through the park, but if this shaman really did need me for something, I couldn't refuse her. "We have time, don't worry." I turned and addressed the North shaman. "Lead on."

We followed the two shamans for some time before we arrived at a small house in Quadrant Two. Following the women, we came into a large living room. I pulled my hood down as I gazed around in amazement. It was much bigger than our house.

Raikidan moved closer to me, uneased by something. I looked up at him, but his hood remained up, obscuring his eyes and hindering me from getting a good look at him beyond his expressionless features.

"Please, make yourself at home," the North shaman said as she pulled down her hood, revealing her short, light-red hair and fair, freckled face. "Most of our people are out in the city, so we'll be alone for some time."

"We shouldn't stay long," I said.

She placed her hand on the slave girl's back. "I'll get this young woman settled in while Tla'lli speaks with you, then, so as not to delay you too long."

It wasn't until the pair was out of sight did the South shaman speak. "As Fe'teline stated, I am Tla'lli. As you may have guessed, I'm from the South Tribe, and I have been searching for you, Eira."

I crossed my arms. "How come?"

"My father had a vision of you and your friends. He was told of what you all were doing and sent me to speak with you. We want to help."

"You can't."

"We want to."

My jaw set. *As useful as shamans would be in getting a leg up on Zarda, the penalty of them breaking the pact...* I refused to budge on this. "No. Do you realize what would happen if you were caught? Do you realize the suffering it will cause your tribe? I won't allow it." I turned to Raikidan. "We're leaving."

"My people used to be proud." I stopped to listen to her. "We used to be strong—and looked to by the other tribes for help, even though many of us were also druidic. The dominant shaman's job was a Guard. We never hid our faces outside our villages. We proudly showed them. Now we are nothing. My tribe lives in fear that one day the pact will break, and the soldiers will come. They fear all outsiders and send them away. We now hide like the other tribes.

"My father, the chief of our tribe, sent me here to find you. We are tired of living in fear. We want to help end this. Say yes and I will convince the other tribes to help. If they are willing to smuggle out refugees, then why wouldn't they be willing to help in other ways?"

I placed my hand on the frame of the stairway and sighed. "I understand why you want this. I really do, but I can't say yes."

"Eira is an ancient name. One that translates to 'peace.' That is what you're trying to attain."

"I don't deserve my name. I can't live up to its meaning. My goal isn't as straightforward as you want to believe. This makes me an unfit candidate. You're better off hiding than dying unnecessarily and dooming your entire people."

"Laz…"

I turned to face her. Tla'lli gazed at me with pleading eyes, but when I refused to budge, she let out a defeated sigh. She removed the bow and quiver from her back and walked over to me. "My father wanted me to give this to you. He said it would help you at some point and would be a nice gift from us to you. Please just think about our offer. I will talk to the other tribes. The North Tribe has already shown interest, thanks to Fe'teline. If they all agree, maybe you will change your mind."

I took the bow and quiver and examined them. The bow was made of black ivory and engraved with shamanic and druidic symbols. The quiver was made of fox hide. Taking out one of the arrows, I noted the obsidian arrow heads. Sliding the arrow back into the quiver, I went to sling both over my shoulder, but Raikidan took them from me.

He briefly looked at them before he slung them over his back. Leaning close, he spoke low in my ear. "You should at least think about it."

"You should stay out of this," I murmured.

"As your Guard, I'm supposed to give you advice. Isn't that correct?"

"You are a Guard in training. Stay out of this."

Raikidan pulled away from me and repositioned the bow and quiver with one hand.

"Please just think it over, Laz'shika, Shaman of the Rising Sun from the West Tribe," Tla'lli begged.

"I will think it over when I have time on my hands." Tla'lli smiled, but then frowned when I continued. "But don't think it means yes."

"So, you're leaving." I looked over to the other side of the room, where the other shaman, Fe'teline, stood. She smiled and walked over to us. Grabbing my hand, she dropped three leather pouches into it.

Curious, I opened one of them and found a blue-and-black glowing orb. "Portals?"

"They may come in handy," she answered. "Be careful when using them, though. They're outlawed in this city, so use them only in an emergency."

"How would they know?" Raikidan asked.

"Psychics," Fe'teline and I replied in unison.

Fe'teline smiled at me. "Psychics can detect the dimensional distortion these portals make."

"We won't have a problem," I assured her.

"I hope so. Now you should be on your way. The girl, Jenifer, is all settled in and safe. I will attempt to find the mother she has been willing to speak about. It may help her, and get one more human into a better, safe life." She smiled at me. "If you ever require our aid, you know where to find us, and please, think over the offer Tla'lli presented. We really want to help."

I pulled my hood over my face. "Farewell."

I motioned to Raikidan to follow, and the two of us left. Once the door shut, Raikidan spoke to me. "That hurt, you know."

"What are you talking about?"

"You saying I had no place to speak. You were stripped of your shaman title and yet are addressed and speak as if you are one, but you claim I can't speak because I'm not a Guard."

"Just because Maka'shi claimed to have stripped me of my name and title doesn't make it true. Once you are a shaman, you are always a shaman. You were never trained how to be a true Guard."

"I was evaluated and approved of by that friend of yours."

"Just because we set up 'proper' evaluation to pass Maka'shi's inspection of your use of the outfit, that doesn't make you a real Guard. You have to take a rigorous training to qualify. Until then, you're a Guard in training at best, and have no place to speak. Ken'ichi would have even told you that."

When he didn't reply, I walked off. We needed to get back to the house, and at this point we wouldn't have time to go through the park—not that I wanted to go with him now. Raikidan caught up to me but stayed silent.

Glancing up at him, I studied his features. At first his face appeared expressionless, but as I examined him, I noticed the small downturn of the corners of his lips. I looked at the ground. I really had hurt his feelings. I had only spoken the truth, but maybe in this instance, the truth wasn't the best thing to go by.

I sighed quietly. I wanted to say something, but I wasn't sure what to say. I never said things right, and I knew if I tried to make things better, I'd just make it worse. So instead, I just kept quiet and let us walk home in silence.

My head rested comfortably on the cushion of the couch as I laid there with the Library access book Shva'sika had given me. I wasn't searching for anything in particular, so the book would start to read off something, and if I found it interesting, it would keep going, and if not, it would find something else.

Rylan sat on the other side of the couch, reading a magazine with the latest high-tech cars he would never be able to afford in a million years. Neither of us had been able to sleep. I had been restless for—the gods only knew why—and even though he had a rough night at the club, he hadn't been able to sleep long himself.

There was a comfortable silence between us. In the past, this was how I had spent my time with him, and even with the time that had passed, nothing had changed. We knew how to enjoy each other's company without the need for words.

That was where most people stopped understanding our relationship. People were so used to relying on their voice that they couldn't comprehend this ability. I smiled slightly. It was nice being able to just jump back into the day-to-day routine with everyone without any issues.

"What are you smiling about?" Rylan asked me.

I shrugged. "Just thinking."

"You, think?" Rylan joked. "That's a surprise!"

I stuck my tongue out at him and he laughed. Rylan was always good to me. Although he would get angry with me over some things, he would never do anything bad to me. He taught me so much and I would never deny I was close to him. This closeness is what made everyone think I had some romantic interest in him in the past when it wasn't true.

Sure, the two of us would pick on each other at times, and to others it might look like flirting or something along those lines, but it was all just good fun. I had no feelings for romance, and to me Rylan was more of an older brother than anything. Had Rylan not developed feelings for me for a time, I know things would have been much different between us.

He had been so direct about how he felt, which made his actions toward Ryoko strange. *He's so apprehensive around her.* It was as though he was afraid she'd say no like I did, but he was so blind to the way she acted that he couldn't see it wouldn't be that way.

A kettle screeched, and Rylan headed into the kitchen. "You sure you don't want anything?"

"Yep."

He came back into the room with a steaming mug and sat back down on the couch. The room was quiet again, and it stayed that way until Ryoko woke up and made herself a cup of coffee. Now she sat near Rylan, looking over some papers.

"So, do you have anything planned for today, Laz?" Ryoko asked, breaking the silence.

I shrugged. "No. You working today?"

She sighed. "Yeah, Zane won't let me have another day off."

I chuckled. "You make it sound like it's the end of Lumaraeon."

"I like having time off." She leaned back on the couch. "And I could use the breaks from all the bad attention I get from customers."

"Wearing more clothes would help," Rylan said. "You'd have fewer issues, and it'd just be overall safer for you."

She crossed her arms. "Maybe men shouldn't act like mindless pigs."

"We're not all like that," Rylan said.

"He's right," I agreed. "Everyone but him, Argus, and Zane."

He laughed, knowing I wasn't being serious. "Her issue is just the soldiers."

I grunted. "Well that's your problem. They're sexually deprived and lack proper social understanding around women." I noticed Rylan struggling not to stare at Ryoko as she continued to keep her arms crossed. "Oh, and Ryoko, don't do that with your arms. They make your boobs look bigger, and I know how much you hate that."

Her arms immediately dropped, much to Rylan's clear disappointment. "Hey, you never mentioned Raikidan when you singled Rylan and them."

I snickered. "It's because I was making a joke. He'd fall under the same umbrella."

"Yeah?"

"I'd have to say she's telling the truth," Rylan said. "I mean, she does share a room with him."

Ryoko pursed her lips, showing she wasn't entirely convinced. This perplexed me. I didn't think Raikidan presented himself in a way that would make her question that. *Maybe it's because she's unsure of him as a whole. He is a bit of a mystery.*

"Let me put it to you this way," I said. "When I gave him a rundown about everyone here and got to the kind of person Blaze is, he wasn't too keen on getting to know him, and that was only after I told him how Blaze is with women." The door of my room opened and then closed. "But, if you don't believe me you're more than welcome to ask him yourself."

"Good idea!" She focused on Raikidan, who looked as if he understood he was somehow part of this conversation but was confused on how. "Hey, Raikidan, you're not a pig, are you?"

Rylan chuckled while I choked on a laugh. "Ryoko, you might want to reword that."

Ryoko looked at me, her innocence clear. "What do you mean?"

I snickered. She was so clueless sometimes. "Your face is priceless."

Rylan chuckled some more. "You'll love Raikidan's expression more."

Letting the book fall flat on my lap, I sat up. I tried to hold back my laughter, to no avail. Falling back onto the cushion of the couch, I held my head and erupted with laughter. Raikidan's face was definitely better than Ryoko's. He clearly wasn't sure if he should be insulted by her question or just confused.

"I still don't get what you mean," Ryoko said.

Her innocence just made me laugh even harder, until I was struggling to breathe.

Rylan also rolled with laughter. "Ryoko, think about your question, out of the context of our conversation. That's what it sounds like to Raikidan."

Ryoko furrowed her brow and thought extremely hard. When the reality of what she had said hit her, she gasped. "Oh no, Raikidan, I didn't mean to ask you if you were a small squealing animal!"

Rylan and I laughed even harder, if that were even possible. Ryoko could be smart sometimes, and it was nice to not have to worry about her, but other times it was worth seeing her mess up.

"Is someone going to tell me what she's blubbering about?" Raikidan asked.

Getting my laughter under control so it was only an occasional giggle and gasp, I pulled myself back up and looked at him. I couldn't get rid of the grin that spread across my face. "She wants to know if you objectify women."

Raikidan responded with a disgusted snort and then he walked into the kitchen.

I shifted my gaze to Ryoko. "See."

She nodded. "I think I can believe it now."

Rylan grinned. "I forgot you could laugh like that, Laz."

My body hurt all over from the excessive laughter. "I did too. I have to admit, it felt good."

"How could you forget?" Raikidan called over to me. "You laughed like that less than a week after meeting me."

I snorted. "It was nothing like just now."

"Close enough."

Ryoko turned and looked at him. "You got her to laugh? You really are something."

"It wasn't that hard," he replied.

I rolled my eyes and went back to reading. Looking up briefly, I noticed Rylan's gaze darting between Raikidan and me. *What's with him?* Figuring it didn't matter, I went back to reading. A dark shadow loomed over me suddenly. I glanced up and then yelped, shooting up into a sitting position as Raikidan jumped over the back of the couch and sat down where my head had been. "What the hell, Raikidan?"

"I wanted a place to sit." He bit into the apple he held in his hand.

"This couch is huge. Find another place to sit. I was laying there."

He leaned back, placing his arms across the back of the couch and his legs up on the coffee table, making himself comfortable. "Too late, I'm already comfortable."

I snorted. If he wanted to be this way, then fine. Pretending he wasn't there, I turned away from him and fell back. My head landed in his lap and he tensed. Ignoring the small amount of pain I received from my hair clip as it dug into my skin, I looked up at him. He was now pinching the bridge of his nose and his eyes were squeezed shut. I smirked triumphantly. Moving myself to get a little more comfortable, I pulled my book up to continue reading. As I did, I noticed Ryoko's and Rylan's expressions. Ryoko was doing her best not to laugh, and Rylan looked as if he was the one who had been hurt.

"What's with you, Ry?" Ryoko asked him through her tight smile. "It's not like she landed in your lap."

"No… but it looked painful nonetheless," he managed to respond.

"Raikidan, I'm surprised you haven't sworn her out yet," Ryoko commented.

Raikidan ground his teeth. "Trust me, it's taking every ounce of restraint I have not to." Once his pain subsided enough, he finally opened his eyes and glanced down at me. "Was that really necessary?"

I gazed up at him, putting on my best innocent look. "Was stealing my spot really necessary?"

"Just move farther down the couch if you want to lie down."

"Why should I? You're the one who forced me to sit up in the first place."

"Move your head off my lap."

"Move your ass out of my spot."

"Move to another spot on the couch." He glared at me. "There are plenty."

I glared back at him. "Take your own advice."

The room went quiet as Raikidan and I stared each other down. Ryoko shifted uncomfortably while Rylan rolled his eyes and went back to reading. With a quiet sigh, Raikidan leaned back and looked away. I grinned in triumph and went back to my book. He wasn't going to move; that much I didn't win. But I didn't have to move either, so I didn't completely lose.

His lap was much more comfortable than I thought it would be. I'd admit it only to myself, but aside from my hair clip digging into my head, I was quite comfortable, so I didn't mind him being my new pillow. As the book read to me, I noticed Raikidan's hand slowly move from the back of the couch and over to the pages of my book. He had barely managed to set his hand down when I smacked it away.

"I'm bored, let me read."

"Get your own book."

"Do you have another book?" When I didn't respond, he snickered and moved his hand toward the book. "That's what I thought. Now let me read."

I smacked his hand away again. "I said no."

He placed his other hand over my eyes. "Then you can't read either."

I sighed. "You really have nothing better to do than to bother me, do you? Or did you really forget I don't read this book with my eyes?"

Raikidan just chuckled and left his hand where it was. That was when I realized what he was doing. In one simultaneous motion, I moved one hand over the book and swatted at his hand that was firmly planted on the pages and moved my other hand to grab his other that was over my face. "I said get your own book."

He grumbled. "What am I supposed to do, then?"

"Figure that out on your own."

Grumbling more, he laid his head back on the couch and stared up at the ceiling. I went back to reading, content I'd won that battle. It was quiet for a time after that.

"How do you work that magic box?" Raikidan finally asked.

I looked up at him, my eyebrow raised. "Magic box?" He pointed to the TV and I laughed. "That's a TV, not a magic box."

"It has tiny moving images of people running around on it. How is it not magic?"

Ryoko laughed. "He's definitely a keeper."

I rolled my eyes and grabbed the remote control. "You turn it on with this remote." I pressed the red button and the TV turned on. "Then you use these arrows to flip through the channels until you find a program you like. The other arrows here are the volume control. Nothing magic about it."

"Then how do you get those people inside it?" Raikidan questioned.

I stifled a laugh. He made this far too amusing. "They're a recording. We use a device to capture the movement and then they're sent to the TV station to be transmitted to TVs in the homes in the city. The TV station gets the videos and transmits them through a tower to the antenna on our roof that then feeds information to the TV. This is also how you get live-cast programs, such as the news. They're sent immediately to the stations through the same network as they're being recorded."

"Still sounds like magic…"

I chuckled and focused back on my book. "Just flip through the channels."

"What if I can't find anything?"

"If you can't find anything out of six hundred channels, then I'd say Laz had better let you have that book, or better yet, let you read with her," Ryoko said.

I laid the book down and gave her a stern look. "Don't say that. Because knowing our luck, that's what's going to happen."

She grinned, her eyes squinting. "You mean your luck."

"It's not luck," Rylan objected. "We all know, no matter how many channels we have, there is barely anything on."

"Yeah, but we're used to all the shows," Ryoko said. "Raikidan isn't a city guy. If he can't find anything that catches his eye, then there's a problem."

Rylan thought this over. "Good point."

I rolled my eyes and went back to reading.

About ten minutes passed before Raikidan started to shift in his seat as if he were uncomfortable. This, in turn, caused my hair clip to dig into the back of my head more. Eventually, Raikidan put the remote down with a sigh and grabbed my head. Lifting my head up, he took my hair clip and gently tossed it onto the coffee table. He then lowered my head back down and went back to flipping through the channels. *Obviously, I wasn't the only one getting uncomfortable with it.*

I lifted my head and pulled my hair to one side. Laying my head back down, I moved around until I was comfortable and picked my book back up. I hated how cozy he was and how willing I was to just lay here. I didn't want to find his lap comfortable and I didn't want to risk getting too close to him. It would just make things worse in the end.

Getting the feeling I was being watched, I peeked over at Ryoko and Rylan. Both of them were engrossed in their reading, although Rylan was taking quick glances at Ryoko and was leaning closer to her than he had been before. *Why can't he just tell her? If he waits too long, he'll miss his chance.* I rescinded that thought immediately. It wasn't uncommon for nu-humans to harbor romantic feelings for another and not act on them for a long time. In many cases, years could pass before anything was done about it. This was because, unlike regular humans, in nu-human courtship, when it happened instead of casual hookups, it would last decades before they'd decide to make their pairing legally binding or not. It was a lot like elves, in a way, now that I thought about it.

Knowing they weren't the reason I was feeling watched, I went back to my book to appear as if I was reading again. Looking up at Raikidan, I raised my eyebrow. "What?"

"Nothing," he muttered as he went back to viewing the TV.

Rolling my eyes, I looked back at my book but casually glanced up through my lashes and caught him watching me again. *What is his problem?* Finally getting fed up with it, I went to ask him, but the sound of someone coming down the hall brought my attention elsewhere. Argus, a pair of scissors in hand, walked into the living room. He rubbed his face to wake up a little more.

"Hey, Ryoko, you mind trimming my hair?" he asked.

She looked up at him. "Um, can I finish reading over these reports?"

"Uh, su—"

"I'll do it," I offered, sitting up.

Skepticism flashed over Argus' face. "Uh, thanks for the offer, but I'd be lying if I said I trusted you to do it."

"I'm not bad at cutting hair."

"Last time you cut someone's hair, it was Blaze, and we had to shave his head because you butchered it so bad," he reminded me.

I laughed. "You do realize I did that on purpose, right?"

His brow furrowed. "Why in Lumaraeon would you do that?"

"Why not? It's Blaze."

"She has a point," Rylan said.

Argus sighed. "You promise you won't make it so I have to shave my head?"

I chuckled and stood. "I don't hate you, right?"

"As far as I know."

"Then you're fine." Jumping over the back of the couch near Ryoko, I pulled a barstool out from the kitchen bar and placed it in front of Argus. He placed the scissors on the counter and went about removing his shirt to reduce the amount of hair he'd get caught up into it. He sat on the barstool with his back facing me. Leaving him for a second, I entered the kitchen and retrieved a bowl from the cupboard. Filling it with warm water, I left the kitchen and set it down on the bar table. I dipped my hand into the water and went to thread my fingers through his hair, but stopped.

I lightly traced the tattoo on his back with my wet fingers. It was a beautiful image of a sidewinder that appeared to be rippling his skin as if it were moving across it. "When did you get this?"

He shivered from my touch. "Shortly after you left."

"Colors look nice still," I said.

"I've gone back to have them enhanced. You like it?"

I nodded. "I think it's fitting, and it's cool too."

Ryoko sighed. "I still think you should have gone with something a little nicer than a snake."

"There's nothing wrong with snakes," I said.

"They're slimy!"

"They are not. They're scaled and smooth to the touch. Well, most of them. Some have a rough texture."

"Still think they're slimy and gross," she muttered. "I hate serpents."

Her comment made me think of Raikidan, and I bit my lip, so I wouldn't laugh. *If only she knew.* Dipping my hand back into the bowl of water, I went to work wetting Argus' hair. While I did, I glanced over at Raikidan. He had given up on the TV and now had my book in his lap.

I shook my head. "Raikidan, could you seriously not find anything to watch?"

"I got bored looking for something," he said, not looking up.

I didn't press him. There was something in his voice that told me not to. I suspected it had to do with Ryoko's comment. Pulling my hair to one side, I grabbed the scissors from the counter and threaded my fingers through Argus' hair more, trimming it. I may not have been a stylist, but trimming his hair wasn't going to be too difficult. I'd had to do more while in the military.

"Argus, you look a little too calm with Eira near your head with scissors." I looked up at the sound of Blaze's voice as he walked down the hallway.

I blinked a few times. "Who are you?"

He gave me an exasperated look. "Don't even start."

I continued my innocent act. "I'm serious. Who are you?"

Ryoko rolled her head back and chuckled. "Go fetch your hat. She might recognize you then."

"Very funny, you two," he replied as he made his way past Argus and me and entered the kitchen.

"I'm surprised you're not bald by now like Zane, what with you rarely removing your hat and bandana," I teased.

"Hey, I'm not bald!" I looked back at the hallway where Zane's voice came from. "I shave my head. There's a difference."

My eyes squinted. "You shave it because you're balding, old man."

He walked up to me and ran his fingers through my bangs quickly. "Oh, I think I saw a gray hair, Chickadee."

I swatted his hand away. "I don't have gray hair, and don't call me Chickadee. You know I hate it."

"That's why I do it." He chuckled. "But you'd worry if I didn't pick on you. Besides, if your mother were to find out I wasn't making sure you were on your toes, she'd... well... I'm not exactly sure what she'd do to me. I'll get back to you on that."

I chuckled. "You don't know what your own sister would do to you? And you call yourself my uncle. I'll tell you what she'd do. She'd haunt you for the rest of eternity."

Zane laughed. "You're probably right."

Ryoko giggled. "I think you guys have gone and confused Raikidan."

I glanced over at him. He was leaning back against the couch again and looking at me with a raised eyebrow.

"What?" I said. "I said he was my uncle the other day."

"Might be because you two don't look similar in the least," Rylan said. "You look more like your mom."

I nodded. He had a point.

"I think she looks like Jasmine," Ryoko said.

Zane chuckled. "Maybe her eyes, but that's about it."

"That's not why I'm confused," Raikidan admitted. "You're all tank-born. How can you have relatives?"

"Just because we're tank-born doesn't mean some of us aren't related, I've told you this," I said. When Raikidan's look of confusion didn't change, I sighed. "The nu-human DNA gene pool used to make us is well mixed, so many experiments are cousins, nephews, or any other distant relative of each other. Zane, my mother, and Jasmine are siblings. They took the same strand of DNA and experimented on them in three different ways to see what would happen. Although their skills were different from each other, Jasmine being smart enough to be made a geneticist and Zane and my mother being soldiers for different talents, they still retained human sibling traits many other experiments lost."

Raikidan rubbed his temples. "I shouldn't have asked. This stuff just gives me a headache."

Zane chuckled at his comment. "You'll get the hang of it eventually." He looked at me again. "I still say they experimented with your mother's DNA the most. How else would she have gotten such a strange hair color you both shared?"

"It's because she was an elementalist," I said as I concentrated on Argus' hair.

"You learn that on your 'vacation?'"

I nodded. "The shamans say the wielder's body has a tendency to change features as a side effect from so much power. Most of the time, it's the hair color. That tends to match their element or show signs of it, like Rylan, Mom, and Jasmine. On rarer occasions you'd never know because they show very little to no physical signs, like some shamans I've met."

From the corner of my eye, I noticed Zane rub his mustache. "That makes sense, I guess, but I still don't know how my sister, a water elementalist, ended up with a child like you, a fire elementalist with violet hair."

I shrugged. "I blame Jasmine. She was the one who was tasked with my creation, after all."

"You're too kind to her," Argus said, a grin on his lips.

I flicked his ear and finished up with his hair. Brushing off the hair that had landed on his shoulders, I moved to the front of him and I ran my fingers through his hair to make sure it was even for the style he usually chose.

I went behind him again and grabbed the bowl of water. "Now go get rid of that stupid skinny caterpillar on your upper lip."

Argus smoothed his mustache. "I like it."

"It looks stupid on you."

"I second that," Ryoko piped in.

Argus sighed and stood. Dusting his hair free of loose strands, he picked up his shirt and headed down the hall.

"Grow a beard instead!" Ryoko called after him. "Well, a managed one. Nothing crazy. You'd look good with it. And don't forget to slick back your hair."

He waved her off and continued walking. I chuckled and went about cleaning the mess I'd created. He didn't have to do any of that of course if he didn't want to. I'd merely been teasing him. He used to have strong options against facial hair in the past. Ryoko on the other hand... she was more than happy to tell people how to present themselves visually. I was half surprised her nose wasn't deep in some fashion magazine right now. *Or a car mag.*

I sat down next to Raikidan on the couch and grabbed the remote.

"Do you mind putting on the news?" Rylan requested. "Same channel as before you left."

"Sure." I pressed a few numbered buttons and let the TV do the rest.

Placing the remote back down on the coffee table, I leaned back on the couch and watched. It wasn't all that interesting, so my attention waned rather quickly. When I couldn't force myself to watch any longer, I slyly glanced Raikidan's way. He was engrossed in the book, and I grinned. I snatched the book away from him.

"Hey!" He glowered at me. "I was using that."

"Not anymore."

"I couldn't find anything to watch on your magic box, so you owe me."

I sighed. "For the last time, it's a TV, and you were too lazy to go through all the channels to find a program you liked, so therefore I owe you nothing."

He growled and tackled me. Sticking my bare foot in his face, I pushed him off of me. He forced my leg out of the way. Putting most of his weight on me, he tried to grab the book again. "Give it back."

"No."

His warm bare chest made this incredibly awkward and uncomfortable.

"Get a room, you two," Blaze grumbled as he ate some of his cereal.

I tilted my head up. "Bite me."

He grinned. "Tell me where."

Zane smacked him on the back of the head and exited the kitchen.

"Hey, that hurt!" Blaze grumbled.

"Oh well," Zane replied casually.

Using the distraction to his advantage, Raikidan took hold of the book. I yanked, but he proved to have a good grip. My eyes narrowed, and I yanked again, but he refused to let go.

"Can't you two just share it?" Ryoko asked. "It's just a book."

"The books struggles with two simultaneous users," I said as I continued to struggle against Raikidan's grip. "They need special training with the two users to work right. Otherwise it gets confused and doesn't transfer information correctly."

She rolled her eyes and went back to watching the news. I latched onto Raikidan's hand and tried to pry him off of me, to no avail. He shook my hand off and then reached out and pinned it to the couch. He tugged on the book but found my grip on it to still be nice and tight.

"You had your time to read it. Now I want something to do," Raikidan grumbled.

"Watch the news, then."

"You watch the news."

"Hey, hey, turn it up, turn it up!" Ryoko screeched. "Something happened!"

Raikidan and I both stopped, but unfortunately for Raikidan, he was unbalanced and fell on the floor. Ignoring his misfortune, I snatched the remote and turned the volume up. Everyone's attention focused on the newscast.

The video wasn't a pleasant one. Crumbled buildings stretched for blocks and soldiers scrambled everywhere.

"As you can see, there is a lot of devastation from this attack," the newscaster informed. "Seven military and nine civilian buildings have been destroyed. The dead count is sitting around one hundred, with hundreds more injured and missing."

Buildings crumbled to pieces everywhere.

I blinked and looked away from the TV.

The smell of burning bodies and screams of people dying filled the air.

"Many claim this is another rebel attack, while others disagree, due to the civilian losses. Although there is a lot of disagreement at this time, the biggest question everyone is asking is why? Why did they do this? What purpose does this serve? This is Eliza Dresh with the morning news, and we will bring you more information when more light is shed on this disastrous situation."

I held my head.

Soldiers rushed through the city, looking for any signs of life, and eliminated it.

"Rebel attack, my ass," Blaze retorted through a mouthful of cereal. "We don't hit civilians."

Rylan nodded. "We've passed up quite a few opportunities in the past due to the threat of civilian losses. Laz, you okay?"

"Yeah, just a small headache," I said. "Nothing to worry about. Our main concern is this attack. Our cause was easily targeted by many civilians. I don't like this."

"Neither do I." We all turned and looked at Genesis, who now stood in the hallways. She walked into the living room and climbed up on the couch next to Ryoko. "That attack was stationed in Sector One. Due to the poor state it's already in, the Council tries to avoid sending teams in there. I'm having Seda look into it now. In the meantime, it'll be in our best interest if we keep a low profile. I'll also relay this message to the rest of the Council."

"I agree," I said. "Although I'd like our efforts to proceed faster, with this situation it could cripple us if we don't tread carefully."

Genesis nodded. "I want you and Raikidan to get jobs. It'll help with the finances since we now have two more mouths to feed, and it'll keep you both low on the radar. We don't need the military to get suspicious."

"They can work at the shop," Zane offered. "They've already been seen there, and if we're to work with their alibi, it'd be best to ease them into the city life. It'll help us out, and once they're seen enough, they can find another job to better help with the finances."

326 ❦ SHANNON PEMRICK

"I'm fine with that," I agreed.

Raikidan didn't respond, but Genesis took his silence as an agreement and hopped off the couch and left the living room.

"That is still weird," Raikidan murmured as he climbed back up onto the couch.

"What is?" I asked.

"Seeing a child talk to you all like that."

I shrugged. "You get used to it."

He opened his mouth to respond, but a knock at the front door stopped him. No one reacted. It was quite early, so we couldn't figure out who would be paying us a visit. Another knock was heard.

Slowly Ryoko got up and headed down the stairs. "General Zo, what are you doing here?"

My blood froze. My eyes darted to Rylan and then Zane. They, too, weren't thrilled at hearing Zo's name and didn't show any signs of knowing why he was here.

"I'm here to speak with Zane and the boys," Zo informed Ryoko.

"Um, okay, come on in," she said.

Quickly I put my hair up and then grabbed my book. *Enemy.* The book wrote out text in response to my alert to appear like a normal, aged book. Raikidan moved his arm around the back of the couch as he leaned in closer to pretend he was reading with me. I glanced up as Ryoko led Zo and two other soldiers up the stairs and into the living room.

"Zo," Zane greeted with a nod.

"Sorry to drop in on you like this, Zane," Zo stated. "But we're in need of your help."

Zane's brow rose, his skepticism clear in his eyes. "What kind of help?"

"I see you have the news on, so I know I don't need to tell you the events that transpired earlier today."

"I have a feeling I know where this is going, and my answer is no," Zane replied.

"Zane, please, be reasonable," Zo urged. "We need you and your boys' expertise on this."

"I'm retired," Zane said. "I solve mechanical problems for you in regards to your vehicles and repair and upgrade weapons when I really have to, but that is the extent I will go to for the military now."

"Just hear him out, Zane," I urged. He eyed me skeptically. "You could at least find out what he wants. He came all this way to ask it."

He sighed. "All right, fine."

Zo grinned. "Thank you, sweetheart."

I forced a smile in response.

"Go get Argus," Zane ordered Rylan.

Rylan nodded and set a brisk pace down the hall. Figuring I should make it look like I was uninterested, I focused on my book.

"That's a fairly large book," Zo commented.

I looked up and smiled at him. "It's really old, too. It's the only book I have that has been helping me recover what I lost."

"How's that going for you?" he asked.

I shrugged. "Decent, I guess."

He smiled at me. "Good."

I went back to my book. Raikidan tried to turn the page on me, but I slapped his hand.

"Slowpoke," he muttered.

I nudged him. "You had a head start. Don't complain."

He grinned. "I will complain. It's not my fault you chose to talk to a stranger."

"At least I try to socialize."

He grunted. "Just hurry up."

I chuckled and pretended to read some more. Ryoko leaned over the couch to take a peek. "Whatcha reading about?"

"Our village's customs," I said.

"Oh, sounds interesting," she said. "Can I read it too?"

"After we're done you could." I shot an accusing glare at Raikidan. "It's hard enough with two people trying to read."

"M'kay." She slipped around the couch and sat back down in her original seat.

"Village?" That got Zo's attention.

I peered up at him. "Yeah, I thought you figured that out when we first met since we had never seen each other before."

"I assumed it was because you were kept up in here," he replied.

I shook my head. "I came to the city without memory."

His brow furrowed. "Then why come here?"

"Because the village was pressuring her to remember." Raikidan didn't look up at Zo as he spoke. "This pressure was making her recovery process hard, and ultimately crippled it, so I brought her here."

"Well… that was… thoughtful of you," Zo replied. There was something in his voice I didn't like, but I couldn't place what it was.

I smiled more and looked at Raikidan. "Rai is the best. He's always looking out for me."

Raikidan wrapped his arm around my neck and head, pulling me into him. "And I'm glad that is one memory you retained from the start. I would have hated to have to remind you of that."

I laughed as I struggled against him until he let me go. Looking down at the book, I glanced at the last two lines of the page and turned it.

"What took you two so long?" I glanced up again when Zane spoke. Rylan and Argus were now in the living room.

"I filled him in on what happened, since he was shaving during the newscast," Rylan informed.

Zo looked Argus over. "Good to see you cleaned your face up, Argus."

Argus grumbled, his eyes flicking to me. "Happy?"

I smiled. "You didn't have to. I was joking."

Ryoko looked up at him "I wasn't. You look better."

"All right, now that we're all here, what do you want with us, Zo?" Zane asked.

Zo reached into a small bag tied to his belt and pulled out a small cylindrical object. "This is one of the few undetonated bombs we found after the attack. We've already determined it's a dud, but we've never seen anything like it. We were hoping maybe an older generation of soldiers may know. The few older gen still in active service have never seen them."

Zane took the bomb and inspected it. "I've never seen anything like this. What about you, Blaze?"

He snorted. "I punch things, not blow them up. Your guess would be better than mine."

"Argus?"

Argus took the bomb and inspected it. "I've never seen anything like this before. What about you, Rylan? You're a bit younger than us. Maybe you've come across something like it?"

Rylan shook his head. "Nothing is ringing a bell. Ryoko?"

"Nope."

"You haven't even looked at it."

She snorted. "I smash things and fix things. I know nothing about bombs."

He shook his head and then looked at me. "Since you two aren't from here, maybe you might know?" He glanced at Zo. "If that's okay."

Zo sucked in a tight breath and gave a curt nod. Rylan tossed it to us and Raikidan caught the bomb. The two of us inspected it, my mind racing with ways to use this. None of the boys would lie about this, but we all knew something had to be done to take the heat off our operation. Rylan trusted me to either let this go or fabricate something based on my alibi, and lucky for him, I could.

Raikidan and I glanced at each other and I nodded before looking at everyone. "We do."

Zo's posture straightened. "What can you tell me?"

"This is common on the west side of the Larkian Mountains," I said. "They're used for mass clearing of land. Extremely destructive on their own, it only takes a handful to level a mountain."

One of the soldiers spoke. "How easy is it for someone to get their hands on one?"

"Anyone can, with the right knowledge," Raikidan said. "Most are made right at home."

Zo looked between us. "Do you two know how to make them?"

Raikidan shook his head, as did I, before I responded. "No. My father taught my brother, but he wouldn't teach me."

"My family didn't have a need for them," Raikidan added.

Zo focused on me, as I hoped. I wasn't sure how much Raikidan could handle the grilling and working with our alibi. "Did you father or brother come with you to the city? I'd like to speak to them."

My eyes lowered and lips slipped into a frown. "They're... both dead..."

"Nice going, General," one of the soldiers muttered.

"I... I'm sorry..." Zo managed, his voice giving away his awkwardness in the situation. "I... didn't mean to upset you. Is there anything else you can tell me about these?"

Wow... That was the most unsympathetic apology I'd heard in a long time. I peered up at him. "I'm assuming you've opened these up, since you confirmed it a dud?"

He nodded. I turned it on its side, listening to how the components inside moved. I'd noticed that same sound before, when the bomb was passed around. I twisted the end cap off and poured some of the contents into my hand. "While I don't know the exact formula, I know how it's detonated, and I've heard of what some of the components were. It requires an electrical charge, and if the contents aren't packed right, that charge won't detonate. This is coming out too loose for it to have ever had hope of working."

I sifted through the contents on my palm and my brow furrowed when I found some metal that reminded me of a synthetic metal no one outside of Zarda's forces should have access to. "This is weird. A lot of these components look like what I've heard should be in here, but there are other contents that look to be wrong, and there are pieces of metal mixed in. I think they were trying for extra shrapnel damage, but these bombs don't need that when made right. Adding it in would increase the chance for a dud."

Argus waved me over. "Let me look."

I nodded and walked around the couch. Argus sifted through the pile in my hand and pulled out some of the metal. He inspected it and then ran off. "I'll be right back."

I looked at the boys, the soldiers, and then down the hall. *Looks like I may be right about my find.* I poured the contents back into the bomb shell while we waited.

Argus returned a little over five minutes later and addressed Zo. "You have a problem. The metal she found is a classified synthetic. No one without proper clearance should be able to get their hands on it."

Zo's eyes darkened. "Shit, means we have a leak somewhere."

"Question is, what kind," his subordinate said. "We know this weapon style isn't from this region."

He not-so-subtly looked my way. I placed my hands on my hips. "Excuse you? Why the hell would you think I'd have anything to do with it?"

"Because you know so much about them," he said.

Shit, this guy is way too suspicious. Well, can't go back now. "Apparently you weren't listening when I said so does half of Lumaraeon! We aren't the only immigrants in this city, or the only visitors. And it most certainly doesn't mean someone from this city couldn't learn how to make these." My eyes burned into him. "On top of that, why the hell would I tell you all of this if I had something to do with the attack on the news? That's completely idiotic!"

Zo held up his hands. "Easy, both of you. Even if it's suspicious she knows, it's no grounds for accusations."

"Knowledge of this construction is near ubiquitous outside of Dalatrend, therefore correlation cannot imply collusion," Argus said, attempting to help me. *Geez, Argus, couldn't use stupid-people words?*

"Besides, she's been here all morning," Rylan said. "We all can vouch for her."

The soldier's eyes narrowed. "Like your friend said, just because she wasn't part of this attack doesn't mean she's not involved. We don't know how dangerous she could be."

"You want dangerous?" I took a step forward, my real anger running a little out of control. "I'll give you—"

Rylan grabbed a hold of me and pulled me back. "Easy."

"No, no," Ryoko said. "Let her. I want to see the show."

The soldier snorted. "You really think she could do anything to me?"

Raikidan closed the book with a heavy *thud*. "She beat a man sense-less with a shoe once. He cut, hauled, and sold lumber for a living."

Ryoko burst with laughter. "I'd have loved to see that!"

I relaxed, using it as a way to calm my image and my real emotions. "I did that?"

"Yeah, about a year before your accident. Your brother and I found it too amusing to stop you."

I crossed my arms. "Now that I can believe."

Zo cleared his throat. "I think we've gotten enough information here. Thank you, Eira, for your assistance in the matter."

I looked at him. "If you want my opinion, which you didn't ask for but I'm going to give anyway, you have either an infiltration issue, or someone isn't as loyal at they claim. My guess is that it's the latter." I glanced at the soldier throwing around accusations. "An *outsider* would be *smart enough* to not use that synthetic metal. They'd know it'd cause stability issues. These are destructive enough without it."

Zo nodded and took my hand, much to my distaste. "I will consider what you have to say." He planted a firm kiss on my hand. "Thank you again."

"Don't let him touch you! Kill him."

I forced a smile. "You're welcome."

"We'll show ourselves out." The three of them turned and left.

Once the door shut, everyone relaxed.

I rubbed my hand on my pants. "Disgusting."

Zane rubbed his head. "Eira, you have to be the craziest woman I know, going toe-to-toe with them when you should be playing it cool."

I scratched my head. "Yeah… sorry about that. Got a little carried away."

"I don't see the issue," Ryoko said. "No civilian, even a timid one, would take that kind of treatment. And even if we wanted Laz to play down her more 'aggressive' side, that's just only going to go so far with her. We all know her better than that."

Raikidan closed the book. "From an outsider's perspective, I'd agree with her."

Ryoko held out her hands to emphasis a silent thank you.

"Either way, that was one heck of a story you crafted," Argus said.

I leaned on the back of the couch. "Wasn't hard. It's a real bomb, and it's most common on that side of Lumaraeon."

Raikidan nodded. "You'll see them most often in the mountainous regions."

Rylan rubbed the back of his neck. "Glad I went with my gut instinct to pass it to you. None of us were going to be able to come up with anything to throw them."

"It was a good call," I agreed. "Even if we didn't have anything, we tried in the very least."

Ryoko leaned on the couch. "Argus, was that synthetic really in there?"

He nodded. "Yes. It is a problem, too." He held up Rylan's arm. "It's this one. Near impervious to fire and heat once hardened, and the only type Brutes even as strong as you struggle to break. Only a select few people have the clearance to touch it. No one in the resistance can even get their hands on it."

Her brow furrowed. "Just great. So not only do we have the military on our ass, we have to worry about someone framing us, too."

"It makes sense they would, though," Blaze said. "I mean, if the military is looking at us as the culprits, then they can get away with more of these unknown agendas they have."

"I know, but I don't like it," Ryoko said.

"It is concerning," I agreed. "What could they gain for causing such destruction?"

"Hard to say without knowing who is doing it," Argus said. "We'll just have to hope more information can be dug up in time. Not ideal, but not much else we can do."

Zane clapped his hands together. "He's right. So, we need to focus on getting through the day." His eyes flicked to me. "I hope you remembered something from the last time you worked in my shop. I don't intend to spend forever teaching you all over again."

I grinned. "I'm confident my time in the wild hasn't affected me that bad."

He clapped me on the back as he laughed. "Good. Now go get something work-appropriate on." He gave the boys a sidelong glance. "I don't need another walking accident on my payroll."

Ryoko got off the couch. "I'll get you some good shoes. Boys, see if you have any extras that'll fit Raikidan. We'll have to go out later and get his own pair."

I went to my room to change into a tank top and jeans. Nothing fancy, but practical, and made sure to keep my jewelry to a minimum and not hanging from my body.

Ryoko came into my room after knocking on the door twice and sighed when she saw me. "Please tell me you plan to wear a different bra."

My brow rose. "What's wrong with the one I'm wearing? It's practical."

"Sports bras compress you too much, making your boobs smaller."

I rolled my eyes. "And? Not like I've got much to compress."

She placed her hands on her hips. "Don't you start with that. You know you're not as small as you like to claim."

"Whatever. Can I have those shoes, or am I going to have to dig through the bottom of my closet?"

She handed me the boots. "You really should consider what I'm saying. We get tips, and as much as I hate it, it does help."

I slipped a boot on. "If they want something to look at, they should head down to Midnight. I'm not a piece of ass they can get their hands on."

"With an attitude like that, it's going to make them want you more."

334 ❦ SHANNON PEMRICK

"Well, good thing no one wants me."

Ryoko's gaze darted away. "I wouldn't say that."

I narrowed my eyes. "What are you talking about?"

"Zo seems pretty taken with you."

I snorted. "Oh, please."

She placed her hands back on her hips again. "I'm serious. He'd be a horrible choice, because I know how he treats women, but I've never seen him act this way before. Could you really not tell how jealous he was getting when you were paying attention to Raikidan?"

I tied up the boot on my other foot. "I'm too smart to fall for your trick."

She smacked her forehead. "C'mon, Laz! I know you hate this topic for various reasons, but you seriously can't be *that* blind. Every time your attention went to Raikidan, he tried to get it back. Every time you two showed how close you were, he got uncomfortable. He kissed your hand as a thank you for a military related issue you shouldn't have even been around to hear as a *non-military* personnel, for Satria's sake. Last I knew, he has never done that to any woman."

"Raikidan and I aren't close," I corrected. "We were acting."

She threw her hands into the air in defeat. "I give up. You can't admit you have a different type of bond with Raikidan than you do with everyone else, and you can't get it through your thick head that someone could actually show interest. You'll see it eventually."

I sighed. "I don't have a bond with Raikidan. Why can't you understand that?"

"Oh, for the love of the goddess! You're so stubborn. The two of you fought over a damn book. Instead of inflicting pain on him or chewing him out for trying to take it, you let him fight with you for it. On top of that, you allow him to stay in this very room. Obviously, with the way you deny your bond, he does sleep on the floor as you claim, but the fact you let him stay in here at all is the part that baffles me! If that isn't a bond of some sort, I don't know what is."

I sat back on the bed and crossed my arms. I refused to look at her. She was wrong. There was no bond. There was only basic trust, and the knowledge that he was a dragon. That's all there was to it. He just enjoyed pushing my boundaries for his own amusement. That was the reason it looked like something else. There was no bond... right?

Ryoko sighed. "You know what? It doesn't matter. At this rate, Zane is going to chew us out for being late."

We left the room to find Argus and Rylan heading downstairs, with Raikidan following. Zane was already gone, no surprise there, and Blaze was stuffing his face with cereal.

He looked me over. "Damn, I was hoping she'd convince you to dress like her."

I scoffed. "Not with you around to make comments."

"C'mon, you'd look great." He grinned. "You could even pass off as her hot older sister."

I glanced to Ryoko and tossed my thumb toward the basement door. "I'm getting out of here before his stupidity damages my brain."

She nodded and followed. "Don't leave me with him."

"Oh, don't be like that, ladies," Blaze said. "It's a compliment. Ladies?"

We continued down the stairs, wanting no part in his kind of "compliments."

"Oh c'mon, don't ignore me. Dammit…"

The two of us snickered and then continued to the garage for a long day of work.

24
CHAPTER

Fussing with my tightly pulled-back hair, and then my form-fitting uniform, I looked myself over in the bathroom mirror. The bright lights harshly outlined my facial features, threatening to mess with the illusion of brown eyes given me by my contacts. I narrowed my eyes at a strand of dark brown-dyed hair that'd fallen loose and toyed with it some more. This bit really didn't want to cooperate with me, which didn't do me any favors on this mission.

Someone rapped on the bathroom door and a mousey woman poked her head in. "Um, hey, you good to go? The guests are arriving."

I continued to mess with my hair. "I will be once this one strand is taken care of. You know how this tycoon is. If anything is out of place, there will be too much attention on us."

The woman glanced about outside the room before slipping in and closing the door behind her. Her demeanor changed to one of confidence as she rushed over. "Let me help. The sooner we get out there, the sooner we can get this done and slip out."

I didn't stop her. I could use the help to ensure this plan went as smoothly as possible.

This would be my first assassination mission since I'd returned, and it was far more involved than I'd expected it to be given right out of the gate. It also happened to be my least favorite type of mission—I preferred to take out my targets without witnesses. But the Council didn't want to lose out on this opportunity. Duard had a lot of pull with Zarda loyalists. His money funded a lot, and if we could take him out, it should have a rippling effect on Zarda's support. Of course, he was rarely ever alone, so it was decided that we should infiltrate one of his infamous parties and send a message at the same time.

Duard had an ego, thinking himself invincible. The security detail he paid for may have been trained to look out for our type of infiltration, but it wouldn't be as tight, looking more to cover his physical person and act as a status boost. The fact I wasn't working alone helped in this manner.

The companion fixing my hair, Evynne, was part of Team One, the rebellion's assassination team. Naturally, for the sake of safety, we were to use cover names, *if* we needed to talk to each other. We agreed, even out of the eye of our target and his guests, verbal communication would be to a minimum. This would reduce the risk of drawing attention to ourselves and jeopardizing the operation.

Evynne finished helping me with my hair; this time the strand stayed put. I let out a deep sigh. "Thank you."

She nodded. "Now let's get going before anyone notices our tardiness."

I agreed and followed her out into a tastefully decorated hallway, watching her posture switch back to her more unassuming, shy disguise. I took a quiet breath and relaxed my shoulders. *I can do this.* I'd appear like any other wait staff and blend in by hiding in plain sight.

We slipped into a large room, crowded with people and expensive artwork. A large crystal chandelier hung from the ceiling and ornate sconces peppered the walls. Men and women in tailored suits stood still along the walls, keeping an eye out. It was easy to tell these were Duard's security. He'd have no reason to disguise them as attendees.

I could only spy nu-humans amongst all the attendees. I didn't expect anything less. Duard was a known nu-human supremacist. He wouldn't be caught dead associating with non-humans. However, due to the high maintenance of the party goers, even nu-humans were working in place of Duard's typical base human slaves.

Evynne and I split up, she slipping into the kitchen, while I accepted a serving tray from an overwhelmed wait staff carrying two plates of appetizers. The man gave a grateful smile and we went in separate directions. I offered my tray to any well-dressed individual I came across, casually eavesdropping on their conversations. While this was a secondary aspect of this mission, the Council knew Duard's party guests weren't large gossipers in circles we needed information from, so they wouldn't penalize us for not picking anything up. And without fail, this was the case.

Most bragged about their achievements or something that put them in a better position over the "common man." I relied heavily on my training to keep my face neutral and not react. Those of Quadrant Four typically looked down on those without wealth and power. This wasn't anything new, and reacting would draw too much attention.

Once my tray had been emptied, I slipped into the kitchen to obtain another and take stock. The moment I opened the door, heat from the stoves and kitchen staff rushing around slammed into me. I grabbed another tray, handing my empty one off to a dish washer to be cleaned. My eyes took in the meal-prep chaos. I didn't envy these people one bit. My understanding was that Duard was not only a neat freak, hence my fussing earlier, but he also had particular food tastes. And if anything wasn't exactly how he expected it, a civilian could see their life ruined in an instant—cruel and uncalled-for in my book, making me even less remorseful of pulling this assignment off.

One chef moving about caught my attention. She didn't perform with any sort of certainty, unlike the other cooks. Due to Duard's high demands, only the best were allowed in his kitchen, and that meant only the most confident in their skills ever took the jobs. *A spy, no doubt.*

Duard may think this one spy, along with his master chef, who was a bleeding loyalist, would keep him safe from any of his enemies attempting to poison him during this party, but my accomplice and I were far too skilled to be outsmarted that easily.

I left the kitchen, my tray scraping against the rings on my fingers. While the wait staff had a rather basic dress code, some jewelry was allowed to make Duard's guests feel more *comfortable* around the work- ers. Evynne and I had each been given a special ring to execute the assignment, and to be sure no one suspected us, we'd both chosen to hide our rings amongst others.

Partygoers casually partook of the appetizer platter I carried around. I didn't see Duard anywhere, but it was only a matter of time. I had no doubts he was mingling in this room. He couldn't possibly resist the chance to show off.

Thirty minutes passed before I found him, though only because of his commanding voice calling out to me. "You, woman, over here."

I turned to see a handsome gentleman of tan complexion with salt and pepper hair, wearing a dark tailored suit, staring right at me. He had an intense aura, his dark, unwavering gaze adding to his overall imposing presence. Duard was known for intimidating any opposition that dared to stand against him. I could see how a civilian would buckle under his kind of pressure. Of course, it helped he was an old soldier from Lord Taric's reign. It was rumored he assisted Zarda in his coup.

Tucked around his arm was the hand of an alluring woman with umber skin and intense golden eyes. Her dark, wavy hair curled past her shoulders over the leather mini-halter dress covering her curvaceous form. Strappy stiletto heels accentuated her shapely legs. *Assassin.*

To most, she'd appear as any perfect eye-candy to work with Duard's status. But my trained eye caught the subtle practiced hints of her training. I didn't expect him to have an assassin in his employ, but as long as my comrade and I were careful, she wouldn't be a problem. I had faith in my abilities, even if I was a bit out of practice.

"Well, hurry up, woman," the lady snapped. "Don't keep Duard waiting."

I forced myself to swallow and hurried over. Offering up the tray of wine, Duard and his company each took a glass. I made sure to keep eye contact to a minimum, especially when it came to Duard and his lady assassin. When everyone had a glass, I began to turn away to leave so I wouldn't overstay any welcome, but Duard spoke again. "Wait."

I faced him again, looking him in the eye for a brief moment before forcing my gaze to lower submissively. "More wine, sir?"

"No. Go find out what time dinner will be served."

I nodded and backed away. "Right away, sir."

I pivoted on my heels and hurried toward the kitchen, only stopping to exchange my half-full tray with Evynne, whose tray was now empty. She gave a questioning look, knowing it was forbidden for the waitstaff to speak in front of the guests unless offering something to one of them or Duard himself, and only when spoken to. The right side of my lip twitched and I blinked once before heading to the kitchen with my new tray. A non-verbal warning to her now passed along—the lip twitch a signal about Duard, and the blink meaning an assassin—I could focus on the task Duard handed to me. It would not do me well to stall.

The kitchen was a little busier than before. People with empty plates, glassware, and utensils ran out a different door, connected to the dining hall. Others worked to put food on serving plates. It appeared the first course would be ready shortly.

I found the head chef, who was not pleased with my interruptions. "What do you want? Can't you see I'm—"

"Duard wants to know when dinner will be served." I was in no mood to be chewed out by some pompous chef because I had slightly inconvenienced him.

The man swallowed visibly. "Soon. Five minutes at most."

I nodded and spun on my heels. Unfortunately, before I could take a step, someone crashed into me. I gasped when glasses filled with wine splashed all over me and the floor. Glass shattering hit my ears, but that was of little concern to me. Wine now stained my uniform, and there was no way I could leave this kitchen.

The woman who ran into me backed up, her hands covering her mouth. "I'm so, so sorry."

I took a controlled breath and did my best not to freak out. Evynne came into the kitchen just then. Her eyes went wide at the sight of me. I pointed at her. "You. Relay to Duard that dinner will be served in five minutes."

She nodded and scurried off. I looked around. "I need a towel… and a mop for this mess."

A towel was tossed to me by one of the kitchen staff, and the woman who'd caused this mess ran off to get the mop. I dabbed the towel on my uniform, soaking up what I could, even though I knew it wouldn't save me in the end. I didn't have a spare, but if I couldn't work, it'd put me in a bad position. *Stay calm, this can be salvaged.* As long as I could be allowed to work in the kitchen, that is.

Before that could happen, I found myself in the way of those trying to get around the kitchen. It wasn't safe for them to walk through the mess, though, so I acted as a liaison to pass objects back and forth. Until a strong hand and angry voice stopped me. "You!"

I was spun around and found myself face to face with Duard's secret assassin. "How dare you send someone in your stead when Duard gave you a direct order!"

My eyes widened at the ferocity in her voice and I shrunk back. "I'm... I'm sorry. There was an accident, and—"

"Don't give me any of your excuses!" Her piercing gaze bore into me. She grabbed me by the arm, her sharp nails digging into my skin. "When Duard gives you a task, you do it without question. You—"

"Bryna, there you are." Duard's voice rang out over the chaos of the kitchen. Everything stopped as all in the room turned to look at the man now standing in the doorway.

The assassin, Bryna, released me. "Sir."

"I admire your passion, always, however, I do think you could stand to stay controlled more often."

Bryna dipped her head. "I will remember that next time, sir."

His gaze flicked over to me, his eyes narrowing. "I see she did in fact have quite the accident."

I nodded, forcing my gaze to fall to his feet. "I... apologize, Mister Duard, sir, for not giving you the message myself. I thought it best not to in my current condition. I didn't want to offend you or your guests."

"See to it that you don't leave this kitchen unless you've cleaned up." He turned. "Come, Bryna. We have guests to entertain."

The lady assassin cast me one last dark glance before joining the tycoon. I let out an audible sigh, as did half of the staff in the room. A woman near me approached. "You're lucky. The last party, she ripped a woman's hair out for stepping out of line."

I dabbed my clothes with my towel again, making it as though I was trying to calm myself. "Is it common for her to do this?"

The woman nodded. "Sadly, yes. She picks a random woman to torment all night. Sometimes Duard steps in, like tonight, and sometimes she's allowed to take her sick twisted pleasure out on us."

I took a deep breath. "Then let's not give her reason to come back in here. What can I do here in the kitchen?"

She smiled at me. "I'll have you help me."

I nodded and joined her in setting food on serving plates and placing lids over them. As I assisted, an idea formed. While we had the assas-sination plan laid out, we hadn't factored a kink in our delivery. With my comrade and I posing as wait staff, it should have been easy. Slip into the workforce undetected, get a hold of a platter or drink specific for Duard, poison him with minimal casualties, and get out. Then we got here and found out just how difficult that'd be.

Drinks were off the table of choices. There would be no way to guarantee Duard would be the only one poisoned. And the food situ-ation would be difficult to say the least. Only the kitchen staff were allowed to set the meals. And they covered them soon after. Evynne was confident she'd be able to slip the poison into our target's per-sonal meal tray, but until now, I was skeptical. However, now that I was working with the food, I may be able to work it to our advantage.

"How many courses in this meal?" I ask the woman, watching her dip a ladle into a soup pot.

"Four, three if you don't count the appetizers that have gone out to the guests already. These soups will go out with salads, and quickly after, we'll offer them the main dish, then desert."

I took a moment to think about this. That didn't give me a lot of time. And as it stood, I wasn't even close to working on my target's dishes. That was reserved for the head chef alone. "Does that include dessert? Duard doesn't come off as the type to offer something so frivolous."

The woman gave a closed-mouth chuckle before scooping more soup. "Bryna has quite the sweet tooth."

I nodded slowly, getting the bigger picture here. At first, I thought maybe I'd slipped up and she'd become suspicious of my presence, using my relay as an excuse to test me. But now, it made more sense why she hung off his shoulder. "It wasn't coincidence she targeted me."

"No, it's not." It was the head chef who spoke, surprising me. He'd just arrived back from announcing dinner was ready. "You just so hap-pen to be the first female server Duard spoke to in Bryna's presence. She gets"—he paused to think—"territorial."

The woman I worked with sputtered a laugh while my lips pressed into a line. That was one way to put it. If Duard treated her well, I could see why she'd want to ensure that position by his side wasn't stolen from her. A brief pang of sympathy hit my chest, realizing I'd be taking him from her. It quickly passed, of course, given that Duard was a horrible person and that I didn't quite care much for Bryna.

Though the fact he spoke that way so freely about the assassin is what caught me. This man didn't come off as anything but arrogant at first. It wouldn't make sense for him to engage in conversation. But maybe he was just stressed under the pressure of ensuring Duard's food was perfect, and took it out on those around him when he shouldn't. *And it seems Bryna's behavior has given others little reason to like her.*

"That's good to know," I said. "Though I doubt it'll save me tonight."

"If you stay here and do everything we say, like Duard ordered, you'll be fine," he said before going back to prepping Duard's main course meal.

Wait staff took the prepared soups and filed out of the kitchen into the dining hall. I finished my last soup prep and handed it to an older gentleman. He shuffled away.

"How much food should I expect to see wasted?" I asked, jumping into setting up serving plates for the kitchen staff.

The woman glanced at me, her brow cocked. I ducked my head, as if embarrassed. "Sorry. Was just curious. My first time temping one of these jobs. If I'm out of line, just let me know."

She gave me a sympathetic smile. "No, you're fine. It may not be as bad as you think, but there will be quite a bit."

We continued to work getting the main course meal ready. I was kept to the easy jobs, but interestingly enough, the head chef enlisted my help with Duard and, as I found out in the moment, Bryna's meal. This boosted my spirits about the potential for success of my mission.

Around the time the kitchen staff finished prepping the main meal, wait staff brought in the half-consumed bowls of soup, while others filed out with the main meal. The head chef rolled Duard and Bryna's meal out on a cart and I let out a deep relaxed breath, the kitchen now in a small lull.

I played with my special ring. I'd done it throughout my time working in the kitchen until the false gem faced under my palm. That's when I noticed a tray with two covered soups left off the side from all the clean-up. "Should those be disposed of?"

The kitchen staff woman I worked with turned her gaze to find out what I mean. "Oh, no. Duard and Bryna don't eat much of their meal during dinner. However, they will finish after the party."

Perfect! Everything was falling in line. If I could just get my hands on his dessert, I could get this assignment over with. But even if that failed, I could use the confusion of the kitchen cleanup to poison his leftovers. Granted, I'd have to do so with Bryna's, too, to ensure he didn't grab her intended plate, but that was a casualty I could live with. Beyond my personal dislike for the woman, as an assassin, she did pose a serious threat.

The head chef returned, let out a breath, and looked around. "You all have five more minutes to breathe."

The rest of the kitchen staff took full advantage of this. While cleaning didn't stop, it wasn't at such a rushed pace. The five-minute lull was over before we knew it, and the kitchen was full speed getting the dessert ready again. Unfortunately, the head chef wasn't allowing me to assist him much this time. It seemed like I was going to have to go with Plan B. As much as I wanted to ensure he'd die before I left the area, and with fewer potential casualties, I had to work with the situations presented. The Council would either understand, or be forced to understand. They were the ones who wanted his death to be handled this way, with such a light infiltration team to begin with.

In theory they were easy, but small changes could make or break the success when you had strict parameters. It was a hazard of the job—not something Zarda ever understood, that was for sure.

Wait staff entered the kitchen, carrying the remains of the main course meal. I rushed around, placing the plates of round cake-like desserts on serving trays for the wait staff to carry out. The one time the food wasn't covered, and I couldn't touch Duard's plate.

I froze when the head chef's voice bellowed. "Where is Duard's dessert?"

The chef I worked with and I glanced at each other, her eyes fearful, and we both looked to the head chef. Where Duard and Bryna's desserts should have been, there was now an empty counter and a clearly pissed-off chef. A wait staff ducked out and returned almost as quickly to confirm neither person of importance had their dish. I swallowed. Someone was going to be in trouble if that wasn't found.

I turned to the woman I worked with. "Do we have more of those cakes?"

She shook her head, her eyes wide with terror. "We only made enough for each person in attendance."

Well that wasn't good. Movement caught the corner of my eye. I glanced that way and noticed Evynne had slid into place with the other wait staff, awaiting direction. When she noticed my attention, her tooth caught her lower lip before she resumed her personality cover. *Ah, I see.* Whatever my accomplice had done with the two desserts, it was now on me to capitalize on the situation. *But how? Think, Eira, think!*

My mind wandered to my time in the West Tribe, to when Daren went on his dessert-making kicks—days of special occasions—days he hounded me to find out my birthday so he could make me something special every year. My thoughts went to one dessert I particularly enjoyed. *That's it!*

"Do we have pudding?"

The head chef looked at me, his brow furrowed. "Pudding? Why are you asking that at a time like—"

"I'm trying to help!" I scanned the prep stations. "Obviously something happened to the prepared dish. So now we have to make a new one and fast, or we're all more than just dead."

Fear flashed across his eyes. "You have something in mind?"

"I'm not a culinary queen, but my step-dad was a pastry chef. He also knew how to make some good, simple desserts. I learned one that will look fancier than it is."

"What do you need for it?" the woman next to me asked.

"Pudding, sweet crackers or cookies, crumbled, and whipped topping and strawberries."

She nodded and glanced to the head chef. "We have pudding left over from two days ago and cookies from yesterday."

He took a breath. "Based on what she listed off, I have a good idea of the dessert. It'll work." His eyes flicked to me. "Barely."

"I'd rather barely save our necks, than not at all."

A wait staff ran into the kitchen. "Duard is not happy he hasn't been served."

"Apologize to him, there was an issue with his food, it'll be out in a moment," the head chef relayed.

The chef next to me jumped into action, getting supplies alongside some others, while I searched for a fancy-looking cup. I found some clear ones that would have to do. A blender went off, and I turned my attention to see the head chef dropping cookies into it. My heart raced and I played with my ring again. This was it. This was my chance. I had to deposit the poison without being noticed. I couldn't blow this.

Setting the cups on the counter the woman chef returned, two bowls in hand. One contained a pale semi-liquid and the other a dark one. "Bryna prefers chocolate, while Duard is less than a fan, so we'll need to work with that."

Perfect! This couldn't go any better. Now I didn't have to worry about needing to apply the poison twice.

I nodded in response and she set the two bowls of pudding down. The head chef joined us, carrying a bowl filled with crumbled cookies. I scooped a spoon into the cookie mixture, filling the bottom of each cup before grabbing two spoons to scoop the vanilla pudding first. Holding one spoon at an awkward angle to scrape the pudding off into the cup, I positioned my fingers to disguise my next action. Twitching my nail against my ring, a tiny latch came loose. The false gem hinged open, allowing the secret pocket of powdered poison to disperse over the pale treat. White in nature, this vanilla pudding was the perfect way to disguise it.

I shut the ring and pulled the spoons away, opting to throw them into the sink myself. I didn't need any cross-contamination risks. When I turned around, the head chef had swooped in to finish my impromptu dessert by sprinkling the cookie crumble over the top and dapping a whipped topping over that. The other chef handled Bryna's treat. I hurried over to a plate of chocolate-covered strawberries laid out and chose the best two I could see, handing one off to each chef working on the individual cups.

Each chef added the fruit, and the female chef scraped two curls off a chocolate bar to add to Bryna's dessert. The head chef snatched both treats. "Good enough."

He rushed out of the kitchen, and after a moment of not hearing any screaming, the kitchen erupted with a collective sigh. I leaned over the counter, playing with my ring again to keep up the illusion of my presumed nervous habit. That had been far too stressful for my liking. No one noticed my poisoning, else it would have been called out right then and I would have been toast. Now we had to wait for it to take effect. As long as he got a decent amount, it wouldn't take too long.

A soft hand touched my shoulder. I glanced up at the chef I'd assisted all night. "That was some quick thinking."

I gave a weak smile. "Thanks. I'm just surprised you both let me help."

She shrugged. "You seemed to know what you were doing and there wasn't time to fuss."

Her words gave me pause. I hoped I didn't blow my cover. I'd been so focused; I may have taken too much charge, forgetting about keeping myself in check.

However, I was glad I didn't have to cook anything. There'd be no way I'd have made anything edible. Glorified sandwich-making was much easier to accomplish. *Thank you Daren, for teaching me things even when I tried to stubbornly refuse.* I would have never guessed his lessons would have ever come in handy like this.

The woman cocked her head. "You look exhausted."

I chuckled, hanging my head. "Today has been far more stressful than I signed up for." I took a breath. "Add that to my stressful week of long hours trying to scrounge up enough to pay the bills—I think I could sleep for a week after this."

The woman laughed, but it was cut short when someone entered the room. I looked up to see the head chef standing in the kitchen. I remained silent, feeling it was best to let him speak first.

The man crossed his arms, eyes pinned to me. "You saved our necks."

Another round of sighs filled the kitchen, though my brow rose instead. "Not just your neck?"

Surprisingly, he shook his head. "No. Duard knows my work. Your contribution was a little too sloppy for me to consider passing it off as mine." If I didn't agree with his assessment, I would have found his words offensive. "Not that I was going to take all the credit even if I could pass it off. I appreciate you jumping in where you didn't need to. The missing dessert would have fallen squarely on the kitchen staff alone, especially me. Yet you were willing to take a risk for us, and I've returned the favor."

I swallowed. I didn't like where this was going. "What do you mean?"

"Duard would like to speak to you personally after the dinner."

Murmurs erupted through the kitchen. That was exactly what I thought was going on. As long as he did in fact eat part of the treat, and the poison took hold, I wouldn't have to deal with this, but I'd now have to prepare extra work for myself if he didn't consume enough. *And then there's Bryna…*

348 ♀ SHANNON PEMRICK

The head chef eyed me. "You don't look excited."

I pressed my lips together. "It's because of Bryna. I don't like the idea I might not have hair by the end of the night."

The man's head flew back as he belted out a hearty laugh. "Don't worry. I'll be with you, and Duard would not tolerate the behavior."

I let out a breath, unconvinced. "Alright." I glanced down at myself. "I should probably try to clean myself up some more. What a day to have an accident without a spare uniform."

Evynne stepped out from the shadows of the other staff, still keeping her mousy persona. "I–I could help you. I know a thing or two about dealing with wine stains."

I smiled. "Thank you, I appreciate the offer."

We slipped out of the kitchen through a back door leading to a long hallway. The two of us didn't speak, and kept our steps normal. We didn't need to draw attention to ourselves before slipping through our planned escape route.

"Where do you think you're going?" A venomous voice hissed before we made it far.

The muscles in the back of my neck tightened. *Oh, no…* Evynne and I turned to face Bryna, but before I could get a good look at her, she pushed my comrade to the floor and grabbed me by my hair bun, slamming me into the wall. I cried out, forcing it a bit to make me sound like a soft civilian, even though her slam felt weak.

My hand reached up and grasped hers, my eyes pleading with her. "Please… please let me go."

"You conniving little bitch," she seethed. "How dare you think you're so special you could worm your way into Duard's good graces over me."

"W–what?" My lip quivered. "I don't know what you're talking about. Please. Please let me go."

The assassin's grip on my hair tightened. I winced and whimpered, begging her again to release me. She reached behind her, her posture tilting as if she were lifting weight off one foot, and then before I knew it, she held a small triangular knife-like weapon up to my neck. No doubt it'd been stowed between the heel and the counter through a special slit. It allowed the tiny dagger to be concealed along the shank. Most assassins had them for shoes like hers. Even the ones Ryoko had bought me "just in case" had been modified in the same fashion.

"D–don't hurt her," Evynne stammered, trying to help without blowing her cover. As difficult as it would be to believe for a civilian, this was still under control. I could break free before she even twitched the knife on my skin.

The assassin pointed the dagger at my comrade, setting a malicious gaze on her. "You, stay out of this, or your pretty little neck is next."

She flinched back, trying to scoot on her rear farther away Bryna. The assassin threatened my neck again, but before she could say anything, a male voice bellowed, "What the hell is going on out here?"

All of us gazed back toward the kitchen to see a handsome man in a well-made suit, though not Duard, standing in the hall. The head chef peered out with a worried gaze. It seemed we'd stalled her just long enough.

The well-dressed man narrowed his gaze at the lady assassin. "Bryna, what the hell do you think you're doing? Duard specifically told you to not touch her again."

Bryna's grip tightened and her lip curled. "She's not to be trusted. Her words—her posture—all so non-threatening and practiced, to lull you into a false sense of security." *Ah shit, she's figured it out.* This was bad. "Well I won't fall for it. She won't snake her way into Duard's graces over me."

Or, I'm wrong. She was just a jealous bitch.

The man's expression remained hard. "Do you even hear yourself? You're being ridiculous. Do you really want her to be the cause of you being reprimanded for insubordination?"

If the situation weren't such a tense one, his insensitive words would have been an issue.

The assassin's grip tightened around my bun a little more before she threw me to the ground. I took a moment to prop myself up onto my forearms and slowly look up at Bryna. A hideous scowl marred her face. "You'd best watch yourself, bitch. Do anything out of line and I will make you regret it."

She then stormed off, though the man grabbed her by the arm when she tried to pass through the kitchen. He leaned close to her ear. "You need to start keeping yourself in check. Your obsession with Duard is going to be your downfall."

Bryna scoffed and ripped her arm free. She disappeared into the kitchen. He shook his head and looked our way as I was pulling myself to my feet. "I'm sorry about her. It won't happen again. Here, let me help you."

I scrambled to my feet faster and moved away from him, as did Evynne. He stopped his approach, seeming to understand even his presence made us uncomfortable. My comrade grabbed my elbow and encouraged me to follow her, barely passing the man a glance. "Let's get moving. We now have more of you to clean up."

To emphasis her point, a strand of hair fell in front of my face. I pressed my lips together and then nodded.

"How's your head?"

I rubbed the back of it. "Hurts. I think I'm lucky I'm not bald."

She chuckled.

The man sighed behind us. "I wasn't going to harm them."

The head chef grunted. "Might be going out on a limb here, boy, but maybe it was because you prioritized Bryna's insubordination over the poor woman's life?

The young man let out a breath. "Yeah, you're probably right. Wasn't thinking, given how out of control Bryna was. She's getting worse."

Before more was said, a shrill scream pierced the air. My comrade and I halted and looked at each other before glancing back. Both the well-dressed man and the chef stared into the kitchen, postures alert. A woman continued to scream, then a voice in the kitchen called out, "Duard's collapsed!"

Both the chef and the man rushed to find out what was going on. Evynne and I glanced at each other before booking it down the hall. We took a corner, then slipped out a window we'd left open earlier that night. We were on the second story, but it wasn't that difficult of a jump for us.

Pushing as fast as we could, we ran across the lawn and scaled the tall fence. When we reached the top, a raged cry filled the air. I glanced back to see Bryna leaning out a window, staring at us. I grinned and flipped her my middle finger before jumping off the fence.

My comrade and I raced through the neighborhood, trying to put as much distance between us and our would-be pursuer. Easier said than done with all the land the lavish estates took up, but we managed.

"Next corner, we'll run into a comrade, Vek," Evynne said. "He was standing by in case we needed a good out if this went weird. He'll get us out of here no problem."

"What do we need to do?"

"Just hold onto him."

My brow rose, but when we rounded the corner, the unspoken question was answered. A young man with dark hair and tawny-beige skin walked the street in front of us. He wore a leather jacket and tight pants, and had a few piercings. From what else I could spot, he wore a blindfold. *Ah, that explains it.*

His arms lifted into the air, sensing our presence, but didn't stop talking. Evynne and I caught up with him, and he wrapped his arms around us when we made contact.

"Now, be good for me," he messaged telepathically. *"I'm doing you a favor helping you out like this, Commander."*

"And how exactly are you helping?" I asked him, fighting off the wave of awkwardness from the close contact.

"Just a simple cloaking. Of course, you're going to want to sway your hips, as that's what an escort does."

"A what?" Heat rushed to my face and I looked down at myself. My stained uniform was now a skin-tight miniskirt and midriff-exposing halter, and my work shoes now looked like thigh-high boots. Glancing at my accomplice, she too had been disguised.

Vek chuckled, patting my shoulder where he gripped me. *"Don't freak out. It's just for show. I'm not going to pull any fast ones on you."* I could sense his focus moving to Evynne. That's when I noticed he'd placed his hand on her hip. *"There's only one woman I'm interested in right now."*

I ground my teeth together, but didn't say anything. I couldn't afford to lose this protection right now. *It's only a disguise. You can do this.*

Minutes passed, and we did run into a search party, but our disguises worked like a charm and they left us alone. By this point I expected our psychic friend to lead us toward Quadrant Three, but we continued through the estates until we came to a large gate belonging to one. My brow ticked up in interest.

Vek flicked his hand and the gate opened. Before I knew it he had ushered us in. My two comrades visibly relaxed once the gates closed and Vek spoke out loud. "Now that I can use my abilities freely here, hold tight. This will be quick."

Before I could begin to question him, my body lifted off the ground and the three of us shot across the grounds. Then, we were at the front door of the mansion within the grounds. I blinked and gazed around, trying to take this all in. Why were we at such a luxurious place?

Evynne giggled. "This is where we live."

My eyes went wide. "Seriously?"

Vek ran his fingers through his hair. "Yeah, my brother and I inherited it after leaving service with Lord Taric. Worked different odd jobs until we found ourselves working for an old business tycoon. We hit it off well, and without any kids of his own to take the business over, he just took us under his wing and showed us the ropes. He left us everything when he passed and we found ourselves CEOs."

I let out a low whistle. "Damn. So you must funnel some of that money into the cause, yeah?"

He opened the front doors with his psychic power and ushered us inside. "About sums it up. Wouldn't make sense to give this all up and fake my death to be more involved."

Evynne winked. "And he has me to help out as his personal secretary when I'm not on assignments."

I snickered. "You mean his personal booty-call?"

She smirked. "That's just an added perk."

When she walked into the foyer, Vek not-so-subtly checked out her backside.

"Besides," she continued. "It's no secret in the company we have a relationship, and that's how I got the job in the first place, so no use trying to shy away from the facts. But enough about that—we need to inform the Council about the success of the mission. Along with the added body count."

My brow furrowed. "What?"

She winked at me. "Your little assassin issue is all taken care of."

My eyes widened. "What did you do?"

She shrugged. "Continued with my plan in case yours wasn't able to be executed, even with the added benefit of you being stuck in the kitchen." She grinned. "I just so happened to be the one to give Duard and Bryna their wine during dinner. And given the trouble she was causing, I took it upon myself to add poison to her drink alongside Duard's. Now they can be in the afterlife together."

A twisted grin spread across my lips. "Thanks."

Vek held up his hands. "Hold up. Didn't the Council say no casualties?"

She nodded. "Yes, and there weren't. It was only Duard and his assassin, who acted like a crazy jealous ex, all because he asked Eira to perform a standard wait staff task. So, no casualties in my book."

He grimaced. "Fair enough."

Evynne waved me to follow her. "Room leading to the Underground Tunnels is this way in the study. It's behind a book—"

Vek tugged her into him with his powers. His hands rested firmly on her hips and he bent close to her ear. "Eira can handle the debrief."

I rolled my eyes. "Let me at least leave, loverboy, before you get all hot and heavy with her."

He chuckled and turned his head to look at me. "Don't be jealous." He tapped his eye covering. "You'll have this, too, in due time."

I scoffed. "Yeah, right."

Evynne giggled and bubbled with excitement. "Oh really? Our famous, love-impervious assassin? Tell me more!"

Vek shook his head. "You know I'm not supposed to talk about those things."

She leaned into him, her teeth catching her bottom lip. "I'll make it worth your while."

I gagged and walked away. "Leaving now."

Vek chuckled. "I wasn't kidding, Eira. He's a lot closer than you think."

I flipped him my middle finger. As if that'd ever happen. Besides, I had more important things to concern myself with. Like debriefing with the Council, and ensuring they agreed with my idea of smuggling out Duard's slaves now that he'd been dealt with.

CHAPTER 25

Darkness and fog clouded my mind, my body heavy and nearly numb. Something pressed on my shoulder, I thought. The numbness ebbed after a moment, and then, something muffled hit my ears. Over time it became louder and clearer—a male voice. "Eira. Eira, wake up. Wake up, Eira."

My eyes fluttered open, Raikidan's blurry form leaning close to my face.

"Eira, you have to wake up."

The fog in my head refused to clear. "Huh?"

"You have to wake up," he repeated.

Inhaling deeply, I rubbed my eyes and then turned my head to look at my alarm clock, but it was missing. My head cleared a little and I remembered I had broken it. The other night I had grabbed it during a nightmare and smashed it against the wall. Unfortunately, I had woken up halfway through that process and had no time to stop myself. Everyone was sure to have a good laugh at me later that morning. Raikidan, on the other hand, didn't find it as funny—well, at all, really. He never told me why. It didn't matter to me all that much, but I had been slightly curious.

Slowly pushing myself into a sitting position, I rubbed my eyes and stretched. I glanced up at the skylight and noticed the sun was barely lighting the sky. "What time is it?"

"Too early for you," he teased. "C'mon, you need to get up."

"Why?"

"Some soldiers are here." I almost panicked, but Raikidan made a low hushing sound along with a hand gesture. "Calm down. They're just here for the inspection. You can go back to bed when they're gone."

"Oh, okay."

He was doing well staying calm, although I figured he had no idea what an inspection was. I forgot to mention them to him when we got him settled in a few days ago. Me, on the other hand, I knew what it was. They weren't common, but with the bombing a few days ago, it would only be a matter of time before they sent out groups of soldiers to search houses. Slowly I scooted to the edge of the bed.

"Do you want help?" he asked.

I shook my head. "No, I'm fine."

Placing both feet firmly on the floor, I stood and tried to walk. Unfortunately, my feet had other ideas. Raikidan caught me as I fell, and chuckled. "Let me help you. You're too tired to move right."

"No, Rai, I'm fine." I pushed away from him and dragged my heavy feet toward the door. Raikidan stuck close, catching me by the hip when I wobbled.

These past few days at the shop had taken their toll on me. The kind of constant work required of my body wasn't like what I'd needed when I was on the run. On top of that, I'd also had two assignments to deal with, one of them the assassination assignment dealing with Duard. All of it combined made me feel like I'd let myself become lazy, when that was far from the case. I couldn't wait for my body to finally adjust to the workload.

We walked past a woman whose face flushed several shades when she laid eyes on Raikidan. For a moment I wasn't sure why, then my head cleared a bit and I realized he was walking around only in flannel pants. *Predictable.* I'd started to grow accustomed to the reaction when he had to interact with women, but for some reason I could never shake that annoyance I felt when it happened. *It's not logical…*

"You can search the room now," Raikidan told her.

I was surprised he acknowledged her. Like all the other women who had this reaction, he didn't seem the least bit interested in her presence.

"O—of course." She made her way into the bedroom and went to work.

The two of us stood a few feet outside my room in the living room, soldiers going about their search task. I didn't see a psychic with them, and sent a prayer of thanks to the gods. It meant Seda could hide a few particular things from them without issue. Thinking of her got my bleary eyes to look around for her, but she was the only person in the house not in sight. *Hiding herself somehow, no doubt.*

Unable to shake the fog in my head, I rested my head against Raikidan's arm. The warmth of his skin made it difficult to fight the urge to rest more of me against him. My eyes closed and Raikidan rested his hand on my head for a brief moment.

"Eira, you okay?" Ryoko asked.

I nodded. "Just tired…"

Several soldiers came into the room and reported to one man, telling him the rooms they checked passed. The room grew progressively quiet, even the sounds of the others breathing faded. That should have alarmed me, but my exhausted state kept me from caring. *I just want to sleep…*

I jolted when a hand shook my shoulder and my eyes flew open. Raikidan pulled away. "Easy, I just had to wake you back up."

"I fell asleep?" My voice came out groggy, partial proof that I had. "I didn't even realize, sorry."

That's when I noticed the ranked soldier standing in front of me. His eyes were sympathetic, but his posture read he needed something from me. "Miss, do you need a moment to clear your head before I ask you a few questions?"

What did he want with me? I rubbed my eyes. "This is as awake as I'm going to be. I had a ten-hour work day and maybe only three hours of sleep at this rate."

He frowned. "My apologizes. I'll try to make this quick." He held up a box containing several of my daggers. Alarm flared up in me. "Why do you have these?"

I rubbed my eyes to keep up an innocent appearance. "I have permits for those."

"So I've been told," he replied. "One of your housemates is retrieving the paperwork, but that's not what I asked you. What use do you have for such weapons?"

Raikidan went to speak but I stopped him. "We're immigrants. I used them daily outside this city."

"What possible use would you have for weapons like this?"

I pointed to them as I spoke. "Hunting—hunting—skinning—gathering—and that one is for protection."

He scrutinized me. "Protection from what?"

"Wild animals? People?" I placed my hands on my hips, my tired state ebbing. "I may be nu-human, but I'm no soldier."

"Why bring them here? You have no use for them here."

My brow rose. "Because they're mine, and according to this city's laws, I'm allowed to keep them as long as I have the proper paperwork."

Zane walked into the room just then, a soldier close behind. It made sense that he went to retrieve the papers. He liked holding the key to all the important documents. "Which I have here, so stop harassing her."

The commanding officer stared me down, which I challenged with my own stare, unflinching, before going over to Zane. I allowed myself to relax some, my weariness making it hard to keep myself strong, and leaned against Raikidan again. Raikidan turned a bit, tucking his arm behind me. This allowed me to lean against him more, but I tried my best to resist, only allowing myself to lean my forehead on his muscular chest. I shouldn't have even done that, but my tired state mixed with this inspection had me all out of sorts.

It wasn't long before I couldn't fight anymore and leaned against him fully, Raikidan resting his hand on my shoulder to help keep me up. *I can just utilize the alibi.* No one could poke fun of me then.

Zane's voice kept me awake. "As you can see, she's done all the paperwork required to keep the knives in question."

"Knives would not be a sufficient assessment for some of these," the commanding officer grumbled. "There's also no reason for her to have these, especially since these documents indicate she's allowed to open-carry them."

I snorted, fixating one eye on him. "Like this place is some sort of utopia where everyone is safe and there's no risk of being harmed by some stranger. I wasn't born yesterday."

Blaze leaned back against the couch. "Just give it up. We have the proper documentation, so you can't confiscate the weapons or take her in for illegal possession. We'd like to go back to bed. Some of us have important jobs in the morning."

The officer scowled, but knew he couldn't do anything. He had rules to abide by, and wrongly arresting a civilian didn't warrant a punishment he'd want to endure. He handed the box of blades back to the female soldier. "Return them to where you found them and then meet us outside."

The officer left without giving the typical disruption "apology," leaving the other soldiers under him to clean up his mess. Once they all left, including the woman who lagged behind, the air in the house relaxed.

"What was that all about?" Rylan asked. "He was way out of line."

"Who cares?" I said. "It was irritating. I'm going back to bed before another situation comes up and I'm too tired and irritable to keep myself in check."

"Don't forget your walking pillow," Ryoko teased.

I flipped my middle finger at her and headed for my room. Unfortunately, I didn't take more than three steps before I tripped over my own foot and stumbled. Raikidan reached out and tucked his arm under me in time to keep me upright.

"Okay, strike two, you're done." He reached under me and hauled me up with one arm.

"No, Rai…" I sighed and leaned my head in the crook of his neck, my weariness getting the better of me. "Okay, whatever. I just want to go back to bed."

"Wow, this is a day for the history books, folks," Ryoko said. "Never thought I'd see the day she wouldn't fight that kind of help."

"Can we also add his unusually high strength for a civilian in there too?" Blaze asked. "And how lucky he is to get her to cuddle up to him?"

I flipped him my middle finger as well, and he chuckled. "Well if you want to, I won't say no."

Blaze yelped when someone hit him, and then Zane spoke. "I'm giving you tomorrow off, Eira. You need the rest."

"Thank you."

"Night, pumpkin," Ryoko called out.

"Not a pumpkin…" I mumbled. She used to call me that in the past when I was overtired. Said I had to go to my pumpkin patch before midnight or I'd turn into a monster.

Raikidan shut the door behind us and carried me to my bed. When he made it in the few steps required, he leaned over to drop me, but in my tired state, it sent an unusual signal to my brain, locking up my arm around the back of his neck. Not expecting this, Raikidan jerked forward with my extra weight pulling him down, and he fell on top of me. A pitiful squeak escaped my lips.

He pulled himself up, as far as my stuck arm would allow, hovering over me. The two of us stared at each other for several moments before I managed to get my arm to work again.

I immediately pulled it close to my chest, my heart's pace thumping harder against it. "Sorry about that. Wasn't intentional."

"It's my fault. I shouldn't have tried to just drop you."

He stayed where he was, his eyes locked with mine. The longer this continued, the harder my heart pounded. An unfamiliar sensation crawled over me, warm and uncomfortably... pleasant? *Most definitely not!*

I pushed my hand against his chest, an action that intensified the new feeling. "You can move now."

He stared for a moment longer, blinked, and then pulled away quickly. "Right, sorry."

I pulled myself back toward my pillows, trying to put some space between us. "It's fine."

Raikidan sat down at the foot of my bed, facing away from me. "Can I ask you something?"

I yawned. "Depends."

"What was this inspection that happened?"

I laid back on my mountain of pillows. "It's a mandatory check by the military to ensure citizens aren't part of the rebellion, harboring criminals, smuggling illegal products, or anything along those lines. Generally, they only happen twice a year, otherwise the citizens feel oppressed, shattering the utopia image Zarda wants to keep them controlled. But with the attack the other day, and the rebellion's continued existence, the military will stop by more often to flush out anyone who gets careless. It's a spontaneous search, so it's difficult to figure out when they'll show up. We just have to be on our toes."

"All right. Now you can go to sleep."

I snuggled into the soft pillows beneath me. "Good night, Raikidan."

I stared into my pillow, surprised by my words. All this time I'd been around him, I had never said good night to him. It showed connection, and I couldn't allow that to exist. Raikidan didn't respond. Instead he shifted back into his dragon form and laid his head down. I chose not to dwell on my words, rationalizing it as me adapting to his constant presence, making it an inevitable side effect. Instead, I let my tired state pull me into unconsciousness.

26
CHAPTER

Cool, refreshing wind tugged my hair as I sat on the sill of the open window, drowning out the heat of the midday sun. The soft strumming of Argus' and Rylan's acoustic guitars filled the room, and the smoothness of their voices filled my ears. With a quiet, relaxed sigh, I leaned back and gazed past the small balcony and watched the people of the city drift by. This is what it had been like all day. I forgot how slow life was when you had nothing to do.

Growing bored with the environment outside, I paid attention to life inside the house instead. Zane and Blaze were at the shop, doing some extra project work when they should have been utilizing the one day the shop closed every week, to do something else with their lives. Ryoko sat with Genesis, near Argus and Rylan, and casually watched them play. Seda meditated in the corner close to me, and then there was Raikidan. He sat on the corner of the couch closest to me and read. He had stolen the book from me when I hadn't been looking, and it was the only reason I was by the window. I hadn't felt like fighting over it with him. It was a waste of energy I just didn't have.

Readjusting to a "normal" life was much harder than I thought it would be. Genesis was even surprised and insisted I not take any assignments until I'd recovered. I was on my third day of rest now, and it didn't feel like I was doing much recovering. *I have to go back to working tomorrow. I can't just let myself sit like this.*

I went back to looking outside, although it wasn't all that great to look at. Everything here was lifeless and dull. It smelled bad, and the small amount of plant life that was spread about looked dead compared to life outside the city walls. The ground was covered in hard asphalt, and the dirt you could find was soiled with who-knows-what.

I missed the forest. I missed the bird songs and the softness of the grass between my toes. I missed the sounds of the rain splashing against the leaves and the endless room to run without stopping. I missed the crunch of the leaves underfoot and the feel of winter snow that came up to my hips. The city was never really my home, but then again, neither was the forest.

I had only small amounts of time to enjoy so many simple things in life. I would relish the day I could have those again, but deep down I knew that would never happen. *It's… not my destiny…*

The sound of tiny fluttering wings echoed in my ears. Turning, I spotted a small songbird perched on the railing of the balcony. Slowly moving my hand out, I called to it quietly with quick tweeting whistles. The little bird tilted its head back and forth and jumped about on the railing until it fluttered over to me. It landed on my fingers and chirped at me. I could feel the fragility of its legs and the quiet beat of its tiny heart. With a small smile, I brought my hand closer to me and gently stroked its chest. The tiny bird chirped and puffed itself out in delight. A happy giggle escaped my lips, catching the attention of the others.

Genesis gasped quietly. "Eira has a birdie."

Slowly she slid off the couch and made her way over to me. She placed her hands on my leg and peered up with her curious child-eyes. I lowered my hand so she could get a better look. She lifted her hand, but stopped and looked at me apprehensively. I nodded and she reached out and stroked the bird's belly the same way I had done. The bird closed its eyes and puffed out more.

"You really like birds, don't you?"

Genesis giggled in delight. "How are you doing this? How are you able to keep such a timid animal so calm and get it to sit on your hand?"

"Want me to teach you how to do it?"

I shrugged casually. "Just a trick I was taught."

"By a friend from outside the city?"

By Xye... I smiled at her. "Yeah, by a friend."

The bird stretched its wings and fluttered off my hand. I bit my lip and held my hand to my mouth.

Raikidan slowly lifted his gaze from reading to me. "That bird is on my head, isn't it?"

I nodded, trying hard not to laugh. He really didn't look at all amused, and I had to admit he looked absolutely ridiculous with the tiny creature perched there.

"Get it off," Raikidan ordered. I couldn't help but laugh now. Not only did he look stupid with it there, but he refused to remove it himself. "Eira, I'll kill it if I try, and I don't think you want that."

I sighed. He was a stick in the mud.

Getting up, I moved over to him and attempted to convince the bird to hop back on my finger. The little bird puffed out and moved around on his head, attempting to dodge my hand. I narrowed my eyes and whistled to it. The bird didn't respond.

Raikidan growled. "Get it off now!"

Startled by Raikidan's anger, the bird flew off his head and flew into the kitchen.

"Nice job, Raikidan," I muttered before going into the kitchen.

The tiny bird sat in a far corner, its flight instinct in full control. I whistled to the little creature several times, but it remained unresponsive to my coaxing. Thinking of another strategy, I reached within myself, finding a warm pulsating sensation.

"Why do something like this for a silly little bird?" the voice hissed. *"It's just a stupid bird."*

Whenever I reached for this energy, the voice always had something to say. I didn't care what it thought of the bird.

I whistled again, but this time laced a little spiritual energy into the sound. *That should get it to calm down.*

The enhanced sound traveled and twisted its way around the tiny creature, calming it. I approached and coaxed the tranquil animal onto my hand, where it chose to go about preening itself.

Genesis beamed a smile at me when I exited the kitchen for the windowsill again. I ignored Raikidan's gaze and sat back down. Genesis leaned on my leg to watch the cute creature in my hand.

Once the bird was satisfied with its preening job, it chirped once and then flew out the window.

Genesis pouted. "Aw, bye birdie."

The two of us gazed out the window, watching the tiny bird disappear into the distance. She then ran off suddenly, making a dash for my room. My brow furrowed. *What is she up to?*

Today had been a bit difficult for her. She was having one of her "child" moments, where she struggled to act more than her perceived body age. It happened quite often in the past, and I was a bit disappointed they still hadn't figured out how to prevent it at this point.

Genesis returned, a small oak box in her hands.

"What did you take from my room?" I asked.

She shoved the box into my hands and then pulled her hands behind her back, looking away as if embarrassed. Brow raised, I focused on the wooden container, running my fingers over it. It was beautifully crafted, and the gloss coating barely existed now, showing its age. I ran my fingers over the symbols engraved on the curved lid and flat face of the body. I didn't know what they said, but they looked nice. *They remind me a lot of the special code Jasmine developed for me to use...*

I opened the box. It was lined with violet silk, and inside rested an object wrapped in more silk. Reaching in, I pulled out the object and removed the cloth. In my hands I held a beautifully crafted pan flute with symbols carved into it similar to the ones on the box.

I tilted my head at Genesis. "Why did you dig this up?"

She gazed at her feet, digging her toes into the floor. "I want you to play it. You only play it when you're in a good mood, and I thought the bird put you in a good enough mood to play a song." She looked up at me with big pleading eyes. "Please?"

I smiled, unable to refuse. "Okay."

Closing the lid, I placed the box on the floor and held the flute up to my lips. Exhaling slowly into the pipes, I began playing a tune.

At first the notes were random as I tried to recall how to play. As I remembered, the notes changed into a melody. Argus and Rylan put down their guitars and sat back in their seats on the couch to listen while Genesis sat down happily under the sill to watch. I closed my eyes as small bits of my memories flooded to the front of my mind. As they did, the tune of my playing matched the memories. The song was about my life. It was about all the hardships and trials I had gone through. It was about the good times with my comrades and the bad times with blood staining my hands.

It was the only thing I could think of to play. I didn't mind much. Although I hated my memories, I knew bottling them up was killing me more than actually remembering them. Playing them on this pan flute allowed me to tell others without verbally telling them. I didn't have to worry about their responses or whether I'd be ridiculed. I didn't have to worry because most didn't know what the song meant.

The song continued, much like my endless story, long into the remainder of the day.

I placed the box carefully into the drawer of my long dresser and ran my fingers over the engraving one last time just as my bedroom door slammed shut. *Oh boy, what's wrong with him now?*

"Where did you get it?" Raikidan demanded.

I turned around and cocked my head. "Get what?"

"You know what I'm talking about."

My brow furrowed. "Are you talking about my flute?"

"Of course I am!"

My brow remained creased. "Why are you yelling?"

He looked taken aback by my question, hesitating before offering an answer.

I pursed my lips and then started rummaging through my dresser. "Are you still mad about the bird situation?"

"What? No—what is with you and that bird? It's just a stupid bird."

"Eira, why do you like birds so much?"

Xye's words so many years ago came unbidden, like so many other memories did from time to time. But it was Raikidan's words that halted my rummaging. "Birds aren't stupid."

"What?"

"They're free."

I resumed my aimless searching, but at a slower pace, dark emotions twisting in my chest. "They can fly where ever they want. They don't have to listen to anyone. They don't have to sit in some cage as a pet for another's amusement. They're free." I closed the drawer and changed my clothes into something more sleep-oriented before I headed for my bed, not looking at him. "That makes them smart."

"And animals in general are kinder than most other sentient beings."

Raikidan remained silent, his intense gaze following me.

I jumped onto my bed and got comfortable. "Now, based on your silence, are you calm enough to tell me why you're so uptight about my instrument?"

Raikidan's brow furrowed. "I'm sorry. I didn't mean to upset you."

"That's not what I asked from you." I didn't care for his "apology." I didn't believe it for one second. *It's not like he really understands how it feels to be caged.*

Raikidan frowned at my rejection and then leaned against the door. "Those symbols written on the box are in my kind's tongue."

I leaned my hands over my knees, slightly interested, though trying not to be so obvious about it. "Okay, so that justifies getting angry at me?"

"I wasn't…" He sighed. "I wasn't angry. I'm sorry. I should have approached that better. Our language is predominantly spoken, so it's not common to find items with our language on it." He looked at me. "Would you please tell me how you got it? It's important to me."

"Eira, dear, I have something for you."

"My mother gave it to me. She found it on some excursion. She thought I'd like it."

"Mother, it's lovely, but what is this written all over the box and flute?"

"Words, written in another language. They have a meaning. I wrote it down on a piece of paper. Let me find it…"

Raikidan nodded. "I see."

"Can you tell me what it says?" I knew I shouldn't engage in this conversation, but I couldn't help myself.

"On the box is, 'Lazmira *sa xruzk*.' On each pipe of that flue, '*zity, gyexy, lgunum, ziaeza, lynyvuma, ziaeza, fulkis*.'" Raikidan paused for a moment. "It translates to, 'Lazmira, my child,' meaning the box is for a female dragon as a gift from their parent. The flute words are 'love, peace, spirit, loyalty, serenity, strength, wisdom.' Single words that go together in some way I don't understand at the moment."

"This isn't from you, then."

"Your father sent it for you. He thought you'd like it. The language makes it an extra special find."

I curled up. "Well, now you have your answer. It's just a coincidence that I have it."

Raikidan sighed and flipped the light switch, plunging us into darkness. I closed my eyes, a lingering memory haunting me before unconsciousness took me.

"Special, right. He couldn't even have the common decency to have the box made in my name."

"Dear, that's not..."

27
CHAPTER

ine. I will protect what is mine. You are mine.

My eyes fluttered open. That dream… It had been such a long time ago. I thought I had forgotten about those types of memories. *Why had I dreamt of that day?*

I stretched a little and yawned. My eyes fluttered as I snuggled deeper into my pillow. As I reopened my eyes, something blue on my bed caught my attention. I let go of my pillow and reached out and grabbed it. Flipping on my back, I gazed at the stem of the pretty blue flower I now held. *Where did these come from?* As I thought about it, one being came to mind. *It couldn't be… could it?*

"Human females like flowers, right?" I sat up and looked at Raikidan, who sat on the windowsill. "It makes them happy, right?"

I avoided his question. "Where did you get these?"

"So, I'm wrong? They don't please you?"

There's that weird 'pleasing' phrase again. I pursed my lips. "No, I never said that."

"But you avoided my question."

I regarded him for a moment. *I don't think he realizes he gave me forget-me-nots.* I inhaled their sweet scent. "I like them."

Raikidan gazed at me hopefully. "But that doesn't excuse your behavior last night."

His expression dropped, and he looked at the floor. *Interesting.* As I studied him, it didn't look as though my words were what disappointed him, but the actual rejection. *Why do I care?*

I crawled out of bed, changing my clothes into something comfortable and casual, and snatched up my hairclip before heading for the door.

"I'm sorry," Raikidan said.

I continued on, ignoring him, until he made it so I couldn't. He closed the distance between us and pushed me against the wall, resting his forehead on mine as he pinned me. His breath came slow and deep, and he kept eye contact with me. My heart pounded in my chest. "I said I'm sorry."

"Raikidan, let me go."

"Not until you listen to me."

I gulped as a warm feeling began to rise up through my body. "I'm not kidding. This is pushing my personal space to a whole new level. Let me go."

"I'm sorry," he repeated, ignoring my demands. "I really am. I shouldn't have yelled. I don't even know why I did. There was no reason for me to. I wasn't even mad. And I shouldn't have insulted something you obviously took interest in, no matter your reasoning behind it."

I closed my eyes and did my best to pretend I wasn't in this situation—my heart thundering in my ears. "Please, Raikidan, let me go."

Slowly Raikidan pulled away, allowing me to breathe. I didn't open my eyes until my heart returned to a normal pace. When I did, I glanced at Raikidan apprehensively. He was acting really weird. I didn't like it.

I took another breath. "You can't do that to people. That's wrong on more levels than you understand. Don't ever do that again."

His shoulders sagged. "I just wanted you to stop and listen to me."

"I did listen, I just didn't acknowledge."

"Why? Why is my apology not good enough?"

"Just because you apologize doesn't mean I have to forgive you." I placed the tips of my fingers on my chest. "I may have screwed-up emotions, but I do have some. And even if I didn't have any, it doesn't give you the right to be insensitive."

He frowned. "I understand that. That's why I'm trying to apologize. It's a sincere apology."

Raikidan reached out for me but I pulled away. I didn't want him touching me. *No connections. No close contact. No stupidity.*

"Dragons touch to help reconcile after differences drive them apart. It doesn't matter the scale of the issue or the sex of either dragon," Raikidan said. "I don't know how to reconcile with you if you won't allow touch and won't listen to words."

I held my arms close to my body and avoided eye contact. Was I being too stubborn about this? *Of course, I am...* I was so concerned about keeping this professional and without any strings that I was being a jerk. *More than a jerk...*

I held out a hand to him, my eyes unable to meet his.

"You mean it?" he asked.

I nodded. At the very least, I could allow some standard body contact. His hand grazed mine, but then touched my forearm. My eyes widened when he yanked me forward and wrapped him arms tightly around me, keeping me close. My body tensed, and he rested his chin on my head.

What is he doing? What was I doing? My whole body stood rigid and all words stuck in my throat. *It's just a hug, Eira.* Nothing wrong with a hug... right?

"Thank you..." he mumbled. "I know this wasn't what you were initially offering, but I swear to you, this is a better way to reconcile."

I swallowed and wiggled my arms free, wrapping them around him, though my grip wasn't as tight as his.

"Thank you," he repeated.

"You're still a stupid dragon," I muttered.

Raikidan's grip tightened, which surprised me. "And you're a silly human."

I sighed and tried to pull away, but Raikidan's grip stayed the same. "Raikidan, let go."

Chuckling, he did as I asked. "I'm surprised you let me do that."

My eyes darted away. "Don't get used to it. It was a one-time deal."

He smirked. "Sure it was."

I rolled my eyes and reached for the door knob.

"Wait," he said. I sighed and stopped. "Do the flowers actually please you?"

I turned and raised my eyebrow at him. "Why is that so important to you?"

"Just answer my question."

I pursed my lips. "Yes, I like forget-me-nots. Yes, it was an interesting choice of a flower to give me as a way to tell me you were sorry. No, I won't tell you of a flower that would have been a better choice. I'll let you figure that out on your own."

Raikidan gave me a confused look, making me laugh before I left the room. I needed to get out of there before any more weird things happened.

"Finally, you're awake!" Genesis exclaimed. "I need to talk to you."

"I already told you, she's going to say no," Rylan said.

"Hush!" Genesis hissed. "Let her hear me out first before you make assumptions."

I didn't like this. I looked at Genesis apprehensively. "I'm listening."

"I need you and Rylan to reconnect your bond."

I laughed dryly. "No way in hell."

"Told you," Rylan replied.

Genesis sighed. "Please? It could help us."

"I said no!" She flinched at my sharpness. "Do you think I enjoy having some tiny sensation in the back of my head telling me what Rylan is feeling? Do you really think I enjoy feeling the same pain as him? I'll pass, thanks."

I jumped over the back of the couch and sat down next to Ryoko. She smiled at me, but refrained any comments. She knew better with Genesis bringing up this topic.

"I don't see a problem with it," Genesis said. "Besides, it's still there. It's just broken down with the time you've been apart."

"If you had to deal with it, you'd be glad it's broken down," I muttered. "Now lay off."

"*Laz.*" I turned my gaze over to Seda, who sat in her meditation corner. "*This is not just a request from Genesis. This is also a request from me.*" I glared at her. "*Yes, I know how much you hate it, but hear me out. I have been getting a bad feeling lately. It is the reason for my extra meditation. I cannot figure it out, but I feel as though we need to prepare for it, and strengthening your bond is one way to start. When this is all over, we can figure out how to sever it for good.*"

I glanced away from her.

"*Laz, you know I would only ask this of you if it was the only thing I could think of.*"

"Seda, we both know I'm not basing my decision on me. This is about Rylan. This bond was the reason our friendship was nearly ruined. It's the reason he felt something more than what was really there. I can't put him through that... I won't hurt him again."

"Laz, his heart has moved on. You know it has. You have felt it because of the bond. You saw it before you left us. I have watched him carefully since then on your behalf, and I can say bringing the bond back will not change anything. He will still feel the same about Ryoko no matter what."

"And Ryoko? What is she supposed to think? She has a hard enough time believing me that there's nothing between me and Rylan in the first place. How is she to feel when she knows I know how Rylan is feeling without trying? How is she to feel knowing the two of us have a type of closeness she can't have with him?"

"She will be fine. I will make sure of it."

"I can't believe that right now." I sighed. *"This isn't just my decision. Rylan has to agree to it. If he does, I'll go along with it."*

Seda was quiet for some time. *"He wants to talk to you in private."*

I looked over at Rylan and nodded. Both of us slipped off the couch, and I followed him.

"Where are those two going?" Blaze asked, looking up from his magazine, but no one answered him.

I closed the door of his room and leaned against it. The two of us remained quiet for several moments.

"Well?" Rylan finally asked.

I crossed my arms. "This is up to you."

"It's up to you, too, Laz."

"No, it's not. This is all you. You know what happened last time."

"It won't happen again."

"Are you sure, Ry? Are you really sure? How do you know it won't?"

"It's not like you to be so apprehensive."

"I don't want you getting hurt again." I avoided his gaze. "I can't do that to you again..."

Rylan approached and pulled me into his arms. "Just trust me on this. Things will be different this time, and after this is all over, we can figure out how to sever the bond for good."

I nodded slowly. "Just don't have any unnecessary feelings, okay? I don't want it to affect me."

He chuckled. "I won't promise anything."

"Seda, are you listening?" I thought in my head.

"I am. I have relayed your choice to Genesis."

"Good. Make her aware this is because you asked, and not her. Also, please don't allow anyone to disturb us. We need absolute silence in order to ensure the bond repairs correctly."

"I can assist with creating a barrier for you to block out sound elements. Good luck."

I took a deep breath and nodded to Rylan. He backed up farther into his room, stepping around the mess of clothes and instrument parts, and sat down on the floor. I came up to him and sat down, straddling him. Instinctively, he rested his hands on my hips.

Discomfort plagued me as I settled. This was one other reason I wasn't keen on doing this. The bond required such an intimate position to connect correctly.

"Relax," Rylan said with a calm done. "You know I'm not going to do anything."

I took a deep breath to calm myself and then rested my forehead on his. Rylan responded by pulling me closer, holding eye contact. The two of us synced our breathing until a familiar pressure pulsed in the back of my head. The sensation sent a wave to the front of my head, and I closed my eyes.

The heat in my chest boiled and the temperature of my skin rose. The ashy taste of smoke hit my tongue as I breathed. At the same time, a cold nip from Rylan's breathing hit my neck. The sensation in my mind pulsed hard, sending a ripple of shorter pulses rushing after it.

My skin grew hotter and Rylan's chilled. My hands clenched his clothes as the heat of my fire burned under the surface, threatening to burst out of me. Embers licked my lips and I swallowed hard to keep them at bay.

Cold crept up my skin, locking me in place, and heat seeped out of my body, trying to fight it. The pulsating in my mind increased to a hard pressure. This wasn't anything like the first time we cemented the bond. It'd been uncomfortable, almost wrong, but this time, it felt worse.

Then a new sensation crept in—dull at first, then it grew and centralized around the back of my head. A relaxing, coaxing feeling. Rylan was calling to me through the bond. The bond was nearing completion.

I took a calming breath, the taste of ash thick in my breath, and willed my body to calm. The fire burning inside took advantage of my state and burst out, licking my skin and sizzling against the ice Rylan created.

Then I felt nothing. My head no longer hurt. The fire no longer burned. The ice faded away.

Staying relaxed, I searched for him. An image of him formed and I reached out to him. He took my hand and smiled. "You'll never be alone. I'll be there for you when you need me. I won't fail you this time. I promise."

I smiled back at him. "You're mine to protect."

His image snuffed out in a bright flash, forcing my mental eyes closed. My true eyes snapped open, and the two of us sat in his room, breathing heavy; no signs of our elements raging out of control. *A mind trick.* I should have known. The first time we'd sealed the bond, there had been some elemental forces at work, but a majority of it had been all an illusion created by the power of our minds connecting.

The pressure in my head was gone, and in its place, a familiar, soothing bubble in the back of my mind. It had always been there, but now it was stronger.

I slid off Rylan to put some space between us, and he didn't fight me. "You okay?" he asked.

I nodded. "Just getting used to the feeling in my head now."

Rylan stood and held his hand out to me. "Let's get you a drink, then. It'll keep your nerves down to help adjust to it all."

I took his offered hand. "How can you act like it's not affecting you?"

"Because we both know my side of this has always been stronger. Even with the breakdown due to distance over these past years, I doubt it became as dull of a presence as yours."

I stared at him. "You could still sense me even at that distance, couldn't you?"

He nodded. "As you moved farther away, it became harder, but it never went away. It helped me stay positive with you gone. But please don't tell Ryoko. I kept it a secret for her sake."

I nodded, understanding the importance of that secret. She wasn't happy about the existence of the bond.

We left his room, and all eyes in the living room fell on us. I stared at them while Rylan went into the kitchen to pour me something.

"What?"

Genesis raised an eyebrow. "It's all done?"

I gave a curt nod. "Yes. We're now in an adjustment period."

The sound of Rylan rummaging through the cabinets and glasses clanking drew their attention to him.

Genesis' forehead crinkled. "What are you doing in there?"

"Finding out what we have for options in the mixed drink department," Rylan said without looking away from his task. "I know we have beer in the fridge, but Laz isn't a huge fan of that option."

"Oh, but I'd love that option," Ryoko called out.

Rylan smiled at her, the bond in my head bouncing a bit, indicating how much he enjoyed this interaction with Ryoko. "I'll get you one once I'm done taking inventory," he laughed.

"I'll take one too," Blaze called out.

Rylan nodded, taking note.

"Wait, wait." Genesis held up her hands. "You're going to drink this early in the morning? You can't wait until noon?"

I leaned on the bar and smirked. "We're rebels, what did you expect?"

The room erupted with laughter; even Raikidan found it amusing. Genesis shook her head, knowing it was pointless to talk sense into us, and went back to going over her reports.

Rylan finished pulling out drink components and then rummaged through the fridge for the beers. "Laz, take a look at what we have, and I'll make what you want."

I entered the kitchen, passing him as he left to hand Ryoko and Blaze their drinks. I perused my alcohol and mixer choices as Ryoko cracked open her beer can and took a few gulps.

Rylan noticed Raikidan take interest in the choice of drinks. "You want one?"

Raikidan's nose scrunched. "I don't ingest anything that smells foul."

"Tastes good," Ryoko said. "Promise."

"I'd disagree," I said, separating my least favorite alcohols from my favorite. "It tastes worse than it smells."

She stuck her tongue out at me and then drank some more.

I mixed up a drink for myself just as Rylan came into the kitchen. "I was going to do that for you."

I shrugged. "I felt like doing it."

"Don't tell Azriel you can do that. He'll try to hire you."

"I wouldn't mind." I grinned. "Means I get to see him all the time."

Rylan crossed his arms. "You're not a people person. Seeing Azriel will not make you feel any better about the job."

"How is he, by the way?" I asked as I mixed up another drink, one I thought Raikidan might like. "Better question, does he even know I'm back in town?"

"Oh, he knows," Rylan said, pouring himself something. "He's just been busy, and he knows you have been, too. Of course, he thinks you should stop by and pay him a visit in your free time, too."

I chuckled. "He's not wrong. Maybe sometime this week I could swing by." I gave Rylan a sidelong glance. "Or he could step away from his club for more than five minutes."

Ryoko laughed. "And mess up his hookup streak? You should know him better than that, Laz."

She had a point. "He still going on the same one?"

"No, he's restarted a few times," Rylan said. "Longest he's gone is seven months." He chuckled. "Don't tell him I told you. He'd assign me to tasks I'd rather steer clear of."

I grinned. "Okay, I'll rat you out next time I see him."

Rylan smacked me in the arm, and I chuckled before taking the two glasses I'd prepared into the living room. I maneuvered around the coffee table and sat down next to Raikidan. I pushed his to him and sipped mine, reacquainting my taste buds with the sweet taste and the alcohol.

Raikidan looked at the offered drink, his brow creased. "What's this?"

"Something a little less foul tasting, with a lot more alcohol."

I could see the mistrust in his eyes. "I'll pass, thanks."

I shrugged and pulled it in front of me. "Okay."

Couldn't make him try it. It'd be ideal, as undercover assignments may put him in a situation where he'd need to consume it, but there were ways around that.

"Well, if he won't have it, I'll take it," Blaze said, reaching for the glass.

"Blaze—no, don't!" Ryoko put her hands up to stop him, but it was too late.

Watching him reach for the glass I'd claimed as mine, something snapped in my head. Without any control over my body, I grabbed his hand, clenching and twisting it into the coffee table, while I grabbed him by the back of the neck with my other hand and slammed him into the wooden surface. An inhuman growl, sounding almost like a hiss, came from my throat.

Ryoko and Genesis sat up and Rylan ran into the room. Even Seda focused on me.

"Laz, calm down, it's okay," Rylan said. "It's okay. You can let him go."

I knew everything was okay, but my body didn't agree. It was as if someone else controlled me while I watched myself do awful things.

"Eira, I'm sorry," Blaze said in a strained voice. "I didn't realize you claimed it."

Rylan came up behind me, pushing on the bond's presence in an attempt to calm me. A fuzzy feeling fell over me and I realized Seda was trying to help by placing me under an artificial exhaustion.

Between the two of them, my body relaxed, and I was finally able to detach myself from Blaze and sit back. "Sorry…"

Blaze twisted his neck. "It was my fault. I know better than to take things you deem as yours. I just didn't use my head."

"No surprise there," Ryoko jeered. He shot her a dirty look, but she ignored him and focused on me. "Are you okay now, Laz?"

"I'll be fine." I pushed the extra glass away. "I'm no longer claiming it."

I picked up my glass and sipped the drink, hoping it'd wipe away some of the tension still in me. Between the bond coming back and that relapse, I needed the help.

"So, I noticed how Rylan was helping you calm down," Blaze said. "Was that you using that bond thing you all keep talking about?"

Rylan nodded as he sat down next to Ryoko. "That's right."

"What is it, exactly?" Blaze asked. "You all talk about it a lot but have never outright said what it is. What does it do?"

I pressed my glass to my lips and stared off at nothing. "It's a feeling. A kind of awareness of each other's condition."

Rylan nodded, grabbing a magazine from under the coffee table. "That'd be the best way I could explain it. We weren't told much about it, because the experiment was deemed a failure soon after Laz's release. We also weren't told we had to deal with it for the rest of our lives. We don't even know what made it fail. I suspect this was Zarda's attempt at creating psychic-like connections without the experiments obtaining telekinetic abilities. That made the connection rather weak in comparison. It only allows feelings to be communicated, instead of words. Based on how the two of us reacted to each other after the connection, it was deemed as too distracting in battle, especially if the two individuals weren't compatible personality-wise."

Blaze furrowed his brow. "So, you're in each other's head?"

"In a way," I mumbled. "If either of us is in some sort of trouble or if either of us was in pain, the other party would know."

Ryoko held up her fist at Rylan. "So, if I punched him, would you feel it?"

Rylan leaned away from her and held up his hands defensively. "Ryoko, don't! It doesn't work like that. Please don't hit me!"

She rolled her eyes. "I wasn't going to hit you hard."

"Even when you don't try, you hit like a train," Rylan said.

Idiot! Ryoko slammed her beer can on the coffee table and stormed off.

"Ryoko! Ryoko, I didn't mean it like that!" Rylan called after her.

Ryoko slammed her door, and it cracked down the center from the force.

"Nice going," I said. "You know how sensitive she is."

Rylan sighed. "I didn't mean it like that."

I scoffed and shot him a sarcastic glance. "Then tell me, how did you mean it? Because I can't think of any other way for it to have meant."

Rylan took the magazine on his lap and tossed it on the coffee table with a sigh. He made his way over to Ryoko's door and banged on it. "Ryoko. Ryoko, open up. I didn't mean it like that." He received no answer. The crack in the door would allow her to hear him, so it was obvious she was ignoring him. "Ryoko, please."

When he didn't receive a reply, he jiggled the handle. It was locked. He called her name again to receive no reply. Turning around, he leaned against the door and stared up at the ceiling. He breathed out slowly and ran his fingers through his hair before slamming his head against the door.

"Dude, just leave her alone," Blaze told him. "She obviously doesn't want to talk to you."

"Look who decided to use his brain," I teased.

"Shut up."

I shook my head and chuckled. Placing my glass down on the coffee table, I made my way to my room. Rylan wasn't going to get anywhere unless he talked to her face to face. Ryoko held grudges, and if he didn't patch this up now, he'd be on her list for some time. Rummaging through my nightstand, I found my lock pick set.

Making my way out of my room, I pushed Rylan aside and inserted a lock pick into the keyhole to Ryoko's door. It wasn't long before the lock clicked open audibly. Turning the handle, I pushed the door open. Ryoko was lying on her bed with her arms crossed, brooding darkly.

When she heard the door open, her head turned. Ryoko's mouth fell open. "Laz, you traitor!"

I grinned and grabbed Rylan by the shirt. "Go get her, loverboy."

Shoving him into her room, I shut the door and headed for my room again. I tossed the lock pick set into my room carelessly to deal with later. Turning around, I noticed Raikidan inspecting the drink I'd made him. He sniffed it and then gave it a small sipping taste. His face scrunched, and I thought he may not like it, but he tried it again. *Ah, he's unsure.* I didn't blame him. If he'd never consumed alcohol before, this would be an interesting new experience for him. I figured it best to leave him be and headed up to the roof. I needed some time alone to reflect on my earlier actions.

I sighed as the wind toyed with my hair. I had been up here most of the day now. I had checked in on my plants in my greenhouse at some point, but that was the only time I had left this spot. Ryoko had done a nice job keeping my plants alive this whole time, and for that I was glad. It had taken a lot of time finding the different species, and then even more time caring for them properly.

The sound of a door opening caught my attention. I looked up to see Raikidan walking through the door. He grinned. "Hey there, Butterfly."

I groaned. "Not you, too. I hate pet names."

He snickered and sat down next to me. "Well, since you hate them, I guess I'll have to keep using it."

I sighed. "Why 'Butterfly,' then?"

He brushed my bangs with the back of his fingers. "Beautiful and distracting." He chuckled, a grin slipping up his face. "And toxic."

My eyebrow rose in question. "Toxic?"

"You appear harmless on the surface, but in reality, you're deadly."

I rolled my eyes. "Whatever. Just don't call me that."

"What, you'd rather me call you something else?"

"Yeah, my real name."

"Well, that's not an option."

I shook my head. Raikidan looked at me and touched my bangs again. I furrowed my brow and pulled away. "Why are you doing that?"

"Sorry." His gaze fell away. "It's just not every day you see such exotic-colored hair. I'm still not used to seeing it."

I snorted. "I doubt you ever will." He looked at me again. "Hair with shades of blue will be the most exotic colors you'll see naturally on any human, elf, or dwarf, and most of them are elementalists, shamans, or soldiers. Violet naturally on its own is just as common as green hair."

"Green dragons have green hair," Raikidan said.

"They don't count."

"And why not?"

I lowered my head to look at him with a stern expression. "They're dragons?"

He snorted. The two of us went quiet. I stared up at the sky as it slowly changed with the setting sun. I frowned when I realized how discolored the sky was. The city air was so polluted.

"Why so sad, Butterfly?"

I rolled my eyes. Him and that stupid name. "I'm not sad."

"That's not what that frown says. What's bothering you?"

I shook my head. "It's nothing."

"Tell me."

"It's nothing!"

Raikidan ran his fingers through his hair. "Can I ask you something?"

"You asked me a question to only ask permission to ask another one?" I chuckled. "You do that a lot. You're really strange."

He looked at me shyly. "So, is that a yes?"

"You figure it out."

Raikidan sighed and was quiet for a moment. "Why did you harm Blaze earlier?"

"Oh, that…" My eyes fell elsewhere.

"If you don't want to talk about it, just tell me."

It was true; I didn't want to talk about it. But I couldn't think of a good reason why it would hurt to tell. He'd probably just forget later anyway. "Have you ever known what it was like to go hungry?"

"A few times."

"Have you ever known what it was like to be weak due to starvation?"

He didn't answer this time.

"A common tactic Zarda used to control us was starvation. Our bodies are so modified that we require large quantities of food to keep us going. This quantity is significantly higher than that of the average nu-human, and it helps with identification if necessary. Because of our food dependence, Zarda would cut our supply and use what we were missing as a reward. Many times, Zarda would just not allow us to eat or drink for days, sometimes weeks."

"And this method worked?" Raikidan asked.

"This method was only effective for certain experiments. It forced them to be loyal, and once they showed him this loyalty, their food rations were never cut. Other experiments, such as myself and the others downstairs, didn't give in. It didn't matter how weak we became from hunger, we refused to give in.

I pressed my lips together. "Unfortunately, this method had many negative effects for those who fought. It was common for experiments to become aggressive over food, and those who had been born with a high aggression over food became worse. I'm one of those experiments. I was always possessive over certain things I'd claimed as mine, and when someone tried to take it, I became very aggressive. That possessive nature worsened because of the treatment. I don't mean to act that way, it just happens..."

"How bad can such aggressive tendencies get?"

"I've watched experiments kill each other over scraps."

Raikidan's brow furrowed. "I don't see how that's unusual. Dragons do that all the time when food is scarce in areas."

"But humans don't," I said. "Humans will go elsewhere if there's no food. A normal human would avoid violence at any cost, at the risk of a serious injury."

He nodded. "All right, I can see that, but what about you? You said you require a lot of food, but I've seen you go a day on only an apple, if that. I don't understand how that statement can be true."

I scratched my head. "There was another side effect I developed from the deprivation that other experiments only sometimes did. Many experiments' bodies couldn't handle the lack of food, and when they were finally given consistent meals, they required even more to keep going.

"Ryoko is one of those experiments. It's the reason we don't have food in this house very often. She had already required a larger quantity due to her extreme enhancements, but that increased drastically after the starvation process. My body, on the other hand, had a much different effect. This effect was much rarer than Ryoko's."

I gazed up at the sky. "My body became so used to the lack of food, it adapted. It learned how to survive and function normally when food was scarce. Over time, it's been able to function like a normal nu-human's would, and at times, I won't feel hungry for days. My appetite has become… situational. I guess that's how you could put it."

"I never thought such incredible adaptation was possible."

"Join the club," I responded with a smirk.

"What in Lumaraeon is a club?"

I shook my head. "Forget about it. It's just an expression."

Raikidan stood. "Very well, Butterfly."

"Stop calling me that!"

"No. I'll stop calling you that when I feel like it. Now go to bed. You'll be going to work tomorrow."

I threw my head back. "Yes, boss."

I then jumped down onto the fire escape and headed into my room.

28
CHAPTER
(RYOKO)

I opened the door to the basement and headed down, Rylan close behind. Laz handing out instructions hit my sensitive ears. She'd taken Raikidan down here earlier to train him with close-quarters combat, and I was curious how well it was going. He was a capable guy from what I could tell, but our training regimens could be difficult on non-experiments. *And knowing Laz, she's not pulling any punches.*

Just then my ears picked up something slamming into a heavy weight bag and then Laz chastising Raikidan. "No, no, not like that."

I snickered. *Sounds like it's going well.*

Making it halfway down the stairs, I spotted the two at the hanging heavy bag. Laz readied herself, punched it three times, and then instructed Raikidan to repeat. He pulled himself into a bad form, to which she sighed and corrected him, and then he hit the weighted bag. She shook her head and pressed on his core, reprimanding him again about his form and the importance for doing it. *Oh, Laz, we all can see you're just using it as an excuse to touch that fit body of his.*

The pair stopped their task and looked at us when Rylan and I made it to the bottom step. I grinned. "Looks like you two are having fun."

Laz scowled. "Fun isn't a word I'd use."

"She's being a pain in the ass," Raikidan said.

She smacked him in the abdomen. "No, that's you. If you'd pay attention for once, you'd get this right."

He rubbed where she hit him. "I am paying attention. You're just too picky."

I half smiled, throwing my thumb behind me. "You want us to leave so you can have your lovers' quarrel in private?"

Laz glowered, and Raikidan looked confused. Rylan snickered behind me. "Quite the mixed response."

He then slipped past me, heading for a closet. "Why don't we show him something more practical? He may learn better that way."

Laz nodded. "Can't hurt to try."

Raikidan narrowed his eyes at her but kept his mouth shut. *Interesting.* Their relationship confused me to no end. I needed to know more about it. And that meant getting to know Raikidan. He was the biggest unknown in all this. *But how?*

Rylan and Laz pulled out mats from the closet and laid them out on the floor. Raikidan stayed out of the way, watching with great intensity. I sat down on a nearby table, content to take it all in. I'd love to join in on the spar, but no one could handle my strength. I doubted even Raikidan, as strong as the simulation claimed to be, could hold his own against me.

I did my best to not sigh out loud. Being strong was useful, but my kind of strength just got in the way most of the time.

Rylan and Laz got into position and she went about telling Raikidan the basics. Based on his bored expression, she was repeating herself. I giggled. He should have just listened in the beginning. Then she wouldn't be going back to square one. *He's lucky she's not teaching grappling. He'd find that instruction even more of a snore fest.*

Laz got a few punches in on Rylan before he went at her, showing a few other types of strikes not in her current "lesson." Typical Laz, she chose to "reprimand" him by striking him with a few non-lesson strikes of her own. *Hypocrite.*

Not surprising, the verbal lesson didn't last long, and Laz and Rylan went in on a full-on sparring match. Raikidan watched the pair intently, his tensing muscles catching my eye. Either this sparring excited him, or something else was up.

My attention was pulled away when a flicker of fire caught the corner of my eye. With fire-consumed fists, Laz threw a punch out at Rylan, who blocked with a small ice shield on his arm. *Really, you two?*

I could understand getting excited to spar, but adding in elements was a bit overboard. *No, I'm not jealous they can use elements and I can't. That'd just be silly.*

Laz landed a few good hits on an ice shield Rylan created on his arm, but when she hyperextended on the last one of the form set, Rylan ducked under her. He grabbed her extended arm and rolled her over his shoulder, slamming her onto the mat. *Wow, nice move, Ry!*

My excitement turned to surprise when Raikidan slammed into Rylan. *What the—*

"Raikidan!" Laz shouted.

Raikidan towered over Rylan as he lay on his side cringing. "That was Raikidan? I thought Ryoko slammed into me."

My back straightened. Did he really hit that hard?

Laz jumped to her feet and tried to push Raikidan. Keyword was tried. He didn't move at all. Laz wasn't the strongest out there, but even she could push most heavyweight civilians around. *What is he?*

Laz smacked his arm. "Knock it off!"

Raikidan's attention snapped to her, his eyes so intense I thought he'd light her on fire. She didn't back down. *Wow these two are intense. Wait...*

A grin spread across my lips as my eyes narrowed. "Someone is being protective."

Laz's eyes snapped to me, but Raikidan's didn't. He focused back on Rylan, who was now getting back up. Rylan backed up a few steps, gauging Raikidan, who remained still, intent on him. My grin widened and Laz's eyes narrowed. She was so in trouble. No way she could convince me I was wrong. All that tensing he'd done was because he didn't like Rylan hurting her, even if it was agreed upon. Which meant there was something there, even if small. *I just have to figure out how to get the truth to surface.*

Rylan rounded his shoulder. "Are you going to keep acting weird?"

"Don't hit her again," Raikidan warned.

My brow rose, and Laz's attention snapped back to him. "Excuse you? Just because you won't hit a woman, doesn't mean everyone else has to abide by that rule."

He won't? I sat back. Meant I wasn't going to get to test out his... strength. *I'm sure Laz does when no one is looking, though.*

Raikidan scowled at her. "I don't approve of this treatment."

386 ☙ SHANNON PEMRICK

Laz crossed her arms. "And I'm supposed to care? Get out of my way and let me get back to my sparring."

She tried to get around him to square off with Rylan, but Raikidan stepped in her way. Laz sidestepped him, but he grabbed her by the waist and pulled her back a few inches. I grinned. This was amusing.

Laz ground her teeth. "You know what, you spar with him, then."

"Wait, what?" Rylan said.

"He needs the practice, and if he's not going to let me spar with you and watch how it's done, then he can get hands-on experience."

He sighed. "All right, fine. But you owe me."

She waved him off as she walked over to me. "Yeah, yeah." I smirked at her when she sat down, and she narrowed her eyes. "Don't you start."

"Oh, you're no fun." I nudged her. "You can't be all that mad at him. It's an admirable trait."

"It's an annoying one." She gave me a sidelong glance. "Not even you can come up with a reasoning that doesn't scream, 'because you need to be delicate and protected like some useless flower.'"

She had a point. I didn't understand the moral stance much better than she did, especially so when it got in my way of getting things done. If I were in her shoes I'd be just as irritated.

Rylan pointed at her. "That's not why we're like that. I've told you that over a hundred times."

"Yeah, whatever."

Rylan frowned, and even Raikidan looked back at her. Neither appeared to understand her reaction to the behavior. *So clueless.* No matter how many times we explained it, not even Rylan understood why we had such an issue with the stance. I didn't lie. I did find it an admirable to have as a trait, but there was a line to be aware of. *And by how Raikidan is acting, this isn't a line he grasps at all and is well beyond crossing.*

The two men squared off. Not understanding where Raikidan stood with fighting experience, Rylan took a more defensive stance, using the time to analyze him. Raikidan, on the other hand, took a more reckless approach, swinging at Rylan, trying to find weak points.

"Use your head, Raikidan," Laz chastised. "You waste energy and allow your opponent to find your weak spot in your defense."

"Like right there," Rylan announced before slamming his fist into Raikidan's side.

Raikidan grunted in pain and threw out another attack, still no tactical thought being put into his swings. Laz sighed but chose not to scold him again.

I rested my arm on Laz's shoulder and leaned my head on her. She glanced at me. "Liking the view?"

Rylan got another good shot in on Raikidan. I grinned. "I'm watching two hot guys working up a sweat by beating on each other. What's not to enjoy?"

Her brow rose. "You have some weird tastes."

I winked at her. "More like fun."

She rolled her eyes and focused on the men again. *Damn.* I needed to figure out how to engage her better, or I wasn't going to get my desired answers.

I leaned on her more. "I mean, the only thing that could make this better is if they lost the shirts."

Her face scrunched. "Please stop sharing your weird fantasies with me."

I chuckled. "You could always share yours instead."

Her eyes narrowed. "I don't have any."

"To share? Oh c'mon, Laz, don't be shy."

She pushed me off her. "Knock it off, Ryo."

I huffed. There went that idea.

Raikidan finally landed a hit on Rylan, and, from the way Rylan cringed, it was a good one. *I wonder how strong this guy is.* I really wanted to go toe-to-toe with him. He owed me a match anyway.

Laz praised Raikidan, though Rylan grumbled about not receiving any when he did well. *Aw, someone's a little jealous.*

The two men exchanged several more blows before Raikidan gained the upper hand and hauled Rylan over his shoulder, tossing him on the ground about three or four feet away. *Not bad.*

"No, not like that, Raikidan," Laz scolded. *Of course Miss Perfectionist found something wrong.* "You can't lift someone like that. You'll hurt your back."

I couldn't argue that. It was a smart thing to nitpick.

He held up his hands. "What are you, my mother?"

I fell on Laz as I laughed. She sucked in a tight breath. "You make me feel like I am."

My laughter continued. This was too amusing.

Rylan got back up to his feet, his breath heavier than I expected. Raikidan had to be putting him through a lot for that to happen. Rylan wiped beads of sweat off his brow and tugged at his shirt. *Oh wait.* I paid more attention to the air, and realized it was a bit hot in here. Wearing so little clothing myself, plus my higher-than-average body temperature, I only really ever noticed when the temperature dropped. *Plus, Rylan is more susceptible to heat due to his element.*

"Rylan, do you want me to turn the thermostat down?" I called out. "I'm not sure what's up with the hike in temp, but it's not a problem to adjust it." I glanced at Raikidan and Eira, who appeared unfazed. "These two won't complain either way, I don't think."

Rylan pulled his shirt over his head and discarded it on the floor. *Oh my.* "No, I can handle it. Thanks, though."

A thin layer of ice formed around his hands and spread up his arms, right up to his torso, the heat of his body melting it little by little. Rylan relaxed as he cooled down, his head hanging back a bit. When he'd cooled off enough, his muscles flexed, and the ice shattered. His body glistened. *Oh, Satria, take me now!* This was getting to be a bit much for me. I joked about them taking their shirts off to get a rise out of Laz, but I wasn't actually prepared for Rylan to go beyond that.

Raikidan crossed his arms. "Are you done yet? Or do you need some more time to pamper yourself?"

Laz snickered next to me.

Rylan scowled and readied himself. "Watch it. Your cockiness is going to be your downfall."

Raikidan pulled himself into a poor stance. "We'll see."

I clapped my hands together. "And fight!" They both glanced at me, their brows creased, and I laughed. "Sorry. I watched Argus play one of his fighting games the other day."

Rylan shook his head, a small smile on his lips, and then used Raikidan's distracted state to gain the upper hand on him. *Smart!* But Raikidan had some good reflexes and managed to evade the surprise attack. Rylan, not to be outdone, refused to be shaken off that easily and closed the gap between themselves and grappled Raikidan.

Raikidan's strength proved superior and he easily escaped, but Rylan had a trick up his sleeve. He grabbed Raikidan's shirt and pulled it over his head, twisting the garment at the same time, trapping his unsuspecting victim.

Laz and I rolled with laughter as Raikidan struggled to free himself, having to resort to removing the shirt entirely. That was too funny of a power play.

Raikidan, displeased, tossed the shirt at us. Laz managed to dodge, but I wasn't so lucky. "Ah!"

I pulled the large shirt from my face, but not before I got a good whiff of his scent. *Man, he smells good. Wait! Brakes! Back up!* I couldn't think that way. I needed Laz to be the one who thought he smelled nice.

"Don't laugh," Raikidan said. "It wasn't funny."

Laz snickered. "Just because you didn't enjoy it, doesn't mean it wasn't funny."

Raikidan's eyes narrowed as he pointed at her. "Do you want to do this sparring thing instead?"

I leaned on her and waved at him. "No, no, keep going. I'm enjoying this view." I glanced at Laz. "Aren't you?"

She looked at me, her eyes impassive. "What view?"

"Oh c'mon, Laz. Look at Raikidan's bod! Those abs are so flat and yummy, you could eat off them."

"And what about Rylan?" She grinned at me. "You could wash your clothes on those abs."

I did everything in my power to not react and to block out the tantalizing mental image of running my hands over those amazing abs of his. *Or eating off them. Stop it!*

I had planned this to get a rise out of her, but she was managing to get a leg up on me. *She does that to me so easily.* She hadn't blinked or hesitated at all. When did she learn to dish out this kind of comment? *Why isn't she reacting at all to what I say?*

I needed to up my game. She should at least get flustered with these kinds of comments. I grinned wickedly when something came to me. "You're avoiding my question. Do I need to drag Rylan away to allow for you and Raikidan to have some alone time? Time to learn how to eat something delicious off him?"

She jerked back, surprise and repulsion clouding her face. Still there was something else—a slight bit of reddening to her cheeks. *Bingo!* "What compels you to have and share such outrageously weird fantasies?"

I wagged my finger at her. "Not weird. Delicious. And I know you think so, too."

She pulled back more. "Can you not be so bizarre for once?"

"Oh, don't be shy." I looked to Raikidan. "You wouldn't mind that, would you, Raikidan?"

The two men stared at us, Rylan looking irritated for some reason, and Raikidan, well, he looked clueless. *How does he not understand? That wasn't a very subtle topic.*

I flicked my hand, dismissing them, and sighed. "You're no help. Well, go on you two. Go back to doing your manly thing and beat each other up some more."

The two glanced at each other and shrugged, going back to their sparring. Their actions remained the same for a bit, Raikidan swinging wildly while Rylan showed his more refined prowess. I shamelessly ogled. Laz watched with a critical eye, calling out Raikidan's improper moves to correct him. I didn't get it. How could she act like this wasn't fun to watch? How could she act so indifferent to men?

I knew this wasn't how she used to be. I knew that person; the woman who ultimately found herself shoved in a cage and hidden away for her own safety. She still had to exist in there, waiting to be released again.

Raikidan landed a solid hit on Rylan, pulling my attention back. Raikidan's posture had changed. It wasn't a mood shift, but a focus shift. It matched more what I'd seen Rylan holding. *Wait a minute.*

I watched closely as Rylan threw out a strike and Raikidan deftly moved out of the way. Rylan tried again and Raikidan blocked the attack, as if anticipating the move. Laz leaned forward as the pair circled the mat, Raikidan watching Rylan carefully; even adjusting his stance. *She also sees it.* Raikidan was mimicking Rylan.

Wait... Raikidan ducked a perfectly timed attacked from Rylan and struck him in the side with a good punch. *He's not just copying.* Raikidan was finally using his head and learning from Rylan—and maybe a bit from Laz with her back-seat coaching.

Raikidan blocked three consecutive attacks and deflected another without blinking an eye, his focus serious, and intent on following Rylan's moves. This was quite fascinating to watch.

I focused on Laz. "He learns fast. I didn't expect him to pick up any technique from one sparring match. Yet he's gone beyond that and has figured out how to execute well-thought-out strategies on the fly."

Laz nodded, but her focus on the match kept her from saying anything. I didn't blame her at this point. Raikidan's improvement was important. I'd have to hold off on my teasing and testing of the waters until these two calmed down a bit.

Rylan came in for another attack, which Raikidan blocked. It appeared as if he was about to follow up with a left hook, and Rylan readied to deflect, but Raikidan feinted and landed a right-handed blow to Rylan's gut.

I couldn't help but cheer. "That was amazing, Raikidan! You're picking this up so well."

Raikidan nodded, acknowledging my praise, and continued his attack.

"He's actually giving Rylan a run for his money," I said to Laz. "If I didn't know his fighting skill, I'd have thought Rylan was the amateur fighter."

"Raikidan is always full of surprises," Laz said.

I grinned, my eyes narrowing. "I'm sure he is."

Laz completely ignored me that time.

Raikidan ducked under a punch and jabbed Rylan in the jaw with a perfectly timed hit. Rylan staggered back and fell on his ass. The stunned and confused face he made sent Laz and me into a hysterical fit of laughter.

Rylan caught his bearings and glowered. "Stop laughing."

"Your face was priceless!" I said through my fit. "Raikidan, that was an amazingly timed hit." I wiped a tear away. "Ry, I don't know how you managed to let him do that to you."

"You think it's easy fighting him?" Rylan got to his feet. "He's a reckless, unpredictable powerhouse."

I waved him off. "Oh, don't be so dramatic."

He stared at me in disbelief. "Dramatic? You're not the one sparring with him." He held up his hands and then pointed at her. "You know what, you spar with him, then tell me I'm being over dramatic."

I jumped to my feet, excitement bursting through me. "That's a great idea!"

Raikidan took a step back. "No."

I placed my hands on my hips. "You promised we'd have a match to prove who is stronger. This is that time."

"I didn't agree to hit you. I agreed to do something to test our strengths in other ways."

"Oh really?" I winked at him. "Sounds even more fun."

His brow rose, his eyes showing he wasn't getting my teasing impli-
cation. *Wow, he's a new level of clueless.* Rylan glowered but clenched his
jaw shut. *What's with him?* I shook the thought from my head. He was
just mad at me for my earlier comments, though I couldn't understand
why. It's not like he cared I was talking about Raikidan so much. *Right?*

I took a deep breath and stood my ground. "I want to spar with
you. I can hold my own against you."

Raikidan crossed his arms. "Not happening."

I turned to Laz. "Laz, make him spar with me!"

She held up her hands. "What do you expect me to do? He wouldn't
let me spar with Rylan. I can't make him do things. He's not some pet
on command."

He could be your hunky pet if you tried harder. I stomped my foot. "He's
the only one who might be capable of holding his own against me,
and I really want to spar."

Laz sighed and beckoned Raikidan with a finger, walking away to a
corner. He followed and I shamelessly eavesdropped.

"I don't know why you want to talk to me over here," he said. "I'm
not doing it. No matter how much she carries on like a child."

Rude!

"Just this once." She placed her hands on her hips. "It's not going
to kill you."

I stifled a chuckle. *Depends on how excited I get.*

"I don't hit females."

My brow rose. That wasn't the first time I'd heard him using strange
words. *He really is an odd guy.* I grinned. Perfect for our odd ex-assassin.

Laz pinched her nose but then straightened. "Then don't see her
as a woman."

Excuse you!

Raikidan's face scrunched. "What?"

"If seeing her as a woman is the only issue here, don't see her as
one. Just see her as a person. Even pretend she's your mortal enemy.
Whatever gets you to forget she's female for maybe ten minutes."

Yeah, like he's going to last that long.

Raikidan's lips pressed into a line and his shoulders tensed. *Man, he's
yummy.* How could Laz ignore that?

Her eyes softened and her posture drew inward, giving her a less authoritative and more gentle presence. "Please. Just this once. For me."

I stared at her. I couldn't believe she was trying that tactic.

Raikidan hung his head and sighed, the pitch telling me he was giving in. "Okay. For you." He held up a finger. "But just this once."

A smirk spread across my lips. *Nothing between them, my ass.*

Raikidan faced me. He didn't look happy, but at least he was finally going to give this a try.

I pointed to the mat. "So, we going to go at it, or not?"

Rylan choked at my wording, Laz pinched her nose as she sighed and Raikidan... looked more clueless than ever. *I don't know why, but that clueless reaction is fun to see after making comments like that.*

"Let's get this over with," Raikidan said, taking up position on the mat.

Giddiness fell over me and I bounced over to him. Laz returned to sitting on the table, and Rylan joined her. I pulled myself into a fighting stance and waited. Raikidan appeared unsure, but after a few moments took some sort of fighting stance.

We stared each other down until my impatience took over and I slammed my fist into his chest. He crashed to the ground on his back, gasping for air. Laz smacked her forehead. *Dammit.* I didn't even use a whole lot of strength in that blow. I thought he'd be able to handle it.

Raikidan caught his breath and pushed himself into a partial sitting position. "I was not expecting that. Are you sure you're a woman?"

I looked down at my enormous chest and popped on my toes, making them bounce, as well as sending a bit of discomfort through me due to their weight. "I'm pretty sure that's what these indicate, and they're one hundred percent natural."

Raikidan gazed at me with a puzzled expression and Laz laughed. I glanced her way to find her holding her sides, and Rylan hiding his face.

My brow rose. "What's the matter, Ry?"

"It's nothing," he mumbled.

Laz continued to laugh. "He's lying. He's so lying."

Rylan smacked her but didn't stop hiding his face. Warmth spread over my cheeks. Did that really get to him? *Duh, Ryoko, he's a straight guy, and not a clueless one like Raikidan.* Raikidan's reaction actually interested me. Unless he was only into men, that should have gotten a much different reaction, even from someone as clueless as him.

Raikidan stood. "I'm guessing that was supposed to be some sexual joke?"

"Man, you are clueless," I blurted out without thinking.

Laz laughed more and Raikidan look unamused by my insult. *Oh well.* Even clueless, he was a good match for Laz. I could feel it. There was something about him that made him different, and not because he was able to get up after being hit hard by me.

I waved him to come at me. "Now you hit me."

Raikidan took a deep breath before throwing a punch at my arm. When his fist met my arm, I frowned. "What the hell was that? The old lady down the street could hit harder than that!"

He pulled back. "It just... isn't right to hit you."

"Isn't right?" My eyes narrowed, rage boiling in my chest. "Isn't right? I can take a hit! I'm not fragile and in need of coddling."

"Ryoko," Laz warned, an edge to her tone. "Keep your anger in check."

I didn't listen. "You agreed to spar with me. That means you don't get to hold back. Take your stupid moral code and shove it up your ass!"

My unchecked anger took over, and I grabbed Raikidan's arm. Using all my strength, I flung him into the wall behind me. Raikidan crashed through and the bricks fell on him.

Laz gasped. "Ryoko!"

My anger ebbed and then I reeled back. "Oh no! I didn't mean to do that. I'm sorry!"

Rylan jumped to his feet. "Sorry doesn't count if he's dead."

My anger flared up again. "I said I didn't mean to! His refusal to see me as an equal pissed me off."

"We're not treating you as if you're unequal."

"Yes, you are! By refusing to treat us like you would some guy, you're saying we're not deserving of equal treatment. Why is it so hard for your ice-encased brain to understand that?"

"Why is it that you can't understand it's not like that at all!"

Laz watched us bicker, her eyes showing her clear discomfort and inability to figure out how to stop it.

The sound of moving ruble caught our attention. Raikidan pulled himself out of the wall, groaning with effort. *Damn, he really is made of tough stuff.*

"No way he's human." Rylan's gaze snapped Laz. "No ordinary person could get up from that."

"He's not ordinary." She didn't look at Rylan as she spoke, her eyes pinned on Raikidan.

Raikidan's eyes snapped to me and his lip curled back into a snarl.

"Raikidan," Laz warned. "Keep your head clear."

He either didn't hear or didn't care to listen, because his eyes showed his livid state. He charged before I could think to react and slammed into me full force. Pain raked across me as I slammed into the ground, but so did excitement. He was strong!

I pushed myself into a partial sitting position, my head spinning a bit. "Wow. That was a nice hit."

Raikidan blinked and then took a step back as if only now registering he'd hit me. "I'm sorry. I shouldn't have done that."

"No, you should have!" Excitement built up in me and I jumped to my feet. "You did exactly what Laz said, and forgot that I was a woman. You were hit hard, so you hit hard back. That's what I want. What *we* want. For you to stop treating us like we're different and can't handle the same things."

I looked myself over. "Look at me, barely a scratch. I'm made of tough stuff, just like you. You're the first to be able to keep up with me! Not even most other Brute experiments can hold out like you. It's exciting!"

I watched him think this over. Whatever controlled him to be careful around us women had to be rooted deep. This wasn't going to change overnight for him, and I was starting to realize that was why Laz told him he only had to fight me once. She already knew he was like this before she brought him here. She knew it'd be a struggle but was willing to either overlook it or work on it with him if he was able to bring other kinds of advantages to the table to aid us.

I punched the air. "C'mon, let's keep going! This is fun. I want to see what tough stuff you're made of."

Raikidan watched me, and then nodded, his hesitation melting away. Maybe I'd finally gotten through to him in some way.

The two of us went at it some more, Raikidan taking a defensive stance more often than not. He appeared to be fighting with his weird moral code, but kept up with my hits well. I could tell they hurt him, but he wasn't complaining. *Very impressive.* If I had any reservations about wanting to get to know him, they were gone now. He was something else.

Oh, that's it! If I were to get him and Laz together, I needed to know him. I needed to try to get close to see how she'd react, and so I knew what I was dealing with. He wouldn't be an anomaly anymore.

The door to the living room opened. We all looked up to find Genesis carefully making her way down the steep steps. Halfway down, she poked her head under the banister. "I have—what happened to the wall?"

"Ryoko," Laz said.

I crossed my arms. "Rat."

Genesis shook her head. "As long as you get it fixed, I won't get on your case. It's not a major support wall, so I'm not too worried about it. And these assignments I have for all of you are more pressing."

I placed my hands on my hips as I relaxed out of my fighting stance. "What kind of assignments?"

"Surveillance for Eira and Raikidan, and some undercover work for you and Rylan."

I tapped my lips, trying to quickly come up with a way to utilize this. "Can I swap with Laz?"

Her brow furrowed. "Well, I picked this pairing because of the simulation results. I would like to test them to determine the accuracy."

"I get that, but I think it's a good idea if more than just Laz works with Raikidan. I mean, we're a team, and she's the only one who knows him all that much." *And I really don't think it's a good idea for me to work with Rylan.* My stupid misplaced feelings would not work well with that set up, especially with today's constant bickering.

Genesis switched her gaze to Laz. "What do you think?"

I turned to face her to find her in thought. Rylan next to her looked irritated but I couldn't be sure why. Laz nodded. "I think her reasoning is sound."

I glanced to Raikidan. "You're okay with it too, right?"

He nodded. "I don't see why it'd be an issue."

I smiled. *Perfect.* I was a bit disappointed Laz wasn't insisting on keeping the assigned teams. I wanted her to show some sort of jealousy or claim to him. But I could live with learning about Raikidan for now and getting under her skin another day.

I hooked my arm into Raikidan's. "Okay, *friend*, let's go find out what we're doing."

He merely nodded and let me drag him to the stairs.

Laz snickered. "Ryoko, making friends one broken bone at a time."

I couldn't help but laugh. It wasn't my goal to make friends that way, but it did seem to be a theme for me over the years. And I liked the idea of being friends with Raikidan. *Now if only I could get Laz and him past that part.*

29
CHAPTER
(EIRA)

The days had grown hotter as summer came closer, making working in the shop a pain, but work was work. It beat some of the other jobs I could be doing to bring in income for the rebellion.

Wiping the sweat off my brow, I pulled on the wrench one last time to finish tightening the bolt. Raikidan leaned on the car as he watched me. Stretching, I sighed and tossed the wrench down on a workbench. Raikidan sighed, and with his shirt, wiped away the beads of sweat that had formed on his brow and then pulled his shirt back down and tugged on it a few times to help cool it off.

"You know you can remove your shirt, right?" I told him.

"Why would I do that? You're always getting on my case about clothes."

"Because it's hot?"

"Why don't you remove your shirt?"

"Because I'm a woman."

"So, men can remove their shirts, but women can't? That doesn't make sense."

"All done?" Ryoko asked as she walked over, saving me from that unwanted conversation.

I nodded. "What's next?"

"I need to go grab a few things so we can get the engine and wiring harnesses hooked up. Then we can get the custom fiberglass paneling back on the car."

Sitting down on the top of the workbench, I watched her head to one of the shelves with supplies. Raikidan pulled off his shirt and tossed it on me.

Grunting, I balled it up and tossed it back at him. "Ass."

He grinned with a chuckle and tossed his shirt onto the workbench.

"Reaching over you," Rylan informed Ryoko as he walked over to her.

"O–o–okay," she stuttered as he pressed his shirtless, walking-work-accident self against her and reached for a tool chest above her.

I bit my lip and pressed my fist against my mouth in order to suppress a laugh. I could see the gleam in the corner of his eye. He was doing this on purpose. This whole time, I figured he wasn't coming on strong to her. I had been so wrong.

Ryoko gulped and tried her best to focus on finding the tools she needed. I shouldn't have found her situation funny, but I did, and I had no regrets.

"That's quite the scar on Rylan's back," Raikidan said. "How'd he get it?"

My body moved, and my vision faded in and out, as did all my other senses. People screamed. Blood splattered. Bodies fell.

I didn't answer him. I had been doing my best not to think about that scar, but now that he had mentioned it, it was hard not to. The scar went from Rylan's right shoulder blade down to his left hip, and you could tell the wound had been deep. Looking at it brought back that painful memory.

Rylan ran through an open door and came right toward me. My vision faded in and out.

"Eira?"

"I don't want to talk about it."

I couldn't take control. My vision faded and then came back just as I was slicing him across the back with a dagger.

"Eira, Are you okay?"

"I told you, I don't want to talk about it," I repeated as I rose to my feet.

Raikidan grabbed my wrist and forced me to face him. "Eira, what's wrong?"

His body lay on the ground, unmoving, and bleeding out. My vision faded in and out. What had I done?

I looked him in the eye. "He got that because of me."

His brow rose. "You gave him that?"

I pulled my arm from his grasp and let my gaze fall elsewhere. "I told you—I'm a monster."

"Eira—"

"Hey, Raikidan," Rylan called over to him as he finally pulled the tool chest from the shelving. "Come with me. I'll need you to grab the new engine for that car the three of you are working on. We'll find out if you can handle the weight."

Raikidan chuckled at his challenge and followed. Sighing with relief, I walked over to Ryoko. I was safe from his questions for a little while.

"You shouldn't call yourself that," Ryoko said.

"I'm not going to talk about this. What do you need help finding?"

She placed her hands on her hips and faced me. "Well, I do want to talk about it."

"And I don't, so drop it."

"It wasn't your fault."

I snorted and grabbed a gas line.

"Laz, seriously. Why do you blame yourself for it?"

"Why?" I threw the line back into the shelf and rounded on her. "Because I lost control, that's why! I should have been able to stop myself from attacking him, but I couldn't. He almost died because of me. It was my fault!"

Ryoko took a step back and gazed at me with sympathetic eyes. "Laz…"

I didn't want to hear it. I pushed past her in anger, snatching up a few tools in need of reshelving, and headed to the back of the shop to put them away. I took my time in hopes it'd help me calm down, but my anger remained.

I stopped when someone grabbed my shoulder. I glanced back to see Zane and then went back to my task. I didn't want to talk, but he wasn't going to take no for an answer.

"Chickadee, you need to let it go," he said.

"It's not something that can just be forgotten."

"I'm not saying to forget. I'm telling you to stop blaming yourself for something that was beyond your control. To stop comparing the person you once were to the person you are now."

I sighed and looked at him. "I'm the same person, Zane."

"I disagree."

"Nothing has changed. I still have the same thoughts and the same bloody past, and the same dark cloud following me everywhere. I still fight the same demons. I've remained the same."

"You're wrong, Eira. You're not the same person. I've seen you at your worst. I feared for your life at that time. Everyone did. We thought we had lost you." He cupped my face with his hand. "But the darkness that lay in your eyes then is gone. In its place is a light I never thought I'd live to see in you again. Between Ryder coming into our lives... and whatever happened to you while you were away, it has changed you. I know you can move on from the past, but you have to let the past go first. You need to stop blaming yourself."

Ryder. Zane saying his name made me wonder how he was doing. I wished there was a safe way for me to contact him, so I could find out.

Zane took the remaining tools from my hands. "Now, why don't you go help out Argus? We both know he won't bother you, and you're pretty good with the projects he does."

I sighed and nodded. Heading back to the front end of the shop, I located Argus at his work bench and sat on a stool next to him as he soldered a wire to a gun. Once he was done, he sat up and lifted his face mask.

While tilting his head, he grinned and handed me the soldering tool as he rested his elbows on the workbench. "I could use the extra help."

"I could use something to distract me," I replied as I took the tool.

He chuckled. "I can tell. Just make sure you solder the wire and not my fingers in your anger."

I laughed. "Won't promise anything."

I pulled down my goggles and went to work. It wasn't long before we were interrupted. I did my best to keep my attention on my task. I honestly didn't want to get Argus' fingers, and I wasn't particularly interested in the customers Zane was now greeting, at least not until a familiar laugh rang through my ears.

"Zo is here," Argus muttered.

"I noticed."

He snickered. "And here I thought you were his number one fan."

I snorted. "Please. All he does when he's here is bother us."

"You mean bother you."

I sighed and he snickered. "It's not funny. I was hoping it was Ryoko being... well... Ryoko."

"It's not a bad thing."

I stopped soldering and looked at him.

"There are benefits to being in the good graces of a ranked officer. We could potentially use his interest to our advantage at some point."

"I suppose..."

"Eira, I know it's non—"

I wasn't going to find out what he wanted to say. Zane strolled over to us with Zo and three other soldiers. Argus and I sat up as they approached.

"I told Zo his weapon still wasn't ready, but he insisted on looking at it anyway," Zane explained.

Argus gestured to the unfinished gun. "What you see is what you get."

Playing on my supposed innocence, I giggled at Argus' words. Argus lifted up his mask and grinned at me. The exchange attracted Zo's attention.

"I'm still surprised it's taken you this long," Zo said.

"Well, you want me to change a rail gun to a plasma gun, which still hasn't been perfected on its own, and on top of that, you want several other modifications," Argus replied. "It's also mostly just me working on this."

Zo crossed his arm. "You shouldn't take Eira's help for granted."

Zane laughed. "Eira doesn't help him much, only when she's angry at everyone else and doesn't wish to work on the car she's assigned. Isn't that right, Chickadee?"

I lifted my goggles and smiled in response.

Zo chuckled. "You don't come off as the angry type, Sweetcheeks."

I forced myself to continue to smile instead of retch at the name he'd started using since my third "official" day working here. I opened my mouth to reply, but the sound of someone walking up behind me pulled my attention. Turning, I leaned back and grinned at Raikidan. He responded with his signature cocky grin as he carried a large car engine on one shoulder. Obviously, he had proved to Rylan he could do it, which would be a major feat for the nu-human he was supposed to be pretending to be.

"C'mon, Butterfly, I need your help. I'm giving this over to Ryoko and then I have a list of parts we need to go grab for her little project."

I narrowed my eyes and stood. "I told you not to call me that."

He continued to grin. "You also haven't given me a good enough reason not to."

Rolling my eyes, I pushed him sideways and headed over to Ryoko, who now stood by a custom car.

He stumbled but caught himself with ease and caught up with me. "That wasn't nice."

"You didn't give me a reason not to do it."

Raikidan chuckled and then pushed me sideways with his elbow. Stumbling, I righted myself and pushed him for a second time. "Asshole."

He smirked at me but refrained from any more comments.

"Don't keep her too long," Argus called after us. "She was actually being helpful."

Raikidan waved him off and the two of us met up with Ryoko. Raikidan made his exchange with her and then pulled out a scrap of paper with a bunch of scribbles all over it. Raikidan just stared at it in confusion, piquing my interest.

Ryoko glanced at the paper and laughed. "Good luck reading that."

"Let me guess, Zane wrote it?" I said.

Raikidan nodded. "I assumed it'd be legible when Rylan handed it to me, so I didn't think to look at it beforehand."

"I'm sure we can manage," I said.

"Yeah, and if you have any trouble, let me know and I'll help where I can," Ryoko said. "I know what I need for this job anyway. I just need to focus on getting this engine lowered in before I can give you a hand."

Raikidan nodded and then led the way to the back of the shop, where we stored all the ordered-in parts. We grabbed the largest parts first and brought them over to Ryoko, who was now being assisted by Rylan, and then went to work on the parts that needed a ladder to access. Well, Raikidan needed a ladder. I was too stubborn to use one, and just climbed up and down the shelves.

"You really should use a ladder," Raikidan said as I made my fifth trip up. "You can carry more and it's less dangerous."

I reached for a few tools. "I'm fine."

"Eira, really. You should—"

"Rai, stop wor—" I gasped when my foot slipped, but I caught myself and sighed quietly before going back to my job.

Raikidan sighed in aggravation. "See, you need to be more careful! You could have fallen."

I snorted as I grabbed the last tool I needed and began climbing down. "I'm far more skilled than that."

When I was only a few feet off the ground, I decided to jump down to save time. I turned and let go of the metal shelves, only to run into Raikidan as I landed. My heart stopped as he caught me and rested his hands on my back. The shop slipped away as we stared at each other, and the longer we remained this way, the more I noticed that strange feeling trying to surface in my body again.

Suddenly, my senses came back, and I snapped myself out of the bizarre trance. I pushed Raikidan away. "You need to watch where you stand. I could have landed on you."

"Yeah, sure," he said slowly.

I shook my head and headed for Ryoko and Rylan's location, only to nearly run into her as we both decided to round the same corner.

"Oops, sorry," she said.

I shrugged. "Don't worry about it. No harm done. Whatcha need, these tools?"

She shook her head. "No, I was going to come grab Raikidan, so he could help me fetch lunch."

I skirted around her. "Oh, well he's all yours."

"C'mon, Rai, let's go," she said.

"Whoa, wha—"

I set the tools down on the work bench and watched as Ryoko dragged Raikidan out of the shop by the wrist. He started laughing when she didn't let up, even after asking her to, and a strange feeling bubbled in my chest. It was different than the one I had felt moments ago. It was fairly negative and a bit possessive, and I had experienced it before, but a long, long time ago. *Jealousy?* That didn't make sense. I couldn't possibly see a reason for that emotion to surface.

"Where are those two going?" Rylan asked, pulling me out of my thoughts.

I shrugged. "She said something about getting lunch and needed Raikidan's help. I'm actually surprised she didn't ask you."

He nodded and looked toward the door they had left open. "She always asks me first, and it wasn't like I was busy doing anything."

The bond flared up in the back of my head and I eyed him. *That's what she's up to.* When she opted to go on a mission with Raikidan the other day instead of me, I knew she was up to something. It made sense for her to want to get to know Raikidan, especially after I finally got him to spar with her. But I knew something else was up, especially when the bond started tugging at my mind as Rylan watched them head upstairs. It had flared up a few times before that when she wouldn't stop talking about Raikidan. "Disappointed? Or maybe you're jealous?"

He grunted. "No, just confused."

"Right."

He nudged me. "And what about you? The bond was acting up for a little while."

"*Tch*, this is me we're talking about. I couldn't care less."

"Yeah, sure."

We both glanced behind us when someone approached. It was Zane, and he was deactivating his communicator. I then realized Zo and his goons were gone.

"What's up, Zane?" I asked.

"Genesis needs you to go do something," he said. "You and Raikidan, but Ryoko ran out before I could stop them."

"I'm sure she has her communicator on her," Rylan said. "I'll give her a call."

Zane nodded and then looked at me. "You'd best get home quick, so you can find out what she wants. She wouldn't say on the line."

I nodded and headed for the door. It wasn't a surprise Genesis wouldn't reveal anything over the line. With us being in a public area, she wouldn't want to risk the wrong person overhearing somehow. It was best if I just headed home quickly to hear her out myself.

Sweltering heat clung to me as I walked; the low, late afternoon sun did nothing to quell the unusual oppressive spring weather. My brow furrowed as I took in my surroundings. The assignment Genesis had given me when I arrived back at the house was simple. Pretend to get lost, and accidentally make my way into a restricted area to teach Raikidan where the boundaries were and how to handle soldiers if any were encountered, including getting information out of them without them realizing what happened. Easy and low-profile, as most missions come, but evidently, in my pretending, I had ended up really getting lost.

The sound of flapping wings echoed through the street and I looked up. A large crow perched on the top of a building and gazed down at me. *There he is.* I continued on. Raikidan hadn't made it back to the house by the time my briefing was over, so Genesis assured me she'd brief him and then send him after me. I was glad she chose him for this type of mission. At least he couldn't make fun of me for getting lost, because he would have no idea.

The sound of approaching footsteps caught my attention. I took a deep breath and started tugging on my fingers. I tightened my shoulders as I bit my lip, making myself look like some worried mess.

"Halt!" I stopped and glanced up to see two armed soldiers approaching me. *Shit.* Neither of the soldiers wore helmets, and I recognized one. He was the soldier Raikidan and I had met when we had arrived at the city. Thinking hard, I remembered that his name was Amon.

"This is a restricted area," Amon said. "State your business."

Wow, I was that lucky? What were the odds? I wrung my fingers together. "I'm lost."

Amon snorted. "Likely story."

The other soldier with him held up his hand. "Don't dismiss her words so carelessly."

"I might as well. This is a restricted area."

"I'm sorry. I didn't know this area was restricted. I really am lost," I said. *Seriously, loser, I'm that much of an idiot today.*

Amon stalked up to me and grabbed my arm. "Stop lying."

"Don't touch her, you vile cretin!"

I flinched at his grip. "That hurts, stop!"

His grip tightened.

"Please..."

He bent close to my ear. "Tell me the truth and I'll stop hurting you."

"Amon, knock it off," the other soldier warned. "You're going too far."

I tried to struggle away. "I'm telling the truth! Please let go of me!"

"What's going on here?"

I stopped moving and looked up at the approaching soldier. My eyes grew wide. "General Zo…"

It was just my luck I'd run into him. I couldn't escape this man. One glance at me, and Zo looked at Amon with confusion. "What is going on, Amon?"

"She was trespassing," he defended.

I struggled against his grip again. "I told you, I'm lost."

Zo glanced to the other soldier, who nodded. "He hasn't given her any time to explain beyond those words."

Zo focused on Amon. "Let her go."

"Sir?"

"She's telling the truth."

Amon hesitantly let go. I stumbled, as I was still struggling against him during the exchange, but refused to fall over, and glared at Amon as I rubbed my arm.

Zo held out his hand. "Come with me, Eira."

Amon's eyes widened, and I childishly stuck my tongue out at him as I made my way over to Zo. As I did, he folded his outstretched arm and had me tuck my arm around it.

"Thank you, General," I whispered.

He grinned. "Please, just Zo."

I nodded. "Okay, I'll try to remember that."

"What are you doing here?"

"Getting lost."

He belted out a hearty laugh. "Shouldn't you be with someone so that doesn't happen? I doubt your overprotective friend would agree to you wandering around by yourself."

I shuffled my feet, my eyes falling away. "I, uh, kinda snuck out without Rai knowing. I wanted to see if I could follow a route Ryoko showed me. I think I need to practice it a little more before I try again on my own."

Zo chuckled. "Cities can be confusing. How's your arm?"

I glanced down at it. "Hurts a little. It'll probably bruise since my skin is so delicate, which means Zane and Rai are going to have a fit."

He flashed me a brilliant smile. "They can give Amon as much of a thrashing as they wish, after I'm done with him, of course."

I giggled and then looked around. "So, is this the way to get back to a main road?"

He shook his head. "You're looking a little pale. We need to get you something to drink before you pass out."

I smiled at him. "Well, if I had known I was going to be manhandled today, I would have brought a bottle of water."

Zo laughed at my joke and led me into a small building. The building had only one room, with shelves lining the wall and a large oak table with a dark finish in the center. Several soldiers lounged about, and I recognized a few of them as moles but paid them no mind. They returned the favor by paying only as much attention as the loyal soldiers.

Zo pulled out a chair at the large table and motioned for me to sit. I sat obediently and watched him walk to a small fridge. My gaze wandered around the room but snapped back to focus on Zo as he returned. With a smile, he handed me a bottle of water and pulled up a chair for himself.

Holding his gaze, I took a quick sip, and then more once I realized how thirsty I truly was. I stopped dead in the midst of a gulp when the water lodged in my throat. Swallowing hard, I beat my chest and coughed violently. Zo stared in shock for several moments.

Regaining his composure, he placed his hand on my shoulder. "Are you all right?"

I coughed a few more times and nodded. "I think my lungs were thirsty, too."

Zo laughed. "Well, it might be a good idea to lecture your lungs on the negative aspects of that wish."

I chuckled and coughed one last time.

"Feeling better?" he asked.

I nodded and smiled. "Yes, and I think I'll stay better as long as I'm not jumped by any more soldiers."

He chuckled. "Now care to tell me how you got in here?"

"I walked?"

Zo frowned. "Eira, this is a restricted area. It's lined with fencing. Now just tell me the truth and everything will be fine."

"I just walked around," I insisted. "There was no fencing anywhere."

He sat back in his chair and rubbed his chin. I kept eye contact as much as possible. I was being honest with him for once, and if he couldn't believe a real truth over a false one, I was going to be really irritated.

A tall, tan young man with short blonde hair walked over to us with a metal box that was only the size of his palm and placed it down on the table. "It is a possibility there is an area where the fence is gapped."

"There shouldn't be," Zo said. "Those fences were carefully placed."

"But there is a possibility someone didn't complete their job, or a problem group took it down and we never noticed, because we've never had someone trespass before." The young man pressed a button on the side of the box, and a large holographic map of the city transmitted from the top. "If we can pinpoint her start point and the path she took until she became lost, we can get a rough idea of where the fence break might be."

Zo rubbed his chin some more and nodded. Leaning over the table, he pointed to a small area on the map. "She started here."

The young man apprehensively looked up through his lashes at him but knew better than to question how Zo knew. I leaned on the table and took a close look at the map. I could make out the building that was our home, and all the main and side streets that connected to each other. Although I was well aware holograms could create amazing detail, the amount of detail this hologram showed off for its size and object scale surprised me.

"I went this way." I traced my finger on the path I had taken, causing the image to distort every time I accidentally touched it. I stopped when I got to the point where I had started to get lost. "I think this is where I lost my way. I was supposed to take a left, and I took a right. Then it went downhill from there."

Zo nodded. "You went through many back alleys. I suppose it is possible a fence might have been forgotten. Corporal."

The young man stood. "Sir?"

"Take a group of men to search the area."

He saluted by placing his arm on his chest like all other soldiers would. "Yes, sir."

"Oh, and bring Amon with you," Zo instructed as the young man turned to gather some other soldiers. "If you do find a break, I want him to be the one to tell me."

The young man, although confused, nodded and went about his

duty. Zo grabbed the hologram box and turned it off. Standing up, he placed it in one of the small leather pouches tied to his belt and extended his hand to me. "Shall we be off?"

I gave a small smile and accepted his offer. Making sure I had my bottle of water, I followed him out of the building. The sound of a crow call echoed through the alleys as Raikidan flew from his perch on top of the building Zo and I had just been in.

When we were out of sight of the other soldiers, I glanced up at Zo. "What was that place?"

"A command post."

"Is that why this place is off-limits?"

He nodded. "Yes. All the buildings you see here are military, and no, I can't tell you what they are used for. That's classified information."

I pouted. "Fine, be mean."

He chuckled but refused to tell, not that I was surprised. *Not like I'm good at getting men to do what I want by batting my eyes and saying please. I'm not Ryoko.*

The two of us grew silent. I knew I should work the civilian cover and attempt some more information baiting, but I couldn't think of anything to get Zo to spill without causing a problem. So instead I searched for Raikidan. I couldn't find him, although I had a strong feeling he was still around, as if he were lurking in the shadows.

Zo cleared his throat. I snapped my attention back to him to find him looking at me expectantly. I realized he was waiting for me to answer a question I hadn't heard him ask.

I ducked my head and looked away shyly. "I–I'm sorry. I got distracted and missed your question."

He chuckled. "I asked how your memory was doing."

"Oh… o–okay, I guess," I replied. *Think of something fast, stupid.* "I unfortunately had a regression period last week, but the other day I made some more progress. I've also had a small breakthrough with my personality, which I think made Rai happy."

"I noticed," Zo remarked. "I must say, I do enjoy the extra attitude, and if you say it was only a small breakthrough, I will have to admit you could give some soldiers a run for their money when it comes to your full personality."

I smiled at him. If this went well, I might be able to act more like myself in time. I wasn't sure if I could keep up the sweetness act for the duration of this rebellion.

He scratched his head. "This next question might seem odd, but why do you call him Rai when everyone else calls him Ray?"

I was wondering when this question would come up. Took him long enough. I smiled. "That's because when we were younger, I wasn't able to say his name right, and it just kinda stuck."

"I see."

Zo suddenly frowned, which confused me. "What's wrong?"

He shook his head. "It's nothing. I shouldn't even be thinking about it."

I nudged him. "You can tell me. I'm good at keeping secrets."

He sighed and rubbed his neck. "Don't take this the wrong way, but your friend, Rai, is a strange one. He's overprotective, and from the sounds of it, only wants you the way you used to be, instead of embracing the person you are now."

I shook my head. "No, no, no. It's not like that at all!"

Zo tilted his head, as if urging me to explain. I shoved my hands in my pockets and exhaled slowly, as if I were trying to figure out how to word myself right. "Rai and I have known each other since we were kids. Our friendship was that type of bond where we knew when the other was in trouble and would come to their aid even if we were miles apart. Rai has saved my neck so many times that I owe him more than just my life. Rai is overprotective because he cares. He doesn't want me to get hurt, and frankly, I don't mind. I like knowing someone is looking out for me no matter what."

"All right, but that doesn't excuse his actions for wanting you to be someone you're not."

I shook my head. "You misunderstand. Rai was happy because I was. He told me the type of person I used to be, strong and independent. That's not the person I am anymore. I don't like being this pathetic, timid..." I scrunched my hands in front of me as the right word escaped me. "...*thing*. Knowing that I'm on my way to being the person I used to be makes me happy. Rai just wants me to be happy, and he will do everything in his power to ensure I am."

"You sound quite fond of him."

I smiled. "He's the greatest friend I could ever ask for. It's... probably more than I deserve..."

Zo looked down at the ground. I waited patiently for another question. He had to have at least one more. "How did you lose your memory?" I frowned and had my gaze fall away. "You don't have to tell me if you don't wish to." He lightly touched my shoulder. "If it's too much to think about, it's not a big deal."

"It's okay. In order for me to move on and regain what I lost, I have to face the past. I can't run from it." I paused for a moment as I conjured up the made-up story I had rehearsed. "I lost my memory in a fire."

Zo's eyes widened, but he remained quiet and listened. "My family and I were trapped inside the building. I went to find a way out in desperation, when a support beam fell on me. Rai had gone out hunting that day, and he wasn't expected to come back for some time, and I wasn't sure how many villagers would be able to help. I didn't think I'd make it. Then, out of nowhere, Rai showed up and saved me.

"I passed out before he got us outside. Because our village is so small, we don't have the same type of medical facilities this city has, so no one was sure if I'd make it. The healer we had at the time did what he could, which, sadly, wasn't much."

I pressed my lips together to make it seem as if I were fighting with the memory. "When I woke up, Rai was there. He hadn't left my side the entire time. I remembered him. He was the only one I remembered." I shook my head. "I couldn't remember what had happened to me, where I was, and could barely remember who I was, for that matter. The healer figured the memory loss was due to trauma. Unfortunately, it wasn't just the accident I had forgotten. I couldn't remember much past my adolescent years. Rai was determined to help me as much as possible, and promised he would do what he could to make sure I stayed safe from then on."

"What happened to your family?" Zo asked, his apprehension to push that line clear. "I know you mentioned the other week your brother and father weren't alive anymore…"

My frown grew deeper. "None… none of them made it. Rai tried to go get them after I was safely outside, but… it was too late."

"I'm sorry."

"Me too…"

The two of us fell silent. Zo believed every word, and I didn't blame him. I had almost convinced myself it had actually happened.

"Here." Zo reached into the leather pouch he had placed the hologram box in and pulled it out. He took my hand and placed it in my grasp. "I grabbed it for you, so you wouldn't get lost again. It will show you all the restricted areas so you don't wander into them again. I'm not supposed to give this out to nonmilitary personnel, so don't tell anyone, okay? I could get into a lot of trouble."

I smiled. "Your secret is safe with me. And thank you. I'll make sure to have it on me at all times. But what if someone thinks I stole it?"

He smiled back at me. "Just tell them to take it up with me, okay?"

I nodded. Although his offer contradicted what I was promising to hide, I didn't say anything.

I started to look around when I recognized a few landmarks. This allowed me to note the darkening sky. I then spotted the house. "I see the house. Thanks for bringing me back this far. I should be able to make it from here."

Zo shook his head. "It's my duty to make sure you arrive safely. You're stuck with me until we get to your front door."

I forced myself to smile. To a normal person, it would seem like he was just being a good soldier, but to me, I found it creepy and it made me uneasy. As we came closer, I made out a small outline of a person by the front of the house. I squinted and noticed it was Raikidan. I wondered how long he had been standing there. He stood extremely still, with his arms crossed over his chest, and could almost pass as a statue.

He looked up as the two of us approached, his expression cold and hard.

"Hey, Rai…" I mumbled.

"Where have you been?" he demanded.

I flinched. "Um, around…"

He snorted and my gaze fell. "I'm sorry. I didn't mean to upset you. I just wanted to see if I could do this on my own."

He sighed and his expression softened. He lightly grasped my arm and pulled me into him, resting his forehead on my head. "I'm not upset. I was just… worried."

I grinned. "You suck at being mad."

"I can never be mad at you," he muttered. "No matter how much I try."

"Pushover."

He held me out at an arm's length and tapped my forehead with his finger. I rubbed it unhappily. Raikidan glanced at Zo. "Looks like you need to brush up on your navigational skills."

I giggled. "I need to learn the city better before I try going around on my own again."

He addressed Zo. "Thank you for bringing her home."

Zo nodded. "It was my pleasure."

I didn't miss the hint of irritation in his voice. Glancing up at Raikidan, I could tell he hadn't missed it either. Raikidan wrapped his arm around my shoulders. "Let's head inside. Ryoko turned into a bigger mess than me."

I groaned. "Perfect."

"Eira." I looked at Zo before I opened the door. "Do be careful. It may be wise to make sure you're with someone at all times while in the city. It's not safe for a young woman to walk around by herself."

I smiled. "I'll keep that in mind. Thank you for your help, Zo."

He nodded and watched Raikidan and me head inside before leaving. Raikidan let go of me once he shut the door, and the two of us sprinted up the stairs. The others were now all home and waiting eagerly.

Ryoko was grinning like mad. "Did you have fun getting lost?"

"Hardly," I muttered.

"Did you at least learn anything?" Genesis asked impatiently.

"No—"

She sighed. "That was the whole point of me sending you out to do—"

"Genesis, will you shut up and let me finish?" She sucked in a tight, annoyed breath, but didn't say a word. "I didn't learn any information, but"—I held up the hologram box—"I did obtain something of interest."

Argus sat up and took great interest in the box. "Is that what I think it is?"

I pressed the button and the hologram map appeared. "I don't know, you tell me."

Ryoko squealed with delight and jumped over the back of the couch to take it from me. "How did you get it?"

"It was given to me."

"Who gave it to you?" Genesis asked. "One of our own?"

"Zo," Raikidan said.

Silence enveloped the room for a moment.

Ryoko giggled as she examined the device. "What does it matter? We now have something that can really help us."

"I suppose it doesn't really matter, but I'm quite curious," Genesis said. "Zo could get into a lot of trouble for handing something like that out. How did you get him to hand it over?"

"Sympathy card," Raikidan and I replied in unison. My eyes flicked to Raikidan, an uncomfortable sensation rolling through me.

Genesis, unaffected by the awkward unison response, looked at the map. "Ryoko, Argus, I want you both to work with this to see what we can learn from it. I suspect this map will have some secrets we can utilize." Ryoko and Argus nodded, and then Genesis focused on me again. "You can take the rest of the day off. Raikidan, you too."

I nodded my thanks and headed to my room to relax. I needed it. Once my head hit my pillow, I looked at my arm. I could already see the skin starting to discolor.

"How's your arm?" Raikidan asked.

"Fine, I suppose. It doesn't hurt, but that could change in the morning. It'll bruise for a little while at least."

Raikidan chuckled. "Just say the word and I'll kill him for you. Zo did give me an open invitation."

I laughed. "That's quite all right. That lowlife isn't worth the effort."

"If you say so."

I closed my eyes and relaxed, only to open them again when Raikidan started going through the drawer of my nightstand. "What are you doing?"

He pulled out my book. "Reading."

I shook my head and closed my eyes again. The pattering sound of rain echoed through the room, along with Raikidan's footsteps as he walked over to the window. It was going to be another night of rain, but I didn't mind. Old injuries might protest, but otherwise I'd enjoy it.

"Thanks for what you said about me," Raikidan said quietly.

"Don't mention it," I replied. At least I knew he'd stuck around for that part of the assignment. He must have arrived back at the house just in time to look like he had been waiting for a while. "I couldn't go about saying I hang around a total ass."

"You made me look like some kind of hero."

I thought about it for a moment. "I suppose I did, but I don't see you complaining… not that it really matters."

Raikidan muttered something in his tongue. I shrugged it off and listened to the patter of the rain now falling from the sky until it soothed me into unconsciousness.

30
CHAPTER

Heaviness permeated my mind as I roused from my slumber. The sound of the rain quietly enveloped my ears. Something felt different about my sleeping arrangement, but my groggy mind couldn't place it. *Is it warmer in here? Why does my bed feel less soft?* Stretching, I realized there was something definitely different. My bed didn't just feel harder—it was. The air was also quieter than usual. There wasn't the normal heavy breathing of a large dragon in the room. Instead, there was the sound of steady human breathing. *And it's close.*

I opened my eyes and found I wasn't facing down on my bed, but curled up against a body—Raikidan's body. I bolted upright.

He chuckled. "Morning."

I pinched the bridge of my nose and forced myself to stay calm. "What... is... your... problem?"

He held up a hand in defense. "Hey, don't go pointing fingers at me. I just relaxed here after I couldn't sleep anymore. You're the one who curled up to me in your sleep."

"I told you to stay off my bed!"

"Why should you be the only who can lay on something so comfortable?"

I pinched the bridge of my nose again. "You have your own bed in your own room. Use that."

He smirked. "That's not as fun. Especially with the way you react."

I glared at him. "If you want entertainment, go watch TV."

Raikidan sat up. "I had thought about it, but Blaze brought a friend home, and neither seemed interested in going to his room."

I hid my face in my hand. "You didn't just tell me Blaze was messing around with some bar floozy in the living room."

"Not familiar with that term, but if you mean he's pinning the woman to the wall and mauling her face with that thing you call a kiss, then yes, I did just tell you that."

I groaned. "That didn't mean you were supposed to tell me!"

Raikidan chuckled. "Your reactions to such things never cease to amuse me."

I glowered at him. "You know what? For that comment, you're getting mandatory training with Ryoko for the next two weeks."

His expression dropped to a scowl. "No. We had an agreement the one time would be it."

"You're right, we did agree, but you're being an asshole, and there are plenty of benefits to you fighting her."

He held his stance. "I don't fight females. There's no negotiating this."

I relaxed my shoulders and rested my hands in my lap, trying to keep myself from blowing up at him. He was as stubborn as me, and that wouldn't do in this situation. "Raikidan, that's the problem here. I'm not telling you to do this because it'll keep you in shape. I'm telling you to do this, because you need to learn how to fight women. There will be a time where a battle will force you to decide to take a women's life, or risk losing your life, or the life of a comrade you're sworn to protect."

I tilted my head when he looked away. "Do you understand what I'm saying?"

"Yes."

"But you're still not going to budge on this, are you?"

His lips pressed into a thin line. "You don't understand just how difficult it is to say yes to this idea."

"You're right, I don't. But that doesn't mean you can't try. Besides, this is a good way to get to know Ryoko, too." I chuckled. "I don't think you'll enjoy going shopping with her, so this really is your only option right now."

His brow rose. "You want me to know her?"

"It can't hurt to make a friend or two." I shook my head. "Even if you don't want human friends, getting to know everyone should be on your to-do list. It'll make it easier for you to work with them."

Raikidan stared at me and then sighed. "Fine, I'll try this, but on one condition."

I pursed my lips. "What's that?"

A smirk spread across his face, and a dreadful knot formed in my stomach. It made him look appealing, and dangerous.

Raikidan leaned closer, reaching out and lifting my chin with his index finger. The touch brought my heart to a screeching halt. "Blaze and his 'friend' reminded me I still haven't found out what a kiss is like."

My heart's pace kicked back into gear, skipping right into a racing speed that thundered in my ears. *He did not*— I shoved him away. "Nope. You're not going to find out with me. Not happening."

Raikidan frowned, his brow creasing. "Why not?"

"Because I said so." I climbed out of bed. "If you want a kiss so bad, go find a hooker, or better yet, go ask Ryoko. She'd be more than happy to oblige."

"But not you."

"I will not be involved in your little experimenting phase. So, do not ask again."

My artificial clothes changed into typical day wear, and I left my room before Raikidan could make this even more awkward. *The nerve of him!*

"I told you not to trust him."

He could ask anyone else for that and wouldn't have an issue. So why did he have to pick me? With those striking eyes, and strong jawline, he could just... lean in and—heat flared in my core when the image of him leaning in close to me entered my mind. I shoved the image away. *Snap out of it!*

What the hell was wrong with me? This had never been an issue before. *These thoughts...* I shut it all out. I couldn't go there. Not with a human, and most definitely not with some dragon. *That would be the most stupid decision I could ever make.* I knew better than to make that mistake...

I entered the kitchen, looking for something to eat. I wasn't hungry, but I hadn't eaten much yesterday, and I needed to eat something.

Small feet pattered on the floor down the hall, and before I knew it, Genesis poked her head around the corner into the kitchen.

"Ah, you are awake," she said.

I pulled out a bowl for some cereal. "What's up?"

"I got a call from Council member Hanama. The assassins are running low on supplies for poisons and other such materials, and our usual supply locations for the more exotic items are tapped out at the moment. Do you think shamans would carry anything we could use?"

I leaned against the counter. "Depending on what it is, they may have to bring some in, but they would carry a lot of what the assassins use for natural-based concoctions. Of course, they'd only sell those kinds of herbs to a shaman, so I'd have to obtain them."

Genesis nodded. "I'll write up a list and get the funds ready for you."

"Take your time. I need to eat first anyway. Plus, I'd like to add to the list, as I've learned a few concoctions in my absence."

"See me when you're ready to add to the list." Genesis ran off, and I finished prepping my quick meal.

As I placed the empty used cereal bowl in the sink, Raikidan came out of my room, clothed in his Guard outfit. "I overheard your conversation with Genesis. I figured you'd ask me to join you for this new task of yours."

"Thank you for saving me time." I walked past him, pushing away a strange feeling that flared up into me when my arm brushed his by accident. "I'll be ready in a moment."

The sun had reached its zenith by the time Raikidan and I made it to the sector where the shamans should be selling their wares. It took me three different soldiers to find anyone with relative knowledge of their current whereabouts. *Now we just have to track them down.*

The clopping of hooves on asphalt caught my ears. I turned to find a small covered wagon pulled by two large horses, coming down the quiet road. Two cloaked figures sat on the driver's seat. *Oh, finally!*

One of them waved to us and I waved back, waiting for them to draw closer. Once they came into better view, I identified them both as male, one a Guard, one not, both from the North Tribe.

The non-guard pulled the wagon to a halt in front of us. "Good afternoon. Are the two of you looking for the rest of the caravans?"

I nodded. "We are. I needed to gather a few supplies, and I've forgotten where the setup was for today."

He chuckled. "I know who you are, Laz'shika. You're going to be out of the loop a lot, with how often we move around these days." *Well, at least my name is known in a way that isn't causing them to tell me to get lost.* The man gestured to the back. "My wagon is full of new supplies, so I can't offer you a comfortable seat, but you and your Guard are welcome to hitch a ride on my back step."

I smiled. "I appreciate the offer."

Raikidan and I made our way to the back, hopping up on the steps leading into the closed-up back. Raikidan tapped the side of the wagon when we were ready, and the wooden vehicle lurched forward.

The city rolled by, everything rather quiet. A few civilians poked their heads out of windows or turned to stare as we passed, their eyes curious about the wagon, but none bothered us. When I started to think this driver was as lost as me, we turned a corner and came to a street filled with wooden wagons. Some remained bundled up tight, while others were open for customers to buy or trade.

Our wagon pulled to a halt and the two of us jumped down, making our way to the front. The shaman driving the wagon was just hopping down as we made it to him.

"Thank you for the ride," I said. "I do appreciate it."

He smiled. "I'm happy to assist. If you need any more help, you know we'll be more than willing."

I caught the implications from his tone. He had to be one of the North shamans siding with Fe'teline. Not wanting to entice any unwanted excitement, I pulled out the list of items Genesis gave me, and held the paper up. "I could use some assistance, actually. I need to find some herbs that are hard to obtain in this city. Do you know who can assist me?"

The shaman took the paper and read it over. His expression didn't change, so he either had no idea what I needed them for, or didn't care. "There's only one person here who will have even half of these. Her name is Se'lata. She's a spice trader from the East Tribe."

The man handed the paper back to me. "You'll find her halfway down this street. Your nose will find her before your eyes do."

I chuckled. "Thank you. Have a wonderful day."

"And you, Laz'shika." He grinned. "And as I said before, if you ever need any assistance, call on us."

"I will keep that in mind."

I led Raikidan down the bustling street, taking in everything going on. Civilians mingled about with shamans, buying, bartering, even arguing. Shamans did the same with each other. It was an interesting sight to see. The shamans had done well over the decades, integrating with the cities and towns on this side of Lumaraeon.

They could be a valuable asset in defeating— *No, don't go there, Eira.* I knew better than to involve them in this.

Raikidan nudged me and then pointed. Following his gesture, I spotted a covered wagon set up with plants on display as well as some bottles with sticks burning in them. A moment later the strong scent of burning incense slammed into my nose. It wasn't a pleasant mix, either.

I scrunched my nose. "I think we found her."

"You don't like the smell?" Raikidan asked.

My brow rose and I looked at him. "You do?"

He nodded. "I think it's nice."

"To each their own, I guess."

We approached the wagon just as a cloaked woman with dark skin exited the back. The ornate designs on her cloak, and the way vines and flowers clung to her and her cloak, screamed East Tribe. They were known to be a bit… eccentric.

She smiled when she spotted us. "Oh, hello there. May I help you?"

I did my best to ignore the smell of her burning products. "Hi. My name is Laz'shika, and this is my guard Raikidan. Would you happen to be Se'lata?"

"Yes, I am she." She frowned. "Are you all right, dear? Are my incenses bothering you?"

"Just a little bit, but I'll be fine."

"I'm sorry. Most love this mix."

I gestured to Raikidan. "He likes it, so don't worry about it too much."

"If you say so." She clapped her hands together. "What can I do for you?"

I held up my shopping list. "I was told you may be able to help me track down these herbs."

Se'lata took the list and read it. "Some very exotic and unusual requests."

I was struck with the realization that not all shamans would be okay with providing such ingredients. I wasn't sure why I hadn't thought of it. *Probably because I'm so used to the laid-back attitude of the herbalists in the West Tribe.* I had worked with many of them, even having had the chance to teach them what I knew. The open exchange had been nice, but easy to take for granted.

Se'lata smirked. "But I wouldn't expect much different from the infamous Laz'shika."

I choked. "Infamous? Since when?"

She chuckled and turned to look through her stock. "I've heard the rumors. A protégé fire elementalist. One of a kind."

My gaze faltered. "I wouldn't agree, but that's what's been said in the past."

"Humble, too. The tales don't lie. I'm interested to see you grow. But enough about that. I happen to have all of these ingredients. Some are rare, so they cost a pretty copper."

I nodded. "I assumed as much."

"Good, good. Let me retrieve the requested quantities."

Se'lata disappeared into the wagon. I waited patiently, while Raikidan found interest in her offered products. I used the time to analyze his curious nature and those around us. Raikidan proved more interesting, with his constant inspection of plants and his desire to pick up every spice jar to get a better look at the contents.

Se'lata returned after some time, a large leather sack in her arms. "Here it is. I did not have a high enough stock of everything requested, so I've added larger quantities of other items on the list of similar or equal value." She then took interest in Raikidan's search. "Need something, dear?"

"I'm just looking at the moment."

"Very well." She focused back on me. "Now, let's discuss payment."

She explained what she'd changed for quantities on my list and then we discussed cost. Her first offer came in much less than Genesis' calculation, but higher than mine. We went back and forth with the haggling until we came to an agreed two hundred gold price. A lot for herbs, but not only had I acquired a lot, some were highly lethal on their own—so much so that she probably shouldn't even have brought them into the city.

Once the exchange had been completed, we focused on Raikidan, who now inspected a small container of ground red spice. He looked at us when he realized we'd stopped speaking. "Um, I'd like to purchase this as well."

This piqued my interest. "I'm sure I have enough money to spot you."

Raikidan came over and held out the jar for Se'lata to see. She nodded. "That's not a commonly purchased spice in these parts. Am I safe to assume you've come from the west side of Lumaraeon?"

I looked to Raikidan. Knowing this kind of insight would be helpful for me.

"No, but close," he said. "I grew up right against the Larkian mountains, on the East side."

Se'lata nodded. "That explains it. A great deal of cultural crossover on both sides of those mountains."

I found myself a bit disappointed. I'd really hoped he'd been from that side. There wasn't a lot of communication between the two halves of Lumaraeon because of those mountains. I'd been out West once, during my stay with the West Tribe, and it'd been quite the eye-opening experience.

Se'lata handed the spice jar back to Raikidan. "A jar that size is ten gold."

Raikidan looked to me and I nodded, digging out the ten gold from my pouch. No need to haggle that price. Se'lata had been more than generous to sell me my poison herbs and not make as large of a profit she could have with a less experienced haggler.

She accepted the payment, and a warm smile spread across her lips. "A pleasure doing business with you both. Take care now."

Raikidan and I thanked her one last time, Raikidan taking the large sack from me to carry, and we headed off.

"So—curious inquiry—what was with the spice purchase?" I asked Raikidan once we'd left the crowded street.

"My mother liked to mingle with humans, and would bring back trinkets of all sorts to share with me. This spice is one of the edible ones she'd obtain as a treat. It's been a while since I've had it."

His mother mingled with humans? Then why didn't he know anything about us? "Very interesting. If you're not sure how to cook with it, talk to Ryoko or Seda. They're both good cooks."

"What about you?"

I snorted. "Trust me, you don't want my cooking. I'd be better at poisoning someone than satisfying them."

"I doubt that's true."

"Ask anyone I know, and they'll give you the same warning. Trust me."

"Trust a protégé fire elementalist, she can't cook?"

I chuckled. "I'm really not *that* special. People just like to talk."

"I don't know. I've seen what you can do with fire, and I've got a feeling that's only been scratching the surface."

A tinge of warmth fell on my cheeks. *Dammit, him and that well-timed flattery of his.* "Trying to butter me up? Won't work."

He chuckled. "Was worth a shot."

"Careful, don't end up on my bad side now."

"I thought I was always on your bad side."

I couldn't stop the laugh. He had a bit of a point. He did seem to be feeling my wrath a lot. But if he didn't push my buttons so often, it wouldn't have been the case.

"Thank you for including me today." I looked up at him to find him staring at his spice jar. "And for buying this. It means a lot to me."

I didn't need to see his eyes to know what it meant for him to have that jar. If I had a food that reminded me of my mother, I'd sure as hell try to get it as much as I could.

I smiled despite myself. "You're welcome."

31
CHAPTER

I pulled out another bundle of preserved meat and placed it onto the pile of other food I had already started. When Daren had said he had given me a lot of food, I didn't think he meant this much. Raikidan and I had eaten quite a bit while we traveled, and there was still enough to feed an army.

Someone rapped on my door.

"Come in."

The door opened and Ryoko strolled in with a smile. "Checking to see what you're up to."

I pulled out another bundle. "Just seeing what's in here."

She raised her eyebrow. "You don't know what's in your own bag?"

"I didn't pack it."

"Fair enough. Need help?"

"I don't *need* help, but you're more than welcome to."

She smiled and sat down on the bed with me. Together we pulled out more food, full meals and single-wrapped meat alike. "Geez, how much is in here?"

"A lot, that's all I can say. Daren didn't want us to go hungry, but even I know this would be overkill. But that's him for you."

"Who is Daren?"

"The Inn keeper at the West Shaman Tribe. Nice guy."

"How nice?"

I rolled my eyes. "Don't even go there."

"Too old for you?"

I sighed and ignored her. Ryoko reached into the bag and pulled out another fur bag. She looked at me and I shrugged. She took out the contents and laid them across the bed.

I stopped what I was doing to pick up a few of the photographs she placed down and inspected them. "I've never seen these before…"

"Some of the people from this West Tribe you mentioned?" Ryoko asked.

I nodded. There were so many photographs. I had no idea there had been any type of camera around for most of them.

Ryoko laughed and held out a photograph. "Who is this guy with the chicken?"

"Nice tae meet ye, lass. Name's Daren an' this here be ma inn. She ain't nae five star hotel in some big ol' city, but she's got fine rooms an' comes with three square meals a day."

I chuckled. "That would be Daren."

"He looks a little too happy to have the chicken in his hands."

I shook my head, a smile on my lips. "That's Daren for you. He is always happy and becomes happier when he gets gifts, like that chicken."

Ryoko chuckled and picked up another photograph.

The woman smiled. "You know me, don't you, my dear?"

"Your face. I've seen it somewhere before."

"That's Shva'sika," I said.

Ryoko looked at the photograph closer. "She's really pretty." I nodded and ate a few pieces of dried meat. She picked up another photograph of Shva'sika. I was also in it. "She was your teacher, yes?"

I nodded again. "I couldn't ask for a better one. Del'karo taught me how to use fire the way I do, but Shva'sika taught me everything else. I owe them a lot."

Ryoko smiled and shook her head. "Who would have thought?"

I furrowed my brow. "What are you talking about?"

"Remember when we always teased you that you'd end up being a shaman one day?"

I blinked.

"Oh c'mon, you have to remember. You were so good with controlling fire right off the bat, and would claim you'd see things no one else did so much that we teased you, and you hated it! We told you, you had to be a shaman, and you kept telling us we were wrong. Who's wrong now?"

I laughed. "I'm not a full shaman. Just half."

Ryoko threw her hands up. "Who cares if you're a half shaman or a full shaman?"

"There is a difference, Ryoko. I don't have all the skills a full shaman has. There is still so much for me to learn."

"Like what?"

"I still have to learn more about using fire and trying to tap into my opposite element if it's possible. Not to mention I have almost no ability in communicating with spirits."

She tilted her head. "Not communicating with spirits is a bad thing?"

"Communicating with spirits is what separates shamans from stand-ard elementalists, though shamans do have a tendency to have a better innate control over their element than elementalists."

"Oh, okay. But wait. I thought people went somewhere when they died."

"They do, but they can come back for a short period of time when we need guidance or when they feel the need to give us a push in the right direction. Some also just like to talk. Either because they're bored or they want to feel like they're part of the living again."

"So, are wandering spirits real?"

I nodded. "Yes, and hell is a real place, too. Wandering spirits refuse to move on, just as old tales claim. Mainly, they're unavenged and angry, but others just want to keep living. They search for bodies that have just lost their host and try to live a new type of life or look for those who can tap into the spiritual plane and use their life force to have a physical form again."

I ate some dried meat. "Hell is where people are sentenced to if they made a pact with Nazir or are just extremely horrible people. Restless spirits who cannot be convinced to cross over also end up in hell, as their refusal to move on slowly corrupts them. Because of their obvious corruption, they are deemed unworthy of peaceful rest and sentenced to an eternity of restlessness."

Ryoko shivered. "Those sent to hell can't come back, right?"

I shook my head. "No. They are imprisoned there."

She sighed with relief. "That's good. Makes wandering spirits a little less scary. Is it hard to communicate with the spirits?"

I nodded. "You have no idea. Between the mental training and physical training to handle the stress of going between the planes, it takes a lot out of a person. On top of that, you have to be willing to face any spirit that exists. There is no picking or choosing. The spirit who can give you the answers will come to you no matter your relation with them."

"So, you could be forced to speak with someone you killed?"

I nodded again. "That's why I couldn't do it. It's why I'll never be able to be a full shaman."

"You feel regret again?" I looked at her, brow raised, and she crossed her arms. "Don't be like that. We both know you felt regret at first, but Zarda tortured it out of you."

I reclined on my bed and gazed up at the ceiling, sighing. "Yes. I don't regret killing in the moment, but after it's all said and done, and the act has settled into my brain, I do."

Ryoko smiled at me. "I know this may sound awful, but I'm glad. I like seeing you come back to the woman I once knew you to be."

I shook my head. I hadn't changed. And if I had, not to that person again. She was stupid and naïve. Sitting up, I decided to pile up the photographs one by one. I stopped when I picked up one particular photograph with me in it. I held it carefully as if I was afraid it would disappear, as if it had never truly existed.

"You probably already found out my name, but I figured I should tell you myself."

"Oh, who's the cutie?" Ryoko asked as she leaned over to take a closer look.

I didn't respond. Ryoko snapped her fingers and my eyes fluttered. "What?"

She sighed. "Who is he?"

"Xye." I handed the photograph over to her as if it no longer mattered to me.

"He a friend of yours?"

I snorted. "Hardly."

"Oh, I forgot, you don't have friends."

"You're my friend."

Ryoko looked up at me with a furrowed brow. "You once told me you didn't have friends. Friends lacked true trust."

I gazed down at my hands in my lap. "Friend means you have an attachment. You are my friend and my comrade. I am attached to you, and you have my trust."

Ryoko smiled. "So, he is your friend."

"No." She gave me a stern look and I sighed. "Yes, he was my friend."

"Was?"

I looked at her. "He's dead."

Her ears drooped. "Oh… I'm… I'm sorry."

I piled up more photographs. "Don't worry about it. It happens."

"So…" A mischievous glint came to her eyes. I didn't like it. "Were you just friends or more than that?"

I glared at her. "You know the answer to that."

"I do?" She tilted her head to emphasize her fake innocence.

"Ryoko."

"Okay, okay." She held up her hands in defeat. "Can't blame me for trying."

"I beg to differ."

She looked at the photograph again, ignoring my stubbornness. "He is cute, though. His ears are a little odd. They're not the full length of an elf or nu-human, but not short enough to be a regular human. Is he a halfling?"

"Don't call him that!" I snapped.

Ryoko flinched. "What? What did I do wrong? We're halflings too."

I sighed. Of course she wouldn't know. "Sorry. It's just being outside these walls you learn things. Even though two millennia have passed since the War of End, *halfling* isn't a good word out there. It's used by those who still see those of mixed blood as abominations."

"Oh…" Ryoko's ears drooped. "I guess the story of Peacekeeper Ryoko is true, in that aspect at least. Sorry, I had no idea."

"It's okay. You wouldn't have known since you never leave the city."

Ryoko placed the photograph on top of the pile of photographs and clapped her hands together. "All right, what's next?"

I shrugged and reached into my bag. "Looking through my treasure trove some more, I suppose."

My brow furrowed when I touched a small bag containing a hard object. Pulling the bag out, I opened it. My eyes grew wide when the bag fell down, revealing a bright red gem the size of my palm.

Ryoko leaned closer, her eyes sparkling. "Wow. It's so beautiful."

"It's called the red dragon's eye. It's extremely valuable, and powerful if used correctly."

I reached into the bag and felt around. If this one was in here, then so was the other. I smiled when I located the leather bag. Pulling it out, I opened the bag, revealing a large green gem.

Ryoko's eyes grew larger. "Another one?"

"There are three in total. This is the green dragon's eye. It's just as valuable and powerful as the red."

"How did you get them?"

My throat tightened a little. "They… they were gifts."

Ryoko's expression softened. "Laz, what happened between the two of you?"

There was no point trying to fool her. She knew Xye had given at least one of these to me. I tied the bag tightly over the green gem. "I don't want to talk about it."

She frowned. "It's the same situation as Rylan, isn't it?"

I sighed and cradled the red gem in my hands. "It was the most valuable thing he owned. I tried to refuse it, but he insisted I think it over."

"Think what over?"

I looked at her. "He asked me to marry him." She placed her hand over her mouth, her eyes filled with sympathy. "Elves don't give rings like humans. They give their most valuable possession to show their commitment. I tried to tell him I wasn't interested, but he wouldn't listen. He was so infatuated. He would do anything for me. It's what got him killed. I'm… I'm the reason he's dead…"

"Laz…" She moved closer to me and embraced me in a tight hug. I didn't fight it. A dark, suffocating feeling gripped my chest. But her hug made me feel a little better. "Let's go do something fun."

I tilted my head. "Like what?"

She grabbed my hand and pulled me to the edge of the bed as she moved. "Let's go downstairs and clean the vehicles."

I rolled my eyes. "You can't stay away from those for more than one day, can you?"

She laughed. "Zane thinks I bleed oil."

"I believe it. But I should really get this all situated."

Ryoko tugged harder. "Do it later! You have all the time in Lumaraeon. I want to do something with you for a change. Just the two of us."

I smiled. "Okay, okay. I'll go with you. It's not like this food can go bad."

She squealed and pulled me out of my room. She nearly ripped the basement door off its hinges when she opened it and flew down the stairs. I laughed at her excitement. She finally let go of my hand when we rounded the corner and crossed the invisible line that marked the garage.

My eyes skimmed over all the cars we owned before Ryoko tossed me a rag and container of wax. I nodded my thanks, and she walked over to her favorite car. It was a beautiful sapphire blue with white racing stripes. It was sleek and sexy, and she made sure it went fast. Knowing her, I figured she had added more up-to-date modifications to it, but from an outside look, it appeared exactly the same as it had when I left. It still had the same hood scoop, tinted windows, and the same style spoiler. It wasn't as modern looking as most of the other cars in the garage, but Ryoko was a fan of the classics. Of course, that wasn't to say she didn't have a few modern-looking vehicles hanging around.

Leaving her to her car, I searched for my motorcycle. If I was lucky, it would be in the same place I had left it, and it would have its tan cover over it. Finding it, I pulled the cover off and furrowed my brow. "Ryoko, where's my bike?"

She looked up. "Isn't she right there?"

"No, this is Rylan's."

She stood and scratched her head. "I could have sworn I put her right there after I tuned her up after you left. No one touched her after."

"What are you two looking for?" I looked up as Zane spoke. I hadn't heard him come downstairs.

"My bike. Have you seen it?"

He smirked and flipped a light switch on the wall next to him. I turned around as a small overhead lamp turned on and illuminated a covered motorcycle tucked away in the back of the garage by itself. Tilting my head in curiosity, I slowly made my way over to it.

I grabbed the cover and pulled it off the motorcycle. "Zane, I think you need to have your brain checked. This isn't my bike."

"Are you sure?"

I inspected the bike. The sleek style was similar to my motorcycle, which had been uniquely designed to fit my body shape, but the color was different, along with how low the rider needed to lean over to steer.

Feet thundered down the stairs, echoing through the garage, but I paid it no mind. Slowly I walked around the bike, allowing my index finger to trail along the body. She was mostly ruby red, with blended black portions and a black seat that allowed for two riders.

Zane walked over to me. "So, what do you think?"

"She's beautiful, but I'm still lost. This isn't my bike," I said.

Zane chuckled. "Yes, it is."

I thought this over while I rubbed my hand over the gas tank.

"We've been working on that thing for months," Blaze called over. "Zane made it our main priority when we weren't under a lot of heat with the military and Ryoko wasn't around. You can thank us now."

I glanced over at Zane. "Why?"

He folded his arms over his chest and smiled. "You always said she could be improved, so I figured I'd give you that just in case you decided to come back."

I smiled. Zane was so thoughtful. He had no idea I was coming back, but used up what little free time he and the boys had to improve my motorcycle in ways I had only dreamed of.

Argus strolled over, leaned on the motorcycle, and gave her a quick look-over. "She's still not finished, but she's highly functional."

"She looks finished to me."

"We wanted to add more to the color and add more to some of the advanced features we installed, but you came back, so we had to finish up and move her back here before you noticed she was missing," he explained.

I was curious about these advanced features Argus mentioned. I knew he wouldn't tell me outright, so I placed both hands on the handlebars and swung my leg over the body of the motorcycle. I left the kickstand down and focused on getting comfortable, which wasn't hard to do. They really had done a spectacular job with styling this to fit me comfortably, which was saying something, because I had thought she had been comfortable as it was.

Letting go of the handlebars, I ran my hand over the gas tank, looking for the keyhole. Suddenly a blue light flashed quickly, and a section of the tank flipped over to a digital reader. I stared at it, my interest in this upgrade intensifying. Ryoko, now curious herself, tossed her rag on the floor and made her way over.

I hovered my hand over the reader, and it responded to my touch. I peered up at Zane curiously. He smiled and nodded, so I placed my hand on the reader and watched it scan my hand.

"Rider accepted."

I pulled my hand away as the screen flashed. The engine of the motorcycle roared to life, startling Ryoko. I laughed at her, and she glared at me but didn't say anything. I placed my hands on the handlebars and twisted the throttle, the motorcycle roaring to life in response. Slowly I let it die down to a quiet purr.

"So?" Zane asked.

I smiled. "She sounds nice. Much better than before. I like the hand-scanning feature. That's quite inventive. Is that the only new advanced feature you boys added?"

He chuckled. "Place two fingers on the scanner."

I did as he instructed, and the reader responded by projecting a small blue beam vertically into the air. I pulled my hand away and watched the reader go to work. A small ball was projected from the beam. As I waited, the ball became bigger and more detailed. "A map?"

Zane nodded. "We figured it'd come in handy. You can use your hand to zoom it in and out, and to navigate anywhere you wish. Since you only recently brought back that new handheld map device with updated landmarks and such, we haven't had a chance to update this one."

"I'm working on getting a tracking feature to work in it, but I'm still getting the kinks figured out. Everything I've tried shuts the bike down," Argus added. "I've installed one in Rylan's favorite truck and it works well, but I can't figure out what is causing the issue with the bike."

I smiled. "You'll figure it out."

"It's an interesting feature." Raikidan pushed his way closer. "But wouldn't that stick out a little too much and cause unwanted attention? That reader in general would attract attention, not to mention the addition to that floating map."

Argus nodded. "Rylan voiced that same concern. Since this is new tech, and I don't want to go through the current hassle of a patent just yet, I've worked on something that should keep this under wraps for longer. Eira, cut the engine, will you?"

"One-finger touch," Zane whispered to me.

I did as instructed and the engine cut off. Argus walked off and disappeared around the corner. His quick footsteps sounded on the stairs as he made his way up. While he was gone, Raikidan moved closer and examined my motorcycle. He appeared curious, and I didn't blame him. Vehicles were still a new thing to him, especially motorcycles, since they never came into the shop for work.

"How do these things normally start?" he asked.

"Keys." His brow rose in question and I sighed. "There's normally a slot you insert the key in, which you then turn and that starts the engine, just like a car. I like this reader more, though. It makes it harder to steal, right, Zane?"

He nodded. "If you're not registered into the computer, you can't start it."

"Who else is registered into it?"

"Just you and me. Rylan was, until testing ceased. Figured you didn't want so many people being able to steal it on you."

Due to the body style, only Ryoko would be able to effectively take it, but the boys would think to pull an immature joke. I smiled my thanks.

Ryoko stood over the front tire and leaned on my handlebars. "So, this is the secret project you guys were working on? Why didn't you let me help?"

"Because you can't keep a secret," Rylan teased.

"I can too!"

Zane, Rylan, and I gave her a stern look and she huffed.

"So, Zane, anything else I should know about this?" I asked.

"Well, there's a defensive mode that is activated with the palm of the hand. And that's all I can think of. Other adjustments Argus planned either haven't worked, or he hasn't revealed them to us. I'll have you try out the defensive mode later."

I nodded. "Okay."

Everyone was quiet as we waited for Argus.

Finally, he came down the stairs and around the corner. He held a small, black, flat object in his hand. I held out my hand as he handed it over. I could tell by the weight that it was made of carbon fiber. "A helmet?"

Argus smiled. "Just put it on."

Shrugging, I placed the object behind my head and pressed a flush button all helmets had on the underside. The object responded by expanding around the side and top of my head until it formed into the shape of a helmet. A dark visor slid down from the inside of the helmet, covering my eyes. The helmet was snug, but comfortable even with my hair still up in my hair clip.

As I sat on my bike, the visor came to life and reflected several types of readings, the way a communicator would. Then the visor glowed, and a beam of light scanned my eyes.

"Rider accepted."

The motorcycle revved to life and purred as it idled. I grinned, my eyes darting to Argus. "Impressive, even for you, smart-guy."

He chuckled and rubbed the back of his neck. "Thanks."

I analyzed the readings and struggled to figure out how the helmet worked. "I'm going to need an explanation of this piece of equipment."

Argus nodded and went to explaining these new fancy and "bleed-ing-edge" features—Ryoko's words. He'd installed a communication system, much like soldier helmets, but since he didn't have the plans for one, he'd built it from scratch. He had created it using a new tech he designed, capable of detecting brain waves instead of verbal com-mands, allowing the user to merely think of the desired feature and the computer inside would do the rest.

He'd also added a map feature I found fascinating. Ryoko did, too, when she insisted on checking it out herself and then located the house in her "playtime."

To hide it all, he'd modeled the visor after two-way mirrors.

Argus sat back on the seat as I took in all the newness. "So, what do you think?"

I ran my hands over the handlebars. "It's all wonderful. Thank you."

Zane patted me on the shoulder. "Why not give her a test run? There's only so much we can test without your input."

I nodded. "Yeah, but I want to see if we can do something. Argus, you said the truck can use the tracking feature for the map without issue, right?"

"Well, very few issues is more correct," he said. "It's still buggy."

"What about this helmet?" I asked. "Does this have the tracking feature?"

"I've got it installed but not working yet. I've been a little more focused with getting the feature on the bike to work."

"Could you rig it up so that someone can feed me tracking information?" I asked. "This feature sounds really handy, and I think it'll be more useful for a helmet than the actual bike."

He thought for a moment. "You know, I might be able to."

"How long do you think it'll take?"

"A few minutes, maybe."

I used the helmet to turn the motorcycle off before compacting it and handing it over to him. "Get to it."

He nodded and ran off, with Rylan close behind to give him a hand if needed. Not long after, they were back and Argus was grinning. "Done."

I was impressed. "Really?"

"Yeah, it was actually a lot easier than I was expecting. Good call."

I smiled. "Thanks. If the feed works well on this test run, I'm sure you'll be able to figure out how to get it to work independently."

Argus nodded and Ryoko jumped up and down. "I'm going with you guys."

Rylan held up the keys. "I'll drive."

"Shotgun!"

Everyone then looked at Raikidan, whose brow rose in response. "What?"

"You're coming with us, right?" Ryoko asked.

"I guess?"

I chuckled and patted the part of the seat behind me. "Jump on. You're going to need to learn how to ride on one of these sooner or later, and I doubt you want Rylan teaching you."

Ryoko giggled and Rylan rolled his eyes. Raikidan remained fairly expressionless, not understanding the tone and meaning of my joke, and climbed onto the motorcycle. Zane tossed him a helmet while Rylan and Ryoko ran to the truck. Putting mine back on, I started up the motorcycle again.

"You won't be able to communicate with Rylan," Argus said to me.

"And you won't be able to relay traffic conditions if you run into any problem areas, or get directions to him if you two get separated. You're completely dependent on him."

I nodded. "I'll try to remember that."

Argus nodded and then backed away, allowing me to pull out of my parking space quickly when Rylan's truck roared to life. Raikidan, who had only been resting his hands lightly on my hips, grabbed a tighter hold and I chuckled quietly.

"Not funny," he muttered.

"For you, maybe."

The room became darker as we made our way from the lit center of the garage to the ramp entrance.

As we came closer to the end of the ramp, I forced my helmet to make frantic calculations and commands. Within seconds, the roof pulled away and we flew out of the mouth of the earth and down the street.

"So where are we going?" he asked.

"I don't have a destination in mind. I'll just cruise around to get the feel of these new changes."

"What about your friends?"

I could hear Rylan's truck engine and exhaust roaring behind us. "They'll follow us for a bit. Once Rylan wants to try out the tracking feature, he'll activate it in my helmet and we'll go from there."

"Anything I need to do?"

"Just remember to keep your balance, and when we make turns, big or small, you'll need to lean with me, all right?"

"Sure."

I set a leisurely course through the city until my visor started to flash. I watched as the transparent map appeared. The map was a bit distracting while driving, and it took me a minute or two to actually get used to it. I'd have to let Argus know about that.

Two dots suddenly started to flash on the map and it didn't take me long to note one was me and the other Rylan. They continued to flash as I drove, but began to change from a green color to a yellow as the road became a bit more congested and then red when we reached a traffic light. *Neat feature.*

When the light turned green, the traffic moved again and a line appeared on my map. It started on my dot and traveled different streets.

"Looks like we're going on a treasure hunt," I said.

"Huh?"

I shook my head. "Never mind. Just lean with me when I take some turns soon."

"Sure."

I wove through the traffic and followed the route Rylan had laid out for me, and Raikidan managed to do as I asked. But I was also aware of how tight his grip was on me. "You okay?"

"I'm fine."

"You sure?"

"Yes."

He was lying. I just knew it. I had a feeling he was scared, though I couldn't understand why. This couldn't be much different than flying… right?

I noticed a curved road ramp and decided to deviate from Rylan's route. "We're going to take the freeway."

Banking a quick and sudden right, the two of us zipped up a long, curved ramp. Raikidan leaned perfectly with me as we took the tight turn.

"Well, you once asked what a freeway was, and I promised to show you at some point, so here it is," I said when we pulled out on the long stretch of road high above the city.

Raikidan shifted around as he looked. "Not what I was imagining, though I honestly had no idea what to expect."

I was having a hard time hearing him over the wind, but I thought I heard him right. "I'm not surprised you expected it would be something more. Based on the name, many would. Man, this wind is bad! Argus really needs to work on these helmets more."

"Huh?" Raikidan asked. "I had a hard time hearing you."

I laughed. "Exactly!"

I glanced to my left when Rylan pulled the truck up next to us. The lift in his truck raised him too high for me to see him, but I spied Ryoko. She waved. She then spoke to Rylan and then focused back on me. She pointed to something near the center of the dash of the truck and then shrugged. While I couldn't see what she was pointing at, I figured it was the map and she was questioning why I had changed the course.

I shrugged in response and then kicked the motorcycle into a higher gear and sped off. I found myself grinning as I wove around the other cars. The motorcycle was handling exceptionally well for my speed, and I had one more gear I could go up to.

"Why are we going so fast?" Raikidan asked.

"Why not? I'm supposed to test this baby out, after all. Don't tell me you're scared."

He snorted. "Yeah, right."

Now I know he's lying. His voice had a slightly raised pitch to it. And his grip—it tightened just enough in his response for me to notice. "It's not much different than flying."

"It's nothing like flying."

"Remove your helmet, then. Might feel like it then."

"I'm not asking for a death wish."

"Now I know you're afraid."

Raikidan's grip tightened in annoyance, and then slowly, one arm released. He held a tight grip on me with his other hand, using me as a brace as he reached back and forced his helmet into its compact shape.

I waited a moment for the wind to fly past him for him to feel the full effect before I spoke again. "See?"

Raikidan secured his free arm around my waist again. "Still not like flying."

"Well, it's the closest thing you'll get unless you sprouted wings right now and took off."

"You once asked me what flying was like. And your comment now has me thinking humans don't have the means for flight. Is that true?"

"Yes. Long ago they did, but then, during the War of End, those means of flying disappeared, along with the knowledge of how."

"How often have you wondered what it was like to fly?"

I didn't reply right away. "Every now and then."

Raikidan loosened his grip around me again, and before I knew it, he reached up and forced my helmet into its compact form. The wind hit me with ferocity, startling me. It whipped my bangs and teased my clipped hair. I blinked to keep my eyes from drying out. I expected Raikidan to grab hold of me again, but I was proven wrong when he reached for my hair clip.

"I wouldn't do that if I were you," I said.

He leaned closer to me and spoke into my ear. His hot breath made me shiver slightly. "And why not?"

"Because my hair is long enough where it'll whip you in the face, and I can guarantee you it won't feel great."

He chuckled. "I'll take my chances."

Something in his words made my cheeks flush. Then he freed my hair of its restraint. It whipped around wildly. Raikidan slipped his arm securely back around my waist. I wanted to know what he did with my hair clip and both helmets, but that wasn't my main concern at the moment. What was my concern was his calm demeanor as he rested his chin on my shoulder. "Do you mind?"

"What?"

"Remove your face from my person."

"Why should I? It's more comfortable than sitting up straight."

He finds me comfortable? My cheeks flushed again, which frustrated me. What was this dragon doing to me?

"I figured you'd be bonier," Raikidan teased, "what with how little you eat."

I kicked him. He grunted and tightened his grip, forcing his body closer to me. I grumbled unhappily.

We zipped past a large vehicle and I glanced down at my speedometer. "Shit!"

"What?"

"That was a military vehicle and I'm going over the allowed speed limit."

"So, what do we do?"

"Well, I'm supposed to slow down and pull off to the side for them to talk to me and possibly even fine me, but…"

"But you're not going to, are you?"

"Well, I kinda forgot to grab my identification card, so if I pull over, I'll be in more trouble than for a simple speeding violation."

"Identification card?"

"It's a device that's used to identify the people of the city. Everyone has one. Citizens born inside the city are made one on the day they're born, and those who migrate here are given one upon citizenship. Temporary cards are even given to visitors. The cards have specific types of information on them with data regarding our identity and allowances in the city. If you're cleared for certain high-risk jobs, temporary city leave, or have even cleared the proper driving courses that allow you to drive a vehicle, it'll be on the card. It also shows what you're not allowed to do. We're actually supposed to carry them on us at all times, but most soldiers are pretty relaxed about it, so those who don't do anything stupid tend to just leave them at home."

"Do I get one of these cards?"

"We're in the process of forging one for you now. It's a harder process than you might think."

"No, it sounds complicated to me."

I swiveled my head back and forth when two motorcycles pulled up next to me. The riders were clothed in military uniforms, and when I glanced in my mirror, I saw another one being let out of the back end of the military vehicle I had passed. He'd catch up quick, and then I'd be boxed in. It was no secret the military had better vehicles than civilians. They needed the power to keep us in line. But that didn't mean we didn't like to listen and do illegal upgrades.

The rider to my left motioned for me to slow down. When I glanced at the other rider he did the same.

Raikidan chuckled in my ear. "Let's see if this thing can out run them."

"What, not afraid anymore?"

He snorted. "I told you, I was never scared."

"Sure you weren't."

"Are you going to go faster, or are you going do what these guys are trying to tell you to do? Because they don't seem to be very happy you're ignoring them."

I glanced at one of the soldiers and he told me to slow down again, but I just grinned and kicked my motorcycle into its highest gear and sped away. The soldiers picked up speed to keep pace, but my motorcycle's enhancements were far better, and I was able to keep some good distance from them without pushing the motorcycle to the limit.

My heart started to race when each soldier's motorcycle had an arm extend out of the side. Each arm wielded a gun, and it didn't take a scientist to know they were loaded.

"Dammit."

"What?"

"They're going to shoot at us."

"What? What kind of lunatic force is this?"

I laughed. "The one Zarda commands."

I ducked instinctively when a gun went off. I peered through my mirror and noticed a gun pointing toward the sky. *Warning shot.* I needed to think fast on what to do or we'd be dead.

"There's a defensive mode that is activated with the palm of the hand."

That's it! I threw my palm down on my scanner. My heart thundered hard in my chest as it took several painstaking moments to read the command. The motorcycle started to make some strange clicking noises and I was taken by surprise when the bike began to morph. Raikidan and I both watched as a protective carbon fiber and glass shell formed over us and I nearly jumped when a bullet bounced off the glass portion.

I laughed. "I love my boys!"

"Looks like it works."

I nodded. "Now that we're protected, let's get out of here."

"What do you have planned?"

"To get off this freeway first," I said as I activated the map on the scanner. "The closest exit ramp I find will be our escape, and I'll try to lose them in the city."

"Will that work?"

"I hope so."

When I found an exit ramp, I cranked on the throttle to force the motorcycle to its max speed and flew down the freeway. I could see the military falling behind, unable to keep up with my speed, and I hoped this escape would be easy.

When we made it to the ramp, I slowed the motorcycle down and deactivated my map. I sent a prayer to the gods as this one curled under the freeway, hiding us from the military, and deactivated the defense shield. The soldiers had fallen so far behind us I doubted they saw us exit, but any cover would help.

I was hyperaware of everything as I drove through the city toward the house. We were lucky there were a lot of motorcycles out today, but that didn't give us full cover.

"Here, take your helmet," Raikidan said when we stopped at a red light. "It should help us."

I took it gratefully, as well as my hair clip when he ended up handing that to me as well. It was a good idea he had come up with. I wasn't sure why I hadn't thought of it myself. "We should be home soon."

"Okay," he replied.

Ten minutes passed, and I finally pulled down the dead-end street for the garage. My helmet made its calculations and the false road pulled back. I cut the engine and knocked down my kickstand when I found a good place to park and let out a sigh of relief as I removed my helmet. It turned into a giggle when Raikidan snickered, and before I knew it the two of us were rolling with laughter.

Raikidan leaned his head on my shoulder in his fit, but I didn't do anything about it. I was too preoccupied with my failed attempts to calm myself down. When I finally managed to control myself, I glanced back at him and smiled.

He grinned and we stared at each other for a moment before Raikidan pulled away and spoke. "Thanks."

I tilted my head. "For what?"

"For including me on this. I thought it was strange you humans found enjoyment in driving these machines around, but I can see why. This was rather fun, and our run-in with those soldiers was rather exhilarating. I didn't think you'd be capable of such risky choices."

I chuckled and slipped off the motorcycle. "You obviously don't know me, then."

He watched me instead of replying, making me feel a bit strange. His stare was also rather intense. It was so intense I was sure it'd make women like Ryoko swoon. I didn't get that about them. I didn't understand how intense stares made a man more attractive. But, as I held his gaze, I started to wonder if I could see that. I could see how being the only person focused on with such intensity could make someone feel so... special.

A warm feeling began to well up in my body, and I could feel my cheeks warming up the longer he watched me. I felt awkward and rather self-conscious, and I didn't like it. *Don't ever go back to that place, Eira.*

I tore my gaze away and focused on my motorcycle. "It's rude to stare, you know."

Instead of replying, Raikidan climbed off my motorcycle, but his foot caught. I gasped and tried to help right him before he fell, but Raikidan grabbed me instinctively and we fell to the ground. I lay on top of him, momentarily stunned. When I finally regained my composure, I found myself staring into those sapphire pool eyes of his—our noses mere inches from each other. My heart thundered in my ears and my cheeks burned.

I quickly jumped to my feet and went back to looking over my motorcycle. It hadn't fallen over, much to my relief, so it wouldn't have obtained any damage from that, but I wasn't sure if it received any from our little run-in with the military. It was best to go back to my check-over just to be sure. *Nice excuse, Eira.*

My gaze was ripped away and forced toward the basement when two pairs of feet stormed down the stairs. Both Zane and Argus ran into the garage soon after.

"Are you guys okay?" Argus asked. "Ryoko called us, saying you had a run-in with the military and then disappeared."

I grinned. "Oh yeah, we're fine. Thanks to that defensive mode you installed."

Zane stared at me. "What did you do to need that?"

I shrugged. "I didn't think it was a good idea to pull over for a speeding fine when I didn't have my ID on me."

He smacked his head. "That's what I was forgetting."

I chuckled. "You'll be happy to know it works great, though you might want to check for damage just in case." I pointed at Argus. "But your helmet needs work. It couldn't block out wind on the freeway worth shit."

"How bad was it?" Argus asked.

"There was a lot of heavy interpreting and guesswork involved," Raikidan said.

Argus nodded. "Okay. I'll work on that and see what I can do to fix it."

Zane waved us to follow him as he headed for the stairs. "Let's get you two upstairs and on the horn with Ryoko so she knows you both are safe. You may be able to convince her to pick us up some dinner."

"Let me guess, your attempt failed?" I teased.

He pouted a little. "Yeah. She said your safety was more important than my stomach."

I laughed. "Well, I think your stomach's need is more important, so I'll see what I can do for you."

He chuckled and patted me on the back before letting me lead the way up the stairs.

32
CHAPTER

Ryoko stood in front of me with her arms crossed, and I narrowed my eyes at her as I leaned against my bed. Genesis had given us a simple surveillance assignment earlier this morning, but it required us to be disguised. Ryoko, of course, was insisting I wear something I wouldn't be caught dead in—a sundress.

"C'mon." She held out the dress again. "It's not that bad."

"I said no."

She sighed. "It's not like anyone will recognize you after you use the temporary dye in your hair, and the colored contact lenses. What's the harm?"

I turned my back on her and stalked over to my closet. Moving clothes around, I sighed and searched my dresser. I cursed when I found nothing. Ryoko chuckled, but I wasn't about to wear that dress. I would use the armor clothing if necessary. Before Ryoko could attempt to convince me to wear the dress again, someone rapped on my bedroom door.

"Come in," I called.

The door opened, and Zane strolled in. "I don't mean to interrupt you two, but I think the boys are in need of some help."

Ryoko and I looked at each other and shook our heads with small smiles. Getting the guys to blend in was not going to be easy. Ryoko discarded the dress on my bed, and I followed her out of my room. No sooner had I taken two steps out of the room, I was hit by Raikidan's annoyance.

"What the hell is this stuff?" He was holding a small bottle with colored liquid in his hand.

"It's hair dye."

"It smells awful! You expect me to use this?"

"Sure do." I spun him around and pushed him toward the bathroom. "Let's go."

"Hell no. I'm not using anything that smells this foul."

"If I have to, you have to." I shoved him into the bathroom. Raikidan attempted to force his way out, but I pushed him back in. "Ryoko, give me a hand, will you? I need you to keep him still."

Ryoko pranced into the room and forced Raikidan to sit on the toilet. He struggled against her, but their evenly matched strength kept him from breaking free. I shut the door and squeezed out the dye from the bottle.

Raikidan began to struggle again, and Ryoko rolled her eyes. "Don't make me sit on you."

I snickered when he looked at her as if he wasn't sure to take that as a threat or not. Ryoko stared back at him as if to challenge him, but he took her words as not meaning much. Because he was a dragon, it didn't surprise me that he wouldn't think it would be awkward for Ryoko to sit on him. Of course, he probably wasn't capable of imagining how she planned to do so.

He squirmed in his seat, and Ryoko made good on her threat. She plopped right down on his lap and hung her arms over his shoulders—their faces rather close.

Raikidan stared at her wide-eyed, and Ryoko grinned. "I told you I was going to sit on you if you didn't behave."

Raikidan only stared at her in response. I found myself frowning and not liking what I was seeing, but I couldn't understand why. There was nothing wrong with what she was doing. It was keeping him still, and it wasn't like she hadn't warned him. With him also being a dragon, he wasn't reacting to the situation like a human male would.

"Now, are you going to be good, or am I going to have to continue to sit here?" Ryoko asked Raikidan.

"Get off me."

"Swear to cooperate and I will."

Raikidan stared at her for a moment longer and then looked at me, exasperated, but I didn't do anything to help. He sighed. "Fine."

"Fine what?" Ryoko challenged.

"Fine, I'll sit here and let you punish me."

"Punish you?" She giggled and stood. "Is that what you think we're doing to you? Honey, if I was punishing you, it'd be a lot different." She winked at him. "And way more fun."

"Why else would you be doing this to me?" He clearly missed her sexual implications, disappointing her.

"Because we have an assignment to accomplish?" I said, my tone sarcastic. "Everyone is wearing hair dye, so quit being a baby and suck it up."

He glared at me but didn't say anything more, allowing me to lace my fingers into his hair and coat it with the foul, sticky liquid. Once I was sure his hair was thoroughly dyed, I applied some to his facial hair before stepping back and allowing him to look himself over in the mirror while I discarded the gloves used to protect my hands.

"What did you do to me?" he asked, his eyes wide with shock.

I shrugged. "Just changed your hair color. You won't see the results until we rinse your hair in a few minutes."

"Should we be doing something else?" Ryoko asked.

I stared at her reflection in the mirror. "Do you have something specific in mind? "

She strolled over and lightly grabbed his chin. A negative and slightly possessive feeling welled up in the pit of my stomach as she leaned on him and looked him over. That was not a comforting sign. "We could shave his facial hair."

Raikidan pushed her away and growled. "I will not."

She blinked in surprise. "What's wrong with that suggestion? If you like the style, you can grow it back out after. It's not like it'll kill you."

I figured it was best if I swooped in. "Ryoko, why don't you go see if Rylan needs any help?"

Her brow creased. "You sure?"

I nodded. "I can handle it from here. Including my own dye job."

"All right, but you'd better not color your hair in a way that won't go with that dress."

"I told you I'm not wearing that!"

Raikidan raised his eyebrow with interest. "You were going to wear a dress?"

I sighed and rummaged through the small closet for the hair dye. "Ryoko, just leave."

She grasped the door handle. "All right, but I'm not giving up on that dress."

I rolled my eyes and grabbed the box I was looking for. Ryoko left as I ripped open the box. Taking my hair out of my hair clip, my shirt changed into a small tank top and I went to work lacing the dye into my hair. Raikidan sat back down and watched me.

"You know, you didn't have to snap at her. She doesn't know your hair won't grow back."

Raikidan sighed. "I know. I just get defensive sometimes while keeping my secret."

"Try to work on that if you can. It's easier to come up with half-truths than full lies. Like this one. Tell people you have a slow hair growth issue, so you like to keep drastic changes to a last resort if you can. Everyone will accept it and leave you alone."

"I will keep that in mind. Thank you. And thank you for keeping this secret from the others."

"You don't have to thank me for that. It's not my place to tell them." I turned to face him. "You're lucky it's me who knows, though. I'm good at keeping secrets, and even better, trained to come up with half-truths and lies. If you need one, just talk to me."

Something flashed in his eyes. *Shit, did I just give too much away?* Raikidan then nodded. "Thank you. I'll keep that in mind."

I discarded the gloves I used for my hair. "All right, let's rinse your hair out."

"Wha—"

I grabbed him by the shirt and pulled him over to the shower. Sliding open the glass door, I ran the water and dunked his head under.

"You know I can do this myself," Raikidan grumbled.

I let him go, but shoved him into the running water. "All right, then you do it. I'll go lay your clothes out on your bed."

"Eira!"

I sprinted out of the bathroom and slammed the door behind me before he could think about grabbing me. Ryoko poked her head out of Rylan's room as I laughed and made my way over to Raikidan's room.

"You pushed him into the shower, didn't you?" I nodded and continued to laugh as I opened the door. "I knew you were up to something. You're so mean."

I shut the door and gathered myself before I rummaged through his closet. His selection amazed me, and this wasn't even what he had in his dresser. When it came to clothes, Ryoko really knew how to shop.

Pulling out a brown leather jacket and a white turtleneck, I laid them out on his queen-sized bed and went over to his dresser. Footsteps thundered down the hall and were followed by the sound of the bedroom door opening and then slamming shut. Raikidan's breath came slow and deep. I grinned and continued to pretend he wasn't there.

"I should make you pay for that!"

I turned my head and smirked. His hair was now a deep brown, although it was hard to distinguish it from black since it was still wet. He clutched his drenched shirt in his hands and his soaked pants clung to his muscular form. He looked as if he hadn't bothered using a towel to dry himself in the least. *Lucky Ryoko isn't here to make her stupid comments.*

"I suppose you should, but you won't." I turned my eyes back to the dresser and pulled out a pair of denim pants for him.

"You'd better hope this color doesn't last."

"Calm down. The next shower you take will rid you of the color. You have nothing to worry about."

"Good, but that doesn't mean you're safe. Why the hell did you push me into the shower?"

I shrugged. "Because I felt like it. Do you have a problem with it?"

"Yes, I do," he breathed in my ear.

I forced myself not to tense. I hadn't heard him move. The heat of his body teased my skin. He wasn't touching me, but that didn't make me any less uncomfortable. Instead of focusing on how close he was to me, I pulled out a pair of boxers and socks for him. "What are you going to do about it?"

"Nothing. I'll be changing out of these wet clothes, so there's no point in making you pay. Plus, I still owe you for respecting me and not forcing me to change my physical appearance when I don't want to."

I turned and handed over his clothes. "I would hope you'd extend the same courtesy when the situation presents itself."

Raikidan took the clothes, but also captured my hands with his in the process, holding eye contact with me. "Of course I would. It's because of your respect I do, and why I made the changes to myself as I have. I did that for you."

My pulse slowed. I didn't know what to say. A part of me didn't like how that sounded. The other part didn't mind at all. This was not a comfortable situation.

I pulled away. "You shouldn't say things like that."

His brow furrowed. "Why not? It's the truth."

I turned away. "It... reminds me of memories I'd rather not remember..."

"But—"

"I made it clear to you back at the village I didn't want you to make personal decisions because of something I may or may not want. I want you making a personal decision because you really want to." I headed for the door. "But I should go and finish getting ready."

"I"—he sighed—"I suppose you should."

Once my hand wrapped around the doorknob, I stopped and glanced back at him. "For the record, the style does look good on you. I didn't lie about that. And the color, as much as this will look good, I prefer its natural state. It suits you better, in a good way."

Raikidan went to say something, but I left his room before he could. When I entered the bathroom, I found Ryoko sitting on the sink. Her hair smelled of the foul dye, and she grinned at me as I entered. "I saw the color you used."

I chuckled. "Is it going to be a problem?"

"Not at all, Ginger. As a matter of fact, I had an idea that would work out perfectly."

"You want to look like twins, don't you?"

"You bet!" Her grin grew wider. "So I grabbed the last box of the same color."

I smiled and shook my head. "This doesn't mean I'm wearing that dress."

She sighed. "Well, if you're not going to wear that, what are you going to wear?"

I grinned. "Let me rinse out my hair and you'll see."

She blinked but didn't say a word as I made my way over to the shower and rinsed out my hair. Once I was certain I had done a thorough job, I turned the water off and dried it with a towel.

"Okay, your hair is now the color you need it to be. What are you going to wear?" Ryoko demanded to know.

I grinned and let the image of my desired outfit run through my head, my armor responding in turn. My tank top changed into a loose off-the-shoulder shirt with a light red and orange flower, and my sports bra switched to a strapless one. My denim pants changed into black leggings, while long black knee-high socks and boots formed on my bare feet.

Ryoko's eyes sparkled with delight. "Wow, this is better than what I wanted you to wear! A little work with your hair, and a little makeup, and you'll look like a completely different person. You won't even need the colored contact lenses."

"I'm not wearing makeup."

"Oh, yes you are. You need to look as little like you as possible. It won't kill you, I promise."

"What are you planning to wear?"

"Well… um…" She chewed her lower lips. "I haven't figured that out yet. You know me and normal clothes. It's hard to get them to fit right."

I sighed. "Go get some armor. I'll put you in something that will look good."

Her brow rose. "You?"

"I may not be as fashion inclined as you, but at least I have an idea that I know will work."

She sucked in a tight breath, her eyes going wide for a moment, showing she didn't believe me, and then left the bathroom. A few moments later, she came back with the cloth in her hand along with a small wooden box.

"Close the door and put them on." She looked at me apprehensively and I gave her a stern look. "Ryoko, it's me. Just change."

She sighed and did as she was told. When she finished, with her clothes sprawled out around her feet, I motioned for her to come to me. Once she was in range of my touch, I grasped her clothing. Thinking hard, I forced the cloth to bend to my will and change.

Her bikini top transformed into a fitted bra and a brown lace-edged tank top. A denim jacket formed over her shoulders and framed her body perfectly. The shorts she was wearing extended into denim pants, and her boots transformed into black laced stilettos. I allowed her to keep her goggles since they added to her look, although I changed the style just a little bit, just in case.

Smiling at my handiwork, I spun her around to face the mirror. "See? What did I tell you?"

Ryoko looked herself over. Her face creased with concern. "I don't know... I feel like it makes my breasts look even larger, and shows off too much cleavage."

"And the bikini showed less?"

She chuckled, her cheeks tinting. "I guess you're right."

"Now rinse your hair and we'll dry and style it."

"We'll style yours first," Ryoko insisted as she forced me to sit on the toilet and plugged in the hair dryer. "Mine needs to be in a little longer."

I muttered to myself but didn't protest. Ryoko grabbed a large round brush out of a drawer and went about doing my hair and then applying way too much makeup from the wooden box she'd carried in. "There, all done."

I looked myself over in the mirror. My hair was a flaming orange and curled just above my shoulders. The round brush Ryoko had used made my hair look layered and wavy, and it was full of volume and bounce. I couldn't stop myself from running my fingers through it. The cover-up she had applied thinned the amount of freckles shown on my face, and my eyes, aside from the color, looked as if they had been taken from a different person. They appeared larger and more feminine.

Ryoko smiled. "You look nice."

"Uh, thanks."

"Laz, what's wrong?"

"It's nothing. We should get you ready, so we can head out."

She shoulders sagged. "Laz, don't take what I said the wrong way. You look great without all this treatment, too."

"Let's get you ready."

She sighed and went to rinse her hair. Once she was done, I dried it with the hair dryer and brush. Grabbing a few pins from the wooden box, I gently pinned her sensitive ears into her hair. "Where are the prosthetic ears?"

"On the second-to-top shelf in the closet."

I left her side and searched for the ears. Once I found them, I secured them to her head and tucked them behind her goggles as an extra measure. Once that was done, I quickly applied her makeup and added a beauty mark by her right eye. Once I was sure her makeup was on point, I grabbed blue contact lenses out of the wooden box and placed them in her eyes.

Ryoko stood and looked herself over when I was done. She smiled in approval. "What do you think?"

I shrugged. "I prefer you with dog ears."

She tilted her head. Realizing what I meant, she smiled. Ryoko tugged my arm and I allowed her to pull me next to her. She beamed at the sight. Aside from the eyes and other small feature differences, we did look like twins, or in the very least siblings.

Ryoko pulled the wooden box closer. "You're going to want to switch up some of your earrings and maybe use some other jewelry."

I nodded and went to work on my ears. I decided to take most of the earrings out and swapped my bell earring for a long hanging earring. I placed its partner earring in my other ear for consistency. Ryoko offered a few metal bracelets and I gladly accepted them. They were of varying sizes, causing them to overlap as they hung around my wrist. I dug out two clip-on earrings for Ryoko and helped her add them to her prosthetics.

"Ready?" I asked. She smiled and nodded, and the two of us left.

Zane whistled low as we entered the living room. "You two sure know how to make a disguise."

Blaze snaked his arm around Ryoko and me. "I'll say."

I elbowed him in the stomach. "Answer is still no."

He grunted and rubbed his stomach. "Aw, c'mon, Eira. Twins are always the best in bed."

Ryoko flicked her hair dismissively and walked away from him. "Who cares? Answer still hasn't changed."

"Fine." Blaze sat down on the couch and flipped on the TV.

Once he was no longer looking, I took a quick glance at him to make sure he was ready. His hair was now a dark blonde, wavy, and pulled back into a ponytail, revealing his pierced ears. He wore a navy-blue shirt and denim pants. Sunglasses were perched on his head instead of a hat and bandana, and from the looks of it, he was wearing green contact lenses. He still wore his favorite accessories except for his glove, which had been replaced with a black wristband. He was all set to blend into a crowd of people.

I peered down the hall at the sound of approaching footsteps. Rylan and Raikidan approached and scrutinized us; Ryoko and I did the same to them. Rylan's hair was now a rich black and wasn't styled with any cream or gel. His eyes were chocolate brown, which matched his brown leather jacket. He wore a red shirt under the jacket, and denim pants. He no longer sported his chain or lip piercing, although his gauges and clamp earring remained.

Raikidan looked normal enough, even with his hair still styled in the manner it usually was. The clothes I had chosen for him fit well, and although they didn't fit who he was, they would do for an undercover disguise.

"You look different," Raikidan said.

I chuckled. "That's the point, stupid."

Raikidan crossed his arms and narrowed his eyes.

"So, whose idea was it to look like twins?" Rylan asked.

"Mine!" Ryoko claimed. "Like it?"

He chuckled. "It's interesting, although I would have used the idea on a more involved assignment."

Ryoko shrugged. "I suppose it would have been a smarter choice to do that, but I couldn't resist. It's not like we can't still use the idea later."

Seda walked down the hall and greeted us with a small nod. "If you are all set, Genesis has said you may leave."

I glanced around. "Where's Argus?"

"He's not going," Blaze said. "Said something about working on some important project, so Genesis told him he could work on that instead."

I shrugged. "All right then, let's be off. Make sure you guys stay in the area you've been assigned, and keep your ears open for any useful information."

Seda held up her hand to stop me. "Hold on, Laz, you forgot about your necklace."

I looked down at my necklace and touched it. "Oh… right… I suppose it would be best to take it off."

"Let her wear it," Rylan said. "It won't harm anything."

"Yeah," Ryoko agreed. "It's never caused a problem in the past, so why would it now? She could play it off as some trinket a traveling merchant sold her if asked."

"Very well," Seda responded before walking off.

Ryoko hooked her arm around mine and dragged me toward the basement door before any more time could be wasted. "Let's take your car, *Sis*. I'll drive."

I smirked. "Lead the way, *Sis*."

"Anyone else find Ryoko's fake ears weird on her?" Blaze asked. The guys murmured in agreement, and I hoped Ryoko heard. It would make her feel a little better about herself if she did.

"So, you know what I wish for?" Ryoko asked me as we headed down the last few steps.

"A million gold pieces?"

She laughed and let go of my arm as we walked toward the garage. "Well, duh! But that's not what I would wish for right now."

"Then what would you wish for?"

"That epic music played in the background of my life."

I laughed. "You've been watching too many action movies."

Ryoko laughed with me. "True, but you have to admit it would be pretty cool, especially in this type of situation. Like epic spy music or something."

I smiled. "Yeah, I suppose."

The two of us rounded the corner and walked through the garage until we came to a sleek black car with red racing stripes. Grasping the handle of the passenger-side door, I pulled the wing door out and sat down in the seat. Ryoko sat down in the driver's seat and started up the vehicle. The car roared to life, and once our doors were shut, she pulled out of the parking spot quickly. "You think this will go as well as Genesis hopes?"

"Personally, I doubt it. She hopes for more than what's possible most of the time, although I do hope this won't be a waste of time."

She smiled and nodded. The garage door opened, and we sped out into the open city. I stared out the window, taking in the city that passed by.

The hot water splashed over my skin, running orange as I laced my fingers through my hair and scrubbed out the hair dye with the special shampoo designed to remove it faster. The assignment had been a complete waste of time. There had been no soldiers to spy on, and no civilian chat worth overhearing. Blaze had become so bored he had walked from his post over to mine and Ryoko's to chat. Others from our team and from other teams we ran into indicated they were having the same problem all over the city. It was as if the soldiers didn't exist.

Sighing, I lathered up my hair with my conditioner and allowed its sweet scent to flood into my nose. Once my hair was rinsed and clean, I turned off the water and dried off with a towel. Grabbing a small washcloth from the drawer under the sink, I wiped away the steam that had collected on the mirror and began washing the makeup off my face.

My lip gloss had faded away during the day, and removing the cover-up and eyeshadow required little effort, but the eyeliner and mascara were much harder. I dabbed and I pulled, but neither would come off onto the washcloth. Irritation flared up in me. *She would use waterproof makeup.* I rummaged around the closet until I found the small bottle of makeup remover.

I stood in front of the sink and dabbed the remover onto the wash-cloth. When I looked up at my reflection, I nearly jumped out of my skin. Standing behind me was a sultry woman around my height. She had tan skin, piercing golden eyes, and luscious red lips. Her red and black wavy hair grew past her shoulders, and black wings grew from her back.

I spun around but found no one behind me. I cranked my neck and listened carefully, only to find myself to be the only one in here. There wasn't a trace of that woman. *Who was she and where had she come from? And where had she disappeared to?*

Taking a deep breath, I decided I had imagined her. I don't know why I had, as I was sure I'd never seen anyone like her, but that was the most logical explanation I had. Turning around, I went back to removing the remainder of the makeup from my face until I was sure my skin was clean. Content, I disposed of the cloth in a clothes basket and headed to my room.

Raikidan sat on my windowsill when I entered. He was still in his undercover clothes, and his hair had yet to be rinsed out. The light from the setting sun scattered across his skin, accentuating his unnatural perfection.

"Shower is free for the moment, so if you want to wash up, grab it now before someone else does," I advised him as I walked over to my dresser.

His gaze followed me. "What did you do to make yourself appear so different earlier? Besides the hair dye?"

I turned and leaned against the dresser. "I just used makeup. I guess you've never come across it in your life?"

Raikidan pursed his lips. "I'm not overly familiar with it. I think my mother would use it now and then, particularly when she went to interact with humans." He shook his head. "I've never seen you use it though."

I shrugged and went back to putting my things away. "I'm not a fan of the stuff. You'll only find me wearing it during assignments, and even then I like to keep those moments to a minimum."

"I see. What's so special about your necklace?"

I rested my hand on the top of my dresser. "It was... a gift."

"So was your earring with the bell, but you take that off."

I sighed. "The tooth is Rylan's. When he lost it, he made it into a necklace and gave it to me. I promised I'd never take it off."

"That's a strange gift to give someone."

I shrugged and placed the earrings I borrowed from Ryoko on the top of the dresser. "We didn't have much back then, but he wanted to give me something."

"You don't find it weird that it's his tooth?"

I shook my head. "No, not really."

"What did you give him?"

I frowned. "That promise. He knew that I couldn't give him something in return at the time, so I gave him that promise."

"But you did take it off. You didn't have it when we met."

"I had taken it off to replace the leather. It wasn't in the greatest condition when Rylan gave it to me, and after wearing it for so long, it had worn down to nothing. I was replacing it when the village came under attack."

"So, you ended up leaving it behind?"

I nodded.

"And you still insist there's nothing going on between the two of you?"

"Just because someone gives you a gift doesn't mean there is anything but friendship behind it. Rylan is like an older brother to me, nothing more. I've told you this."

I stiffened and an uncomfortable feeling rushed through me as Raikidan snaked his arm around my waist and pulled me into him. I couldn't believe he could walk so quietly.

He chuckled low into my ear. "That's a thoughtful promise to give to him. Now why don't you make me a promise?"

"Why would I do that? Especially when you're doing something I've told you not to do."

I felt his grin on my ear. "Because it'd be beneficial to us both."

"I'm listening."

"Don't wear that stupid stuff you call makeup again," he murmured. "I prefer you this way, without it. You're perfect as you are."

My mind went blank and my mouth went dry. *How am I supposed to reply to that?* I tried to think of something but failed. I couldn't figure out what was wrong with me.

He chuckled low in my ear and let me go. He left my room, but I still didn't move. I wasn't sure if I could. Something in his words stirred the memories of the tank's voice as I had grown.

"Perfection is the desire of your maker. Imperfections will be removed from the equation."

And Zarda's awful voice when he saw me the day I came out of my tank and I wasn't to his exact specifications.

"...Disgusting..."

But all of this was becoming drowned in those words...

"You're perfect as you are."

CHAPTER 33

My body shook and a low, muffled sound penetrated my sleeping state, but I didn't heed either. I wanted sleep. I wanted the darkness to soothe and lull me. The shaking happened again, and the sound became louder. It was someone's voice. I rolled over in an attempt to rid myself of the pest, but they followed me. "Go away…"

"Wake up." It was Ryoko.

I moaned. "Let me sleep."

"Wake up!" She shook me harder.

I groaned and reluctantly sat up. It was dark in my room, which confused me. "What time is it?"

"About ten p.m."

"What?" I fell back on my bed and pulled a pillow over my face. "Wake me up when it's daytime, you jerk."

She pulled the pillow away. "C'mon, I want to ask you something."

"It couldn't have waited 'til the morning?"

"Just hear her out," Raikidan muttered.

I sat up and looked at him. He sat motionless on the windowsill. Even in the little available light in the room, I could tell he was scowling. "She wake you up too?"

He snorted. "I thought she was going to break down that damn door. I don't know how you slept through it."

I yawned. "I was in a deep enough sleep, I guess. Now what is it you want, Ryoko?"

"Do you want to go to Twilight?" she asked.

"Huh?" My head was still slightly foggy with sleep, so I wasn't sure if I had heard her right.

"Do you want to go to Twilight?"

"You woke me up to ask me that? What the hell is your problem?"

She frowned. "Well, you went to bed early, so I didn't get to ask you earlier. If you don't want to go, you don't have to. But you didn't need to be so mean."

I sighed. She was right. I shouldn't lash out because I was tired. "No, I'll go."

She perked up. "Really?"

I shrugged. "I might as well, since I'm already awake."

Ryoko squealed. "Raikidan, you wanna come too?"

He raised a brow in question. "Do what now?"

I chuckled and nudged Ryoko off my bed. "You go pick something out for him to wear. I'll do the explaining. It'll give me time to wake up." She nodded enthusiastically and ran for the door. "Oh, and, Ryoko, does Genesis know about this?"

She shook her head. "No, she's asleep, but if she finds out, we'll tell her it was to talk to Azriel. You know she won't be too happy to find out we went there for fun. She's a bit too serious sometimes."

I shook my head. I knew there had to be a reason she wanted this so bad. Ryoko left and shut the door behind her. Yawning again, I looked at Raikidan. "Basically, what she asked was, do you want to go to the club?"

"I figured that much out. I remember being told Twilight was a club you guys owned. But what is a club?"

"It's a place you go to for dancing, drinking, and having fun. Human stuff."

He raised an eyebrow with interest. "And you do this?"

"Not unless I'm told to. But Azriel is there, and I'd like to stop in and see him."

"All right, now tell me why is it that Ryoko has to pick out my clothes?"

"Because Ryoko thinks we need to wear a specific style of clothing while at clubs. I've learned not to question it and accept it, so you should, too."

Raikidan shrugged. "All right, fine. What do I have to do?"

"Nothing more than to act normal. Follow Rylan's lead if you need to, but honestly, it's not that hard to fit in. There are a lot of different types of people who congregate there."

"Sounds good to me. But pretending I'm someone I'm not isn't easy for me," he admitted.

"You get used to it."

He raised an eyebrow at me.

I sighed. "Undercover missions, remember?"

"Right."

Ryoko tapped my door before strolling in. "His clothes are all laid out. Rylan said once Raikidan's ready, they'll head out and we can meet them there."

"I don't like the sound of that." I scooted to the far side of the bed. "I don't like the sound of that one bit."

She smirked. "Don't worry, Laz. I'll be good."

"No, you won't. You're never good."

She laughed. "You're right. Oh well, I promise I won't put as much makeup on you as I did for the mission."

Raikidan growled quietly as he reached the door. "No makeup. She doesn't like it and she doesn't need it."

Ryoko blinked. "It won't be a lot. Just enough to enhance her already great features."

"No."

Ryoko cocked her head. "How about a compromise? I'll limit it to eyeliner and lip gloss, with maybe a little eye shadow. Makes her stunning eyes stand out"—her eyes narrowed and her lips slipped into a devious grin—"and make her lips temptingly kissable."

I blanched at her insinuation, though, unsurprisingly, it was lost on Raikidan. He blinked and then shook his head. "You need to consider what she wants."

Ryoko smirked. "What she wants, or what you want?"

Raikidan left the room without indulging in the conversation more. Ryoko shut the door and looked at me, a grin spreading ear to ear. "He likes you."

I rolled my eyes. "When are you going to give this up?"

"What? He voiced how much he likes you without makeup. He fought with me over it, in a way. I think that merits liking."

"Please, it just means he hates makeup as much as I do."

"But he said nothing about me wearing it."

"You didn't say you were going to. Now, are you going to pick out my clothes, or am I going to have to guess what would be good?"

"No, I'll do it. I want you to look amazing and make the men drool."

I spun my finger in the air. "Oh, I can't wait."

She laughed and went to work. It wasn't long before I was in a form-fitting, one-sleeved forest-green shirt that showed off my midriff, tight, blue, low-ride denim pants, and cork platform shoes. Instead of my typical arm sleeves, I wore the metal bracelets Ryoko had allowed me to wear earlier on the assignment. My lips were coated with lip gloss and my eyes were lined with black liner, while various spots of bare skin were coated in a thin layer of roll-on glitter. My hair was brushed and, to Ryoko's delight, teased to perfection. I was ready, and so was Ryoko.

I had helped Ryoko choose her outfit, and although she liked it as a club style, I had to fight to get her to wear it. Her shirt was a shiny blue halter that cut low in the front and had no back except for a string that was tied to keep it from falling open. She wore blue low-rise denim pants and black knee-high boots.

I clasped a black choker around her neck at the last minute, and stood back to take her in. "Perfect."

She looked herself over the best she could without a mirror and fidgeted. "I'm not so sure about this."

I sighed and pushed her out into the living room. "You look perfect. You'll have the men drooling in one glance."

"But I don't want men drooling over me."

I grinned. "You're right. You only want one particular man to drool over you."

Her cheeks flushed several shades of red. "Laz!"

I chuckled. "Don't even try to hide it with me. You know I know." I leaned closer to her. "And trust me, he'll be drooling."

She didn't say anything, but then again, she didn't have to. Her thundering heart said everything for her.

"Have fun, you two." Argus waved at us as I pushed Ryoko toward the basement. He was sitting on the couch with a strange watch-like object in his hand and tools spread across the coffee table.

I tilted my head. "Guess you're not coming with us?"

"Nah, you know me. The club scene isn't really my thing."

I chuckled. "Right. Your thing is working out at a gym or fiddling with some sort of gun or gadget."

"You know it. Hey, Ryoko, catch." He tossed a small blue object to her. From the looks of it, it was a compacted helmet. "Zane did a little work on your bike. I made you a new helmet to go with it. You should also be able to communicate with Eira. Let me know if it works if you get the chance to try it out."

"Um, thanks?" Ryoko said. "When did you two start doing this?"

He shrugged. "A little after we started Eira's. You rarely use it, so we figured you wouldn't notice it missing. When Eira told me her helmet's features worked fine, but the communication was an issue, I changed the structure design back to an original helmet but added a communication feature instead. I then made your helmet and connected the two. If they work together, they should also work with the communicators with some minor tweaks."

"When do you find time to do all this?" she asked.

"I... I don't sleep much these days..."

"That would explain why you're awake now, wouldn't it? Well... have fun. We have our own fun to have."

She grabbed my arm and pulled me down the stairs. Ryoko let me go to allow me to make my way over to my motorcycle. My helmet was compacted and sitting on the seat of my bike. I snatched it up and placed it behind my head. Holding up my hair, I pressed the button, and the helmet formed around my face.

I sat down on my motorcycle and watched as my visor slid down over my face and made rapid calculations. Once the readings accepted me, my motorcycle roared to life.

"Can you hear me, Laz?" Ryoko called in.

"Loud and clear, Ryoko."

"Great! This is a neat invention Argus made. I see a lot of potential coming from it."

I murmured a low agreement and revved the throttle. Hearing Ryoko rev her motorcycle in response, I pulled out of my parking space and zipped through the garage. Ryoko pulled up beside me, and together we raced out into the city.

The ride to the club was easygoing—low traffic and no crazy drivers, surprisingly. When the lights started to change from the typical streetlights to neon, I knew we were getting close, that is, if the beat of the music playing at all the clubs hadn't been a giveaway on its own. It pounded in my chest as it rushed through the ground. I would hate to be the poor souls who were forced to live in the area. I could only guess what their sleep habits were like.

"Think your boyfriend will be waiting for you?" Ryoko teased.

I snorted. "He's not my boyfriend, Ryoko."

"Obviously he is if you know who I'm talking about."

"How could I not when you're always assuming he is?"

"Damn, I can't argue with that."

The club came into view, and I chuckled when I caught a glimpse of the boys. "Hey, Ryoko."

"Yeah?"

"I think your boyfriend is waiting for you."

"Laz, he's not my boyfriend!"

"No, but you want him to be."

She muttered quietly, making me laugh.

"Do me a favor when we park?" I said.

"What's that?"

"Remove your helmet by pulling it off."

"Why? All that'll do is mess up my hair."

"Just trust me, all right? If there's one thing I was forced to learn from Shva'sika that wasn't shaman related, it was how much she knew about how to get men going."

"But—" She sighed. "This is all embarrassing, that's all. It's hard being the only woman in the house that seems to be able to have feelings for someone else. Not to mention that someone else is supposed to be my comrade and second-closest friend."

"But you do want to catch his attention, don't you?"

She sighed. "Yes…"

"Then as your closest friend, trust me on this one. Your hair will get thrown around a little when you remove your helmet, which will show your femininity. While you walk, sway your hips more than normal and look as confident as possible, even if you don't fully feel it. This'll give you a sexier look. If you do this, you'll keep his attention on you for quite a while."

"Hearing this from you is a little weird. Figured I'd share that."

I laughed. "The feeling is mutual."

"You'll do this with me, right?"

"Sure. I may not have a reason to, but if it will make you feel better, then I will," I said. "Gives me some practice for certain assignments later in the very least."

"You have a reason."

"Oh yeah?"

"Yeah. He's a tall, mysterious guy whose name starts with an R and ends with an N."

I chuckled. "You know Rylan's name is like that too, right?"

"Oh shit, you're right."

I laughed.

"But I still stand by my statement, for the most part at least," she said. "He is tall and mysterious and should be a reason you do this with me."

I sighed. "We've been over this. He is not a reason for any of my actions or thoughts, and never will be. Just like any man"—*or dragon*—"who will come into my life. End of story."

"That'll change; I'll see to it. Just you wait."

I shook my head. She was too stubborn for her own good sometimes. This wasn't a battle she was going to win. She just couldn't understand that my heart couldn't beat for anyone. And even if it could, Raikidan was a dragon. And humans and dragons weren't compatible. *She's lucky I care about her as much as I do, else I wouldn't put up with this as well as I do.*

Ryoko and I pulled up to the club on the opposite side of the street. There was a long line to get in, but that wasn't unusual. Twilight was one of the most popular clubs in the city, although it wouldn't be a problem for us.

I kicked down my kickstand and listened for Ryoko to do the same behind me. My motorcycle engine cut as I swung my leg over my motorcycle and removed my helmet. My hair sprang free and flowed across my shoulders. *I need to remember to cut my hair. It's getting too long.*

Resting my helmet on my handlebar, I glanced at Ryoko with confidence and grinned. She looked at me slyly and grinned back. She was doing exactly what I had asked, and as long as she kept her confidence this high, she would be golden.

Together we strolled over to the entrance. Trying to appear indifferent as usual, I allowed myself only brief glances at the boys. Blaze visibly swallowed, and Rylan also looked taken aback by what he saw, although his reaction to the situation was much more reserved. Typical of him, but it worried me that Ryoko wouldn't notice his reaction.

Raikidan, as I expected, appeared unaffected and uninterested. At least that would prove to Ryoko that there really wasn't any hope, if nothing else. I could just tell her he was a dragon and put it to rest once and for all, but it wasn't my place to tell.

"Boys," I greeted as we walked past them.

None of them uttered a word as we walked by, that is, until Blaze saw Ryoko's backside. "Nice ass, Ryoko."

Ryoko rolled her eyes and shook her head with a grin but took it in stride. If he had mentioned her breasts, I was sure her reaction would have been much different and less confident. The shirt I had picked out, while nice, really was a risky move due to her chest size. I only hoped it wouldn't become a problem if she hit the dance floor.

The two of us walked up to the roped-off door, where a tall, muscular, dark-skinned man stood. He glanced our way with his golden eyes and grinned. I waved my fingers at him as we strolled up.

"Well, well, well, if it isn't my favorite ladies, Eira and Ryoko." His voice was deep and silky smooth. "Been a long time since I've seen you around here, Eira."

I smiled and hugged him around his neck. "It's good to see you too, Orchon."

"Where have you been, girl?"

I shrugged. "Around."

He laughed. "Obviously it was important for you to not show up all this time."

I nodded. "You know me, always busy with important things."

He chuckled. "I suppose you want me to let you in?"

I smiled. "If you're nice, you will."

He placed his hand around my shoulder. "I'm always nice to you two ladies. Besides, Azriel would have my head if he found out I made you wait."

I winked at him. "Thanks, Orchon, you're a doll. Mind letting the boys in, too?"

He glanced over to the men. "I can do that, but I have a question about the new face."

"A new friend. Don't be too harsh with him. I like this one."

He chuckled. "Sure thing. Just do me a favor in return and don't get into trouble, all right?"

Ryoko and I smiled at him. "All right."

Orchon lifted the rope to let us by. A bunch of waiting citizens protested, but I ignored them. It wasn't my problem they didn't have VIP privileges.

The music was loud, and the bass thumped in my chest as the two of us descended the stairs leading into the club. The place smelled of alcohol, people, and horribly chosen cheap perfume. It wasn't the most pleasant mix of smells, but as long as I was here, I'd have to deal with it.

Ryoko nudged me. "You like your new *friend*, eh?"

I rolled my eyes. "Don't start."

She narrowed her eyes but didn't press… for now.

Ryoko and I walked up to the bar. It was a large area, fit for accommodating up to five bartenders. Liquor and juices of all colors and bottle sizes lined shelves in a particular color-coded pattern. Clean glasses were stacked up neatly on shelves in front of a large mirror.

I leaned against the bar. There was a tall, muscular man with two sets of ears, wearing a black long-sleeved shirt and black denim pants working it, but his back was turned. "Hey there, stranger."

The man turned around and blinked. He had olive-tan skin, short dark-brown hair, chocolate eyes, and well-kept facial hair. A pair of silver dog tags hung around his neck, and a single earring pierced one of his ears. He held a glass and rag in his hand. I assumed he had been cleaning it before I disturbed him.

His back straightened. "Laz?"

I smirked. "Hey there, Azriel."

Placing the glass and rag down, Azriel rushed over to our side of the bar and embraced me in a tight hug. "I'm so glad you're safe. I've done nothing but worry since you left."

I chuckled and hugged him back. "No scolding for not coming by sooner?"

He pulled away and flicked me on the nose. "I was getting there."

I rubbed my nose and grumbled.

Azriel slipped behind the bar again. "So, what can I get you?"

I sat down on the barstool. "You know what I like."

Azriel looked at Ryoko, who smiled. "Surprise me."

He turned his back to us again and went to work. Raikidan sat down next to me, his eyes darting as he made himself comfortable. He had his arms crossed on the bar and leaned close to me. This was the first time I let myself have a good look at him. He was wearing his typical layered men's tank look with cargo pants, but he had a leather jacket over that and instead of boots he sported standard sneakers. Although simple, it fit him, and I couldn't lie to myself. I liked the look—a lot.

"Just relax, will you?" I whispered.

"This place is weird. It's loud and smells funny."

I chuckled. "You'll get used to it. Just put up with it tonight and I won't make you come back here again."

Raikidan grunted. Azriel turned back around and gave Ryoko and me our drinks. His focus switched to Raikidan, a grin slipping up his handsome face. *Oh boy, there's that look.* Things were going to get interesting.

He leaned against the bar, his full attention on Raikidan. "Well, who do we have here?"

"This is Raikidan. I'm sure you've been told about him once or twice by Rylan or Genesis." I looked to Raikidan and gestured to Azriel. "Raikidan, this is Azriel. I mentioned him before."

Azriel feigned hurt. "Only mention? You wound me."

I smirked. "I just thought it'd be better to introduce you two, as your vibrant personality likes to speak for itself."

He chuckled. "Cheeky. I've missed that." He focused on Raikidan again. "Now, is there anything I can get you?"

Raikidan's expression remained impassive. "No, I'm fine."

"Really?" Azriel leaned closer. "Nothing at all?"

Raikidan's brow twisted and he looked to me for clarification. I snickered and Ryoko flat out rolled with laughter. Rylan shook his head and ordered some scotch from another bartender working.

Azriel looked to me for answers and I snickered some more. "You're not going to get anywhere with him. He's quite clueless in that department."

A devious smile spread across his handsome face. "I could teach him a thing or two."

Raikidan jerked his head back, now more confused than ever, and I couldn't stop the laughter. Ryoko was even laid out on the bar, losing it.

When I got myself calmed, I leaned closer to Raikidan. "He's flirting with you, dummy."

His brow remained creased. "Why?"

Ryoko's laughter got louder. "I can't take this! He's too adorable."

"I'm not adorable," Raikidan muttered.

Azriel grinned. "I think you are."

Raikidan gave him another confused look and Azriel sighed. "I give up. I can see my charm isn't going to work on you."

I snickered. "You'll find a replacement by the end of the night."

He smirked. "True. But this just means he's all yours."

I snorted and sipped my drink. "Pass, thank you."

"Careful now, he might take offense to that."

Raikidan grunted. "I know her enough to not find it offensive in the least."

"Smart." Azriel grinned, an unusual look in his eyes I couldn't interpret. "Well, as I asked before, are you sure you don't want a drink?"

Raikidan hesitated, unsure what to say, and this time I swooped in to rescue him. "He's not accustomed to our drink consumption yet."

Azriel nodded. "Fair. Is there anything you have had outside the city? I'm sure I've got it. I stock my bar with some uncommon product for those adventurous types."

"Dwarven ales from the cask," Raikidan said. "They're all that I've had."

My brow rose. "Explains why you thought Ryoko's beer smelled so bad the other day."

Ryoko stuck up her nose. "There's nothing wrong with what I drink."

Azriel chuckled. "Except your beer smells like metal and mine doesn't. So lucky for him, I've got just the thing."

He reached out and flicked a switch under the back bar. The mirror behind him lit up, several colored lights turning on either side, revealing a large cask behind it. *A two-way mirror?* Azriel moved an out-of-place bottle of colored liqueur, something I always found peculiar, as he had a particular placement for all his bottles based on color, revealing a tap connected to the cask.

"Well, aren't you snazzy," Ryoko said.

Azriel bowed. "I aim to please."

He then pulled out a ceramic stein and went to pour from this fancy hidden cask, but I stopped him. "Hey, whoa, what are you doing?"

He turned back with a raised brow. "What do you mean?"

"You know not to skimp on the good stuff with us, Az. Raikidan is no exception."

"Whatever do you mean, my dear?"

"I know you hide the good stuff for those who are in the know." I grinned. "Don't try to deny it. You do, and I'll ruin your streak. And I know it's not as good as you'd like me to believe."

Azriel shot a dark look at Rylan, who shrugged. "Don't look at me. I didn't say anything to her. She just knows you."

"While I'm not doubting she does, I know you'd tell her that," Azriel said.

I leaned on the bar. "And if you retaliate in any way, I'll ensure you won't have a streak for the next three months."

Azriel's eyes narrowed and then he started laughing. "You never change!"

I leaned back, smiling. "I can't go changing on you. You'd be unhappy if you couldn't take the credit."

He winked. "I'll always take credit."

Azriel then ducked under the bar and rummaged around. When a minute or two passed and he continued to search, the four of us exchanged glances. I leaned over the bar. "Everything okay, Az?"

"Everything is fine. Just have to figure out where I stored it. I could have sworn—ah, here it is!"

He popped back up, a tiny wooden keg in his hands. We watched Azriel pop the cork and pour all the dark liquid into the stein he'd pulled out earlier.

He pushed it to Raikidan. "Try that. I imported this brew from Azrok."

My brow lifted. "And how did you manage that? Not only are the import laws with them complex, but getting a dwarf from up there to talk to you for business is next to impossible."

Azriel grinned. "Threw your name around enough with the right individuals."

I shook my head. While rare in numbers, I'd met a few dwarves in my years, but there was one family I'd gotten along with well. I had a suspicion it was the same family that hooked him up. "I'm surprised you got such a small keg of it."

"Oh, I didn't. I had to buy fifteen casks. I kept one, filling these kegs for easy dispensing, and resold the rest to other vendors in town. I didn't expect it to be such a hit with some of the restaurants, otherwise I would have ordered in more to capitalize on the investment."

I grinned. "No one says you couldn't now."

Azriel chuckled and went to cleaning up. I focused on Raikidan, who was now inspecting his drink. He smelled it, his eyebrow ticking up for some reason, and then he took a small taste test. I guessed he approved, as it didn't take him long to take a big gulp of the ale after.

I looked around when I realized we were missing a person. "Where did Blaze run off to?"

Rylan shrugged and pressed his glass to his lips. "I think he said something about a hot chick and then ran off."

I snorted. "Typical."

Azriel leaned against the bar. "If he ran off, then it's safe to guess you're all here on leisure and not because Genesis has something crazy cooked up?"

Ryoko smiled wide at him. "You got it!"

Azriel looked at me. "And you came willingly?"

I shrugged. "I wanted to see you, and I get a few free drinks in the process. Win-win."

"I see how it is. Take advantage of my hospitality."

"More like cashing in on all the favors you've asked of me."

He chuckled. "Careful, I'll add to that list if I know you like it." His gaze switched to Ryoko when he noticed her staring. "What is it, Ryoko?"

Ryoko shook her head. "Oh, it's nothing."

"C'mon, just say it."

Ryoko rested her cheek on her hand and played with the umbrella in her martini. "It's just, looking at your dog tags around your neck makes me miss mine."

I snorted. "What, having your number engraved in your skull isn't enough?"

Ryoko sighed. "I don't want them because of the number. I just have some fond memories mixed in with the bad. Those tags would remind me of them." She smiled in some weird way I couldn't interpret. "Plus, I think they look cool."

"Tell you what. I'll talk to Jaybird and see if he can scrounge around to see if he can find yours. Or in the very least, have some official ones remade. How does that sound?"

Ryoko's eyes lit up. "That would be amazing! Thanks, Azriel." She placed her empty martini glass down and grabbed my arm. "Okay, now it's time to dance."

"Screw that," I said as I grabbed onto the bar. "I'm staying right here."

"Oh, c'mon, Laz! Lighten up and have some fun."

"I don't dance." My gaze slid to Azriel. "I do, however, like to drink, and would like another."

Azriel chuckled. "Coming right up."

Ryoko sighed and slipped off her seat. "Fine, I'll go dance by myself. Maybe I'll be able to convince you to join me when you've had enough to drink."

I shook my head and consumed my drink, ordering some food for those of us who preferred to sit this out. Of course, Rylan's wandering gaze as Ryoko sauntered away didn't escape my eye. "You could go dance with her."

"I'm fine," he said before sipping his drink.

I shook my head. "Whatever."

I didn't understand those two at all. I didn't understand those feelings. *What's the point figuring it out?* If those two wanted to play stupid games, it wasn't my job to get in the way. *It's not like I could ever feel them.* Not that I wanted to. *Stupid lies…*

I munched down on the fries I ordered and had to verbally give Raikidan permission to try some of the food. I didn't get him.

Azriel engaged in light conversation when he wasn't called away, catching up with me. It sent a bubbling sensation into my chest. I'd missed him.

Ryoko eventually returned, beads of sweat building up on her skin. "You all should really think about hitting up the dance floor. Azriel has some good DJs on tonight."

I grumbled about passing on the offer, and Raikidan didn't respond.

Rylan looked at her, and his eyes showed he wanted to, but in the end, he said, "I might in a bit."

Ryoko held his gaze for a moment and then shrugged. "Okay. I'm going back now."

She then disappeared into the crowd. I clamped my mouth shut. It wasn't my place to get involved. I set up the bait for him, but if he wasn't going to bite, then there wasn't anything for me to do. *Of course, there's Ryoko in all this...* I suspected she thought I was pulling her leg at this point about Rylan, and I felt a bit guilty. I was getting her hopes up without following through with the promise to help.

"You should have taken up her offer," I finally said to Rylan. "I know it's what you want."

He pressed his lips to his recently refilled glass. "I'd like to not talk about it, thanks."

I shrugged. "Your choice, but for your information, she got all dolled up so you'd notice her."

He remained silent, his eyes falling on his glass. The bond tugged, the idea of her dressing up for him flaring up bits of desire in him, but died soon after. So quickly in fact, it was if he smothered it on purpose. *What's up with him?*

My attention pulled to my left when a woman appearing in her mid-twenties came up to the bar and not-so-subtly put herself between Raikidan and me. She had a horribly done fake suntan, bleached blonde hair, so much makeup she could give a clown a run for his money, and tight clothes that clung to her tall, slim form. She also smelled of heavy perfume. *Woman, did you bathe in it or something?*

She ordered two drinks, and her eyes darted to Raikidan several times as she waited. He paid her no mind and reached in front of her to snatch up a few fries from the plate of food I'd forgotten to push to him earlier. Her eyes darkened when they darted over to me, and my brow rose as I lifted my drink to my lips. What issue did she have? It wasn't like I was getting in her way. Raikidan was more than capable of rejecting her all on his own out of sheer cluelessness.

Azriel finished her drink requests and she left, but not before purposely brushing against Raikidan's arm. He stopped mid bite for a moment, but only a moment, and went back to eating, not passing her a glance. I sputtered out a laugh, and even Rylan found the exchange amusing.

"You think that's funny?" Azriel said. "I've been watching her and her table mates. They've all been giggling and eyeing him from afar. That one was the only one brave enough to test the waters, and I don't doubt she'll be back."

"I hope not." We all looked at Raikidan as he stuffed his face some more. "She smells funny."

I threw my head back as I laughed. "That's the only reason? You are something else."

"Well, I didn't like how she looked at you."

He noticed that?

"None of them like her," Azriel said, picking up a glass to clean. "They're under the impression she's going to get in their way of impressing you."

"You got that from watching them?" I said.

"I've been doing this a long time. I know a lot more than I probably want to."

I shrugged and ate a chicken finger. "Rai, if you need any help getting rid of her if she comes back, shoot me a look. I don't mind helping."

"Thanks, I guess."

I didn't get halfway through my chicken finger before the woman returned, this time on Raikidan's other side.

She leaned on the bar, being extra sure to tuck her arms under her chest as if that'd grab his attention. *Desperate much?*

"Hey."

Raikidan stopped mid-bite into a breaded cheese stick and glanced at her. "Uh, hey."

"Name's Malia."

"Uh, Ray."

A coy smile spread across her painted lips as she tilted her head and leaned a bit closer. "I couldn't help but notice you've been sitting here a while. My friends and I wouldn't mind if you joined us for a bit. We're a lot of fun."

Lady, he's got no idea what kind of fun you're trying to allude to.

Raikidan looked at his food, her, me, and then her again. "I'm here with my friends, so I'm going to pass. Sorry."

Unsurprisingly, she wasn't deterred. She continued to smile and readjusted herself, so her cleavage was easier to see. "Well, then maybe I could stay here and keep you company."

Raikidan lifted his stein and then darted his eyes over to me. "I already have good company."

Malia's eyes darkened when she glanced my way, but wasn't ready to give up on what she wanted. She reached out and lightly caressed his bicep. The sight of this action stirred up a negative, possessive feeling in the pit of my stomach. *Jealousy.* There it was again, just like when Ryoko had dragged Raikidan away that day we had all been working at the shop. It didn't make sense for me to be jealous. It wasn't logical, but it was there nonetheless. Why was I feeling this way?

"Are you sure—"

I let out a loud groan, tired of all this. "Geez, bimbo, take the hint already and get lost."

Raikidan's gaze flicked to me, his eyes wide, while Rylan and Azriel lost it. Rylan hid his face in the palm of his hand as he rested his elbow on the bar and laughed, while Azriel kept his back to the club as he cleaned glassware to help conceal his bias in this situation.

Malia sucked in a tight breath. "No one was talking to you. So why don't you mind your own business?"

I put my drink down and let my hand fall onto the bar harder than needed. "Maybe I didn't make myself clear. *Or* maybe your bleach job also got to your brain." Rylan and Azriel snickered more, Raikidan continuing to stare as if unsure what to do. "Either way, I'll repeat myself one more time. He's not interested and has made that clear. So, go march your tiny little ass back to your friends and look for another guy to bring you home tonight and treat you like a temporary toy."

She gave a smug smile. "Your jealousy is amusing. It's not my fault your average looks can't land you a man."

I grinned and leaned back in my chair. "At least I don't have to stuff my bra."

Malia straightened and sucked in a tight breath, her gaze flicking between Raikidan and me. He showed no signs of defending her and she took great offense to it, storming off in a huff.

Rylan rested his forehead in his arms as he laughed into the bar. Azriel allowed himself to laugh louder with the patron gone, and Raikidan remained confused. Based on what he told me about dragons and females fighting, that small altercation put him in an uncomfortable position.

Azriel set a new drink down for me. "This is for you, because you were so wonderfully catty just now. It was refreshing to see from you."

I chuckled and accepted the drink. "Don't worry. You'll remain the queen of catty for some time to come."

He gave a flourished bow. "Thank you."

His brow furrowed when something caught his eyes behind me. My brow creased as well. "What's wrong?"

"Ryoko appears to be having some trouble."

I whirled around and scanned the dance floor. I found her trying to refuse the attention of two men who didn't want to listen to her protests. My eyes narrowed. *Not on my watch!*

"Make them pay for their insolence."

Rylan also noticed and went to go help her, but I threw my arm out and stopped him. "Don't even think about it. You didn't have the balls to go dance with her, so you don't get to play white knight."

Irritation bubbled in the bond from Rylan as his eyes narrowed at me, but I couldn't have cared less.

I cracked my knuckles. "That's going to be me. I'll be right back."

34
CHAPTER

I pushed my way through the throng of people, the bass of the music pounding in my chest, my eyes pinned on Ryoko. She wasn't doing well with staying polite anymore, not that I believed she should with how little these "men" were listening.

When she was within my reach, I latched onto her arm and pulled her close. "There you are! I've been looking everywhere for you."

Ryoko looked to me and smiled. "Sorry. I got a little caught up."

I noticed the two men's growing interest in my presence and needed to defuse this ASAP. I tugged Ryoko away. "Well, let's go. Everyone is waiting."

"Wait, hold on." One of the men stepped in my way. I glanced up at him through my lashes. Yellow-tan skin, dark eyes and hair, he was a good-looking man and the sly smirk he was flashing me screamed heartbreaker. Or maybe it was the dog tags. I was always suspicious about soldier's intents when it came to the affairs of the heart. "No need to run off so quick. We were just asking your friend here if she wanted to dance with us. You're more than welcome to join us." The soldier stepped behind me, resting his hand on my lower back. "I'd be quite happy if you did."

"Don't let him touch you!"

I pulled away and tugged Ryoko with me. "I'm going to pass. Our friends are waiting for us."

He snaked his arm around me again and bent close to my ear. "You don't have to be scared, baby. I don't bite... too hard."

My eyes narrowed, and I shoved him away. "I said no. Now leave us be."

He scowled and I spun on my heels. I didn't make it more than four steps before a deeper voice spoke. "Hold on, sweetie."

A large, strong hand grasped my wrist, but that wasn't what my mind focused on. A crunching sound hit my ears, and I stilled. Ryoko's ears twitched and she zoned in on me just as the pain slammed into me. I screamed as I turned to see what happened, my body locking up in various places.

"Eira!" Ryoko shrieked. Her shout got the others around us noticing the issue and even the music stopped, the entire club going silent.

My assailant was an enormous man, like some freak out of a movie. Dog tags hung from his neck, identifying the reason why. *He's like the soldier Raikidan and I ran into the day we visited the temple.* Were the two related in some way? If they were, were they the new experiments I'd heard about? If they were, it was obvious Zarda no longer cared about an experiment's appearance as long as they had the modifications he needed. He would be able to use the looks as a reason to get rid of them in the end.

That didn't matter at the moment. The throbbing pain in my arm, as well as the numbness ebbing over my hand did.

The man who grabbed me let go and pulled away, his buddies staring at him. "What did you do?"

The hulking man took a step back. "I'm sorry, I didn't mean to. I–it was an accident."

"You idiot!"

I stared at my arm, cradling it gently. *He crushed it. He crushed my wrist. "Make him pay!"*

"You asshole!" Ryoko roared. She launched herself at him, slamming her fist into his chest as hard as she could, uncaring if it harmed him or not.

The man stumbled back, coughing. *He's a Brute class. No doubt about it. He can take those hits.* Ryoko's rage blinded her, and she continued to assault the man. But her attacks weren't hurting him like it would another person, not even any Brute I knew. Something was not right.

The hulking man grabbed her and threw her to the ground, but she bounced back and body-slammed him. The other two men talked to each other, trying to figure out what to do—and figure out how Ryoko was able to stand up to this Brute. *You'd think everyone in the military knew her.*

People behind the soldiers pushed their way through, their dog tags clearly identifying them. One look at Ryoko engaging with the Brute, and then me holding my arms, they knew what went down.

One looked to the man who had accosted me. "What the hell happened here?"

"I don't know. It happened so fast," he said. "Who is that woman?"

The first man's brow rose. "How do you not know of Ryoko? She's one of the best former Brutes we've ever had in the military."

The man who had accosted me swore, the name now ringing bells.

I glanced behind me when patrons shuffled away and watched Raikidan and Rylan push their way through. Raikidan reached me first and looked at the way I held my arm. The immediate pain had dulled to a throbbing, but I also couldn't feel my hand at all. His eyes darkened, and his lips curled back into a snarl before he focused on the man Ryoko was beating on.

Before I could think to stop him from getting involved, he charged over to the man just as he threw Ryoko off him. Raikidan's fist slammed into the hulking soldier's gut. He choked and then fell to his knees, struggling to breathe and holding his abdomen. Raikidan pulled his arm back and then threw his fist into the man's face, my ears picking up the snapping of his nose. *Ouch, nice hit.*

Raikidan continued to hit him over and over again, his face filled with rage. An odd feeling fell over me as I watched him beat this man up because of me. It was warm and had some sort of pulling effect toward him. It confused me. Most feelings were confusing for me, but I'd never experienced this one.

Blood splattered across the floor. No one jumped in to aid the Brute, and the Brute soldier couldn't catch his bearings between Raikidan's swings. *If this continues, Raikidan may just kill him.*

"Rai, stop," I called out.

He halted mid-swing and his attention snapped to me. His muscles tightened when his eyes landed on my held arm.

"Please, no more. He gets it."

Raikidan looked down at the Brute, now spitting out blood on the floor, and hit him one last time before stalking back over to me. Azriel, along with what appeared to be his entire bouncer staff, pushed their way through the patrons. He assessed the damage and barked out orders to get the soldiers out. Rylan left me to give a hand. Ryoko offered to help, but Azriel declined and requested she help me. She nodded, but upon seeing Raikidan reaching me, she winked and stayed put for a bit longer. *Thanks, Ryo…*

Raikidan gazed at my arm and scowled. "How bad does it hurt?"

I averted my eyes. "My… body is in shock. I can't feel my hand and there's a dull ache in my wrist. Pretty sure he crushed it. If I don't get it fixed up before the shock wears off, I'm going to be in excruciating pain."

His lip pulled back and some sort of sound came out of his mouth, but I wasn't able to discern what. I assumed it was some sort of Draconic. "What needs to be done to heal that right? I can go find—"

I let go of my bad arm, flinching from the slight movement, and placed my good hand on his chest. "It's going to be okay. Azriel is a former military medic and has many medical clearances. I'm sure he has something here. And if not, we can talk to some other unconventional contacts."

"Why did you have me stop? How can you be so calm after what he did?"

"Because I didn't want you to kill him. It's not worth going to jail for."

He held my gaze. "Yes, you are."

My heart skipped a beat and my face warmed. *What?* I looked away and went back to cradling my arm. He was wrong. Whatever messed-up reason he had for saying that, he was wrong. *I'm not worth anything.*

Ryoko came up to us then. I suspected she'd seen enough and didn't want things to get anymore awkward between us. "Ray, you should go give Azriel a hand. Some of the soldiers aren't cooperating, and I think having the guy that beat up a Brute could spark them to listen." She placed her hand on my back. "I'll get Eira situated in Azriel's office for when he can tend to her."

Raikidan nodded, giving me one last look before walking off. Ryoko gave me a gentle nudge and the two of us headed through the club to the back.

Azriel's office was just down the hall, past the kitchen. It was a rather large room, with a mahogany desk and comfortable chair, couch for lounging, and a few bookshelves filled with various items.

I sat down in Azriel's chair while Ryoko fetched some towels. When she returned, she created a comfortable rest for my arm and then pulled up a chair for herself. "How are you feeling?"

I shook my head. "I don't know. I don't know what to make of what happened, and I'm feeling pain and numbness in different parts of my arm."

She nodded. "From the sound of it, he got you good, but it didn't look like he grabbed you all that hard."

"I saw another Brute like him in the city my first week back here. He smelled like tank water. If it weren't for the smells here, I'm sure I would have gotten it off him, too."

"So, a new Brute. Why would he be here, then? It's protocol for them not to be in such settings with civilians until five years after release."

I grunted. "My guess is the group assigned to show him around wanted to have their own fun when they weren't supposed to, and hoped he'd behave himself."

Ryoko snorted. "That wouldn't surprise me." She looked at my arm. "As bad as it is to say, I'm glad it was you that he grabbed and not some civilian. There wouldn't be a way to save their limb."

I agreed. Civilians, as advanced as they were compared to an ordinary human, didn't take too well to the types of accelerated medical treatments we experiments could.

Ryoko's eyes softened and her ears drooped. "Sorry I was the cause of this."

I shook my head. "Not your fault they wouldn't listen."

"Yeah, but you had to jump in."

"Well, I didn't have to. Rylan was going to, but since he decided not to take you up on the dancing offer, I thought it wouldn't be right for him to play 'white knight.'"

She shrugged. "He didn't have to. He's not interested. It is what it is."

"Except he is." I pointed at her when she went to open her mouth. "Don't even try to say he's not. I know what I saw when we first arrived." I pointed to my head. "I know what I felt. He just has far more control than Blaze."

She pursed her lips, and then smiled wickedly. "Regardless, had he jumped in, then your hot date wouldn't have been able to swoop in and beat the snot out of that guy."

I narrowed my eyes. "Ryoko, he's not my date."

"Not with the way he looked at you when we first arrived."

"He didn't look at me any different than he does every day. Indifferent and uncaring, as he should."

She nudged me. "Stop being a pain and just admit that some guy likes you and you're totally okay with it."

I let out a long sigh. "Ryoko, I'm in too much pain to deal with this right now. Just stop for once."

She frowned and studied me. "You're not telling me something. Something about him."

My mouth spread into a thin line.

"What? We always tell each other stuff." She thought for a moment. "Does he have a girlfriend?"

I sighed. "No. And he's not into men as far as I know, so I wasn't lying to Azriel, either."

She chuckled and then leaned forward. "Then tell me what's going on."

I frowned. "I'm sorry, Ryo, but I can't. I gave him my word it'd stay between the two of us."

"Oh…" She sat back up. "Okay then."

She accepted that a little too easily. I knew Ryoko far too well. Despite her placating tone, this topic was far from done with in the future.

The door to the office flew open and Azriel strolled in, a medical kit in hand, and Raikidan close behind. The latter looked extra-irritated. Azriel, on the other hand, appeared excited. "All right, doctor is here!"

Ryoko and I laughed. That explained it.

He came up to me, placing the medical kit on the desk. "Now, be good for me, Laz, and I might give you a lollipop."

I snickered. "No promises."

Azriel rummaged through his kit, pulling out various tools and devices. I noticed Raikidan take up position by the door, leaning against the wall, as if he were expecting trouble to come through any minute.

Azriel pulled out a cylindrical object from the kit. "Let's get a good look at what we're dealing with."

He pressed a button on the side of the object, and used both hands to pull it apart. Thin rods of metal on the top and bottom connected the two parts, and a hologram projected in the center. He held the object over my wrist. The hologram distorted and displayed an x-ray view of my bones. As I thought, there wasn't a single bone that had more than an inch of unbroken length.

He sucked in a tight breath. "That's... bad. I'm going to use a regenerative serum. It's the only way you're going to get that fixed at this rate."

I chewed my lip, not liking the idea. This wasn't like the virtual simulation. "How much better is that serum than in the past? I know natural healers that would make this process better than that stuff."

"Don't worry. It's leaps and bounds better than when we were active military. Nowhere near as painful, and does a better job. Will still take about an hour with the damage you sustained."

Ryoko let out a low whistle. "Not even I knew it improved that much. That's amazing!"

I agreed, but still didn't like the idea of using the serum. Azriel didn't care. He rummaged around through the medical kit, pulling out a small gun.

"Grab her! Don't let her get away."

I watched him carefully as he searched for more items and pulled out a small cloth, a bottle and a vial of clear liquid, and a needle sealed in a bag, aware of my increasing heart rate.

"No, don't!"

"We're not here to hurt you. This will help you."

"Leave me alone!"

I swallowed, unable to look away from the needle. *It's okay, Eira, it's not like that. It's more like virtual training. I can handle this just like I can there.* But even so, I wasn't going to enjoy this.

"Stop this right now! This isn't going to do her any good."

"She needs these."

"No, she doesn't!"

Azriel soaked the cloth with the liquid from the bottle and lightly wiped it over my wrist. He was gentle, and the strange-smelling liquid left my skin more numb than it had been before. Perspiration dripped down the back of my neck. Azriel then loaded the needle and small vial into the gun. I tensed.

"Let me go! Let me go!"

Ryoko got to her feet and rested her hands on my shoulders. "I've got you."

I looked away from Azriel and my arm. "Thanks…"

"Please, don't…"

Azriel grasped my arm gently and pressed the gun to my arm. My free hand clenched tightly, and I flinched from the pain when the gun silently went off. Although the numbing solution did well for numbing the top layer of my skin, it did nothing to numb everything underneath. I felt the needle slice into my flesh and the solution spread through my arm as Azriel continued to press the trigger. It wasn't a pleasant feeling, to say the least.

I counted until the vial was empty. I knew because I felt the needle retract, and Azriel let go of my arm. I took a deep breath before I turned my head back to him. Azriel ejected the vial and needle, placing them in a bag to be disposed of. He put the gun back into the medical kit and pulled out a roll of white bandages. Picking up my hand, Azriel quickly and precisely wrapped up my arm.

"That should do it." He set down my arm. "In an hour, you shouldn't have anything but a small scar to show for this night."

My pulse started to slow back to normal. Ryoko let me go and stepped back. "So, that's it then? She was the last thing to be dealt with?"

"Well, no." Azriel began to pack up. "I'm waiting for those boys' commanding officer to show up. Actually"—he looked at her—"if you'd be so kind as to help me with that, I'd appreciate it." He glanced at Raikidan. "Your new friend here was more interested in beating up the soldiers than helping. Of course, since this is because of Laz, I can't say I blame him. So, I thought it best he keep an eye on her instead of getting into trouble."

Ryoko grinned. "I'd be happy to assist."

While I agreed with Azriel's perspective, I knew what Ryoko was up to, and I didn't like it. She went over to Azriel, a skip in her step. Azriel tucked his medical kit under an arm and then allowed Ryoko to hook her arms into his free one.

He glanced back at me as they left. "Behave now, you two."

I flipped him my middle finger just before he shut the door. Raikidan came over and sat down in Ryoko's chair. An air of silence fell over the room. I focused on my arm, playing with a part of my cloth wrap as I thought about recent events. This Brute we dealt with was an anomaly. Ryoko wasn't the toughest Brute out there, but she ranked near the top, and even he had outclassed her. And if my suspicions were correct in his relation to the other Brute Raikidan and I ran into, I wondered if these were some of the new soldiers we were told about by Aiden. If so, Zarda wasn't keeping to any visual appeal standards. *I wouldn't doubt he's using it as an excuse to get rid of them later when he's bored.*

Raikidan looked at me. "You don't expect me to talk, right?"

I chuckled. "No. I much prefer comfortable silence over idle chit chat."

He nodded and silence fell over us again. That is, until my arm spasmed. The uncomfortable sensation made me cringe and instinctively I grabbed the good part of my arm.

Raikidan bolted out of his seat. "What's wrong?"

I shook my head and waited for the episode to subside before speaking. "Nothing's wrong. That's just the effect of the serum. It's mending all the tissue and bone damage incrementally. I'll be fine."

He sat back down and then frowned. "I'm sorry I didn't get to you sooner. I thought you'd be fine to handle the problem."

I chuckled. "Trust me, I didn't expect this, either. You have nothing to apologize for."

He pulled his chair closer and rested his forehead in the crook of my neck. "Yes, I do. I need to keep you safe. I failed to do so."

I sat there, rigid from the close contact. But as uncomfortable as I was, a strange sense of calmness spread over me. No, calm wasn't the right word. I felt more okay with this than I thought possible. *What's going on with me?*

"R–Raikidan, what are you doing?" I finally managed to ask.

He pulled away, a frown on his lips. "It's a calming gesture for us dragons. I guess humans don't work that way?"

My lip twitched. "It might work for a normal human, since they're okay with being close to others. But I'm not normal."

"So that didn't help you at all?"

I shook my head. "No."

His brow knitted as he went to thinking. "Can… can I do it again? It helped me."

I chewed my lower lip. Was it okay? He wasn't human. Nothing weird would happen because of that fact. "Sure."

He rested his forehead against my neck again and took slow breaths. I focused on my wrist, a pulsating sensation making its way up my arm. *I'm going to be hit with another spasm.* As if on cue, my arm twitched as a healing spasm took hold. The sensation of pain shot through my arm, and I clamped down on my lip so as to not cry out.

I exhaled when everything subsided. Raikidan's arm reached around me suddenly and pulled me closer, burying his face deeper into my neck. An uncomfortably warm sensation flooded over me.

"R–Raikidan, what are you doing? We didn't agree to this."

He didn't respond, and his grip remained tight.

I glanced back at him. He didn't look at me and his whole body appeared tense. My brow knitted. "Is this situation really affecting you that bad?"

He nodded.

"Why?"

He tilted his head to look at me, those deep sapphire pools snaring my gaze. "Why wouldn't it? I failed to keep you safe when I told you I would."

"No, you told me you'd help me get revenge."

"And as a Guard, I swore to protect you. I'm not going back on that while I remain here."

My cheeks burned, and my mouth dried a little, and I didn't know why. I didn't understand what this dragon did to me. No one had been able to get me to react like this. *That's a lie.* I pushed the memory away. I told myself to never think on that. It was for the best…

I averted my gaze. "I'm not worth getting upset over."

His grip on me tightened and he pulled me closer. "I disagree."

My heart rate picked up and I pulled on his arm with my good hand. "Please let go."

"What is wrong with what I'm doing? I get you're human, but this is normal for dragons."

"It's not normal for humans." I pulled on him some more. "It's… a possessive action. Please let go."

He listened this time. "How possessive are humans?"

I glanced at him and then focused on my healing arm. "Depends on the person and what the object of their obsession is. Some get annoyed when something happens to the object they possess or want to possess, and some... get violent."

Raikidan leaned on the desk, his arms crossed. "Sounds like us dragons."

I looked at him. "How often do you get violent?"

"Well, it depends, but if someone doesn't have expressed permission, whether that object is inanimate or living, like a dragon or non-dragon, that's the more likely state we'll be in."

My brow furrowed. "Non-dragon? Like humans and elves?"

He nodded. "It's most common for reds, as they like to mingle and live amongst the non-dragons, but it can happen to any color. Even a black, believe it or not."

With what he told me about black dragons, I found it hard to believe. "Why people?"

"The dragon forms an emotional bond with the being, attaching to them enough to see that living being as a treasure. They'll then protect them with their life."

I glanced down at my hand. "Must be nice having a dragon protecting you like that."

"I watch your back."

"Not like that." I fiddled with my cloth binding. "I'm no treasure. A muddy rock at best."

"No, you're not."

What did he know? He was a dragon who claimed to know little about humans. I looked at him, only for those captivating eyes of his to snag me. My pulse slowed, and everything around us disappeared. I tried to say something, anything that would bring me back to reality, but the words didn't come.

Raikidan moved, breaking the eye contact, and rested his chin in the crook of my neck. He wrapped his arms around me again and I resigned to this fate. He wasn't going to listen, and if I was honest with myself, it wasn't really all that bad. I did feel calmer, safer even. Allowing myself to look at this objectively, it wasn't as alarming as I'd let myself believe.

Raikidan tilted his head, and still it was okay. I found myself reaching up and resting my hand on the side of his face. He didn't pull away, and still, everything remained okay. It didn't make sense to me. *It has to be because he's a dragon.* I wouldn't have given such lenience to a human.

Azriel's office door flew open, and the two of us jumped. I immediately regretted it and cried out as excruciating pain shot through my arm. Raikidan reacted by placing his hand on my shoulder and looking at me with worry. I gave him a reassuring smile. It was my fault for not being aware of my surroundings.

Azriel's voice carried into the room. "Eira, are you okay? Do you need some painkillers?"

"I'm fine. I just need to not be surprised by sudden entrances, thank you." I looked up, only to be taken aback by the familiar man standing in front of Azriel, our hasty door-opening culprit. "General Zo?"

He stood in the doorway, staring at me. Unlike when I'd seen him before, he wore standard civilian clothes, but dog tags hung around his neck. This was standard attire for soldiers, playing off the lie that their service wasn't forced. A stupid façade. The majority of civilians didn't care that we had no say in what we did or that we only served orders every hour of the day. *But I guess it helps soldiers get through their miserable lives by pretending they can have normal lives sometimes, so there's a plus there.*

Zo took another moment to speak. "You're the injured civilian?"

I looked to Azriel. "No one else was hurt, right?"

He shook his head. "Just you."

I focused back on Zo. "Then, yep, that's me."

Zo glanced to Azriel. "Then who beat up one of my men? You said he was in here too."

Azriel pointed to Raikidan. "He is."

Zo's brow rose. "A civilian beat up a Brute? You expect me to believe that?"

"I do, since he's my newest bouncer." *Azriel, what the hell are you doing?* "Ryoko recommended him to me because of his strength. He got his chance to prove it today." Azriel looked to Raikidan. "And yes, Rai, per your earlier request, you're getting off-time pay for assisting me earlier with the corralling."

"Better be," Raikidan muttered. "And it's Ray. Only Eira calls me Rai."

Azriel huffed. "I don't get special treatment, too? What is this?"

I giggled. "Because it's fun to hear you whine."

He pointed at me, his eyes narrowed with mischievous intent. "Watch it, young lady. I can mess with your hours now that I'm your boss."

I stuck my tongue out at him and Zo chuckled. "You two seem to know each other well."

I nodded. "Azriel and I met… three days after Rai and I arrived in the city." I grinned Azriel's way. "He was all bummed out he'd lost his good streak."

"I did not," Azriel said, crossing his arm. "It was only delayed."

I waved him off. "Yeah, yeah."

Zo approached and sat down on the desk, his eyes focused on me. It made me uncomfortable. "As amusing as this banter is, I do need to ask you a few questions."

"I'm more than happy to answer your questions, General."

He tapped my chin with his knuckle. "Just Zo, remember, Sweetcheeks?"

I laughed. "Right—I forgot, sorry."

"Now, tell me what happened."

I gave him a quick but thorough explanation of the events that transpired, and then gazed at my bandaged arm when I came to the end. "Then the big freaky guy grabbed me and this happened."

Zo's brow furrowed. "Azriel said he harmed you, but didn't go into detail."

"Well, he—" My arm spasmed and I cringed.

Zo jumped off the desk and stared wide-eyed at Azriel. "You gave a civilian regenerative serum? Are you insane?"

Azriel crossed his arms. "Your Brute completely crushed her wrist. It'd take several surgeries and weeks, if not months, of healing for her to maybe get full use of that hand back had I not. I tested her to make sure she was compatible, and then gave her a low dose determined safe for civilians. I know what I'm doing." Azriel looked my way. "That was your third spasm, correct?"

I nodded, wincing—this pain the worst of them yet—and he nodded back. "I thought so. Everything is happening on time. You'll have one more in ten minutes. That'll be the last."

I let out a small breath of relief when the spasm died down. I hated this stuff. Improved or not, I should have sought out a shaman to give me proper healing. "It's fine, really."

Zo sat back down on the desk and brushed my bangs out of my eyes. "Are you sure?"

I nodded, using the motion to pull away a bit and tried to flex my hand. It hurt to try, but my hand moved, showing the serum was working. "See? I'm a lot tougher than you think."

He chuckled. "I suppose so." He turned his head and brushed my bangs with his fingers again. My brow furrowed and he smiled. "Sorry. Your hair color fascinates me. I—"

I held up a finger, finding this the perfect opportunity to throw off any suspicion about my identity. "Don't say you think it's natural. I'm so tired of hearing that." Zo blinked as I ranted. "Who in their right mind thinks purple hair is natural? I mean, c'mon!"

"Well, uh, you have a good point," he managed. "What color hair do you have naturally?"

"Red," Azriel said as he walked over to one of his bookshelves. This pulled Zo's attention from me, allowing me to give my friend a questioning look when he turned around with a picture frame in hand. Azriel walked over to the desk and handed it to Zo, winking at me when Zo's eyes fell on the photo.

Zo chuckled. "You two are something else."

I leaned to the side to look myself to find it a photograph of Azriel and me. The two of us were pulling on each other's faces to make each other look as ridiculous as possible, and my hair was in fact red in this image. And not an orange kind of red like I had for that failed mission with Ryoko. This red was a typical shade a fire elementalist had, and the color Raikidan sported in his hair. *I remember that day.* It was about a week before I'd gone on the run. I had just finished an undercover assignment and he'd stopped by for a visit. *Azriel, you are a genius.*

Zo looked at me. "You look good with red, but I think you pull off this violet color well. You should keep it this way."

"She'll color it as she pleases," Raikidan said.

My eyes darted to him to find a clear scowl directed at Zo. *What's up with him?*

Zo cleared his throat and passed the photo back to Azriel. "Of course. My comment was merely a suggestion."

I pushed Raikidan by the shoulder, though he didn't move much.

"Don't be mean. Or I'll let Azriel get creative with his work punishments."

Azriel grinned. "Please do."

Raikidan glanced at me. "I'll give him the same permission for you."

I stuck my tongue out at him. "He loves me too much."

Zo looked intrigued. "You're going to be working here as well, Sweetcheeks?"

I went to open my mouth, but Azriel beat me to it. "Yes. She's my newest waitress."

Zo focused on me, his eyes showing his clear interest in the matter. "Really?"

Azriel, I'm going to kill you! I forced a smile. "Yeah. I needed to try something different, and since Rai was coming to check out open positions, I tagged along."

"Well, you're in good hands with Azriel." He tapped my chin with his finger and then stood. "I need to get going. Stay out of trouble from now on, Sweetcheeks, you hear?"

I chuckled. "Trouble is my middle name."

He chuckled and touched my chin again before leaving. Azriel followed him and had a quick conversation before closing the door.

He looked at me with a raised brow. "Sweetcheeks?"

I hung my head. "Don't get me started. It's not my idea to put up with it." I then pointed at him. "Speaking of not my idea, how about consulting us next time before you spontaneously hire us."

Raikidan nodded, agreeing with me.

Azriel held up his hands. "Sorry, but I didn't have time to consult you. Zo showed up quicker than I expected, and I needed a legitimate excuse to why Raikidan was able to beat the guy up. All my bouncers need to have exceptionally high strength to handle the clientele I bring in. You know this."

"And what about me? It's not like Raikidan said I was working here, just that he would convince you to dish out creative punishments."

"I figured you two came as a package deal." He smiled. "Plus, I'm sure the shop doesn't pay as well as I can."

I sighed. He wasn't wrong. At the rate the projects were crawling in, Zane wasn't able to technically pay all of us individually, plus fund the rebellion. It was why we had a shared fund stashed away in the house.

Azriel came over to me. "How's the pain?"

"I'm coming out of shock slowly, so the pain is increasing, but not as bad as it could have been had I let it be."

The door of the office opened, and Rylan and Ryoko strolled in. Rylan looked... confused. "Azriel, have you seen Blaze? I looked everywhere for him."

"He left with four young ladies before the incident happened," Azriel said.

Rylan pinched his nose. "I knew he was up to something. I shouldn't have let him hold onto the keys."

"No use getting worked up about it. This is Blaze, after all," I said. "Nothing we can do to stop him. We'll just use the bikes."

"But you—"

"I'm almost healed up. I can drive."

Rylan crossed his arms. "Even if your bones are fixed, you shouldn't put too much tension on them for a few more hours."

I looked to Azriel, who shrugged. "I don't see an issue with her driving. It's not like she's using that wrist to twist the throttle."

"To add to that, Raikidan can't drive a motorcycle," I said.

Ryoko's hand shot up into the air. "I can drive him!"

While Rylan didn't physically react to the excited offer, the bond tugged hard on the back of my head. That didn't please him in the least.

I shook my head. "I'm more than capable of driving him."

She winked at me. "I'm sure you are."

I rolled my eyes and went to spit out a retort, but my arm spasmed. Luckily this wasn't nearly as painful as the last three times.

"And that's four," Azriel said. "You're good to go. Your arm will hurt for a few hours, but by the morning, you should be as good as new."

I flexed my hand, the pain a dull ache. "Thanks for patching me up."

"I'll always help you, Laz, you know that."

I smiled and then stood. "We should head out."

Azriel sighed. "And I should go make sure the dance floor has been properly sanitized. One thing, though, Laz."

"Yeah, what's up?"

"Watch Zo's hands when he's around. He's an ass grabber."

I pinched my nose. "Perfect. Thanks for the warning."

We said our goodbyes, and left the building. I noted, besides the closed-off dance floor, everything had returned to normal in the club. When we reached our parked motorcycles, Raikidan climbed on behind me. I secured my helmet and then started up the machine. I planned to wait for Ryoko and Rylan, but the two insisted on arguing who would drive.

"We'll see you two lovebirds at the house." I shifted the motorcycle into gear and drove off.

"Lovebirds?" Raikidan said. "As in the small tropical birds that mate for life?"

I nodded. "Yeah. Humans use the expression to tease others who care about each other a lot. Especially if they're too stubborn to make anything official between them."

"I see. So, it's in no way a reference to the bird's life mating?"

I shook my head. "No. I told you before, most nu-humans don't mate for life. Not anymore, at least."

"I see. Thank you for answering me freely."

Why is he thanking me? He'd been acting weird all night since the incident.

I shook the questions from my head and focused on driving. It wasn't anything to be concerned about.

The rest of the ride was quiet. Ryoko and Rylan never caught up with us, so I suspected either they continued to argue long after we left, or they took a different route.

The garage door opened at my command when we drew near, and I parked my motorcycle in its usual spot. As we hopped off, the sound of Ryoko's motorcycle echoed through the garage. I waited for them to pull up beside us, finding out that Rylan had managed to win their mini-argument.

"I thought you two were going to be there all night," I teased.

Rylan snorted as he cut the engine. "She's stubborn, but not your kind of stubborn."

I noticed Ryoko's good mood when she removed the helmet and grinned. "So, what did you bribe her with?"

He hung his head. "Ice cream."

I laughed, and Ryoko smiled wide as she hopped off the motorcycle. "Any kind I want, too!"

"Well, I hope you're not thinking of having it now. It's a bit late," I said as I headed for the stairs.

She held her head high. "If I want ice cream at one in the morning, I will."

I glanced back at her. "What, some guy break your heart, so you need to watch sappy love stories and mend your soul with ice cream?"

Ryoko laughed and caught up with me, leaving the confused men behind. "You're too funny, Laz."

The two of us were ascending the stairs by the time they caught up. When I opened the door to the living room, we stopped short. In front of us stood a very angry little girl.

"Where were you?" she demanded.

"Uh, out?" I pushed past her and called out down the hall, "Seda, I need a communicator."

"Yes, I'm aware you were out," Genesis said. "And I know exactly where you were, because I was awake when Blaze came home an hour ago."

"I guess his escapade didn't last as long as he'd hoped," Ryoko mumbled.

Rylan snickered, and Genesis' eyes darkened more.

I leaned against the back of the couch. "And what's your point, Genesis? We're allowed to go out and have fun every now and then. It's called a morale boost."

She opened her mouth to speak, but then noticed my bandaged arm. Her eyes went wide. "What happened? Blaze never mentioned anything about you getting hurt."

"Probably because he was too focused on the four girls he left with to notice the real issue that happened," Rylan said.

Genesis' face scrunched. "I didn't need to know that detail, thank you."

Seda came out of her room just then and sashayed down the hall. I took the communicator from her and placed it on my head. The visor slid across my eyes, and I searched for a particular communicator signal.

"Whatcha need, babe?" Aurora asked when I connected.

I could tell she was typing away at some project, and I ended up shaking my head with a chuckle. "Do you ever sleep?"

She laughed. "Sometimes I wonder, but that's what happens when you have insomnia."

"Fair enough. I need files."

"All right, what type of files?"

"I need as many files as you can get on these new experiments coming out."

Her end was silent for a moment. "Any particular reason?"

"I ran into one a week or so ago, and we ran into another one within the past few hours. There's something weird about them. Those files will help me figure out what to plan."

"All right, if you say so." She typed some more on her keyboard. "I'll see if Arnia can sneak them out. Anything else?"

"No, that's it. Have fun not sleeping."

She laughed and then cut the line. I handed the communicator back to Seda and stretched.

"So, what is going on?" Genesis asked.

"We ran into some freak show of an experiment at the club," Ryoko said. "Some super-strong Brute class. He snapped Laz's wrist as if it were made of paper, and even I had difficulties with him."

Genesis placed a hand over her mouth. "That's horrible."

I shrugged. "Azriel patched me up, so I'm okay. Now we just need more information on him and another one Raikidan and I ran into outside the club."

She nodded. "Agreed. We need to know what kind of trouble these Brutes could cause us. I'll leave you all to rest, then."

She walked off and Ryoko looked at me. "You gonna take a shower?"

"That was the plan."

"Okay, I thought about taking a bath, but I can wait."

"Or you can take your bath and I can take my shower. They are two separate units, after all."

Ryoko shrugged. "All right. Just knock before you come in."

I headed for my bedroom. "Sure."

I didn't bother closing my door after I entered. I knew Raikidan would be in shortly after, and if I was going to take a shower, I wouldn't be in here long. I took off my jewelry and laid the pieces down next to my daggers on my large dresser. I picked up the armor cloth, so it would be a fast switch to my nightclothes and turned around.

As I did, I noticed Raikidan sitting on my windowsill. He leaned on his arms, with his jacket under them, and watched me. I was really confused. I hadn't heard him walk in, and as I glanced toward the door, I realized I never heard him close it.

His gaze was intense and I couldn't look away. Slowly I walked closer to him. He stood and met me halfway, paying no mind to his jacket as it fell to the floor. He stared down at me as we stood close to each other and I stared back. I wasn't sure what was going on with me.

Slowly he lifted his hand and touched my chin with his finger. In an instant I felt self-conscious and a little uncomfortable. "W–what are you doing?"

"I don't like his scent on you."

I blinked slowly. He didn't like a scent on me? Was he talking about Zo's? It made sense. Zo had touched my chin multiple times. But if that was true, why was he touching my face?

Raikidan touched my bangs in the same fashion Zo had, and it clicked. He was covering Zo's scent with his own. Raikidan touched my chin once more, and as he pulled his hand away, I grabbed it with mine. I pulled it back and forced him to cradle my cheek.

I closed my eyes and opened them a moment later. "I'd prefer your scent on me over his."

Without warning, I let his hand go and walked out of the room. As I made my way to the bathroom, I thought deeply over the situation I had just been in. I couldn't figure out why I had been unable to look away. It was like some stronger unseen force was compelling me to do it. It was like the second day I had been with him at the waterfall. That compelling sensation was the same.

With an ordinary person, these reactions I was having would have been disturbing to me, but they weren't with Raikidan. He hadn't reacted when I placed his hand on my face. He had reacted only when I spoke. I felt the brief stop of his pulse before I let his hand go. His reaction was primal—almost subconscious. It wasn't a reaction a human would have had. A human would have reacted to the touch.

Did my reaction to him really have to do with the fact he was a dragon? Was Ryoko right in claiming I had some sort of bond with him? Would I ever find out? How would I react if I did?

I knocked on the door and then entered the bathroom. Peeling my clothes off quickly, I jumped into the shower stall and let the steaming water wash over me. As I stood there, my mind went back to those questions. But then, one bigger one came to mind.

Do I want to find out?

35
CHAPTER

K eeping low in the shadow of the building, I listened carefully. Genesis had sent me out on an assignment in Quadrant Four to snag a few documents from some business tycoon deeply involved with Zarda. The building was said to be heavily guarded, but as I listened, I wasn't so sure about that.

I decided to take a peek, only to find the grounds empty. There wasn't even a heartbeat reading on my modified sunglasses. *Strange...* For such a wealthy woman with connections, I couldn't understand why there weren't any security guards or soldiers, either patrolling or just hanging around pretending to do some important job. I knew better than to trust this situation, but I had to do this assignment, so I slunk around until I found a window leading to a dark room on the first floor to pry open.

Once I was inside, I listened only to find the place as silent as outside. I proceeded cautiously and found every room I entered to be as dark and empty as the last room. I stopped abruptly when I caught sight of a security camera and pressed against the wall, out of view. The camera had been strategically placed in the foyer leading up to the next floor. There wouldn't be a way to get around it without disabling it, and even though it may alert some sort of security system, I had to take the chance.

Quietly rummaging through my supply pouch, I pulled out a special finger gun and a supply of darts. Removing a dart from the container that carried them all, I pressed a button on the side of it and then loaded it into the gun before peeking around the corner and aiming for the camera. The recording light stopped blinking when I fired the dart and it landed in the wiring, but I didn't move. I waited to make sure the light didn't come back on. Some cameras were equipped with a backup power source because of this type of disabling technique.

When the light didn't come back on after several minutes of waiting, I moved on and up the stairs to my target room. I took a left at the top and kept my ears peeled for any sounds as I searched for the room. I ducked into a dark doorway quickly when I heard something, but then ventured on when nothing happened.

I was cautious when I finally made it to the room I needed to be in. This room was also dark, save from the light filtering in through the window from the crescent moon, showing just enough to identify the room as a study. It was also quiet, but that didn't mean it was safe. *I'm no amateur.*

Careful to not disturb much in order to keep my presence a secret, I searched for the documents Genesis and the Council wanted, but I kept getting distracted by various priceless objects that seemed out of place in this room. Rings, necklaces—all expensive looking and very shiny. *Focus, Eira.* I couldn't afford to be distracted by such trivial things, but as I filed through documents that looked to be of importance, I couldn't stop glancing at the jewelry.

One necklace in particular caught my eye, even though it wasn't something I'd wear. In the end, I picked the necklace up, but caught myself and set it back down immediately. *You dealt with this childish habit before—focus!* I really wasn't sure what was up with me. I hadn't been so easily distracted by such things in a long time. Why now?

I groaned inwardly when I touched the necklace again and decided to stow it in a pouch. *Might as well get something out of this...* I continued searching and found the papers I was looking for, along with some other pieces of jewelry, including a large diamond ring I was sure I could pawn off for a good sum of money.

Just when I thought I had finally accomplished my assignment, I stopped moving and listened. Something in the air didn't feel right. As if... as if I wasn't alone anymore.

I narrowly dodged the claws that sliced through the air near my head
I retreated to the far end of the room and eyed the two men nearby.
With deformed ears and noses, fangs, and talon-like hands, neither
man was exactly pleasing to look at. *Hunters.*

One snickered. "Look at what we have here. A little mouse?"

"More like a fox," the other said. "I knew I caught a strange female
scent here. Our mistress will be pleased we stopped this one."

Great. It would figure this business woman would use Hunters to
guard her estate. They were almost as stealthy as well-trained assassins, and if an intruder got away, they'd just be tracked down and
dealt with anyway. It made sense now that intel warned us about the
security, and it made sense that I had been picked to do this job. I
may not like killing, but I had no quarrel killing Hunters. I never had
the greatest... past with them.

"This one is rather cute," the first Hunter said. "I'm going to enjoy
killing her."

The other Hunter glared at his companion. "Oh no you're not. You
got the last one. I'm killing her and giving her to the mistress."

I rolled my eyes as the two squabbled. Typical Hunter behavior. It was
why it was never recommended to have any of them work together.
Neither wanted to share a reward or take turns with receiving one.
This drawback had become my benefit.

Taking advantage of their complacent states, I drew a dagger and
attacked. The Hunter closest to me was too slow to dodge and choked
as my dagger plunged into his chest. He attempted to attack me with
his claws, but I was quicker and withdrew my blade from him as I
evaded his counter. I then plunged the dagger into his back. He fell
to the ground with a *thud*, and I removed my dagger from his body
as I focused on the other Hunter.

He was already coming at me, trying to catch me off-guard, but I
was far too experienced for him. I ducked under his arm and sliced
my dagger through his throat—blood splattering everywhere. The
smell of his sweet blood enticed my senses. I ignored it. I couldn't
allow myself to be consumed by that side of me.

Although bleeding out profusely, this Hunter wasn't going to go
down without a fight. He held his neck and sliced his talons at me.
I stayed light on my feet and out of reach as I danced around him,

looking for an opening. *There.* I went for his exposed side and sliced into his body. Quickly removing the blade, I sliced his arm as he whipped around to defend himself. Looking him in the eye, I knew this wasn't going to be easy. He was bleeding at a rapid pace, and yet was showing no signs of going down. I suspected he had enhanced pain suppression or had a rare ability of rapid blood replenishment. It didn't matter, though. I needed to take him down and get out of there. For all I knew, more would be coming, bringing up another issue I'd have to address after this.

Drawing another dagger, I launched a furious attack on the hunter who struggled to keep up. I sliced into his body over and over and slowly wore him down until the Hunter was on the ground and unable to get back up. He was still alive and struggling, but he wasn't a threat—not at the moment, at least.

My eyes scanned the room as I thought of a plan to cover my tracks. If this woman had two hunters, she either had more or could at least get more; especially if it was found out I had taken important information. Snatching any papers I could, I crinkled them up and placed them strategically around the room. I then moved around the house and did the same.

Once I was sure there was enough, I breathed a small flame into my hand and tossed the fire about, lighting drapes and the wads of paper. Moving quickly through the house, I set more paper and cloth-like material ablaze until I made it back into the study. I only briefly looked around before igniting this room as well.

The living Hunter breathed heavily on the floor and glared at me—his neck wound preventing him from speaking. I grinned at him and then jumped out the window. Rolling on my landing to absorb the impact better, I took off for the back of the yard. I hoped the burning smell would mask the scent trail I left from entering and exiting the home, but to be sure, I ran through the city at a fast pace to hopefully throw off any would-be followers later that night.

I slipped into my room through the window and tossed my spoils onto the bed. *I'll put them away later.* My first order of business was to wash up. No one paid me much mind when I entered the living room.

Raikidan stared from where he sat on the couch, but I ignored him. I was sure he was noticing the blood on my clothes, but he would have to learn that this was what I was designed to do, whether I liked it or not.

Entering the bathroom, I turned on the faucet and did my best to wash up. My skin was easy enough to clean, thanks to a special soap we had for such times, but my clothes proved to be more difficult. My belt and boots cleaned up okay, but nothing worked on my denim jacket or low-rise jeans, and my white midriff-cut tank top now had large pink splotches as if it had gone through the wash with some red clothes and bleach.

I was a bit irritated by this. I liked this set of clothes, and I knew I should have prepared for a worst-case scenario similar to what had transpired, but it didn't make me feel any better knowing I might have to throw them out because of the stains.

With a sigh, I gave up and put on the armor clothes I'd grabbed before my shower. I headed for my room to hide my new jewelry, but just as I reached the doorway of my room, a door flew open down the hall, and tiny feet stomped into the living room. "Eira, are you ready for another assignment?"

I looked back at Genesis. "I'm always ready."

"Good, because I need all of you on top of your game." She was in a foul mood, which told us this was a big deal. "Team Four had been assigned a simple mission, but, come to find out, it wasn't as simple as it had been first thought to be, and now they've come under some heavy artillery."

"Where is this happening?" Argus asked.

"Sector Three, on the line of Sector Four."

"All right, everyone get ready," I instructed.

"She hasn't given us any other information," Raikidan said.

"She doesn't need to. We know the location, what team needs to be helped, and that there will be enemy fire. Those three pieces are all we need. Moles assigned to fight against us won't shoot us, just in our general direction, and are aware they're not going to be given similar treatment from us due to various reasons."

Raikidan grunted. "If you say so."

Ryoko jumped to her feet. "Guess I'll go change."

Rylan, Argus, and Blaze looked at each other. "As will we."

I sat down on the back of the couch to wait, since there was no need for me to change. I glanced over at Raikidan when I realized he had yet to move. "Aren't you going to change?"

"Why would I need to?" he asked.

"Same reason we change our appearances for undercover work. So we're less likely to be identified."

"Okay, that makes sense, but I don't know what to wear."

Right. I had gotten into the habit of picking everything out for him. I looked him over. What he was wearing would do fine for the most part. "Tatter up your tank top and pants, add a vest and boots on those bare feet of yours, consider some gloves, fingerless or otherwise, , and you should be good. Gives the military the idea we have less funding that we do."

"What about my face? You have those weird things on your head."

"They're sunglasses, and you'll get a pair as well. Since we'll be in close proximity, we won't need the communicators, so we'll use these special glasses. They work like the communicators except for the communication part."

"All right."

As I expected, he was wearing the armor cloth already, and it changed at his will. He seemed to like the armor more than normal clothes, although I wasn't sure if it was due to their convenience or because it felt different than regular clothes.

When he had the clothes I instructed, he looked at me. I nodded in approval. The cover of darkness would also aid in his disguise.

Ryoko came out of her room with a smile. She had pulled her hair back into a loose pony-tail and had added a blue plaid zip-up jacket over her top and shorts. She also wore what appeared to be fingerless gloves that cut off mid-forearm and were strapped at the top with three belts, but I knew better. Argus had worked on that glove design. It would cushion the impact of her close combat blows for her only, improving her chances to maintain her stamina in a dragged-out fight.

Tied to her back was a holstered wrench almost the size of her. To most, that would be odd to look at, but there was a reason. The wrench was actually a siege weapon Argus crafted for her. He chose the shape design for kicks, and made the joke that our living siege weapon needed to carry a siege weapon of her own.

Argus, Rylan, and Blaze came into the living room soon after. They all had chosen a similar look to Raikidan's, only Blaze had chosen a sleeved jacket and Rylan had chosen to go with a T-shirt and long coat.

Ryoko headed for the basement door. "Laz, choice of weapon?"

"Pistol and finger gun."

"Close range combat?" She laughed. "Daring tonight, aren't we? You, Raikidan?"

"Carbine, I suppose."

She nodded and dashed down the stairs. Rylan followed to give her a hand. While they were gone, I made my way to my room and grabbed the rest of my daggers since I had made the risky choice of only taking one with me on my prior assignment. I made sure I had my special one strapped to my arm. I was going to need it. By the time I came back out, Rylan and Ryoko returned.

Ryoko tossed me a pistol and finger gun, which I caught with ease and strapped to my thigh and hand. I then watched Raikidan carefully as he loaded his carbine. It had been a while since he had done so, so I wanted to make sure he'd be all set.

Ryoko tossed a small pouch to me. I opened it and nodded when I noted the contents. Inside were an extra clip of rounds for my pistol and finger gun, and several magazines for Raikidan's carbine. Even though I wasn't planning on running out of ammunition, Raikidan more likely would, and there would be only so much he could carry.

Strapping the pouch to my belt, I glanced up as Seda approached with sunglasses in her hands. Using her psychic power, she handed them off to everyone but me. "Be careful. It is not the numbers of the opposing army that is hindering the other team. It is the choice of firepower. The last report indicated the military had two tanks at their disposal, and the other team is running low on ammunition. It would be wise for someone to carry extra to hand off to a few of them."

"I'll do it," Argus offered. "I'll grab a pack full of what I can find and toss it off as we get there."

Seda nodded. "Very well. Others of our team will join in, so you will not be the only reinforcements."

I looked to the others. "Our main priority is disabling those tanks. If we do that, our chances for success increase exponentially."

"I will be watching and helping where I can," Seda said.

"Thank you. Let's move out."

I led the way to the roof, and the others quietly followed. We waited for Argus to join us, and once he did, we took off on the rooftops to the battlefield.

We knew we were getting close when we came to a point where the buildings were too demolished to continue by rooftop. The air was thick with the smell of fire, gas, and gunfire. We could hear the gunfire in the distance, and as we progressed at a rapid pace, it grew louder rather quickly.

"I see something," Rylan called out. "Ryoko, mind giving me a small lift to the top of one of those broken buildings?"

She nodded. "Sure thing."

Rylan made sure his rifle was secure on his back and he jumped into the air near Ryoko. Ryoko put her hands together, and as his feet landed into them, she launched him into the air. Rylan landed safely on one of the buildings and searched for a good spot to hunker down.

"I see a tank," I said. "Ryoko, I want you to focus your attention only on disabling those. I'll watch your back."

Ryoko grinned and her skin hardened. "I like the sound of that."

"Blaze, Argus, I want you to get that extra ammo to the other team. Then you can take out what you wish."

"Right," they agreed.

"Raikidan, watch our backs."

He nodded.

"Everyone has their assignments. Let's go."

Ryoko and I picked up our pace. I drew my dagger and willed it into a kusarigama, spinning the blade and chain to the side of me in anticipation.

Ryoko pulled out her large wrench and threw it like a boomerang. "Heads up!"

Several members of the other team looked back at her call and ducked down in time as it flew past them. The wrench swung into the barrel of the tank, denting it severely, and clattered to the ground. The two of us ran past our confused allies and focused on the tank.

I swung my kusarigama out at every enemy I could as Ryoko rushed the tank and slid underneath it. The creaking of metal sounded, and soon enough, the tank slowly lifted into the air. The soldiers inside scrambled out in fear. Ryoko grunted with her effort, and she raised it as high as she could. She turned until she found the other tank.

Raikidan's carbine fired several times, and I watched a small group of soldiers around Ryoko fall to the ground. I was thankful Raikidan had our backs. My current weapon wasn't doing as well for me as I had hoped, so I chose to go for a closer and more preferred range of combat choice. I willed my weapon into my favored reverse blade dagger and split it into two weapons.

Bullets bounced off my armor as enemy soldiers attempted to take me out during my moment of weakness. I faced them and they backed up, their eyes wide with fear. With extreme speed, I closed the distance between us and sliced through their flimsy armor and into their flesh. They screamed in agony and fell to the ground.

Ryoko heaved with all her might and tossed the tank into the other. Soldiers from the undamaged tank scrambled out just before the two tanks collided. The tanks exploded on impact, creating a wave of shrapnel and fire. I braced myself for a direct impact, but none came. Ryoko had jumped in front of me and took the full blow. I placed my hand on her shoulder, and she glanced at me with a smile. She was tired from throwing that tank, I could tell, but she wasn't out of this fight just yet.

"Raikidan is out of ammunition," Seda informed me.

Quickly unzipping the pouch, I tossed three magazines to him. "Raikidan, catch!"

He caught them and reloaded his gun. A loud boom echoed through the street, and Ryoko and I barely managed to jump away from another tank's fire. I glanced at Ryoko, who nodded. Returning my weapon to its compact dagger size, I let the fire burn in my throat. I pulled it into my hands and ran at the tank. The tank fired at me, but I was too quick and dodged the attack. Jumping up onto the tank, I ran up the barrel and forced a wave of fire down inside. Ryoko peeled open a section of metal near the gas tank, and the two of us widened the distance between us and the tank. As we ran, I turned back and unleashed a ball of fire into the open hole.

I was forced to the ground as the tank exploded, but it wasn't the wall of energy that did it. I could feel Ryoko next to me, meaning it wasn't her who had knocked me down. I looked up. "Raikidan?"

He chuckled as he laid over us protectively. "You should be more careful."

"But you wouldn't come to our rescue if that were the case," Ryoko toyed.

He chuckled again and allowed us to jump to our feet. I assessed the situation. The soldiers were now starting to fall back. The loss of their three tanks had damaged their morale severely, along with the armed fighting force Argus and Blaze helped rebuild.

Raikidan exhaled a stream of smoke. "Let's show them what we're made of."

I grinned. At least he was just as into this as we were. Ryoko rushed off alone into a crowd of soldiers, unleashing a wave onto them from her rail gun. Thankful I had a small ember still burning on my fingertips, I forced it to burn into a large flame and unleashed it on the opposing army. Raikidan spewed fire from his mouth, and together, we pushed back a portion of the army. Once that task had been done, we separated as I went to give Ryoko a hand. She looked at me gratefully as I pushed back the force with more fire.

"Laz, Raikidan is surrounded!"

I turned back to see Raikidan taking on more than he could chew. He wasn't able to put out enough fire to quell the mass. I watched one soldier aim for Raikidan's head, but before I could move, the soldier fell to the ground with a large bullet hole between his eyes. I sent a silent prayer of thanks to Satria for Rylan's aim.

I unleashed a wall of fire and encircled it around Raikidan as a protective barrier. It was a thick fire, so as long as he stayed within it, he would be safe from basic firearms. Raikidan's gaze flicked to me, but I turned away before I could see his expression. Instead, I unleashed balls of fire onto the enemy and forced them back further. Argus and Blaze came up behind me and gave me a hand.

"Fall back!" a general yelled. "Fall back!"

What was left of the army listened to the general's command, and it wasn't long before the street was abandoned. The team we had helped grouped up and assessed the damage to their members. Our teammates who'd flooded in to aid them grouped up as well. Ryoko and Raikidan maneuvered their way through the rubble over to me as I gazed around and studied the damage.

Both civilian and military buildings were reduced to rubble. Bodies were strewn everywhere, and the ground was stained with blood and other viscera. As I gazed about, I couldn't shake the feeling we were being watched, but the thick scent of blood masked any indication of someone still lingering.

I greeted Rylan with a nod as he picked his way over to us. He rested the stock of his rifle on the ground and checked everyone's condition.

"Eira." I looked over as a tall man with dark skin and dark eyes made his way over to us.

I nodded in greeting. "Ven."

"Thanks for the help." He glanced back at his team. "You came just in time."

"What's the damage to your team?"

"We lost two when they brought the tanks in. The rest have mostly minor injuries, with just a few severe ones," he assessed. "Not as bad as it could have been, though."

"You should have abandoned the mission. It could have been avoided."

"I don't run, Eira."

"There is no shame in it. It allows you to fall back, regroup, re-strategize, and go back for more without major losses."

Ven snorted but didn't voice an argument. He was a stubborn man and was stuck in his ways. He wouldn't look like a coward in the least. Ven pulled out his gun and aimed when he heard movement behind a broken wall of a building. I chuckled and forced the gun down. His brow furrowed. "There's something over there."

"I know." While we had been talking, I had caught the scent I had been searching for. "Ryder, come on out."

A young boy, no older than ten, poked his head out from behind the broken wall. He had crew-cut white-blue hair and dual-colored eyes, the left being green with a golden ring around the pupil and the right being a bright blue with a silver ring around the pupil. A smile was plastered on his face as he ran over to us, unfazed by the devastation around him. I knelt and embraced him in a hug.

"You're back!" he exclaimed.

I smiled. "I'm back."

He buried his face into my neck. "I knew Ryoko was wrong. I knew you'd come back. You always keep your promise."

I chuckled. "Yeah, Ryoko was wrong. I would never dream of breaking my promise to you."

He pulled away and held up his pinkie. "Swear by it?"

I smiled and grasped his pinkie with mine. "Swear."

A wide grin spread across his face and he hugged me again. "I missed you."

"I missed you too, Ryder," I mumbled. "There wasn't a day I didn't think about you."

"Really?"

"Yeah, really."

"I'm glad." He looked at my arm where my preferred dagger was sheathed. "You still have the dagger I made you!"

I chuckled. "Of course, I do. I rarely go anywhere without it."

"That makes me happy."

I smiled more. I was glad he was okay. I was glad I had made the right choice. "You've been good, right?"

He pulled away, his gaze falling to the ground.

"Ryder?"

"They've been telling me to fight..."

I sighed. "You haven't been listening."

He shook his head. "I don't like fighting."

I placed my hand on his head and rubbed it. "I know. You like to build stuff, but you can't just go around disobeying orders."

"But you did."

I frowned. "Yes, and it got me into the situation I don't want you in. You need to start listening. I can't protect you all the time anymore. If something happens, I can't guarantee I can save you, and I don't want that. Do you understand?"

He nodded slowly. "Yes."

I lifted his chin and smiled at him. "I'm glad you're okay, though. That's all I can ask for."

He grinned. "I'm glad you're okay, too. When can I come live with you again? Can't I just come with you now?"

I shook my head. "Not yet. It's not safe for you to come with us."

"But it's not safe for me here, either."

I chuckled. "I can't believe I'm going to say this, but it's safer for you to stay where you are. As long as you do what they say, you'll do fine. You're too young for them to expect much from anyway."

Ryder frowned. "Okay, if you say so."

I patted his head. "It'll be over soon, all right? Then it'll be like I promised."

He nodded enthusiastically. "Okay! That's a promise, so you can't break it."

I laughed. "Right." I peered up as a young woman approached us. She carried a handful of dog tags in her hands. I furrowed my brow. "What are those for?"

"If he's going to have an excuse to give for not retreating with the others, then he'd best have a good one," she said.

I nodded. *Smart.* He would be seen highly in the eyes of the other soldiers for such an honorable deed, and it would give him the correct excuse. It might even help him win points with the higher-ranking officers. If he was lucky, they would more than likely keep him out of battle.

The woman handed the tags over to me, and in turn, I handed them to Ryder. "Take these back with you. You'll be less likely to get into trouble. Also tell them we hung around for quite a bit of time, preventing you from going anywhere. Got it?"

He nodded. "Got it. This means I have to go now, doesn't it?"

I kissed him on the forehead. "Yes."

He sighed unhappily. "All right. When will I be able to see you again?"

My eyes softened, and my chest tightened. "I'm not sure. I'll try my best to do it soon, okay?"

He nodded. "Okay! But if not, I'll understand. Jaybird says it's really hard to get information back and forth without being caught. I guess it would be the same when it came to seeing you."

I nodded. "Yes, but I promise I will try."

He smiled and gave me one last hug before running off. I stood and watched him go, my heart heavy. A lot had happened these past few weeks. This win from a perceived loss would improve the rebellion's morale, but we still had much to do. Raikidan's help had been invaluable, and while I loathed to admit it, my mistake that landed me in his path proved to be the key we needed. I just hoped he'd continue to be useful and that I'd not made a mistake by placing my trust in him. *Maybe soon, Ryder and I can have the life I always promised him.* My gaze faltered. *As long as this path doesn't lead me to the fate I've tried to change.*

The others around me dispersed to go about their business before we headed home. Raikidan, on the other hand, moved closer to me. "Who was that boy?"

I continued to stare long after Ryder had disappeared from sight. "My son."

Moonlight filtered through the barred window as I opened my eyes. "Ryder..."
I hoped he wasn't involved with this mistake I made. I prayed he was safe. I
curled up against the stone wall when the clomping of boots echoed down the hall.
My life may be in the balance, but as long as he was listening to what I had told
him, he would live a full life, and that was all I could ask for in a time like this...

GLOSSARY CHARACTER

DALATREND

LEADERS
Taric – Former ruler of Dalatrend, nu-human, deceased
Zarda – Ruler of Dalatrend, nu-human

MILITARY
Zo – Nu-human experiment, general, interested in Eira

REBELLION

COUNCIL
Genesis – Oversees Team 3, first nu-human, necromantic abilities
Hanama (*HAH-nah-mah*) – Oversees Team 1, nu-human experiment

TEAM 1
Assassin based
Evynne (*Ev-een*) – Nu-human experiment

TEAM 2
Recruitment based

Dan – Nu-human experiment, former lieutenant to Eira

TEAM 3
Income based, former Brute and foot soldier mostly

Argus – Nu-human experiment, inventor

Aurora – Nu-human experiment, Underground computer tech

Azriel – Nu-human experiment, former medic, night club owner: Twilight

Blaze – Nu-human experiment

Eira (*AIR-uh*) – Nu-human hybrid experiment, battle leader, former commander, assassin, fire shaman. Alt names: Laz, Laz'shika (*laz-SHEE-kah*)

Orchon (*OR-con*) – Nu-human, bouncer at Twilight

Raikidan (*RYE-ki-DAN*) – Black and red dragon, Guard in training

Rylan (*RYE-lan*) – Nu-human experiment, experimental shapeshifter: wolf, former captain, artificial mental bond with Eira, ice elementalist, interested in Ryoko

Ryoko (*Ree-OH-koh*) – Half-wogron experiment, clone of Peacekeeper Ryoko, Brute, former lieutenant, best friend to Eira, interested in Rylan

Seda (*SAY-duh*) – Nu-human experiment, psychic: Seer, twin to Nioush

Zane – Nu-human experiment, uncle to Eira, brother to Jasmine, former soldier, mechanic

TEAM 4
Reconnaissance based

TEAM 5
Psychic based

Vek – Nu-human experiment, psychic: Battle Psychic, registered

TEAM 6
Research and development based

TEAM 7
Reconnaissance based

Chameleon – Nu-human experiment, molecular fusion ability, former assassin

Doppelganger – Nu-human experiment, temporary cloning ability

Ezhno (*EZ-no*) – Nu-human experiment, Underground computer tech

Mocha – Nu-human experiment, anthropomorphic: cat

Nioush (*NEE-oosh*) – Nu-human experiment, psychic: Battle Psychic, twin to Seda

Raynn (*rain*) – Nu-human experiment, battle leader, former general, clone of Peacekeeper Raynn

MOLES
Arnia (*ARE-nee-ah*) – Nu-human experiment

Jaybird – Nu-human experiment

SHAMANS

NORTH TRIBE
Fe'teline (*fey-TELL-een*) – Nu-human, fire shaman

SOUTH TRIBE
Ne'kall (*nay-CALL*) – Elf, son to Del'karo and Alena

Tla'lli (*teh-LAH-lee*) – Elf, chief's daughter, wind shaman

EAST TRIBE
Se'lata (*say-LAH-tah*) – Elf, spice merchant, earth shaman

WEST TRIBE
Alena – Elf, wife to Del'karo, mother figure to Eira, mother of Ne'kall and eleven other sons, healer

Daren – Human, Valene's adopted father, inn keeper, former partner to Valessa

Del'karo (*del-CAR-oh*) – Elf, mentor and father figure to Eira, husband to Alena, father of Ne'kall and eleven other sons, fire shaman

Ken'ichi (*ken-EE-chee*) – Nu-human, friend to Eira, Guard and healer

Maka'shi (*mah-KAH-shee*) – Leader, half-elf, ice shaman, widow

Mel'ka (*mel-KAH*) – Elf, elder, storyteller, earth shaman

Shva'sika (*sh-VAH-see-KAH*) – Elf, sister to Xye, mentor and adopted family to Eira, lightning shaman

Valene (*Vah-LEEN*) – Human, daughter to Valessa, Eira's and Daren's adopted daughter, plant-based earth shaman

Valessa – Human, mother to Valene, former partner to Daren, earth shaman, deceased

Xye (*zeye*) – Half-elf, brother to Shva'sika, attempted to court Eira, healer, deceased

GODS

Anila (*ah-NEE-lah*) – Goddess of air

Arcadia (*are-KAY-dee-ah*) – Goddess of spirits

Genesis – Goddess of life, partner to Zoltan

Gina – Goddess of health and healing

Halcyon (*hall-SEE-on*) – Goddess of the sea

Imera (*eye-MEER-ah*) – Goddess of literature and knowledge

Jin – Goddess of refined earth

Kendaria – Goddess of water

Koseba (*koh-SAY-bah*) – God of shapeshifting

Le'carro (*ley-CAR-oh*) – God of lightning

Lunaria – Goddess of the moon

Nazir (*nah-ZEER*) – God of death and corruption

Phyre (*fire*) – God of fire

Raisu (*RAY-sue*) – God of dreams

Rashta (*RAH-sh-tah*) – Goddess of judgement and rebirth

Rasmus – God of love and fertility, partner to Savada

Satria (*sah-TREE-ah*) – Goddess of war

Savada (*sah-VAH-dah*) – Goddess of sex and seduction, partner to Rasmus

Sela – Goddess of psychics, sister of Tyro

Solstice – Goddess of ice and winter

Solund – God of the sun

Tarin – God of nature, partner to Valena

Tyro (*TIE-roh*) – God of psychics, brother of Sela

Valena – Goddess of earth, partner to Tarin

Zoltan – God of life, partner to Genesis

MISCELLANEOUS

Rosa (*ROH-sah*) – Succubus, mated to Zaedrix

Voice – Mysterious voice that speaks to Eira inside her head. Malevolent

Zaedrix (*ZAY-driks*) – Incubus, mated to Rosa

SPIRITS

Amara (*ah-MAR-ah*) – Nu-human experiment, general, water elementalist, deceased

Jade – Nu-human experiment, former soldier under Amara, deceased

Jasmine – Nu-human experiment, aunt to Eira, sister to Zane, geneticist, deceased

Tannek – Nu-human experiment, former soldier under Amara deceased

Zeek – Nu-human, former soldier under Amara, deceased

PEACEKEEPERS

Assar – dwarf, deceased

Pyralis (*PIE-ral-iss*) – Red dragon, deceased

Raynn (*rain*) – Human, deceased

Reiki (*Ray-KEY*) – Green dragon, deceased

Ryoko (*Ree-OH-koh*) – Half-wogron, earth shaman, deceased

Varro – Elf, healer, deceased

GLOSSARY LANGUAGE

ELVISH

Elvish is an eloquent language, light on the tongue with an airy sound. Even the usual consonants of common don't hold the same harshness in Elvish. Many elves and other humanoids raised with Elvish as their mother tongue carry this light speech over in their common.

While not the easiest language to learn, Elvish is a favorite among the linguistically gifted. Those who seek to learn this language seek out elves before any other race and are taught by full immersion. Some elves will provide a few words for the humanoid to start with but it's not common to do so. The elves believe this technique is the best way to learn and creates a better understanding of the language for everyday use.

Written Elvish is just as elegant as spoken, usually written in script by native speakers. Non-natives tend to forgo the script, which is accepted by native speakers, though the handwriting is still expected to be neat, and flourished on important documents. Sloppy writing is considered an insult.

DRACONIC

D raconic is a guttural language made up most of grunts and growls with the occasional tongue flick, exhales, or teeth clatter. It's difficult for a non-dragon to learn, as the formation of these words are foreign to most humanoids. Some sounds are impossible for non-dragons to create so other sounds are substituted as an alternative. Even dragons taking a humanoid form must make these changes. Rarely is a humanoid able to perfect the speech, even when raised among dragons.

Those attempting to learn are always taught single words before attempting sentence structures. Draconic sentence structure is similar to Common, but with a possessive edge due to the mindset of dragons. There are no contracted words in Draconic, as such, dragons who don't speak common often, tend to use the same sentence structures of their mother tongue when they do speak common.

It's not common for dragons to write in the current age but there is a basic written form of the language that was used more extensively in the past. This written form is comprised of glyphs easily created with dragon claws and easy to decipher for most dragons no matter the cleanliness of the script. Non-dragons find this writing easier to learn than the spoken language and most of the time will stop learning after they've master it.

Phrases translated to Eira in the series:

Ion cuvk – Our kind
Lazmira, sa xruzk – Lazmira, my child
Zity, gyexy, lgunum, ziaeza, lynyvuma, lmnyvwmr, fulkis – Love, peace, spirit, loyalty, serenity, strength, wisdom